Praise for the novels of
MICHAEL HIEBERT

Dream with Little Angels

"Hiebert's first novel courts comparison to the classic
To Kill a Mockingbird, but the book manages to soar as
a moving achievement in its own right. In Hiebert's
hands, psychological insight and restrained lyricism
combine to create a coming-of-age tale as devastating
as it is indelible."
—*Publishers Weekly* (Starred Review)

"Readers who enjoy literary fiction depicting small-
town life in the tradition of Harper Lee's *To Kill a
Mockingbird* may want to try Hiebert's debut."
—*Library Journal*

"Michael Hiebert's debut delivers . . . a breathless,
will-they-get-there-in-time affair, with a heartbreaking
resolution."
—*Mystery Scene*

Close to the Broken Hearted

"Hiebert does a masterful job of building suspense."
—*Publishers Weekly*

"A very good, sometimes emotional, mystery that will
stay with you long after it's over."
—*Suspense Magazine*

A Thorn Among the Lilies

"Engaging . . . Readers will keep guessing whodunit
to the end."
—*Publishers Weekly*

Books by Michael Hiebert

DREAM WITH LITTLE ANGELS

CLOSE TO THE BROKEN HEARTED

A THORN AMONG THE LILIES

STICKS AND STONES

Published by Kensington Publishing Corporation

STICKS
AND
STONES

MICHAEL
HIEBERT

PINNACLE BOOKS
Kensington Publishing Corp.
www.kensingtonbooks.com

PINNACLE BOOKS are published by

Kensington Publishing Corp.
119 West 40th Street
New York, NY 10018

Copyright © 2016 Michael Hiebert

All Kensington titles, imprints, and distributed lines are available at special quantity discounts for bulk purchases for sales promotions, premiums, fund-raising, educational, or institutional use. Special book excerpts or customized printings can also be created to fit specific needs. For details, write or phone the office of the Kensington sales manager: Kensington Publishing Corp., 119 West 40th Street, New York, NY 10018, attn: Sales Department; phone 1-800-221-2647.

This book is a work of fiction. Names, characters, businesses, organizations, places, events, and incidents either are the product of the author's imagination or are used fictitiously. Any resemblance to actual persons, living or dead, events, or locales is entirely coincidental.

PINNACLE BOOKS and the Pinnacle logo are Reg. U.S. Pat. & TM Off.

ISBN-13: 978-0-7860-4182-4
ISBN-10: 0-7860-4182-X

First Kensington trade paperback printing: July 2016
First Pinnacle mass market paperback printing: July 2018

10 9 8 7 6 5 4 3 2 1

Printed in the United States of America

First Pinnacle electronic edition: July 2018

ISBN-13: 978-0-7860-4183-1
ISBN-10: 0-7860-4183-8

For Natalie . . .

PROLOGUE

Alvin, Alabama, 1974

The Stickman.

Harry Stork.

A year and a half of Detective Joe Fowler's life.

Joe Fowler: one of the two main officers working the Alvin Police Department, and the only detective. The other cop is a tall, lanky man with a bad comb-over whose name is Strident. Officer Peter Strident. Strident has the eyes of an arctic wolf—that crisp morning sky blue—and when he looks at you, it feels like he sees right *through* you. Nobody interrogates a suspect like Strident.

What Fowler lacks in his eyes, he makes up for in gumption.

A year ago February, the first evidence that Harry Stork would eventually come onto Detective Fowler's radar appeared when Stork's first victim turned up beneath the tracks at Finley's Crossing. A black male, mid-thirties, turned out to be one Waylon Ferris. Ferris's body was found shirtless. His hands and feet hog-tied behind him, putting him in an almost reverse-fetal position. A thirty-eight-caliber bullet hole entering the back of the skull, a big exit hole in the front.

Even more horrific, a wooden stave was hammered through Ferris's chest, staking him into the ground. On a piece of paper affixed to the stave, a drawing of a stickman made in black permanent marker.

Lack of blood and brain matter at the crime scene and evidence from the ligature marks on his wrists and ankles suggested Ferris was shot somewhere else, somewhere he had spent a day, maybe two, before his killer put the bullet through his brain.

For the press release, Fowler held back the stake and the paper attached to it.

Waylon Ferris was victim number one.

A succession of killings followed, all inside of or circling the small town of Alvin, each with the same MO: shirtless victims inversely hog-tied with a .38 Special-caliber slug entering the back of the skull. Victims ranged in age from mid-twenties to early forties, mixed men and women, black and white. Each one staked to the ground with the picture of a stickman. Women stickmen had circles for breasts, hair rising to tips on either side of the head.

Every killing brought more cops into the mix. Fowler created a task force and managed to continue holding back the staked paper with the stickmen from the press. Until the information leaked out after victim six. Someone on the task force talked. Someone obviously needed cash.

Almost immediately, the killer was tagged the Stickman by the media. Fowler hated the name. Thought it trivialized everything, almost turning it into a game.

The case was long and arduous. Too many victims. Too many pieces of paper with bloody stickmen.

Nine in total, that is, *if* Fowler knows about all of them.

Nine bodies, almost a year and a half away from his daughter—Leah—and his wife, Josephine. Because Fowler is *like* that. Even when he's home, if he's on a case, he's *still* on the case. He lets them get to him. They pick away at his bones, eating him up until he solves them. They take their toll on his family, especially on his daughter, Leah. He worries about her and how she's affected by his stress. It's the part of the police game he hates most.

Harry Stork.

The Stickman.

It took Fowler too long to figure out they were the same man. When he did, Stork disappeared.

That was almost a month ago.

But tonight, Fowler and four other officers surround an abandoned shotgun shack with Stork inside. He'll be taken either alive or dead. It's all up to him now, how he plays it.

The dilapidated shack is set back in the woods, flanked by tall oaks, their boughs heavy with Spanish moss. Fowler's positioned at the shack's rear door. Fog and a light mist cover the ground, making the dense forest ghost-like. If not for the band of stars and the silvery gold of the moon overhead, Joe Fowler wouldn't even be able to see his own hands.

The rest of the officers are broken into two teams of two, waiting at the shack's front for Fowler's instructions. Team A will batter down the door, Team B will rush in and clear the front room. Team A will move on to clear the rest of the place.

Joe Fowler is Team C, protecting the only other exit,

other than a window. Stork won't have time for windows.

Pushing his fingers through his short, graying hair, Fowler feels sweat pop onto his forehead. He brings the blow horn to his lips. "Come out, Harry!" he yells into it. "You're surrounded. Come out or we're coming in! And if we come in, it could go bad." He rubs his chin, feeling three days' worth of stubble. He wonders if maybe Stork wants it to go bad, wants to go out in a blaze of glory.

A fitting end to the Stickman? Maybe.

From the windows, the occasional flashlight beam dances erratically into the night, the only indication Stork's still alive. He silently moves from room to room.

Fowler counts to five. Stork stays quiet. Stays inside.

"All right," Fowler says. He tosses the blow horn onto the loamy ground, lifts his walkie-talkie. "Team A, go! Team B, ready! Team C is ready!"

Dropping into a crouch, Fowler pulls his weapon, readying himself in case Stork's stupid enough to come out shooting.

There's a *boom!* as Fowler hears the front door go down. "Front clear!" Someone shouts.

"He's running!" Someone else.

It all happens in a blur. The back door bursts open, and Harry Stork appears, silhouetted by the flashlights from the cops in the hall behind him. Fowler sees the gun in Stork's hand, tightens his grip on his own weapon—a snub-nosed Colt Cobra revolver—and readjusts his crouch, balancing his weight on the balls of his feet.

"Drop your weapon!" Fowler screams. "Drop your weapon or I will shoot!"

Stork hesitates while his eyes adjust to the darkness.

He must've dropped his flashlight in the scramble. He sweeps his gun blindly in front of him. Fowler sees the barrel tremble. "Don't kill me!" Stork yells, panicked. "I was set up! I'm a fuckin' patsy!"

"Then drop it, Harry!" Fowler calls out. He notices a slight shake in his own hand. Arthritis. Doc gave him the news six months ago. He readjusts his grip and the shake goes away, replaced by a tingling pain shooting up his right arm. Fowler knows too well what it means: He's getting too old for this game.

He pushes the thought away, focuses on Stork. Everything becomes a tunnel around the man. Stork hasn't dropped his weapon. "Drop your gun!" Fowler shouts again.

But Stork doesn't. Instead, no longer blinded by the night, Stork levels the barrel straight at Fowler. There's little choice left. In that split second, Fowler reacts on instinct, pulling off a .38 Special round destined straight for Harry Stork's heart.

Fowler wanted to hit the man's gun arm, but overcompensated, too afraid he might miss. Too afraid Stork wouldn't. Fowler's shot clips the edge of Stork's lower left ventricle, the kind of shot there's no coming back from.

The gun barrel goes limp in Stork's hand before falling and rattling on the broken wooden porch at Stork's feet. Stork falls right behind it.

And that's how it happened the night the Stickman went down and Joe Fowler gave his life back to his wife, Josephine, and his daughter, Leah. The daughter who would one day follow in her pa's footsteps.

CHAPTER 1

Fifteen Years Later

Summer came to Alabama the way it always did, like a twister out of the east. The heat from the early morning sun pounded down on the red maple and black gum trees out along Cottonwood Lane. Officer Leah Teal drove by these trees every day on her way to work, but this was the first day she could remember in a long time it being so hot at only half past seven.

Everything was alive in vivid colors. Alvin looked like a picture book filled with images of white clusters of berries bursting on the mayhaw, and yellow, green, and orange flowers popping out of the tulip trees, late bloomers. Even with her window rolled down, the air lay in the car like a dead animal, making the heat even more intolerable. As she came to her turn, the smell of sweet bay magnolias trying their best to bloom wafted inside. Drifts of cottonwood fluff fell like snow onto the brown hood of her Bonneville as she turned down the hill.

As she drove, Leah hummed a tune, unsure of what it was. She was in good spirits lately—ever since Christmastime, really, because of a man she was rapidly falling for: a detective out of Birmingham whom she'd met on her last big case, a case that started with a psychic—of all things—and ended with a serial killer.

Things were never dull for long around Alvin.

The detective's name was Dan Truitt and he was different from any man Leah had ever met. She hadn't dated a lot of men in her life. In fact, Dan was the first in over a dozen years since her husband, Billy, died in an automobile accident.

For too long she had let that accident spin her life out of her control. Now she felt like she was finally taking her life back. And Dan Truitt was helping her do it. No, more than that, he was making her *want* to do it. She was starting to admit to herself she was falling in love.

Pulling her sedan to a stop at the curb outside the Alvin Police Station, Leah exited the vehicle and was immediately overwhelmed again by the melting, stagnant heat. Honeybees buzzed around the red buds on the sweetshrubs planted in front of the station's windows.

She picked up the *Alvin Examiner* from in front of the station door on her way inside. The station was locked, which meant she'd beaten Officer Chris Jackson to work. Officer Jackson was the only other cop at the Alvin Police Station apart from the chief, Ethan Montgomery. Jackson was also black, which caused quite a stir in this little community when he first came on the force, but that quickly faded. Now he was respected as much as Leah or Ethan.

After putting on a pot of coffee, Leah took the newspaper she had tucked beneath her arm, pulled the elastic off it, and unrolled it.

She read the front page and her happy demeanor immediately changed.

The headline read: *15 Years Later, Stickman Strikes Again*.

The photograph beneath the headline could've been a lot more gruesome than it was. It was taken some distance from the crime scene, which left out a lot of the details described in the article. It didn't matter; Leah knew immediately what the actual scene would've looked like. The victim, unnamed in the paper, would've been shirtless with her ankles and wrists bound together behind her back. Her body would be staked to the ground, through the chest, and attached to that stake would be a piece of paper with a stickwoman drawn on it. But that's not what would've killed her. A gunshot wound to the back of the skull would've done that job. Leah didn't have to see it all in a picture; she could imagine it pretty well. She'd lived it.

Scanning the photo, Leah made out strangler fig and cypress trees. The dirt looked soft. She guessed the body was found near water. Indeed, the article confirmed it had turned up on the bank of Leeland Swamp, an area surrounded by forest just outside of the ranch lands in the northwestern corner of Alvin.

And then the rest of the train caught up with her thoughts and she realized what this really meant. It made her breath catch and her heart tumble into her stomach.

She had lived the case vicariously through her pa, Joe Fowler, fifteen years ago when he spent a year and a half hunting down a serial killer. But—

Her pulse quickened.

Heat rose to her face.

This, all because there was one thing Leah knew with absolute dead fact: *But . . . what I'm looking at, it's . . . it's impossible.*

Her pa killed Harry Stork, the man who earned the

nickname "Stickman" in papers from one side of Alabama to another. Shot him through the heart. The *Birmingham News* had called it "The Shot Heard 'Round the World." It made the front page. Suddenly everyone knew about Alvin, a town with a population of just over six thousand people almost nobody in Alabama had ever heard of.

She glanced up to the newspaper's date, hoping for some bizarre reason to find the paperboy had accidentally delivered a paper from 1974, but today's date stared back at her under the black script headlining the *Alvin Examiner*. She hadn't *really* expected to see anything else.

But how . . . ? The more she thought of it, the more impossible it was.

The door opened and she jumped. It was Chris. He took one look at her sitting on the edge of her desk, paper in one hand, forgotten coffee mug steaming in the other, and closed the door quietly behind him. "How you doing?" he asked in his low-timbered voice. Chris spoke slowly, and with near on perfect enunciation. It made him sound as though he was a man who chose his words carefully and said them with reverence. "I see you got the coffee started." He smiled, wiping his brow with his uniform sleeve. "Man, is it hot."

Leah said nothing back, and he realized she was reading the paper.

"Oh," he said, with a big sigh. His smile faded quickly as he plunked into his chair. "So you know." He ran his dark fingers through his cropped black hair. Sweat, even at this early hour, popped over his hand. He looked like he wished he would've called in sick.

Leah snapped the front page of the paper toward him. "This can't be the Stickman," she said. "The Stickman was Harry Stork and my pa *killed* Harry Stork fifteen years ago."

"Yeah, I know," Chris said, "but he shows every sign of having come back to life."

Leah bit her lower lip. It couldn't be Harry Stork. She remembered her pa on that case like it was yesterday. He would come home physically exhausted most nights, but mentally he stayed on the job twenty-four/seven. His brain never stopped trying to solve it. It took him near on a year and a half to finally do it, and, near the back side of it all, Leah and her ma both thought he would be needing intense therapy. It all tied up because of a lucky break, an anonymous tip called in to the station—although he would never use the word *lucky*. Leah could hear him in her mind. "No," he'd say, "lucky would've been catching him 'fore anybody had to die. This ain't luck, Leah, after all this time, this is God throwing down justice." Back then, he had told her she was too young to understand, but one day it would all make sense.

He lived long enough to get her on the force after he left, but not long enough to find out exactly how much sense his words would one day make.

She was more like her pa than she ever cared to admit, but Police Chief Ethan Montgomery constantly reminded her. Like her pa, she took full responsibility for everything that happened during any of her cases. Any blood spilled was spilled on her own hands. She took everything personally, same way he had. And, like him, it wore on her. She wondered how much of the stress contributed to the cancer that finally took him.

Leah's son, Abe, had been six when his grandpa died. Leah always consoled herself with the fact that he at least got to know his grandpa those half-dozen years. Not like Abe's own pa, Leah's husband, Billy, who died in an early morning head-on collision that took him out of not only her life, but Abe's, and her daughter, Caroline's, life, too. Billy left them all far too early. Leah doubted, if not for the shoe box full of photos she had given him, that her little Abe even remembered what his pa looked like. He was only two when Billy passed.

Now Abe was thirteen and Caroline turned sixteen this past Christmas, and Leah wondered how different things would be for them if they hadn't lost their pa twelve years ago—if Billy hadn't decided to pass that eighteen-wheeler in front of him.

But there was no point in thinking about it, some mistakes you just can't come back from. Billy's decision to pass that truck that fatal morning was one of those mistakes.

She still missed Billy and her pa, but her pa was different. Somehow, she still felt him with her some days. She even found herself talking to him during those times when she could badly use his sage advice. Of course, he never answered, but it still usually helped to ask the questions.

Ethan Montgomery had hired Leah's pa and he'd also agreed to bring Leah on when her pa suggested it. And after all this time, he was still working at the station, although every year he seemed to come in later and later. These days, he rarely arrived before eleven. Leah expected he would just keep being later until there was no time left in the day and that would be when he retired. Until then, he spent most of his time behind a ridiculously large desk in a squeaky chair watching the Crimson Tide stop the Auburn Tigers from making any yardage.

Because of the connection her pa had to Ethan, Leah knew she was treated differently than Chris. She was made "detective" not just to walk in her pa's footsteps, but also to allow Ethan to pay her a higher wage. She and her two kids needed all the help they could get. This was something Ethan and her pa arranged without her even knowing, but now it was pretty much common knowledge. At least Chris didn't seem to hold any animosity toward her because of it. She wondered sometimes, though. Especially on those days when Chris sat at his desk doing nothing but crossword puzzles his entire shift. Even if the phone rang, there were days he'd wait for her to take the call.

She didn't mind so much. Chris was more of a desk cop anyway. That's how he was cut. According to Ethan, Leah was different. Chris did have some special talents, though, like his uncanny ability to unearth the details of juvenile records.

"I see your mind moving," Chris said to her. His regulation boots were up on his desk and the coffee he'd fetched for himself was sitting beside his hat. Leaning back in his chair, he put his arms behind his head. "What I don't see are the details moving around. Care to let me in?" He spoke tentatively, almost like he was scared.

Leah looked back at the paper. "This is impossible."

Chris just shrugged.

"It's a copycat. It's gotta be. But why would someone copycat a case they had to dredge up from fifteen years—"

Chris cut her off. "I know what you're thinking, but it's not a copycat. It can't be."

"Yes, it can, Chris. Remember, the holdback about the stakes with the drawings was leaked. That's how Harry Stork *became* the Stickman."

"I know," he said. "But the staked stickman page wasn't the only holdback. There was another. A *big* one. And it wasn't leaked."

A thought suddenly came to Leah, one that probably should've come long before now. "Wait a minute. Why am I just reading about this now? Which police department was on the scene last night? Last time I checked, Leeland Swamp was in *Alvin*."

"Yeah," Chris stumbled. "That . . . I . . . we . . ." He glanced at the door to Ethan Montgomery's office. It was mainly glass, like the walls, but brown blinds hung down that Leah couldn't remember ever seeing open. She could only imagine how much dust was collecting inside them. Of course, now the door would be locked. Leah glanced at the white clock hanging in front of her desk on the wall between the door and the window. It was twenty past eight. They wouldn't see Ethan for another two or three hours.

"What time did you get the call?" Leah asked. She remembered Chris was still at his desk when she left. She doubted he would have stayed much longer than fifteen more minutes, and she had gotten home just after five.

"What call?"

"Whoever found the body. I'm guessing it must've been around five?"

Chris scratched the back of his head. "Ethan called me at home," he said.

Leah tried to process this. "Ethan was still here when it came in? That's"—*a miracle*—"unusual."

"Yeah, um, the body hadn't turned up yet."

Narrowing her eyes, Leah asked, "What do you mean? Wait, if this holdback you're talking about was so secret, how come you know about it?"

"Ethan told me about it yesterday. What matters is, it

wasn't a copycat kill. It's more than that. Ethan was pretty clear."

Leah felt the heat rise in her skin. A trickle of sweat ran down the back of her blouse, tracing a line from the bottom of her bra strap, along her vertebrae, and right into her brown pants.

"Sure is hot out there," Chris said, looking out the window.

Leah snapped the paper at him. "What aren't you telling me? What do you mean 'the body hadn't turned up yet'? What's this super-secret holdback and why did Ethan tell *you?*"

Chris took a deep breath. "Leah, it was a long night. We searched that swamp for three hours before finding the body."

"What are you talking about?" The hair rose on the back of her neck. "I wasn't called in on any search last night."

"That's on account of we didn't know how you'd react to it. With what happened with your pa and the Stickman fifteen years ago and all . . ."

Leah's stomach roiled. Anger swooped in like a hungry vulture. She did her best to hold it back, but heard the edge it put on her words when she spoke. "If you hadn't found a body, how would you know . . . ? Wait, I am missing something here. What made you even know to *look* for a body? What aren't you telling me?"

Chris said nothing, just shifted uncomfortably in his seat.

"Someone had to call someone," Leah said. "I don't . . ." No matter how much she tried to make sense of things, nothing worked.

Chris let out a big sigh. "Man, it's hot."

Leah's anger swelled. "I am getting mighty pissed off

about talking about the goddamn weather, Chris. If there's something you're not tellin' me, I'd best be making your mouth start going sooner rather than later." Both Chris and Ethan knew Leah had a temper. Neither of them ever wanted to push the envelope and find out how bad it really was.

When she looked back at Chris, he had seemed to take a sudden interest in the floor.

"Okay, first things first," she said. "Tell me about the stuff."

"What stuff?"

"The super-secret stuff that actually *was* held back from the press throughout the Stickman murders."

Chris sighed again and took a big drink of coffee. He was running out of stall tactics. "Well, for every victim, this station—well, your pa—was given a letter."

Leah cocked her head. "Letter? How was it given? Who gave it?"

Chris shrugged. "Apparently it came from the Stickman. It would be left in an envelope with no postmark or address, simply your pa's name written across the front. Inside there was always a single piece of paper folded three times. It had a drawing of a stickman, a time, and a location."

"A time and location of the killing?"

"Yeah."

"Sounds weird. Why didn't my pa just show up and arrest the Stickman then?"

"The locations were general. Like the one last night simply said *Leeland Swamp, 8:30 P.M.* That's a large area to search in two and a half hours. Not counting travel time. And we had to assume it could also mean somewhere in the surrounding forest."

"So the time in the letter designates when the body will be dumped at the secondary crime scene?"

"According to Ethan it's more like the maximum time in a range. So, when the letter comes in they knew they had from whenever it was opened until the time it said before the body was staked."

Leah thought this over. "If the staked drawings were leaked, this letter thing could easily have been, too."

Chris held up his palm. "I know what you're thinking, but listen. Not every cop on the task force knew about the letters. In fact, Ethan said other than him and your pa, there were four other detectives in the loop, each handpicked by Joe. After the first leak, he wasn't about to take any chances."

"And forensics said all the letters were written by the same person?" Leah asked.

"All except the last one. They had a weird slant to the left."

"And what was different with the last one?"

"The last one was the one that came the night your pa shot Stork. Mobile said the handwriting didn't match the rest. It could be the same person, but if so, he wanted it to seem like someone else."

"The night my pa shot Stork? There was no victim that night."

Chris put his feet back up on his desk. "No, the letter was for Stork. It had the address of the shotgun shack. The actual address. There was no time. Harry was holed up there. He was there when your pa and Strident arrived with the other officers. And there was one more difference."

"What was that?"

"The letter had the initials *H.S.* written on it."

"Harry Stork?"

Chris nodded. "One would gather, yes."

"I thought Stork's whereabouts came from an anonymous call?"

With a shake of his head, Chris said, "That's the story your pa made up. He didn't want to release the holdout."

"Why not, if Stork was dead? The Stickman case was solved."

Chris shrugged. "That, I don't know. I asked Ethan that exact question and he didn't seem to know, either. He just said your pa asked the other four cops to keep the letters secret. Said your pa always said the case felt 'unfinished'."

Leah considered this. He did always go back to the case. Even years later, she remembered him bringing home Stickman files and staying up late some nights poring over them. She hated those nights. "No wonder my pa got so wrapped up in that case. I always thought he seemed to take it particularly personal. Now I understand. It *was* personal. He was getting letters addressed directly to him."

Chris nodded. "Can't get much more personal than that. Plus, Joe was the one being quoted in the papers and being interviewed on the news. He was the face of the Stickman task force."

It was Leah's turn to sigh as her eyes went to the clock. "I don't suppose we're goin' to see Ethan anytime soon. You'd think he'd want to tell me all this himself," she said, trying to keep her anger and frustration out of her voice. Truth was, she also felt a bit betrayed by her pa not confiding in her about the letters all those years.

"So," Leah said, "the letter came last night after I left?"

"It came after I left, too," Chris said. "Ethan found it on his way out jammed halfway under the door. He called me right after I got home. Said he almost didn't open it. Figured it was probably another thank-you card from the Ladies Auxiliary for your helping out with their Mother's Day parade."

Leah gave her coffee mug a half turn where it stood on her desk. "Mother's Day was at least a month and a half ago. Besides, this one didn't come to me. It came to you and Ethan. Or . . . ? Who was it addressed to?"

Chris took a deep breath and blew it out slowly. Sweat was dotting his forehead. She didn't bother following his gaze when it shifted to the window.

"Well, you know . . . that doesn't really matter." Chris stood from his chair, walked over to the coffeemaker, and poured two new mugs full. To one he added three teaspoons of sugar and some cream. He left the other black and handed it to Leah, nodding to her half-filled one. "I think that's probably getting cold," he said and sat back down.

Without saying thanks, Leah took the mug. She stood there silently, holding it and slowly shaking her head.

"What?" Chris asked.

Her emotions rose to the surface. "The letter wasn't goddamn addressed to you *or* Ethan, was it? Christ, no wonder he's not here yet. Chickenshit."

Chris scratched the back of his head again. "It was just like all the other times," he said. "The information was delivered to us. The police."

"Last time it all came to my pa. Exactly *who* was this new letter addressed to?"

Chris didn't answer. He sat in his chair and ran his fingers once more through his hair.

"Who was it addressed to, Chris?" Leah said, louder.

"You," Chris said, almost too quiet to hear.

"Who? Say again?"

He swung his chair toward her. "You. Okay? The letter came addressed to *Leah Fowler,* so obviously whoever is behind this doesn't know you were married."

"Or he wants to drive home a point," Leah said in a clipped tone before falling silent. When she spoke again, it was quiet and pensive. "Otherwise, did Ethan say it was exactly like the other ones?"

"Yes. Exactly." Chris took a swig of coffee and turned back toward the window. Leah was pretty sure *he* couldn't wait for Ethan to get into the office, either.

"And you didn't call me in?" she asked. "You and Ethan decided to just handle this alone like a couple of cowboys?"

"We thought you might freak out," Chris said. "You have in the past."

"You could have *used* me," Leah said, growing louder again. "You needed as many cops as you could get. I should have been called, goddamnit!"

"Well, Ethan said not to."

"Well, Ethan and I are goin' to have some discussion when he gets in." She looked at the clock again. That big black minute hand was inching its way closer and closer to twelve. "That is, *if* he ever gets in."

Chris took a big, calming breath. "Don't you find it hot today?"

"Show me the letter," Leah said, trying to remain calm. "Surely you thought to make a copy of it."

"Of course, but it will only make things worse."

"Show me the goddamn letter!"

"All right." Chris reached into a file folder on his desk and pulled out a piece of paper. Leah could tell it was a photocopy because it had no fold creases.

"Mobile has the original?"

"Yeah. Their forensic experts are goin' to see what they can get off it. Maybe a fingerprint—I don't know. There won't be nothin' on it. We all know that. This guy's smart." He stopped mid-sentence and corrected himself. "*Was* smart."

"Yes, *was,* because this guy is *not* the Stickman, Chris! Are you not hearing me? The Stickman was Harry Stork and Harry Stork is dead. The dead don't come back."

"Well, this time, maybe one did," Chris said.

The time and place on the paper was 8:30 P.M. Leeland Swamp. The stick-figure drawing had breasts and hair. It was female.

"What time did you get to the swamp?" Leah asked.

"Around ten after six."

"So you had under two and a half hours to try to save this woman's life." She looked once again at the photo on the front page of the *Examiner,* her brain automatically filling in the missing details. A hideous sight. "Does she have a name? Our victim? Or do you just want me to keep referring to her as 'she'?"

Chris wiped his forehead with his right hand. He was starting to sweat in his uniform, even though Leah hadn't noticed an increase in temperature. "Abilene Williams. Married with two kids. She went missing around eight-forty-five after dropping her son off at school."

"So one of you at least went to her house and told her husband what happened?" It actually surprised Leah that they didn't leave that fun bit to her.

"Of course. Here." He handed the rest of the file folder to Leah. She flipped through it quickly. Copies of photos and sketches made at the scene. Reports. "It's all in here. Her husband was pretty frantic when we got to their house."

"That surprises you?" Leah knew what it was like to lose a spouse. Frantic didn't even come close to describing it. "Two and a half hours isn't nearly enough time to search that swampland, especially not for two people," she snapped. "You would've had a lot better chance with me helping. I should've been called."

"In retrospect, I agree."

"In retrospect, you and Ethan are assholes. What you two did last night is wrong on so many levels. The letter came to me, I should've been called *then*. And if not, once you opened it and you saw what it was, there should've been no question."

"I didn't open it, Ethan did."

Leah bit her tongue. "I know."

"We don't always make good decisions, Leah. We aren't perfect."

She let out a fake laugh. "No, you definitely aren't goddamn perfect. Don't worry, I know you wasn't the one making the orders. It's Montgomery who's goin' to get a piece of me. *If* he ever comes in."

Chris smiled. "He's probably 'fraid to."

"Don't smile. There ain't nothin' funny. A woman is dead, possibly because of dumb decisions made by this department."

Chris sipped his coffee. "Sure is hot outside," he said absently.

Leah just slinked down in her chair. "I should've been goddamn called."

CHAPTER 2

It wasn't long after Leah stopped being angry at Chris that the phone started going crazy.

Leah took the first call, from a woman who said she lived in Cloverdale and wanted to know if she should lock herself and her family in her house until the Stickman was caught. Leah did her best to console her, but the call kind of blindsided her. In hindsight, she should have expected it. And the twenty-five or so other ones that had come through since. Alvin was a small town. The Stickman was big news fifteen years ago. Folks were panicked then, and Leah certainly should have realized they'd panic now.

"No, I don't think there is any reason to be too concerned," she told the woman. "But yeah, I understand how you feel. No, right now we only have an isolated instance. We don't know for sure what we're looking at yet. No, I don't reckon it's the same Stickman. Yes, I am well aware that Harry Stork is dead. Well aware."

Two phone lines came into the station, and there were times when Leah and Chris had them both on hold while they tried to settle down. Near on every call went almost exactly the same way. That was until around twenty after nine. Then the real calls started coming in. Calls from the newspapers, radio stations, and the television news programs. Some from as far north as Huntsville. Everybody wanted an official statement about last night's murder. *Is this really the return of the Stickman? Did Joe Fowler—my very own Pa . . . could he possibly have killed the wrong guy?*

"That's it," Leah said to Chris after fumbling through a conversation with Nick Danger, a newsman from WAFF News, channel forty-eight out of Huntsville. Danger asked a lot of the same questions Leah had been asking herself. *Why have the murders started up again? Why a fifteen-year absence? Who really is the Stickman?* Of course, Leah had no answers. Her official statement was that she'd "release an official statement soon."

"Soon, as in hours? Days? Weeks?" Danger asked.

"I don't know right now."

"Well, people want to know what's happening."

"I realize that," Leah said. "We're being inundated with calls. Right now, we really don't know much more than you people do from reading the paper."

"Folks aren't goin' to find that very comforting."

"I'm afraid that's the way it is. I'm sorry, there's really nothing I can do other than tell you what you already know."

Danger eventually got off the phone. Reluctantly.

"What's it?" Chris asked. Both HOLD buttons were flashing.

"I can't do this anymore, Chris. You've gotta handle the calls. I need to read over the file you gave me from the murder last night. I need—I just have to stop talkin' to people. I'm goin' to lose it."

"So you expect *me* to take all the calls?"

"You know, it's kind of a little like justice after what you guys pulled last night."

"I thought we were past that," Chris said.

"Handle the calls and you'll be headin' a long way to getting there."

Chris's shoulders heaved while he let out a big sigh. "Fine."

Leah took the folder he'd given her and rolled her chair over to the coffee table. It probably wasn't as comfortable as sitting at her desk, but it was a few feet farther away from the phone. That counted for a lot.

She started going through the folder's contents, first looking at the sketches Chris had made of the scene and comparing them to the Polaroids. She could see where Abilene Williams's body had been found, staked into the soft dirt beneath a particularly large cypress tree about six feet from the edge of Leland Swamp. Unlike in the *Examiner,* these photos showed all the gory details. Leah's stomach clenched. The phones continued to ring as Chris answered one line, only to have to put it on hold to answer another. She tried to block him out, but between the telephones ringing and the gruesome photos and the nagging thought that her pa might've killed the wrong guy, Leah was having a hard time holding things together.

The Polaroids felt familiar after having listened to her pa talk about the crime scenes for so long. Many times, she listened from her room as he and Peter Strident spoke either in person or over the phone. Her pa always kept his voice low, almost in a whisper, but Leah had good ears and heard pretty near every word.

So she wasn't surprised at the grotesque way Abilene's body was wrenched backward and held up with the wooden stave. The top of the stake was mushroomed.

Even in the soft earth of the swampy edge, whoever killed her used something heavy to hammer it in. Maybe a rock. Maybe a sledgehammer. Leah looked closer at the Polaroid. The stake hadn't been driven into the dirt at all. The ground was probably too soft to hold the body up. Instead, the killer had hammered it into one of the gnarled roots of the cypress tree.

No wonder its top had been so mushroomed.

Just like the murders from fifteen years ago, there wasn't near on enough blood for the body to have been killed at the scene. She was shot somewhere else, a primary crime scene. What her pa used to refer to as "the slaughterhouse." It was the one piece of evidence he had so wanted to find and the one that wound up eluding him. According to his notes, finding the primary scene was the key to unlocking everything.

Leah wondered if that was still true and, if it was, how would she be able to find it when even her pa failed to? This part of the Stickman case reminded Leah of her last big case—one involving another serial killer. Only that one came to be known as the Maniac Tailor case on account of the way the killer stitched up the victim's eyes.

A shiver pulsed through her veins, like the feeling you got when you touched an electric fence. She was glad the Tailor case was behind her. Only, did anything ever really get left behind? For some reason, she could never put anything fully into the past. There were always parts dragged along behind her, like a heavy chain that only grew heavier and longer as new cases came up.

That chain added an intensity and a focus to her work that became sharper as time went by.

She went back to the report.

Chris noted that along with the blood, pieces of her

skull and other internal parts were missing, as well. Leah remembered what he said about her dropping her son off at school. That's when she'd gone missing, eight-thirty in the morning. The killer had lots of time to hog-tie and shoot her before bringing Abilene to that swamp.

In some ways, that made Leah feel a mite better about last night. Odds were, nobody could have found her alive, because she probably hadn't been alive when the letter was left at the door. But they still would've had a better chance of catching the son of a bitch.

Leah wondered how the killer had brought Abilene's body into the swamp area. It was surrounded by twisted cypress and strangler fig that fell hard against a dark and dense wood of birch and poplar. There was no way to drive in. The body would've had to have been carried, or brought in on a dolly or something like that.

She found more of Chris's notes explaining that there was a trail that opened near where they'd found the body. He'd figured that was the way the killer came in. The trail ran for five country blocks until finally leading out to one of the old logging roads still accessing parts of the forest. Chris walked the trail back to the road. Near the site, for about a block or so, it was narrow and he guessed the killer had carried Abilene through that part. But after that, it widened and Chris found a fresh wheel track running along it. In the photos it looked almost sunk into the moist, brown ground that was littered with pebbles and bits of broken stumps. Immediately, Leah suspected the same thing Chris had: The killer threw Abilene in a wheelbarrow after taking her out of his vehicle and wheeled her until the path became too narrow, then carried her the rest of the way, leaving the wheelbarrow behind to be fetched on his way back.

Chris and Ethan hadn't made out any tire tracks on

the side of the logging road. The gravel and dirt had been too hard-packed, so there was no guess as to what sort of vehicle the killer drove. Of course, depending on the size of the wheelbarrow, it could even be tossed into a trunk if the trunk was left open and tied down with bungees.

They did find boot prints. Not on the trail, but in the mud around Abilene's body. To Leah, the sole cast looked like some kind of hiking boot or maybe even a combat boot. They certainly weren't galoshes or anything like that.

Chris hung up the phone. For once, it had stopped ringing. "Oh my God!" he said. "Do you hear that? It's the sound of silence." He smiled.

Leah looked back at the photocopy of the Polaroid. "You got Mobile working on these boot prints?" she asked him.

"Yep. That's why you don't have the original Polaroid. It went down with all the other evidence we found. Not that there was much."

Leah found another Xerox of a Polaroid. "This a fingerprint?" she asked, squinting at it. The fact that it was a black and white copy made it hard to tell.

"We're not really sure. It looked like it might be, so we thought we'd give it a shot. If it is, it's only a partial."

"Better than nothin'."

The phones rang again. Leah gave Chris a sympathetic smile. "Just think how much character this is building," she said.

"Yeah, I could do without character." He picked up the phone. "Alvin Police. This is Officer Chris Jackson."

Leah rolled her chair back to her desk so she could

get her empty coffee cup. She was just about to roll it back to where she'd set up camp when Chris held the receiver away from his mouth and said, "Hey, it's Jacqueline Powers from the *Examiner*. She wants to speak to you."

Biting her lower lip, Leah looked past Chris to the framed newspaper page hanging on the wall. It was the front page of section two, where the *Alvin Examiner* always ran their "Spotlight on Success" article on Sundays. Each week, they picked some resident of Alvin and did an interview with them. The people were typically blue-collar workers and their stories usually revolved around what they did for work. A week and a half ago, Jacqueline Powers interviewed Leah, and Ethan had been so proud he immediately framed it. Ironically, much of the article was Leah talking about her pa. She'd even mentioned his success at finally solving the Stickman case. Ms. Powers thought that must have been his crowning achievement. Thinking about that now brought Leah a sigh. She hoped it would turn out to be a crown and not a jester hat.

Most of the article consisted of anecdotal bits. Jacqueline asked Leah how she managed to juggle the busy life of a cop with raising kids, to which Leah had responded that most of her time wasn't spent solving cases but going through files and doing data entry. Jacqueline laughed at this. But the reality was, in a small town like Alvin, there was a lot of downtime.

Then Ms. Powers asked about holidays, saying she knew at least one officer had to be assigned to work during things like the upcoming Fourth of July celebration.

Leah responded the truth, that usually those jobs fell to her, which meant for a long day spent without her family. She usually checked in to the station around eight and found herself back there after the festivities had mostly wound down, twelve to fourteen hours later.

It made for a very long workday.

As she responded, Leah felt a flip in her stomach because she knew her kids didn't *like* her being gone on special days. She hoped like heck Chris would actually be slotted for the Fourth. For once, she'd like to spend a holiday actually relaxing. Of course, she said none of that to Jacqueline Powers. Instead, Leah told her about how supportive and great her children were.

After that, thankfully, Powers's questions went back to things like police procedure and different cases Leah had worked on. Of course, she asked about the Cornstalk Killer and the more recent Maniac Tailor case. Like her pa before her, Leah *hated* the names the press liked to paste on things without thinking. The "case of the Maniac Tailor" bordered on ridiculousness.

But in the end, the published article not only put Leah and her pa in a very nice light, but it also did a good job of showcasing the entire Alvin Police Department. Now Leah felt like she owed Jacqueline Powers and felt obligated to talk to her.

"I'll take it," Leah said, resignedly. Lifting her phone's receiver, she took the call off of HOLD. "Hi, Jacqueline. It's Leah. How are you today? What do you think of this weather? Hot, hey? I've noticed a wind's picked up, though."

Right away, Leah knew Powers had no intention of talking about the weather. She got straight to the point. "Leah, I need you to answer some questions about last night's murder. Turns out the article we ran this morning scooped everybody else and now my phone's ringing off the hook for more details. I don't know what to tell anyone—"

Leah cut her off. "*Your* phones are ringing? You ain't heard ringing till you've come down here. It's nuts."

"Well, I guess my first question is, when will we get an official statement from your department?"

Leah let out a breath. "I really don't know. When we've got somethin' to state. Right now, we don't know any more than you do."

"I see. Do you think this is the same Stickman that was killin' folk fifteen years ago?"

Leah's head was shaking even though Powers couldn't see it. "I don't—no, I don't think it is. But it *could* be. I can't really give you an opinion on that at the moment. Again, we really don't—"

"Leah?" Powers asked, cutting her off this time.

"Yeah."

"Can we talk, like, off the record?"

"Um, sure. What's up?"

"You guys have to give the public something, or you're goin' to have hysteria on your hands. Everybody's thinking the worst. Like it's goin' to be a streak of killin's like before."

"There is no evidence to support that."

"The public doesn't care about evidence. They care about you telling them that they're goin' to be safe. If you can't, things will get out of control. Even if you have to lie, tell folk they're goin' to be safe. Do you understand what I'm sayin' here?"

"Yeah, I think I do. Point taken. I'll try to put a statement together."

"Good. In the meantime, do you honestly think this is *not* the same Stickman as before? Still off the record, of course."

Leah thought this over while her eyes scanned her "Spotlight on Success" article. She got to the part where

Powers referred to the case as her pa's "crowning achieve-ment," and she knew the answer to the question. "Yes," she said. "I honestly think this is *not* the same man. Harry Stork was the Stickman, and Harry Stork is dead. My pa killed the boogeyman. I'll issue a statement be-fore the end of the day."

Jacqueline Powers thanked her and Leah hung up the phone. *Even if you have to lie, tell folk they're goin' to be safe.* The words still rang in her ears.

Ethan finally decided to show up. He came in quietly (which wasn't hard with all the telephones ringing), opening the door slowly. Not that it mattered; Leah's desk sat eight feet from the door. She'd spotted Ethan through the window as he walked past on the sidewalk. At least he was earlier than his usual 11 A.M.: The clock had just clicked past nine-twenty-five.

Without so much as a "good morning" or even a "hello," Ethan marched straight past Leah and Chris and unlocked his office door. Leah thought she'd never seen a man move so fast while still give the semblance of walk-ing. His office door *clicked* quietly closed behind him before she heard the strain of his desk chair and the an-noying and unique squeak it made as he sat back in it, probably letting go of a deep breath he hadn't known he'd been holding.

Leah realized Chris was probably right: Ethan really was scared about what she was going to do. And well he should be, she thought. Ethan was in a bit of a tight squeeze. He couldn't very well fire her, not because she wasn't in the right for what she was about to do (she knew she was on pretty firm ground with this one), and not just because she was one of the only three people in all of Alvin trained to be a police officer. The big reason she felt so secure in her job was on account of Ethan and

Leah's daddy being such good friends while her pa was alive. So close, they were almost like blood. You don't fire blood. You get mighty pissed off at it sometimes, and may say things you later regret, but blood is blood. At the end of the day, you go home happy, and you've always managed to say your piece and clear your chest.

Leah's anger about what happened last night had all but dissipated while she had been performing the job of inputting data, but seeing Ethan strut right past her without saying a word brought the irritation right back like a wet slap in the face. Pulling one of her blond bangs down over her face, she let go and felt it spring back into place. Her time to act had come. She had a piece or two to say and some chest clearing to do.

But first things first. She stood and brought her empty mug to the coffee machine, which Chris had so nicely just brewed. Since this morning, he'd been on his best behavior, even doing data entry alongside her instead of crossword puzzles. In fact, since they finished their talk, both his boots had remained on the floor instead of up on his desk.

Carrying her mug of fresh coffee with her, Leah started for Ethan's door.

Chris hung up the phone. "Oh, I'm about to hear some cussing and screaming, aren't I?" he asked.

Leah stopped and looked back. "No, you're about to hear someone get blamed for somethin' they did wrong. I realize people make mistakes all the time, but some mistakes you can't come back from. Like this one. We have a dead woman on our hands who very well might still be alive if that one little mistake hadn't been made."

CHAPTER 3

Carry and Jonathon relaxed under the cherry trees in Carry's backyard. The boughs were hanging low from the weight of cherries. The fruit was plump and in bunches. Some had fallen, littering the ground. The sun gleaming from their skin made them look like perfect rubies. Abe had recently mowed the lawn, and the smell of fresh grass hung in the air. A crow flew across the open, clear sky cawing all the way. Off behind the yard a yellowhammer darted in and out of the oak trees, probably on the lookout for insects.

The still air that had started the day had changed. Even though it was later, the heat was much more tolerable on account of a wind that had picked up. It kept blowing Jonathon's red hair all sorts of different directions. Both he and Carry were wearing shorts and T-shirts. Carry's shirt was navy and she had on yellow shorts. Jonathon's shirt was black and he wore red shorts with white stripes up the sides.

"What a lazy day," Carry said. A burst of wind erupted and blew a pile of cherry leaves from beneath the tree into a small eddy before letting them land again. "Windy," Carry said, "but lazy." A cherry dropped from the tree, barely missing her head. She tucked a blond lock of hair behind her ear that had come free from her ponytail.

"I love lazy days," Jonathon said. Leaning over, he gave her a kiss. Not a kid's kiss like he'd given her six months ago when they first started dating, but a full-on relationship kiss, openmouthed and everything. Carry loved the way he kissed.

"Wow," Carry said, a smile spreading across her face. "Now I love lazy days, too." Above her head, a blackbird sat among the branches and leaves of the tree, singing a blackbird song. Every few minutes a gust of wind erupted and blew back its feathers.

"It really is beautiful to be alive in the summer, isn't it?" Carry asked.

Jonathon took a look at her, from head to toe. "*Now* it is. You make summer beautiful."

Carry playfully punched him in the stomach. "You are such a flirt. You always know exactly what to say."

"Well, that's good, isn't it?"

"I guess. Sometimes I think you've had a hundred girlfriends to practice on, you're so good at it."

"Yeah, that's me. Mr. Hundred Girlfriends." He leaned back. "Nope, I just fly by the seat of my pants. Besides, I told you, my family comes from a long line of romantics. Wait'll you meet my grandpa."

"I'm goin' to meet your grandpa?"

"Yeah, I think it's time."

"Well, you've definitely made my mother fall in love with *you*," she said.

The blackbird hopped to a lower branch, still singing.

"Can I ask you something?" Carry said.

"Anything, my love."

"Why do you never talk about your folks, only your grandpa?" She hesitated, then added: "If it's some sort of touchy subject, I'm really sorry for asking. I can't believe I've never asked you before."

"No," he said, sounding somber, "you're allowed to ask anything you want." He clapped his hands together. "Let's see, where to start? Well, my father is a drug addict. I have no idea where he is, but my ma took me away from the run-down little town we lived in up in Mississip and brought me here to Alabama. So I got away from Mississip *and* him. I don't reckon he has any clue what part of the country I'm even in."

Carry frowned. She wished she hadn't asked him. "That's harsh. So what about your ma?"

With a *click* of his tongue, Jonathon answered. "She was fine for a while, looking after me, getting me to school, holding down two jobs so she could afford rent and groceries, but it became too much for her. She had a nervous breakdown. She's in Satsuma in a long-term care facility. I see her sometimes. Like, every month or, I don't know, two. I can't even remember if I've seen her since we started going out. It's fine. She has her own life and I don't mind how it worked out. I like living with my grandpa. I think you'll like him, too."

The wind picked up again. Suddenly, a loud noise rose from the other side of the house. It sounded like a jet engine. The blackbird jolted out of the tree and flapped away.

Carry's heart hammered in her chest. Both she and Jonathon got up to a sitting position. She looked at him and saw the same thing she felt: terror.

Then something did come over the house. At first it came so quick Carry couldn't make out what it was. Then she started to calm down. It turned out to be the most bastardized version of a kite she had ever seen.

"What in God's name is that?" Jonathon asked, getting up. Carry stood beside him.

They watched the thing quickly soar above the oak trees out back, growing smaller and smaller. The yellowhammer darted away. A flock of sparrows burst from the trees like black darts being thrown across a clear blue sky.

"I don't know, but I have a pretty good idea who's behind it," Carry said once her heart slowed down.

Both of them ran to the front of the house. They went so fast, Jonathon hit his side on the handlebar of Dewey's bike. When they made it to the front yard, sure enough there was Abe and Dewey standing with their eyes focused over the house. Dewey had a roller in his hand. There was no string on the roller.

"What the hell are you doing?" Carry asked Abe.

"We just built Dewey's newest invention and it actually worked!"

"It was a kite!" Dewey said. "A really good one! Did you see it go?"

Jonathon came up, still holding his bruised side.

"What happened to you?" Carry asked him.

"I hit Dewey's handlebars on my rush around the house."

"You okay?"

"I will be. Just give me a minute."

"Want me to kiss it better?" Carry asked.

"Maybe later," Jonathon said.

"I think the kite worked a little *too* good, Abe," Dewey said.

"What do you mean?"

"Look." He showed Abe the empty roller in his hand. "I'm not sure if the string just wasn't tied to the roller or if it just snapped when it got to the end."

"You mean you don't have control of it?"

"No, it's gone."

"What the hell was that thing made of?" Jonathon asked. "It sounded like a damn lion coming over the house."

"We constructed it from cedar two-by-fours and industrial-strength plastic we found in Abe's ma's garage," Dewey said.

"And you managed to get it to fly?" Jonathon asked, still holding his side.

"I knew it would. I did the calculation."

"How much did it weigh?"

Dewey did another calculation. "I reckon 'round 'bout five, maybe six pounds."

"And you no longer have the end of the string?"

"No," Dewey said sullenly. "I don't think I calculated string tension properly."

"That kite's goin' to come down and kill someone!" Carry said.

"It's definitely goin' to scare someone," Jonathon said. "I sure hope it doesn't hit anyone or come down on a car or nothing. Especially if someone's driving when it happens."

Carry walked over to Jonathon and hugged him from behind. They all just stood there, looking at each other.

Abe turned to Dewey. "I think we should go see my ma."

Dewey looked away. "Do I have to come?"

"You're the *reason* we're goin'. To find out what to do about your little 'invention'."

CHAPTER 4

Here we go, Leah thought. *You have something to say, girl, and it's best be said. No point in letting rust grow on it.*

She opened the door to Ethan's office without even knocking—something she *never* did. Ethan Montgomery was a big man, with a full head of brown hair and sideburns. The rest of his face was clean shaven. He had a big voice to fit the rest of him, and when he was mad, you knew it. Right now, his voice wasn't so big.

"Since when in hell do you have the right to just march into my office?" he asked Leah. He sat behind his huge oak desk. So big, Leah often wondered how it had ever fit through the door.

"Well, I guess we've all just stopped following rules, maybe? You reckon so, Ethan?"

"Now, what in the Sam Hill are you talking about?"

Leah still held her coffee cup in her hands. She was standing, looking down on him in his plush and noisy chair. "You know exactly what I'm goddamn talkin' about. I'm talkin' about a dead woman who might not be dead today if our 'police chief' had more brains."

Ethan pointed a finger at her. "Now, you just watch

your respect, little girl. And for Christ's sake, close the door. Chris doesn't need to hear all this."

"I agree!" Chris yelled from his desk.

"Oh, I already gave him a piece of my mind." A phone started ringing. Leah heard it mainly from her and Chris's desk outside of Ethan's office. The phone on Ethan's desk rang much quieter than the other two.

"*Please* close the door?" Ethan asked, and gestured toward the two empty chairs across from him. "And have a seat, for Christ's sake?"

She paused a moment and decided to acquiesce. She closed the door so hard the blinds on it shook. Only the outside wall directly opposite Ethan had its blinds open. Sun flooded the front of the office like water pouring out of a summer sprinkler. The view showed a portion of the sidewalk, Main Street, the edge of Applesmart's Grocery, and a lone fig tree planted just outside the glass. That fig tree had grown immensely since Leah first joined the force thirteen years ago.

To Ethan's left bookshelves spanned the entire wall, covering the blinds and any view of the outside. Law books stuffed those shelves, not quite as tightly as the binders in the main office. Leah reckoned Ethan hadn't ever opened even one of those books. They were there to make him look smart. She wondered if it fooled anyone.

Usually, other than the pictures, Ethan's desktop was kept clean. Today it had a foot-high stack of file folders on it. Leah decided not to ask about them. She was too pissed off.

The *real* telltale giveaway about the man was the television mounted on the ceiling in the far corner of the room. Ethan sat in his office watching sports of every assortment near on all day long. The thought struck Leah that maybe she was the only employee who took her police work seriously. She decided to leave this thought to herself, though. Things were about to get pretty bad, and comments like that would just cause the fire to blaze even higher.

Currently the television set was dark and turned off. But then, she'd only given Ethan a few minutes to get comfortable.

Leah sat down, choosing the seat closest to the door. It didn't really matter which one she'd picked—both were uncomfortable and low, especially compared to the plush chair Ethan sat in. Maybe he thought it gave him an air of authority. Well, today she'd show him what authority really meant even without a cushy chair.

Ethan leaned back with a loud squeak. Today, that squeak especially bothered her. "When are you goin' to fix that GD chair of yours?"

"What's it to you?"

"I have to sit here and listen to it, that's what it is to me. Christ, if you won't do it, I'll call someone in to do it this afternoon. Or maybe tomorrow before you get in. That would give him *lots* of time."

Something flashed in Ethan's eyes, and she knew she'd hit a nerve. He leaned forward with another squeak. His big arms came halfway across his desk, which had pictures of his family and even some of Leah's family sitting along the edge. That's how close Ethan and Leah's pa had been. Almost family.

"Now, you listen here, Leah," Ethan said, lowering his voice and keeping it calm and steady. "I know you're mad, but I will not take you talking to me in this tone. Now, get on with whatever you came in here to get on with so we can just move past it."

Hearing him talk so quiet and calmly practically unnerved Leah. It was almost enough to make her apologize for wasting his time and ask to be excused so she could go back to her desk.

Almost, but not quite.

She did find herself shaking slightly, though, especially the hand holding her coffee mug. She decided the quicker she finished drinking it so she could set the mug on the floor, the better.

"You let a woman die last night," she said. "Well, she was probably already dead, but you had a chance of catching the killer."

"No, we didn't *let* anything happen," Ethan said. "We found her too late."

"You should've called *me.* Christ, I could've called Dan down. God knows he can get here in an hour the way that man drives. You and Chris didn't have time to search that swamp by yourselves."

"This isn't part of Dan's jurisdiction," Ethan said at last. He swallowed and Leah could tell his mouth was dry. She bet he wished he'd gotten a coffee on his way in after all.

"When in hell's name did we start worrying about jurisdiction? I thought we was here to *save lives.* Seems to me, if that's our main objective, we failed pretty much completely last night. And you didn't *have* to."

"You're right, we didn't. But we decided not to call you out of respect for your daddy."

"First," Leah said, "there is no *we,* Ethan. You call the shots, so take responsibility for it. *You* decided not to call me. And how in the hell was that respecting my pa at all?"

"We thought you'd get too emotional. We know how much your pa and the rest of you at home were affected by the Stickman the first time 'round."

"By 'the rest of you' I'm assuming you mean my ma on account of there was nobody else around?"

"Now, don't go making trouble where there is none. I didn't leave your ma out as any form of disrespect. I apologize for the oversight. Now, we were talkin' 'bout the Stickman murder last night?"

"This *isn't* the Stickman. The Stickman is *dead,* Ethan. I all but saw the body, I heard my pa tell that story so many times."

"Well, if it ain't the real Stickman, it's someone who knows his MO perfectly *and* his signature. I assume Chris told you about the letter?"

Leah nodded. "He did. Glad *someone* did."

"Figures. Well, whoever killed this victim also knew to send the letter ahead of time, something we managed to conceal from the press."

"You mean the letter addressed to *me?* The one *I* should have opened?"

Ethan let out a huge sigh. "It's more complicated than that. And you weren't here to open it."

"How in God's name could this be any more cut-and-dried? You went on a hunt with two-thirds of your team when you didn't *need* to. I should've been called."

Ethan swiveled his chair sideways. It was hot in his office. A wooden fan spun slowly from the ceiling's center, but so slowly it didn't seem to offer any breeze. And it always spun, whether it was winter, spring, summer, what have you. Leah often wondered the purpose of it.

She took a big sip of coffee and looked back out at the street. A mockingbird sat on one of the boughs of the fig tree, its white wing patches and feathers standing out brightly in the summer sun.

Ethan gently drummed his fingers on his desk. He

hadn't responded for a while, and if he was angered at all by what Leah was saying, she couldn't tell. She was calming down. "Well then," she asked, "tell me, who do *you* reckon did it?"

"At this point, we have to believe it's the same Stickman we were after fifteen years ago. Everything about the killin' matches perfectly. I haven't heard back from Mobile, but to me, even the handwriting in the letter matches."

This struck a part of Leah's brain like a mallet hitting a timpani. "How can you—whoever's doin' your 'handwriting analysis' in Mobile . . . He's *in* on the secret. He has to be."

Ethan ignored her. "We're not talkin' 'bout that. We're talkin' 'bout the Stickman."

"The Stickman was Harry Stork and Stork's dead. My pa shot him."

"I agree that your pa shot Harry Stork. What I'm starting to reckon is that maybe Stork wasn't the Stickman after all."

Leah's "tone" came back. "Yes, he was. My pa was certain of it. He was on that case goin' on the long part of a year and six months. He got it right."

Ethan put up his hands. "I am not putting down your daddy in any way. That case near on killed him. Every new death weighed him down. In the end, the total was what? Nine victims? That's a lot of extra weight to be carryin' around."

"And then," Leah said, "Pa shot Harry Stork, and, lo and behold, the killin's ended. There were no more Stickman murders."

"Until last night." He lowered his voice. "There's more you don't know. Stuff nobody knows except me and your pa and, I think, Peter Strident."

Leah shook her head, slack-jawed. "How much stuff am I goin' to get dumped on me today?"

"This is stuff your pa just didn't want anyone to know on account of how it would've made him look. In fact, I can tell you right now, after it all went down, your daddy started wondering if he'd made a mistake. The kind of mistake you don't come back from."

"And what mistake might that be?" Leah asked.

"Shooting Stork dead. Your pa started thinking later that maybe he wasn't the Stickman."

"He never told me that. Besides, he shot out of self-defense. Harry pointed his gun at him."

Ethan leaned forward and whispered, "The gun's magazine was empty. No bullets. Not one."

"What?" Leah asked, astonished. Why had her pa never told her this? "Did he have one chambered?"

"Nope. Empty magazine, empty chamber." Ethan dropped his voice even more. "There's more," he said.

"I don't know that I can handle much more, Ethan."

"The last thing Harry Stork said before dying was that he had been set up. That he was a patsy."

"Then why did he continue to point his weapon at my pa? Unloaded or not? My pa had no way of knowing that."

Ethan shrugged, shaking his head. "That's a question your pa tackled with many years after that night at that shotgun shack."

Leah took another drink of coffee, considering everything she just heard. "Okay, so let's say for argument's sake Harry Stork wasn't the Stickman and the real Stickman's still out there. Why did he wait fifteen years to start killin' again?"

"I can't answer that, either. All I can say is the MO

and signature were perfect. Dead-on," Ethan said. "No pun intended, by any means."

"Maybe Harry Stork told someone how he did it before he died?" Leah offered.

"Maybe. Or maybe Harry Stork wasn't the Stickman. Leah, the simplest answer is usually the right one. It's why folk like things simple. Why complicate it? Harry Stork wasn't the Stickman. Your pa shot the wrong guy."

"I can't accept that." She felt tears sting the back of her eyes. "I can't accept that what Jacqueline Powers called 'the Holy Grail of his career' might be a . . . a mistake. This is my pa's legacy you're running down. I can't accept it." She shook her head, trying not to cry. "I can't, Ethan. I just can't."

"Well, until we capture whoever murdered that woman last night, you're goin' to have to consider the possibility. But for God's sake, don't let this case eat your life away like your pa did."

She wiped her eyes. "You keep puttin' down my pa and I'm goin' to quit."

Ethan raised a palm. "For Christ's sake, Leah, I'm not puttin' Joe down. He was one of the best men I've ever worked with. He just let things get to him the way I've seen them get to you. You've got to be able to go home and take off the badge."

"The letter was addressed to me, goddamnit," Leah said. "I should've been called."

"I know. And now I wish we had."

"I hope you do, because in my opinion, some of that poor dead woman's blood is on your hands for making stupid decisions."

"Again, I ask you to watch how you respect me."

Leah hesitated and took a deep breath. "You know, I'd like to call you a horse's ass right now."

"Well, I appreciate you not doing that," Ethan said. "Fighting ain't goin' to get us nowhere. Anyway, there's somethin' else I wanna tell you. I assume Chris told you about the final letter fifteen years ago?"

"The one with Harry Stork's initials on it?"

He nodded. "The letters always pointed to victims. Dead ones. But there was no victim in that shack, Leah. Just Stork. And I have a theory 'bout that."

"What's your theory?"

"That the tenth victim was Harry Stork."

A laugh escaped Leah's lips before she could stop it. It sounded nervous. "You mean it was all a game? He *knew* he would be shot?"

"Or someone did, and set him up. Someone convinced him the police were goin' to kill him whether he surrendered or not."

"So he committed suicide by cop?"

"Pretty much, yeah. Your pa was already after him. Stork knew that. Maybe he *was* the Stickman and he'd had enough of being a slave to his emotions. Maybe he just wanted the madness to stop and figured death was the only way out. Maybe he just got tired of looking over his shoulder, hoping Joe Fowler wouldn't be there, ready to take him down. If that's the case, he became his own victim."

"Okay," Leah said, watching the fan on the ceiling slowly turn. "I can buy most of this. But it still doesn't explain who's doing the killin' now. Besides, Chris told me Mobile figured that last note was written by someone else."

Ethan turned up his palms with another shrug.

"Knowing that Harry Stork got his wish when my pa shot him down really does nothin' to progress the case. What drew my pa to Stork in the first place?"

"Lots of things," Ethan replied, tapping the foot-high stack of folders on his desk. "Two eyewitnesses reported seeing his company truck at the scene of the ninth victim. We found tire marks in the mud at two other scenes that turned out to be potential matches for that same vehicle. Before that, someone who knew Harry's twin brother, Tommy, reported seeing him at a scene. The fact that he saw Tommy in profile and couldn't remember seeing the scar on his face made us figure they might have been describing Harry. He later pulled Harry out from a photo lineup."

"Harry Stork has a twin brother? Identical twin?"

Ethan nodded. "Except Tommy has a scar on his face and is missing two of his fingers. That's why I mentioned the witness reported only seeing him in side profile. He wouldn't have seen the scar. You'll see it all in the reports. That whole family looks the same, even the old man. There's more evidence supporting Harry being the killer. Here's a big one: Victim number four all the way up to the last, every single person killed worked in hospitals. Harry had a waste removal company that did jobs for four of those six places." He tapped that big stack of files again and repeated, "You'll find everything in the reports."

"Those are all the case files?"

"Pretty much everything you'll want is here. Pictures of evidence, witness reports, background checks, medical records, pictures of the crime scenes, notes your daddy made over that year and a half, everything. You name it, it's here."

"That's a lot of paperwork."

Ethan nodded again. "I pulled it all for you last night. All the physical evidence is down in Mobile, but there's copies of everything they had on microfiche that we didn't. You should be fine with just this."

"'Just this,' hey? I'll be lucky to get through all that by Christmas."

"I agree, it's a lot of work."

Leah looked back out the window behind her. The mockingbird in the fig tree was gone, and now the tree just stood all alone, bending slightly in the wind. At least the air wasn't still anymore. Christ, looking at the leaves blowing along the sidewalk, it looked downright windy.

A thought struck Leah. "I was only eighteen during the original Stickman murders, but Pa used to come home and talk about nothin' else. Do you remember a guy who came forward claiming to be the Stickman? I don't think he was ever taken seriously."

"Yeah," Ethan said.

"What was that guy's name? It was something like . . ."

"Thomas Kennedy Bradshaw," Ethan said, flatly. The name had obviously crossed his mind lately for him to pull it from his memory banks so easily. "And he didn't just come forward once, he tried to convince us of his guilt three separate times. The last one was just after we searched Stork's house and your pa put out a statewide search for him. About a week after that, Stork's truck— camper and all—was found in the bottom of Cornflower Lake. We *still* have no idea why it was there or who put it there. We're assuming it was Harry."

"Weird. Why was Bradshaw not taken seriously?"

"Simple. We asked him to show us the murder weapon.

We knew what we were looking for; if he had it, we'd have believed him."

"But he didn't?"

Ethan shrugged. "Said he did. Said he'd bring it in with him and then we wouldn't see him again until the next time he decided to go wacko. There were other discrepancies, too. We did a handwriting analysis on him, comparing his writing to the letters coming in."

"Not a match?"

"Not even to a blind man. And he hadn't even truly done his homework by reading the papers. Simple details about the case that were public knowledge he couldn't answer. We told the papers we found the actual gun during the raid on Stork's house, but when Bradshaw came in that last time he still told us not to worry, he'd come back with the murder weapon. Of course he didn't, and that was the last we saw of him."

"So, it wasn't a hard leap to decide that—"

Ethan nodded, cutting her off. "Deciding that he was nuts?" he asked. "No, not at all. I think he finally did go to the joint eventually, for armed robbery or somethin', but it had nothin' to do with the Stickman. If I remember, they put him away for six years, probably did four if he behaved himself. I'm sure it's in the reports, but just for clarity reasons, ask Chris to get you new information."

"I am capable of doing paperwork," Leah said.

He slowly shook his head. "This is goin' to be a big case, Leah. You are starting out so far behind the eight ball. You have a year and a half of killin's and investigation and evidence and all sorts of things you need to concentrate on. Use Chris all you can. The man's good, at his desk. He's not as good as you are in the field."

"Thanks. I just had a thought. What if Bradshaw actually *was* the Stickman, and had some disorder that made him confused?"

"Anything's possible, I guess," Ethan said. "Anyway, you'll find some information about him in the files, but there are lots of files and they all date back to 1974. Make sure you get Chris to pull something recent before you go confronting Bradshaw."

"Well, since I had no suspect when I walked in here, I think Thomas Kennedy Bradshaw just rose to the top of my list."

"I don't think he'll stay there long. He's been out of the bucket for years, unless he went back. Why start up killin' again, now? Besides, I'm willing to bet you still find him nuts. That boy was nuttier than Christmas cake." Ethan turned his chair with another annoying squeak.

"You really need to fix that if you want me to keep coming in here."

"Right now, I'm on the fence 'bout that."

Leah let a deep breath go. "All right, so just so I'm straight on this, you don't think the Stickman slaughtering nine, well, ten, now—maybe—you don't think that's nuts?"

"Different kind of nuts than Bradshaw. The Stickman knew what he was doing. His crime scenes were always carefully set up. Rarely did he make a mistake and leave any viable evidence behind. He was what those FBI guys call 'organized.' Probably the two biggest leads we had in the case for the longest time came from rounds that had become lodged in two victim's skulls and Norm was able to retrieve them."

"Norm, the ME?" she asked. "He was the medical examiner even back then? How old is that man?"

"I dunno, I think we're having a contest. Who can just work his entire life and die on the job first. Some days, I believe he's gonna win."

"So what kind of nuts is Bradshaw?" Leah asked.

"I doubt the man could operate a Slurpee machine without assistance."

Leah laughed. "Well, if what you're saying's all true, and this is the work of the actual Stickman, there's been two injustices done," Leah said.

"You think? And what might those be?"

"A woman died last night whose killer might very well have been captured if you'd called me in to help, and Harry Stork might possibly have been wrongly accused, hunted, and shot for a crime he didn't really commit."

Ethan paused at those words. "With that last one, always remember that your pa made decisions based on evidence and his protection. We had a lot of evidence against Stork, and when it came down to that fateful night, your pa had absolutely no way of knowing Stork hadn't put any bullets in his gun.

"And even Stork yelling for Joe not to shoot, telling him he was a patsy being set up—it didn't matter, Stork still didn't drop that weapon. Your pa thought his life was in danger. He did what the book says to do. And the fact is, he wasn't trying for a kill shot, at least that's what he told me and I have no reason to believe otherwise. He was trying for Stork's arm—the one holding the gun."

She shook her head. "This unloaded gun thing doesn't sit well with me at all. Why would Stork even bother carryin' a gun with no bullets? It makes no sense. And if it's unloaded anyway, why not just drop it?"

"Your pa gnawed on that very question a lot throughout the years following Harry Stork's death. Said he'd never felt closure on the case, figured he'd missed something. Something big and maybe obvious, I don't know."

"Maybe Stork wasn't aware the magazine was empty."

"You've felt the weight difference between a loaded nine millimeter and an empty one. Pretty easy to tell."

Leah clacked her tongue. "So, we're right back to square one," she said. "If not Stork, then who? From what I've heard, I tend to agree with you about Bradshaw. Of course, I haven't met him yet, that could change. Like you said, even with the penitentiary sentence, it leaves a whole lotta years unaccounted for. So either an old killer has suddenly come back to once again take up his long-forgotten hobby, or a new killer has started up out of nowhere. And from what I know about profiling, one of the first things you want to establish is the event that caused the behavior to start. Nobody just gets up one day and thinks, *Gee, I think I'll buy a gun and take up a new hobby. I like to travel.* And another thing: Did the police ever establish motive with Harry Stork?"

Ethan took a deep breath. "We managed to assemble enough evidence to satisfy a judge into issuing a warrant. We tossed his house and found the murder weapon."

"Do you remember the evidence that got you the warrant?" Leah asked. "Just give me the high points." She had her notebook in her lap and was taking a lot of notes.

"Well, let's see. Harry's business handled medical waste management and he had a handful, I don't know— maybe a half-dozen, major contracts with hospitals around Alabama. Now, don't quote me on this, but I believe every victim from number four onward worked in hospitals or in the medical field somewhere."

A tingle ran up Leah's neck. The evidence against Stork was growing. She wanted to see how big of a pile it would make. "And Harry Stork did work for all those different places?" she asked.

"No," Ethan said, bringing his palms down on his desk. "There were two hospitals we weren't able to link him to. The others he had contracts with and did work for them on a fairly regular basis."

"Okay, I'm startin' to see how you got the warrant."

"Well, what really nailed that for us were the statements we got from those two independent eyewitnesses. They claimed to have seen Stork's work vehicle parked along the edge of Tucker Mountain Pass way down south. The time correlated with the guesstimate made by the medical examiner as to when the body was dumped. The location where the eyewitnesses claimed to have seen Stork's truck was right beside a path leading into the woods we'd already determined the suspect had carried the body down."

Leah took this all in. "That *is* a lot of evidence, for sure. Enough that you've managed to pretty much convince me that this'll all work out fine. Harry Stork had to be the Stickman. This new murder is someone else."

"Just wait," Ethan continued, "there's more. Like Stork going sub rosa immediately after we tossed his house and found the murder weapon. Forensics determined it to be the one used to kill all nine victims."

"He just disappeared?" Leah let out a slight chuckle. "Isn't that practically an admission of guilt?"

Ethan's eyebrows went up.

Leah thought all this over some more. "So, I s'pose my job is to prove Harry Stork *was* the original Stickman and to figure out how our new guy got inside information and why."

Ethan nodded. "Might be a fine approach to it. But, word of advice." Ethan began carefully selecting his words. "Try not to be too influenced by your not wanting any tarnish to fall upon your pa's legacy. We all know solving the original Stickman case was his biggest success. Christ, you made sure everybody knew that during your interview with the *Examiner*."

"Yeah," Leah said quietly, scanning the floor at her feet. "That's goin' to be the tricky part. It's hard not to be biased."

"Well, if it helps, I reckon we'll find out this is a different Stickman. Fifteen years is just too long, unless this guy spent it locked away somewhere doing time for another crime and only just now got out."

"Not a bad theory," Leah said.

Ethan let out a big breath, his fingers tapping on top of his desk. Leah could tell he was trying to decide whether or not to tell her something. How much more could there be?

"What?" she asked.

"I dunno. It's just something your pa told me a couple of days after Stork went down. He told me he didn't feel right 'bout the way the case wound up. Too many loose ends were left untied."

"Like why Stork said he was set up?"

"Yeah, there's that, and . . ."

"And . . . ?"

"And your pa never did find the primary crime scene where the victims were kept and, as far as the medical examiner was concerned, were killed. Your pa always thought the key to breaking the whole thing wide open was to find that primary scene. He kept calling it—"

"The slaughterhouse," she finished, cutting Ethan off.

Ethan sat back. "Now, how'd you know what I was goin' to say?"

"Remember, Ethan, I lived through that case, too. For a year and a half it consumed my pa's life. I couldn't help but absorb some of it, just by pure osmosis."

They both sat, silently thinking for a moment.

"You know," Ethan said, "if I were you, I'd check all the nearby federal penitentiaries and correctional institutions. Just ask who's been recently released."

Leah wrote this on her pad.

"'Course, there is yet another possibility."

"What's that?" she asked

"We're seeing the work of someone taught to kill by Harry Stork before Stork died. Someone he'd confided in."

"Another interestin' idea. How do I cover that?"

Ethan shrugged. "Ask around at these same institutions. Ask if they have any talkers who like to collect information. There's usually one or two inmates with a knack for gettin' other criminals to cough up details of their crimes. 'Talkers' like these then squirrel that information away somewhere until the time comes when it might be valuable."

"Thanks. That's good advice. Only, I doubt any of 'em will talk to me."

Ethan shrugged again. "You've got nothin' to lose. You're gettin' better at interrogatin'." Leah's station only recently added an interview room, and she still hadn't done any sort of *real* interrogations. "Just try your best," Ethan added.

"My best isn't so good." Her confidence in the matter was a mite shaky.

Ethan went on. "Just try to get names. Then check them out, thoroughly. I still reckon your best bet, though, is to find which inmates were recently released, say, in the past six months or so. I figure the killer would need time to adjust to freedom before startin' to kill again."

"Yeah," Leah said. "I like that. It's not a bad theory."

"We run this shop on 'not bad theories,'" Ethan said.

Leah laughed a little, surprised her anger had faded so quick. "I told Jacqueline at the *Examiner* I'd issue a statement before the day's end."

"What the hell will you say? We're as befuddled as everyone?"

"No, Powers read me the riot act. Said folks will grow hysterical if I didn't say something soon. She said even if I have to lie, I gotta make everyone at least *believe* we're on top of things and that they're all safe."

"She's a smart one," Ethan said. "I'd advise listenin' to her."

"I know, I just hate making stuff up. Seems so . . . dishonest."

"Well," Ethan said, "maybe now you'll find out the truth. Get Chris to run some checks on Thomas Kennedy Bradshaw. Everything he can find: background, medical, employment, anything applicable. Also, you'll likely find a fair bit on the man in here." Again, he placed his hand on top of the imposing stack of reports. "His damn *name* makes him even *sound* like a serial killer."

Leah finished her coffee. It had gotten cold. Outside, the mockingbird returned, along with a friend. Now there were two.

"Findin' out the truth," Leah said with a sigh, allowing the idea to settle in.

Ethan nodded. "At the end of the day, truth's all we're ever really looking for. Funny how elusive it can be, yet it shouldn't. Just remember, usually the simplest answer's probably the right one."

Leah bit her lower lip. "Know what?" she asked. "I reckon, I might not be ready yet to know the truth."

CHAPTER 5

Me and Dewey rode our bikes to the police station to tell my mother that Dewey might have killed someone with his kite. I figured it was something she should know about, not just because she was my mother, but also because she was a police officer.

The ride along Cottonwood Lane and down Hunter Road was nice, although I could tell Dewey felt uneasy. Alvin was a really pretty town. I doubted many other towns were as pretty as Alvin, but then I hadn't been to many other towns except Satsuma, and all Satsuma did was remind me of middle school, which I didn't want to go back to after summer break. It wasn't that I hated school, it was just that it took up so much of my time. Especially the bus ride there and back. Me and Dewey could always find things to do that would be better than that bus ride. Heck, hunting squirrels with slingshots was better than that bus ride.

Hunter Road was such a steep hill we just coasted down it. Pretty little houses nestled in the woods on either side. Most had old-fashioned porches and window shutters. Near on all of them had gardens full of flowers. We rode past Mr. Harrison's Five-and-Dime and rang our bells to say hello, but I don't think he heard us, on account of he never came out and waved. He was probably with a customer.

At the bottom of the hill, we took a left on Main Street and rode on to the police station, passing by the library first. The Alvin Library looked very similar to the Alvin Courthouse at the other end of Main Street—both had big white marble steps that led up to brick buildings— only there were no lion sculptures at the library, just a statue of someone sitting and reading a book. Apparently, it was someone famous, but I couldn't remember who.

Most all the shops down Main Street had their doors open, probably trying to take advantage of the wind that had finally picked up. That same wind may have caused someone to die from Dewey's killer kite.

I wasn't too worried about coming clean to my mother about Dewey's kite. After all, it was his idea and his fault the string broke. What kind of a moron goes to all that work to design something like that and then forgets to figure out what weight of string he'll need?

Dewey, that's what kind.

We arrived at the police station and set our bikes up against the shrubs that grew along the outside window. A butterfly had been fluttering about them and flew away when our bikes came down on the branches. Those shrubs always seemed to attract lots of butterflies.

When we walked inside, I could tell my mother was stressed about something. Now I was a little worried. Generally she didn't like being bothered when something else was on her mind. Maybe this wasn't such a good idea after all.

"What are you two doin' here?" she asked. There was

no "happy to see you" in her voice and I really got the feeling we maybe should've waited.

"Um, we came to tell you somethin' that might be important," I said.

Dewey just looked at his shoes.

"Dewey," my mother said. "Why in God's name are you dressed for a Siberian winter?" She had finally looked up from the huge stack of folders she had in front of her.

"It's all the clothes his ma washed," I said.

My mother rolled her eyes. "Aren't you sweatin' buckets?"

Dewey said nothing. Just stood there, sweating buckets.

"Well, what's so important?"

"Well . . . I think Dewey should tell you."

But Dewey just stood there, studying the floor.

"Come on, boys," my mother said, "I haven't got all day."

"We built a kite," Dewey mumbled, so quiet I barely heard him.

"You did what now?" Leah asked.

He finally looked up and into my mother's eyes. "We built a kite."

I didn't like the "we" he kept throwing into his sentences. So I clarified. "Dewey *made* us construct a kite," I said. I noticed I was talking a mite fast.

"I didn't *make* us do anythin'," Dewey said.

"Will one of you tell me why you're here about a kite?"

"Well," Dewey said, "this wasn't no regular kite."

"We built it out of two-by-fours we found in the garage. And used some of the industrial-strength plastic he had lying around."

"Okay. So you made a kite too heavy to fly. That was silly." My mother went back to the papers in the top folder on that ridiculously high stack. There must've been fifty of them. Well, at least a dozen. "Still doesn't explain to me why you're here," she added, without looking up.

"The kite wasn't too heavy to fly," Dewey said, pulling out his notebook. "I made sure I did all the calculations necessary. And we caught a good wind."

"Your kite flew?" my mother asked absently. "I'm impressed."

Dewey scratched the back of his head. "Tell her," I said.

"No, *you* tell her," Dewey said back.

Finally my mother looked up at us again. "Will *one* of you please tell me? I'm quite busy, as you may or may not have noticed."

"Dewey's kite took off like a twister. It went way above the oaks in our backyard. It went so fast it ran out of string real quick."

"And . . . ?" my mother asked.

"And the string broke from the roller," Dewey said, again examining the tiles on the floor. "Or it was maybe never attached. I dunno."

There was a hesitation while my mother processed this information and I knew we were in for it.

"What did I tell you about following stupid, Abe?" she asked. "And I'm sure Dewey didn't *make* you do nothin'."

I kicked at the floor. Behind me, the watercooler burbled.

"It went really good," Dewey said, apparently trying to impress her before she got mad.

"I don't care how it went. How much did it weigh?"

"Five or six pounds," Dewey said, almost sounding delighted he finally had a question he could answer.

"And the string snapped when?"

"Right at the end of the roller," Dewey said. "Three hundred feet out."

"First," my mother said, "get that smile off your faces, both of you. Second, that puts our danger zone into Blackberry Trail, which is nicely populated with Douglas fir and pines, so you might've gotten lucky. I'm goin' to send Chris out to see if he can find it." She turned to Officer Chris. "Can you do that for me? I need to keep working on finding an answer to someone else's mistake."

I wondered who she was talking about, but from her tone of voice I knew it was best not to ask. It was almost like she was mad at Officer Chris for something. I think we picked a bad day to have a kite catastrophe.

"What about the phones?"

She shook her head. "Just let them ring. We're on a phone break."

"All right," Officer Chris said slowly. "I guess I'll go kite huntin'." He spread his hands wide. The tips of his fingers were almost pink.

"And please, take the boys with you," my mother said.

He picked up his hat from his desk. "May I ask why?"

"Two reasons. First, they saw what direction it took off in, and second, and most importantly, they deserve to spend the rest of their afternoon bored. At least you're paid to look up in trees. They're not."

"Understood," Officer Chris said.

CHAPTER 6

Once Chris left with the boys, Leah decided not to think about Dewey's damn kite any longer. She had enough on her plate with this new Stickman murder. There were so many questions going through her head, it felt like it might explode. And now she had to come up with some sort of official statement about the murder scene she didn't even get called in on last night.

She needed some advice and, probably, some emotional backup, too. So, after pouring herself a fresh cup of coffee, she called the man she'd been dating the past six months, Detective Dan Truitt, from the Birmingham Police Station.

"Well, hello, sexy," Dan said, answering her call. Obviously he had caller ID on his phone, something Leah didn't have the luxury of yet.

"I'm afraid this isn't a social call, Dan," Leah said.

"What's up?"

She told him about last night's murder.

"Yeah, it wasn't in this morning's paper, but I just heard about it on the news. I thought your pa killed the Stickman?"

Leah took a sip of coffee. She set her mug on her desk. "So did I. Apparently, he doesn't die very easily."

"You thinkin' copycat?"

"Possibly, although there's evidence against it."

"What kind of evidence?"

Leah hesitated a moment. Should she be letting out the one thing her pa had managed to hold back from the press? At this moment she questioned how much she trusted Dan Truitt. She decided to go with her gut. That usually helped her out. It's what Chief Montgomery said made her a good cop.

"There was stuff held back from the press on the original killin's. It's part of this new guy's MO and signature, too."

"I thought the holdout got released? I barely remember that case. I was just a beat cop, two years on the squad."

Leah watched the second hand tick off two on the big white clock. "No, there was more that was held back."

"What was it?"

Here it goes. Go with your gut. You trust him. "Every time the Stickman murdered someone, my pa was given a letter with a drawing of a stickman and a time and place the body would show up. We're pretty sure the victims are already dead when they're dumped at the crime scene."

"So you get an address? Or . . . ?"

"No, nothing that precise. More like an area. Usually, a frustratingly *big* area."

"Wow, no wonder *that* was held back. And last night's?"

"We got the letter. Only it came addressed to me, instead of my pa. Leah Fowler, though, not Teal."

"That's scary. Almost like it's personal."

"Yeah, well, with my pa, it became personal fast. I get the feeling that's what this guy's planning this time around, too. My pa was the face of the task force, though. Ultimately, he was the one who killed Harry Stork."

"So Harry Stork wasn't . . ." Dan hesitated mid-sentence to gather his thoughts. "You think the Stickman was someone else?"

Outside, the sun glimmered off the leaves of the sweetshrubs. The red flowers looked like little spotlights. "I don't know. Why would he wait fifteen years without a single kill?"

"Maybe there were two Stickmen. Harry Stork and someone else. Maybe it took fifteen years for this guy to find a new partner."

Leah took another sip from her mug. The coffee was still hot. "See?" she asked. "This is why I call you. You come up with things I never think of." She hesitated again, but decided she had to say the rest: "You realize I told you about the letters we received in confidence, right? You can't tell no one. Only a handful of people know."

Now it was Dan's turn to hesitate. "You don't trust me? After six months?" Leah heard disappointment in his voice.

"No, I do, it's just—ever since Billy died, I have a hard time trusting anything, not just people. I trust you more than I've trusted anyone since."

"Don't worry, your secret's safe. You really *can* trust me. I thought you'd know that by now."

I hope so, Leah thought. *And that goes for my heart, too.* Some things were just so easily broken.

"So what do you think?" Leah asked.

Dan, in his ever-overreaching patois, replied, "I don't know. It stinks like a festering carbuncle."

"And I have to give a statement to the press today. It's goin' to be mostly fabricated."

Dan hesitated, then: "You do what you gotta do."

"If I don't make somethin' up, I got nothin' to put in it that everyone don't already know. We're worried people will panic."

"Yeah, I understand. Don't sweat it. We lie to the public all the time." She could hear him smiling. "It's part of our job. So, what's your next step?"

"Ethan says I should contact the federal penitentiary and all the correctional institutions and find out who recently got out."

"That's not a bad idea," Dan said. "Listen, I have some vacation time coming up. How about I come down and give you a hand on this for, say, four weeks or so?"

Leah's heart rose. "Four *weeks?*" she asked. "It better hell not take us four weeks to figure this out."

"The first time 'round didn't it take your pa near on a year and a half?"

A spike turned in Leah's chest. It *had* been almost that long. She didn't have that kind of time. She couldn't go through everything she'd watched her pa go through.

"You there?" Dan asked. "You don't want me to come? Why do I keep hearing phones ringing?"

Leah took a breath. "Forget the phones. And Dan, I would *love* for you to come down. But . . . four weeks? Can you really get that kind of time away?"

He laughed. "They owe me nine. I never take holidays."

"Can you actually get—I mean, won't they miss you if you're gone that long?"

"Nah. I've been pretty much on glide for the past

three weeks already. I'll have to check with my boss, but I think he'll be happy I'm finally taking off some of that time. Besides, I can work while I'm down there. I do most of my work at night. In the wee hours."

Leah knew this about him already. She also knew he did most of his work in those wee hours accompanied by a bottle of bourbon. "You've been doing nothin' for three weeks?" Turning around, she sat on the edge of her desk, coffee mug in hand.

"Well, whenever one of us isn't assigned we're sort of expected to reassign ourselves to this ongoing . . ." He paused. "You heard 'bout the Cahaba River Strangler? We all take turns at bat trying to crack that one. It's sort of become a back burner, which is really a travesty."

"I read about the Cahaba River Strangler," Leah said. "There was an article about it in the *Examiner*."

"Yeah, I'm sure there was. Most folk around here have gotten used to it now, but it's so frustrating. We've had five victims actually get away from him, we've got a blood sample, a partial fingerprint we managed to lift from a victim's chin, if you can believe it, but nothin' ever seems to cut us a break. Our best chance came about three years in. I remember it because it was Christmas Eve. The victim screamed so much some guy came running to her rescue and beat the shit out of the Strangler with a tire iron. Smashed up his fingers, his arms, and his back before he managed to get away. We put out a bulletin asking the public if anyone knew anything, but other than a few crazy reports, we got nothin'."

"This has been goin' on for some time, hasn't it? Musta been five or six years ago I read that article."

"Over ten years," Dan agreed. "He actually went dark for four of them—well, at least we didn't find any victims matching his MO. I'm sure we got some missing persons during that time, so who knows? There's been some disappearances around the area we reckon are probably Strangler victims we just never found."

"Sounds horrible. Lots of victims?"

"Sixteen that we *know* about. Another almost half dozen we're pretty confident went his way."

"The Cahaba's a long river to search." Leah took a drink of coffee and set the mug down beside her.

"Longest river in Alabama. Goes all the way from the Piedmont and the Cumberland Plateau until it finally empties into the Alabama. So far, though, the Strangler has been centering 'round the Birmingham area, or at least we think so. Haven't heard about any bodies turning up near other parts of the river. None that match the Strangler's MO, anyway."

Leah let out a big sigh. "Him 'going dark,' as you say, sounds a bit like the fish that just hit my plate. Only mine appears to have gone dark for fifteen years. It just—it seems too impossible. At least to me. With you on the Strangler case and all, you sure you can get away?"

"Yep, let me just clear it with my lieutenant. This mystery has lasted ten years. Taking some time away from it ain't goin' to make much of a difference. Besides, like I said, I can go through files and stuff while I'm down there."

Leah sat on the edge of her desk and took a gulp of coffee. "Another thing Ethan wants me to do is find out who the talkers are in these same institutions and interrogate them. Find out if anyone's been yakkin' about the Stickman lately, or giving out his MO and his signature." She paused before adding, worriedly, "I'm not a great interrogator."

Dan ignored her last statement. "Another good idea," he said. "There's always squealers. Serial killers like to talk once they're in the can. Has this guy done any time?"

"Not that I know of. I still need to go through the files. There are a lot of files."

There was a pause before Dan spoke again. "I think going around to these places isn't a bad idea at all. I can come with."

"Yeah, but what'll make anyone want to talk to us?"

"Oh, don't worry 'bout that. They'll talk to us. Hang on a sec." Leah heard Dan speaking to someone. She couldn't make out the words, they were muffled. Dan's hand must've been over the receiver. A few minutes later, he came back on the line. "I'll be down day after tomorrow. That sound okay?"

"That sounds great! Oh wait, there's one more possibility I haven't mentioned," Leah said. She finished her coffee and set the mug down on the table beside the machine.

"What's that?" Dan asked.

"The letters we received—the signature that wasn't leaked—there *were* some people who knew about it: a few select cops from my pa's task force that he hand-picked on account of him *absolutely* trusting them. But you never know, could be that he was wrong and we're looking at the work of a dirty cop."

Dan sighed. "Now *that's* a tougher one to act on. A lot of those guys will be either in the upper ranks by now or retired. And if your pa handpicked 'em, you gotta think they're pretty much stand-up guys. But—"

"But you never know," she said, finishing his thought. "So what do we do about it?"

"We approach that one carefully. *Very* carefully. That is, if we approach it at all."

* * *

Hopping on to her computer, Leah decided to get the press release she had to write out of the way. She already pretty much knew how it would read. She just needed to write it. The fact that Dan so easily approved of her "slanting the facts" helped give her the confidence to get it done. That and the constant ringing of phones motivated her like nothing else.

PRESS RELEASE

Alvin Police Department

Update on the Recent "Apparent" Stickman Murder

Wednesday, June 14, 1989 (FOR IMMEDIATE RELEASE)

This release is in regards to the recent victim that was discovered on the bank of Leeland Swamp yesterday, Tuesday, June 13, 1989.

The victim was thirty-six-year-old Abilene Williams. The condition of the victim's body and the way it was found was congruent with the Stickman serial killings that happened from February 10, 1973, running until July 22, 1974, when the then Stickman, Harry Stork, was shot dead by an officer from this department.

This new incident is currently under investigation. Alvin Police want to assure the public that its safety is the number-one priority at this time and precautions are under way to assure this "new Stickman" doesn't kill again. Confidence is high that evidence found at last night's crime scene will lead to a quick arrest.

The Alvin Police have discerned that, other than in a superficial way, this new incident is in no way related to the incidents of 1973/74. The public is safe from Harry Stork and the police are doing everything possible to bring this new suspect to justice.

Anyone with information regarding this incident is urged to call the Alvin Police. Information leading to an arrest could be eligible for a cash reward.

She sat back and read it over. It was good. And really, at this point in time, there might actually not be any falsities to it. Leah simply didn't know. And that made her somehow feel a little better about it as she printed it out before faxing it to the local papers, radio stations, and television news shows.

Officer Chris Jackson returned to the station with Abe and Dewey in tow. They managed to convince him to stop at Igloo's Ice Cream Parlor on their way back so they both had ice cream cones. In this heat, they were melting pretty fast, so Abe and Dewey were licking them up as quick as they could. Leah took one look at them and made sure they knew she wasn't impressed.

"What can I say?" said Chris, "I'm a pushover." He picked up the press release that was still sitting beside the fax machine. "Evidence from last night?"

"Don't start. If we're lucky it will put an end to the phone calls. Did you find the kite?" Leah asked. "You were gone awfully long."

"Yeah, it was up in a Douglas fir on Blackberry Trail just as you thought. Nobody was hurt and it's far enough back that I think it's best to just leave it there. It takes a while to look in trees. Try it sometime."

"So, Dewey," Leah asked him while ice cream dripped from his hand, "what have you learned?"

"That two-by-fours and industrial plastic make amazing kites, ma'am." His face was covered in ice cream. He looked ridiculous.

Leah sighed. Then to Abe, she said: "Will you go over and grab that boy a paper towel before he gets ice cream everywhere?" The paper towels were on the same table as the coffeemaker. Abe grabbed three pieces off the roll and an extra piece for himself. He handed the three to Dewey, who used them to wipe the ice cream from his face.

"Okay, Dewey," Leah said, "now try again. What did you learn?"

Dewey looked at Abe. Abe just rolled his eyes.

Turning back to Leah, Dewey said, "That I should take the tensile strength of the string into account next time?"

With yet another sigh, Leah said, "One more time."

"Um, I don't really know what you're lookin' for, ma'am. Is it that kites shouldn't be homemade in Alvin?"

"Oh thank goodness, you got it."

"Okay, but I still feel the experiment was a huge success. I—"

"Dewey?"

"Yes, ma'am?"

"Shut up while you're ahead."

"Um, okay . . ."

It took all she had not to laugh out loud.

CHAPTER 7

Leah was back at the station for another day, feeling antsy because Dan was arriving tomorrow. He always kept her on her toes. She never knew what the man was going to say or do next. Sometimes, the most inappropriate things came out of his mouth (usually at the most inappropriate of times). Strangely, she found herself loving it.

After work last night she had stopped by Tuesday's crime scene and checked it out. For a good hour, maybe hour and a half, she walked around the markers indicating where the body was found and looked for anything Ethan and Chris might have missed. She even walked the trail Chris had reported searching and, other than the wheelbarrow track, found nothing new. By the time she left, she felt confident that everything that needed to be documented had been documented. One thing positive she could say about her two workmates, when they did a job properly, they covered their bases. Her anger about not being called in for the search had diminished substantially.

After pouring herself the day's essential first cup of coffee, she took a seat at her desk. The clock said ten o'clock. Ethan's office door was closed, of course. "He in yet?" she asked Chris.

Chris sat at his desk doing the crossword from today's paper. "Not yet," he said. He had barely said anything to her but a quiet "good morning" since she came in. "Oh, this is for you." He handed her a two-page fax.

"What's this?"

"The report you asked me to run on Thomas Kennedy Bradshaw," Chris said, actually looking up from the paper. "Better known as 'the Buzzman'." He laughed and went back to his puzzle.

"That was quick." She had asked him to get it for her shortly after leaving Ethan's office yesterday.

Chris shrugged.

Leah skimmed the report. Ethan was right, Bradshaw's name *did* make him sound like a serial killer. But he was never caught killing. He certainly wanted to be, though. Three separate times, he came forward to Alvin Police stating that he was the Stickman and, all three times, police decided he wasn't. The final time, they had him taken to a psychiatric hospital for a review.

However, on October 10, 1974, Bradshaw finally got his wish when he was sentenced to five years at the Federal Correctional Institution at Talladega and wound up staying for every single day. The last Stickman murder happened on June 16, 1974—near on four months earlier—so, theoretically, Bradshaw could've been responsible.

He now lived in the suburbs of Satsuma, where he'd lived since leaving Talladega.

Sipping her coffee, Leah read on.

Evidently, Thomas Kennedy Bradshaw walked into a Shell station one evening wearing a balaclava, a black-and-red checkerboard shirt with a white T-shirt underneath, a pair of army boots, and a gas-powered chain saw. Pulling the saw's cord, it roared to life as he held it above his head, yelling, "I am the Buzzman!"

Luckily, nobody got hurt. Bradshaw got away with eighty-seven dollars and change from the register and three bags of assorted candy. In fact, police reports made at the scene established the candy was what got him caught. The clerk hit the store's silent alarm while Bradshaw rummaged through Tootsie Rolls and gummies, giving law enforcements time to show up and cover the store's exits. Bradshaw waltzed out eating a Mars bar and was immediately taken into custody.

The history of the Buzzman was short and sweet. Even still, given his history of claiming to be the Stickman, Leah decided to drive out to Satsuma and see what the man had to say.

Bradshaw lived in a fairly run-down clapboard house. The wooden siding had once been white, but the paint had long ago begun to peel. One of the shutters framing the bedroom windows had pulled from its hinge and hung at an angle. A short, gravel driveway ran down the left side of the house and a beat-up red Chevy pickup was currently parked there. Leah left her Bonneville on the side of the road out front.

Like the other houses she had passed driving in, Bradshaw's home was nestled in a wooded area, with a small front yard of sparse lawn and dusty patches of dirt. Douglas fir and oaks loomed from the back and sides of the house, nearly suffocating it. The boughs of the fir trees, heavily laden with Spanish moss, hung over the driveway and pushed against the house's side.

Leah walked across the yard, and, not seeing a doorbell, knocked hard on the wooden front door. From inside came a loud *bang* and then heavy footsteps. Slowly, the door opened, revealing a man who stood probably six feet tall with unkempt dishwater blond hair. He probably weighed around 240 pounds, Leah guessed, and wore a stained, gray T-shirt and baggy, black track pants. His socks had holes in both big toes.

"H-hello," the man stammered, his gaze dropping to the floor, "w-what can I help you with?" Leah wondered if he had a speech impediment.

She flashed her badge. "Hello. I'm Detective Leah Teal from the Alvin Police. I am looking for a Mr. Thomas Kennedy Bradshaw. Would that be you?"

"I—I am him . . . he."

Leah put away her badge, pulled out her pad, and started taking notes. Bradshaw's eyes went back to the floor and he rocked slightly from foot to foot.

"Is something wrong?" Leah asked.

"No, I j-just don't like getting company."

"May I ask why?" Leah said. And just to see the response, added, "You're not going to invite me in?"

Bradshaw's eyes flashed upward, momentarily locking with hers. "Wh-why? Wh-What does this have to do with?"

"The Stickman."

Again those eyes darted to Leah. This time, for a brief second, she saw an emotion but couldn't place it. Panic? Anger? Fear? His eyes once again went to his carpet, and the rocking came back.

"What do you want to talk to me about *him* for?" he asked, almost mumbling.

"Well," she said, "there was a time you told authorities that you were, in fact, the Stickman." She consulted her notes. "I believe you did this three different times during 1973 and 1974, the last being after police issued a statewide manhunt for Harry Stork. You came into my station and told Joe Fowler personally that Stork was innocent and you'd been responsible for all the Stickman killings." She paused as Bradshaw continued going from foot to foot, even more pronounced now. "You told Fowler, 'You're after the wrong guy,' according to the report I read this morning. Got me thinking, with this most recent murder you may have heard about, that maybe there was something to this, after all."

Once again, Bradshaw's eyes came up, this time staying there. "What recent murder?"

"Two nights ago a victim was found in Alvin. The crime scene looked remarkably similar to the old Stickman murders."

Bradshaw stepped sideways, his gaze again dropping. "I—I know nothin' 'bout that. I'm—I'm not the St-Stickman."

"Oh right," she said, turning quickly to catch his gaze, dipping her head to see his face. His expression looked like a wild animal caught in front of a car on a dark road. "I forgot. You're just the Buzzman."

Their eyes gripped each other again for a moment, then he looked away. Leah nodded, unable to hide her smirk. "The Buzzman," she said quietly.

"Look, lady, I'm—I'm not anyone now. I'm just Thom-Thomas Bradshaw. I paid for what I—what I did. I did my time."

Leah couldn't help but smile grimly. "Glad you dropped the Kennedy," she said. "Makes you sound less like a serial killer. Of course, that might be on purpose." She was intentionally trying to push buttons. She still didn't know how to assess his reaction to her showing up.

"No—no, ma'am, I'm not a s-serial killer."

"Detective, if you don't mind."

"What?"

"Call me detective."

"No, Detective, I'm—I'm not the Stickman."

"But you *are* the Buzzman."

"That—that was five minutes of my life. I was very con-confused."

"Would you like me to leave, Mr. Bradshaw?"

He looked up, pleadingly, and quieted his voice. "Yes, please?" It came out almost like a question.

"Do I make you feel unsettled?"

"Yes, ma—Detective."

"If you're not guilty, then why?"

"Be-because, ever since get-getting out of Talladega, I don't like cops—I mean, the police. And I-I'm *not* guilty. I promise."

She hesitated. "'Cops' is fine. It's not derogatory, and I think most serial killers would promise that. Why should I believe you?"

"I-I don't know," Bradshaw asked.

"Where were you Tuesday night? What were you doing?"

"I was here."

"Can anyone corroborate that?"

"What?"

"Can somebody confirm you're telling the truth? Did a friend come over? Did you call someone?" By his actions, Leah suspected the man didn't have a lot of friends and probably few telephone conversations.

"No, but I was here. I'm not—I'm not lying."

"Again, I think a serial killer would say that."

His eyes met hers, searchingly. "I'm not a serial killer. I'm not. I'm—I'm just a man."

This conversation hadn't brought a lot of notes to Leah's pad, but she did have a strange feeling about Bradshaw. During the ride here, she had almost convinced herself the man wasn't a suspect, but now she wondered if that came from the fact that her pa had ruled him out. Now, based on his reaction to her, she second-thought that. Bradshaw was definitely staying on her suspect list. "Tell you what, Mr. Bradshaw," she said. "I'm goin' to leave now, but I want you to be available for questioning. If you suddenly disappear, you will be found. Do I make myself clear?"

A look of relief washed over him. "Yes, ma'am—I mean, yes, Detective."

Leah turned and the door closed quickly behind her. As she walked to her car, she could almost feel the woods take the opportunity to tighten even closer around Bradshaw's house.

CHAPTER 8

That afternoon, once she got over her experience with Bradshaw, Leah decided it was time to seriously dig into the Stickman files. It wasn't going to be easy; there were lots of them. She figured her best bet was to make a duplicate of everything and take one set home so she could work here and there without having to lug them back and forth. What she didn't count on was how long it would take to copy every piece of paper in those files. Near on two hours went by as she stood by the Xerox machine, putting page after page onto the top, closing it up, and pressing the green button.

When she was done, she poured herself a new coffee and returned to her desk.

Her feelings for this case were different from most. Even though Ethan accused her of always getting too emotionally involved in her work, this one felt extremely close to her. Probably because it had been so important to her pa. She wanted to make sure she missed nothing. Wanted desperately to be certain that, once everything was solved, she got it right.

So she read slowly, taking everything in. It would take a long time to get through all the information. She looked at the two identical stacks of folders on her desk and figured she'd be putting in a lot of overtime at home. She wouldn't get paid for it—not in money, at least—but it was an investment in how she would feel when the whole thing was finally over.

The top folder was simply labeled *STORK* in capital letters and, after a quick scan through its contents, seemed to contain various reports and statements regarding the members of the Stork family. Leah hoped this might fill in some of the blanks she still had in her head. She already knew some of the stuff, mostly from remembering back when her pa was on the case, but also from her recent chat with Ethan.

Right at the top of the file were pages and notes about Harry Stork, along with a copy of a photo Leah presumed had likely come from the DMV or somewhere like that. Harry Stork had a round face, wide nose, and full lips. His hair was black with signs of early graying around the sides.

The report echoed what Ethan said, only it did so more formally. Harry Stork had a monogenetic twin brother named Tommy, and a pa named Noah. Harry's ma, Sally-Anne Stork, was already dead when the report had been issued, June 20, 1974.

His birthday fell on July 7, 1943. The report was disturbingly quiet about the first twenty or so years of his life, until August 10, 1964, when the army conscripted Harry and flew him to Vietnam to fight for his country. He returned near on exactly three years later with an honorable discharge. Due to, it said, psychological trauma.

Leah had a yellow pad she was taking her own notes on as she read. That fact was put down on it.

After he returned home, Harry's medical records listed a series of visits to a psychiatrist named Dr. Edwin

Freeman, who remained Harry's doctor until 1971 when, for reasons unknown, Harry began seeing a new psychiatrist named Dr. Leanne Swift. Swift remained his doctor up to the date of the report, likely right up to his death, on July 22, 1974, a date Leah knew by heart. You couldn't have grown up in her house while her pa chased the Stickman and *not* have memorized that date.

Leah couldn't find any long-term hospital stints or anything like that from his records, so whatever "psychological trauma" Harry suffered from must have been somewhat in control, or at least his doctors thought so.

For most of his life following his army discharge, Harry was on a 300-milligram dose of a drug called chlorpromazine. After switching doctors, Leah noted his prescription was raised to 500 milligrams. Leah had never heard of the drug before. It went down as another note on her yellow pad.

On November 1, 1967, just three months after coming home, Harry started his own company, a medical waste management corporation called Stork Sanitation and Waste Removal. From what Leah could glean, he continued this work up until this report was issued, with surprising success. Beneath the company's name, Leah's pa had written a list of Stork's major clients, along with the dates they signed contracts with Harry's company.

Springhill Memorial Hospital, November 1967
Searcy Hospital in Mount Vernon*, December 1967
Providence Hospital (Mobile)*, February 1972
University of South Alabama Children's and
      Women's, March 1972
Mercy Medical in Daphne*, May 1974

* * *

Well, he couldn't have been too messed up to run such a company, Leah thought and wondered about the asterisks her pa had put by some of the names. Obviously, those were separated out for a reason.

She came to a handful of pages that were copied straight out of Harry's P&L books. It showed all the jobs Harry did since Stork Sanitation opened its doors, most of them being for the hospitals Leah's pa had listed. There were others, maybe a half-dozen smaller places, including a dental office, but Stork didn't work for these on a regular basis. Just one or two times each.

Following the information taken from Stork Sanitation's ledger book was a copy of the company's legal documents, including the original filings for incorporation, name registration, certificate of formation, annual reports, all that sort of thing.

Stork Sanitation and Waste Removal was incorporated in Alabama on October 25, 1967. Leah looked over the minutes from that filing. Something popped out at her: They listed Noah Stork as not only the registered agent for the company, but also the primary director. She flipped through the rest of the corporate documents, including the issuing of one hundred common shares—the total shares available—to Noah Stork. Harry Stork's name appeared nowhere in any of the legal documents. She made a note of this as a puzzle to be solved later. Surprisingly, she didn't find any notes by her pa about it.

As far as police records go, Stork's history couldn't have been more spotless if someone went at it with a mop and a bucket of Mr. Clean. Not even a tussle with the cops showed up anywhere. The only thing Leah found was a two-word question her pa had posed at the bottom of a page of unrelated notes. It said: *Juvie record?* But nowhere was there any other indication that an attempt to find such records ever even happened.

Leah looked to Chris. "I need you to do something for me. You know—with your weird 'expertise'?"

He narrowed his eyes. "Okay . . . what expertise is that?"

"You know. That thing you can do with juvie records."

"You mean, like actually *find* them?" he asked.

"Yeah . . . and, somehow, uncover all the details. I have no idea how you do it. From what I know, juvie records are s'posed to be sealed except in situations where—"

Chris stopped her. "Nothing's really ever *sealed*. Folk just make a half-ass attempt at making them hard to find."

Leah raised her eyebrows. "Obviously not. I've seen you do what you do too many times. I'm just sayin' that's the way they're s'posed to be. I have no idea how you get your information."

Chris paused for a sip of his coffee. "And you don't want to know, either," he said, with a wicked little grin.

"I'm sure I don't. Anyway, here." She handed him a report on Harry Stork.

"Harry Stork? You think he might have a blemish or two from his childhood?"

"Well, if you look here"—she pointed to her pa's note—"my pa left a note about potential juvie records." She started flipping through the rest of the documents in the folder on top of the stack. "But I can't see anywhere he actually *got* the information."

"Does it matter?" Chris asked. "I mean, with him being dead and all."

Leah shrugged. "I can't answer that, yet. Obviously, it mattered to my pa. I just want to cover my bases."

"Maybe your pa already found out and it's just not in the file. Ask Ethan about it."

"Ethan already told me, twice: 'Everything's in the files'."

Chris laughed. "Well, there you go."

"Just humor me, okay?"

"Sure. I'm on it."

Just as Leah was about to dive back into her *STORK* folder, the phone rang. She decided Chris had done enough answering. "Alvin Police, Detective Teal," she said, raising the receiver.

"Detective Teal. It's Chuck. From Mobile?"

She widened her eyes at Chris to get his attention. "Yeah . . . Chuck. How're you?"

"Fine, fine. Just wanted to get back to y'all about the Polaroids you sent down here Tuesday night? The partial finger and the boot print?"

"Right. Find anythin' interesting?"

"Well, I'll tell you where we stand right now. We ran the print through AFIS, and so far haven't found a match."

"AFIS is your print database, right?" Leah asked. "How far does it go back?"

"The FBI's been usin' it for well on ten years now. We've had it for a few. We have some other ways of comparing matches, too. We're still workin' on it, it's just goin' to take some time."

"What about the boot?" Leah asked.

"You might've gotten lucky with the boot," Chuck said. "It's not so common. From what we can tell, you're lookin' at a size nine 'jump boot'."

"What's a 'jump boot'?" Leah asked.

"A type of combat boot, normally worn by paratroopers and airborne units. Some special forces, too. They're designed by the Cove Shoe Company, one of their divisions, the Corcoran and Matterhorn Company, to be precise. They have the exclusive contract with the Department of Defense to artifice and supply them."

"Okay, so we're lookin' at someone in the military?"

"Likely, or someone who got them from someone in the military. Likely someone with parachute skills. They're traditionally worn with dress uniforms."

Leah wrote down everything he said. "Got it, Chuck. Anything else?"

"No, that's it for now. I'll let you know if we find a match on the print, but I'm not holding my breath." There was a pause, and then Chuck seemed to stumble. "Um . . . actually . . . Leah? Would it be possible for me to speak with Ethan for a moment?"

That was an odd request. Chuck had been working as her forensics liaison goin' on six years now, ever since the last one, Markus, had left Mobile. Never once had he asked to speak to Ethan until now. Leah thought she knew why, but she decided to play it out just to prove she was right.

Putting Chuck on hold, Leah went and quietly rapped on Ethan's door.

"Come in!" he yelled from behind his desk.

She opened the door and popped her head in as the blinds hanging down the back side rustled. "Chuck from Mobile forensics wants to talk to you." She almost didn't add the rest, but something made her say it. "Pretty sure it's got somethin' to do with handwriting analysis on the super-secret letters." She gave Ethan a patronizing little smile.

He shook his head. "For Christ's sake, Leah. Just come in here. Take a seat while I take the call."

"Ethan Montgomery," he said, after taking Chuck off hold.

Leah listened to Ethan's side of the call, a pause after each sentence he said as he listened for Chuck to respond. "Uh-huh. Yep. Got it. That's what I figured. Yeah, I know, it's gonna be another tough ride I'm thinkin'. All right, Chuck. How's the wife? Kids? Yeah? Excited 'bout the Fourth? Yeah, no . . . not me. I don't really change my routine much for holidays. Me and Betty just . . . you know, hang out. Yeah, we should. One of these days. All right. Take care."

Ethan hung up the call. "Now, you need to promise me one thing," he said, pointing a thick finger at Leah. "You all but forget what you know about Chuck, you understand me? By no means, and I mean absolutely none, do you tell even *Chris* that you've got a hunch Chuck's one of the secret circle."

"Why? Why's it such a big deal?"

"I can't explain it to you without telling you too much. But it goes far beyond this case."

"Why don't you try."

"Let me think about it."

Leah wondered what sort of reaction she was going to get when she came in and actually told Ethan she needed the *names* of what he called the "secret circle." She had a hunch she was in store for a pretty big argument.

"So," she asked. "Am I allowed to know?"

"To know what?" Ethan said gruffly.

"'Bout the handwriting analysis. I'm *assuming* that's what you were just talkin' about, other than the crap about your family and kids and holidays and getting together."

Without looking up at her, Ethan answered. "It's a match. The same person wrote this letter who wrote the other nine."

"For certain?" Leah asked. Disappointment twisted inside her stomach. "This still doesn't mean it's the same guy doing the killin's," she said. "Could be different people back then writing the notes and slaughtering folk."

Ethan took a big breath and spread his palms on his desk. "Sure, Leah, anything's possible. Just don't let your bias toward wanting your pa's legacy to remain intact act out in how you investigate this case, okay?"

She just stared at him without replying.

"I said, okay?"

"What, you want me to promise that, too?"

He nodded slowly. "Yep, I do. And I know you keep your promises."

She looked at his bookcase full of law books and thought this over. "Fine," she said after a while. "I'll do my best to keep my pa's memory out of my work."

"Thank you. Now please go back to your desk. You exhaust me."

With a huff Leah got up and left Ethan's office, making sure to gently close the door on her way out. She had no idea what had made her so upset. Was it the secrecy? The fact that she wasn't let in? Or was it the idea that her pa may have messed up after all this time? Or was it just . . . everything? As she sat back in her chair, Chris asked her what was going on.

"What did Chuck have to say?"

She brought him up to speed.

"Well, I reckon that's great," he said when she finished. "I see on this report that Harry Stork was drafted for 'Nam."

Frowning, Leah shook her head. "Yeah, for the *army*. Nothin' in the file 'bout him bein' a paratrooper, though."

"Still . . ." Chris said, not wanting to give it up. "Seems like a coincidence."

A stone turned in Leah's stomach at the use of the word. One thing she hated was coincidences.

Setting all of Harry Stork's paperwork aside, she came to a single page with the date June 2, 1974, written at the top and the name Noah Stork written beneath it. The handwriting didn't belong to her pa. Leah guessed it was Officer Peter Strident. Below Noah Stork's name, Strident had written his address, which, at the time, was a remote part of Alvin, to say the least.

On clear days, from the rail bridge above Finley's Crossing, you could see the Nashoba hills rising bald from the fan of trees that thickened as it spread out, covering miles upon miles of Alvin until finally coming up hard against the southern edge of the Anikawa. It was known as the Lusa Forest, a name, Leah suspected, that it had been given long before any white person ever stepped foot in North America.

Back when these notes about Noah Stork had been made, that's all it was. Just a mess of old-growth trees, densely packed hardwood all trying to choke out the rest. The only roads running through the forest would've been hard-packed logging roads, and even those would've been few and far between, each one cutting a path necessarily windy due to having to dodge timber much too big to ever consider chopping it down. Noah Stork would've lived in one of probably only a dozen or so homes in all those miles and miles of trees.

The address Strident wrote down was 7 Rural Route 1, probably the main road through those parts back then.

Things were different now. Two years or so ago, fueled by the rise in Alvin's population, folks suddenly became more interested in the Lusa Forest. Slowly, the logging roads were overhauled and new roads were added, and the area became an almost popular place to build new homes. It was given the title Blue Jay Maples, despite the fact that there really weren't many maple trees. The majority of the forest was by far made up of gigantic poplars and imposing oaks. Leah wasn't even sure if the maples could grab third place.

Quite a few places still existed in Alvin where one could build a home and still feel safe that nobody else was about to come along and squeeze a new house in right beside you, but none held the guarantee of that not happening like Blue Jay Maples.

Those woods were best described as tangled and snarled and as thick as they were dense. When the kids were younger, Leah sometimes took them on hikes through the Lusa Forest, following trails that could've very well been first made over a hundred years earlier. Many followed the Taloa River as it splashed and spilled while winding and weaving southward from the Anikawa. Some of the biggest cypress Leah had ever seen clung onto the soft sloping banks of that constricted little river.

After pulling the phone book from her bottom left drawer, Leah searched and found a current listing for a "Noah Stork." Sure enough, his house number had gained in status to 749 and he now lived on a road called Woodpecker Wind, which meant she probably was right. He hadn't moved, time had just moved everything around him. The area where his house stood now had an actual name, Blue Jay Maples, and consisted of many roads cutting twisted swaths through all those trees.

Leah had only driven through the area twice, and both times she wound up lost. Nowadays, Blue Jay Maples was like a maze of new roads and, to make things worse, each one was named after a different type of bird.

She wrote Noah Stork's "new" address in the margin beside his old one. Then she looked for the same note in her Xeroxed stack so she'd have a record of it at home, too. Just to be safe. She actually came to Tommy's report before she found the note and noticed he had the same address as his pa.

"Huh," Leah said.

"Huh, what?" Chris asked.

"Tommy Stork lived with his pa sometime."

"Is that relevant to somethin'?"

"I don't know yet." At any rate writing the new address here was just as good as writing it on the note. The two stacks of folders didn't have to be *exactly* the same. So she did and then carefully squared up that pile to make it easier to lug home.

Strident's notes from talking with Noah Stork were sparse. Leah realized they were just from a quick conversation they'd had after Strident arrived to bring Tommy Stork back to the station for questioning. As she'd already discovered, back then, Tommy lived in his pa's house. The rest of the notes related to a few questions Strident asked Noah regarding Tommy's whereabouts at certain times and whether or not Noah could provide some kind of alibi for his son, but Leah didn't read anything too conclusive.

Setting the notes down on top of the stuff she'd already gone through, Leah moved on, coming to a bunch of stuff relating to Tommy.

Just like she'd found with Harry Stork, there was a copy of a photo of Tommy looking like it came from his driver's license. She pulled Harry's photo back out and compared the two. The resemblance was astonishing.

Nobody would ever question whether or not they were twins. Same round face, same lips, same wide nose. Even their hair had the same streaks of gray in roughly the same places. The only real difference between the two photos was the scar slashed across Tommy's face, starting just above his upper lip and tracing a crescent shape upon his left cheek before coming to a stop just below his eye. It wasn't a nice scar, if there was such a thing. Leah set both pictures aside and moved on.

The date on Tommy Stork's police and medical reports was May 30, 1974, two days before Strident picked him up and talked to his pa. She flipped through the police report and, just like with Harry, nothing too interesting stuck out for her. Then she looked over his medical history.

Like Harry had after returning from East Asia, Tommy also saw a psychiatrist. The difference here, though, was that Tommy started seeing his at the age of twenty, and his report actually listed his diagnosis as schizophrenia. Tommy's doctor tried him with a number of different medications throughout the years, including a regimen of chlorpromazine, the same medication Harry had been on. Tommy started at 500 milligrams and eventually moved up to 750.

After being diagnosed, Tommy's medical history showed him in and out of psych wards at a number of different hospitals around Alvin and other parts of Alabama. Apparently, his medical disorder was considerably worse than his brother's.

Tommy worked in construction from age nineteen until he was twenty-one. Then, all vocation history for him came to an end. The date was September 20, 1964, to be exact, the day Tommy Stork lost two fingers from his right hand while at work. Six months after that, his address changed, becoming the same as his pa's. That's where he'd lived ever since.

Unlike Harry, Tommy wasn't drafted into the war. He was labeled F-4 on account of his accident.

Two years later, on September 20, 1966, Tommy wound up in a bar fight and he received that gash across his face Leah had seen in the photo. The police showed up and threw Tommy in the drunk tank for the night, but no charges were laid. The bar, some place called the Three Little Pigs, was ten miles out of Birmingham.

One page of notes made by Strident was all that remained in the *STORK* folder. He'd taken them while interviewing Noah when he went to pick up Tommy. They all pertained to Noah's wife, Sally-Anne, and her suicide, which happened back on February 5, 1973. Cause of death: an overdose of barbiturates. Maiden name: Delford. Strident noted that Leah's pa had been the first responder at the scene. He also commented that, should they need it, a proper police report would be filed somewhere in their archives. The archives being the rows upon rows of binders and folders stuffed across the station's back walls. Leah had no doubt the official report was in there somewhere, but that didn't mean she'd ever find it. She decided if she needed anything further on Sally-Anne's death, she'd just get it straight from Noah.

Leah glanced at the clock. Half past three.

Her knees popped as she got up from her desk and lifted the Xeroxed stack of files she'd made to read at home. "I'm takin' off early," she told Chris. "I figure the kids deserve a home-cooked supper for once. I can sift through all of these just as well there as I can here . . ." The stack was heavy and she nearly dropped it while struggling with the door.

"Need some help with that?" Chris asked.

"No, I'm good." She got the door open and read-justed her grip on the bundle. "Don't forget about my juvie records."

"I won't," Chris said. "You don't have to tell me twice. Have I ever failed you?"

She pretended to think on this. "If you did, I no longer remember it. Listen, though. I'm probably goin' to be a little late tomorrow. I plan on interviewing Noah Stork, Harry Stork's pa, on my way in. You should see me be-fore Dan shows up, though. But just in case . . ." She didn't know how to end that sentence.

"Just in case . . . what?"

"I don't know. Just . . . let him sit in my chair until I get here, I s'pose."

"I can do that. Have fun with your interview. Hope it goes as well as Bradshaw's did this morning." Chris smiled, the fluorescent lights gleaming in his dark eyes. She had told Chris the details of her bizarre encounter with Thomas Kennedy Bradshaw upon returning to the station this morning. She was certain interviewing Noah Stork would be much more normal.

"I'm mostly worried about finding the place," she said. "He lives in Blue Jay Maples. Some road I never heard of called Woodpecker Wind." She pronounced it as rhyming with "sinned."

"Woodpecker Wind? What kind of a name is that?" Chris went to take a sip of his coffee, realized his mug was empty, and set it back on his desk. Leah was just about out the door when he told her to wait. Still awk-wardly holding the stack while balancing the door on her ass, she backed up.

"What?" she asked.

"I bet it's not wind. It's probably wind." The way he

said it made it rhyme with "kind." Then he said, "All those bird roads down there twist and turn like crazy. Wind makes more sense."

Leah wanted to explain that she'd be reading the sign, not listening to someone yell it at her, but instead, just replied, "Yeah. You're probably right."

CHAPTER 9

Leah awoke Friday morning refreshed. She'd set her alarm for nine-fifteen and woke up ten minutes before that. As the sun streamed into her bedroom, slicing a path through the gap in her curtains, Leah yawned and stretched. Then everything about this new case came back to her. All her doubt and worry descended like flies on a dead carcass. The hole that had been forming in her stomach throughout the last few days ripped open again. One single idea filled her head: *Could my pa have shot the wrong man?*

She wished she was still asleep.

When she had arrived home last night, she had felt exhausted, despite how little work she'd actually accomplished. Feeling like she should trudge on, after fixing the kids some dinner, she hit the paperwork again, forcing her way through everything, outlining from what led to the police obtaining a warrant to search Harry Stork's house up to and including the details from the night Stork was shot.

He hadn't been home when police raided his house on June 24, 1974, and found, among other things, a gun forensics would later confirm as the murder weapon likely used on all nine victims: a Smith & Wesson Model 10, a revolver chambered for .38 Special caliber rounds, a gun also known as an S&W Victory.

After his house was tossed, Stork disappeared for near on exactly a month before Leah's pa and his small team surrounded him in that shotgun shack. Nothing in the reports mentioned any letters coming into the station, but Leah had already expected that.

She set the files in her "done pile" and decided she'd done enough work for the day. Needing to wind down, she sat in the living room and watched television with her daughter, Caroline.

And now it was morning again, another hopeful day. So, she pushed all the doom and gloom out of the way, clearing her head enough for her to run through the day's plan. She had two interviews to do: one with Harry Stork's pa, Noah, the other with his twin brother, Tommy. She didn't know what she was looking for, but it was a good-to-go after yesterday's strange experience with Thomas Kennedy Bradshaw. She still hadn't decided what to make of Bradshaw's strange behavior. Her gut told her he was guilty, but guilty of what, exactly? She was only sure of one thing.

Her gut was rarely wrong.

By the time Leah found Noah Stork's house, she was quite certain Chris had the pronunciation of the street right. This was only her second time driving through Blue Jay Maples, but it brought back her last experience quite vividly. Every single road zigged and zagged along ridiculous paths through a tangled forest. Mostly oaks and birches, but also the odd maple and gum. Without the maples, the name would have been odd. The woods were thick and grew right up to the edge of the deep culverts dug out on either side of the roads. The ditches looked at least six feet wide and God only knew how deep. Leah drove carefully. The last thing she needed was her Bonneville sticking ass-up in one of them.

Every road was named after a bird. She got lost twice, both times ending up on a particularly nasty stretch of gravel with the delightful name of Mockingbird Lane. She also drove down Cardinal Road, Chickadee Road, Finch Drive, and Hummingbird Highstreet. There were more, but by the time she managed to find Woodpecker Wind, she'd successfully blocked them from her mind.

This had to be the worst part of Alvin to drive through, yet the area was being actively developed. Most of the roads were fairly new, and she passed many houses either recently built or in the process of being constructed. Noah Stork lived practically in the middle of it all, his area still rustic. In fact, she drove a mile before finding his house without a neighbor in sight.

Stork lived in a baby blue clapboard-style home with white trim. The house and yard were well-kept. Every window but the living room picture window had white shutters, and an old-fashioned porch wrapped around half the house. The shuttered windows had flower boxes, overflowing with red and yellow tulips. A short, paved driveway ran alongside the home, separating it from a separate garage painted the same baby blue as the house. A white Hyundai Excel was parked in the driveway. The lawn in the small front yard looked like a putting green.

After exiting her vehicle, Leah traversed the driveway and went up the porch step and rang the bell.

The door was answered by an older gentleman with

gray hair and green eyes. Leah knew from his report that
Noah was sixty-five, but he barely looked a year past
fifty. She immediately saw an acute resemblance between him and the Xeroxed photos of Harry and Tommy
she found in the files yesterday. The eyeglasses with
thin gold frames Noah wore were the only real thing
separating him from looking exactly like his sons. He
had on a blue collared shirt tucked into eggshell-white
Dockers and stood slightly taller than Leah, probably
around five ten.

"Noah Stork?" she asked.

"That's me."

"I'm Detective Teal from the Alvin Police Department, I'd like to ask you a few questions if I may, regarding—"

"The new Stickman murder?" he asked, without letting her finish. His smooth voice articulated every con-
sonant of his words, making him sound almost like
Chris, but with a confidence even Chris usually lacked.
To Leah, he sounded like a radio disc jockey.

"Good guess," she replied.

"I read the papers, Detective. I keep up. I am also
fully aware of what transpired all those years back when
my son was accused of being the Stickman. I assume
now, with this newest murder, his record has been exon-
erated?"

"Well, that's still remainin' to be worked out. Obviously, it's still pretty early in the investigation, but I'm
hopin' you might be able to shed some details on a few
things. Maybe save me some time."

"Why don't you come inside?"

This was a surprise. Very rarely did anyone invite
Leah in when she showed up unannounced to ask questions. She liked doing it this way. She felt it gave her a

strategic advantage, like yesterday, when she saw what her surprise visit had done to Bradshaw. It obviously stirred up some emotions—she just had yet to interpret exactly what those emotions were.

"That would be nice," she said to Stork. "Thank you."

She followed him inside, stopping at the threshold to remove her boots.

"Just leave them on," Stork said. "Tomorrow's cleaning day."

He led Leah into an expansive living room that had a nice view of the front porch. A burgundy davenport accented in cherry sat beneath the window. A stone fireplace stood opposite, with two wing chairs on either side that matched the davenport. Along the third wall, cherry shelves had been built that ran the entire length, floor-to-ceiling. They were near on full of books, the shiny spines of which reflected brightly in the well-lit room.

Leah had never seen so many books, and she took a minute to study the spines, noticing that the shelves' edges were labeled by subject. Books with authors like Kant, Descartes, Nietzsche, and Freud were in the philosophy section. Titles such as *The American Revolution, Reign of Terror: Stalin and the USSR,* and *World War II Frontlines* sat in history, and spines reading *Shakespeare's Complete Works, Chaucer,* and *Divina Commedia* had been relegated to fiction. This last one gave Leah pause.

"Do you read Italian?" she asked Stork.

"I do," Noah said slowly, following her gaze, "but that version's actually in English. I don't know why they didn't translate the title, probably just to be pretentious." He laughed. "But the rest of the book's an English translation of Dante's poem."

"I don't think I've ever seen this many books outside of a library or a store before now," Leah said, and actually thought he might even have more than Hemingway's, a bookstore downtown.

"Reading is good," Stork said. "Keeps the mind active and supple. It's always good to keep things working. I believe the mind is much akin to an automobile in that respect—if you don't keep it tuned up, it slowly wears down."

Leah considered this and nodded. She was surprised at Stork's ability to set her at ease. She had shown up wanting the advantage of surprising a man whose son was taken from him by her very department, expecting to find him bitter and resentful, but found herself surprised by how calm and good-natured he seemed.

Stork gestured to one of the wing chairs. "Sit. Please. Would you like something to drink? Perhaps some sweet tea? I have some already made."

"Sure," Leah said, "that would be nice." She took a seat, her attention remaining on all those books.

Stork returned from the kitchen, a cup of sweet tea in his right hand. He gave it to Leah. "Thank you," she said. "Aren't you having some?"

"I am," he said. "Mine's still in the kitchen."

He went back and got himself a cup, carried it back in, took a seat on the davenport across from Leah. He placed his cup of tea on the cherry coffee table in front of him.

Leah's eyes remained on all those books, but Noah Stork brought her back to the subject at hand.

"So," he said. "I am sure you will get around to

telling me sooner or later, but, may I ask, what details do you reckon I might be able to help with?" His right arm went up along the davenport's top.

Shifting in her chair, Leah met his eyes. "As you might guess, there is a lot of paperwork to go through regarding the murders from 1973 and 1974. I've only just begun to go through everything."

"Why don't you tell me about this newest murder?" Stork said. "That might allow me to best comply with whatever it is you need."

"Well, honestly, there isn't a lot to tell you don't already know. The victim was found pretty near in exactly the same state as all the victims from fifteen years ago. Whoever killed Abilene Williams wanted us to believe he was the old Stickman."

"But you reckon he's not. I read your 'official statement,'" Stork said, "I felt it came off rather vague."

The hole in Leah's stomach tore open again. She really didn't want to discuss her bogus statement. She had hoped nobody would see through it, but obviously she hadn't done a great job. "Mr. Stork," Leah answered. "As much as I don't want to offend you or make you angry, I've looked at the evidence surrounding the old case, and everything I've seen supports the fact that your son committed those crimes. So, yes, I believe this new murder is the work of someone else."

"Hmm," he said, with a slow nod. "You also indicated in your release that evidence turned up linking this death to a potential suspect. May I ask what that evidence entailed?" He took his arm down from where he'd laid it, leaned forward, and lifted his cup of tea from the table. With a big drink, he set the cup back down and returned his arm to where it was along the davenport's top.

"I'm afraid I'm not at liberty to say," she came back with, probably a mite too quick.

"I see. Well then, why don't you tell me what we *can* talk about?"

Pulling out her pad, Leah flipped to her notes.

"I'd like to first discuss Harry's tour of duty in Vietnam. What, exactly, led to his honorable discharge?"

Stork stared right into her eyes, never once flinching. "According to the army, he couldn't perform his duties due to psychological impairment."

"Yes, I garnered that much from the report, but what exactly *was* his 'psychological impairment'?"

"This is where the army and I don't see eye to eye," he said, and Leah could hear an edge to his voice. "According to them, Harry wasn't right even before they dropped him in East Asia, but that's a lie. Harry was as bright a bulb as any one of them soldiers. What messed him up was what they made him do. He came back with severe PTSD—post-traumatic—"

Leah cut him off. "I'm familiar with PTSD," she said. "Your other son, Tommy, he also has psychological issues, does he not?"

Leaning back on the davenport, Stork let out a little laugh. "One could say that. He's been in and out of hospitals a lot. Suffers from bad schizophrenia. Looking back, he probably had it from birth, but he wasn't diagnosed until his late teens."

"Is he doing all right, now?"

Stork's attention drifted to the wall of books as he answered almost offhandedly. "Oh, he's up and down. Goes through stretches of being okay, but sooner or later his illness once again gets the best of him."

"I noticed for some time, he and Harry were on the same medication. Do you think there's any chance Harry might've also suffered from schizophrenia? I understand doctors believe it can be genetic."

Stork's eyes locked again with Leah's. "I just said, Detective, the army brought on Harry's 'illness,' and it has nothing to do with schizophrenia. That's just the doctors looking for an easy scapegoat. The army broke Harry. Before then, there was nothing wrong with him. Even after he came back with PTSD, he still managed to start his own company and work. Not like Tommy . . ." He drifted off.

"Yes, from the reports, I reckon Harry's company did quite well."

"Very well, Detective. I am rather proud of him for it. Did you see the photo on the mantel?" He nodded toward it. "That was taken just after he became incorporated. I helped with the logo design."

Leah stood and took the picture from where it sat and studied it. Harry Stork and his father stood in front of Stork's truck shaking hands and smiling. At the time the photo was taken, Noah wasn't nearly so gray, and the resemblance between the two of them was uncanny, although the father stood two inches or so taller than his son. Harry's truck was a red pickup with a white camper on the back. A logo was written across the side of the camper. Although the two of them were in front of it, Leah could make out enough to fill in the blanks.

Stork Sanitation and Waste Removal
THE COMPETITION CAN'T TOUCH OUR JOBS

"I came up with the slogan," Stork said with a smile. "Do you get it? The waste products Harry handled were toxic. So you couldn't touch any of it. I thought it was clever." Leaning forward, he again took a sip of his tea.

Leah nodded. "It is." She set the photo back where it had been and sat down again. "May I ask you about your wife?"

Stork put his right arm along the top of the davenport again. "Not much to tell. She was a good woman, just had to deal with too much. It was one thing putting up with Tommy's problems, but when Harry came back it just became too much. Still"—his eyes gleamed, and Leah realized tears now stood in them—"I never thought she would . . ." He faded out, wiping his eyes with his right forearm. "I'm sorry, Detective. It's still hard."

"Please don't apologize," Leah said. She was starting to feel bad about disrupting this man's day. "I haven't got to the report yet concerning the details of what, exactly, happened to her. I understand it was . . . sleeping pills?"

"Yeah, almost a whole month's prescription." Stork seemed to have regained most of his composure. "We'll never be sure what time she did it, but Tommy found her in her room around about three o'clock. I was down in Mobile at the time. Didn't come back until two hours later. Tommy was out of his skin by then. He had no idea what to do. He hadn't even called the police."

"I see," Leah said, jotting down some notes.

"Tommy was living here at the time?" she asked. "Does he still live here?"

Stork sighed. "Not anymore, but yes, he did live with me quite some time after the government funding he got from his accident ran out."

"This is the construction accident?" Leah asked. "When he lost his fingers?"

"That's the only 'accident' my son ever had, Detective."

"Oh, I was referring to the . . . his face. You know, the—"

"I wouldn't call that an 'accident.' Tommy liked to fight and he picked fights on purpose. I believe he deserves that gash as much as any Boy Scout deserves a merit badge."

Leah raised her eyebrows. This response surprised her.

Stork obviously read her face. "Oh, don't get me wrong, Detective. I love—well, in Harry's case, I guess 'loved' is more accurate—both my boys as much as any man can. And God knows their ma liked to dote on both of them. But I won't lie. When you spend as much time as I have living with your grown-up child, certain . . . *animosities* is the word, I suppose . . . begin to arise. It's unfortunate, really. Tommy and I rarely talk anymore now. I'm lucky if I see him even once a year. There was a time I saw him near on every single waking hour of every day. It was too much, I reckon." He paused for a moment and then changed topics. "You know something? I've been sitting here trying to figure out where I've seen you before. I just figured it out. You're the one who was interviewed in the *Examiner* a couple weeks back, right?"

Leah felt her cheeks redden. "That was me, yes." She smiled thinly.

"It was a good article. I remember now. You talked a lot about your pa. He was the man who shot my boy, isn't that right?"

Leah narrowed her eyes, trying to discern even the slightest hint of anger in his response. She couldn't find any. "Yes, that's right," she said quietly.

Shaking his head dramatically, Stork said, "Well, isn't that something. Sure is a small world. Now there's a new Stickman case and you're the one investigating it. Doesn't it feel like things have come full circle?"

Once again she raised her eyebrows. "I . . . I guess it does. Haven't had time to really think about it that closely."

"I remember the piece in the paper. You have two children, right?"

Suddenly, Leah felt like she was the one being interviewed. "That's right."

"And if I'm remembering correctly, you lost your husband, too?"

"You have a good memory, Mr. Stork."

"Eidetic," he said then clarified. "Photographic."

Leah nodded. "I know what *eidetic* means."

"Sorry," Stork said, raising his palm. "No offense intended."

"None taken. And yeah, so because of losing my Billy, I can sympathize pretty well with what happened to your wife."

His lips tightened. He dropped his gaze to the coffee table. "It was a goddamn shame," he said. "She was a good woman. You know"—his eyes lifted to Leah—"you don't really know how good some things are until they're gone."

Leah stared past him out the window and allowed her mind to settle on Billy for a second or two before coming back to the room. "How long ago did Tommy move out?"

"Oh, let me think. I believe he left summer of 1978."

Leah smiled at this. "Thought you had a photographic memory?"

"I do. For important things. Exactly when Tommy left isn't that important. What is, is that he did."

"Where did he move to?"

"Oh, up near Birmingham. About ten miles outside of town."

This surprised Leah. "Why Birmingham?" she asked. "Why didn't he stay in Alvin? Far as I could tell from the reports, up until the time they were issued he'd spent his whole life here, hadn't he?"

"I honestly don't know what goes through that boy's head, but I have some guesses. First, he went up that way quite often even while he lived with me. I asked him what the hell he did there, but he never gave me a direct answer. For a while, I thought maybe he had a girlfriend that a way, but he's not really the girlfriend type. I think, maybe, he felt the strain on our relationship just as much as I did, and he figured he should just get away. That's my best guess."

Leah got ready to write. "Can I have his address?"

"Well, he's not in Birmingham anymore. He actually did eventually come back down here. I assume you want his *current* address?"

"Yes," Leah said. "Please."

He gave it to her, right off the top of his head. Tommy lived in the northern part of town, on Rodman Road, an area about as far away from his pa's as you could get and still be in Alvin.

"And his telephone number?" Leah asked.

"That one I can't give you. It keeps changing and, last I heard, his service was cut off again, so he's either still without a phone or he has a number he hasn't given me yet."

"How long ago was it you last heard from him?"

"October of last year. He never contacts me, I always have to go to him. Even when he was up in Birmingham, I had to take the initiative to visit and call him when I wanted to talk. He's not that social, if you know what I mean."

Leah nodded.

A pregnant silence followed, feeling awkward as Stork's attention went up to that photo on the mantel. Leah knew his thoughts had gone back to Harry. "You know, there are days I sure do miss him," he said.

"I understand that," Leah said, trying to sound sympathetic. Reality was, she did feel sorry for him.

"You know, your department brought Tommy in for questioning two weeks before they went for Harry. I had no idea what was going on. It sure felt like the police had singled out our family." He paused, pulling his eyes away from the photo and bringing them back to her. "Still does sometimes."

"Yes, well, a witness who knew Tommy gave a statement saying he saw him at one of the murder scenes." Leah didn't want to stumble over the fact that she didn't know the exact details of what happened during that interview—why, exactly, her pa's suspicions fell away from Tommy and settled instead on Harry.

"I know, Detective. But that witness and Tommy had a long history of not liking each other very much. He was part of that bar fight Tommy got in—a friend of the one who gave my boy that scar."

"So this . . . acquaintance, this witness . . . you think he lied in his statement?"

Stork nodded. "I would say so."

Well, Leah knew something had changed her pa's mind about Tommy, and what Leah just heard could very well be true. She stood from her chair. "I think I've taken up enough of your time, Mr. Stork."

He waved the comment away. "Think nothing of it,"

he said. "I like the company. I don't spend a lot of time talking with folk. Not since Tommy left."

She smiled sadly. "I'm sorry your relationship with him isn't as good as it could be."

"Oh, it's not as bad as I am probably making it seem. I just . . . ever since Harry's death, I can't help but keep comparing the two in my head. They're just so different. You know, Tommy would've been drafted, too, if he hadn't been designated 4-F on account of his accident."

Leah nodded. "I read that."

"You realize he got that accident ten days before Harry was drafted. Sometimes I think about that a bit."

"How so?" Leah asked.

He raised a dubious eyebrow. "Seems a bit of a coincidence to me, is all. I'm not a man who likes coincidences, Detective."

And on what turned out to be a string of points, Leah once again found herself agreeing with what Noah Stork said. She walked back to her car, thinking over how much she'd felt drawn to him. They had a lot in common, a lot of similar views.

She wondered if she'd feel anywhere close to the same about Tommy when she interviewed him.

CHAPTER 10

Dan Truitt, detective from the Birmingham Police Department, arrived at the Alvin Police Department. Leah had just gotten back from her interview with Noah Stork. She had only taken two sips of her coffee when her paramour from up north showed up.

It wasn't even noon.

"Knock, knock," Dan said, opening the door. "The party's here."

"I wish you wouldn't do that," Leah said.

"Do what?"

"Drive like an imbecile. Being an hour later wouldn't have killed you." She had called him just before leaving the house this morning and he had told her he was just about to head out. That was almost ten o'clock.

"Yeah, well, just be glad I'm not drunk. Then I would've been here a half hour ago."

She hit him in the chest. "You're such an idiot."

Dan Truitt wore a white collared shirt tucked into olive drab khakis. His hair, though thinning, was a very light blond, so it was hard to see the baldness from the hair. His eyes were a translucent blue that Leah often found herself getting lost in. Dan always reminded Leah a little of the Professor from *Gilligan's Island*.

"You alone?" he asked her.

Leah looked toward Chief Montgomery's office, where the door was closed along with the blinds. "Ethan's in there, probably watching whatever sport is on right now. Chris is out for lunch, I believe. I actually just got here. I was on an interview. Why?"

Dan took her in his arms and for a moment they shared a kiss. They'd been in a relationship since Christmas, and there was no longer any point in trying to hide it, even though they still did their best.

The kiss lasted a good minute.

"That's why," Dan said.

"I think Chris should go for lunch more often," Leah said. "I like the way you kiss." She walked over to the coffee machine. "Want a cup? I just brewed a new pot."

"Sure. It's not a bad day for coffee. Been cooling off since Wednesday."

"I hear they're calling for rain tomorrow," Leah said, pouring two mugs full. She added cream to Dan's and brought both mugs back to where he was standing in front of her desk. She handed the cream-filled one to him.

"Rain," Dan said. "I'll believe it when I see it." They both looked out the window. The sun twinkled brightly off the chrome of a light blue Buick parked outside the station.

"One of the weather channels said thunderstorms, actually," Leah said.

"Well, that's probably more likely. The Lord seems to hate Alabama. We'll probably get smited by a twister in four days."

"Don't say that. Stranger things have happened. And I think the word is *smote*."

Dan walked around and took a seat in Chris's chair. Leah sat in hers. "So," he said, "I'm dying to know what's happening in your case."

"Not much. I made some calls and confirmed that, in the last few months, nobody's been let out of a local federal correctional institution or the Louisiana State Penitentiary or the Federal Penitentiary in Atlanta. At least nobody they suspect would be a serial killer."

"They said that? Nobody we *suspect* would be a serial killer?"

"No, not in so many words."

"Thank God. For a moment there, I thought the world went crazy. Nobody *expects* people to be serial killers. They're usually the ones you expect the *least*. The quiet ones who keep to themselves."

"At any rate, I didn't come up with any names or anythin'," Leah said.

"Well, it was a good try." Dan took a sip of his coffee before placing the mug on Chris's desk.

"Ethan and Chris lifted a print Tuesday. Mobile's still looking for a match with anyone in the system. Probably be a while till they're done."

Dan picked up his mug again, went to take a sip, but instead returned it to the desk. "Do you have to brew this so hot? There should be a setting for temperature on those machines."

Leah was already nearly done with hers. "It's not that hot," she said. "I even put cream in yours. You're just a baby."

"I'm *your* baby," he said, the fluorescent lights glimmering in his eyes.

Leah felt that pang in her stomach. The *I'm in love* pang she hadn't felt for so long. "Yes," she said, "I guess you are."

They both fell silent. Leah's gaze fixed on her coffee mug.

"What's wrong?" Dan asked.

"I dunno," she said. "Just . . . I keep thinkin' about, what if my pa was wrong? What if he shot an innocent man?"

"Now, you don't know Stork was innocent, yet. He had a gun and he was runnin'."

Her chest heaved. She lifted her eyes back to Dan's. She felt tears come to them. She didn't want them to—didn't want Dan to see her get emotional—but she couldn't stop them.

"Come here," Dan said, getting up. He knelt down beside her chair and took her in his arms. "It's goin' to be okay."

She pulled away. "How? How is any of this okay? What if my pa shot the wrong man?"

"What if? Listen, we're goin' to catch this guy," Dan promised. "Whether he's the original Stickman or a copycat killer, we're goin' to get him."

Leah pulled away. "And what if it takes *us* a year and a half and he takes nine more victims like happened the first time 'round? I can't deal with that, Dan."

"Yes, you can. It's your job."

"I can't do it. Too many people die."

"Leah, listen. You can't save the world. The best you can do is the best you can do. The rest of the time you need to let it out of your head. Otherwise it'll drive you crazy. Why do you think I drink so damn much? I know sometimes it's hard not to take things personal."

She looked at him, knowing her own blue eyes were

swimming in tears. "This one *is* personal. At least it *was*. Personal between my pa and Harry Stork . . . A man who wasn't even . . ." She paused, unable to finish the sentence. "And now the letters are coming to *me*. With *my* name on the front. Don't you understand, Dan? This is as goddamn personal as it can get."

Her words broke apart again. Dan Truitt pulled her in close and ran his fingers through her hair. There was nothing left to say or do. He just knelt there and let her cry herself out.

"We'll figure it all out," Dan said. "It's just goin' to take a little time. But we'll figure it out."

"Well, we need to answer some questions. Two big ones, to be exact," Leah said. "One: Why did the killin's stop after my pa killed Harry Stork? Just to make it *look* like he was the Stickman? And two: Why have they started again now, fifteen years later, seemingly out of the blue?"

"Yep," Dan said, "those *are* the big questions. Maybe we'll have some luck finding answers with the squealers Ethan wants us to interview."

"I sure hope so, Dan." Leah felt a stone turn in her gut at the thought of her pa killing an innocent man, especially on a case that, for many people, was his legacy. "I sure hope so."

At that moment, Chris walked in the door.

"Hey . . ." he started, then noticed the state Leah was in. "Everything okay?"

Dan nodded. "Yeah, we're just havin' a moment."

Chris walked around to the other side of his desk. Dan moved around Leah so Chris could get in his chair. Lifting Dan's mug, Chris asked, "This belong to you?"

"Yeah," Dan said, taking it from him. "Thanks."

Leah wiped her tears away.

"You goin' to be okay?" Dan asked.

She nodded, her lips pressed into a thin line.

"I might be able to cheer you up a bit," Chris said to Leah. "I have some news."

"What's that?" Leah asked, her voice still tearstained. She hated feeling weak.

"You asked me to check for any juvie records for Harry Stork? Well, I did that this morning. And sure enough, bogies hit the radar."

Dan's eyebrows went up. "Thought his record was spotless?"

"His adult record is," Chris replied, lifting a paper full of scribbled notes from beside his keyboard. "Turns out he did a year at the Mobile County Youth Center in 1960. He actually went before a judge twice that year, both times for breakin' and enterin'. First time he got a year's probation. Then, exactly three months later, neighbors reported seeing him climb through a window after he smashed it. Cops chased him down the street while he ran from the sirens, a stereo system in one hand, a crowbar in the other." Chris laughed.

Dan lifted his hand to his chin, obviously thinking about something.

"What?" Leah asked.

"Just . . . well . . . it just makes more *sense,* now."

"What do you mean?"

"It just didn't sit well with me that someone would go from having no record to slaughterin' folk for fun."

"Dan, he boosted a stereo. That's hardly the same as—"

"Doesn't matter. He did time. Bein' in the joint changes a person. Especially when you're young. Even in youth detention centers."

"Yeah, well, after that he got drafted for 'Nam. I

talked to his pa this morning. Said Harry came back a lot different from how he was when he left."

Dan looked at the floor, his face rigid. "How so?"

"Well, his pa said he had PTSD, but he was honorably discharged for psychological problems affecting his ability to do his job. They reckoned he already had them before the war. So I think it's something more than just PTSD."

"There's no 'just' PTSD, Leah. PTSD is a *huge* thing."

"Yeah, but . . . his brother. His twin . . . they're identical. He's got schizophrenia or somethin'. Apparently, pretty bad. That sort of thing can be genetic."

"But it doesn't *have* to be."

"No," Leah said. "You're right. Chris, have you found out how likely it is for twins to both have schizophrenia?"

"Jesus," Chris said. "How much do you want from me in twelve hours? I can only do one thing at a time."

"Okay, okay," Leah said. "I just thought you might've looked into it."

"I know I might look like Superman—I mean, if Superman was black—but I don't have any real superpowers."

Dan took the scribbled notes. "I dunno," he said, looking them over. "Getting juvie records like this? I'm goin' to have to disagree."

CHAPTER 11

After spending a couple of hours with Dan at the station, Leah sent Dan home to her house with her key. She'd already set out some blankets and a pillow for him this morning before she left. Dan would be sleeping on the sofa. It had only been six months, and Leah still felt uncomfortable about sharing a bed with the man while her kids were home. Dan had started to argue the point, but quickly acquiesced. "Besides," he had said, "I do have to get some work done. And I like to start after midnight. Probably a time you like to be sawing logs."

Leah had laughed and said, "Yeah, probably," but inside she felt conflicted. She already knew from experience that Dan's idea of working involved not only late hours but a half bottle or so of Jim Beam.

At first, she didn't think about it, but the more she had to deal with his obvious addiction problems, the harder it became for her to wear the happy face. Oh well, he'd be out in the living room on the sofa and the kids would be in bed by then. *So,* she thought, *out of sight, out of mind.*

Leah pulled to the side of the road right out front of

Tommy Stork's shotgun shack on Rodman Road. His house looked out of place here, surrounded by fields of ranchland. Most of the structures she passed on her way up were farmhouses and barns set way off from the road behind fields of cattle, cotton, and corn. Tommy's shack looked like a pimple ready to pop on an otherwise clear porcelain doll–like face. The land surrounding it was flat and full of witchgrass and stretched way back to a tree line far off in the distance. It brought a memory of a picture she'd formed in her head one night while her pa thought she was sleeping and had what he assumed was a discreet conversation with Officer Peter Strident about some details of the night he shot Harry Stork dead.

Tommy's house looked a lot like the one she imagined Harry in. There was no driveway, and a pomegranate-colored Ford Fairmont was parked on the ground between the road and the house. The shack's wooden siding was a faded pale green and the door was a rusty red. Leah walked across the dusty ground, avoiding the car. Up close, she noticed cracks in the door where the original light brown wood showed as deep splinters.

She knocked.

It took so long for anyone to answer that she was on the verge of turning back to her car when she heard a slide lock on the other side. The door opened, revealing a man slightly taller than herself with sandy black hair and green eyes she felt she recognized as being the eyes of Noah Stork. Only these ones belonged to his son. They were the spitting image of each other except for the gash running down the left side of Tommy's face. Although she'd seen the photograph in the files, nothing could really prepare her for what the scar looked like up close. It hadn't healed well, and Leah hoped her face managed to hide the visceral reaction it brought to her.

"Mr. Stork?" she asked. "I'm Detective Teal from the Alvin Police Department? I was wonderin' if we could talk for a spell?"

"Yeah?" Stork said. "Was wonderin' when you'd show up."

"You were figuring I'd be comin'?" Leah asked. "Now, why's that, Mr. Stork?"

"You're here 'bout that murder, ain't ya?"

Leah stared into his eyes. Although they were clear and bright, she got the distinct feeling nothing else about the man was. It was near on the exact opposite of the way she felt about his pa. "I am," she said. "What do you know about it?"

"Just what's on the TV."

"And what's that?"

"I dunno. Seems like another Stickman killin'."

Leah nodded slightly. "It does, but it's not."

"I heard your report. I think it's full of shit."

"Why's that?"

"On account of if you had evidence pointin' directly to a suspect, you would be questionin' him, not me."

"So why do you reckon I've come to your door?" Leah asked.

"Because, just like last time, y'all is graspin' at straws. And back then it wound up not bein' me. And this time it ain't neither."

Leah couldn't imagine Tommy living with his pa. Having now met them both, they were nothing at all alike. She could see why Noah was frustrated.

"Do you miss your brother?" she asked.

"What kind of question is that?"

"Seems like an easy one."

"'Course I do. Been a long time, though."

"It has. Funny how a new murder matchin' the old Stickman ones just popped up after all this time."

She waited for Stork to respond, but no response came. Finally, he just shrugged. Leah's eyes were drawn to the man's right hand, where his middle finger and index finger didn't go any farther than the lower knuckle. Tommy saw her studying it and put both hands in the pockets of his dungarees.

"I understand you suffer from mental illness," Leah said.

Another shrug. "Dunno 'bout that."

"Your pa says you do."

"My pa says lots of shit."

"What about the doctors?" Leah asked.

"What about 'em?"

"What do they say?"

"I reckon they ain't that smart." Tommy pushed himself up on his toes and scanned the horizon behind Leah. She took a quick glance behind her, trying to figure out what had his attention, but there was nothing there. Just an old timber-framed barn that looked as though at one time it had sheathing covering the clapboards. Now, from where Leah stood, the sheathing was mostly gone and time had turned the siding a dark gray. It stood two empty fields away, surrounded by dirt that was overgrown with witchgrass.

"You still on medication?" Leah asked Tommy.

"I don't reckon that's any of your business, ma'am."

"When was the last time you had an encounter with the police, Mr. Stork?"

He thought long and hard, and again his attention went to an area behind Leah. "I dunno. I s'pose right before y'all killed my brother."

"And before that?"

He dropped his gaze and looked at her. "Probably when I got this," he said, and his left hand came out of his pocket and traced the scar from the top of his lip to where it ended just short of his eye.

"Bar fight up near Birmingham, right?"

"You seem to know a lot 'bout me already."

"Just what's in the reports. How did you get the . . ." She accidentally stumbled and started over. "What was the cause of your scar?"

"I gave the bastard a left hook and went in for a right, but he came up with a broken bottle."

"What started the fight?"

Stork inhaled deeply, stuffed his hand back in the pocket. "Him and his friend were makin' fun of me. They's sayin' I lost my fingers on purpose so I wouldn't have to go fight in 'Nam."

"Do you *always* get violent when people make fun of you?"

Stork thought for a moment, scratched the back of his neck, and replied, "I was pretty drunk that night."

"I see. How often do you drink?"

"Not so much now. With my meds, I tend to fall asleep if I drink too much."

"So you are on medication," Leah said.

"S'pose so."

"When was the last time you were hospitalized for it?"

Another pause went by while he considered this. "I don't reckon I can recall," he said.

"In the past year? Two years? Surely you have some idea."

His eyes gripped hers. "I said I don't recall, ma'am."

"Your pa says you get hospitalized a lot."

"Yeah, well, *he's* the one who's schizo. Not me. He just likes to *tell* people that. Like the doctors."

Leah narrowed her eyes. "Now, why would your pa make up something like you havin' a medical disorder?"

"On account of he doesn't care so much for me. He uses it as an excuse as to why I ain't perfect like him or like Harry was before he came home all messed up."

"When you say you're not perfect, what do you mean? Not perfect at what?"

He scratched his neck again. "Behavin', I guess. Harry never got into no fights or nothin'. Well, 'cept for when he was in 'Nam, but that's different, least to my pa it is."

"You lived with your pa quite a while, didn't you? Seems strange to me you would stay with someone you feel so strongly about."

"Yeah, back then I didn't know how much of a liar he is. Practically everythin' comes outta his mouth is a lie. I ain't got no 'mental illness,' I just have problems. Normal problems. Everyone's got problems."

"Okay." Leah decided to drop the schizophrenia for now and try a different tack. "Do you own a gun, Mr. Stork?"

A long time went by as he carefully studied the world off in the distance. Finally, he said, "Nope. Sure don't."

"For certain?" Leah asked. "You seemed to think on that a long while before answerin'."

"I'm sure. I ain't got no guns."

"Not even a shotgun for huntin'?"

Something flashed in his green eyes. He once again fixed his gaze on Leah. "I told ya! I ain't got no guns!"

"I can come back with a warrant, you know."

Again he fell silent. This time he studied the floor while coming up with a response. "No guns," he said, looking back up. "Just like I told ya, I ain't got no guns."

"What were you doing Tuesday evening between five and nine?" Leah asked.

This time, Stork answered right away. "Was sittin' on my couch watchin' the TV."

"You came up with that pretty quick. You sure you were here? Don't want to think about it a bit?"

"No, damn straight I know where I was," he said. "I watch *Mod Squad* Tuesdays. It don't end till eight-thirty."

"You watch it *every* Tuesday?"

"That's right."

"Can anyone confirm you were here watching television?"

"What do ya mean?"

"Did you have anyone with you? Did you call anyone on the phone during that time? Did anyone happen to come to your door?"

"Nope. I told ya. I was watchin' *Mod Squad*. I wasn't talkin' to nobody."

Leah let out a big breath. "I see. One more question. Do you own any boots?"

Stork's eyes partially closed while he examined Leah's face. "That's a strange question to ask someone," he finally replied.

"Can you please answer it?" Leah asked.

"Of course I own boots. Who the hell doesn't own boots?"

"How many pairs of boots you own?"

Leah had been holding her pad the whole time she'd been talking to Stork, but so far she'd only written but a few notes. There really wasn't much to write. Now she thought she might be coming to something of value.

"Three, I reckon."

"You're not sure?"

"Do you count hip waders?"

Leah shook her head. "No, just proper boots."

"Three then," Stork said. Then: "No, wait, four. I still have my old Timberlands with the sole comin' off. I haven't tossed 'em yet. So it's four."

"Can I see them?"

He blinked. "You wanna see my boots?"

Leah nodded.

"All of 'em?"

"Yes."

He shrugged. "Okay, hang on a minute."

Leaving the door ajar, he walked down and disappeared in one of the rooms in the center of the shack. Leah could hear him start rummaging. It sounded like he was pulling stuff off of shelves or going through a cluttered closet. She took the opportunity to reach out and push the door open wider. Craning her neck, she took a look inside the first room of the shack. It was a living room with two worn sofa chairs, one forest green, the other a beige. Both were torn in several places and the stuffing popped from the armrest of one. The beige had been repaired several times with silver duct tape.

A small round table stood between them, and across the room a twelve-inch TV with rabbit ears sat upon two upturned crates. The television was turned on and the picture was fuzzy. Tommy had been watching an *I Love Lucy* rerun. Now that the door was open, Leah heard Ricky Ricardo's distinct voice and the ubiquitous laugh track coming from the set in a wave of static.

The room was a sea of empty bottles—mostly beer, but Leah also made out at least a dozen wine and alcohol bottles, too. They covered the table and the floor. Pizza and other takeout boxes were scattered among them. One empty pizza box balanced open wide on the back of the green sofa chair. There was a distinct smell of sourness, like when milk turns. Flies buzzed around and the dead air hung hot and heavy inside the room.

Leah shook her head, once again comparing in her mind the difference between this place and Noah Stork's spotless home. She could not get her head around what the two living together could possibly have been like.

Hearing Tommy's rummaging come to a stop, she quickly pulled the door back a bit and stood up straight. He came down the hall awkwardly carrying eight boots. It seemed especially awkward for him on account of missing those two fingers.

Arriving at the threshold, he simply dropped everything in his hands. The boots hit the wooden floor with a *bang*. "These are all my boots," he said, his breathing labored.

Leah crouched down and went through them, setting them up straight and pairing them together. When she was done, she discovered he had a pair of gum boots, cowboy boots, and two different sorts of work boots. She took the left one of each pair and looked at the soles, trying to remember the sole of the "jump boot" print Ethan and Chris had put in the file.

The gum boots definitely weren't a match. Neither were the cowboy boots—they had a slight heel. The work boots she wasn't sure about. One pair had *Timberland* written in the center of the sole, but the rest of the tread could be a match. Sure enough, the sole of Tommy's right Timberland boot was barely hanging on to the rest of it. She doubted he would've been able to walk in it.

The other work boot was leather and looked fairly new. The boots and the soles were tan-colored and the tread looked to Leah like it was similar to the one in the Polaroid. She looked inside the boot for the brand and the size. They were US Men size eight and made by Tomis. The company name didn't sound familiar, but Leah couldn't exactly remember what Chuck from Mobile had told her. She also wasn't entirely sure what a "jump boot" looked like, so she wrote all of the boot information on her pad.

Standing back up, she thanked Tommy for being so forthcoming with the boots.

"Why'd you wanna see my boots? What did you write?"

She shook her head. "Nothin' important."

"You wrote somethin'."

"Really, it's nothin' important."

Stork sighed but gave up asking any more questions.

Leah poised her pen over her pad. "Do you have a telephone number I can call you at if I have any more questions?"

Stork shook his head. "Phone's disconnected."

"Okay then, I suppose if I need anything else I'll just have to drop by again. You're okay with that? Not planning on leaving town in the next while or nothin'?"

"No plans."

"Good. Well, Mr. Stork, I reckon that's about all I have to ask you today. I hope you have a good afternoon."

Leah took one last look at her pad where, at the top of the page, she'd written Tommy Stork's name. Now she circled it. Twice. Then she put the pad back in her pocket and said good-bye before turning around and heading back to her car. Behind her, she felt Tommy's gaze leave her before he closed the door.

As she got behind the steering wheel of her Bonneville, she thought about what she learned from this interview, deciding she only knew one thing for certain. And that was the fact that Tommy Stork lied at least once.

He definitely owned a gun.

CHAPTER 12

One of the perks of having Jonathon as a boyfriend was that he had a car. A silver 1982 Nissan Sentra, not the greatest car in the world being seven years old, but it sure beat having no car at all. Even still, Carry and Jonathon did a lot of walking. Carry liked walking because he would hold her hand the whole time. In the car, he occasionally held her hand, but it didn't seem as intimate.

Today, they were in Jonathon's Sentra, but Carry had no idea where they were headed. Jonathon refused to say. After she got in, he started driving.

"Why all the secrecy?" Carry asked. "Where are we going?"

They drove past a lot of pines with little houses squatting among them. Many of the homes had pretty gardens, many still in bloom. An Eastern redwood went by, full of beautiful clusters of pink flowers. This area of town was well-kept and looked nice despite the rain pattering the car's windows. Over the weekend, clouds had rolled in, and by early evening Saturday, rain pounded Alvin like Sandy Koufax firing a fastball into the catcher's mitt. Now it was Monday, and the rain hadn't taken a break since. Carry cracked her window, letting in the smell of fresh, moist air.

Jonathon took another turn. "We're going to my house," Jonathon said. "Well, it's not exactly *my* house, it's my grandpa's. But it's where I live." He smiled.

Excitement pooled in Carry's stomach. "So it's today? I get to meet your grandpa today?" She'd heard a lot about the man since meeting Jonathon. He owned the restaurant Jonathon worked at, Raven Lee's Pizza on Main Street. "So, your grandpa," she asked. "I assume his name is Raven Lee?"

"Raven Lee Emerson," Jonathon corrected. "He's part Choctaw."

This grabbed Carry's attention. Native culture and art had always fascinated her. "How much?" she asked.

"How much what?"

"How much Choctaw is he?"

"I believe one half."

"So that makes you . . ." Carry tried to do the math.

"I don't know," Jonathon said. "I can never work it out properly. I think one eighth."

"That's pretty cool," Carry said. Jonathon reached over and intertwined his fingers with hers.

"There's a lot more to his name and heritage that's cool about my grandpa," he said.

Now Carry was riveted. "Like what?"

Jonathon kept taking his eyes off the road to look at her while he talked. "Like he's a total romantic," he said. "He believes in eternal and everlasting love. My family comes from a history of romantics. We all should've been born in the early 1800s, we would've definitely fit in better. Nobody's romantic anymore. I think that's a shame, don't you?"

"Yeah," Carry said and smiled. "I think *I'm* a romantic. Only problem, didn't most of the romantics die at very young ages?"

Jonathon took another right. They were in the western part of town. Carry couldn't remember the last time she had been this way.

"I'm *definitely* a romantic," Jonathon said. "And I had no idea about the lifespan thing. But I'll tell you something. I'd take thirty or forty *good* years over eighty crappy ones any day." He braked for a squirrel leaping from across the road. He smiled at Carry again. "There's even more to my grandpa than just the romance."

"Like what?"

"I'll let him tell you. He loves stories. Just remember, you're the one anxious to see him, so don't complain if you're stuck listening to him go on and on."

Carry wiggled excitedly in her seat. "I so won't."

"Good. Anyway, see that white house with the green trim? That's mine. We're here."

Jonathon pulled into the driveway of a beautiful little home, and Carry waited for Jonathon to open her door before she got out of the car. In front of the house, two magnolia trees stood in a garden that almost covered the yard. A stone path wound around huckleberry, hydrangeas, and other bushes that broke for small areas of rock gardens and colorful bursts of flowers all surrounding a koi pond with a small, wooden bench.

"This is so beautiful," Carry said. She had the feeling she was going to like Raven Lee Emerson.

A lot.

CHAPTER 13

Leah and Dan decided to check the Federal Penitentiary in Atlanta first, their logic being that anyone knowing anything about the Stickman could, quite practically, be doing pretty big crimes himself. If someone had information about a serial killer's MO, this was a likely place to find them.

Much to Dan's chagrin, Leah drove, insisting that it was *her* case, so traveling duties automatically fell to her. During the long drive, which was mainly through woodlands, she felt Dan's impatience growing. It radiated from him like skunk on a coon dog. The forest finally started to break, and Leah glanced at the clock on her dash. The penitentiary should be coming up soon.

Before they had set out from the station, Norman Crabtree, the medical examiner, had called reporting his results from Abilene Williams's autopsy.

"I figure she was dead probably five or six hours before you found her," Crabtree told Leah.

Leah almost said *she* hadn't found anything, but managed to hold it back while Crabtree continued.

"She died from a gunshot wound to the back of the head. My best guess here is a nine millimeter at close range. The wound's circular, blackened, and seared. Usually that indicates the barrel was probably pressed right against the skull."

So, once again, the Stickman had a new weapon. From what little she'd read in the files, Leah knew the original Stickman killed his victims with an unregistered Smith & Wesson Victory .38 Special revolver, the gun police found when they raided Harry Stork's house. Ballistics confirmed a match using the two rounds recovered from victims' skulls. A month later, when Harry Stork made his last stand, he had wielded an unloaded Beretta 92 with the serial numbers sanded off.

Hearing about this new firearm made Leah wonder if the gun Tommy Stork denied owning happened to be chambered 9 mm.

But that was a question for another day, and the answer would likely involve having to collect more evidence against Tommy that supported Leah's "hunch." She didn't think a judge would issue a warrant based solely on her gut feeling, despite how right that usually turned out to be.

The penitentiary came up on Leah's left.

"Wow," Dan said. "Been a while since I've been here. Don't remember it being quite so big." The main prison building encompassed hundreds of acres.

"I think I read somewhere there's upward of twelve hundred inmates locked away inside," Leah said.

"Makes you wonder, hey?"

"I suppose. Not sure about what, though."

"About why so many people have so much trouble living life the way we've come to think they ought to."

She slowed down as they drove along a wrought-iron fence that ran around the whole compound, and found somewhere to park. Exiting the car, the two of them headed for the main gates, where a tower stood topped with a US flag. The flag snapped loud in the wind and the rain.

They had to state their business and show their badges to get through the gates. Then they followed down a long walkway to the penitentiary's central entrance. The building had an almost baroque feel to it, with the main entrance built forward from the rows of cells spread out on either side. Arched windows loomed down at Leah as they walked beneath a tympanum supported by two white columns. Upon going inside, Leah and Dan once again had to flash their badges.

Two desk officers were working the front. One was already dealing with a dark-haired boy. He had on a blue shirt that hung loosely down around his oversized denims, and was in bad need of a shave. The other officer was free. A young woman with short brown hair and big hazel eyes, she smiled at Leah as she and Dan approached. "I'd like to talk to the on-duty lieutenant," Leah said, again holding up her badge.

The officer picked up the receiver of a black telephone and dialed two numbers. "Who should I say is askin'?" she said to Leah while propping the receiver between her chin and shoulder.

"Detective Leah Teal and Detective Dan Truitt."

"And where you from?"

Leah pointed to herself, then Dan, and said, "Alvin and Birmingham."

"Alvin?" the officer asked. "Didn't you just have another Stickman killin'?" Until now, Leah had grown used to folk never having any clue as to where Alvin was. Nobody other than residents usually ever heard of it. Funny how one dead body can put you right back on the map.

"That's right," Leah said. "That's actually why we're here."

The officer spoke into the phone. "Detectives Teal and Truitt wish to speak with you. From Alvin. Something 'bout that Stickman murder."

Hanging the phone up, she gave Leah another smile. "He'll be right down."

"Right down" turned out to be twenty minutes later, when a Lieutenant Sanders appeared and came over to where Leah and Dan had been sitting, waiting in two very uncomfortable plastic chairs. They stood and both shook Sanders's hand.

"What can I do for you?" he asked, first looking to Dan and then to Leah. "Somethin' about the . . . Stickman?"

Leah explained Ethan's theory, how they might be able to get some useful information out of an inmate if they might be allowed to interview one.

"We've got over a thousand choices for you," Sanders said. "I don't know how you're goin' to pick one out."

"Isn't there usually someone who sticks out a bit from the rest?" Dan asked. "You know, a 'talker'? A sort of social butterfly who's into everybody else's business?"

Sanders rubbed his chin. A tall, lanky man, he must have stood six-four. His eyes were hard and gray. "Yeah," he said. "Come to think of it, I think I know a guy inside just like that. Goes by 'Scoop'."

"The nickname sounds promising," Leah said.

Sanders cocked his head, giving it a quick shake. "He's got attitude, though. Don't reckon he's goin' to want to tell you much. And . . ." He inhaled a breath through his teeth.

"And what?" Dan asked.

"And he can be a mean son of a bitch, sometimes. Gotta warn you."

"Can we at least *try?*" Leah asked.

The lieutenant leveled his gaze at her. Slowly a smile crept across his face. "Certainly," he said. He picked up a receiver on the wall above the row of chairs and made a quick call. After hanging up, he asked Leah and Dan to follow him to an interrogation room.

After a bit of a walk that provided a tour of some of the facility, they came to Interrogation Room 1A. Sanders stopped at the one-way window looking inside, where a man was already seated. He was in one of two metal chairs that stood on either side of a metal table. The rest of the room was white, with walls of concrete. To Leah, the starkness made the room appear lonely and cold.

The man inside had dark brown hair tangled in a messy, wild clutch. His eyes were dark and his wrists and ankles were shackled. Two scars on the left side of his face crisscrossed into a deeply cut *X*. He wore the standard inmate orange suit. Tattoos done in jailhouse blue adorned the backs of his hands and arms leading right up under his sleeves. More tattoos were on his neck.

He turned his face toward the glass, almost as if he could feel them watching. His gaze chilled Leah and, even though she knew all he saw was mirror, she had to glance away. Something in his eyes scared her. It was like looking at some kind of wild animal. A jackal, maybe.

"He *looks* mean," Leah said with a swallow. Inside her head she talked herself down. She needed to gain some confidence before going in.

"Yep," Sanders said. "Told you."

"Shackles, eh?" Dan asked.

"The man's like a tiger, Detective," Sanders replied. He rubbed his hands together. "So, you both goin' in? I'll need to get another chair . . ."

"No," Leah said, trying to keep her voice calm and steady. "Just me."

"You sure?" Dan asked.

Leah hesitated, twisting her bottom lip between her teeth. "Honestly?" She let out a big breath. "No. I'm not sure. But I won't ever be able to look at myself again if I don't at least try."

Dan gave her a thin smile. "Alrighty, then."

Leah took another big breath. "Okay, here we go."

Dan wished her luck as she walked away and turned the corner toward the door. She entered the room, closing the door behind her before sitting down across from Scoop. Then she realized she had no idea what the man's *real* name was. Did the lieutenant just expect her to call him "Scoop," she wondered.

"Hi," Leah said. Scoop's eyes were nearly black as he glared upward at her. One wandered lazily and disconcertingly to the right. He said nothing.

Leah placed her palms on the cold metal table. "So," she said, hearing a bit of a quiver in her voice. "I hear you're the man to talk to for inside information." She instantly regretted the statement. Made her sound like a schoolgirl.

Scoop spat something on the floor and then once again resumed his dead-eyed, Manson-cold stare.

"I, um, don't know what your name is," Leah stumbled. "I was just told you were known as 'Scoop'."

His stare continued in silence.

"Anyway," she said, "I'm wonderin' if you might know anythin' about a killer called 'the Stickman'?"

Again Scoop spat, and again he came back with that stare.

Leah let out a breath and glanced toward the mirrored glass of the one-way window. She didn't know what to do. She turned back to Scoop. "I'm sorry," she said. "Do you . . . What can I tell you to make you talk to me?"

This time he didn't spit. He continued staring for at least a dozen seconds until finally saying, "Get me a cigarette." His voice was jagged and edgy.

"Um." Leah shrugged and gave another lost look to the mirror.

Dan stood beside Sanders watching everything go down, feeling worse and worse for Leah. Finally, he turned to the lieutenant and said, "Pull her out."

Sanders had his hands behind his back and Dan noticed he was chewing gum. A smirk adorned his face. "Why?" he asked, sarcastically. "This is some of the funniest shit I've seen in a long time."

"I said, pull her out!"

The smirk went away as he threw Dan a last look before going inside the room and whispering something to Leah. She stood and actually thanked Scoop before leaving the room with the lieutenant. Dan continued watching the evil smile come to Scoop's lips as he sat among those four white walls alone once more.

Leah walked to his side, looking relieved. "Was it as horrible from out here as it felt in there?"

"Like watching an appendectomy in slow motion," Dan said. He turned to Sanders. "Mind if I give it a try?"

The lieutenant's smirk came back as he made a *be my guest* gesture.

"Please do," Leah said. "I want to see how it's s'posed to be done."

Dan smiled calmly. "I'll do my best." Dan blew on his

hands then rubbed them together before disappearing around the corner and entering the room. Leah still felt shaky as she stood with Sanders looking on.

"Scoop, Scoop, Scoop," Dan said, fumbling with something by the door. "I'm turning off this crummy camera and recorder. Guys like you and me, we don't need things recorded, do we? We like to do things off the record."

Leah realized now that was what he was doing by the door. Sanders, after checking something out down the wall a ways, came back and clarified. "He was just pretendin'. Recorder's still runnin'."

But inside, Scoop looked slightly on alert.

"You know what else we don't need?" Dan asked. "This chair." Picking up the empty metal chair Leah had sat in, he fired it across the room, where it made a helluva *clang* as it struck the concrete wall. Scoop scooted back in his own chair, his shackles rattling. A trickle of sweat ran out of his mess of hair, continuing down the side of his face and into the crisscrossing scar.

"In fact," Dan said, "even this table is really just in our way." Dan threw the table. It crashed against the wall with a *bang* before rattling atop the upturned chair.

"What's he doing?" asked Sanders. He looked agitated.

Leah kept her smile to herself. "Hell if I know," she said, "but he's already gettin' a better reaction than I did."

More sweat dotted Scoop's forehead.

"Have you *ever* interrogated anyone before?" Sanders asked Leah.

"Not really."

"And you picked a *federal prison* as the place to start. Good idea."

Their attention went back to the room, where Dan was still hard at work.

"And there's one more thing I don't need, 'Scoop.' Guess what that is?"

In a blur, Dan grabbed Scoop by his throat with his right hand and pushed, sliding him and his chair straight back until they slammed into the wall. Leah thought Scoop's head might knock against the concrete, but Dan kept it forward with his grip as he pulled Scoop up to his own height.

Scoop was sweating something fierce. "I'll tell you what I don't need," Dan continued. "I don't need some goddamn convict who thinks he's better than I am. Now, you wanna answer my questions, or should I start clubbing you over the head with that chair I tossed back there?"

Scoop was trembling, his hair drenched with sweat. It streamed down his face.

"I gotta put a stop to this," Sanders said, his hand coming up to the window.

"Please don't?" Leah asked, resting her hand on his. "Just give him five more minutes. He knows what he's doing."

"Sure as hell doesn't look like it! This sort of thing could put us in major shit."

"Just a couple more minutes?" Leah asked again and followed with a comforting smile. She was happy Sanders didn't move from the window.

"Wh-what do you wanna know, man?" Scoop asked, his voice shaky.

"I wanna know what *you* know 'bout the Stickman," Dan replied, the words sounding like they came through his teeth.

"S-same thing everyone knows, man. The Stickman's

dead. He was Harry fuckin' Stork and you guys put a bullet b-between his eyes at least a dozen years ago . . . man, *everybody* knows this. Everybody."

"And that's *all* you know 'bout it?"

"Th-that's it, man, seriously. That's it. What else is there to know? Other than what I just told you, I don't know shit."

"What about a new Stickman killin' in Alvin a few days ago?" Dan asked. "Hear anything 'bout that?"

"S-sure man, I read the papers. But . . . but it's a copycat, right? I—I mean, Harry Stork's dead, man."

"Anything else you wanna add?"

Scoop stared at him, wide-eyed. "N-no, man, I'm good."

"Okay." Dan released his grip and Scoop fell back into the chair, his shackles sounding like a hammer on an anvil so loud Leah thought even those concrete walls might shake.

"Well, that was a waste of a drive," Dan said. They were back in Leah's Bonneville and headed toward Alvin.

"Not for me." Leah smiled. "I got to see my man in action. You were incredible in there."

Dan grinned. "Thanks."

"No, really. I thought Scoop was goin' to crap his pants." She laughed.

"What's so funny?"

"Just thinking. 'Scoop poop'."

Dan had complained before getting in the car, saying Leah should give him the keys. "We'll get home an hour early."

But she had insisted on driving. "I don't wanna get

home an hour early in this rain, I'd rather just get home alive."

Now, though, she kind of wished he *was* driving. After the thrill of watching him with Scoop, she figured she could stand a little more action. "You know what I can't stop thinking about?" she asked.

"What's that?" Dan rolled down his window and rested his arm on the bottom of the frame. The smell of the rain filled the car.

"Ain't your arm getting soaked?" she asked him. "My seat sure is."

"It'll wipe up," he said. "I like the rain. Cools me off. What can't you stop thinkin' 'bout?"

She put her attention back on the wet road. "That thing you said about there maybe being two Stickmen working together and Harry Stork was just one of them. I reckon there might be something to that."

"I'm not just another pretty face," Dan said, looking ahead.

"But you really think it would take the other one fifteen years to find a new partner?"

"Hell if I know, it just occurred to me. I only gave it maybe two seconds' thought. I'd have to look at all the reports."

"You've got your own case to work on," Leah said. "I'm the one who's gotta look through a mountain of reports. I don't know if I'll get through everything before Halloween."

Dan gave a little laugh.

"I'm serious. I need to not only read them, but analyze them. I need to know this case as good as my pa did. And he knew it inside out."

"Just don't go making yourself sick about it," Dan said.

"What's that s'posed to mean?" Leah asked, glancing his way.

"Now, you know exactly what that means. Try to keep some distance."

Leah let it lie and they drove for a while in silence until Dan finally broke it. "Can you break the speed limit a *little* bit?" he asked. "For me?"

Leah did eventually get them back to Alvin alive and well. She decided the day had been long enough and they would just go straight to her house. She had copies of everything she needed to study there, anyway, and that's where Dan's work was, too. Before they got there, though, Dan made a request she had been expecting.

"Do you mind stopping at a liquor store somewhere for me? I got a lot to get through tonight."

She almost let out a big sigh but caught herself. She didn't want to get into an argument about anything, not now. Right now she needed to concentrate on the Stickman. Besides, she still hadn't made up her mind about how much his drinking was affecting their relationship. So, hiding her emotions as best she could, she answered. "Sure. There's one on Main Street."

"Thanks," Dan said. And the rain from outside continued to come down through his open window, soaking him and his seat.

CHAPTER 14

" . . . so you were *really* in the Mafia?" Carry asked Jonathon's grandpa, Raven Lee Emerson. When Jonathon introduced them, his grandfather had asked Carry to just call him Raven. She thought Raven was a cool name.

They were sitting in the living room of Raven's small house. An old sofa, nearly bloodred, sat at an angle in one corner of the room. Beside it were two dark brown wooden chairs. One had a wicker back. Carry couldn't tell what the back of the other looked like on account of the blanket draped over it. Like the sofa, both chairs faced the small TV across the room. The black iron feet of a potbellied stove stood on a wooden board beside the television. A rug knitted rust red and hunter green covered most of the dark oak floor.

Carry and Jonathon were nestled on the sofa. Raven was seated on the chair with the wicker back. The blanket covering the other chair was a dazzling tapestry of colorful animal totems. Carry recognized a frog, a wolf, and a bear.

Raven had long black hair that hung straight down his back, falling past his shoulder blades. He wore a leather vest with his arms bare, displaying his tattoos: more native art colorfully inked along his bicep and forearm. His pants were black with little feathers hooked down the outside of either leg. On his feet, he wore leather sandals. Carry had never met a real Indian before. She was delighted. Just sitting here made her happy.

Once she had started looking around, she found the room held more surprises. She especially liked the two wooden aboriginal masks hanging on either side of the room's picture window. One looked like an eagle, the other a bear. Their empty eye sockets seemed to stare right through her.

"Well, I worked *for* the Mafia," Raven replied, answering Carry's question. "There is a slight difference," he replied. His voice was raspy and low, with a light aboriginal accent. Carry could tell he'd lived an eventful life just from the room and the way he was dressed. He was obviously a man proud of his heritage.

"Wow, that's still quite a story," Carry said. Her blond curls were free today. She had decided against the ponytail, so when she laughed they sometimes fell forward, cascading over her right eye, and then she'd have to push them back. "That's a beautiful blanket," she said, nodding toward the chair beside Raven.

"Thank you," the man replied. "My ex-wife made it."

"Wow, that's awesome."

He nodded.

"Tell her some of the things you did," Jonathon said, getting back to the Mafia story. "Some of the things that happened to you." He took a drink of the herbal tea Raven had made them both when they arrived. Carry's mug was on the chipped coffee table in front of the sofa. Jonathon held his in his hands.

"I was once the front man for a tavern. Police always raided it, all the time. And each time, I'd just crouch behind the bar and wait."

"Wait for what?" Carry asked.

"For the shooting to stop."

"Was this during Prohibition?" Carry asked.

Raven laughed. "No, this was in the sixties. It was a go-go bar. The cops hit us all the time because of all different reasons: prostitution, drugs, money laundering, everything. You name it. All the bars were the same like that. Just fronts with men like me who made them appear legitimate."

"But behind the scenes . . ." Jonathon started.

"Behind the scenes we peddled in everything."

"Tell her about the hotel," Jonathon said.

Raven looked away, smiling. "That was before all this stuff."

"Tell me about the hotel," Carry said, repeating Jonathon. She couldn't help getting caught up in all Raven's stories.

"Not much to really tell. The Drisco Hotel. Biggest hotel in town. A friend told me my first wife was there sleeping with another man, so I shot it up."

"You shot up a hotel?" Carry asked, unable to hold back a smile.

"Yes. And that didn't go well with the sheriff. He came after me, but luckily my brother was waitin' down the road with a getaway car. He drove and I stood on the sideboards shooting backward at the sheriff chasin' us."

"Holy cow!" Carry said. "What happened?"

"It took some time, but I managed to shoot out his tires."

"It's like a movie," Carry said.

Raven smiled. "After that, for years, I had to sneak back when I wanted to go to town."

"How many years?"

"I don't know. Three or four. The sheriff finally forgave me."

"What great stories!" Carry said.

"Told you," Jonathon said.

"Did you ever get caught sneaking around?" Carry asked.

Raven waved his palm. "No, that sheriff was not what you'd call swift." He laughed. "But my wife used to say it was excitin' to drive into town in the early mornin' hours, especially when we had to hightail it out of there once the cops got wind of me bein' back again."

"Why did you keep going back?" Carry asked.

"It was the only town within a hundred miles of where we lived. We needed groceries." He laughed and looked away again. "And booze. Always we needed lots of booze back then."

"This would be your second wife, I presume?" Carry asked and laughed.

"Yes," Raven said. "And I only had two." He held up two fingers, like a peace sign. "The second one was like solid gold."

"Where is she now?"

"She's moved on to a better place," Raven said, solemnly.

"Oh, I'm sorry," said Carry.

"Omaha," Raven said. "She works in a casino." A pocket of silence followed until Raven finally laughed. Tears stood in his eyes. "No, I'm just jokin' you. She died five years ago. Life's a lot less excitin' without her, that's for sure." He looked at the potbellied stove, but his eyes seemed focused on something farther away behind it. Carry sensed he was getting lost in time and memories. "A lot less," he repeated after a bit.

"I can understand that," Carry said, and sighed, hoping her question hadn't brought the man any sadness. "I lost my pa when I was six. Death sucks." She scrambled to think of something lighter to talk about, changing the subject. "So what's Raven Lee's Pizzeria a front for?" she eventually asked.

Another burst of laughter from Raven. "Nothin'," he said. "You think I'm crazy? Those days are over. In the past where they belong. When your car gets blown up and someone burns down your neighbor's house, you know it's time to move on."

"Did that really happen?"

"Yes, but those are stories for a different time. Tell me how you and Jonathon met. I know that day cost me a fortune in pizzas."

Carry glanced to her boyfriend. "I walked into him while he was carrying the pizzas. I guess I wasn't paying attention to where I was going."

"No," Jonathon said, "*I* wasn't watching where *I* was going and I walked into *you*."

Raven said, "You don't agree? I already see the making of a great relationship."

"I think we'll both agree the two pizzas we ate that day were the best two pizzas we've ever had," Jonathon said.

"For sure," agreed Carry.

"Then I'm glad that day cost me an extra seventy dollars," Raven said, standing from his chair. "Before you go," he said to Carry, "I have something I wish to give you."

"Give me?" Carry asked. "You don't need to give me anything. I just loved hearing your stories."

"Just one moment." He left the room, heading down the hall. Carry looked questionably to Jonathon. He returned the look with a shrug. A few minutes later, Raven returned with something in his hand. "I want you to have this."

Carry took it. It was a carving of some kind of bird hung on a black leather string. "Did you carve this?" she asked, turning the bird over in her hands. The detail was exquisite.

"Yes, of course. It wouldn't carve itself. I tried to make it do so, and it flatly refused." Raven smiled.

"I can't accept this," Carry said.

"Why?" Raven asked. "Is it no good?"

"No, it's amazing, it's just—"

"Just take it," Jonathon said. "He won't take no for an answer."

"I really liked meeting your grandpa," Carry said on the way home.

"Yes, I could tell. He liked you, too."

"I can't believe he gave me this carving." She held it out from where it hung around her neck.

"It's a hummingbird. It's considered good luck."

Trees rushed past Carry's window in her periphery. "How long did it take him to carve it?" she asked.

"I don't know, a month probably."

"A month? And he just *gave* it to me?"

"That's the way he is," Jonathon said. "I told you. He's a romantic. He and my grandmother were together fifty-five years before she died of a stroke a few years back. I thought for a while her death was going to take him with her; he got so sad. It wasn't a good time. But he's pretty near bounced back again now."

"Wow. That's a long time to be together," Carry said.

Jonathon reached over and took her hand in his. "Maybe one day we'll look back and say that."

Carry just beamed, feeling a stupid smile spread right across her stupid face.

CHAPTER 15

The day started off very gloomy. Me and Dewey were sitting on my bed wondering what we could do. Outside, the rain came down like aerial bombs and I could see more war clouds moving in. Things only looked like they were going to get worse. I heard my mother say they expected thundershowers tonight.

I figured they were right. Whoever "they" were.

"What do you want to do, Abe?" Dewey whined once more.

"How many times you gonna ask me that?" I asked. "That's gotta be at least the fifth time, and my answer hasn't changed. There ain't nothin' much *to* do on a day like today. It's just depressin'."

"Wanna go outside and play cops and robbers?"

I was still looking out my bedroom window. The backyard was all gray and glum. I was starting to see how much my summer break could be affected by something as small as the weather.

"No," I said. "I don't feel like goin' outside. It's pissin' like racehorses out there, Dewey. Sometimes I wonder where you get your thinkin' from."

Dewey lay across the width of my bed holding his

chin up with his hands. "There must be *something* we can do 'sides sit here and reckon what it is we can do," he mumbled.

Took me a minute to get my head around that, but I eventually figured out what he meant. "We need fall-back activities for days like today," I said. Outside lightning flashed across the sky. I caught it out of the corner of my eye. A rolling thunderclap shook my window two seconds later. Then the rain really picked up. I actually heard it hitting the glass.

I sighed. "See? You gone and jinxed it."

"That thunder was mighty loud," Dewey said. "I think we're in for it."

"In for what?" I asked.

He looked at me and I could tell there was nothing going on behind his eyes. "I don't rightly know, Abe. Just . . . why do you count the seconds after the lightning until the thunder anyway?"

I shrugged. "Search me. Maybe to see how far the lightning is away?" It made sense to me. Lightning would travel at the speed of, well, light. Thunder was much slower.

"So, what happens when there is no delay? Does it mean we'll be hit by lightnin'?"

I could tell he was now really worried. "Listen, Dewey. I don't think we're in any danger of bein' struck with lightnin'."

"Newt Parker got hit by lightnin'," Dewey said. "Twice."

I stared at him. "Newt Parker did *not* get hit by lightnin'," I said. "Not even once." Newt Parker was a black man who used to live in Alvin before he up and died one day of mysterious circumstances. Ever since I could remember there'd always been wild stories about Newt

Parker. Apparently, some folk said, he liked to barbecue roadkill and eat it, but I figured that was about as likely as the man having been struck by lightning two times.

"I wish he was still alive," Dewey said.

"Who?"

"Newt Parker."

"Why?" I couldn't figure out why he suddenly cared so much about Newt Parker.

"On account of that would give us somethin' to do. We could go spy on him and see what other crazy things he did."

"I don't think Newt Parker ever did *anythin'* crazy," I said. "Folk just like to make stuff up."

"My ma told me some things 'bout him," Dewey said.

"Yeah, well, your ma's just 'bout as crazy as Newt Parker," I said.

"I know," Dewey said and looked away.

Something came into my mind, then. I remembered a present I got for my birthday last March. It was a science kit of some sort called My First Forensics Lab, and it had been in a very big and exciting box that I unwrapped with great anticipation. I remembered reading the back and finding out inside was all the stuff you needed to learn about forensic police work. It came from my mother, who told me she hoped it might direct me toward a promising future. I figured that meant she hoped I'd one day work as a police officer the way she did on account of her pa.

I never actually opened the box. I guess I got so wrapped up in the rest of my birthday that it sort of wound up forgotten. I only remembered it now on account of seeing the big stack of file folders my mother had sitting on the kitchen counter when I let Dewey in earlier today. Those file folders had just flashed in my mind and that somehow led me to the forensics lab kit.

"I reckon I know what we can do!" I said brightly, getting off my bed.

"What's that?" Dewey asked, suddenly with a bit more interest.

"Hang on, I gotta find somethin'." I opened my closet, figuring that would be the most likely place that box would've ended up. The inside of my closet looked like an airplane disaster. There was stuff thrown everywhere. Toys I hadn't played with since I was a little kid. Lots of *Star Wars* stuff. Micronauts. Things like that. I started pulling everything out, trying to get through the different layers, when I realized that box had been so big it would have risen above the litter of toys. I looked up and checked the top shelf, where a number of boxes were stacked, but they were all puzzles and old board games like Pay Day and Monopoly and Risk. I used to play Risk with Carry all the time until she started refusing to play on account of she never won a single game.

She was just a sore loser was all.

Dewey had gotten off the bed and was standing behind me in the pile of toys I'd hauled out. "What are you lookin' for?" he asked.

"I'll tell you 'bout it once I find it."

"If you tell me now, maybe I can help look for it."

I stared at him. "How would you have any idea where anythin' in my room is?" I looked down at his feet. "Hey, you're standing on Darth Vader."

He kicked Vader out from under him. "Sorry."

"That's okay. I don't really play with him much no more anyway. Here, help me throw all these toys back in the closet."

Once we did, I had to close the door really quick to

keep the mountain of junk from tumbling back out. It took three tries, but I finally managed to get the closet to look completely normal from the outside. Now I had to think: *Where would my mother put a big box like that forensics kit?*

I looked around my room and realized there was only one other place it *could* be. Dropping onto the floor, I stared under my bed. The view was obscured by some Hot Wheels tracks and a few books, one being my favorite, *The Sword of Shannara,* the others being the three different *Lord of the Rings* books. I had already read all of them in the last year or so. Dewey tried to borrow the first *Lord of the Rings* but told me he thought reading was too boring. Apparently, Dewey would rather spend rainy days lying around my room complaining that there was nothing to do than read.

I pulled out the orange track and pushed aside *The Return of the King,* and sure enough, the big orange box with My First Forensics Lab written on the side came into view. I could tell it still had its plastic wrap on. Excitement swelled inside me. This could be our savior from wallowing in these wet, watery days.

"Abe, what're you doin'?" Dewey asked.

"I found it, I just can't . . . reach it." I was straining to get my fingers on it, but it was pushed too far back. Then I thought of something. I sat back up and turned to Dewey. "You're smaller than me. See if you can wiggle under my bed and get the box out that's near the back."

"I ain't smaller than you," he said. Looking up at me even though we were both seated.

"Dewey, you're like three inches shorter than me and probably weigh forty pounds less. Just see if you can do it."

He rubbed his nose and considered this. "I'll try," he

said, finally. "But if you can't do it, I don't see how I can. I'm as big as you." This time his voice held no conviction.

I watched him get down on his stomach and slide under my bed, fitting beneath it just like he was made to go there.

"Is it the orange box you want?" he called out.

"It's the *only* box, Dewey," I said.

"But the orange one, right?"

I rolled my eyes. "Yes, Dewey, the orange one."

Two minutes later, he came out with the box. "Here," he said snappily, handing it to me. "But I still ain't no smaller than you."

"All right," I said, turning the box over so I could read all the stuff written on the outside.

"What is it?" Dewey asked, looking on.

I turned it front forward. "What does it *say* it is?"

Dewey read the words out loud. "My First Forensics Lab." He looked up at me. "'Fraid I still don't know what it is. What's 'forensics'?"

"Forensics is police work. It's what a special group of experts down in Mobile do to help catch crooks. With forensics they can check stuff like fingerprints and blood and"—I couldn't think of much else—"and other stuff. You know. Stuff police need to test."

"So you're sayin' this box has stuff to teach us how to work in Mobile?"

Once again I stared at him. "Not *just* Mobile, Dewey. There's forensics experts everywhere. Mobile's just where my ma sends most of her stuff to for testin'."

This seemed to take a while for him to process. While I waited, I pulled off the plastic wrap and slid the top of the box off the bottom, revealing the contents. I couldn't believe all the stuff inside. This present couldn't have been cheap. I felt bad now for having left it waiting under my bed for so long.

Dewey peered into the box, his eyes like hubcaps. "Wow!" he said slowly and with reverence. "Look at all that stuff. Are those two things *real* microscopes?"

"I reckon so," I said. "I don't think they'd bother givin' us stuff that didn't work."

His expression only grew more wondrous, and I couldn't blame him. The inside of this box reminded me of walking into Mr. Farrow's garage and seeing all his tools. It just held so many mysteries. There were things inside the likes of which I'd never seen before.

Reaching in, Dewey took the only thing that didn't look interesting: a small flashlight. "Look!" he said. "A flashlight!" He pushed the button to turn it on and . . . nothing happened. His smile fell. "It's broke."

I shook my head. "Or just maybe it needs batteries?"

His smile came back. "You know, I bet it does!"

I took it from him and unscrewed the front. Sure enough, there was room inside for one AA battery. I knew where my mother kept our batteries, so I ran with the flashlight into the kitchen, opened the junk drawer, and began rummaging through it, reminded of the mess of toys on my closet floor. Only, with the drawer it took me less than two minutes to find a AA battery. Pushing the drawer closed, some paper got stuck sticking out of the top. I didn't care. I was too excited to get started doing forensics. I put the battery inside the flashlight as I walked back to my room.

"Here," I said, pointing it at Dewey's face. "Voilà! A flashlight." I pushed the button and something weird happened. Dewey's face lit up all blue.

"Holy!" Dewey shouted. "It's a blue flashlight."

"Hmm," I said.

"What's it for?" Dewey asked.

I was wondering the same thing. "Forensics, I guess. I'll have to read the book."

Again, his face fell. "There's a book?"

"Tell you what, Dewey. Since you hate readin' so much, how 'bout I read the book and then just explain it all to you?"

This idea brightened his spirits tremendously. He took the blue flashlight from me and kept turning it off and on while pointing it at his chin. "Look, Abe," he said each time. "I'm Blueface."

"I reckon you're an idiot," I said.

I pulled the book from the box. The title was *Understanding Forensics*. It wasn't as thick as *The Sword of Shannara,* a book I'd read twice.

"That's huge," Dewey said. "How long will it take you to read it? My ma wants me home for supper."

I couldn't believe him sometimes. "I can't read all this today, Dewey. It's goin' to take some time." I flipped to the back and read the page number. "It's a hundred and sixty-five pages long."

His frown came back. "We're never goin' to work in Mobile," he said.

"We're not goin' to work in Mobile!" I snapped. "Do you understand this at all?"

"I understand the book is pretty near impossible to read. It might as well be a million pages."

"No, Dewey. It actually isn't that long. Just give me maybe a week, I don't know. Maybe two weeks. Depends how much time I get in. I'll try to read fast."

"So we won't be doin' nothin' till you're finished it?" he asked, reproachfully.

"We can still do stuff. Just not forensics. I'll read it when you're not around."

"Can we pull out the microscopes?"

I thought this through and figured it wouldn't hurt anything. "We need somewhere to do all this," I said, looking around my room. My chest of drawers was too high and my bedside table wasn't near on big enough. "I know, I'll go get one of the foldin' tables my mother uses at Thanksgiving and we can set it up against that wall."

"Need help?" Dewey asked.

"No, I'll be fine. Just . . . don't *touch* anythin' till I get back."

Sure enough, my mother's three folding tables were in the garage right where I thought. I tried to remember the last Thanksgiving my mother invited guests over, and couldn't. It had been a long time. I figured with Dan Truitt now in her life and Jonathon in Carry's, Thanksgiving this year would be bigger than usual. That thought made me smile.

I only banged the walls three times getting the table to my room, and only once did it make a gouge so big my mother might be in danger of noticing it. I wasn't too worried, though. I'd just blame Carry.

Dewey helped me pull out the legs and set it against my bedroom wall. Then he handed me the microscopes and I set them on top. "Wow," I said. "This already looks professional."

Dewey squinted into the lens of one of the scopes. "You reckon your ma got you a box with two of these so we'd each have one?"

"No, they're different. Yours is taller than mine, and look at those silver things at the bottom—they're bigger. I reckon yours might be more powerful."

"Maybe this one's for the really expert stuff?"

"Maybe," I said. "I have to read the book."

Many items were still inside the box, including a real camera. It was a Polaroid, the type my mother had for work. Carefully packed in Styrofoam were vials of different liquids, most of them different colors. They were labeled with words like *phenolphthalein, leucomalachite green, luminol,* and *fluorescein*. Not only had I never seen these words before, I couldn't even pronounce them. Each vial had a picture of a skull and crossbones beneath the label and, in small print, the words: DO NOT DRINK.

I laughed and Dewey looked over to see why.

"How come they have to tell us that?" he asked. "Do they really reckon someone would be dumb enough to say, 'Gee, I'm thirsty. I could sure go for a bottle of phenolphthalein?'" I figured he hadn't even come close to pronouncing it right.

His question actually surprised me on account of the first thing I thought of when I read the warning was that they were put there because of people just like him.

More stuff still remained in the box, including a little packet labeled FINGERPRINT KIT. That one excited me. I found miscellaneous things like small paper envelopes, plastic envelopes, a pair of scissors, and a whole lot more. It seemed like an assortment of stuff that nobody would ever think went together.

"What's all this *for?*" Dewey asked.

"I dunno," I said. "It's why I gotta read the damn book, Dewey."

"You should start now."

I opened *Understanding Forensics* and flipped past the title page and contents and all that. I read the introduction and right away learned something called "Locard's Exchange Principle." It said that whenever a person contacts another person, or a place, or an object, or anything, it resulted in an exchange of physical mate-

rials. It was saying that if I went and petted the Clear-
sons' dog, Mr. Olympus, Mr. Olympus would leave
traces of hair or something on me and I would leave
something from me on him. I don't know what I could
leave, maybe pimples or something. I supposed I would
find out later in the book. But I was excited that I had
only read three pages and was already learning new
stuff. This was going to be awesome.

I tried reading more, but I felt Dewey watching me.
"What?" I asked him.

"Nothin'." He shrugged. "How's the readin' goin'?"

"Dewey, I've read three pages. It ain't goin' like bottle rockets. If you ask me every three pages how my
readin's goin', I'm apt to pitch a fit."

"Hmm," Dewey said. I figured I'd just offended him.

"Look," I said. "Why don't you head home for a while
and let me read. I think I'll go a mite faster if you do."

He frowned. "You're sendin' me home?" He gave me
a look like I'd expect from Mr. Olympus if I ever kicked
him.

I sighed. "Tell you what, why don't I read this later?"

"Okay." He smiled.

"So . . ." I said, setting the book aside.

"So . . ." Dewey answered.

"What should we do?"

"I dunno," he said. "I reckon there's nothin' to do."

The rain still battered against my window, but there
hadn't been any more lightning. "Nope," I said, "there
ain't."

"Sure wish it wasn't rainin'," he said.

"Me too, Dewey. Me too."

CHAPTER 16

All through Dan's entire first week in Alvin, the rain continued pounding down like nails falling from a tipped-over toolbox. Today was Friday. Lightning and thunder filled last night's sky the same way it had since Tuesday. This morning looked a bit brighter, though. The thunderheads had passed. Now it just rained, although it was some of the hardest rain Leah could remember coming down for some time and, every so often, a bitter wind wound up firing it at a slant.

Leah and Dan continued driving from federal correctional institution to federal correctional institution all around the vicinity of Alvin. They limited their searches to facilities within a one-hundred-mile radius of the town. Each place they visited said yes when they requested to interrogate a "talker," and each inmate they spoke to was as frustratingly useless as "Scoop" had been up in Atlanta. Sure, they'd all heard of the Stickman, but each and every one said the police shot him dead fifteen years ago. Leah let Dan handle all the interrogations while she watched, trying her best to learn what she could.

Today, they had one more place to check out, the last

one on their list: the Federal Correction Institution in Talladega. The very same one Thomas Kennedy Bradshaw took up root in for being the Buzzman. Leah remembered how he'd reacted when she called him by that name. She still had some hunches about Bradshaw. Something there didn't feel quite right.

By now, Dan had the whole thing down to a routine. The interviewee this time was named "Duck."

"Why can't these guys have normal names?" Leah asked.

"They think they're above normal names. Besides, their street name usually means something. Duck probably quacks a lot, is my guess. Or he likes ponds. One or the other."

"Maybe someone was always shootin' at him, so he had to duck a lot," Leah suggested.

The lieutenant in charge escorted them to the interrogation room where Duck was already waiting, his hands cuffed behind his back. Unlike Scoop, the rest of the inmates they interrogated weren't shackled, only handcuffed. It made them appear less threatening. Duck actually looked quite civilized even in his orange outfit. His blond hair was combed, parted neatly down the middle, his chin recently shaved. The best word Leah could come up with to describe his face was "squat," as though someone set something heavy on his head and squished it. He reminded Leah of a Muppet, with dark eyes peering out from beneath bushy brows.

"This one's goin' to be different," Dan said to Leah.

"What makes you think so?"

"There's no fear in his eyes. Even Scoop had that wild animal look before you came in and he rattled your cage. Nobody likes going to the interrogation room not knowing what it's about." He took another hard look at

Duck through the one-way window. "No, I have a feeling this one's going to require a bit of finesse."

"Well then, finesse away," the lieutenant, whose name was Stone, said.

Dan walked into the interrogation room and did his "pretend to turn off the recording" thing. Unlike most of the times he used this ploy, Duck didn't seem to care. In fact, before Dan could say anything, Duck took the initiative.

"Look," he said, rather calmly. "I've been in here goin' on four years keepin' my nose clean just doin' my time. I got six left. I hope less with my great behavioral skills. I don't need any shit thrown at me. Understand?"

Dan thought this over. "All right, Duck, I won't throw any shit at you. I won't even play the good cop/bad cop routine. I'll just ask you straight-up. What do you know 'bout the Stickman?"

Duck's laughter echoed in the small room, bouncing off the metal table and chairs and those concrete walls that seemed ubiquitous to all interview rooms. "*That's* what this is about? You think I have some 'inside information'? Well, I'll tell *you* 'straight-up' that I don't. I just know he's out killin' again, so someone fucked up pretty bad when they nailed Harry Stork."

Leah felt the hairs rise on the back of her neck. Her cheeks went flush. She was glad to be out in the hall, watching through the window. Had she been inside, there's no way she'd have been able to just let that one go by.

"What makes you think it's not a copycat?" Dan asked.

There was a moment of silence and then Duck leaned forward, lowered his voice, and said something that made Leah's heart skip. "Have you guys been gettin' the letters?"

A telltale pocket of silence came next, and Leah couldn't blame Dan for reeling. She figured he'd expected that about as much as she had: not at all. "What letters?" Dan said quietly.

Another laugh from Duck. "Oh, don't play stupid, we're both so above that. The letters tellin' you 'bout the killin'? The ones with the stickmen drawn on 'em? Along with a time and location?"

Dan shot a quick glance to the mirrored glass of the one-way window, as if to make sure Leah wasn't missing this. It took him a beat or two to respond. "Okay," Dan finally managed, "I'll play, Duck. Let's say, for argument's sake, we are getting letters. What the fuck do you know 'bout them?"

Duck grinned. "You guys all think the same. How can I know 'bout somethin' that was held back from the press, right? Well, that's just it. Nothin's *ever* held back, my friend. Some things are just kept more secret than others."

Dan's eyes narrowed. "Well, since you're tucked away all nice and neat in here, you can't be responsible for the murder last week. Got any idea who might be?"

"Maybe," Duck said. "One or two. You got a deal you can swing?"

Dan mulled this over. "Sure. I could put in a good word with the district attorney." In truth, that was all the power Dan really had. He couldn't swing any "deals," and the last time he saw the DA was at a very drunken fund-raiser where Dan ended up going home with the DA's date. He doubted his "good word" would mean much to Gary Carmichael, Talladega's district attorney.

"No, I want more than just a 'good word'," Duck said. "I want you to get someone in here who can actually cut a *real* deal. Maybe get that DA friend of yours to take three years off my sentence or somethin'. Maybe throw in a cell with a better view for the rest of my stay, too."

Dan considered his situation. The violence trick wasn't going to work this time. Duck wasn't the same as the other squealers. He was smart. He knew information had value. He'd given out just enough to wet Dan's whistle.

"Let me see what I can do," Dan said. "In the meantime, why don't you start compilin' a list of names for me? People who might also know 'bout this information we 'held back.' People not actively *in* the can. Someone who might've wanted to pick up where Harry Stork left off."

"Come on," Duck said. "You don't actually believe that?"

"What?"

"That Harry Stork was the Stickman."

"It's what the official report says."

"Your official report ain't worth shit."

"So you're telling me this is the *original* Stickman's work we're seeing now?"

"I ain't saying *shit* until you get someone down here to cut me a deal. That's it. Other than that? I'm through talkin'."

"So where to now?" Leah asked as they exited the correctional institution and got back in Dan's car. The rain pummeled Dan's windshield harder than ever.

Dan's car was a green four-door Chevy Nova. It was at least four years old, but looked well taken care of.

Like what most detectives drove around in, it was the sort of vehicle nobody noticed. "Now," he said. "You get to watch me eat some crow." He pulled out onto Renfroe Road.

"How so?" Leah asked, doing up her seat belt. When you drove with Dan, you didn't take any chances.

"You heard 'Duck,'" Dan said. After he had finished the interview Leah and Dan found out Duck's real name was Stanley Bishop. "He wants a deal. To do that, we need to get the DA onside."

"So?"

"So, let's just say me and him have a bit of a 'history'."

"What did you do?"

"Got drunk at a black tie gala and screwed his date."

"*At* the party?"

Dan laughed, taking a turn at the light. "No, I took her home first."

"Great. This oughta be fun."

"What's Duck or Stanley or whatever the fuck the guy's called in for, anyway?"

Leah looked through the papers in the folder on her lap. "Armed bank robbery. Got away with a hundred twenty-nine dollars. Cops nabbed him in the street on his way out. I'm guessin' a silent alarm."

Dan nodded. "Thieves are stupid. Banks have high security, and unless you bust open a safe and take a pile of hostages, you're going to make off with a few hundred bucks, tops. Liquor stores at Christmastime? Now *that's* what they should be hittin'. That's where the *real* money is."

"I see you've put lots of thought into this."

"What? That criminals are idiots? You haven't noticed?"

"This latest one kind of has me a bit perplexed," Leah replied.

Apparently, Dan knew his way around the city. He hung another left at a stop sign. Leah was lost.

"I think we may have lucked out with Duck," Dan said. "'Lucky Ducky,' that's what I'll call him." He laughed and glanced at the file in Leah's lap she was still going through. "They give us everything we need?"

"Looks like it," Leah said. "He asked for three years off his sentence, right?"

"Yeah, but that came from the ether. I doubt the DA will give him more than one. Maybe a nicer cell. I'm sure there's wiggle room in this negotiation." Dan looked at the business tower they were passing. "We're here."

He pulled into the small parking lot, taking the only available spot. Big white letters were stenciled on it that read: RESERVED FOR EMPLOYEES ONLY.

"You can't park here," Leah said.

"I can do anything I like," he answered. "I'm a cop. Laws don't apply to us. If they did, we could never get the bad guys, because they pretend the laws don't apply to them, either."

Leah sighed as she exited the car. "With our luck, it probably belongs to the DA."

"That would be great," Dan said, cocking her a grin.

The DA's office was in a ten-story high-rise. Dan checked the board when he came in. "Of course he's on the tenth floor, the asshole," Dan said. "Room ten oh three. He's such a prick, I bet it's the office with the best view in the entire building."

They got into the elevator and Leah pressed ten. When they got out on the top floor, the décor was much nicer than it had been in the foyer. They walked down a hall carpeted in a lush, deep-pile forest green, complementing olive green walls, to a trio of glass doors. Etched into the glass of one were the words:

GARY CARMICHAEL
DISTRICT ATTORNEY

Beyond the doors was a reception room with a dark-haired woman working behind a large maple desk. "Should we knock?" Leah asked.

"Screw that." Dan opened the door and they entered. The receptionist looked up from her typewriter. Her hair was in a bun and she wore way too much mascara. She was chewing gum while she talked on the phone. A gold-colored placard on the desk said her name was TWILA BROWNING.

"I'll be right with you," she whispered while covering the receiver.

Leah looked out of the glass wall at the back of the room. Dan was right, the view was spectacular. Even the rain didn't look so bad from up here. All of Talladega spread out around this tower, like some sort of living labyrinth. From the ground she'd have never guessed the city could possibly be this busy as she watched tiny cars make their way through narrow streets like rats going through a maze in pursuit of cheese. "The rent on this place must be a fortune," she said.

"Yeah, and you can bet, he don't give two shits," Dan said from beside her.

Leah jumped. "I hadn't heard you walk up." She had Duck's file folder of information in her hand.

"Sorry," he said. "Didn't mean to be so stealthy. It's this thick-pile carpet the bastard probably spent ten thousand dollars of taxpayers' money on."

She turned to him. "You really got something against this DA, don't you?"

"Nah, just that he's the DA and DAs piss me off."

Dan took a seat on one of two black leather sofas in the room, both on either side of a short maple bookshelf with a potted urn plant atop it. The plant's shiny green leaves opened, revealing the pink and violet flowers just beginning to burst from their center. A pile of magazines were heaped on the stand's two shelves, looking as though someone had just tossed them there. They near on destroyed the rest of the room's eloquence. If she hadn't known better, Leah would've suspected Dan had gone over and mussed them up out of spite.

Dan read her thoughts as she sat down on the other sofa. "It's because his clientele don't give a shit 'bout how much his rent costs," he said. He reached over and pulled a copy of *Time* from the top of the mess, opening it to a random page.

The receptionist, Twila Browning, was still on the phone.

Leah grabbed herself a recent issue of *Scientific American,* drawn to the cover subtitle "The Future of Forensics."

She found an article talking about the problem with police finding weapons with unreadable serial numbers, usually due to criminals sanding or grinding them off. Federal law required gun manufacturers to stamp or etch unique numbers on every firearm produced. Apparently, maybe even by the turn of the century, scientists might uncover a way to restore the serial numbers.

Leah didn't understand most of the science. The piece said all metals were composed of grains packed together like a Jenga game and if you looked inside these grains, you would find a crystalline arrangement of atoms all oriented the same way, but not oriented with the next grain packed beside it. This difference created a natural boundary between grains, forming a natural barrier between them, which acted as a sort of record of how the metal originally looked before it was altered.

Using something called an "electron microscope," scientists might someday be able to record how electrons bounced away and scattered from the modified metal, forming a "backscatter diffraction pattern." This pattern would act as a key to restore the sanded-off serial numbers.

Leah didn't even pretend she could follow it. Be nice if she had the ability now, though. She'd love to use it on the gun Harry had aimed at her pa that night. The one with no bullets in it. Someone went to great trouble to make sure those serial numbers couldn't be traced. Made her wonder why.

"DNA," Dan said out of the blue, pulling Leah's attention away from electrons and microscopes and back to him. "That's where the world's headed." He pointed to an article in his magazine. "They say we're 'bout five years out from mapping the entire human genome." His eyes rose to Leah. "Know what happens next?"

She shrugged. "No clue."

"Killer clones. Armies of 'em. And then it's a small step before we've got a tyrannosaurus rex running amok in Wald Park. DNA mapping's like the gateway drug to big scary dinosaurs."

An oval, maple table matching the bookshelf and desk separated them. Leah rolled her eyes. "At least you're not too dramatic. Where's Wald Park?"

"On Montgomery Highway in Vestavia," he said. "One day I'll give you a tour of Birmingham."

"Is it a nice park?"

Dan's eyes went back to the magazine as he turned the page. "Sure, if you like kids. *Lots* of kids. T. rex would have a feast."

Twila Browning finally finished her call. "What can I help you with? Pretty wet out there, eh?" She looked out the glass wall at the rain now falling in sheets.

Standing, Dan closed up his issue of *Time* and threw it back on the pile of other magazines. "Dan Truitt and Leah Teal to see Gary Carmichael." Leah got up and straightened her jacket, which was still wet with rain.

"Do you have an appointment?"

"No, but it's vital that we see him at once. It's literally a matter of life and death. Not mine, thank goodness, but somebody's. Oh, and do me a solid? When you tell him we're here, don't use my name. Just say it's Detective Leah Teal from the Alvin Police Department on urgent business."

"Are you Leah?" Ms. Browning asked Leah, non-plussed by Dan's patter. Leah could empathize. He really was a taste you had to acquire.

"I am."

"And is it *really* a matter of life and death?"

Leah nodded. At the moment there really wasn't anyone's life hanging in the balance. But technically, she supposed, there *could* be.

The receptionist made a call on her phone. "Hi, Gary? There's a detective here wants to see you. Leah Teal. With the Alvin Police. Yeah, I think so . . . hang on." She covered the receiver and asked Leah, "That where that Stickman murder happened last week?"

Leah nodded. "Yep." She looked at Dan and whispered, "Two weeks ago, she'd have never heard of Alvin."

"You're like a weevil in a cotton farm," he said.

"He said he'll see you, but it's gotta be quick. He has to leave in ten minutes for a meetin'. Right now he's just finishin' up a call. Would you like a coffee while you wait?"

"Sure he's on the phone," Dan said. "If he actually is, I'm guessing it's got something to do with a motel and a blonde. That'd be the 'important meeting' he's rushin' off to." Leah was just about to sit back down when Dan strode right past the receptionist's big desk and went down the hall to a closed office door. Leah followed behind him, tossing Twila Browning an apologetic look along the way.

She called out for them to stop, but Dan already had his hand on the doorknob of Gary Carmichael's office. He pushed it open and Leah entered behind him.

Leah's breath caught. The office was even more breathtaking than the reception area. Two glass walls looked out over the city. A third wall was covered in maple shelves and stuffed with law books, reminding Leah of the wall in Ethan's office, only this one looked well dusted. She also guessed the DA probably read some of his books from time to time. She doubted Ethan ever had.

Gary Carmichael actually *was* on the phone, looking quite surprised at seeing Dan and Leah burst in.

"Uh, Roger?" Carmichael said, his eyes locked on Dan. "Something's just come up. Let me call you back in ten, okay? Thanks." He cradled the receiver and glanced to the receptionist, who was now beside Leah.

"I told them you were on the phone," she explained.

"Who's Roger?" Dan asked the DA. "Your pimp or your drug dealer?"

"Should I call security, Gary?" the receptionist asked.

Carmichael thought briefly about her request. "No, Twila," he said with a resigned sigh. "It's fine."

"Don't worry, Twila," Dan said, still looking at Carmichael. "Gary and I go back a long way."

Twila looked a bit shaken when she left the office and returned to her desk.

Gary Carmichael had black beady eyes, short black hair, and a widow's peak, reminding Leah of an extra playing a role on *The Munsters*. Impeccably dressed in a dark blue suit, he wore a white shirt beneath with a red-and-blue-striped tie. His composure came back quickly as he did his best not to appear intimidated by Dan's impromptu visit. He shot his cuffs and set his elbows on his desk.

"Detective Teal," Carmichael said, looking at Leah where she still stood at the threshold. "Come in. As for you, Detective Dan Truitt, didn't I tell you never to step foot within four hundred yards of my office again? Do you want me to get a goddamn restraining order?"

"Rein in the wild horses, Gary. I wouldn't come if it wasn't somethin' important." Dan took the manila folder from Leah.

"And you used this poor young woman as your cover. Nice."

"She's not that young, Gary," Dan said. "And I know you *know* young. Anyway, we need you to cut a deal." He passed the folder to Carmichael, who accepted it with trepidation, almost like it was a live grenade.

"What's this?" he asked, placing it in front of him and gently opening it up.

"We believe that man has crucial information involving the recent Stickman murder," Leah said.

Carmichael flipped through the pages inside the folder, quickly scanning their contents.

He looked back up at Dan. "You expect me to do this as a favor?" he asked. "I owe you nothin'. You owe me—"

"No," Leah interrupted. "I'm hoping you'll do it as a favor to me. And also on account of you shouldn't like people being murdered in a town that's practically in your backyard."

"I wouldn't say you're in my backyard."

"Your backyard's probably a pretty scary place, eh, Gary?" Dan asked. "Got the odd body buried out there? Or is it just a bunch of skeletons that live in your closet?"

Carmichael looked back to Leah. "He isn't helping your case."

Leah gave Dan a reproachful frown.

"Okay." Dan sighed. "I'll try to be civil."

"Thank you," Leah said quietly.

"Tell me about this"—Carmichael flipped back to the front of the documents—"Stanley Bishop. What's he in for?"

"Robbin' a bank with a firearm," Leah said. "Sentenced ten years in Talladega. He told us he'd talk if you reduced it to seven. We reckon he'll probably accept one. He'd also like a nicer cell."

"And what does he know that's so damn important?"

"Information about the original Stickman killin's that was never given to the press."

"I thought the holdback was leaked?"

Leah glanced quickly to Dan before continuing. "Some was, some wasn't. He told us enough to verify that he knows the stuff he shouldn't. He also told us he can provide names of other people who know. One of these people could very well be responsible for Abilene Williams's death a week ago last Tuesday."

Gary Carmichael's eyes went to Dan. His words became clipped. "What's he got to do with this?"

Leah answered. "He's helping me out. And we're . . .

um . . . sort of dating." She blushed and wondered what in hell's name had pulled that out of her mouth.

Carmichael laughed. "That so? Word of advice: Don't take him to any parties. You never know who he'll go home with."

Leah braced herself for Dan's counterattack, but it never came. "I'll . . . um . . . keep that under advisement," she said, trying desperately not to smile. "Anyway, I reckon that file you got has everything you need to know about Stanley Bishop, or 'Duck' as he likes to be called."

"Duck?" Carmichael asked. "He in cahoots with someone named Cover?" He laughed, and when Leah didn't laugh back, he even looked expectantly at Dan. "You know," he explained, "'duck and cover'?" Dan nodded with a pitiful grin. Carmichael's attention went back to the files in front of him. "You guys got no sense of humor," he mumbled.

"This ain't nothin' to laugh at, Mr. Carmichael," Leah said. "We got one dead woman already, and I reckon it's just a matter of time 'fore another body shows up. Time is of the essence. Right now, we have depressingly few leads." She tried to sound serious but found it hard with Dan quietly snickering beside her.

Carmichael sighed and closed the folder up. His eyes met Leah's. "Fine. I'll take a looksie and decide if this warrants a deal and exactly what sort of deal I *might* be able to swing. Just remember, I'm doing this for *you,* Detective, not the prick you're dating. I mean no offense. You seem nice, despite your obvious lack of good taste."

"None taken," Leah said and passed him her card. "Please call me as soon as you've made your decision."

"Just so we're square on this," Carmichael said, taking her card and examining it. "I'm only saying there's a *chance* I'll be able to help. It's not a hundred percent. I have to read the file."

"I understand," Leah said. "But, as I said before, time is of the essence—"

He interrupted her by raising his palm. "In case you didn't notice, the weekend starts tomorrow. Maybe, if you're real lucky, I'll start on this tonight. But the *earliest* you'll hear back from me is Monday. The *earliest*. That's just the way it goes, I'm afraid."

"That's fine," Leah said. "I'll wait for your call Monday mornin'. Thank you, Mr. Carmichael."

"Yeah," Dan said, sarcastically mimicking Leah and sounding like he should be in a grammar school playground. "Thank you, Mr. Carmichael." Then right before they walked out, he added, "By the way, you should feel lucky. She turned out to be a lousy lay. Your New Year's Eve gala date, I mean. She passed out in my bed halfway through."

"That's not saying much about you," Leah said, raising her eyebrow.

Carmichael's laughter bellowed. "Oh, I *like* this one. Don't get rid of her. She's a keeper."

CHAPTER 17

Jonathon showed up at Carry's house expectantly around four o'clock Saturday afternoon.

"What's goin' on?" Carry asked, opening the door. She'd spent the whole day in her pajamas watching cartoons and feeling like she had her old life back, before Jonathon, when everything was unequivocally boring. She hadn't wanted to spend the day like this, but Jonathon told her he was off to visit his ma.

"Why are you dressed for sleeping?" he asked her.

"Why are you even here?" Carry asked back. "Thought you were goin' to see your ma?"

He gave her a half smile. "One of the nurses where she is called and said she wasn't having a good day. Suggested I come another time."

"What does that mean?"

He shrugged. "I dunno. Anyway, you want me to leave? You headed to bed?"

A big smile burst onto her face. "No, I don't want you to leave, silly. You're my pooh bear."

Laughter spilt from his lips. "Your *what?*"

"My pooh bear."

"I don't *think* so."

"I do. I like it. So that's what I'm goin' to call you."

"Whatever. So, have you spent the whole day in your pj's?"

Carry let out a big breath, remembering how much time she'd wasted in her life just strewn out on the sofa staring at the television. Now she spent valuable time usually strewn out on the sofa watching television *with Jonathon*.

"So, you comin' in or what?" she asked. He was getting mighty wet in the rain that had been falling for so long Carry couldn't remember the last time she'd seen the sun. "Or are you *tryin'* to catch pneumonia?"

"No, I came to take you out, but you're . . . not really dressed for it."

Carry continued smiling. "Give me ten minutes. And for God's sake come inside. You're getting soaked."

She turned and ran to her room to change, hearing Jonathon's leather boots on the floor as he came in and closed the door behind him. "Awfully quiet in here!" he called out to her. "Where's Abe?"

"No idea," Carry yelled back. She pulled on her pink shirt with the sequins and stepped into her white capris. She came back into the dining room and found her jacket hanging on the back of a chair. "Abe was here earlier," she said, sitting on the floor and pulling on her boots. "But, to be honest, I try not to think about him that much." She looked up at Jonathon. "You're soaked," she said.

"There's this thing about rain, though," he said. "It dries."

She gave a little laugh. "So, where are we goin'?" Her fingers went to the hummingbird that had been hanging from her neck ever since Jonathon's grandpa gave it to her. "I should leave my ma a note. What time will we be back?"

Jonathon looked at his watch. "I dunno," he said. "Six-ish?"

Carry pulled the piece of paper from the junk drawer where it had been pinched and sticking out all week, took the pen her ma had sitting on top of her stack of files, and wrote a note telling her mother when she'd be home. Using the daisy magnet, she stuck the note on the fridge.

"Okay?" Jonathon asked, his hand on the doorknob. "Ready to go?"

Carry pulled up her hood. "Now I am. God, I hate all this rain."

"Without rain, the crops would die and Alvin would be bankrupt in no time. We rely on rain." He opened the door just as lightning flashed over the rooftops and trees in the west.

"Okay, Mr. Encyclopedia. Remember what I said 'bout not bein' a geek? Don't be a geek."

"Sorry," he said, but Carry only saw his lips move. His voice was obscured as thunder cracked the sky wide open. "Is it just me or was that really loud?" he asked.

Carry's heart had sped up. "It's not just you. That was scary."

Jonathon smiled. "Don't worry. I'll protect you."

She grinned back, her fingers going to the carving hanging around her neck. "You don't need to, remember? I've got my lucky hummingbird."

"I'm glad you like it."

"Are you kidding? I *love* it. My mother thought it was pretty awesome, too."

They walked outside and closed the door behind them.

Holding hands, they walked across the drenched lawn to Jonathon's car. He opened her door and she got inside. He turned on the ignition, and they started down Cottonwood Lane toward Hunter Road, the windshield wipers on high.

"What happened to Alabama?" Jonathon asked as rain splattered the windshield's glass and peppered the hood of his Sentra. "Summer was s'posed to have started three days ago."

"I reckon summer's on vacation," Carry said, then abruptly changed the subject. "You never said where we're goin'."

"It's a secret."

"Won't be for long."

"True."

Carry noticed a small black case on the seat between them. It looked old. She picked it up. "What's this?"

"Oh, it's um . . . one of my hobbies."

She scrunched up her face. They had been dating near on six months now, and she'd never heard him mention any hobbies. "What sort of hobby?" she asked.

"Open it."

She did. Inside were long, thin tools all clipped into place. They all had little hooks and stuff on the end. "I, uh, I'm still not sure what your hobby is. Dentistry?"

"No, it's a lock-pick set."

A school of thought swam through her mind. She wasn't even sure she'd heard him right. Did he say *lock-pick set?* "What . . . what do you do with it?"

He laughed. "What do you think you do with a lock-pick set? You pick locks."

"You pick locks for a hobby?"

"Yeah."

"I . . . I don't know what to say."

"You don't sound too enthusiastic 'bout it."

"Well, I . . . um . . . ." she stammered. "You know my mother's a detective, right?"

Jonathon laughed again. "I'm not a *criminal*. I just like picking locks."

She raised her eyebrows. "Okay. I s'pose that's all right."

"You watch," he said. "I bet it comes in handy sometime."

"Okay," she said, closing the case back up and returning it to where it was. "I'll watch."

He turned left onto Main Street.

"You know," Carry said. "The longer you drive, the more narrowed down the choices are becoming as to where you're secretly taking me for supper."

"Okay, I'll tell you. I thought we might check out that new place, Greek Voyage. Haven't had good souvlaki in a long time. You okay with Greek?"

"Absolutely." Carry beamed. "There isn't too much food I don't like."

Jonathon kept looking up in the sky, as though anticipating lightning. None came. Instead of thunder, all Carry heard was the continuous hollow thumping of rain pelting onto the roof of the car.

They were on Main Street now, and Carry could see the restaurant coming up. She'd never actually *had* Greek food before, but she wasn't about to tell Jonathon that. She wanted to appear worldly.

After pulling to the curb, Jonathon killed the ignition and pulled out his keys. A moment later, he opened Carry's door for her, something she was starting to get used to. She even told her mother about it. She had replied, "Nice to know chivalry's not completely dead.

Wish Dan would take a page or two from the Gospel of Jonathon."

Rain peppered them like buckshot as they hurried across the street to the restaurant. Again, Jonathon held the door open before following Carry through it.

The inside of the place was a surprise. Netting covered the ceiling, holding up oversized starfish, beach balls, lobsters, clams, crabs, and all sorts of other sea-like things. It didn't really remind Carry of Greece, but it was pretty cool. While Jonathon waited at the lectern for a hostess to come and seat them, Carry checked out the pictures of sailboats hung on the wall behind them, colorful ships being tossed on whitecaps. Behind the sailboats, saltbox houses clung to the mountainside like bats.

The pictures looked more authentically Grecian than the plastic crabs hanging overhead.

"Hey," Jonathon said. Carry turned around to see a hostess with two menus standing in front of Jonathon, both of them waiting for her to follow them to a table.

"Sorry," she said. "I was lookin' at the photos."

Jonathon smiled and took her hand. They followed the hostess around an impressive aquarium that stood vertically in the middle of the restaurant, reaching all the way from the floor to the ceiling. An assortment of colorful saltwater fish swam inside, ducking in and out of a coral reef that twisted purple and red from the aquarium's bottom halfway to its top. Big bubbles rose from around the reef, ascending through the water. The aquarium was brightly lit with colors that cycled through an array of violets, greens, and pinks. Its glow glimmered into the restaurant, casting a magical aura across most of the booths.

The hostess was a small girl, probably not much older than Carry, with dark red hair pulled back into a bun and big green eyes. Her lipstick matched the color of her hair, and both shimmered in the aquarium's light. Once Carry and Jonathon were seated across from each other in one of the aquamarine booths, she handed each of them a menu.

"Tammy will be your server tonight. She'll be right by to take your drink orders," the hostess said.

Carry flipped open her menu and started going through it, hoping to find something that sounded at least familiar if not appetizing.

"Um," Jonathon stammered, "before we order, I was hoping we could talk a bit."

A feeling of doom crept its way inside Carry. "Oh," she said, trying her best to hide it. Talking before ordering couldn't be a good sign. She closed her menu, feeling quite conspicuous. "Are you . . . I mean, what do you want to talk about?"

"Us," Jonathon replied. "I think it's time to 'define' our relationship."

Uh-oh, Carry thought. *This* really *doesn't sound good.* "What do you mean by 'define it'?"

"Well, we've never actually talked about it head-on. What exactly do we have? Are we committed to each other completely? If someone asks you out on a date at school or somethin', are you goin' to go? What if you really want to? Should we talk about it before you do? You know, stuff like that. I just want to make sure we're on the same page."

"Um." *Shit,* Carry thought. "You want to go out with someone on a date?"

Jonathon laughed. "Of course not!"

"Then, why . . . um . . . I'm confused."

"Well, I guess, so am I. That's why I want to define things."

Carry fidgeted uncomfortably. Her fingers played with her hummingbird as she glanced at the napkin holder and salt and pepper shakers sitting on the red-and-white-checkerboard tablecloth.

"I, um . . . I thought we had defined it," she said, at last. "I mean, not 'officially,' but I thought we were . . . um . . ."—*damn, what was that word he just used? Oh yeah*—"committed. At least."

Jonathon gave her a big grin. "*That's* what I wanted to hear!" He let out a big breath. "For a minute there you had me on pins and needles. Truth is, I *love* you, Caroline Josephine Teal. And because I love you, I am giving you"—he pulled a little purple case from his pocket and placed it on top of Carry's menu—"this."

Carry was still reeling from the "*L* word." She'd felt that way about him for quite some time, but she never told him because she'd be crushed if he didn't say it back. Hearing it now made her head feel like it was full of helium balloons. Her eyes were fixed on the purple case in front of her. She knew what it *looked* like, but . . . . *It can't be* . . . She thought. *Can it?*

She knew her eyes were as big as the sun in those sailboat pictures as she looked up. "Is that . . . ?" she asked.

Jonathon sat back. "I don't know," he said, crossing his arms. "Open it and find out."

She did. And it was. And her breath caught in her throat.

A ring!

The aquarium's effervescent fairyland lights sparkled from the stone mounted on the golden band inside the small box, making it look deep red at first and then a color closer to purple. Whatever color it was, that color was now her favorite. "Oh my God," she said. "What's this for?"

"For being my honeybee," Jonathon said, smiling. His eyes caught the shimmering lights for a moment and Carry melted in them. "That's my new name for you. None of this 'pooh bear' crap."

"You really don't like 'pooh bear'?" she asked.

"I'm just kidding. You can call me anything you want. But you're my honeybee."

"Perfect," Carry said. "Oh, and I love you, too!" They kissed over the table. Carry couldn't stop smiling.

"It's a promise ring," Jonathon said. "It's promising that one day I'll be able to afford a diamond one. Try it on."

She popped the ring out of its box and slipped it on her finger. "How did you know my size?"

"I played a trick on you. Remember last week? We were playing that game with the string?"

"Cat's cradle?"

"Yeah. Remember when I looped it around your fingers, pretending to tie you up?"

She laughed. "Yeah. You're so dumb."

"No, I'm not. That's how I got your size."

A girl, different from the hostess, appeared at their table, this one with black hair hanging down her back and big blue eyes that looked almost recessed into her heart-shaped face. She wore a white shirt tucked into black pants. "Hi," she said. "I'm Tammy. I'll be your waitress for the evening. Can I start you off with any drinks or appetizers? Dolmathes are on special tonight."

"I'll have a Coke," Jonathon said.

"I'll have a sweet tea," Carry said.

"Do you want any appetizers?" Jonathon asked Carry. "I love dolmathes, don't you?"

"Um, yeah. They're the best." She had no idea what dolmathes were.

"So, one order of dolmathes?" the waitress asked.

"Yep."

When the appetizers came out twenty minutes later, dolmathes wound up being grape leaves stuffed with rice, served in some weird white sauce. Carry absolutely hated just the thought of it, never mind the actual taste. But she pretended to love it and ate half the plateful. Food didn't mean anything to her anymore. The only important thing in her world was the ring on her finger and the fact that Jonathon had told her he loved her.

He'd given her a promise ring. He promised her his love.

Jonathon, her pooh bear.

CHAPTER 18

I had been reading *Understanding Forensics,* the book that came with My First Forensics Lab, since Monday. I'd made it to page seventy-five, which I thought was pretty good since I was reading slowly, making sure I understood everything. Plus, it had some big words I didn't know, so I had to keep looking them up in my mother's dictionary, which she gave me after I kept asking her what different words meant. That all happened days ago, on Tuesday, when we were all sitting in the living room. Well, me, my mother, and Dan were there. Carry wasn't home. She was likely out with Jonathon.

"What does *felony* mean?" I asked.

"Means it's time for us to get to work," Dan said.

I ignored him. I knew he'd never give me a proper answer. I looked at my mother.

"What're you readin'?" she had asked.

I showed her the cover.

"'Bout time you opened that box. I'm surprised you found it."

"I looked in my closet first," I said.

"I'm surprised you found your closet, too. Your room's always such a mess."

"Are you gonna tell me what the word means?"

"Tell you what," she said and got up and left the room. She came back ten minutes later and handed me a book. "Look up any words you don't know in here."

I read the front. "*Webster's Ninth New Collegiate Dictionary,*" I said. "What's *collegiate* mean?"

"Look that up first," Dan suggested. I ignored him, but looked up *felony* instead.

Since then, it feels like I've looked up a hundred words. One thing was for certain, *Understanding Forensics* was adding to my vocabulary.

So far I'd read about "working a crime scene," which was all about gathering evidence and how to understand it after you do. The book said you always have to be careful how you package evidence to make sure it's protected before you give it to a lab to have them analyze it. I had to look up *analyze.* I thought I knew what it meant—and it turned out I was right—but I wanted to be sure.

I also learned there are different crime scenes sometimes, like a primary scene and a secondary one. So if someone was killed in one location and then the body was buried somewhere else, the first place was called the "primary crime scene" and the other was the "secondary crime scene."

The book stressed it was very important to "preserve" a scene. I had to look up all these words. Now I know them all. You preserve a scene by wrapping police tape around it and being careful when you are inside that tape. I also learned that it can be tricky judging the borders of a scene because you have to make sure your "perimeter" held everything important.

One of the most important things was making sure you documented everything. This was why my lab came with the Polaroid camera and also a thick pad of paper and even a little pencil. When you arrived at the scene, you sketched the location of major items on the pad. Then you did something called "walking the grid," where you took one footstep at a time, photographing anything that looked like it might be a clue. All of that became evidence. There are two types of evidence: direct and circumstantial. I'd heard my mother use the word *circumstantial* a lot. Now I finally knew what it meant.

Direct evidence is based on fact—eyewitness statements, confessions, stuff like that. Circumstantial evidence is evidence that infers (another word I looked up) what actually happened. It "hints" at something. Things like fingerprints are circumstantial on account of they infer that the person leaving them was there. It isn't complete proof; it just gives an idea of what might've happened. The book said circumstantial evidence was usually better at telling what happened than direct evidence because eyewitnesses got things wrong a lot. They often identified the wrong person or remembered things in different ways than they actually happened.

From down the hall, I heard someone knock at the door. I thought maybe it was Dewey coming over to do some crime work with me, but it turned out to be Jonathon—I could hear his muffled voice talking to Carry even from my room. So I went back to my book.

It said you collected evidence while you walked the grid and it was important to handle the evidence with care. Fingerprints could be photographed and lifted (using items that came with my kit). Small hairs and other things could be found by using ultraviolet light, which was what the blue-beamed flashlight Dewey liked so much was for. Sometimes police even vacuumed areas and analyzed the contents of the vacuum later. My lab set didn't come with a vacuum, so me and Dewey wouldn't be doing any of that. Well, I guess we *could* borrow my mother's vacuum if we really needed to.

You had to carefully package evidence you took from a scene. Dry evidence was placed in small, folded papers. Plastic bags were also used. My lab set came with both. Wet evidence went in containers that weren't airtight so it could dry. Sometimes, the book said, removing evidence without damaging it was near on impossible.

I read about lots of different ways to analyze evidence. Sometimes you used different chemicals to check whether or not something was a bloodstain, or some sort of drug or something like that. You could compare evidence with things you knew about the suspect—that was called "linkage." Finding a suspect's blood at a crime scene "linked" him to it in some way.

I turned down the corner of the page to save my spot, set down my book, and fell back, letting my head hit my pillow. My mind was swamped with information. It all seemed so complicated, but at the same time, it sure would be fun to play detective with Dewey. We could be like Sherlock Holmes and Watson.

Dewey would be Watson.

I heard Carry go into her room while Jonathon yelled something to her. A little while later, I heard her come back out.

Lightning flashed outside my window, shimmering brightly on the walls of my bedroom. I braced myself and started counting. Before I even got to two, the thunder followed, sounding like a herd of cattle stampeding down a hill.

The back door closed and I didn't hear either Carry or Jonathon anymore. Getting off my bed, I walked through the kitchen and into the living room, but didn't find anyone home. Then I saw a note on the fridge from Carry to my mother, saying she'd be back around six and that she and Jonathon had gone for dinner.

On the kitchen counter, I noticed my mother's stack of files. A small portion were lying across the rest. I guessed those were the files my mother had already read. Walking over, I saw that on the very top was a yellow pad of lined paper with a pen lying across it. The pad was full of notes my mother had made.

Making sure I knew exactly how the pile looked, I took the pen off the top and went through some of the folders, going past the top one about the Stickman killing that just happened so I could read them in order. That one must be last, I figured. After that, the next folder was full of a bunch of reports and notes about people with the last name of Stork.

Then I went to the next page where my mother had written in big letters: *Did my pa shoot an innocent man?*

I got an ache in my stomach when I read that. I didn't rightly know what to make of it. She must mean my grandpa. I didn't know much about the case she was on, only that it was about someone called the Stickman, a name I thought was kind of creepy. So, after double-checking that Carry wasn't home, I dragged one of the chairs from the table over to the counter and started going through the top part of the file, skimming past anything that seemed too boring or didn't make sense. I got confused. Everything was about this "Stickman," but it was all from a long time ago, before my mother was a police officer. Most of the stuff was written by my Grandpa Joe.

I didn't understand. My mother's case was new. Then I found a report by Officer Chris from just a couple of weeks ago, talking about the murder my mother was investigating right now. Sure enough, it mentioned the Stickman, too. Apparently, this case was linked to one my grandpa worked on.

Now I felt excited, but still the ache in my stomach hadn't gone away. What had my mother meant about Grandpa Joe shooting an innocent man?

The next folder had notes written by my grandpa that sort of filled in the blanks for me. He had shot a man named Harry Stork after deciding he was the Stickman, only now, I knew, the Stickman had just killed a new person. So Harry Stork couldn't have been the Stickman, right?

With a deep breath, I thought over the fact that Harry Stork's gun didn't even have bullets in it. Even if he was guilty, there really wasn't any reason for my grandpa to shoot him. There were five police officers against just one Harry Stork. Maybe I just didn't understand things well enough.

That thought made me decide I would read the whole stack, although it would take a while as I could only read it when I was home alone.

For now, though, my head was already too full of facts from *Understanding Forensics* for me to add much more. Setting the files back exactly like I remembered them being before I started going through them, I carefully placed the pen on top of the pad and pushed the chair back to the table.

Next time I got the chance, I would read more of the files. I figured it was important to find out for myself whether my grandpa had murdered someone innocent. Besides, I figured there might even be things my mother would miss. Sometimes she was like that. She needed me to help her out, although she'd never say that out loud.

But I knew.

Outside the kitchen window, the rain came down like marbles spilling from a jar. It had been like this at least a week, and I'd spent almost all that time holed up in my room reading. Dewey had come over a few times, but hadn't stayed long. We were finding out the hard way there really wasn't much to do together when the weather was so bad.

So, despite all the rain, I decided to walk around the neighborhood by myself and see if maybe I could find some kind of forensic evidence lying around somewhere. I figured a little rain never hurt anyone, although that lightning might if it came back. Still, it wasn't often that lightning struck folks, despite what Dewey might think about Newt Parker. As my uncle Henry was fond of saying, that was a bunch of hogwash.

Going back to my room, I pulled my duffel bag from where I kept it in my drawers and packed it up with stuff from my forensics lab that I thought might come in handy. Then I put on my red rain slicker and my rubber boots and carried the duffel back out to the kitchen. Borrowing the pen from the top of my mom's files, I added to Carry's note, just saying that I was going for a walk and would be back at six, as well. Then I put the pen back where it was, careful to make sure it was the same as before.

I checked my watch, a gift from my uncle Henry. It was a hair after five. That gave me near on an entire hour to hunt for evidence and I bet I'd find a lot. Then I could come back and read more of the book before actually analyzing whatever I discovered.

CHAPTER 19

"So the kids are gone for almost an hour," Dan said when he and Leah returned home from a late Saturday lunch and found the kids' notes beneath the daisy magnet on the fridge.

Leah checked the time. "Well, more like fifty minutes."

"Close enough," Dan said. "Any idea what we could spend that fifty minutes doin'? I'm hopin' it's got nothin' to do with your sofa."

For a moment, Leah felt bad having relegated Dan to the living room, but she didn't feel at all comfortable putting him any closer to her room around the kids. She knew the sofa wasn't comfortable—her uncle Hank complained about it every time he came down. He didn't stop coming, though.

She and Dan were standing in Leah's bedroom. "Well, Mr. Detective," Leah said. "Can you come up with some way to fill the time, just the two of us?"

"Oh, I'm pretty sure I might be able to." He smiled.

Leah pulled her shirt out from where it had been tucked into her pants all day and undid the buttons. Removing it, she tossed it onto the pile of clothes at the foot of her bed that had been growing ever since laundry day.

"Caroline stole my dirty laundry bin," she explained.

"I couldn't care less," Dan said, taking in Leah standing there wearing her pants and bra. "I'm just admiring the scenery."

Leah took off her pants and added them to the pile. Reaching both arms behind her, she stretched backward. "My back's been killing me all day. It's all the walking we've been doing. If I see the inside of one more correctional institution, it will be one too many." She gave Dan a sly look. "Don't suppose you'd mind giving me a little massage?"

"Don't suppose I would," Dan said, still smiling.

She lay facedown on her bed wearing nothing but her bra, panties, and socks. "There's some lotion in the top drawer of my dresser," she said.

Rain pitter-pattered against her bedroom window. Her drapes were closed but they glowed with a pale light from outside from the west.

Dan got the lotion and began rubbing it into her back. He concentrated between her shoulder blades and on that spot right at the bottom of her vertebrae that always felt tight. Slowly, his hands started lingering more often around her sides below her bra and the area just above her panties.

Reaching around, Leah undid her bra, letting the straps spill open onto the bed.

"Thanks," Dan said. "That'll make things easier."

Leah smiled. "Let's not throw the word *easy* around."

His hands now came around and cupped the bottoms of her breasts.

Leah let out a small moan.

"Back feeling any better?" he asked.

"Mmm."

She turned over, leaving her bra on the bed behind her, displaying her petite breasts. "So," she asked. "What about the front?"

"A man's gotta do what a man's gotta do." Dan pulled off his T-shirt and got out of his jeans in record time. He even took off his socks. Sitting down on the edge of the bed beside where Leah lay, he gently rubbed her tummy until once again he was lingering higher and lower. This time he didn't stop and soon he had one hand on her breasts and the other down the front of her panties.

Leah reached down and stroked him through his boxers, surprised to find him already hard. "Wow, you're the easy one," she said.

"That's what all the girls say."

"Why don't I get rid of these . . ." Leah tossed her bra on top of the other clothes. Then she did the same with her panties.

Dan took off his boxers. "If I throw these in that same pile, will they become miraculously clean in the next few days?"

"They should." She smiled.

With that, he embraced her, letting her pull him down on top of her. Their lovemaking was all things, sensual, lustful, and passionate. Slow and fast. Back and forth. Dan knew what he was doing when it came to women, and this made Leah feel both good and bad. She felt good because . . . well, it *all* felt good. But she also wondered how many women he had practiced on to *get* this good . . .

Their lips met, open and wet, and his tongue found hers while they continued their rhythm.

After thirty minutes or so, her heart beating strong from two climaxes almost right on top of each other,

Leah fell back into Dan's arms as a bead of sweat ran from under her hair, down the side of her face, and onto him. Turning over, he wrapped her in a hug and she felt his heart, too. Sweat glistened on his forehead. "You know," he said, catching his breath, "even with this rain, it's almost too hot for this. Either that, or I'm out of shape."

"I think it's the heat," Leah replied. "You're in pretty good shape from where I'm lying."

They stayed like that, entangled and naked, another ten minutes, talking about everything they could think of that had nothing to do with the Stickman. Then they both fell silent and content. Leah had needed this. Badly. The sex and its afterglow was probably the best forty-five minutes Leah could remember having had for way too long. Her thoughts meandered through all this until from outside she heard the sound of a car door close.

"Shit!" she said. "That's Jonathon and Caroline. Quick! Get dressed!" She turned over and glanced at the digital clock beside her bed. The green readout said 6:04. They were pretty near right on time.

In no time flat, they were both back in clothes and out in the hallway just as Carry came in through the back door and pulled off her boots. Leah remembered something and glanced back into her bedroom through the open door. Sure enough, Dan's boxers were in a ball at the top of the pile of clothes.

Dan noticed her looking. "Commando," he whispered. "They teach us all about it in basic training."

Leah smiled. "You're such an idiot. But I s'pose I must like idiots." They shared a brief kiss just as Caroline came walking into the kitchen.

"Ick," she said. "Do you guys gotta do that while I'm home?"

"Hey," Leah said. "I put up with you and Jonathon. That's even weirder."

"How's that?" Caroline asked.

"You're my daughter."

"Yeah, well, you're my mother. It's just so . . ." Caroline looked at Dan. "Sorry, but it's really kinda gross."

Dan put his arm around Leah and pulled her to him, tightly. "You don't have to look," he said.

"No, but it's hard not to," Caroline said. "It's kind of like trying not to look at a train wreck."

Leah narrowed her eyes. "Caroline Josephine, you just watch that you don't cross a line."

Caroline rolled her eyes. "Whatever. I'm goin' to go watch some television."

CHAPTER 20

Even with my red rain slicker, the weather sucked. It wasn't the usual warm rain we got in the summertime in Alabama. This had a cold bite to it and a wind that made sure whichever way I turned, the rain's teeth snapped at my face. I decided the best place to look for evidence would be a crime scene. But since I didn't have one, I figured I'd make one up.

That required a bit of thought. I walked aimlessly down my street, thinking hard on it. Finally, I decided what to do and headed down Hunter Road all the way to Mr. Harrison's Five-and-Dime. There usually wasn't a lot of customers there on weekdays, so I had an idea. I just didn't know if Mr. Harrison would go for it.

Normally, this walk was a nice one, but today's weather made it wet and dreary. By the time I got there, I really wished I'd brought my bike. My clothes were pretty much drenched right through my slicker. It turned out to not be very good at doing what it was designed for. Maybe Dewey could invent a better one. I'd have to ask him about that.

Just before I came to Mr. Harrison's, a very wet and dreary and grumpy-looking tabby cat crossed the sidewalk in front of me before scurrying across the road. *Funny,* I thought, *how cats hate the rain just as much as me.* You could tell by its face.

I went inside the store.

"Don't tell me you walked all the way down here for gummies in this deluge?" Mr. Harrison asked with a big smile. I had no idea what *deluge* meant, but I liked Mr. Harrison. He always gave me and Dewey extra candy when we came in.

"Actually, no gummies today. I have a . . . weird sorta question." Outside, a seagull landed on the sidewalk. I was trying to figure out how far that seagull was from any sea. He had a pretty long flight home.

Mr. Harrison slapped his hands on his desk. "Well, my boy, tell me your question and I shall see if I can answer."

The words tumbled from my lips. "Well, see, my mom got me this forensics kit for learning 'bout solving crimes and stuff usin' forensic analysis, and I want to try it out, but I don't have any evidence to try it out on. I was wonderin' if we might fake a robbery at your store and then see what kind of evidence I'm left with and, if you don't mind, maybe I might be able to take that evidence home with me so I can analyze it?" I realized I hadn't taken a breath in a while and took one now.

Mr. Harrison thought this over. "While that does sound like fun," he said, "I'm not sure how you'd go about doin' it. A real robbery would involve a thief, likely wieldin' a gun. Or maybe a baseball bat."

"Do you sell bats?" I heaved my duffel bag full of investigating stuff up onto his counter.

"Nope, no bats, sorry. What you got in the bag?"

"This is all that I need to use in solvin' the crime once we fake it."

"I have a thought," Mr. Harrison said. "We don't sell baseball bats, but we *do* sell peashooters. They're right back here. Let's say your perpetrator robbed my store by threatening me with poison darts."

"Okay."

Mr. Harrison gave me a peashooter and a package of peas. I frowned. "I ain't got no money with me."

"That's fine. Today's robbery is on me!"

"Thank you. That's mighty kind."

"Think nothin' of it. Now, you be the robber and let's say you fire off one pea to show me that they really are poison darts to make me scared enough to give you everything you want."

"Okay." I did as he said and fired a dart right past him. The pea hit the wall behind him so hard it stuck right into it. "Sorry," I said, looking down at my bag.

"Think nothin' of it. Okay, so I say, 'What do you want? Please don't kill me, just take whatever you need'." I was finding out Mr. Harrison was a good actor. He also talked pretty fast, something I never noticed before today.

"Okay," I said, "so I'd probably steal some gummies . . . oh . . . And I s'pose all the money in the register, of course."

"Of course," Mr. Harrison said. And he gave me a bag of gummies.

"What?" I asked. "Can I . . . um, keep these?"

"Of course! I don't want to die!"

I smiled. He was really good at this.

"Now, I'm just going to *pretend* you took all my money," he said. "You don't get to keep *that*." Hitting a button on the till, he opened it with a *ding*. Then he counted the cash inside and said, "Looks like you got away with 'bout eighty-six dollars and twenty-seven cents."

"Actually," I said, "I should open the register, not you. That way my fingerprints will be on it."

"Good idea." He closed it back up and I came around to his side of the counter and he showed me what button to press.

"Now, you better get runnin' on account of I just pressed the silent alarm."

"You have a silent alarm?"

"No, not really. But I do have a video camera." He pointed up to the corner of the ceiling above his head.

"Geez, I should have worn a hood and a mask," I said.

"That's okay, we'll just pretend you did. Do you want the video? It's time for me to change it anyway."

"Sure!" This was great.

He stood up on a stool that was on the floor beside him and ejected the tape from the camera. It was VHS so I could watch it at home. He took a new video cassette from a drawer beneath the register and slid it into the camera and started it back up.

"All right, now that the robbery's done," I said, "it's time for me to start collectin' evidence."

I pulled the Polaroid camera from my bag first. I had to use it and some drawings to document exactly how I found the scene. I took pictures of my muddy footprints coming into the store—which I also apologized to Mr. Harrison for. Then I snapped shots of the video surveillance camera, the cash register button—where my fingerprint was actually *visible;* I must've really pressed it hard—the pea stuck in the wall, and finally, I took a picture of the big cylinder of gummies where the ones I "stole" came from.

I used a set of tweezers to dislodge the pea from the wall so I could analyze the "poison dart." The tweezers came from my forensics kit. When they made it, they pretty much thought of everything. I dropped the pea into an evidence bag, initialing it and dating it just like the book said to do before I placed it in my duffel bag.

I read about the initialing and dating of evidence in the same chapter I learned about something called the "chain of custody." Basically, anybody who handled the evidence had to *always* date and initial it. This kept the "chain of custody" intact. If it was ever broken, there was a chance someone might've corrupted the evidence and it wouldn't be usable in court. I couldn't believe I remembered all that.

"Did I touch the glass counter at all?" I asked Mr. Harrison.

"Yes, I think you did. Why?"

"Because the fingerprint on the register is good, but any I may have left on the counter might be even better." I used the blue flashlight to find the print. Sure enough, it showed up, plain as could be. I used the fingerprint kit to lift both prints. After initialing and dating those, they went into my bag, along with the VHS tape. I didn't put the tape in an evidence bag. It was too big.

"Well," I said, "I think that's it. Now I've gotta walk back home."

"You gonna do your 'analysis' tonight, then?"

"No," I said. "I have some readin' I want to get done. 'Sides, I'll probably wait till Monday when Dewey can come over and help me."

Mr. Harrison grinned. "I wish you the best of luck in solving this crime, young detective!"

I turned right before leaving and waved. "Bye!"

Mr. Harrison waved back.

Once I was out of the store and on the sidewalk again, I started eating my "stolen" gummies. According to my watch, it was ten to six. I was goin' to be a little late gettin' home. I hoped my mother didn't mind.

I started back up the hill just as a burst of lightning lit up the sky overhead. Slowly, I started counting. "One Mississippi. Two—" And that's as far as I got before thunder roared across the sky louder and angrier than any lion I'd ever heard. It was as though the sky had cracked open, releasing all the rain that fell down hard upon me like a million peas being blown from a million peashooters.

Heaving my duffel bag over my shoulder, I tried to speed up my walk, but Hunter Road was steep and I still couldn't go very fast. I could feel myself getting wetter by the minute.

I thought again that Dewey really needed to invent a better rain slicker.

Oh, and something for grumpy wet cats, too.

Jonathon drove past me just as I was coming down Cottonwood Lane toward my house. He honked and waved, so I waved back with a smile. I liked Jonathon. I reckoned he was good for Carry, not like that boyfriend she had a couple of years back. I got the feeling my ma was much happier with Jonathon than that other one, too. So far, at least, she hadn't threatened to "blow his balls off" like she had with the other one.

When I went inside, my mother and Dan were in the kitchen, where my mother was fixing supper. As I pulled off my boots and my slicker, I felt guilty about going through her files and worried that she had noticed. Then I worried that she'd notice I looked all guilty. I wound up with these thoughts circling in my head while I just stood there, dead in my tracks in the middle of the kitchen. It was like all of a sudden I had no idea what to do. Guilt and fear had taken me over.

My mother was at the stove with a frying pan, and the whole kitchen smelled of onions. I guessed she was making hamburger steak.

Dan was leaning with his back against the sink. He looked at me, frozen in place, holding my wet duffel bag.

"What're you doin'?" He laughed. "Why are you just standing there? And your hair is soaked. You look like a drowned possum."

"I ain't doin' nothin' . . . ." I said. "I'm just . . . I dunno. I'm . . . um . . . goin' to my room to read."

"You're sure readin' a lot these days," my mother said without turning around. "I'm guessing you like your birthday present?"

"Yeah, it's pretty cool. Haven't really started usin' it yet. I want to finish the book first so I know what we're doin'."

"We're?" Dan asked.

"Yeah. Me and Dewey."

"Haven't seen him 'round in a while," my mother said.

"Yeah. He was off visitin' his grandma today, and to-morrow his ma says he can't play on account of they'll be busy with church and something else I can't remember. 'Sides," I said, "he doesn't like the rain. Sort of like cats."

"What?" Dan asked.

"Cats don't like the rain," I said again, wondering what part had him confused.

My mother took the pan off the burner and turned toward me for the first time. Again, I started feeling conspicuous. I wasn't sure why I hadn't continued down the hall to my room yet, but my feet were refusing to follow my brain.

"So," my mother asked me, "how was your . . . whatever it was you were doin' out there walkin' around by yourself?"

"My robbery?" I asked. "It went great!"

"Good," my mother said, using a knife to push the onions from the frying pan onto a plate. "Supper will be ready in 'bout fifteen minutes."

I finally got control of my feet and left the kitchen, continuing down the hall, heaving my duffel bag over my shoulder the whole way.

As I entered my room I heard Dan from the kitchen ask my mother, "Did he . . . um . . . did he say 'robbery'?"

I just smiled and closed my bedroom door behind me.

CHAPTER 21

Monday found Leah at the station, waiting for Gary Carmichael's call. She had left Dan asleep on the sofa after reading a note he'd left saying he hadn't gone to sleep until 5 A.M. and not to wake him. She thought the rest of the note said "see you in the afternoon sometime," but it was only a guess. The writing was obviously done in a drunken stupor, emphasized by the empty bottle of Jim Beam Kentucky straight bourbon Dan had left beside the note. Leah hid the bottle with all the others she'd collected each morning, stuffed in a black plastic garbage bag relegated to the kitchen closet where old coats and footwear were stored.

Once again she vowed to come to some sort of decision about Dan's obvious addiction problems soon.

For now, though, she had to concentrate on work. She decided to continue reading through the files. She'd brought her yellow notepad from home. It was the only thing she had to worry about taking back and forth. Xeroxing everything else had been a good idea.

"You're not getting through those files very fast," Chris said. He was being unnaturally quiet today, but Leah had no complaints about that.

"I don't want to miss anythin'," she replied.

"I understand."

She went down the stack of remaining folders, finding the point where she'd read up to. Placing the next folder in front of her, she began to read about victim number four: a forty-three-year-old woman named Maggie Ledbetter.

Ledbetter worked at Providence Hospital down in Mobile, and Leah knew she had found the start of the pattern Ethan told her about. From here on in, all of the victims would be employed by the medical industry.

Leah flipped back to the list her pa had made of all of Harry Stork's major clients. Sure enough, Providence was not only on the list, it was one with an asterisk beside it.

Ledbetter had been missing three days before police found her body dumped down along the edge of the Old Mill River, a deep river that splashed and dashed violently through a narrowly cut gorge all the way down the eastern side of Alvin until emptying into the Anikawa. Cypress flanking the length of the river blocked out the sun, rendering the river near on invisible. The clamorous sound of rushing water seemed to just spring from the blackness of the gorge's bottom.

Five days after finding Ledbetter's body, Leah's pa organized his task force, pulling in four cops and detectives from Mobile.

Coincidentally (a word that made Leah cringe), the fifth victim, a man named Travis Moyer, *also* worked at Providence. His last known whereabouts had been at the Mobile Regional Airport. Security cameras recorded him coming off a flight from Atlanta, where he'd been visiting his mother. Four days later, police discovered his body staked into a field at Shearer's Cotton Farm, a blanket of land that lay along Highway 17 on the outskirts of Alvin.

Later, the medical examiner pulled a .38 Special slug from Moyer's skull, which forensics inferred might have come from a Smith & Wesson Model 10.

At the crime scene, tire marks were found off the side of the road, indicating a vehicle with a 117-inch wheelbase and fourteen-inch tires. Shoe prints, less distinct than the tires, were also discovered. Forensics' best guess was that they belonged to a men's size seven Nike Blazer basketball shoe. On both pieces of evidence, it was indicated that the time the impressions were made could not be discerned with any reliable certainty.

However, an eyewitness driving past the cotton farm around the time the ME calculated the body had been dumped reported seeing a yellow car parked along that area of Highway 17. The witness believed the automobile to be an AMC Rambler. In regard to this, forensics noted that the Rambler's wheelbase was only a hundred and six inches.

This new murder grew the task force by three more, all detectives from Atlanta.

Leah had just come to the end of that file when the phone rang. She looked up to the clock as Chris answered it. It was a quarter of ten.

"For you," Chris said to Leah after answering. "Gary Carmichael? DA from Talladega?"

With a deep breath, Leah lifted her telephone receiver and pressed the HOLD button, taking the call.

"Mr. Carmichael," she said. "Thanks for getting back to me."

"I said I would. I don't say things without following through on them."

"Well, that's good." She felt anticipation course through her. A lot was riding on this phone call.

Carmichael got right down to business. "Now, I know how important what I'm about to say is to you. And I agree with what you said, this new Stickman can't be allowed to continue killin' folk. And *if*—and that's a big if—this Stanley Bishop character or 'Duck Fuck' or whatever he's called can help, then I reckon there should be some sort of deal cut."

Leah let out a relieved sigh. Now she braced herself. She didn't expect him to be too generous. She waited to hear just how bad his offer would be.

"I say we take your advice. Go in with an offer of one year's grace on his sentence and an upgrade to his cell. If he takes that deal, we'll call that our best case. I am, however, given the weight of the situation, prepared to offer a reprieve of two years *if* we *have* to, but I really don't want to. His suggestion of three is out of the question."

Leah's heart leaped into her throat, bouncing all the way back down. This news couldn't be any better if it came on a golden ticket found in a Wonka bar.

Carmichael continued. "I'm heading in to the correctional facility this afternoon to pitch the deal. I would like you there with me. I do *not* want Dan Truitt there, do I make myself clear?"

"Yes, sir," Leah said. "Very clear." *Dan will be so pissed*.

"And, for the record? I'm doing this in memory of your pa. He was a good man, and I don't want to see his name tarnished by some bogus criminal re-creating crimes originally orchestrated by a mastermind only outsmarted by Joe Fowler."

"You think Harry Stork was a mastermind?" Leah asked.

"I'm just goin' on the few times I met your daddy. He was good at what he did. For him to be outsmarted by someone for so long, Stork had to be pretty smart, I reckon. If I was you, I wouldn't worry about tarnishing your pa's name. He shot his man. I'm convinced of that. But you know what? Even if it turns out Harry Stork wasn't the Stickman, at least your pa shot the man he was after. Remember that. And it's not like Stork was some innocent bystander. He was brandishin' a gun. Your pa did what he had to. His life was on the line. Even if this winds up goin' back to court and it's decided Harry Stork wasn't a serial killer, in my mind Joe Fowler still goes down as a hero."

Until now, Leah hadn't thought of the case being retried. The thought twisted inside her like a broken Slinky. What if the courts decided her pa was guilty after all? What would he get? Manslaughter? Now she had worse things goin' on in her head than just hoping her pa didn't turn out to have mistakenly shot the wrong man. She wasn't sure she could handle it if things went that far.

"How long do you think it will take to get here?" Carmichael asked.

"To your office? Dependin' on traffic, three, maybe four hours."

"Okay. Leave as soon as you can. Then we'll head out to the correctional institute together. I reckon this 'Duck' has a better chance of takin' our first offer if there's a woman in the room."

"Why's that?"

"Just a hunch. I work on hunches."

She hung up and Chris must've read her face. "What's wrong?" he asked.

"I just . . ." She picked the receiver back up. "I don't want to make this call."

"Who are you calling?"

"Dan." She dialed her home number.

Abe answered. "He's still sleepin'," he said. "Snoring away. Sounds like a train."

Leah told Abe to wake him up. Dan could always go back to sleep. She just hoped he wasn't still drunk.

"Gary Carmichael called," she said, once Dan groggily came to the phone. Leah detected a slight slur in his speech.

"And?"

"He's willin' to take up to two years off Duck's sentence along with giving him a nicer cell."

"Wow. He must've found a pretty nice hooker last night. Has he offered it yet?"

"No. There's something about that."

"What?" Dan said, still sounding a bit drunk. Leah was glad he'd be staying put.

"He wants me to drive up there now and be with him when he makes the offer."

"Okay, I'll pick you up in ten minutes. Call Gary. Tell him to expect us in three hours, tops."

"Um, yeah, about that."

"What?"

"He said under no circumstances am I allowed to bring you."

"Fuck him, he can't make those kind of rules."

"Dan, he's doing us a *favor*." *Besides,* she wanted to

say, *you're still drunk.* "I'm going by myself. Please don't hate me."

A long pause followed, before, "I could never hate you. I'm going back to bed so I can dream 'bout punching Carmichael's rules right out of his head."

"Okay, you do that, honey. Love you."

CHAPTER 22

Dewey finally came over today, and I eagerly explained to him what me and Mr. Harrison did so we'd have forensic evidence to test out our new lab with. He sat on my bed while I explained everything, pulling each piece of evidence from my duffel bag and placing it on the fold-up table where the two microscopes still stood.

"He just let you keep the gummies?" Dewey asked. "For free?"

"Yep." I'd gone past the gummies two pieces of evidence ago. Dewey hadn't stopped chattering about them since.

"Wish I'd been there."

"Dewey, the gummies ain't what's important. What's important is all this evidence we have to analyze." I showed him all the Polaroid shots I took before extracting the actual PE (short for *Physical Evidence*). "See?" I asked. "These are my muddy shoe prints, and here's the register with my fingerprint. And here's your damn gummies before I ate 'em all. This is the poison dart embedded in the wall."

He stared at that last shot. "That ain't no poison dart. It's a pea from a peashooter."

"I know, but we're pretending it was a poison dart. I fired one off to show him I wasn't just foolin' 'round." I couldn't believe I had to explain all of this.

"Oh. And I s'pose Mr. Harrison *gave* you the peashooter and peas for free?"

"Yep."

Dewey crossed his arms. "Wish I'd been there."

"No, you don't," I said. "It was raining tabbies and poodles. I got soaked. You'd have hated it."

"I like gettin' wet."

I shook my head. "You can be so weird. You know that, right?"

He ignored me. "That pea still in Mr. Harrison's wall?"

I pulled out the evidence bag containing the poison dart. "No, I extracted it."

"Did you shoot any more?"

"Nope," I said. "One was enough to get Mr. Harrison to give me what I wanted."

"What did you want?"

"It was a robbery, Dewey, what do you think I wanted?"

"Gummies?"

"No . . . Well, yeah, I s'pose. But mainly, all the money in his register."

Dewey's eyes went wide. "If he let you keep *that,* I'm goin' to be real mad you didn't call me to come get wet with you."

"No, Dewey," I said, spelling it all out. "We just *pretended* he gave me the money." I read from my notepad. "It came to eighty-six dollars and twenty-seven cents."

"How do you know?" Dewey's eyes tracked a fly buzzing around the room.

"Mr. Harrison counted out how much was there."

Next, I took out the two fingerprints I'd lifted. "Before you ask," I said, "these *are* my fingerprints."

He didn't seem too impressed.

Lastly, I removed the VHS tape from my bag and plunked it down with everything else. This caught Dewey's attention.

"What's that?" he asked.

"It's from Mr. Harrison's security camera. He had to change the tape anyway so he let me keep it. It's got my whole robbery on it."

"And other stuff, too?"

I shrugged. "I dunno. I guess so."

"Let's watch it."

"My robbery?"

"No, the whole thing." He was ridiculously excited.

"Dewey, it's just goin' to be all the same thing, people comin' into the store, buyin' stuff, and then leavin'. How much of that can you watch?"

"How long's the tape?"

I read the label. "Two hours."

"I reckon I can watch two hours of that, no problem at all."

I just shook my head. "Let's analyze the rest of the evidence 'fore we do anythin' with the tape."

"Thought you weren't finished with the book yet?"

"I'm not, but I'm comin' up on page one hundred."

"How we gonna know how to analyze anythin' if you still got sixty-five pages to go?"

I thought this over. He was right.

"So, let's just watch the tape now," he said. "Do you have popcorn?"

With a huge sigh I took the VHS from the table and Dewey followed me into the living room, where I slid it into our machine.

"What 'bout popcorn?" Dewey asked, getting comfortable on the sofa.

"I ain't making popcorn to watch people buy stuff," I said.

"All good movies have popcorn, Abe."

"This ain't no *good movie*. It's a stupid surveillance video from a five-and-dime."

"I think it'll be great."

"I think you're weird."

Carry was out or we would have had a fight on our hands for taking over the TV. It was unusual for her not to be draped across the sofa like she normally was, with her head on Jonathon's lap.

I turned on the TV, switched it to channel three—for some reason movies only worked on that channel—and pressed PLAY on the VCR. Apparently, Mr. Harrison had rewound the tape to the beginning before giving it to me because the screen showed him sweeping up his shop, not my pretend robbery.

"I need to fast-forward it to the part where I steal everythin'," I said. "It's probably at the very end."

Just before I hit the double arrow button that forwarded the tape, Dewey stopped me. "No, Abe. I wanna watch the whole thing."

"*Seriously?* I thought you were just goofin'. You *really* wanna watch Mr. Harrison sweep up the floor for two hours?"

"Yeah. And everything else. People comin' in and buyin' stuff, people leavin', Mr. Harrison stockin' the shelves. I wanna see everythin'."

"You're crazy," I said. "What do you want to watch all that stuff for?"

"It'll be fascinatin'."

"It'll bore me out of my skull."

"Please? You said it's only a two-hour tape."

"Dewey, I am *not* going to watch Mr. Harrison sweep for two hours. That's just plain nutso."

"Let's start watchin', and if you really find it that borin', you can forward it to your stupid robbery thing."

My *stupid* robbery thing? Now I was getting mad. "Dewey, it wasn't stupid, it was fun and you gotta pretend it was real. Remember, I even got free gummies and a peashooter out of it."

He crossed his arms, defiantly. "Whatever. If you don't at least play part of the beginning, I'm goin' to go home and not watch *your* thing at all."

"Now you're just bein' a baby," I said.

Dewey sat there on the sofa, arms remaining crossed. He didn't say a word.

"Fine," I said. "We'll watch some of the beginning. But when I start noddin' off, be sure to wake me up." I left the tape playing and sat in the big chair across from the sofa. On the TV, Mr. Harrison finished up his sweeping and put the broom away in the utility closet. Then he sat behind the counter, drumming his fingers on the top. After a while, he picked up a book from beside the register and started reading. I watched him read for about five minutes before I couldn't stand it any longer.

"Okay," I said to Dewey. "Do you *now* agree this is the most boring movie ever? It's worse than the stuff Carry watches, and that's sayin' somethin'."

"No," Dewey said, riveted to the screen. "Leave it on."

I sighed. I figured there was no point in arguing about it. No matter what I said, I was destined to spend the next two hours of my life watching somebody else work one of the most boring jobs on the planet. I might as well have been working at the store myself if I had to watch Mr. Harrison doing it.

"Look!" Dewey said, stiffening. "Somebody's comin' in!"

The front door opened and three kids entered. I didn't recognize any of them at first because the picture was so grainy, but as they got closer to the camera, I realized it was Tyler Bonnet and two of his friends. I didn't know his friends, but Tyler was in the same grade as me and Dewey, and rode the bus with us to school. On the screen, he was wearing a hoodie and shorts, both different shades of gray on account of the video being all black and white. His friends were wearing T-shirts and shorts. One had a baseball cap on with the Alvin Eagles logo on the front. The other had some kind of picture on his shirt, but the picture quality was too bad to make out what it was.

The kids split up and perused different aisles of the store. I really was starting to feel like I was falling asleep when suddenly Dewey jolted me awake.

"Abe! Did you see that? Rewind it! Play it again! Play it again!"

"What the hell is wrong with you?" I asked.

"Tyler just took somethin' off that shelf and put it in his pocket! He's stealin' from Mr. Harrison!"

"He did not. I didn't see it."

"You had your eyes closed. Rewind it and you'll see."

I got up and hit the double arrow key that made the movie go backward. I went back about a minute and pressed the PLAY key again.

Sure enough, Tyler Bonnet was in the middle of an aisle, looking around to make sure Mr. Harrison couldn't see him right before he nabbed something off one of the shelves and stuffed it in his kangaroo pocket. I couldn't make out what he had taken. We watched that part of the tape four times before we finally figured out what it was he stole. Well, to be honest, it was Dewey who caught it.

"He's in the knickknacks aisle," Dewey said. "He took a hacky sack."

"Maybe he's just puttin' it in his pocket until he gets to the counter," I suggested.

We kept watching. The boy in the baseball cap went up to the register and bought some Action Candy (which, when I was younger had been called Pop Rocks) and a roll of Bottle Caps, but Tyler never approached the counter or put the hacky sack back. After his friend bought the candy, all three boys left the store together. You could see some of the sidewalk through the store's glass front, and, once outside, the boys high-fived each other.

"Tyler *steals* from Mr. Harrison!" Dewey said. "We gotta tell someone."

"Probably Mr. Harrison?" I figured it was the obvious choice.

"Or your ma. She's a law enforcement agent, after all."

"Why don't you just say 'detective'?" I asked.

"What?"

"Nothin'."

We kept watching the tape. I started noticing that when nobody moved in the store and nothing changed, the video stopped recording and skipped to the next point of action, sort of jerking along. Mostly, we only saw the store in the daytime when Mr. Harrison was there doing stuff, but sometimes we'd see a night shot if someone happened to walk by on the sidewalk.

I had no idea how many hours or days went by while the movie jerked along, but, later on the tape, Tyler Bonnet once again came in—this time with just the friend with the baseball cap—and me and Dewey watched, both of us on high alert. Believe it or not, Tyler did it again, only this time he stole a yo-yo. Just like before, he waited till the coast was clear and then stuffed it in his hoodie's kangaroo pocket.

"He's a compulsive thief!" I told Dewey.

"We really gotta tell somebody 'bout this."

"I reckon the best person to pick is Mr. Harrison. He can decide if it's worth talkin' to my mom."

Dewey considered this. "I s'pose that makes sense. Let's keep watchin' and see if he takes anythin' else."

We watched the entire tape, which actually only went to an hour and forty minutes, and Tyler Bonnet came in two more times. The first time, all by himself and he *still* managed to steal some kind of fancy notebook. The second time he was with both friends again and took a whole bottle of Coke from the back cooler.

When the tape got to my pretend robbery, both of us were too revved up about discovering Tyler Bonnet being a kleptomaniac to really care about what I did. I'd never admit it, but Dewey turned out to be right: Watching the tape *was* fascinating.

Deciding this news was too important to wait, I took the tape and we headed out to our bikes so we could go down and tell Mr. Harrison what we had discovered right away.

CHAPTER 23

It was near on two o'clock when Leah finally reached District Attorney Gary Carmichael's office in Talladega. She was so sick of driving, she actually considered getting a hotel room for the night, but was unsure how Dan would react. He was already pissed about having to stay home.

While inside the elevator and heading for the tenth floor, Leah felt the first twinge of relief she'd had since this case fell into her lap. Obviously, Stanley "Duck" Bishop knew something important. His statement could literally break the case wide open if he accepted the deal. Leah was pretty certain he would say yes. He'd pulled the three year number out of his ass. There was no way he *expected* it.

Thankfully, Carmichael suggested they take his car, which turned out to have its own driver. Leah was happy Dan wasn't there when they both got in the back and Carmichael began discussing how things would proceed.

"You talk first," he said. "I want you to tell him how great a thing this is that he's doing before we even mention the word *deal*."

"I don't think he'll care about that, especially if it's *my* opinion on the matter," Leah said. "We all know he ain't doing this because he's a saint."

"Everyone likes to think they have noble intentions," Carmichael said.

"You reckon? Even someone like Duck?"

"Everyone. Everyone wants to believe they're doing things for the right reasons, Leah. When you've been a DA as long as me, you learn these things."

"Wow, you just restored a little bit of my faith in mankind."

"So, you tell him how great he's bein', and the first thing he'll say is, 'Cut the crap, what's my deal?' because even though he might *aspire* to be good, truth is he's just another asshole waitin' out time while stuck in a cell. This'll be where I take over and lay out our first deal: an upgrade to his cell."

Outside, the omnipresent rain came down in a sheen of gray. Leah was getting a mite sick of this damn weather. It especially did nothing to complement Carmichael's little speech he was making her listen to.

"He'll reject offer one," Carmichael continued. "That's when I hit him with what I say is the best we can do: an upgrade to his cell *plus* shave a year off his sentence. It'll take him a while to think this through, but eventually he'll reject it, as well. That's when you and I get up to leave, but just before we make the door, you stop me and ask if we can please sit down and try one last time to work somethin' out. I look at you like you've lost your mind, but I sit. Then you say to him, 'Duck, think about it. You're not hurtin' anyone giving us this information. You're not incriminating yourself or nothin'. There's no backstabbing goin' on here. You're just helping with an investigation. Take the deal. Don't stay behind bars any longer than you *have* to'." Carmichael grinned. "And *that* I believe he *will* buy."

He sat back and smiled.

"So when do we offer the two-year pardon?" Leah asked.

Carmichael just batted the question away. "That's just there on the off chance he doesn't take the year. But trust me, he'll jump at the year. He'll be happier than a hog in shit with that year."

"Wow," Leah said, "you've really played this through."

"I like to be prepared. It's why I win most of my cases."

Well, I guess we'll see, Leah thought.

Carmichael's car pulled up to the front of the Talladega Correctional Institution, and the driver opened Leah's door for her. Leah thanked him. Carmichael stayed seated until the driver came around and opened his door. Not a word of thanks left his mouth. He just grabbed his briefcase from the seat beside him and got out.

Leah and Carmichael went inside, going right past the desk officer without so much as even showing identification. Leah supposed that, when you were with the DA, you got some sort of GET OUT INTO JAIL FREE card.

The on-duty lieutenant was the same one Leah remembered from last time. He took Carmichael off to the side for a few words before they returned and Carmichael told her everything was in order. He rubbed his hands together. "Duck's already waiting for us," he said.

Things were identical to Friday when Leah and Dan had come here, only now an extra metal chair stood at the table. Duck was already seated, same as last time, his hands cuffed behind his back.

Leah followed Carmichael inside the room and they

both sat at the table. Leah carefully picked the seat across from Duck—it being the farthest away from him. Carmichael looked at her expectantly.

Oh yeah, I'm supposed to start this. "I want to begin," Leah said, her voice tentative, "by thanking you for agreeing to meet with us. We appreciate it."

"Where's the asshole from last time?" Duck asked.

Leah didn't know right away who he meant.

"The one who offered to 'put in a good word with the DA,'" Duck explained.

Ah. He meant Dan. "Oh," Leah said. "He couldn't make it. Had other things that needed to be done. But, as you can see, the DA *is* here." She gestured toward Carmichael.

"And," Carmichael clarified, "not in any way because that ass wipe put in a 'good word for you.' Let's get that straight right off the top."

Okay, that was off the script. "Anyway," Leah went on, "I want you to know that I reckon it's a tremendous thing you're doin'. You could save many lives today."

Duck laughed. "Cut the crap. Just give me the deal." He actually parroted the response Carmichael had surmised he would give. "Is this worth my time, or should I go sit on the shitter and count my farts?"

Leah glanced to Carmichael, who had his briefcase on the table in front of him, his index finger tapping the leather top. "Good news, son," he said. "We're goin' to give you a nicer cell. I hear it's got a view of the valley and everythin'."

Pinching her lower lip between her teeth, Leah wondered what valley he meant.

"Now," Carmichael said, "tell us who told you about the holdback?"

Leah realized Carmichael didn't even know what the holdback was. He hadn't asked, so she hadn't said. She was thankful that he never did actually inquire, as it would've put her in an uncomfortable spot.

Duck just stared at him. "*That's* my deal?" His cuffs rattled as he awkwardly stood and gave out a loud whistle. "Guard! Take me out! I'm through in here!"

Carmichael rose halfway from his chair, making a downward motion with his palm. "Now, now . . . Let's just stay seated a while longer and see if we can come up with some *other* arrangement if you don't like that one."

"I'm not goin' to like any one now. You think I'm stupid? You start with 'we'll give you a better cell'? What am I, fuckin' two years old? I'm out of here! Guard!"

"Wait!" Leah said, much too loud. Her voice ricocheted off the cement walls.

Both Carmichael and Duck's eyes went to her. "The best deal you'll get today," she said, "is the better cell and two years off your sentence. That's the God's honest truth. It's the maximum the DA here told me he's willing to go. Take it or leave it. I think it's a good deal, considering you just pulled the three-year thing out of thin air."

Duck absorbed this, nodding slowly. "A better cell and *two years* off my sentence?" he asked.

"That's right," Leah said. She didn't look at Carmichael. She could *feel* how pissed he was. But she knew she'd done the right thing. Carmichael's plan wasn't worth squat.

"Okay, deal," Duck said. "I need it in writin', though, before you get anythin' from me."

With an evil glare to Leah that she quickly looked away from, Carmichael snapped open his briefcase and leafed through a series of pages. He pulled some out that were stapled together and laid them in front of Duck. "Here," Carmichael said. "Read page one and then I'll turn to the next for you." His words were clipped. Leah knew she was in for it all the way back to his office. She felt his silent anger filling the room while Duck read.

Finally Duck said, "Next page," and Carmichael flipped the top one over for him. There were only two pages. "Looks fine to me," Duck said when he'd finished reading. "Get the guard to take off my bracelets so I can sign it."

Carmichael looked at Leah. "Fetch the guard," he commanded.

Leah almost told him to go "fetch" the guard himself, but then decided she wouldn't mind a small respite from sitting beside him.

Returning with the guard leading the way, Leah stood while Duck's cuffs were removed from one wrist so he could sign the agreement. He did, and then Carmichael signed his name before pulling out some sort of official DA stamp and stamping the last page of the document as the guard cuffed Duck's hands again.

"Okay, roadkill," Carmichael said, "*now* it's your turn at bat—it's the duck's time to start quackin'. Tell us what we paid for."

"God," Leah said to Carmichael. "You have absolutely no bedside manners, you know that?"

Carmichael gave her a look like he wanted to decimate her where she sat.

"She's right, you know," Duck calmly said. "You're a prick. Everyone thinks so." Leah nodded in agreement.

A slight smile came to Duck's face. "Tell you what," he said, tilting his head to Leah. "I'm only tellin' *her*. I don't want you in this room anymore, you fat bastard."

A giggle escaped Leah's lips. She couldn't help it. Carmichael was far from fat, but he also wasn't Charles Atlas.

Carmichael's face went red. "You will tell us *both* right now," he said. "We have a *deal!*"

"The deal's just that I'll tell someone," Duck said, serene and quiet. "And really, she's the one who needs the information. Not you. So, scoot!"

Carmichael turned to Leah for assistance. "Just go," she said. "Make him happy. I'll let you know what I find out."

Without a word, Carmichael stood and stomped from the room, letting the metal door slam shut loudly behind him. "That was kind of funny," Leah whispered to Duck. "So, what do you have?" She pulled out her pad and a pen.

"To be honest," Duck said, "I don't know how useful this is actually goin' to be. Hopefully, you can make somethin' out of it."

"Just tell me how you found out 'bout the letters," Leah said.

"Well," Duck said, his voice dropping low, "I have problems. You know . . . mental issues? I get paranoid delusional flashes sometimes. Not fun."

Leah nodded. "I bet."

"So sometimes I wind up in the psych ward. Unless it happens while I'm here. Then they just leave me to work it out in my own irrational head. But what I'm goin' to tell you happened before I got here. Back in seventy-three. I was at Grell Memorial in Montgomery. Stayed four or five weeks. It was a bad one." Pausing, he collected his thoughts. "Anyway, when you're in a place like that, you don't use your real name, just in case it gets out on the street that you're messed up. Can ruin your cred, you know?"

Leah nodded and made some notes.

"So," Duck continued, "I was Billy Boston to all the other patients. Now, some guy goin' by the name Jimmy McNimmy came in a week after me. He was still there when I left. It was this 'Jimmy McNimmy' that told me he was the Stickman—the guy responsible for all them murders on the TV. Of course, I thought he was full of shit. I mean, I'm in the freakin' nuthouse, right?"

He laughed. Leah gave him a sad smile. "When in seventy-three was this?" she asked.

Duck replied immediately. "I was admitted May sixth, 1973. I know the date 'cause it was my ma's birthday. I felt bad 'bout that. Happy birthday, Ma! Your son's loony tunes." He cocked a grin. "Jimmy McNimmy came in, I believe, six or seven days later. Sometime around May thirteenth."

Leah wrote this down. "Thank you," she said. "Please, go on."

"Well, he tells me everythin' about the Stickman, but it's all stuff I already know. He goes on 'bout how he ties up their wrists and their ankles and how he shoots 'em in the back of the head then drives them somewhere, leaving their bodies staked with stickman drawings for the cops to find. And I'm like, 'That's great, man. I can read the freakin' papers, too.' Only then"— Duck's voice grew even quieter and he gave the one-way window a quick glance—"*then* he drops the bombshell. 'Here's something *not* in the papers,' he says, and he tells me, 'For everybody I've killed, I've sent the Alvin Police a note telling 'em when the body will turn up and where they'll find it'."

He paused, letting his words hang there so Leah could feel their weight.

"So," he continued, "as you probably guessed, I don't believe him, so I call him on it. I'm like, 'Then why the *fuck* ain't you been caught?' and the bastard taps the side of his head and says it's because he's smart. 'Smarter than the cops. Smarter than anyone.' 'Course, all I'm thinkin' is, *Dude, you're in the freakin' cracker barrel right now. You're a freakin' nut job.* But then you and that asshole come in and I drop it on you guys, and y'all get that five-pointer-in-the-headlights look. So now I'm sittin' here wondering how nuts that guy actually was. You really *did* get letters, didn't you?"

Leah avoided answering the question. She just kept her pen going as she finished copying down everything Duck had said. When she finished, she asked him, "Any idea if Jimmy McNimmy was his real name?"

Duck shook his head. "No. But I highly doubt it. It's a dumb name."

Leah agreed. "Is there anythin' else you can give me?"

"Nope, I'm 'fraid that's pretty much it. Hope it was worth the deal you threw me."

"I think we did all right. One last thing, would you be willin' to look at a photo lineup to see if you recognize Jimmy McNimmy?"

Duck thought this over. "Guess not. Oh, and I guess I should say thanks for stepping up to bat with fuck face."

It took a minute for Leah to figure out that 'fuck face' was Gary Carmichael. "If I hadn't," she said, "you'd have walked out and I wouldn't have my leads."

"Maybe I would've, maybe I wouldn't have. Maybe I was just rattlin' Carmichael's little chain—and from what I've heard, it's real little . . ."

"No, you were serious. I could see it in your eyes."

Duck hesitated. "What are you, some kind of psycho-analyst?"

"Nope, I'm not. Just a parent."

Before leaving the correctional institution, Leah asked if she could use a phone and their fax machine. She was admitted to a small office and given the fax number. The office had a computer much like the one Leah used in Alvin, a fax machine, and a telephone. She was told to dial nine before calling an outside line.

She found a phone book in one of the drawers and looked up the number for Grell Memorial Psychiatric Hospital in Montgomery.

A lady answered her call, and Leah explained she was a police officer and wanted information. They must've had caller ID showing that Leah was calling from the correctional facility, because the lady believed her and asked what she could help with. Leah asked for the names of all patients admitted in May of 1973 and whether, in particular, there was someone named Jimmy McNimmy.

"I'm just goin' to put you on hold for a minute or two while I run the search, that all right?" the lady asked.

Leah said it was.

When she came back on the line, she apologized for taking so long. "We had no patients in that month by the name of Jimmy McNimmy," she said.

Leah sighed. "I figured so. It's likely a fictitious name. Could you print a list of every patient admitted between May sixth and May twenty-seventh of that year?" That would broaden Duck's estimate of when McNimmy came in by two weeks, giving wiggle room for error. If Duck wasn't thinking straight at the time, he could easily be mistaken.

The phone number for the fax was labeled right on the machine. Leah read the number to the lady. "Might take a bit of time to run the report," she replied. "Probably at least fifteen, maybe twenty minutes? Our systems aren't that fast."

"That's fine," Leah said, thanked her for all her help, and hung up. Then her eyes settled on the fax machine.

While she waited, she wondered how useful this information was likely to be. For certain it would generate more suspects, which was always a good thing, she figured.

Only ten minutes or so went by before the fax machine sprang to life and a page of names crawled out the front. Ripping off the paper, Leah read them over. Thirty-nine in total. Far more than she'd expected. They were sorted by surname and most also had their last known address, phone number, and Social Security number.

Well, she had leads. Only, it was about thirty-five more than she wanted. She needed to think of a way to narrow this list down. She decided to set Chris to the task of tracking everyone down. Some would be harder to find than others. Ten or so had no information other than just their names. Those would be tricky, even for Chris.

Chapter 24

Me and Dewey flew down Hunter Road on our bikes all the way to Mr. Harrison's Five-and-Dime. I had hold of the VHS tape, so I struggled a bit with my trajectory, riding one-handed. Both of us were close to bursting we wanted so much to tell him the news about Tyler Bonnet. When we came to his storefront, we skidded to a stop, my bike actually sliding sideways, leaving a black mark on the sidewalk beneath my back tire.

After leaning our bikes up against the store's glass front, we went into the store. The bell on top of the door rang as we passed beneath it.

We marched straight up to the counter, but Mr. Harrison was busy talking to an old man about some card game. The man was black with graying hair, and he wore big, round glasses perched halfway down his nose. A cane was in his left hand, and a deck of cards was on the counter. I guessed they were for whatever game him and Mr. Harrison were talking about.

I felt my entire life go by as we stood waiting for them to finish their conversation. Me and Dewey didn't have much patience when it came to things like this. In fact, this was worse than usual on account of we felt like *real* detectives. We'd actually uncovered an honest-to-goodness crime that nobody else knew about. Nervously, I tossed the VHS tape back and forth between my hands.

The two men went on about "bowers" and other things I didn't understand. Dewey gave me a nudge. "Just say, 'S'cuse me, but I have somethin' important to tell Mr. Harrison,'" he whispered. "Then we can just tell him."

"That'd be rude," I whispered back.

Dewey looked as though he had to pee. "How long can these two talk about some dumb card game for?" he whined, his voice still quiet.

"Apparently pretty long." I'll admit, I was just as antsy as Dewey.

Finally, their discussion wrapped up and Mr. Harrison rang in the cards. "That'll be two-fifty," he said. The man handed him two singles and two quarters. "Need a bag?" Mr. Harrison asked.

"I'll just put 'em in my pocket," the old man said, reminding me of Tyler Bonnet putting everything in *his* pocket, only he never paid first.

"Sure nice talkin' to you, Phil." Mr. Harrison waved as the old man left, limping as he walked by us using his cane.

"Well, well, well," Mr. Harrison said, bringing his palms down on his counter. "If it isn't my forensic psychologist and his friend."

Both of us started talking at once, saying the same thing. "We have something—" Then we stopped, realizing this was only going to work if one of us spoke.

"Let *me* tell him, Dewey," I said.

"It's because of *me* we know 'bout it," Dewey said. "You only wanted to watch your dumb ending."

"My ending wasn't dumb. Ask Mr. Harrison."

"I don't care 'bout your ending, Abe," Dewey said. "I care 'bout tellin' Mr. Harrison what we found out!"

"Hey, hey, boys," Mr. Harrison said, holding up a hand. "How 'bout *one* of you tells me what in the Sam Hill has you so worked up?"

I nodded to Dewey, letting him say it. He was right— if I hadn't listened to him, we'd never have known about Tyler Bonnet.

Dewey took a deep breath. "Sir, I'm 'fraid to say a great injustice is occurring in your fine establishment."

I rolled my eyes. As usual, he was being weird. I was fixin' to jump in when Mr. Harrison spoke.

"That right?" He leaned forward with his forearms on the glass countertop. "And what injustice is that?"

Dewey glanced at me. "We watched the VHS tape you gave Abe out of your camera."

"You watched the *whole tape?* I only meant for you to watch Abe's robbery." He tossed me a smile and a wink, on account of it being just a pretend robbery.

"Yes, sir," Dewey said. "We watched the *whole thing*. It only recorded when somethin' was happenin', otherwise it jerked ahead to the next interestin' bit."

"That's right," Mr. Harrison said. "It's motion-activated. Otherwise, I'd have to change the tape every two hours."

Dewey nodded. "I only told you because it makes it hard to know how many days we actually watched, but throughout the tape, Tyler Bonnet came in and stole four different things from your store. Stuffed 'em all in the kangaroo pocket of his jacket and just walked out without you knowin' a thing."

Mr. Harrison rubbed his nose, thinking. "Tyler Bonnet," he said, finally. "Now, he's the boy with the black hair always looks in need of a comb? Freckly cheeks? Usually comes in with a friend or two?"

"Yeah!" we both said at once.

"What did he take?"

It was my turn to talk, so I did before Dewey had a chance to answer. "The first time he stole a hacky sack," I said. "Then he took a yo-yo—and it looked like a good one, too. Next, he stole some kind of fancy notebook from your school supplies aisle—"

"You mean my *stationery* aisle," Mr. Harrison corrected.

"Yeah, I guess. The last thing we saw him nab was a bottle of Coke from the back cooler."

Mr. Harrison tapped his fingers on his chin, staring at something out in the street. I turned to look through the glass front of the store, but didn't see anything interesting. A second or two later, his attention drifted back to us. "You're *sure* about this, boys?"

I nodded, holding out the tape. "See so yourself." He took it from me.

"The picture isn't great," Dewey said, "and it's only black and white, but you can definitely see him stealin' everything."

Mr. Harrison sighed. "I'll check it out myself, then I'm not sure what I'll do. Probably best to talk to his parents."

"You could talk to Abe's ma," Dewey said. "She's a detective. She could arrest him for thievery."

Mr. Harrison chuckled. "I don't think I need to go *that* far. He *is* just a kid. Some kids just do dumb things sometimes."

I was in shock. And slightly offended. "This isn't just 'some dumb thing,'" I said. "He's *stealing* from you."

"I'm sorry," Mr. Harrison said. "I didn't mean to dismiss it like that. You're right, it's important to deal with, but I need to deal with it *properly*. Some kids go through phases. I have to consider all the ramifications of any action I take on account of how it could affect whether or not Mr. Bonnet continues stealing the rest of his life or just grows out of doin' it."

I didn't rightly understand what he was saying. I had no idea what *ramifications* meant, but it didn't sound like Tyler Bonnet was going to get in too much trouble. I was about to argue the point when Mr. Harrison interrupted.

"Thank you, boys," he said. "I appreciate you bringin' this to my attention."

Dewey grinned. "You're very welcome."

I let out a big breath and we started for the door when Mr. Harrison called out, "Oh, and boys?"

Both of us turned around.

"Congratulations on the great detective work."

That brought big smiles to both of us. We left the store and got back on our bikes knowing we'd done something good.

Dewey said, "You know, Abe, today we made the world a little safer for common folk."

I thought about this for just long enough to realize how idiotic it sounded.

But I didn't care. Mr. Harrison had called us "detectives."

CHAPTER 25

Leah had driven straight home from Talladega yesterday after she and Carmichael cut the deal with Duck. When she finally made it back to Alvin, it was past quitting time anyway. Now it was near on eleven, and she'd just made it in on account of she spent the morning cooking eggs and bacon for Abe, Caroline, and Dan. Dan had gotten up long enough to eat and then went straight back to the sofa, complaining that he was up until five reading through the Cahaba River Strangler files. Didn't sound like he was discovering any breakthroughs in the case, but, Leah noticed, he did manage to polish off yet another bottle of Jim Beam.

Thankfully, he didn't seem drunk at breakfast.

Setting the fax from Grell Memorial beside her keyboard, Leah poured herself a coffee from the half-filled pot on the table and took a seat at her desk. For once, Chris was typing away on his computer and, Leah realized, he had been the last few times she'd seen him. Normally, the man spent his time with his boots up on his desk doing crossword puzzles. She had no idea what he was working on. It wasn't like he was doing data entry, since he wasn't consulting any data.

She hoped Ethan hadn't given him a special project to keep him busy, since she needed his help narrowing down the thirty-nine potential suspects she suddenly had.

"Whatcha doin'?" she asked him.

"Somethin' for Ethan," he said, his eyes riveted to his computer screen.

Leah bit her bottom lip. *Damn.* A series of characters scrolled up his monitor too quickly for Leah to make them out. "What're all those?"

"Hang on," he said, pointing his darkly creased index finger at the list's bottom as it began slowing down. "I think we're . . . almost . . ."

The data stopped scrolling, and Leah noticed it was a bunch of names followed by numbers. She rolled her chair in closer to Chris's. "What is all that?"

"That . . ." Chris said, his attention still on his screen. ". . . is the result of three solid days of work."

"And? What is it?"

"One sec." He looked over his shoulder to Ethan's office. The door was closed. "Hey, Ethan!" Chris hollered. Leah almost told him to damn well stifle himself. It was one thing for her to be cavalier with Ethan—he and her pa had been friends—it was quite another for Chris to be disrespectful, and quite out of character. Leah sat there shocked.

She heard Ethan's chair squeak right through his closed door as he got off of it and opened his door. Sitting there, she patiently braced herself to hear Chris get yelled at, only that never happened. Instead, Ethan walked over and stood behind Chris, looking at his monitor, his face breaking into a smile. "Please," he said to Chris, "tell me you're finally done."

Chris was all smiles. "I reckon so, yes."

Ethan rubbed his large hands together. Leah noticed age in his forearms and wrists. "So? What's the verdict?"

"Well, if I'm right—and if all the data you gave me is correct—"

"It's correct," Ethan said, cutting him off. "Don't even start with that."

"All right." Chris turned back to his screen. "Then, as of yesterday, I've got Texas at nine to one."

Ethan's hand-rubbing stopped, and his palms came together in a loud clap. "That's what I wanted to hear!" He grasped Chris's shoulder. Leah had absolutely no idea what was going on. "I can't believe those suckers could be so far off," Ethan said. "But I *knew* they were, though. What did I tell you? Huh?"

Still smiling, Chris gazed up at him.

Leah's eyes narrowed suspiciously. "What are you two talkin' about?"

Ethan clapped again and then went back to rubbing his hands together. "We're talkin' 'bout making a fortune because them guys settin' up the odds don't know half as much as we do, ain't that right, Chris?"

"Actually, this is all you. You gave me the data, the only thing I did was compile it. I'm not takin' any responsibility for—"

"Don't be such a candy ass. You know as well as I do that—"

Leah interrupted. "Are . . ." she started then decided to keep going. "Are you talkin' about betting? On baseball?"

"I don't know," Ethan said. "Is it still called 'betting' when it's a sure thing?"

"Last time I checked, there was no such thing as 'sure things,'" she said. "Not only that, but *who* are you making bets with?"

Absently waving her question away, Ethan said, "I got a telephone number from a friend. Doesn't matter who. What matters is they've got the Texas Rangers at fourteen to one. Five points too high. And I figured as much, that's why I got Chris to prove it. Five points high makes Ethan Montgomery a wealthy man."

"You're talkin' about some bookie?" Leah asked. "Isn't that against the law?"

Ethan scrunched up his face. "When was the last time you took somebody in for running a sports book? It's . . . you know. One of them gray areas. 'Sides, I'll call him from home, not from here."

She tried not to laugh. "Last time I checked, making bets with bookies was illegal, from home or anywhere, Ethan. There ain't no gray area about it."

He cast her a sideways glance. "And I'm betting you'd cite someone with an open container for havin' a beer up at Cornflower Lake in the dog days of summer."

"Actually," she said, "I've done precisely that. Well . . . maybe not *anyone*. But last year I busted a half-dozen schoolkids with two cases of Bud."

"But you didn't arrest 'em, you just took away their beer."

"So, you're saying we don't arrest bookies, we just take their money?"

Ethan didn't bite. "You wouldn't even have taken all that beer if they hadn't been under age," Chris said. "Admit it."

She scratched her neck where a mosquito had got her. "I'm not so sure. I find anyone in public with two cases, I reckon I—"

"Just go rain on someone else's parade, would you?" Ethan asked. "We don't come down on bookies because of it bein' a victimless crime."

This time, Leah couldn't hold back her laugh.

"What?" Ethan asked. Both he and Chris watched her expectantly.

"You're goin' to be the only victim—when you lose everything you put down on the Texas Rangers. Texas Rangers ain't winning shit this year."

Ethan shook his head slowly. "It's so sad. You have no idea what you're talkin' about. Nolan Ryan's taking them all the way through the World Series to the grand finale."

Leah rolled her eyes. "You mean this comin' October?" she asked.

"That very one."

"How can you possibly have enough data at this point to figure out who's goin' to win a game come October?"

Ethan tapped the side of his head. "That's where my smarts come in."

Leah laughed again.

"What?"

Smiling, she slowly shook her head. "Just . . . I can't believe it."

"What?" Ethan asked again.

"How much cow shit you two are actually tossin' 'round right now."

It was Ethan's time to squint. Something was going on behind those eyes. "You have no idea what you're talkin' about," he said after a spell.

"Yeah? Remember, my daddy was right into base-ball, too. He'd never tell you to bet on the Rangers.

Maybe if he was drunk, but that's it. And he *knew* baseball. You just sort of watch it."

Ethan held up his palm. "Now, I'd never say anythin' bad about your daddy, God rest his soul, but the one thing I knew 'bout more in this world than that man did was baseball. He was just—"

"What were you just thinkin' before you tried to convince yourself my daddy didn't know shit from a shine box?"

A smile came back to Ethan's face. "Just rememberin' him goin' on 'bout the A's. Every year it was 'Oakland this,' or 'Oakland that.' There ain't no way Oakland'll even get near the pennant this year. The Series? Forget 'bout it."

"Ah," Leah said. "So you *do* remember my pa's thoughts on the sport."

"Like I said, no offense to him. He was a marvelous man. Normally, chock-full of good ideas, too. He only became misguided when it came to the A's."

"Tell you what," Leah said, "how about you and I make a little side bet?"

Ethan mulled this over before holding out his hand. "You're on. A sawbuck?"

"*Only* a sawbuck?" Leah asked. "So you're really *not* that confident, are you?"

"Fine," he said. "Make it twenty."

Leah shook his waiting hand. "You're a fool, but I'll take your money."

"Silly, silly girl," Ethan said and crossed his arms.

Chris sat back in his chair with a satisfied smirk. "Anything else you need?"

"Actually," Leah said, "before you answer that, Ethan, I have somethin' I *really* need Chris's help on. And mine has to do with *upholding* the law, not breakin' it."

"That's fine," Ethan said. "I got what I wanted. I'll be in my office." He walked back, closing his door behind him. Leah heard a loud squeak as he returned to his chair.

Chris lifted a dubious eyebrow her way. "What do you want me to do? Utilize more of my special powers?"

Grabbing the fax from her desk, Leah showed him the list of thirty-nine suspects who were admitted to Grell Memorial in Montgomery around the time Duck said he'd met Jimmy McNimmy. "I want you to find out which of these people have priors. I reckon that's the first step to narrowing things down. They'd be more likely to fit the Stickman profile than the rest."

"How the hell am I goin' to find anything with just this? Are these addresses and phone numbers even current?"

"Probably not. Some'll be in the same place, though. And most of them are listed with their Social Security number, surely that'll help."

Chris counted off some names. "What 'bout the nine who have no address or SSN listed?"

"Yeah," Leah said. "Those ones will be a mite tougher. Just see what you can do, all right?"

He glanced over the three pages that Leah had stapled together before leaving the correctional institute in Talladega. "*Thirty-nine* people? Are you serious?" He looked crestfallen.

"What's wrong?" Leah asked.

"It's just . . . This isn't as fun as the usual stuff you get me to do."

CHAPTER 26

I was on page 120 of *Understanding Forensics,* at the beginning of a new part called "Analyzing Evidence." A subheading beneath that read: "Ballistics: After the Bullet Leaves the Gun," and was all about figuring stuff out from any used bullets discovered at a crime scene.

The first thing you did was measure the bullet's size, which is called its *caliber.* Knowing that is the first step toward figuring out what kind of gun it came from. Some guns ejected shell casings, and if the assailant didn't clean them up, police found them, too. With the casings, police could learn even more.

Most guns were made so that the bullet comes out spinning. This made it more accurate, but it also cut grooves into the bullet. These grooves created a "rifling pattern," which could also be measured, along with "lands," "striations," and "twists." By measuring all of these, forensics experts could actually match a used bullet to a certain gun. The book had an example of one specific firearm having five "lands," or high marks, and five grooves with a left (or counterclockwise) twist.

Along with all these marks, there were other smaller

marks that were unique between every single gun, just like a fingerprint. With careful measurement, police could tell whether or not the bullet came from a specific gun.

Turning the page, I came to the next part, which was all about handwriting analysis. No two people wrote alike. How a person wrote was personal and unique, involving unconscious and automatic actions that were uncontrollable.

To investigate handwriting, you needed several samples before you could fully understand a person's style. Some things forensics experts looked at were the spacing between words, the slants between lines, and the amount of pressure the writer applied to the pen or pencil. Also, the size, shape, and proportions of the letters were all important.

The next part was called "Serology: Blood and Other Fluids." It said blood was the most common bodily fluid found at crime scenes, and by analyzing it, police could match up a suspect.

You needed a good-size sample of blood to properly test it, and it was vital that it was uncontaminated when the forensics team got it. Therefore, how you packaged it at the scene was important. The book also said detecting blood could sometimes be tricky. This was where some of those vials of liquid that came with my kit were used. For instance, with the phenolphthalein, you could perform something called a Kastle-Meyer Color Test by mixing it with the blood and hydrogen peroxide. If it really *was* blood, the liquid would turn dark pink.

You could even find blood in places that had been cleaned up or on walls where somebody had painted over top by using a tiny drop of the vial called luminol. The luminol test was good because it didn't affect the sample as much as other tests did, so that more tests could still be done on the same sample.

The book got pretty complicated after that, when it discussed how to match a blood sample to a specific person. You first needed to find out the ABO type of the blood—whether it was O, A, B, or AB. Then you looked at things like enzymes, proteins, and antigens. I flipped past some stuff I couldn't understand about how to genetically map certain aspects of the blood to a person.

I went on to read about other bodily fluids, but quickly realized I probably didn't need to know so much about those, either, so I just skimmed all that.

Just before I was about to turn over the corner of the page and close the book, I came to the next subheading: "DNA: Life's Building Blocks." We had studied DNA in science this last school year, and I found it fascinating. I decided to keep reading.

DNA was a molecule of smaller units arranged in a double-helix formation that was made up of long strands of chromosomes. My science teacher last year, Mr. Garson, had a 3D model of a DNA double helix that stretched up from his desk in a twisted spiral.

Each strand of DNA was made up of millions of molecules called nucleotides, and those had four kinds of nitrogen bases, designated by the letters *G, C, T,* or *A.* These codes could join together in tons of different ways, making a unique instruction for different parts of the human body.

Every person's body had around six billion codes in their DNA, that could all go together in different ways, allowing for a huge number of potential sequences. Except for the case of identical twins, everybody's DNA was different from everybody else's. In fact, the book said DNA was even *more* unique than a fingerprint or an individual snowflake.

To analyze DNA, first it must be lifted from the material containing it. This was done by breaking down proteins and releasing the DNA.

After that, using a recently discovered technique, the sample of DNA could be amplified by causing a polymerase—a word I could barely sound out and that wasn't in my dictionary—chain reaction, often referred to as just PCR. Through PCR, technicians could re-create as much of the DNA as they liked, something called short tandem repeats, or STRs. I didn't quite understand it all.

Then, by comparing "markers" between a sample of DNA and a potential suspect, forensic experts could calculate the likelihood of whether the suspect was the one who had left the DNA behind at the crime scene.

It sort of made sense, but it also made my head feel like the Liberty Bell was being rung inside it. I turned over the corner of the next page and closed the book, setting it on my nightstand. The end was coming up soon. I doubted I'd finish it today, though, since I also wanted to read more of my mother's Stickman case files before she got home. I didn't want her to find me reading them. I figured she'd probably get mad if she did, but I wasn't worried too much about that. Now that I'd learned all this stuff about police work, those files gripped me like nothing else I could remember.

Excitement pooled in my stomach and rippled through my skin. I checked the time. My mother wouldn't be home from work for at least an hour, probably even two. That gave me plenty of time to read more files. I had a goal now, too. Ever since seeing my mother's note about my grandpa Joe maybe killing an innocent man, I'd been trying to find evidence in all them papers proving that he didn't. So far I hadn't been able to, but I still had a lot of that stack to get through.

I had read a bunch of stuff about some suspects, and also the report of what happened the night my grandpa Joe shot a man named Harry Stork, who, at the time, my grandpa thought was the Stickman even though it turned out Harry Stork's gun didn't have any bullets in it. Now, after carefully making a sketch in my notebook about how my mother had left the stack of files with the pen on top, I took everything I'd already read from the top and started in on the next file, which was all about the very first time the Stickman ever killed anyone. His first victim was a black man named Waylon Ferris who had been unemployed at the time, but previously worked for Built-Right Tool and Die in Alvin, a shop I couldn't remember ever seeing myself. Maybe it wasn't around anymore.

Waylon Ferris's body was found on February 10, 1973, at Finley's Crossing, hog-tied backward—something I had a hard time visualizing—with a wooden stake hammered through his chest straight into the ground. A piece of paper with a stickman on it was attached to the stake. I decided I didn't *want* to imagine that, so I pushed it from my mind and quickly went past all the photographs in the file.

I'd been below the tracks at Finley's Crossing before—me and Dewey rode there a few times on our bikes. It was dark down there even in the daytime, on account of all the trees sort of snarled and tangled up around where it had been dug into. The sun never shined down there. I can only imagine how black it was that cold night in February at ten-thirty at night. That's when, according to the reports, the police found Ferris.

The whole thing put a "twist in my tummy," as my mother used to say when I was younger. It seemed so senseless, like the Stickman did it for no reason other than to just be able to say he killed someone. And then I realized he couldn't even tell nobody on account of they would go to the police, so it made even less sense then. Ever since the time I saw the hollowness of Mary Ann Dailey's eyes, the way the life had been sucked out of 'em as though they'd been replaced with the black button eyes of a rag doll.

It made me wonder about people. I guess I wasn't old enough to really understand, because even if I hated someone, I couldn't take all that away from them. And I knew that a lot of the killings my mother had investigated were done by folk who never even knew the people they killed, so they couldn't even have hated them. They just . . . I don't know. Again, I figured I just wasn't old enough to understand.

Part of me hoped I never would be.

From what I could tell from the file, the only evidence found at that first crime scene that police thought might be important were the tire tracks of a vehicle parked nearby. There were photos of the tread marks, along with measurements. The notes said the imprints were likely made by a truck with a 132.9-inch wheelbase and 16.5-inch tires. Even I realized this wouldn't really help in finding the killer. There were a lot of trucks in Alvin, and I bet a lot of them had the same wheelbase and tire size. Not only that, there didn't seem to be any proof the truck was there when Waylon Ferris was put there. Those tracks could've been made near on any time before that.

I moved on to the file for the Stickman's second victim.

Veda Gamble was a thirty-eight-year-old white woman who worked as a waitress at Camponi's Italian Restaurant on Main Street, yet another place I'd never heard of. I was starting to realize how much things changed over time. Made me wonder if things might be always changing and you don't really notice until you look back. I decided to pack that one away and think on it when I had nothing else to do. Right now I wanted to keep going through these Stickman files. It wasn't so often I found myself alone enough to chance reading them.

Around seven o'clock in the evening on March 22, 1973, according to a statement written by my grandpa Joe, Veda Gamble's body was found deep in the woods in Cherry Park Forest. She had gone missing the day before around noon when she had gone out by herself to meet a friend by the name of Veronica Stetson for a coffee at—and I was starting to think this was like an episode of *The Twilight Zone*—*another* place in Alvin I never recalled having seen in my life, some place called Beans & Co. on Main Street. According to her friend, Veda Gamble never showed up.

That was pretty much everything I read that was really important. There were pictures, of course, and sketches of the crime scene, but no mention of any solid evidence or anything like that. I found it sad that she didn't have more stuff in her file. It was like her life just ended, and that was all there was to it. She deserved at least to have a story.

Victim number three's body showed up around noon in one of the fields way up along First Road. My school bus took that way to get out of Alvin on our way to Satsuma every single day, so I knew that area pretty well. Of course, all them fields looked exactly the same, and they went on for miles before you finally came to forests again. I wondered where exactly in those fields the victim had turned up, but I wasn't good with addresses. Besides, it was only an estimated guess, as the report said the land he was found on belonged to the county. There were no buildings on it, just witchgrass and dirt.

His name was Lafayette Eagan, and he had been white. I wondered why the reports always had to say what color of skin the victim had. Seemed strange to me, as my mother always told me I shouldn't even look at skin color, I should be looking at the color of the heart beating underneath all that skin and whether or not that heart was made from steel or flesh. I realized there wasn't anybody with a *real* steel heart; she was using the term "metaphorically," something we just learned about in English class right before summer break started in May.

Mr. Eagan was thirty-nine and it had been April 30, 1973, when my grandpa and someone named Officer Peter Strident found him in the field. There were tire marks found in the soft earth running between First Road and a very broken fence from what I could tell in the file's pictures. They didn't look like great tire impressions, at least not from what I knew about them based on *Understanding Forensics*. According to the report, though, police were able to discern they were made by a vehicle with a 132.9-inch wheelbase and 16.5-inch wheels. Someone had made a check mark beside these two facts and written the initials *H.S.*? I wondered if that was my grandpa's writing I was looking at. And what did *H.S.* mean? My guess was Harry Stork.

I thought those numbers seemed familiar, so I quickly went through the stuff I'd already read and, sure enough, in the reports about the first victim, Waylon Ferris, police found these exact same tire prints. I looked at the two photos but couldn't tell whether the tread was the same or not. The Polaroid from this new file didn't show near on enough details. I squinted best I could, and from what I could tell, the actual marks on the tire weren't the same. But it seemed awfully suspicious that the numbers were. At least to me, but then, I'm naturally suspicious. At least that's what my mother says.

Just like in Waylon Ferris's file, this report said the wheelbase and tire width was *indicative*—a word I had to sound out and still didn't know what it meant; my dictionary was in my room, and I didn't feel like fetching it—of a truck, in particular a four-by-four half ton. Once again, it occurred to me that there were a whole mess of trucks in Alvin. That really didn't narrow things down too well.

Lafayette Eagan was last seen at—and you're not going to believe this—*another* place I'd never heard of, called the Just Around the Corner Mercantile. It was on Hunter Road, just like Mr. Harrison's Five-and-Dime. My mother sometimes referred to Mr. Harrison's as "the mercantile." Made me wonder if this place used to be where Mr. Harrison is now.

Anyway, the clerk at the mercantile, a man named Joseph Connelly, was showed a photo of Lafayette Eagan by my grandpa, and the clerk remembered him. Said he came in for a pack of cigarettes and had mentioned he was walking—not driving—and that he was on his way home. That made me wonder where he lived.

I lived within walking distance of Mr. Harrison. Lafayette Eagan might've been my neighbor if the Stickman hadn't got him.

That thought made me sad.

Then I heard something that made my heart slam against the inside of my ribs, and it kept slamming again and again like a manic jackhammer somebody lost control of. It was the sound of my mother's car door closing. She was home. Panic welled up inside me. I quickly looked at the sketch I'd made of how the file folders had been before I started, and in a flurry of paper, I tried my best to put it all back as it was. The pen she always set on top of the stack went flying off behind me in the process. I was just about to start crawling around the floor in search of it when I heard something else. Something I couldn't believe I hadn't noticed before.

Dan was snoring in the living room. Only, it wasn't the normal freight-train snores he made; this was just a soft and easy snore. My eyes were wide and I felt sweat collecting on my head and under my arms. The whole time I'd been in the kitchen going through my mother's notes and files, Dan had been just two rooms away. He could've easily come in and found me. I was so stupid.

My brain was spinning like the back wheels of a Formula One race car trying to get out of a sandpit. I still had the chair at the counter. I quickly pulled it across the floor, banging it against the tiles twice with two very loud *thuds!* I froze, halfway to the table, listening to see if I'd woken Dan up.

I didn't hear anything. Not even his quiet snores. I quickly slid the chair the rest of its way back to its spot at the table where it was when I came in the kitchen. I had just squatted down to get on my hands and knees and search for the pen when the back door opened. My mother came right through the dining room and into the kitchen without even taking her boots off.

She smiled at me. "Well, how are you?" she asked.

I stood there, feeling shaky, my eyes glued halfway between the floor and hers. I didn't know what to do. Without moving, I let my eyes rove around the kitchen floor looking for that pen.

"What's . . ." she started, trailing off. "What are you doin'?"

"Nothin'!" I said, a mite too loud.

She narrowed her eyes. "Why are you being so weird?"

"I'm not. I'm normal. Just . . . doin' normal things. It's a normal day."

"Where's Dan?"

I just stood there, not knowing what to say. Out of the corner of my eye, I saw the pen! It was right in front of the fridge.

"Is Dan *here?*" she asked.

I still didn't answer, just started trying to sidestep slowly toward the pen. So slowly she wouldn't notice I was moving.

"Abe," my mother said. "I asked you a question. Is Dan here? His car's outside."

"He's in there," I managed to say, nodding my head toward the living room on the other side of the kitchen wall.

"He's not *still* asleep, is he?"

Continuing to move sideways so slow I couldn't be seen by human eyes, I just shrugged.

My mother let out a big breath, shaking her head. "I'll handle this," she said and stomped into the living room. Her voice rose and snapped as she accused Dan of sleeping the entire day away, adding something about a hangover. I tried not to listen.

Quickly, I took the opportunity to dive for the pen, coming down on my knees before my hands got in front of me. My leg hit the pen and I desperately grasped for it as it rolled forward, my fingers a fraction of a second too late to stop it from going under the fridge.

I swallowed hard. Sweat clung to the inside of my T-shirt. There was nothing left to do. My fate was sealed.

I was doomed.

CHAPTER 27

Holding hands, Carry and Jonathon walked down Hunter Road toward Main Street. They had no real destination; Main Street was just somewhere they could go where Carry could window-shop. In reality, she just liked walking with Jonathon, holding his hand.

It was somewhere around one in the afternoon, and the rain still fell, although not near on as hard as it had some of the past days. The sky remained gray, but it was a solid shade of gray, without the thunderheads from a few days ago. The color was a lot closer to white than black and it glowed bright, almost like the sun wanted you to know it still lived somewhere behind the thin layer of stratus. This was a definite improvement as, for the past two weeks, it was as though the sun had come down with chemical depression and given up completely, deciding to spend the entire day in bed feeling sorry for itself.

They strolled beneath the boughs of a series of red maples, the trees' buds gleaming even in this dreary light. Soon they would be in full bloom. The trees were on the other side of a white cedar fence, but their branches spread out past the edge of the sidewalk. The lawn along the underside of the fence was in need of trimming. Rain-soaked tufts of grass burst from the bottom of the fence posts like green hedgehogs out for blood.

"So," Jonathon said, "what did you do for fun before I came along?"

Carry laughed. "Life wasn't fun before you came along."

The fence they'd been following ended, and the road-side became sparsely wooded. Pepper trees, black walnut, poplar, and even more maples now lined the side of the road. These maples weren't of the red variety, though. They didn't quite have the same effect.

"Oh, come on," Jonathon replied. "You know that isn't true. You had Abe and Dewey to entertain you." A squirrel darted out of the woods carrying some sort of nut, took one look at the two of them, and scurried back the way it came, dropping its nut before leaping off the sidewalk.

Carry laughed again, this time even louder than before. "You find Abe and Dewey entertainin'? I just find 'em as annoying as hell." She looked back. The squirrel returned to grab its dropped treasure.

"I find them fascinating."

"Squirrels?" Carry asked.

"No. Abe and Dewey. *Especially* Dewey."

"Well, you can find them fascinatin' on your own time. This is my time, and I'm sick of all of our conversations windin' up being about my dweeby brother and his dweeby friend."

"All right then," Jonathon said. "If you didn't rely on them for fun, what did you do?"

Carry thought about this. "You know, the regular stuff

everyone does. Watched TV, sometimes read a book, wrote poetry, hung out with friends, occasionally went out for dinner—"

"Hold up," Jonathon said, cutting her off. "You write poetry? Why am I only learnin' about this now?"

"You never asked before now."

"Are you a good poet?"

She laughed yet again. "No, I'm a crappy poet. But I am—or at least was—fairly prolific. I used to write two poems a day. One just as I was wakin' up and another just when I was goin' to bed." They passed a bunch of hydrangea bushes. A yellow and black butterfly was flitting around the branches and leaves dodging raindrops.

"You'll let me read them, right?" Jonathon asked.

"Hell no! You'd just laugh at me."

"I would never laugh at you."

"You still aren't reading my poems, they're kind of personal. Besides, they're mostly depressin'."

"Why's that?"

"Because my life was depressing before I met you."

"Have you written *anything* since meeting me?"

They stopped, and Carry stared into his eyes, feeling the day's glow glimmering in her own, making her blink. "Honestly?" she asked. "I haven't. I don't think. Um . . . No. I really haven't." She smiled.

"But you'll let me read some you wrote before, right?"

"I don't know."

"Come on, you gotta."

"Why do I gotta?"

"It's part of you. I want to know all the parts I can."

She sniffled as rain dripped off her nose. "Let me think 'bout it, okay?"

"Okay," Jonathon said. They walked on, continuing

their way down Hunter Road, walking past Raven Lee's Pizzeria before turning onto Main Street.

"How come you never work there anymore?" Carry asked.

"My grandpa's pizza shop?"

"Yeah."

"He hasn't asked me to. I really didn't ever work there a lot. When we met, I was just helping him out over the Christmas holidays. They're a busy time for him."

Carry scrunched up her face, thinking this over. "People eat more pizza at Christmastime than other times?"

Jonathon just nodded.

"Weird," Carry said. "Why?"

Jonathon shrugged. "I don't know. Maybe it's festive."

"I don't remember Baby Jesus ever eating pizza," Carry said. "Come to think of it, that's what one of the wise men should've brought. The guy who brought the myrrh. He should've brought a pepperoni, bacon, and mushroom sixteen-inch pizza instead." She smiled at Jonathon. "You could've delivered it. Nobody really likes myrrh." Main Street looked washed out as Carry stared through the drizzle at the rows of shops growing smaller and smaller toward the horizon's vanishing point.

"So, is your ma still busy goin' after that Stickman guy?" Jonathon asked. "Or is that all done now?"

"She's obsessed with it. I can't believe you don't know this and you actually come to my house."

"Her and Dan are never home. Not when I'm there, anyway."

Carry watched the sidewalk in front of them. "Still," she said, "don't you think you'd have heard if she'd caught him yet?"

Jonathon shrugged. "Two weeks ago it was everywhere, all over the papers, the news, everything. Now it's like it never happened. Funny how quick people forget stuff like that. Stuff that seemed so important, like, just a breath or two ago, you know?"

"I guess. I'm not like that. Well, I guess I kind of am. My interests change."

"What do you mean?"

"Well, I used to collect fairies and dragons. Now I'm not so interested in fairies and dragons."

She glanced down to her left hand, where a drop of rain had collected on the dark purple stone of her promise ring, making it appear even bigger. She smiled, but kept the smile to herself.

"What do you mean you 'collected fairies and dragons'?" Jonathon asked.

"Statues. I'll show you when we get back to my place."

"How many of them do you have?"

"Actually, now, just one of each. I had a few dragons and five fairies at one point, but I gave them away to my cousin. She just turned thirteen. I thought she'd give them a better home than I could."

"Why did you keep one of each?"

"They were my favorites. Even when you outgrow things, you still have favorites that you loved the most. It's like anything. If you loved something and then it's gone, you don't stop loving it." Carry thought over how to explain what she meant, but didn't come up with much. "You just learn to love the memory of it, I guess."

Jonathon gave her a smile. "You really *are* a poet."

Carry felt herself blush. "I was just tryin' to explain why I still have them. You asked."

They kept walking along Main Street without talking. All Carry heard was the sound of the rain, that soft, ambient hush that makes you know nature's still out there, even when things are shrouded in gray.

After a while, Jonathon spoke again. "You said your ma brought down the Cornstalk Killer, right? From a couple of years back?"

"Yeah." Carry sighed. "Don't even remind me. That was no fun. Don't you remember the stupid curfew she put in place?"

"I do. I remember complaining to my grandpa about it. Telling him I was fifteen and should be allowed to stay out as long as I wanted." He gave her a smile.

Carry shook her head with a sarcastic laugh. "The curfew wasn't even the worst of it. For you, at least, you got to stay out 'til then. Abe and I? We couldn't leave my mother's sight. She even had my uncle come down here and babysit us."

"How old were you?"

"I was fourteen," Carry said after a slight hesitation.

"Wasn't he snatching up fourteen-year-old girls?"

Carry frowned. "Yeah, I guess."

"Your mom was just worried about you. Wouldn't you try and keep your kid safe if you'd been her?"

Carry looked up at him. "Don't do that."

"Do what?"

"Talk to me rationally about something I have a completely irrational viewpoint on. I like my irrational viewpoints, thank you very much."

"Okay," Jonathon said.

"You know," Carry said after another round of silence. "I actually keep waiting for her to do it again."

"Who? Do what?"

"My mother. I keep waiting for her to tell me and Abe we can't go outside because the Stickman might get us."

Jonathon shrugged again. "The Stickman hasn't gone after any kids, has he?"

"Do you think that matters?"

"What?"

"That he hasn't killed a kid yet? Do you think he actually *cares* who he kills?"

Jonathon appeared to think this over for a bit. "I don't know. I've never had the urge to kill someone, but you gotta think that somewhere in his mind, somethin' is making him do what he does. Isn't that how they always catch the killers in the movies? Because of patterns that come out in their crimes? Hard to control behavioral patterns. They're subconscious." Jonathon wiped the rain dripping from his nose with his arm. "It would be weird for him to suddenly start killing kids if he hasn't done it yet. At least I think it would. I don't know. We should ask your ma. She'd have a better idea."

They passed by Madame Crystalle's Psychic Shop with the creepy frog statue outside. Again, neither of them said a word for the next block. Then Carry asked, "Please don't, okay?"

Jonathon stopped walking. "Please don't what?"

They stood facing each other, Carry's left hand in his right, her right hand in his left. "Don't ask her about the Stickman? My mom. Please?"

"Okay," Jonathon said. "But why?"

Carry sighed. "Because she'll think it's a big deal and that you're either freaking out about it or secretly rooting for him. Or . . . something like that. She makes a big deal out of things that aren't such a big deal."

"I think a killer runnin' around Alvin is a bit of a big deal."

"Yeah, I guess," Carry said, "but it's . . ." She sighed again. "Just promise me you won't mention it to her? As a favor to me? Please?"

Jonathon thought a second before answering. "Sure," he said finally, then went back to walking.

They passed the hardware store and Mel's Pop Shop before Carry stopped again. "You really want to read some of my poems? Honestly?"

"I do."

"Okay," she said with a big breath. "Let me think on it. It's just . . . I've never showed them to anyone before. It's weird." She tried to reconcile the emotion she felt about the whole idea and found no word to describe it.

"I know," Jonathon said.

"What if you laugh at 'em?"

"I won't."

"I know you won't, but my stupid brain doesn't."

"That's your problem," Jonathon said.

"What is?"

"Thinking with your brain. I stopped doing that real quick after we met."

"So, you just don't think?" She laughed. "Not sure that would help matters at all for me."

Jonathon smiled. "No, I still think, only not with my brain. The brain's not so great at figurin' out stuff when it comes to love. You have to go deeper."

"Deeper? To what?"

"Your heart, silly." Jonathon laughed. "I can't believe you didn't see that coming." A bird flew from a pepper tree down onto the sidewalk in front of them. With a shake, it tossed all the rainwater from its feathers. Jonathon gestured toward it. "Even the wren knew where I was headed."

Carry laughed.

"See, that's the big difference between you and me," Jonathon said. "You're a poet and I'm just some corny guy with sappy lines."

Carry decided right then, next time he came over, she'd probably let him read one or two poems.

CHAPTER 28

Police Chief Montgomery called Leah into his office, not even bothering to open his door or turn down his television as he did so. All she heard was a muffled "Leah!" over the sound of whatever sport he was watching. Her guess was baseball.

"Jesus," she said to Chris while getting off her chair. "You'd think the man could get off that big ass and at least open his door."

Chris just laughed.

Straightening her black shirt, Leah walked over and let herself into the chief's office. "You call, Master?"

Ethan's gaze was fixed on the television hanging from the corner of the ceiling. Turned out he was watching baseball. Texas Rangers playing the Cleveland Indians, if she was right. In fact, she was pretty sure Nolan Ryan just threw a strike over the plate, putting Joe Carter out.

"Damn, that boy can pitch!" Ethan said. "You missed the Rangers going 'round the horn just a minute ago." He shook his head. "Amazin'."

Leah pressed her lips into a thin line and just nodded.

"I don't even know what that means. That why you called me in? Give me an education in baseball?"

"No," he said, still watching the screen but using the remote to mute the sound. "Have a seat."

Leah did. "So, what's up?"

Finally pulling his eyes from the screen, Ethan looked at her for the first time since she came in. "I remembered something from the old Stickman files. Not sure if you've come across it yet or not. I know there's a lot of crap to go through."

"You could say that. It's a bit dizzying."

"I'm sure. Anyway, after you told me 'bout the squealer who knew 'bout the holdback. Whatshisname? Goose?"

"Duck."

"Duck. Yeah. What'd you say his real name was?"

Leah blinked. She actually had to think hard to remember, she'd gotten so used to just referring to him as "Duck."

"Stanley Bishop."

Ethan's eyes were back on the TV screen as he pointed to her. "Yeah. I knew I'd heard it somewhere before. You'll find it in them folders sooner or later."

This got Leah's attention. "Duck's in the old files?" she asked, wishing Ethan would focus on her, dammit. This could be something important. In fact, it almost *had* to be. "Where . . . how does he fit into the old case?"

"Oh!" Ethan screamed, his arms going up over his head. "He was tagged. That was a *bad* call!"

"Ethan," Leah said, trying to stay calm. "Can you please finish with me, and then I'll let you alone to holler at the umpire all you want."

"Sorry," he said, and actually turned off the set. "That was rude of me."

"So . . . Stanley Bishop?"

Ethan snapped his fingers. "Right. He was here. Your pa questioned him."

"Duck?"

"Yeah. It all came out from two witnesses coming forth and describing the same car being parked near one of the crime scenes—I think that's the body we found in the back of Full Gospel." He shook his head. "That was something, let me tell you. Seeing that body staked in the goddamn middle of the night among all them crosses and tombstones. It was a clear night, too, with practically a full moon. Just the shadows cast in the glow of that bone-white moon were enough to give me nightmares." He gave a dramatic pause before continuing.

"Anyway, one of the witnesses got a partial plate, and both said the color of the vehicle was yellow. Got a hit with Bishop's vehicle—he drove a yellow 1968 Dodge Charger, a car you didn't see a lot of around Alvin. So we followed it all up, but it turned out to be a dead end. Figured I'd let you know before you read about it and got too excited, involving your witness and all."

Leah fidgeted in her chair. She was still trying to recover from finding out her pa and Duck had crossed paths. "Wait . . . what kind of dead end?"

"He had an alibi. It stood up."

She shook her head. "Listen, Ethan, either I need more coffee today or you're being annoyingly vague. Can you give me the whole story? I *haven't* read the report, remember? It must be near the bottom of the stack."

"Sorry. The Charger looked like a good lead. It even

matched some of the tire marks found at other scenes. But with just the partial plate, there really wasn't anything conclusive we could hang Bishop on." Ethan glanced up at the dead television. "Love to have that car now."

Leah couldn't help but feel her pulse in her wrists. It was too much to be just a coincidence. "This could be exactly the break we need," she said. "He knows about the holdback." Her eyes drifted to the wall behind Ethan. "Why the *hell* didn't I think of this before now?" she asked, more to herself than Ethan. "He goddamn lied when I interviewed him. He didn't meet the Stickman in the psych ward at all. He knows about the holdback because he *is* the friggin' Stickman!"

Ethan held up a thick-fingered hand. "You're not listenin'. We checked out his alibi. It was good. You'll see the statements and shit in the file. Him and a friend or some guy he worked with were at the bar all night. Closed the place down."

"How do you know?"

"Jesus, Leah. It was a bar. People *saw* him there. The barmaid specifically said she noticed him. He sort of stood out. She said all his type did. Called him 'weaselly.'" Ethan laughed. "'Weaselly.' Isn't that rich? I thought of a lot of people that could describe—"

Leah stopped Ethan's tangential thought. "But . . ." she started. "Even if it was just *his* car at the scene and he hadn't been driving it—especially if it was also at other scenes. That could—"

"His car was at the bar. They were at Bell's Tavern. You know that place? Been there since the invention of fire?"

"The one about ten miles west? Looks like someone

dragged it kickin' and screaming from the back of a train?" she asked.

Ethan nodded. "Seen the inside?"

"No. Never had the urge to get that close to it."

"Probably just as well." Ethan's mouth formed a thin line.

Something else struck Leah. "Hold it. Why was he so close to Alvin?" This seemed like another unnerving coincidence, although she realized she didn't know where Duck actually was from before getting thrown in the box.

"He lived here," Ethan said, plainly.

"*Here?*" Confusion fell over her. "In *Alvin?*"

Ethan nodded as though she should've known this already.

Leah's mind revved into high gear. Coincidences didn't exist, not to her. This was too much. She'd found her killer.

"Leah," Ethan said, obviously noticing her mind had gone off through a field picking wildflowers. "He's *not* your man. He wasn't back then, and he couldn't possibly be now."

That was true. Be pretty hard to kill someone from behind bars in Talladega.

Leah bit her lower lip. "It's too much of a coincidence," she said. "I—"

"Don't believe in coincidences," Ethan said. "I've heard that before. Many times. You know from who?"

Leah shrugged.

"Your pa."

"Yeah?"

Ethan batted her question out of the air. "Shit, half of what comes out of your mouth sounds just like him."

His face looked at his desktop, but his eyes looked up at her from under his graying brow. "That's why you're good, you know. You got his blood."

Her mind still sat in Duck's car that night parked out front of First Gospel. "Did y'all ever find any other vehicle matching the description and tire marks and partial plate and all that?"

Ethan leaned back in his chair with a loud squeak. "Nope. Remember, though, we found other tire markings consistent across murder scenes that didn't fit that Charger."

Leah hadn't had a chance to actually put together a timeline to look for patterns. She'd wanted to look through everything before she did that.

While she thought that over, Ethan turned the television back on but left the volume muted. "Figured you'd get all excited over this," he said. "That's why I wanted to tell you 'fore you stumbled on it yourself, on account of I honestly don't think there's anything there."

"How about my pa?"

"How 'bout what?"

"How did he feel about it?"

Ethan laughed, his eyes on the TV. "Oh, he, of course, was all brimmin' over about it, too. Eventually, though, even he had to admit there wasn't anything to it. Anyway, it's in the files I gave you." Suddenly, he yelled, "Yes!"

Leah looked at the TV. The Rangers were up by four and the bases were loaded. "I assume we're done?" she asked.

"Yeah, I think so," Ethan said, his eyes locked on the game.

A thought passed through Leah's mind. "Actually, we're not."

Ethan's eyes quickly met with hers. "What do you mean?"

"I need to ask you for somethin'. You're not gonna want to give it to me."

"What's that?" His eyes wandered up again.

"The names."

"Names? What names?"

"The other detectives or officers or whatever they are 'sides you and my pa who know about the letters."

Ethan's tongue clicked, and his gaze slowly fell and settled on Leah. "Figured that was coming sooner or later."

"I need to cover all the bases."

"Your pa handpicked these people, Leah. You questioning his judgment?"

Leah shook her head. "No . . . I . . . I dunno. Maybe. I mean, it's startin' to look like he might've shot himself the wrong guy. I'm starting to question everything."

"If I give you those names, what are you goin' to do with 'em?"

Leah took a big breath. "God's honest truth?"

"Mmm." Ethan sat back, crossing his arms. Of course his chair squeaked.

Another deep breath. "Probably at least give them each a call. Maybe meet with them. Ask them some questions."

"You'll piss everybody off if you do that."

"What's important here, Ethan? The feelings of—"

He held up his hand. "I don't need to be preached at. Let me think 'bout it a spell, okay?"

She started to object, but he once again cut her off.

"I told you I need to think on it. Respect that."

With a big sigh, she said, "All right." Ethan's attention once again fixated on baseball. "I'll see myself out," she said.

Chris was playing some game called Super Slither on his computer when Leah got back to her desk. She thumbed through the small pile of folders she still hadn't gone through, until she came to one labeled *Bishop, Stanley*. Without even looking through it, she tossed it right on top of Chris's hands and keyboard. She had another copy at home she would study over this weekend.

"Hey!" Chris snapped. "What the hell?"

"Stanley Bishop," she said. "Better known in the pen as 'Duck.' Find out everything you can on the guy, and I mean *every single thing,* Slither-King."

CHAPTER 29

Monday morning, Leah sat at her desk still going through the old Stickman case files. She decided she had to finish them today. She was down to victim six. There wasn't a lot left to go. She was already at least two-thirds done.

Then it happened.

She started looking at the report for victim six—a woman from Montgomery named Geneva Wade—already expecting to see that Geneva was working at a hospital. Ethan had told her victims four onwards all did. He'd also said two of them worked at places Harry Stork didn't have contracts with.

This was one of those victims. Only—

Only what she read couldn't be right. It was way too much of a coincidence, and it made Leah's brain go on the offensive.

Geneva Wade was a psych nurse at Grell Memorial, the same hospital Duck reported meeting "the Stickman."

"This is impossible," she said.

"What?" Chris asked. He had been on the phone and his computer nonstop since Leah came in.

"You know that list of witnesses I gave you from Grell Memorial Hospital in Montgomery?"

"Yeah, I'm workin' on it. Hold your horses."

"No, I'm not rushing you. I've just . . . The original Stickman's sixth victim—she *worked* there."

"No shit," Chris said. "Didn't you say Harry Stork had a medical waste company or something?"

"Yeah, but—" She flipped back to the list of major contracts her pa had made. Grell Memorial wasn't there. Then she scanned all the pages from Stork's books listing every job he did, once again noting that a handful had asterisks beside them that Leah guessed came from her pa. But not a one was for any job at Grell. "He never did any business with Grell."

"Creepy coincidence," Chris said.

"Too much of one," she said.

She came to a note regarding her pa's task force growing by three more detectives working out of Montgomery. Now there were twelve and, Leah knew, it was one of these twelve who had leaked the original holdback to the press, tellin' 'em all about the stake with the Stickman drawing. Sometime, a day or two after Geneva Wade's lifeless body was found, the killer—presumably Harry Stork—became an overnight sensation and earned himself the name of "Stickman."

Then a thought struck her about this particular murder. She quickly went back to the description of the crime scene. "Wait a second," she said aloud, more to herself than Chris.

"What?" Chris tried to read her face.

"Nothin', I don't think . . . Well, it just . . ." She paged through the rest of the file looking for any note regarding the weird change in MO between this victim and all the rest she'd read about so far. She didn't find one. Maybe it wasn't a big deal, but any change in suspect behavior should've been at least noted. She read the scene again, remaining just as puzzled.

"Are you goin' to tell me?" Chris asked.

"It's probably nothin', it just seems weird that . . . well . . . the sixth victim wasn't staked into the ground like the rest. Her body *did* have a stake through it, but it was found floating in Beemer's Bog."

"Oh my God," Chris said. "Of all the places I don't want to end up dead, Beemer's Bog takes the prize. Have you driven up that way? The stench is . . ."

Leah skimmed through the report. "Never mind," she said. "Says here that there was evidence that an animal pulled the stake free and dragged the body into the bog." She looked up. "They found bite marks on the victim."

"That's horrible."

Leah nodded and went back to the file, flipping ahead to the next victim. Victim seven.

"Okay, this is too much," she said.

"What?" he asked.

"Victim seven, a man named Forrest Ingram, *also* worked at Grell. It's . . . this is making my head hurt. Everything's connected to everything. It's *impossible*."

"Obviously not impossible," Chris said.

This seventh victim was the one Ethan had told her about, the one where the body turned up spiked into the cemetery grounds behind Reverend Stark's Full Gospel Church. Full Gospel was a black church, and for a moment, Leah wondered if there was something to that. Only, Ingram had been white.

Just as Ethan had said, two separate witnesses reported a yellow car parked in front of the church around

eight-thirty or nine, which was close to the time estimated by the ME. Like Ethan said, one witness managed to give police a partial on the plate.

The rest of the file was full of witness statements
from Bell's Tavern, most taken the following day. As
Ethan had intimated, both Bishop and his 1968 Dodge
Charger had been seen at the bar, Bishop drinking and
playing pool from around seven o'clock until closing.

Authorities took photographs of Bishop's car and
showed them to the two witnesses. One was unsure of
whether it matched the one she remembered seeing, but
the other confirmed it looked very much like the car
he'd passed outside of the church.

Across the room the fax machine sprang to life. Leah
looked at Chris.

"That's mine," he said and got up to retrieve it.

Leah went on to victim eight, a twenty-nine-year-old
man with the unfortunate name of Warrick Quackenbush whose body was found in Willet Park. Willet Park
was huge and Leah wondered how long it actually took
them to find Quakenbush's body. Quackenbush worked
at Searcy Hospital in Mount Vernon, one of the hospitals Leah's pa had asterisked.

A single tire-tread mark discovered along the muddy
back roads below the lake appeared to be again a match
for Stanley Bishop's Charger, but there wasn't enough
conclusive evidence for police to go on. A single tread
mark could match many vehicle tires.

In fact, the one witness from the incident didn't report seeing a vehicle at all. He stated that he was fishing
in that far end of Willet lake when he saw Tommy Stork
come out of the woods, crouch down in the water, and
carefully wash off his upper arms and hands. He knew it

was Tommy on account of he and Tommy once worked at the same construction site.

This prompted Tommy being picked up from where he lived with his pa and brought into the station for questioning. Tommy denied being anywhere close to Willet Lake during that time and went on to say he hadn't even been near that part of town for probably a year, maybe more. He was quoted in the report as saying, "I ain't fond of woods or lakes or nothin' in nature. I just like to sit at home and watch television, which is what I was doin' while the Stickman put that body amongst all them trees."

Tommy told police his pa had been down in Mobile on business during that time, so Tommy's alibi couldn't be corroborated. When asked what "business" his pa was conducting, Tommy replied that he had no idea and that he and his pa didn't talk all that much.

There were notes in the file about remembering to do background and medical checks on Tommy Stork, which, obviously, were done, as Leah had read them back when she first started going through all these folders.

With a big breath, she came to the last folder in the stack. Victim nine. The last person the original Stickman ever killed.

Lola Reid worked at Mercy Medical in Daphne, Alabama, and that was the last place she was ever seen until her body turned up in the woods around the bottom of Tucker Mountain, so far north it actually lay outside the boundaries of town.

The medical examiner found a bullet lodged in Lola Reid's skull. That was the second round police managed to procure. Both slugs matched, both being fired from what forensics was now pretty certain was a Smith &

Wesson model 10 chambered .38 Special caliber, a gun popular in World War II.

Leah found a quickly written statement dated two days after the police discovered Lola Reid's body. It looked like Strident's writing, and the statement was made by Leah's pa. Fidgeting in her chair, Leah read on.

Her pa made it into the station first that day to find that sometime during the night, the window had been smashed with a brick and someone had come inside and made off with the entire stack of folders on her pa's desk, which contained all the Stickman case files to date. Of course, they had more copies of everything, but they never found out who broke in or why they wanted the files. Lots of blood was collected from the scene due to the thief cutting himself on jagged glass while climbing in, but a match was never made. On the back was a note in her pa's handwriting saying that the Storks' blood type differed from that of the samples.

According to her pa's notes, Leah could tell that, at this point, Tommy Stork was still pretty high up on his suspect list. That was until a witness named Betty-Lou Panders came forth the same day the station was robbed saying she'd seen a truck parked on the side of Tucker Mountain Road right around the time the ME said the body was dropped off in the woods. The vehicle she described was a red Ford F-250 with a white camper, and on the side of the camper, in big black letters, was the name STORK SANITATION AND WASTE REMOVAL with the slogan below it, OUR COMPETITORS CAN'T TOUCH OUR JOBS.

Well, there can't be too many trucks in the world like that, Leah thought, remembering how Ethan had told her this was the evidence that clinched her pa's decision about Harry Stork.

If that wasn't enough, the next day another witness came forward, this time a woman named Andrea Reinhardt, basically parroting exactly what Panders had stated the day before. Reinhardt again described Harry Stork's truck, right down to the make, model, business name, and slogan.

Harry Stork was then interviewed on June 19, 1974, and Leah's pa posed the question in his notes as to the possibility of the witness from victim number eight mistaking Tommy for Harry. He further noted that, given the witness's statement, he would've been looking at Tommy in side profile—the side without the scar.

Leah flipped to the next page of notes and discovered something odd. On June 20, 1974, Noah Stork, Harry's pa, reported a break-in. Someone had smashed his son Tommy's bedroom window and entered the house. Strident arrived on the scene to find that nothing had been taken and questioned in his notes why Noah Stork had even called the police about the incident.

Four days later, on June 24, 1974, the judge issued police a warrant and Harry's house was raided. They found a Smith & Wesson Model 10 revolver chambered .38 that forensics later confirmed as the Stickman murder weapon. What they didn't find was Harry Stork.

The next day, Fowler declared a statewide manhunt for Stork. The task force had grown to over twenty cops by then, and they scoured every corner of Alabama, without uncovering a single sign of Stork anywhere.

Somehow, he'd just mysteriously disappeared, and from what Leah read, he'd stayed that way while an entire month rolled by.

Then, according to the reports, an anonymous tip led to the abandoned shotgun shack Harry was holed up in the night of July 22, 1974. Of course, Leah knew now it wasn't an anonymous tip, but another letter delivered to her pa, only this one not written by the same person who wrote the other eight. At least that was forensics' opinion on the matter.

She shook her head when she saw the final page left in the file. It was a statement from Thomas Kennedy Bradshaw taken by Ethan, of all people, claiming once again to be the Stickman. This was his third attempt at convincing the police he was guilty, and, for the third time, he was sent back home. Leah thought back to her interview with Bradshaw and wondered how innocent the man really was.

On the inside of the last folder, her pa had written: *Where is the primary crime scene? Where is the slaughter-house?* Once again, Leah was reminded that her pa failed to ever find it and that he reckoned it was the key to everything.

She lifted the pen from her notepad and tapped it against her lips. Where would someone be able to kill ten people without being noticed? Was the "slaughter-house," as Leah's pa so eloquently put it, the same now as it was fifteen years ago? If so, how did it remain hidden all these years? And then came the thought that had kept coming up every time her pa mentioned the Stick-man's abattoir in the files: *How can I expect to ever find it if my daddy couldn't do it? He was a far better cop than I can ever hope to be.*

"You're done?" asked Chris as Leah let the last folder fall closed, obscuring the question written on the inside.

"Yeah," she said, relaxing in her chair. "Still have a lot to process, though, but I think I know the case pretty well."

The phone rang. Leah went to answer it, but Chris beat her to it.

"Yeah, just a sec," Chris said, after answering. He put the call on hold. "It's for you," he said to Leah.

"Who is it?" she asked. "Dan?" When she'd left, Dan was once again at home, sleeping off a hangover.

Chris shook his head. "Don't think so."

Leah lifted her receiver and hit the HOLD button. "Detective Leah Teal."

"Leah! It's Peter. Long time, no talk. How the hell are ya?"

Confusion fell over her. "I'm sorry. I . . . Peter who?"

"Strident. You know, I used to work with your pa?"

She brightened. "Now I remember. I only ever knew you as 'Officer Peter'." She laughed.

"Well, you were a kid back then. Your pa told me you became a cop about a few years after I left for Mobile. I trust things are going well?"

"You know," Leah said. "Up and down. Never dull."

"Yeah. I hear you're at your armpits with alligators on this Stickman case."

Leah paused, suspicion falling over her like a dark shadow. Where would Strident have heard that? And now that she thought about it—

"Officer Strident?" she asked.

"It's actually 'Lieutenant.' I moved to Mobile for the promotion in seventy-five."

"Oh, I'm sorry, 'Lieutenant' Strident."

"And then I retired in eighty-six, so now I'm just 'Strident,' but please, Leah, call me Peter. It's been three years since I've been 'Officer' or 'Lieutenant,' and I'm quite happy to be a homebody now. Now the honorifics just make me feel old. Well, I s'pose I am old, but it makes me feel even older."

Leah gave a little laugh, but part of her was annoyed by the call. A throbbing pain came to the back of her head. She had a pretty good idea why Peter Strident was phoning out of the blue after all these years, but figured she might as well ask anyway. "So, may I ask what I did to warrant your call?"

Strident grew serious. "I'll just be straight with you, Leah. Ethan called me. He's a little concerned. He said you wanted the list of officers in on the 'Stickman letters'."

She suddenly realized what she should've figured out long before now. Strident was one of the 'handful.' Of course, he'd pretty much have to be. He worked directly with her pa. He probably even *found* some of the letters himself.

"I need to cover all my bases, Mr.—Peter. I'm sure you can see that, being the successful cop that you . . . *were* . . . there's really—"

"He's not giving you the list, Leah."

She fell silent and felt a bit like an eight-year-old being sent to her room. "And why are you telling me this and not him?"

"Because he asked me if I would agree to be the spokesman for the group. Let's meet for lunch, and you can ask me whatever it is you want to know."

"What if my question is, what're the names of the other people on the list?"

He laughed. "Well, that one I am not at liberty to answer. Anything else, though, probably won't be a problem. When's good for you? You free Friday around two? I'm up in Selma now, so it's a bit of a drive."

"Well, I appreciate the effort," Leah said. "But I'll be 'straight with you,' Peter. I really don't like the way Ethan's gone around his responsibilities by just having you call me."

"I reckon he thought it was a way to appease your request without pissin' anyone off."

Leah thought about this. Why was she angry about Strident calling her? She wasn't exactly sure. It just seemed to reek of cowardice from Ethan. "Okay, well, I guess I'll take what I can get. Friday at two works fine for me."

"Where would you like to meet? Vera's still operatin'? That's where your pa and I always went."

The mention of her pa caused a strange emotion to stir inside her. She decided the best word to describe how she felt was *anxious*. Peter Strident linked back to her pa in a way few people or things did.

"Yep," she said. "Vera's is still there. And their burgers are better than ever, I'd say."

"Okay, then it's a date," Strident said. "See you at two on Friday. Have a good Fourth."

Leah had almost forgotten tomorrow was the Fourth of July. So many things were crowding for space in her head, that one sort of got pushed to the back. "You, too," she said, and hung up the phone, letting her mind meander back to the last time she'd been in Vera's Old West Grill going on six months ago.

The very first time she ever laid eyes on Detective Dan Truitt.

CHAPTER 30

When I woke up, my mother had already left for work, Dan was still snoring on the sofa, and Carry was nowhere to be seen. I decided it was safe enough to chance finishing up going through my ma's folders. I'd read most of it already. There were just a couple of files I skipped over on account of I hadn't heard her ever talk about what was written on the tabs, so I reckoned they weren't that important to the case. Other than that, I had the newest file from the murder goin' on three weeks ago still to read.

I decided to read the two from the stack I let slip by on my way through. I figured they would be pretty quick and easy.

Except, now, one had me kind of confused.

According to the files, someone named Thomas Kennedy Bradshaw actually *told* police that he was the Stickman. Now, I know I'm only thirteen and all, but why in all the sky would someone admit to something like that unless it was true? They would only end up going to jail for a crime they didn't commit. Who would want that? To me, jail was a horrible thing. You couldn't

go out on bike rides or catch frogs in the pond or anything. You just read all day or made license plates or
something. I didn't really know much about jail, just
that you spent most of your time behind bars in a little
room while you sat around wearing stripey shirts.

So, I figured if Harry Stork turned out not to be the
Stickman, then it *had* to be Thomas Kennedy Bradshaw.
Probably, Mr. Bradshaw was so eaten up by guilt of
what he done that he wanted police to throw him in jail
so he could stop killing folk.

In fact, he tried to tell them he was the one murdering
everybody three completely separate times. And not
once did they do anything to him. He was just sent
home. Well, one time it seemed they sent him to the hospital.

The other file I hadn't read yet was near the bottom
and all about someone named Stanley Bishop. From the
reports, Stanley Bishop lived in Alvin and had no criminal record when my grandpa and Officer Strident interviewed him on April 5, 1974. Originally that day, they
went to his house, but he wasn't home. A neighbor told
them he was at work, so they went there. It was a construction site of some kind, and they found him on the
roof nailing up tar paper.

This was right after they found victim number seven
behind Reverend Starks's church in the little cemetery. I
read the statement by Reverend Starks. He said he didn't
see nothing and appeared very upset about the news. I bet
he was, too. I knew Reverend Starks well and I really
liked his church. I even talked my mother and Carry into
going there with me once, even though it was a black
church. They have much better singers and stuff than
First Baptist, where we usually go. First Baptist is run

by Reverend Matthew and his wife. I like them, too, but I really like Reverend Starks. It kind of upset me to read that the Stickman upset him.

Anyway, once Stanley Bishop came down off that roof, police interviewed him and asked him where he was at the time the body was dumped the night before. He claimed he was at some place called Bell's Tavern. There wasn't much else for them to ask him so, after taking a couple of Polaroids of his car—which was a pretty neat-looking car—my grandpa and Officer Strident interviewed some witnesses from the pub. Two of them were actually back there already that afternoon. Another one, the barmaid from the night before, they found at home. In my grandpa's notes, he says he believed they had woken her from sleep when they knocked on the door.

All the witnesses said the same thing, that Stanley Bishop had been drinking in Bell's Tavern since late afternoon and stayed all the way until it closed at two in the morning. I wondered how reliable statements were that came from people who spent all their time drinking. Not only had these witnesses stayed at the tavern until closing time the night before, they were right back there already drinking again when my grandpa interviewed them.

There wasn't much more about Stanley Bishop. I returned his file, along with all the ones I had out about Thomas Kennedy Bradshaw, back to the stack and straightened everything so it looked the way it had when I first found it today. I never did retrieve the pen from under the fridge and, to my surprise, my mother never noticed it missing. She had just taken another one from the junk drawer and kept going.

Coming to the end of all these files had brought with it a weird sense of sadness. I guess I hadn't realized how much I enjoyed reading *real* police stuff, especially when it involved people I knew like my mother and my grandpa Joe. What I really liked were the handwritten notes I'd find. Sometimes they were written in the margins, sometimes they were just all by themselves. My grandpa wrote most of them; I had figured out how to spot his handwriting.

I sure missed him. I missed my pa, too, but in some ways, I missed my grandpa more, probably on account of I could remember him. I couldn't really remember my pa. He died when I was still a baby.

But me and my grandpa used to do all sorts of stuff together before he died. He even took me to a baseball game once, and we just missed catching a ball that came up into the stands. Well, we were about five rows away from the guy who caught it, but it seemed really close.

Reading my grandpa's notes was like having him back for a while. Sometimes it felt like he'd written them just for me.

Now I opened up the last thing I had to look at—the file from the new Stickman killing. As I opened it, I thought about whether or not Harry Stork had been the Stickman. I had read all the information now and figured I should know one way or the other. Trouble was, every time I thought for sure Harry Stork did it, something came up that made me think it was someone else, someone like Thomas Kennedy Bradshaw.

Throughout the files, there was a question in my grandpa's notes that he kept writing through different files. That question was: *Where is the primary crime scene?* Because of everything I'd read in *Understanding Forensics* (a book I'd finally finished), I knew the primary crime scene meant the scene where the victims were killed. Everybody was pretty much convinced the victims were shot to death before having a wooden stake hammered through their chests at the place where the police found them. I kept waiting for them to find out where the place was. I started getting excited about finding that out as I got closer and closer to the end of the files.

Only, nobody ever did. My grandpa said he figured the real key to unlock the case completely was finding that primary crime scene. From his notes at the end of all the files, I think he was disappointed about leaving that part of the case unsolved. I think he might've even had his own questions as to whether or not Harry Stork was really the Stickman.

Maybe my mother's reports and notes from the new case would enlighten me more.

I looked at all the sketches and photographs taken at the newest crime scene.

The body had turned up in Leeland Swamp, a place me and Dewey had ridden our bikes to a few times. It wasn't as cool as Skeeter Swamp, on account of it wasn't filled with gators the way Skeeter was, but we hadn't really gone near Skeeter for the past two years or so. Not since my mother cracked the case of the Cornstalk Killer, which was a dumb name the papers came up with after she'd finished investigating it.

Too many weird memories blew in the breeze down by Skeeter Swamp for me to go back. Probably Dewey would have no problem with it, on account of he never saw what I saw. But he didn't like going places by himself, so we started visiting Leeland Swamp instead. Still wasn't the same, though.

One thing was for sure. I'd remember Skeeter Swamp as long as I lived.

The victim of the Stickman's most recent murder (which was either the tenth or the first, depending on your view of things) was Abilene Williams, a thirty-six-year-old black woman who worked as a receptionist at the Hawk Ridge Business Center on Main Street.

There wasn't much about the crime scene in the file other than a bunch of pictures (the ones of the dead body I kind of skimmed over—I knew from experience what my memory hung on to and what it didn't), some sketches, and a few pieces of evidence, like a partial fingerprint, some boot marks in the damp soil around the cypress her body was staked into, and a wheelbarrow track going through most of a trail that wound through the woods back to a logging road.

I looked at a picture taken from near on the other side of Leeland Swamp that showed the entire crime scene. I saw all them thick-boughed cypress with Spanish moss draped over their branches like clothes. You could even see the roots where the cypress dug into the edge of the swamp so they wouldn't be thirsty. Then I noticed something else. The trunk of the leftmost tree that grew tight against the edge of the photo, had a carving of a big, giant happy face in it. *I know that carving.* Dewey and I had laughed at it the last two times we visited Leeland Swamp.

This meant that I *knew* where this crime scene was. Not just in general, but exactly. I made a decision right then, and when I did, the sadness of having no files to go through anymore came to an end, replaced once again by excitement and anticipation.

As soon as we could, Dewey and I would be visiting this crime scene. Now that I was done with my book, I couldn't wait. Only, it wouldn't be tomorrow on account of tomorrow was Independence Day.

Me and Dewey would be too busy watching parades and eating burgers till we puked.

CHAPTER 31

In the afternoon, Ethan lumbered from his office and approached Leah's desk, at first saying nothing. Leah looked up from her chair and could tell something was spinning in his head. "What?" she asked. Chris looked up, too.

Rubbing the back of his neck, Ethan glanced at them both. "Y'all know what tomorrow is?"

"Sure," Leah said. "It's the Fourth." She already knew what this was about. Every year, Ethan elected either she or Chris to work Alvin's Independence Day celebration. It was rare, though, that their presence was ever actually needed. The worst thing Leah remembered ever having to do was to get a drunk man down from the roof of the Alvin First National Bank. He'd gone up the fire escape in the back, and Leah deemed him way too wasted to climb safely back down by himself.

It was barely eleven in the morning.

So while he hollered and waved to everyone lining Main Street watching the parade, he also watched as Leah went up and finally escorted him down. She made sure his foot hit a ladder rung with every step. Once on the ground, his wife—who didn't seem to have had anything to drink—did everything but slap him she was so mad. After calling him a bunch of names Leah rarely used, the woman asked if he had to go to the police station or could she just take him home.

Leah figured compared to his wife, the drunk tank would be a vacation, so she let the man's wife take care of doling out any punishments.

She couldn't remember another incident, other than breaking up the odd fight between teenagers or having to confiscate fireworks, which usually belonged to the same kids doing the fighting.

"I got Independence Duty last year," Leah said. "And the two years before that. It's *always* me. It's Chris's turn." Her eyes went to the window outside. The rain had all but stopped. Main Street appeared shrouded in a light mist that clung tightly to the air and appeared bright from the sun struggling to break through the high layer of clouds in the overcast sky. Truth was, with Dan down and all, Leah really didn't want to have to work all day tomorrow. It would be much more fun hanging out with Dan and the kids.

"We don't take *turns*," Chris said. "We draw straws. Whoever gets small straw works the parade and the park."

Each year the parade started around nine in the morning, heading out from down at the courthouse. It continued to the other end of Main Street before turning up and heading to Willet Lake in the center of town. Everyone followed the end of the parade, walking with it to Willet Park, which wrapped around the lake, where there was always a big barbecue and sports for the kids and things like that.

"I know how we do it," Ethan said. "I got the straws." He held up two white straws with thin red and blue lines running along the outside.

Leah narrowed her eyes at him. "Where did you get those from? Steal 'em from Guppies?" Famous for their deep-fried halibut nuggets, Guppies managed to grab the number-one position for fast-food restaurants in the *Alvin Examiner*'s yearly poll.

"It's not stealing when they have them in a dispenser."

She shook her head slowly. "I don't know 'bout you, Ethan. First it's illegal gambling, now drinking straw thievery. I can't help but wonder what's next."

Ethan ignored her. "Just pick a damn straw." He placed his hands behind his back and mixed up the straws. When he held them back out, there was one in each fist, both looking roughly the same height.

"Who's first?" he asked.

"Me," Leah said. "I'll take this one." She pulled the straw from Ethan's left hand and felt a surge of adrenaline go through her. Her choice was the right one.

Just as Leah had expected, Chris started whining. "Ethan, I honestly reckon you should have just as much of a chance as me to work tomorrow. It's *supposed* to be a holiday."

Ethan gave this some thought until he finally put his hands back behind him. "Fine," he said. He brought the straws back out and Chris pondered over which hand to pick for a few seconds. Finally, he nabbed the straw from Ethan's right hand. A smile burst across his face. He'd left Ethan with the short straw.

"Great," Ethan said sarcastically. "There goes my day."

"Spare me," Leah said. "I've never known you to *ever* do it. It's always been between Chris and me."

"I *used* to do it all the time," Ethan said. "Back when it was me, your daddy, and Strident. We'd all draw straws and, pretty near on every year, I got short straw. I'm pretty sure them two cheated, but I never figured out how."

Chris laughed. "It's really not so bad. You kind of get to be part of all the action."

"I'd rather be part of my sofa watching baseball."

Leah rolled her eyes. "I'm pretty sure the Texas Rangers will play the same whether you're watching or not."

Ethan went back to his office.

The fax machine started sputtering as a piece of paper began crawling from its front.

"That's the end of it," Chris said.

"End of what?" Leah asked.

"The research I'm doin' for you. You know, finding out which of your thirty-nine suspects from Grell Memorial have priors?"

"That was fast."

"That's me," Chris said. "Speedy McDeevy."

He went over and tore the fax sheet off, bringing it back to his desk, where he had two more very similar fax sheets. He began going through them all and making marks on a copy he'd made of the list of people Leah got from the hospital.

"Here," he said when he was finished, and handed her the list. "There were seven with priors, but you only need to worry about four."

"Why's that?" Leah looked at the paper. Seven names were circled. Two of those circled were also crossed out. One had a tick beside it.

"Two are dead."

"I suppose that's a pretty solid alibi. What about the third, this one with the tick?"

"Currently doing time. Went in last January. He couldn't have killed our recent victim."

Leah let this swim around in her head.

"What?" Chris asked.

She shook her head. "Nothin', I s'pose you're right."

"Of course I'm right. How could he have murdered anyone?"

"I . . . just . . . I keep looking at this whole thing as two different cases, the *old* Stickman murders and the *new* Stickman murders. I have to get that view out of my mind."

"I don't think you even need to really address the old murders. You're trying to investigate a body found three weeks ago. That's the case, isn't it?"

"I suppose. I just—"

"You just don't like the way your pa's tied up in it. I understand that, Leah. But you can't let that twist your focus on this latest suspect. *This* is the case you want to solve."

"I keep thinkin' about what Dan said, about there being two Stickmen."

Chris shrugged. "Even if there was or is, you still need to concentrate on the newest aspect of the case, don't let your thoughts get dragged through fifteen years of sludge."

"You're right," she said, looking up. "What about the nine without addresses or Social Security numbers?"

Chris shrugged. "I'm not a super wizard. Nothin' I can really do about those nine."

"Okay, I understand," she said. "Hopefully, the one we're after is one of these four."

"Yeah," Chris said. "And here, you'll want these."

"What are they?"

"Their police reports, along with mug shots."

"Wow, this was more than I expected," Leah said. "The mug shots are perfect."

"You goin' to interview them four? Three of them don't even live in Alabama anymore. One's as far from here as Oregon."

"First thing I'm goin' to do is put together a photo lineup for Duck."

"Duck?"

"Sorry, Stanley Bishop. The witness these leads came from."

"His nickname is Duck?"

Leah nodded. "Mhm."

"Why?"

She shrugged. "It's one of the great unknowns."

CHAPTER 32

Leah lay in bed, sound asleep, her quiet snores filling the bedroom's tacet song. When she had fallen asleep, any noise she made had been overwhelmed by the rain outside ping-ponging against the window glass behind the tightly drawn drapes. Now a faint pinkish-yellow glow lit the thin border along the top of those drapes.

The telephone on the nightstand beside her head came alive with a shrill ring.

Jolted from sleep, Leah abruptly opened her eyes. While her heart bounced off the inside of her rib cage, she lifted the phone's receiver to her ear and answered the call.

"Leah, it's Ethan."

She reached out, fumbling with the radio alarm clock that, for some reason, had its green digital time readout turned away from her bed. With a clumsy left hand she accidentally pushed it off her nightstand and it fell down between the back of the nightstand and the wall. "Jesus!" she said as the clamoring sound of electronics tumbling against wood rattled inside her head.

"What happened?" Ethan asked. "You okay?"

Leah pulled herself up to a seated position and caught her breath. "Yeah, I'm fine. Ethan, what time is it?"

"Half past seven."

"Are you callin' me from home or work?"

"I'm at the station. Wanted to get something done before I started my Independence Day duties."

"What's up? Why are you calling me at seven-thirty in the morning?"

She heard him let out a big breath. "We got another one, Leah."

Her brain switched to high alert. "Another what?" Only she already knew what he would say.

"Another letter. Addressed to Leah Fowler. Found it under the door about five minutes ago. Inside it's just like all the others."

Leah's insides went hollow. She knew what it all meant, but somehow she needed to hear him say it. "Man or a woman?"

"Woman," Ethan said.

"Where?"

"The Anikawa."

"The Anikawa? That's all it says? *Just the Anikawa?* That's an awfully long river, Ethan. Does it even say 'in Alvin' or anythin'?"

"Nope."

Leah felt her head spin. She let out a breath she hadn't realized she'd been holding. "How much time we got?"

"Till noon."

"It says that? 'Noon'?"

"Says twelve o'clock."

Leah tilted back her head and thought about this. "Christ, it's the Fourth today. Main Street will be closed. This is going to be a mess."

"I know." Ethan's voice never wavered from its low, lulling tone. He had far better control of his emotions than Leah had on hers.

"And we'll have nobody workin' it. We can't possibly leave someone watching the damn parade when we need to search the whole damn river."

"I know."

"Okay, I'll be there ASAP. Just gotta get Dan movin' and throw on some clothes. Have you called Chris?"

"Nope. I'll do that now. Just get here as quick as you can."

Leah hung up the phone and let everything in her mind settle down before she started the day.

"Goddamn Anikawa," she said. "On the goddamn Fourth."

CHAPTER 33

Despite the way the day started, Leah felt wide awake as she and Dan drove down Hunter Road. Dan, on the other hand, had been strangely quiet since she woke him. The smell of bourbon sweating out of his pores filled the inside of the car. Luckily, the day was beautiful. The near on endless rain they'd been going through finally came to an end. Today the sky was completely blue without a cloud in sight. Leah rolled down her window, letting the summer's fresh air inside to lessen Dan's smell.

She had a hunch he was still drunk. She knew he'd worked into the wee hours of morning, but didn't quite know how wee those were. He could be running on an hour's sleep. That and the alcohol pissed her off. She needed him to be keen and sharp. Twice, she nearly broached the subject of his drinking, but thought better of it. It wasn't a conversation for today. Today they all needed their focus on stopping the Stickman.

Leah had left twenty dollars on the counter along with a note to Caroline explaining that some important police work came up and Leah and Dan wouldn't be able to join them for the Independence Day festivities.

They came to the bottom of Hunter Road but couldn't get near the station. "Shit," Leah said. "They've already got the parade route cordoned off."

"Just park here," Dan said, his words slightly slurred. "It's not that far to walk."

Leah gave him a sideways look before pulling to the edge of Hunter and throwing her Bonneville into PARK. "Sure you're capable of walking?" Leah asked him snidely.

"What's that s'posed to mean?"

"Nothin'," Leah said, her lips forming a narrow line.

"No, you said somethin'. Now tell me what you meant."

"It's nothin', Dan. Nothin' at all." Opening her door, she angled out of the vehicle. A second later, Dan did the same.

They were silent for most of the walk up Main Street. All the stores were closed but had their outsides decorated for today. Many American flags hung from doors or in windows. Red, white, and blue streamers dangled from the eaves of shops and even ran across Main Street, looping above their heads. Leah thought about the kids, hoping they'd have a good time without her.

When they were a half-dozen doors from the station, Dan broke the silence. He must've been thinking about her comment ever since they left the car.

"Don't make it a competition," he said.

"Don't make *what* a competition?"

"You against the bottle."

"Yeah, wouldn't want that. I got a hunch I might come in last."

He stopped, turning to her. "Leah."

"Dan, this isn't the time for this."

"I *have* to drink, Leah."

"Nobody *has* to drink, Dan." She wanted to stop talking and get to the station. Part of her knew, of course, that the victim was probably already dead, but this could be the day they caught the killer dumping the body.

"I do have to," Dan said. "When I don't drink, the world's way too crazy. I can't stand the world. Drinking makes it tolerable and allows me to focus on one horrible thing at a time." He paused and looked up at the sky for a second. "Drinking keeps the monsters from all charging through my head at me at once."

She shook her head. "Okay, I have no idea what to say to that, but we've got a woman's life on the line. *That's* where we need to focus. Understand?"

He gave her a little nod and they continued on to the station. When they made it inside, the clock read ten minutes before eight.

Ethan was filling a mug at the coffee machine. "You guys made good time," he said.

"Where's Chris?" Leah asked.

"He's comin'. I called him right after you. He should be here anytime."

"It's a zoo out there already with all the different sections of Main Street roped off. Luckily they hadn't closed down Hunter yet," Leah said.

The door opened and Chris came inside, his face dotted with sweat. "Sorry I took so long, guys, but it's crazy out there. I had to park on Maple. It almost wasn't even worth driving."

"Don't you live on Maple?" Ethan asked.

"Yeah. I drove down to Main Street and couldn't get any farther."

"Wow," Leah said. "That's quite the walk."

"Yep," Chris said. "And it's already getting hot. Goin' to be a scorcher today."

"Where's the letter?" Leah asked Ethan.

He picked up a piece of paper from her desk and handed it to her. "It's a copy," he said. "I didn't touch the original at all. It's in my office. I'll courier it down to Mobile tomorrow so they can try and get whatever it is they get off of it."

Leah looked at the paper. No surprises, it was exactly as Ethan described it. In black felt marker stood a drawing of a stickman with breasts and hair that came to tips on either side of her head. Two words lay below that: *The Anikawa*. And beneath that was the time: *12:00*.

"I just hope we weren't supposed to get this yesterday and the time means midnight last night," Leah said.

Ethan considered this. "I hadn't thought about that. But really, the whole point of the letters is that we get them. It's part of this guy's game. I'm sure he makes certain the letters will be discovered when he wants them discovered. Your pa even had some come to his front door with a loud knock. When he got to the door, whoever knocked had gone. All that remained was the letter on his porch."

"What?" Leah asked. "When?"

Ethan nodded. "A few times it happened. All during the seventy-three to seventy-four murders."

"You mean, I was at home?" Fear crept its way up Leah's backbone, like a fishing spider inching its way up the trunk of a dark walnut tree.

"Likely in bed," Ethan said. "The ones that went straight to Joe's house were always at odd times when nobody was at the station."

A thought struck Leah. "But . . . today is a holiday. Nobody *should* have come in to work. You just happened to . . . why, again?"

"Why what?"

"Why did you come in to work at half past seven this morning?"

Ethan scratched the back of his neck. "I . . . um . . . needed to call my guy."

"Your guy?"

"You know . . . the 'bookie' guy."

"I thought you said you only call him from home?"

"Yeah . . . well . . . that was a little lie. If I call from home, I might get in trouble. But nobody's goin' to say anythin' about a call made from a cop shop."

Leah shook her head exasperatedly. "Okay, for now, let's just say I have no idea what you mean. My concern is that the killer apparently *knew* you were comin' in early. He had to, or he wouldn't have put the letter under the door."

Ethan's eyes narrowed. "Hadn't thought of that."

Leah looked to Dan. He wasn't helping much. He looked like he wanted to go pass out somewhere. Damn him.

She turned back to Ethan. "Who knew you were comin' in this morning?"

"Betty. Nobody else."

"So what does your wife think about your new hobby?" Leah asked.

"She doesn't know. Told her I was comin' in to catch up on some paperwork. Which is kind of true. It involved papers."

"She's not stupid, you know."

Ethan gave a tight-lipped smile. "I know."

"So, who else knew? Somebody must've."

"Nobody."

Leah thought about this. It didn't make sense, unless the killer didn't know today was a holiday. But who wouldn't realize it was the Fourth, especially if they came down Main Street and saw all the flags and streamers and all? Not only that, but unless that letter was dropped off really early, Main Street was likely closed off. That meant the killer had to walk to deliver the note. Seemed kind of sketchy to Leah. Too many ways something like that could go wrong and he could get caught.

"I don't get it," she finally said.

"Me neither."

"Unless . . ." Leah said.

"Unless what?"

"Unless it was like I already said and the letter came *yesterday* and the twelve o'clock actually means midnight, not noon."

Leah saw an epiphany go off like a Roman candle behind Ethan's eyes. "For shit's sake," he said, finally. "That's just—"

"No," Chris said, cutting him off. "I stayed late last night. I was here until after six. There was no letter."

"Are you *sure?*" Ethan asked.

Chris nodded. "I'd have seen it. I'm positive."

"And if there was nobody here—" Leah started.

"He wouldn't have left the note," Ethan finished.

Everyone fell silent. Leah looked to Dan, wishing he would offer something. When he had the ball, he usually came close to scoring. But today he didn't appear to have the ball at all. Resentment over his drinking festered inside Leah. She couldn't believe he'd basically told her that if she gave him the ultimatum of choosing her or Jim Beam, Jim Beam would be the one he went home with.

The phones rang and everybody jumped. Chris was the only one seated at a desk, so he answered the call.

Leah took another look at the letter in her hand. Even she could tell it was written by the same person who wrote the last one. She didn't need to wait for any "hand-writing analysis." The stickwoman was terribly drawn, her arms and legs all different lengths. Her head wasn't nearly round. Whoever was behind the killings was not an artist.

She thought about the crime scenes, about the way the bodies were backward hog-tied and staked into the ground. It made her reassess the killer. He was an artist, after all, only his best work shone in the macabre set- tings he left behind.

Her stomach clenched. If she kept thinking about the condition of the victims, she would get sick. Already, it rose in her throat. She placed the letter back on her desk and let her attention drift to Chris, still on the phone.

"Slow down," he was saying, calmly, in an obvious attempt to calm down the person on the other end. "Yes, ma'am. I'm listening. It's just hard on account of your talking too fast and too loud. Yes, I *realize* you're a mite upset."

Ethan mouthed to Leah the words, "Missing person." But Leah had already figured that out. "Goddamn it!" she snapped under her breath.

"Okay, Mrs. Hughes, thank you. Yes, I have every-thing written down. I will. As soon as I can. Yes, Mrs. Hughes. Try not to worry, okay? We'll do our best to find her. All right. No, that's fine. Bye, now."

Chris hung up the phone and looked to Leah. "I thought she was never goin' to let me off that phone."

"When did she go missing?"

"Who?"

"The victim. That was a missing person call, was it not?"

"Yeah, but . . . it doesn't automatically mean it's linked to the Stickman."

"Be an awful coincidence if it wasn't," Dan said, crossing his arms, his eyes still bloodshot.

"Thought you'd fallen asleep standin'," Leah said.

"I was just listenin'," Dan said. "How long ago did whatever her name is go missin'?"

"Samantha Hughes. She went missing last night around eight, after attending a workshop about mechanics."

"Mechanics?" Dan asked. "What kind of mechanics?"

"Does that really matter?" Leah asked.

"I'm assuming car mechanics," Chris said, consulting his notes. "I was talking to her mother-in-law, Virginia Hughes. She said Samantha was a mechanic, but currently unemployed. Anyway, she called the company that did the workshop this morning and was told that Samantha had picked up her name badge and lanyard so, they reckoned, she attended the workshop. It let out just before eight. Virginia drove around looking for her this morning and spotted Samantha's Audi parked on Sweetwater Drive just a block away from where the workshop was held."

"So somehow the killer managed to grab her between the workshop and her car," Dan said. "If it was only a block, that's quite a feat. Almost like he was waiting for her. One of us should check the car, see if there's evidence of her having gotten back to it. Maybe he was waiting in her backseat, or grabbed her while she was trying to unlock it."

"I don't think that's at the top of our task list," Leah said. "We've been given a deadline. Every minute we stay here talkin' about everything is one less minute we could be searching for her and her killer."

Dan gave her a look she didn't like at all.

"Shit, it's already quarter past eight. We gotta get movin'."

"We need a plan before we do anythin'," Dan said.

"I agree with Dan," Ethan said.

Leah let out an exasperated breath. "Okay, what's the plan? I really want to get started on this. I've got a lot of river to scour."

"Hey," Ethan said. "Try to remember it's not *just* you. There's me and Chris, too. We're a *team*. Christ, you even have Dan here."

"Sorta," Leah said solemnly, casting a glance Dan's way.

"Just stop," Dan told her. "Please? I'm here. I'm one hundred percent functional."

"Sure you are. I'd rather have a dog hunting with me today, I reckon." She didn't want to pick a fight, so she left it there.

Dan didn't leave it quite so easily. "Who do you think you are? Queen Detective of Planet Earth? We're all here to hunt down your guy. We all want to save this Samantha Hughes woman. The public is countin' on us working together. You don't seem to have any idea what that means. You think it's all about you."

She swung around fast, this time unable to contain her anger at Dan. "That's because it *is* all about me. *I'm* the one everybody expects to fix everything. It's *me* they expect to find their little girls and bring them back home alive. *I'm* the one who gets called to chase down the boogeyman who's been pestering them. And when hookers and junkies go disappearing from the streets, it's *me* they think about. It's all *me*. And goddamn it . . ." Her voice started breaking into tears.

The three men just looked at her, none with any idea what to do.

Leah spoke again, much quieter, her voice choked with tears. "Look," she said. "I'm sorry. It's this case . . . it's gettin' to me. Dredging up memories of my pa, and I feel like if I can't prove he shot the right guy, then . . . well . . ."

Dan wrapped his arms around her, the smell of bourbon almost bringing the bile up her throat again. "Hey," he said quietly. "Just let it all go. You are *way* too tightly wound. You won't be any help to anybody if you can't pull out of this."

"I think I know now why you drink," she said with a smile, the tears still in her eyes and voice.

"Okay," Ethan said. "We all have to work together. So, push any emotional baggage off the carousel for now. You can always go back to that on your own time."

"Well," Leah said. "I s'pose it's best if we break up the search area and each of us take a different piece." She thought about the Anikawa, a river that cut straight across Alvin and kept going, wending and winding its way through steppes and grasslands all the way to the Mississip. "We need to confine our search to the part of the river that's only in Alvin. We don't even really have time to properly search that, let alone any other parts, but given that all the victims up to this point showed up in our town, I think we're pretty safe assuming this one will, too."

"Seems reasonable," Dan said. "So, how do we break up the river so we can search every square mile before noon?"

"That's impossible," Chris said.

Leah leveled her gaze at him. "Today it has to be possible."

"We really need a plan, people," Ethan said. "And time is a tickin'."

They managed to concoct a strategy. Each of them assigned themselves different parts of the Anikawa. Leah took the eastern third of the river that led past Skeeter Swamp and Mr. Garner's ranch, despite the memories she had from that area while investigating the Cornstalk Killer case. Ethan took the central region, where the river ran side by side with Bullfrog Creek. Chris took the western end of the river where it ran out of Alvin and splashed and rolled its way through the ranch lands. Dan would cover the overlapping spots between everyone else's areas.

"The river is high right now," Leah said. "And it's fast. If there's a body thrown in it somewhere, it probably got taken down the current a ways."

"It's not in the MO for the Stickman to leave the body in the river," Dan said. "He always spikes his victims to the ground, doesn't he?"

Leah shook her head. "One of the victims was found floating in Beemer's Bog, but evidence showed she was probably dragged there by a coyote."

Dan gave her a puzzled look. "That's good. A changeup in the MO would be strange. Wouldn't settle well with me. That's why I don't think we're going to find anybody actually *in* the river today."

"We really need more cops," Leah said. "But Satsuma's about the closest place we'll find any."

"Yeah," Dan said. "There's no time. Don't worry, we can handle it."

It made Leah happy to actually hear something positive come out of Dan's mouth this morning.

"Okay, I think we're ready," Ethan said. "And remember, folks, no cowboys. Anything suspicious and you radio for backup, you hear?"

"Of course," said Leah. She kept glancing to the clock,

wanting to get this search underway. Her little break-down earlier had revitalized her and galvanized her drive to find the killer.

She and Dan left the station first, walking down Main Street back toward Leah's car.

"You stink," she told Dan.

"Thanks."

"No, I'm serious. You smell like my uncle Theodore used to smell. It's gross."

"I've never heard you mention your uncle Theodore before."

"I don't think of him a lot. He's an alcoholic." She looked at Dan and added, "Too."

"I see. Well, like I said before, Leah. Don't make it a competition."

She knew. It would be a losing battle and, for now, she'd just let it go.

But not forever.

And as they walked beneath an American flag rippling and tossing in the light wind, the thought crystallized in her mind that soon would come a time when she'd have to decide whether or not she wanted to engage in that war.

CHAPTER 34

Leah started searching, entering the forest that hugged the northern bank of the Anikawa. She followed one of the many trails made throughout time by animals and hikers. She knew the woods were a good third of a mile from the river's edge. The soil—a mixture of dirt and mulch—was still moist from all the rain, and Leah's boots sank into it with each slow step.

Boughs of sumac on either side of her reached up and across, intertwining above her in a knotted canopy of branches and leaves. What little sunlight they allowed fell dustily through the open spaces, bright pockets of green in a shadowy darkness.

A thorny thicket of mayhew grabbed at the side of her pants, pulling her back until she freed herself, pricking her finger in the process. "Damn!" she whispered. Putting her finger into her mouth, she sucked it until the bleeding stopped.

In places, the trail closed in on itself, overgrown elm and underbrush squeezing into the path, leaving Leah little choice but to blindly push her way through all the limbs and leaves until, eventually, the trail opened up again. And always, the smell of wet woodlands, everything still damp from all the rain.

She came to an old rotted log lying in her way. Carefully, she stepped on top of it, breaking the soft wood against the sole of her boot. Her leg fell inside the log. It came down heavy and it was painful. She kicked her other foot forward so it landed behind the log and she managed to clamber over it without stumbling.

But her shin hurt like a son of a bitch.

The trail wasn't straight. At times, it veered to the left, and other times it curved hard to the right. Leah wished she could see the sun so she'd have some idea which direction she was headed. She wanted to know she was still on course for the Anikawa River.

She took another five steps and then, from somewhere off to her left, a twig snapped.

She froze, her hand reaching down and unclipping her gun from its holster. She pulled the weapon and held it away from her body with both hands. Squinting, she tried to peer through the foliage, but the tangle of branches and leaves and chaparral blocked anything from sight.

Something had made that noise.

She went a little farther, her few steps silenced by the velvety leaves scattered on the brown soil, and found a place where the wood thinned and the path widened.

Her fingers tightly gripped the gun's handle, and she had the barrel pointed at a forty-five-degree angle toward the ground.

She still couldn't see what had made the noise. *It was probably a goddamn squirrel*, she thought and took another step. That was when she heard it again. Another snap. This one closer.

She tensed. A rivulet of sweat ran from her hair down

her face. Her heart pounded in her head as she adjusted her stance to get a better view of the direction she thought the sound had come from.

Then, somewhere behind the tangle of branches and leaves beside her, something moved. She saw it in the corner of her eye. A branch shook, or something. She wasn't exactly sure what she had seen, but whatever it was, it was *big*. A lot bigger than some GD squirrel.

Her heart pounded behind her eyes. Her adrenaline kicked into high gear. Dropping into a crouch, she waited, staring at the tapestry of forest, listening for more sound. A ways off, the Anikawa babbled and burbled. Mixed with that, the ubiquitous song of the cicadas rode gently on the light wind.

Leah's eyes searched the scrub of woods where she'd seen movement, but saw nothing. "What the hell was it?" she whispered to herself.

Inside her chest, her heart continued thumping faster and harder than usual. She let go of her gun's grip with her left hand and pulled up the front of her shirt, using it to wipe sweat from her eyes. Then her hand went back to join the other as she readjusted her grip on her revolver.

She counted down from sixty, and still nothing had moved again.

"You're going crazy," she whispered.

She stood up and started to take another step when it happened. From right beside her, a doe burst from the mess of brambles and trees, bending boughs and snapping branches. Leaves fell in the deer's wake, coming down on the trail's floor.

Her heart in her throat, Leah swung her gun around and sighted the deer on reflex. Her trigger finger tightened, and she nearly peeled off a round before realizing what she had in her aim. The deer landed almost directly in front of her and, after regarding her for a half second, fled down the path the same direction she was headed in a flurry of mulch and hooves.

After a few deep breaths, Leah's panic subsided and her pulse went back to normal. She clipped her gun back into its holster and again used her shirt to wipe sweat from her face and neck.

She continued following the trail, seeing the fresh hoofprints embedded into the loamy ground where the doe had dug deeply into the soil. Those tracks went on a good hundred yards before bounding off the edge of the path back into the dense forest.

The trail continued to swerve left and right as Leah walked, but the turbulent water of the Anikawa kept growing louder. She was headed generally in the right direction.

When the forest finally broke, she found herself on hard clay that ran along each side of the ravine cut by the Anikawa. The ravine was deep, probably thirty feet if you counted the depth of the river, and it spanned maybe thirty feet from bank to bank. The river was high and fast, as Leah had expected. The waves cresting in the current couldn't have been more than ten, maybe fifteen feet down, filling up at least half the gorge.

Sunlight glimmered and winked in the cascading water, nearly blinding Leah, whose eyes had become accustomed to the dimly lit forest. Shading her face with the cup of her hand, she tried to get her bearings. She had expected to come out across from Painted Lake, an open body of water surrounded by a rocky black and gray beach, but all she saw now across the flume was more woods, only these looked even more dense than the ones she'd just come through.

A worried sigh escaped her lips. Her watch read 9:05. Only three hours left until her opportunity to catch the killer came to a close. She didn't have time to be lost.

She thought about the layout of the eastern edge of the Anikawa, which was the area she'd picked to search. She reckoned she must have come out of the forest farther east than she expected, since the remainder of the land wasn't nearly as wooded. Her eyes followed the gurgling and grappling course of the river as it rushed around boulders and splashed against rocks, sometimes pouring in little falls over slate edges, sometimes pooling into little eddies, but all the while racing toward the Mississippi, taking anything in its current not rooted down with it.

"If he threw you in here," Leah whispered, "I ain't never gonna find you. You might not even be in Alvin anymore."

She could only see maybe another three hundred yards before the river took a soft left. That was where she expected the tree line to open up to the beach wrapping Painted Lake.

She began walking the edge of the river, following it west to where it bent. Here the water was even louder as it roiled around the bend, tossing water up against the ravine's smooth, curved edge that splashed back down on huge rocks. She followed the edge, twisting through a large S shape before continuing on eastward. With each step she made, the sun seemed to grow hotter.

Again, she wiped away sweat that had dripped into her eyes.

Keeping an even pace, she went as fast as she could without missing something. Always, she looked and listened for the slightest hint of something awry. She didn't know what she expected to hear, especially with the clamorous sounds of the river.

She turned out to be right, and shortly after walking through the bend, the forest on the other bank thinned and finally came to an end on the rocky beach of Painted Lake. The still water reflected the morning sun like a mirror, its light broken into tiny ripples along the penumbra.

A wooden footbridge constructed from rope and planks ran from one end to the other, sagging in a parabolic shape. It was old and, in places, looked rotted. Leah looked ahead where the river continued as far as she could see without any other means of crossing. The forest she just came out of ran right along with it.

She saw no point in searching the woods. In three hours, she couldn't possibly go through even 5 percent of it. If the killer had left her in there, there wasn't much she could do. So she had to assume that wasn't where the body would be left. Besides, the only vehicle access to the Anikawa was Garner Road, a narrow artery of gravel and dirt that came down from Tucker Mountain and led not only to Bob Garner's ranch, but also the other side of the Anikawa and to Painted Lake.

Odds were, if the killer wanted to dump the body as quickly as possible, it would be somewhere on the other side of the river. Along with the river and the lake, there was also Skeeter Swamp, a consideration that cast a black and bitter shadow over Leah's heart.

The thought of the swamp immediately switched pictures in her mind. Suddenly, she was back in time two years ago when the Cornstalk Killer was nabbing fourteen-year-old girls out of the town. Then her mind went even further back to the first incident of the Cornstalk Killer a

dozen years earlier. Ruby Mae Vickers. Leah had promised her ma that she'd find her girl and bring her back
safe and sound. But she hadn't. Instead, she found her
body by Skeeter Swamp beneath the boughs of the willow tree growing between the swamp and Garner's
Ranch. Leah hadn't kept her promise, and the Vickers
family got back a daughter who was irreparably broken.

Leah never got over that case. That swamp and that
willow still gave her nightmares. Especially the willow.

She didn't relish the thought of having to search either of them, yet she had picked this area on her own vo-
lition. Had she subconsciously set things up so they
forced her to face her fears? She didn't know.

At any rate, time was running out, and she was
stalling because her next task was to cross this wooden
bridge where, fifteen feet below, the river smashed and
licked huge jagged boulders thrusting up from the running water like giant teeth waiting to be fed.

She put one careful foot on the bridge. It immediately
began to sway. Closing her eyes, Leah took a deep
breath and took another step, trying to keep from trembling because trembling only made the bridge pitch
even more. She couldn't help it, though. Her legs quiv-
ered involuntarily, nearly buckling her at the knees, and
she continued taking little step after little step.

When Leah made it to the middle of the bridge, its
lowest point, the river spat and spewed up at her, nearly
reaching the planks of wood she stood on. The thunder-
ous roar of the breakers hitting the rocks in a gush of
whitecaps nearly deafened her. Her legs stopped con-
vulsing and fell numb. Fear fell over her. She was too
scared to move.

She shifted her stance slightly and a rotten piece of
plank broke off beneath her boot, leaving a gap big

enough for her to watch its complete fall until the Anikawa swallowed it from sight.

"Okay," she said. "Come on. Pull yourself together. You have to get through this."

After a few deep breaths, she managed another step. Then another.

She was halfway up the other side of the bridge when another rotted piece dislodged from a plank beneath her boots, sending it tumbling into the river's watery depths. This time, she stumbled and, for a moment, thought she would fall. In that instant, the sounds of the river raging beneath her went away, along with everything else. For that moment, everything stopped and became silent as she dropped into a squat and put her hands out, one in front of her, one behind her, and steadied herself on the wooden planks.

Fear and adrenaline tingled as they coursed through her. The sound of the Anikawa came back, more fierce than ever. "Okay," she whispered, "that was close."

Slowly and cautiously, she rose back onto her feet and managed to make her way up the rest of the bridge.

Her legs felt like chewing gum when she finally stepped onto the shore of Painted Lake. Somewhere out on the water, she heard a fish jump, flipping back in with a splash. Searching the lake would have to wait, though. She wanted to walk the full length of her area down the edge of the river. After that, she would search deeper.

From this side, oddly, the river wasn't as loud and it mixed with the cicadas chirping from wherever they were hidden. She walked the river to the end of Painted Lake and still had found nothing. A copse of elm, oak, maple, and pine blocked all but the edge of Skeeter Swamp, and she was happy for it. The small wooded area was a tangle of trees, strangler fig, and thorny vines. She tried to give it a quick search but couldn't find a path. Without one, it was nearly impenetrable.

She followed the river farther, the copse of trees continuing along her left side until it ended at the shallows of Bullfrog Creek, a small tributary that formed a little kidney-shaped pond out behind the marshland and moor of Skeeter Swamp.

She walked down the creek a ways, trying to find an easy way over. This time there was no footbridge. There were, however, big, smooth stones rising from the shallow creek's surface. She found a place where they more or less formed a walkable path from one side of the creek to the other. As carefully as she could, Leah hopped from one stone to the next, slipping only once, but managing to get nothing but her boot wet. After braving the footbridge across the Anikawa, this was a no-brainer.

At just after ten, she decided she'd spent enough time scouring the edges of the river. With two hours left, she needed to widen her investigation. Skeeter Swamp and that willow loomed close. She could almost hear the slip of a dark voice calling out to her, asking her to come and return to this place where all her bad dreams came from.

She forced the voices to quiet as she walked around the chaparral and through the glade that opened onto the moor around the swamp. A blue and red dragonfly nearly flew right into Leah's face and she had to bat it away.

Between the huge cypresses lining its edge, Skeeter Swamp appeared deceptively passive. Deceptive because she knew damn well that beneath the green, murky water lurked dozens of gators. She'd had to wade into this swamp once in her life, and that was once way too much. She had no plans on searching that brackish fen today.

She approached the edge of the swamp, walking across the wet marshland, ever wary for gators. Her gun on her hip was holstered but not clipped. If she needed it, she could have it in a jiffy. As she got close to the swamp's edge and saw the willow tree on the small hill across from it, a strange combination of emotions swept through her. She couldn't pinpoint exactly what it was. Fear? Not quite. Regret? Closer. Guilt? Yes. But, likely, all three.

She searched around the cypress that towered from their fluted trunks, their boughs like the gnarled fingers of some giant hand all draped with Spanish moss. She looked into the nooks that formed between them where their roots split and intermingled, and also around the shallows of the swamp where the trees dug into the water's edge, clamping themselves in place.

She found nothing.

With a heavy heart, she moved on to the willow, the base of its trunk coming into view as she ascended the gentle rise. She had half-expected to find another dead girl propped up beneath it, her vacant eyes pleading to Leah, asking why she wasn't saved.

This was the nightmare she lived through continually. It haunted her at least once a week.

Instead of a dead girl, she found only fresh flowers scattered around the willow's base. Pansies. Pink and blue.

She knew where the flowers came from. And that thought just brought more guilt and shame along with it.

The Cornstalk Killer case had been a bad one. Bad

enough that she almost hung up her badge for good. She still remembered the writing on the tombstone: DREAM WITH LITTLE ANGELS.

She headed across the glade, back toward Painted Lake, her eyes probing the area for any sign of a body as she went. The dirt here was hard and grassy with the odd thicket of shrubs. Another copse of trees, this one much smaller than the other and mostly consisting of maples, stood between her and the river. Leah checked them out, but found nothing.

The smooth stones covering the beach of Painted Lake crunched beneath her boots as she started searching around the water. She hadn't gone even twenty yards when she thought she heard something over the chorale of cicadas and the far-away swooshing sounds of the Anikawa.

She stopped walking and listened more closely, but whatever it was she'd heard was gone. Cupping her ear with her hand, she strained to pick out even the quietest of sounds from all the background noise.

Then she heard it again. The same sound. Only, this time, there was no question what it was she heard.

Again, her adrenaline and her heart kicked into high gear. From somewhere down the river from where she now stood, she'd heard the distinctive *click* of a car door being closed. There were only three places a car could be, and she could see two of them, those being the front of the Garners' house and the hard-packed area just behind her that butted up against the shores of Painted Lake.

The third was hidden from view behind the large copse of trees that was so dense and convoluted she was unable to search it. She knew what it looked like, though. A small dirt road split off from Garner Road before it led to where Bob Garner's farmhouse nestled among a bed of smooth stones on one side and a gentle slope of land on the other. That small road continued toward the edge of the Anikawa, fanning out into a dusty steppe ornamented by the occasional clutch of witchgrass and other weeds. This plain rolled out a fairly large area and snuggled right up against the river's southern bank.

What she just heard could only mean one thing. Someone had pulled right up to the river and opened and closed a vehicle door at least twice, which probably meant two different doors. Or perhaps the second one was a trunk, or a tailgate.

It didn't matter. It all meant the same thing.

As fast as her feet would take her, Leah ran back across the glade the way she had come, pounding the ground with her boots. She didn't even think of the evils of Skeeter Swamp as she hit the edge of the marshland, her feet digging into the moist, soft ground even as her boots sank into it. The morass slowed her, so she pushed harder, coming out of the swamp area just this side of the small wooded area that ran between her and the dusty plain, where she now heard a vehicle engine idling.

She knew she couldn't go through the copse of trees. She'd already tried that once, and now she had no time to even consider it. So she began running around it, racing toward the edge of the Anikawa.

The sun was just a smidgeon out from being straight overhead, looking like a yellow blister in the center of a parched skin sky. Its heat beat down on Leah like the hammer of God pounding against an anvil. Sweat streamed down the back of her neck. Her shirt felt heavy and wet. Her breathing became labored. Her stomach knotted and her chest hurt. The breath wheezed from her dry throat.

But she didn't stop.

As she rounded the copse, the Anikawa spluttered its disdain from alongside her. But she paid it no attention. She just kept running, racing toward that dusty parking lot.

Just when she was nearly past the back side of the chaparral, only a few seconds away from where the short dirt road fanned out onto a wide-open plain, a new sound rose above the scream of the river. The revving of an engine and the squeal of wheels spinning out in the dusty ground. She heard the vehicle start to pull away just as she came out from behind the trees. Throwing her hand up over her eyes to shield the sun, she squinted into the bright light of morning, watching a vehicle quickly pulling away.

Only she couldn't see it. All the dust it had kicked up behind it concealed it from Leah's view. By the time the cloud settled, the car or truck or whatever it was had already made it to Garner Road and taken a turn that caused it to vanish behind a tall row of Douglas fir.

Leah's breath came in convulsions as sweat ran down every part of her body. Bending forward, she grabbed her knees and breathed deeply, waiting for the pain in her chest and the rawness in her throat to subside. Slowly, even the knot in her stomach untied and she was able to think again.

Standing, she scanned the area between the dusty plain and the Anikawa.

Sure enough, she saw what she expected to see: the macabre outline of a shirtless woman's body hog-tied in a disturbing backward thrust, staked into the ground like some sort of ghastly, twisted vampire. From the top of that stake, a white piece of paper billowed in the gentle breeze.

The Stickman had struck again.

Leah's eyes grew dark, and her head snapped to the short length of road the vehicle had sped off on. "He killed you!" she screamed. "My pa shot you! You're goddamn dead!"

But there was nobody to hear her shouts. She stopped yelling and conceded that even though her pa had already killed the boogeyman, somehow or other, the boogeyman had come back.

CHAPTER 35

I woke up excited about the day. It was the Fourth of July, and that meant a whole day of fun. Alvin always had a big Independence Day celebration that began with a parade, which led into a whole day of eating at Willet Park, until finally tonight there would be fireworks after the sun went down. I think the eating was my favorite part.

To top it all off, the rain had finally stopped. I never closed my bedroom curtains before going to sleep last night, and now the morning sun streamed into my room. Then I realized something. My mother never woke me up. Last night she said she would have me and Carry up by eight so we could have a decent breakfast and still make it down to Main Street in time to see the Independence Day Parade. The parade wasn't near on as good as Alvin's Christmas Parade, but it was still a parade. I'd seen enough parades to last the rest of my life. Dewey, it seemed, would never run out adoring everything about them, but these days, I rarely loved watching parades.

I leaned over and rummaged through the drawer in my bedside table, looking for the watch that Uncle Henry gave me. It wasn't easy—the drawer had pretty much become my junk drawer. I threw just about everything and anything inside it, especially important stuff. I knew, if it was in this drawer, I'd never lose it. Things like the pictures of my pa that my mother gave me. Most of them were still in a shoe box sitting on my chest of drawers, but I picked out some special ones I really liked and put them in this drawer for safekeeping. While I tried to find my watch among all the papers, pens, take-out menus, comic books, and other stuff, I began wondering how safe this drawer really was. It seemed like anything I threw inside just got swallowed up.

Finally, my fingers found my watch and I pulled it out. I looked at the face, expecting the worst.

I was lucky. It was only eight-fifteen. That gave me plenty of time to still make it down to Main Street by nine. I put my watch on my wrist, closed the drawer, and got out of bed. I searched through my chest of drawers for something to wear as the sun streamed in through my window. It was still low, barely high enough to shine over the oak trees in our backyard, but at least it was back. There wasn't even a rain cloud in sight. The sun just hung above the treetops all yellow and happy, alone in a clear blue Alabama summer sky.

This was how Alabama summers were *supposed* to be.

It was a big, bright, beautiful day, one of them days that make you happy just to be awake. After stretching with a small yawn, I took a pair of shorts and a T-shirt from my drawers and got dressed. Then I remembered my mother hadn't woken me like she said she would, and I got a bit worried. Carry's bedroom door was still closed when I walked out in the hall. Undoubtedly, *she* was still sleeping, something she did until the afternoon on summer days.

I thought she was crazy. The summer was made for enjoying being out of school. How much could she enjoy that while sleeping? I shook my head. I couldn't believe she didn't realize this herself. For someone older than me, she certainly didn't have my smarts.

A pit formed in my stomach as I looked into my mother's room and saw her bed was not only empty, but unmade. Her drapes were still pulled tightly closed, casting the room in shadow. It felt dark and ominous. A pool of dread filled the pit in my stomach.

"Mom?" I called out, but heard no response. I walked out to the kitchen, my sock feet near on silent on the hallway's wooden floor. The sun's rays poured into the window above the kitchen sink, gleaming off the stove and refrigerator.

My heart fell when I realized I couldn't hear Dan's snores. He *always* snored.

"Mom?" I called out again as I walked through the dining room and into the living room. Sure enough, Dan wasn't asleep on the sofa. His covers and pillow were there, but no sign of him. On the coffee table, a small stack of files and other paperwork lay scattered about.

Nobody except me and Carry were home. I returned to the kitchen, where I found a note on the counter beside my mother's stack of file folders. Beside the note lay two ten-dollar bills. The note said: *Had to go in to work for an emergency. Enjoy the Fourth. Sorry I won't be able to join you. I left some money for you both.* My mother ended it with some *X*'s and *O*'s, but that didn't make me feel any better. I was expecting to spend the day with her. Since she started working on this new Stickman case, I barely ever saw her, and when I did, Dan was always there. She seemed to be too busy for me right now.

I walked back down the hall and knocked on Carry's door.

"What?" she hollered from the other side, with a snap in her voice I didn't like.

"Carry, it's me," I replied, timidly. "You gotta get up so we'll make it down to Main Street in time for the parade."

"I don't wanna go. Tell Mom I'll just meet you guys at the park for lunch."

"Mom's not here. It's just you and me." I paused, thinking how unlikely that scenario was, and added, "And probably Dewey."

"Great," she said sarcastically. "Where the hell's Mom?"

"She left a note sayin' she had to go in to work for an emergency."

"When will she be back?"

I started to become annoyed having to holler through her door. I wished she'd just get up so we could talk like normal people.

"She didn't say," I answered.

"Great," she said again.

"Is Jonathon comin'?" I asked.

She didn't answer, but I heard her get out of bed and open her closet door. I stood in the hall outside of her room listening to her bustling inside. A few minutes later she opened her door, fully dressed in an Auburn Tigers university shirt and orange shorts. The shirt was navy and had orange sleeves. The football team's logo was on the front. I remembered from last time I'd seen her in it that the words, "War eagle!" were on the back.

"You never answered my question," I said.

"What?"

"'Bout Jonathon."

She narrowed her eyes. "What 'bout Jonathon?" She sounded angry and I had no idea why. Probably just because it was so early. Carry and mornings weren't that agreeable.

"I asked if he was comin' along," I said.

"Of course."

"Okay. I have to call Dewey." I headed back toward the kitchen counter for the phone.

"Don't be on it long," Carry said from behind me. "I need to call Jonathon."

I couldn't believe *she* was telling *me* not to be on the phone long. She and Jonathon sometimes talked for hours, even on days when they just finished spending the whole entire day together. I'd never once told her to get off the line. Not even when I desperately needed to call Dewey.

Dewey answered on the first ring and asked why it took me so long to call him. I ignored his question and just told him to come over as quick as he could on account of we had to walk down to Main Street.

"Why can't your ma drive us?" he asked.

"She ain't comin'," I said.

"How come?"

Carry stood tall behind me, her arms crossed. She had no patience, even on her good days. Seeing her like this, woke up so early with her hair all matted and disheveled, I almost got scared.

"Get off the phone," she said slowly, enunciating every syllable. "I need to call Jonathon."

"Dewey, just get over here as quick as you can," I said and hung up the phone.

I went into the living room and switched on the television while I pulled on my shoes and waited for Carry. I hoped she wouldn't be long. Odds were, with the nest of hair she came out of her room with, she would likely be having a shower. I could still hear her talkin' on the phone and wished she'd just hang up and get moving.

I flipped around the channels until I stopped at the first thing I found even slightly interesting—an episode of *Full House,* a show that was as much funny as it was corny. Oh well, it would waste time while I waited for my sister to finish getting ready.

Eventually, Carry hung up the phone and went back down to the bathroom, only a minute before Dewey showed up at my door.

Lots of people stood on the side of Main Street waiting for the parade. The shops were all decorated for the festivities, everything bright and clean in the morning sun. Red, white, and blue were the only colors I could see as I stared down one end of Main Street and then the other. The street was empty of traffic, since all of the parade route had been blocked off. But people swarmed on the sidewalk, some with children up on their necks, some even brought their dogs. I saw Mr. Robert Lee Garner a block down the street, with his coon dog, Dixie. I waved, but he didn't see me. I guess I was too short.

We were about two blocks up from the courthouse, where the parade always started. Every year it took the same route, starting at the far end of Main Street and then turning up Hunter Road and weaving all the way up to Willet Lake, which had a huge park wrapped around it.

We stood right in front of Vera's Old West Grill, the restaurant hosting the lunch and supper barbecue at Willet Park. I loved Vera's and couldn't wait to start digging in to the burgers and milk shakes after we followed the parade up Hunter Road and down Blackberry Trail. I could already taste all the food just from thinking about it.

A trumpet sounded, announcing the beginning of the parade.

People began marching from the side of the courthouse. The Independence Day Parade wasn't near on as good as the Christmas one. It didn't have floats or nothing like that, but it was still fun to watch. Mostly, though, it was pretty near the same year in and year out.

I watched as the beginning of the parade started passing by us. Four girls with red skirts and blue and white shirts twirled batons, throwing them in the air and catching them at the same time. Just behind them, two boys dressed the same played trombone while another boy marched between them playing a snare drum.

"What song is this?" Dewey asked.

I rolled my eyes. "How long you been alive?"

He looked up, as though calculating. He was ridiculous. "I reckon goin' on thirteen or so years. I'm not sure if I should start at zero or one when I'm countin'."

Shaking my head, I said, "Dewey, you're thirteen. Same as me. Are you tellin' me that over the course of those thirteen years you've never heard this song before?"

"Why can't you just tell me what it is?"

"It's 'America the Beautiful,' and my mother would say you should be ashamed for not knowing that."

He didn't look ashamed. In fact, he pretty near lost interest in me before I even finished. He was busy craning his neck to watch a classic dark blue car with no top on it slowly drive a good ways behind the musicians. Small flags mounted on either side of the windshield rippled in the breeze. Mayor Robertson sat in the front seat, along with a driver, waving and smiling to everyone. Only about half the folk waved back. Neither me nor Dewey did.

Two clowns on stilts came out from nowhere, catching up to the mayor's car. They were tossing saltwater taffy into the crowds. Dewey managed to scrummage with everyone else on the sidewalk for however many pieces of candy he could grab. When he stood back up, he was beaming.

"Look!" he said. "I got four! One's even strawberry-flavored!"

"Your lip's bleedin'," I said.

"Yeah, I think someone accidentally kicked me in the mouth."

"Was it worth it?" He touched his bloody lip with his finger, examining it afterward.

"What?" he asked. "Was what worth what?"

"Bleedin'. Was the taffy worth bleedin' over?"

His smile came back. "Shucks, yeah. I *love* saltwater taffy."

I just let that one fall and looked back out to the road, where the members of the Future Farmers of America were now walking by with tall flags announcing who they were. I recognized them from last year. Each of them had red, white, and blue armbands.

After the farmers, people dressed in oversized animal costumes skipped all over the road. One was a dog, another a bird, and the third one was a dragon. I had no idea what any of them had to do with the Fourth of July. But they threw out more candy—this time mints of some sort, all individually wrapped—that Dewey scampered across the sidewalk for, fighting against a flurry of kindergarten kids.

I just let out a breath and shook my head. When he finally came up, his lip was bleeding more than ever.

"Really, Dewey," I said, exhausted from just watching him grab candy from the hands of little kids. "Is it worth it?"

"What?" Again his finger came to his lip. This time when he pulled it away, it was actually bloody.

"Keep that up and you're gonna need stitches," I said.

"No, it's fine."

"Dewey. You just fought six-year-olds for mints."

"I got four." He opened his hand and showed them to me.

"Your lip's bleedin' like crazy."

"No, not really," he said. I watched the blood drip down his chin. His tongue came out and licked most of it away.

"That's so gross," I said.

"Just watch the parade." I could tell he was running out of smart things to say.

Next came the Ladies Auxiliary, all of them wearing bright red berets. One woman marched front and center holding a big American flag that kept catching the wind and snapping from side to side.

Then, with the crash of cymbals and snare drums

came a full marching band made up of kids who couldn't have been much older than me or Dewey. I found this exciting, as I couldn't remember them from any previous Fourth of July parades. Spilling out behind the drummers came at least a dozen other kids, all marching three abreast, each one playing a different musical instrument. There were trombones and trumpets, and flutes and clarinets. At the back came a large boy with his arms wrapped around a tuba. The whole lot of them brought their knees up at the same time and halted on the street as the drummers rat-a-tat-tat-ed a military march on their snares.

The cymbals crashed again, and the band started "The Star-Spangled Banner." Folk all around us on the sidewalk took off their hats and sang along. I couldn't believe how loud it was. It reminded me of the choir at Reverend Starks's Full Gospel Church, only common folk like the ones on the sidewalk couldn't sing near as well as Reverend Starks's choir.

Still, their voices rang out loud, true, and clear, and goose bumps appeared on my arms. The singing rose above the sounds of drums and brass, taking me with it. Something about it made my heart swell, and I actually felt tears sting the backs of my eyes. Something had an emotional grip on me, but I didn't know what it could be.

I assumed the answer would be something I'd discover later in my life. I tried unsuccessfully to hide my watery eyes as the musicians started marching again and moved on down Main Street.

"What the hell you cryin' for, Abe?" Dewey asked.

"I'm not cryin'," I said, wiping my eyes. "It's sweat. It's like a thousand degrees out here. Aren't you sweaty?"

Dewey's eyes narrowed. "Sure looked to me like you was cryin'."

"Dewey. Look at your shirt. You've got wet spots under your arms. You're sweatin', too."

"Yeah, but I ain't cryin' 'bout it."

I took a deep breath. My goose bumps were gone, and I felt kind of sad at the fact. "Just watch the goddamn parade," I said, finally.

"Okay, as long as you ain't gonna cry 'bout it anymore."

I grit my teeth. "I wasn't cryin'. I was sweatin'."

"Uh-huh," he said, not even pretending like he believed me.

I glanced over at Carry, who stood beside Jonathon, holding his hand. Jonathon had a small gray knapsack over his shoulder and his other hand gripped the strap. Carry seemed much more content now than she did when she first got up this morning.

Two girls walked behind the marching band, each holding one end of a banner explaining that they had all come from Murphy High School in Mobile.

"They must've got up really early to make it here in time for the parade," Dewey said. "I'm surprised they look so happy."

"What's not to be happy 'bout?" I said. "It's the Fourth. We get to eat for the rest of the day after this. I love eatin'."

"Eatin' is different than gettin' up early, Abe."

I gave Carry another sideways glance. She was staring at Jonathon so, of course, I didn't exist to be seen at the moment.

"Not everyone hates gettin' up," I said to Dewey. "Just Carry, far as I can tell."

"No, my ma hates it, too. That's why she stopped doin' it."

"Stopped doin' what?"

"Gettin' up. She stays in bed probably longer than Carry now on most days."

I stared at him. "Who makes you breakfast?"

"I do. My ma says I should be able to feed myself on account of wolf cubs my age can without any problems."

I nearly laughed. "What do wolf cubs have to do with you?"

"She always says things would be different if I'd been raised by wolves. I'd appreciate stuff more on account of wolf cubs don't have much. Just a den or whatever they sleep in. She figures I'd have probably been fixin' my own breakfast for years."

"*You* make your own breakfast? What the hell do you make?"

He gave me a look like I should know the answer to such an obvious question. "I don't make nothin', Abe. What do you think? I don't know anythin' 'bout makin' breakfast."

I thought about this and came to the conclusion he was probably right. "What 'bout toast?" I asked. "Surely you can make that."

"Never thought much 'bout toast," he said. "Thanks, I'll keep that in mind." Dewey's gaze drifted back to the parade, where more clowns now filled the street throwing out more saltwater taffy. Four were on stilts and two rode unicycles. Two more just walked normally.

Dewey's face lit up and he jumped up with his hands in the air, trying to make one of the creepy clowns toss candy his way. "Don't you just love clowns?" he asked.

"No, I reckon they're all mass murderers. Why do you care so much 'bout the stupid candy anyway?"

"Candy's good. I haven't had breakfast, remember?"

I had no interest in candy. I was saving all my room for a Vera's Old West barbecued burger. I was *glad* I hadn't eaten anything yet. I wondered about Dewey, though. "How long have you been goin' without breakfast?" I asked him.

"I dunno. A month?"

"A whole month with no breakfast?"

One of the clowns ran up and dropped a fistful of candy into Dewey's waiting hands. The clown offered another handful to me, but I declined. "No thanks," I said. "I'm savin' all my room so I can eat so many burgers there's a chance I might throw up." It probably wasn't the most eloquent thing to say, but it was certainly the truth. Oh, and I'd also be consuming a big bowl of homemade ice cream. The Ladies Auxiliary always handed out homemade ice cream.

"It's not hard to go a month without breakfast, Abe," Dewey said, finally answering my question.

"I guess so," I said, deciding not to spend any more time talking about Dewey's diet. At least I'd given him the gift of toast.

The clowns were now a block past us up the street, and the members of the Rotary Club were now going by. Every one of them held a little flag not much bigger than a deck of cards.

I looked behind them and saw the Boy Scouts coming up next. They walked four across with one in the front holding out another flag just like the woman in the front of the Ladies Auxiliary had.

My stomach gurgled and popped, like the inside of an active volcano. Like Dewey, I hadn't had breakfast, either, only I did it on purpose. Now my hunger was beginning to take precedence over watching any more of the parade. I wanted to get down to eating.

CHAPTER 36

When the tail of the parade finally went by, everyone watching spilled into the street behind it, and followed as it made its way to the library and then up Hunter Road.

The sun had hoisted itself way up above the trees and shone straight into my face, forcing me to squint as we went along. I glanced at my watch. The day already felt near on unbearable because of the heat, and it was just past ten-thirty as we hiked up the long hill toward Blackberry Trail, where everyone would turn to make their way to Willet Lake. A bead of sweat rolled down from my hair, running along the side of my face. I wiped it away with my arm.

"Sure is hot," I said to Dewey. Carry and Jonathon walked in front of us, still holding hands. Jonathon still had his knapsack on his other shoulder. I realized I hadn't heard either of them say a word since we met up with Jonathon around a quarter to nine at the bottom of Hunter Drive. I started thinking maybe they didn't talk much when they were together. That would explain the long phone conversations.

"This ain't so hot," Dewey said.

I wiped away more sweat that appeared on my forehead. "How can you say this ain't hot? By the time we make it up this hill, I'm goin' to be havin' a bath in sweat." I saw two beads of sweat run down the side of Dewey's face. He just left them there.

"I don't find it hot," he said. "Not *real* hot, anyway. I remember way hotter days than this."

"Dewey," I said. "You're sweating pails, just like me."

"No, I'm not."

I shook my head at him. "Why are we even discussin' this? I can *see* the sweat on your face."

He finally wiped it away. "I just don't think it's that hot."

I gave up. As usual, there was no point in arguing with him. I think Dewey liked to dispute everything so he could hear himself talk.

We finally got to Blackberry Trail and made a right, getting off the hill. I was actually a bit out of breath as we walked along. Beside me, I heard Dewey breathing heavy. He had on a white T-shirt that was now soaked, and he kept having to wipe sweat off his face. "You're an idiot," I said to him.

"What?"

I shook my head. "Never mind."

Jonathon stopped walking and actually spoke. "Hey," he said. "I almost forgot." Letting go of Carry's hand, he slipped the knapsack off his shoulder and unzipped it. Then he reached inside and pulled out some lady fingers. "Here," he said to me and Dewey. "I got these for you."

Dewey beamed as he took the fireworks. "Thanks!" he said.

Jonathon looked at me. "Those are for *both* of you."

"Thanks," I said.

Jonathon and Carry shared a glance at each other. Then Jonathon sort of stammered, "Um, maybe don't tell your ma you got them from me."

"Actually," Carry said, "I wouldn't tell Mom you got them at all."

Lunch exceeded all my expectations. Four cooks from Vera's manned the barbecues, where they cooked up a whole lot of burgers. The smell of them sizzling on the grill filled Willet Park, which now overflowed with folk from all over town. Looking around, I imagined near on everyone was here other than my mom and Dan. I had no idea what they were doing or where they were, only that it was some sort of emergency. I hoped everything was okay. I had worried that, without my mother, the day wouldn't be nearly as fun, but it turned out to be all right I figured as I finished my second burger.

"Going to try for number three?" Jonathon asked with a laugh.

I thought this over. "I don't think so. I have just enough room left for a big bowl of ice cream." As usual, the Ladies Auxiliary had shown up with tubs of home-made ice cream that would be the perfect topping for the food already in my stomach.

Dewey stopped eating halfway through his second burger.

"You're not done, are you?" I asked, lifting my can of Dr Pepper to my lips.

"I'm too full," he said.

"What 'bout ice cream?"

He shook his head. "I don't think so."

"But you haven't had breakfast in a month," I said. "You should be starving."

"I reckon my stomach's shrunk."

"Fine." I got up from the grass where the four of us were sitting. "*I'm* goin' to get myself some ice cream then."

"Just do it quick," Dewey said. "I want to set off these lady fingers."

"They can wait," I said. "We've got all day until the fireworks." The fireworks were scheduled for ten tonight. For that, I *couldn't* wait. Next to the food, the fireworks were the best part of the Independence Day celebration. Every year, pretty near all of the shops on Main Street pitched in to buy them. I had no idea how much they cost, but there were always a *lot* of them. They usually went off for near on a half hour.

With Dewey still protesting about me taking time for dessert, I completely ignored him and walked over and got into line at the tables where the Ladies Auxiliary was set up. The sun was right overhead and, I think, even hotter than it had been earlier. I wasn't sweating near on as much as I was walking up Hunter Drive, though.

Across the park, a few boys were throwing a baseball around. I started thinking Dewey and I should've brought our gloves but then figured doing anything in this heat would just be horribly uncomfortable.

A girl walked by with two small dogs. I think they were on their way to snatch the second half of Dewey's burger, the way they marched on in front of her, pulling their leashes tight.

I finally got to the front of the line and ordered my ice cream. I got two really big scoops, one strawberry and the other chocolate. As I made my way back to where we were sitting, the ice cream had already started to melt from the heat of the sun blazing overhead.

Across the park, someone blew an air horn announcing the start of the sack race. Me and Dewey had decided when we got to the park that we were too old for those kinds of things. Well, I did, anyway. Dewey had taken a little more convincing.

"All they got is buttons and flags and stickers from businesses," he had said while we checked out the prize tent.

"What do you expect?" I asked. "It ain't like we're payin' anythin' to be here."

"The Harvest Fair always has cool stuff like thumb locks and goldfish," he said, looking across the grass at all the kids hobbling along in the three-legged race. I didn't think any of them looked older than ten.

"You don't reckon that looks like fun?" Dewey asked.

"Dewey, everybody in that race still goes to grammar school. Some of them don't look older than six."

"Oh." His attention went back to the prizes. "I kind of like the buttons."

They were all advertisements for places on Main Street. The ones he had his eye on said: ALVIN FIRST NATIONAL BANK: SECURITY YOU CAN COUNT ON!

"What do you like about 'em?" I asked. "They're just advertisements."

"I guess." His attention wandered back to the kindergarten kids racing in twos with their legs tied together. "I reckon we could win a lot of those," he said.

"I'd certainly hope so, Dewey," I said. "They're barely out of diapers." I tossed him a snide look. "What the hell's a matter with you, anyway?"

He shrugged, his eyes fixed on the two boys crossing the finish line being announced winners. "We could've beat 'em," he said, longingly.

I just shook my head, but the cogs were spinning behind his eyes, I could tell. "We could win every single prize in that tent," he said at last.

"And what would you do with a thousand buttons advertisin' the bank?" I asked.

"I think you're missing the point."

"Dewey, as usual, there is no point. Come on, let's go find Carry and Jonathon. And 'sides, we have lady fingers. Don't you reckon they'll be a lot more fun than competing against little kids?"

He sounded as though he was being pulled from a dream when he answered. "Wouldn't you just love to have all them buttons, though?"

I ignored him and began heading away from the prize tent, back toward where Carry and Jonathon had claimed a spot in the park's grass. Eventually, Dewey jogged up beside me, apparently having dropped the idea of winning a pirate's pillage worth of banking advertisements.

The day wound down as evening set in and everyone in the park hunted for a good place to sit to watch the fireworks from. They always went off from a small boat anchored in the middle of Willet Lake, which meant there were lots of good spots to sit. Carry and Jonathon led the way to a sandy spot beside a small grove of maple trees.

Me and Dewey had spent most of the day lighting off lady fingers and playing Frisbee. I thought Dewey was going to blow himself up with the lady fingers. He wasn't very good at throwing them once they were lit. We got the Frisbee from a man and a woman with two little kids who wouldn't stop crying and so they decided to go home and told us we could have their Frisbee if we wanted. We had no lady fingers left, so I figured we might as well take it. It was something to fill time before I was ready to eat again.

I managed to consume another burger around dinnertime, just before the four cooks stopped barbecuing and started putting everything away. I almost didn't make it in time.

That was back around seven o'clock. Now it was fifteen minutes before ten and the clear sky had turned a deep violet that slowly dissolved into a black strip in the eastern sky. Above us, the first stars of the night popped out.

Dewey sat cross-legged beside me, a big grin on his face.

"What're you so happy 'bout?" I asked. I still had the Frisbee, and I was flipping it over in my hands, seeing how the night's shadows fell over the scratches dug into its white plastic surface.

"I'm happy 'bout fireworks," he said. "I reckon so far this is the best Fourth ever."

For once, I couldn't disagree with him. The three burgers I ate could very well be the best I'd ever had. Them alone were enough to make the day great.

Out on the lake, I heard a trout flip and fall back into the water. Farther out, a shadowy figure stood in a dory, lifting things from the boat and placing them on the floating platform in the lake's center. That's where the fireworks shot off from.

The moon had barely risen above the trees, and the dory's silhouette bobbed gently on the water beneath its pink grapefruit light.

It didn't take long until the man finished removing all the stuff from his boat.

Then we waited for what seemed like an hour but was

probably closer to ten minutes before classical music erupted from speakers that had to be placed discreetly around the lake. I didn't see them, but I sure heard them. The music came from all around us, echoing out over the lake. Violins grew to a crescendo as the first explosion of fireworks went off above the platform in a shower of cascading silver and gold.

I shifted myself a bit to get more comfortable, my eyes staying glued to the sky above where the dory still rocked on the lake's gentle waves.

Four more bursts filled the sky, these ones all red, white, and blue. The music swelled to a peak and goose bumps came to my arms for the second time that day.

"I love fireworks," Dewey said, his voice barely audible above the rising music and explosive fireworks. Carry sat on the other side of Dewey, and she reached across to Jonathon, their hands meeting as their fingers interlaced. Behind me, the rest of the park looked eerily empty. All of the folk who had scattered the grounds earlier were now nestled on the shore of Willet Lake.

With a sigh, I thought about my mother missing all of this. I had actually expected her to show up sometime during the day once she'd taken care of whatever the emergency was she needed to deal with. I guessed she was likely out with Dan somewhere, and that brought a strange pain to my stomach. I think maybe it was jealousy. I didn't get to see her nearly as much as usual now that he was here.

Above my head, the moon gently rose in a field of thousands of stars all twinkling down from a velvety sky.

"Don't you just love fireworks?" Dewey hollered at me.

I decided it wasn't worth the struggle of trying to

reply above all the noise, so I ignored him and sat back watching as five fireballs shot up in the sky, all popping at once, lighting up the park in an iridescent eruption of bright white light.

My mother was missing the fireworks, and that made me sad. But there was a chance she was looking up and seeing the very same stars as I did twisting brilliantly through tonight's sky.

And as I had that thought, I hoped that she was.

CHAPTER 37

When Leah finally got home the night of the Fourth of July, Abe was already in bed. He'd left his curtains open and, outside his bedroom, a glittering array of stars lit up the clear night's sky. She looked in on him from his doorway, lying on his side, his palms pressed together with his cheek lying atop them. He was beautiful, and in that instant she saw him again as a baby. He was always such a good kid. Even when Leah lost Billy, Abe was always there for her. For those months when all she could do was cry, he'd come over to where she was lying on the sofa and say, "Mommy all right?" It always sounded like "all bright" when he said "all right." Even then, it made her smile through her tears.

Thinking back to that now almost brought them again.

Leah's mind flashed back to the topless body of Samantha Hughes staked there on the bank of the Ani-kawa, a 9 mm bullet hole in the back of her head. Leah wondered if Samantha had children. Were they out there somewhere tonight asking where Mommy was? A pang of sorrow hit Leah's heart. What could anyone ever tell a child to make this okay? How would they ever be able to understand?

She realized she hoped they never would. That was the only way people like the Stickman would ever stop.

Something caught in Leah's throat, and she had to cough quietly to clear it.

Abe stirred. His eyes opened half-mast.

Leah came over and knelt by his bed, gently rubbing the side of his face, his hair falling between her fingers. "You okay?" she asked. "How was your Fourth?"

"It was good," he said.

Leah gave a sad smile. "Did you eat a lot?"

In a tired voice, he replied, "Yeah. Three whole burgers."

"Three whole burgers? Holy cow."

Abe gave her a small smile. "The fireworks were nice."

She continued running her fingers through his blond hair. "That's good, honey. I'm glad you had fun."

He didn't answer, just looked into her eyes, his lips forming a straight line.

"Something wrong?" she asked.

When he didn't reply, she knew there was.

"What is it, my little soldier?" she asked.

"No, I'm not *your* little soldier," he said. "That's what Uncle Henry calls me."

Leah smiled. "Okay, you're my little man, then. What's wrong?"

He brought his right hand out from under his cheek and rubbed his nose. "Where were you today?"

"I had an emergency at work."

"What kind of emergency?"

She hesitated, again wondering how to explain something like today to a thirteen-year-old. She couldn't. Instead she shook her head and said, "Just police stuff."

"Stickman stuff?" Abe's eyes were now fully open. He rubbed sleep from them.

"Shh," Leah said. "It's too late to talk. I just wanted to say good night."

"Is Dan still here?"

Leah's brow furrowed as she wondered where this question came from. "Yeah, he's in the living room."

"What's he doin'?"

"I don't know. Sleeping, probably. He sleeps on the sofa." As she said this, it sounded like she was reinforcing that fact more for herself than him. "Sometimes he stays up late, working."

"I know," Abe said.

"You know what?"

"When he's up. I hear him. He's pretty loud. And he snores."

A big smile came across Leah's face. "He *is* loud, I agree." Then, without giving it any thought, she asked, "Do you like him?"

Abe's eyes searched hers for a heartbeat before answering. When he did, it wasn't an answer she expected. "Do *you?*" he asked.

"Yeah . . . you know? I think I do."

Abe gave her a small smile. "Then I do, too." But Leah got the distinct impression there was something beneath his smile.

"Are you sure?" she asked. "Just because I do, doesn't mean you have to."

He thought this over. "No, he's fine. He's nice. Kind of dorky, but nice."

Leah laughed. "He is. Both. Dorky and nice."

Abe yawned.

"You should go back to sleep," Leah told him. "It's been a long day."

Something seemed to be weighing on him. "Mom?" he asked.

"Yeah?"

He seemed to search his mind for how to form his next thought. "Some folk are sayin' Grandpa Joe killed an innocent man. Did he?"

Leah sighed. This wasn't the conversation she wanted to have tonight. "What folks are sayin' that, honey?"

There was something in his eyes. Leah felt like he wasn't being entirely truthful. "Some kids me and Dewey ride the bus with," he answered. "We saw them today on Main Street and they said it. Is it true?"

Leah took a deep breath and tried to collect her thoughts. "Your grandpa killed a man who was threatening him with a gun."

"So he's not a murderer?"

These words echoed in Leah's mind. "No, your grandpa is not a murderer."

"Then why are folks sayin' he is?"

"On account of they read too many damn newspapers."

"But he thought he killed the Stickman, right?"

She took another big breath. "Yes, honey, he did."

"And was it the Stickman?"

Her fingers slid down the side of his face to his neck. Something caught in her throat. "I don't really know, to be perfectly honest. It's what I'm tryin' to find out."

"Why would he shoot someone he wasn't sure was the Stickman, though?"

She paused to think. "Because, honey, when you're a police officer you have to make decisions. Sometimes those decisions have to be made fast and you don't necessarily always make the right decisions." *And,* she thought, *there are some mistakes there's just no fixing once they're made. You can't always come back.*

"So Grandpa Joe made a mistake?"

She pulled his sheet up to his chin. "Your grandpa thought his life was in danger. He did what he had to do. I think that's enough questions about this tonight, okay?"

He gave her a small smile. "Okay."

Leah pushed his nose gently with her index finger. "Want to know something?"

"What?"

"I love you so much," she said.

Abe smiled a sleepy little smile. "I love you, too, Mom. Good night." He yawned again.

"Night, night, my little man," she whispered and stood. She walked out of the room, pausing in the doorway to look back at him lying there in the glow of the starlight, his palms once again pressed together beneath his cheek. His eyes were closed and she could tell he'd already fallen back to sleep.

With another sad smile, she thought of Samantha Hughes and how, in just the course of a day and a half, her life and the life of her family had completely changed. There was no coming back from it. She thought about what it would be like if Abe lost her, or if she lost him, but she had to bat it away. They were crazy thoughts that only led to one place, a hellish and dark place.

From where Abe lay, Leah heard quiet snores. She took a mental snapshot of him lying there, partially lit

by the light of the night outside, shadows falling softly
from the edge of his face and hands. He looked so
peaceful. So happy. She hoped nothing would ever take
that away. But she knew that was impossible. The world
constantly undermined happiness, as though it was its
greatest mandate.

The broken body of Samantha Hughes materialized
in her head like it had been doing all day since Leah
found her. If she was honest with herself, the vision terrified her. She wouldn't be able to live with herself
much longer if she didn't stop the Stickman. Too much
blood was being spilled, blood that she thought fell on
her own hands. It was *her* duty to stop all the madness,
not Chris's and certainly not Ethan's.

So a war between responsibility and action raged inside of Leah. She felt powerless to stop it. It would continue as long as the Stickman kept taking lives, and
there was nothing she could do about it.

Abe rolled over onto his back, still asleep, and she
watched him, trying to remember back when she was
young and the world felt safe and secure.

She couldn't do it. Too many times, the world had
come up against her, its wickedness and its wiliness.
Trying to outsmart her. Trying to win.

For now, she'd managed to hold it off, but could she
continue doing so? Sooner or later, the world had to
win. And on that day, Leah knew she would lose all her
faith.

Right now, though, she tried to replace these
thoughts with the image of her little boy asleep in his
bed with a puddle of drool on the pillow beside his
head. She hoped, unlike her, that he would remember

this time in his life, a time he felt completely secure and at peace.

He was her little man.

He's not just my little man, she thought, *he's more than that.*

He's my little angel.

CHAPTER 38

The day after Samantha Hughes's death, Leah managed to arrive early to the station. She kept glancing up at the framed article about her in the *Examiner,* thinking how misrepresented she'd been. The story made her out to be a great detective, but the reality was, she wasn't great. If she was great, she would've already stopped the Stickman. If she was great, Samantha Hughes would still be alive.

If she was great, she wouldn't have so much blood on her hands that, like the bloody hands of Lady Macbeth, would not come clean simply by submitting to a wash of soap and water.

She had slept poorly last night. Haunted by nightmares, flashes of which she remembered went way back to the time when she got that call from Bob Garner, showing up only to find the limp and lifeless body of Ruby Mae Vickers tossed in the soil around the base of that willow tree. That vision she knew all too well. It haunted her sleep often, only this time the dream had changed. It now incorporated the busted body of Samantha Hughes, naked from the waist up, spiked on the bank of the Anikawa in that horrible inverse-fetal position.

Leah had heard those car doors literally moments too late to make it on time.

In her dream, she had chased after the vehicle squealing away in that cloud of dust. And, although she ran faster than she ever did before, she could never get close enough to see it. Always, that cloud of dust lingered before her. She breathed it in and began to choke. Then, involuntarily, she fell on her knees, gasping for air, her chest and throat screaming out to her as the vehicle tore away, never once giving her a glimpse of it. In the dream, she never got that close to the killer again.

What followed that was by far the worst part of the nightmare, when the spiked body of Samantha Hughes began shrieking with the voice of a demon, asking Leah why she had to die, asking Leah to loosen the rope binding her wrists and ankles, asking Leah to pull the stake from her chest.

But as much as Leah tried, the dream would not let her walk any closer to Samantha Hughes's howling body. It was as though an invisible barricade lay between them. It seemed like she tried forever until, eventually, the body of Samantha Hughes wailed one last time before a white film formed over her eyes and her ribs and femurs tore through her skin. The skin on her face stretched and tore, revealing the hollow sockets of her eyes and the eternal grin of her skull.

Leah shivered. The life force of Samantha Hughes had been ripped away, taken to the place where the innocent prey of evil must go.

Forced to do nothing but watch, in her dream Leah screamed out helplessly. "I'm sorry," she screamed repeatedly. "I'm *so* sorry."

Then she had called out for her ma to come save her.

Sitting at her desk now, Leah took three deep breaths and tried to forget the nightmare. It wasn't easy. It had been so terrible and vivid that, even as she woke up to the buzzing of her clock radio, it took her some time to calm down and realize it wasn't real.

She needed to distract herself, so she decided that since she'd been through all the Stickman files by now, her next step was to create a timeline of events. She hoped that might reveal something she hadn't yet seen.

Turning to a new page in her legal pad, she started going through the stack of files again, only this time only looking at what she thought might be relevant to her investigation.

She still wasn't sure about the four starred jobs in Harry's maintenance record. Because she was looking at a Xerox, the asterisks could've been in the original file, or they could've been added by her pa. They didn't look exactly the same as the ones her pa had made in the hospital list, but Leah was by no means a handwriting analyst. She decided to include those particular jobs in her timeline and hope that their importance, if any, would come to light in the near future.

STICKMAN CASE TIMELINE

Feb 20, 1959—Harry Caught B&E: Gets One Year Probation

May 20, 1959—Harry Breaks Probation (Another B&E)
  * Sentenced to Mobile County Youth Correctional Institution for One Year

Aug 10, 1964—Harry Is Drafted
  * Harry Stork, 21, drafted into service in Vietnam. Brother, Tommy, 4-F because of accident.

Nov 30, 1965—Tommy moves to Noah Stork's house
- (From notes) Noah not exactly comfortable with situation.

Apr 3, 1966–Apr 24, 1966—Tommy Hospitalized
- (From medical) Admitted to Grell Memorial. Previously diagnosed schizophrenic.

Jan 15, 1967–Feb 7, 1967—Tommy Hospitalized (again)
- (From medical) Admitted to East Point Hospital in Daphne. Medication adjusted.

Jul 6, 1967—Harry Comes Home
- Honorable discharge due to mental conditions affecting ability to perform duties.
- Notes from interview with Noah Stork
- Noah claims Harry was fine until being drafted. Suspects PTSD.

Nov 1, 1967—Harry starts Stork Sanitation and Waste Removal (SSWR)
- Company incorporated under Noah's name.

Leah circled this last point and drew an arrow to it with the note: *Why?*

Nov 1967—SSWR signs contract with Springhill Memorial Hospital
Dec 1967—SSWR signs contract with Searcy Hospital in Mount Vernon
Sept 2, 1971–Sept 16, 1971—Tommy Hospitalized
- (From medical) Tommy hospitalized at East Point. Medication adjusted.

Feb 1972—SSWR signs contract with Providence Hospital in Mobile
Mar 1972—SSWR signs contract U of SAl Children's and Women's

Dec 30, 1972–Jan 13, 1973—Tommy Hospitalized
- Tommy hospitalized again at East Point.

Jan 16, 1973—Death of Sally-Anne Stork
- Sally-Anne suicide by barbiturates. Tommy Stork finds mother's body.

Jan 30, 1973—Stickman Victim #1: Waylon Ferris
- Black male, unemployed, body found under Finley's Crossing, Alvin
- Tire marks @ scene indicate vehicle w/ 132.9-inch wheelbase and 16.5-inch tires.

Mar 20, 1973 (Tuesday)—Victim #2: Veda Gamble
- White female, waitress, body found in Cherry Park Forest, Alvin.

Apr 24, 1973 (Tuesday)—Victim #3: Lafayette Eagan
- White male, notary public, body found in a field out on First Road
- Tire marks @ scene match those found @ scene of vic 1. In report, Fowler writes note: *Harry Stork?*

May 6, 1973–May 27, 1973—Stanley Bishop @ Grell: Claims to have met Stickman

Oct 11, 1973—Harry does work for Providence Hospital, Mobile, AL

Oct 17, 1973—Victim #4: Maggie Ledbetter
- White female, RN @ Providence Hospital in Mobile, body found beside Old Mill River, Alvin

Oct 18, 1973—Thomas Kennedy Bradshaw (TKB) claims to be Stickman
- Alvin Police determine it's a false claim. TKB is sent home.

Oct 22, 1973—Fowler Organizes Task Force
- Consists of 6 officers and detectives.

Dec 6, 1973—Harry does work for Providence Hospital, Mobile, AL

Dec 10, 1973—Victim #5: Travis Moyer
- Black male, Anesthetist @ Providence, body found in field of Shearer's Cotton Farm, Alvin
- Shoe marks @ scene indicative of a men's size seven Nike Blazer
- Front tire marks indicate vehicle with 117-inch wheelbase and 14-inch tires
- ME finds bullet in victim's skull. Probable weapon: .38 cal. S&W Victory

Dec 10, 1973—Witness: Gerard Buchowitz
- Claims to have seen yellow car, possibly AMC Rambler @ scene of vic 5. Forensics state wheelbase and tire evidence does not match Rambler.

Dec 11, 1973—Fowler's Task Force grows to 9

Jan 16, 1974—Victim #6: Geneva Wade
- Black woman, technician @ Grell, body found in Beemer's Bog. Evidence indicates she was staked on edge of bog before wild animals pulled her in.

Jan 17, 1974—Fowler's Task Force grows to 12

Jan 17, 1974—TKB again comes forward claiming to be Stickman
- Again, police determine claim is false. Sent to Grell for examination.

Jan 19, 1974—Someone on task force leaks stake and stickman drawings to media

Apr 6, 1974—Victim #7: Forrest Ingram
- White male, RN @ Grell, body found behind Full Gospel, Alvin

Apr 7, 1974—Witnesses: Tara-Lee Norton & John Donner
- Both report seeing yellow car on road in front of Full Gospel. Donner gives partial plate. DMV search indicates potential match to vehicle

registered to Stanley Bishop. Vehicle congruent with wheelbase and tire marks found @ scene of vic 5. Bishop interviewed, but witnesses support his alibi.

May 1974—SSWR signs contract with Mercy Medical in Daphne, AL

May 27, 1974—Harry works for Searcy Hospital, Mount Vernon, AL

May 29, 1974—Victim #8: Warrick Quackenbush

- Black male, ultrasound technician @ Searcy Hospital, body found in Willet Park
- 14-inch tire mark on roadside congruent with those found @ scene of vic 5. Fowler made note: *Bishop?*

May 30, 1974—Witness: Bodie Applewhite

- Claims he saw Tommy Stork @ scene. Vague when asked how he knew T.S. Claims he saw Stork 8 days earlier & Stork was acting "weird."

June 2, 1974—T.S. Interview

- Strident brings Stork in. Stork denies involvement, but nobody to back up alibi. Stork claims he and Applewhite have long-standing contention from way back to bar fight.
- Fowler circles Stork's name on statement & writes: *Doesn't fit the profile.*

June 12, 1974—Harry works for Mercy Medical, Daphne, AL

June 16, 1974—Victim #9: Lola Reid

- White female, student nurse @ Mercy Medical in Daphne, body found in woods beside Tucker Mountain Pass, just outside of Alvin
- ME finds round in skull matching one removed from vic 5. Same gun.

June 18, 1974—Break-in at Alvin Police Station. All Stickman case files stolen.

- Blood found at scene different type than the Storks.

June 18, 1974 & June 19, 1974—Two witnesses (Betty-Lou Panders & Andrea Reinhardt)

- Both claim H.S.'s work truck parked along roadside where vic 9 found.

Leah left a note to herself after circling these two witnesses' names: *Interview again?*

June 19, 1974—H.S. Interviewed: Denies involvement

June 20, 1974—Bodie Applewhite (witness from vic 8) interviewed again

- Shown photo of H.S. and states he could be suspect he saw @ scene

June 20, 1974—Noah Stork Reports B&E: Nothing stolen or missing

June 24, 1974—Police Issued Warrant to Search H.S. House

- H.S. not home when police arrive.
- Police find S&W Model 10 .38 Special revolver. Matches 2 rounds in evidence. Gun unregistered.

June 25, 1974—H.S. Disappears: Fowler issues statewide manhunt

- Fowler's Task Force grows to its biggest size: 16 detectives and officers

June 26, 1974—TKB Comes Forward Again

- TKB claims he is Stickman for third and final time. Police dismiss him again. He is sent home.

Jul 2, 1974—H.S.'s truck is found in Cornflower Lake

- Searching the truck turns up nothing

Jul 22, 1974—H.S. Shot Dead after Police Receive Note

- Note contains address along with initials *H.S.* Forensics report all notes except this one written in the same hand.

- 4 officers arrive at shotgun shack with H.S. inside. Police force entry after H.S. refuses to come out. H.S. flees through back door.
- Fowler shoots H.S. dead after H.S. refuses to relinquish gun—unloaded 9 mm Beretta 92. H.S.'s last words claim he was set up as a patsy. Nothing found in files regarding what was meant by this statement.

Leah circled the last fact and wrote herself a note: *Was H.S. the wrong guy?* Then, looking at her point about this note being written by someone else, she realized one of the two remaining cops on Ethan's "trusted list" had to work in forensics as a handwriting analyst.

Aug 31, 1978—TOMMY STORK MOVES TO BIRMINGHAM SUBURB
- Noah Stork claims T.S. spent much of his time in Birmingham before move. Unable to offer clue as to why.

Jan 1, 1989—TOMMY STORK MOVES BACK TO ALVIN

Leah circled this fact and the one before it and wrote a question in the margin pertaining to both: *Why?* Then she pulled the file folders regarding the two recent Stickman murders and added that information to the timeline.

June 13, 1989—Victim #10: Abilene Williams
- Black woman, receptionist, body found on the banks of Leeland Swamp, Alvin, first victim in 15 years

- Partial fingerprint and boot impression found at the scene. Forensics determine boot likely a "jump boot" used by paratroopers in WWII.

Jul 4, 1989—Victim #11: Samantha Hughes

- White female, unemployed mechanic, body found south side of the Anikawa in front of Garner's Ranch
- Marks in the dirt indicate victim was dragged from assailant's car.

Leah went back to the report she'd made and remembered what Chris had said when he read it through. "You found drag marks?" he'd asked. She had just nodded.

"This is too weird. First it appears the Stickman can't carry a hundred-and-ten-pound woman down a short trail and would rather push through a clutch of thorny brambles to get closer, and now he can't even carry her thirty feet from his car to the riverbank? Is there anything like this in the reports from seventy-three and seventy-four?"

"Not that I could find," Leah had answered.

Now she wondered about that again. Why was the Stickman suddenly appearing to be so weak? Obviously he had no problem hammering them stakes through his victims' chests.

For now, she let that question go and looked back over the timeline. Leah figured that was about all she had. The timeline spanned three sheets of paper. She took them over to the Xerox machine and made two copies. Then she took her originals and Scotch-taped them together so it was one long piece of paper. She hung this on the wall between the door and the window so she could see it from her desk.

Right away, she did notice something about those four asterisked jobs in Harry's maintenance record. For each one, within two to six days following a victim was killed who worked at that hospital. So, the stars obviously were made by Leah's pa, even though, to her, they looked a bit different from the asterisks he'd made earlier when he flagged the relevant hospitals in Harry's major contract list.

Other than that, nothing really popped off the page and, for the next hour, she stared at the timeline, trying to find a clue as to what she was looking at. Other than Harry Stork, two names seemed to come up again and again on the list: Thomas Kennedy Bradshaw and Tommy Stork. Two Toms.

That thought brought with it the question Dan had posed on the phone a couple of weeks back: What if there were two serial killers, working together as the Stickman? She wondered if Stork and Bradshaw's paths had ever met. How could she find out? Going through her stack of files, she extracted their folders and flipped through everything, unable to find anything to support that the two ever knew each other.

CHAPTER 39

After loading up my duffel bag with all the supplies I thought we'd need, I zipped it closed and bungeed it to my bike. Most of the stuff I shoved inside came from the My First Forensics Lab kit, but there were other things that the book recommended without supplying it in the box. Stuff like airtight containers to store any kind of evidence that doesn't fit in the small envelopes, marker pens to label evidence with, and pencils to sketch out the crime scene. Also, I needed a proper pen and paper to make a report of all the details.

"You sure you know where we're goin'?" Dewey asked as we rode into the sunny morning on our bikes. My stomach let out a little complaint about missing breakfast this morning, but when I woke up I was still full from the three hamburgers I'd eaten yesterday at Willet Park.

The day was bright and a light mist clung to the ground, making everything appear magical. I was glad the sun was back. Now it actually felt like summer.

"Yep, I know *exactly* where we're goin'," I answered. "Way up to Leeland Swamp."

"Ain't that goin' to take us right past Preacher Eli's?"

I found that question a bit strange. We had both been scared of Preacher Eli a year or so ago when he came back here after being in prison, but my mother assured me he was nothing to be scared of. "Now, why do you care 'bout that?" I asked Dewey. "My mom said he's done his time and now we should treat him just like anybody else. She told me he's harmless."

"I don't think he's harmless, Abe. I find him scary. 'Sides, he killed that kid, remember?"

"'Course I remember. But now he's fixed up his relationship with God or something. My mom tried explainin' it to me once, but I didn't quite understand all of what she said. 'Sides, he's too busy buildin' that new Baptist school to take any interest in us. You seen it?"

"The school?"

"Yeah."

"Nope. When did you?"

"About a month after my mom solved the Maniac Tailor case, back when she first met Dan."

"How come your ma's cases always have funny names, like the Stickman or the Cornstalk Killer?" Dewey laughed. "Or the Maniac Tailor? That one's the funniest."

"She don't name them. I asked her 'bout it once, and she said mostly they come from some clever newspaper writer. But 'the Maniac Tailor' didn't. You remember that psychic Carry saw?"

"Sure do." Dewey grinned. "Madame Crystalle—she said I was 'gifted'."

I rolled my eyes. "Yeah, you're the kind of gift that people take back. Anyhow, the *Examiner* found out she helped my mom solve the case and interviewed her. She came up with the 'Maniac Tailor' name."

"Oh," Dewey said. "Still sounds kinda funny."

We turned up the big hill of Hunter Road, the road

Preacher Eli's house was on. It was tough pedaling, but when you're riding with someone else you don't dare get off and push your bike unless he does first. It makes you a weenie. And since Dewey lives by the same rule, neither of us gave in to the hill and we pushed our pedals hard as we could to make it up.

"Nothin' much funny 'bout serial killers, Dewey. Anyway, I was tellin' you 'bout Preacher Eli's Baptist School. A month or two after my mom met Dan, she took me and Carry to lunch with her and him. My mom drove to some little diner in a town halfway between his house and ours. The road we took out of Alvin was Fairview Drive—that's where the new school's bein' built. Looked like it was goin' to be big."

"When's it meant to be done?"

I shrugged. "No idea. I'm wonderin' if maybe we'll be able to go there instead of bussing all the way to Satsuma every day. Sure would be nice."

"I don't know," Dewey said.

"What don't you know?"

"'Bout attendin' school at a place owned by Preacher Eli. He still creeps me out."

I knew what Dewey meant. I somewhat even agreed with him, but I didn't tell him that. We just rode in silence awhile.

We got to the bridge going over Blackberry Springs, and I pulled to a stop.

"Why you stoppin'?" Dewey asked. "Too tired to ride anymore?"

"No," I said quietly. "Listen."

"I don't hear nothin'," Dewey said.

"Listen harder."

"All I hear is the sound of the water rushin' over the rocks," he said.

"That's what we're listenin' to. Isn't it relaxin'?"

"You're full of bull crap. You stopped because you is tired."

"Think whatever you want, Dewey. I stopped to listen to the river. Sounds like it's singin' to me." A cardinal flew out of the poplar trees lining the creek. Its red-and orange-painted feathers soared majestic across a blue canvas of sky.

"It don't sound like no singin'," Dewey said. "Let's get goin'. I want to get past Preacher Eli's place as quick as we can."

He awkwardly started back up the hill. I joined him. When we'd pedaled past Preacher Eli's small house, neither of us said a word about it. I gave the place a quick glance, but I noticed Dewey purposely kept his eyes straight ahead. I really didn't blame him. There were as many rumors around town about Preacher Eli as there were about Newt Parker, and unlike Newt's rumors, the ones about Preacher Eli always involved him killing folk.

About fifteen minutes later, we reached the top of Hunter Drive and knew we could coast the rest of the way down to Leeland Swamp. We were only about five minutes away.

"Whereabouts at Leeland Swamp is the crime scene?" Dewey asked.

"You remember that cypress in the marsh that some kid carved a happy face into?"

"No."

"Sure you do. It's a big happy face. At least this big." I let go of my handlebars and held my palms a good two feet apart.

"I ain't never seen a happy face tree in my life, Abe. Especially one that big."

"Well, I have. And I saw it again in the photos from my mom's files 'bout the Stickman murder that happened a few weeks ago."

"Someone was killed by the smiling tree?"

I shook my head. "Nobody knows where she was killed, but her body was found in the swamp near the tree."

"How come no one knows where she was killed?"

I told him what I'd learned about primary crime scenes and how, according to my grandpa Joe's notes, he was never able to find the primary scene and that always worried him. It was like he figured there was some evidence he needed that could only be found at the primary scene. Some of his notes about it were written weeks after Harry Stork died, almost as though my grandpa was still investigating the case. It made me wonder more about the question my mother made in her notes asking if my grandpa might have shot the wrong guy.

"What if there's more than one tree with a happy face, Abe? That swamp's huge. We'll never find two happy trees."

I sighed. Sometimes dealing with Dewey was just too much work. "I know the tree, Dewey. Don't worry 'bout it. I know pretty near exactly where the police found Abilene Williams's body."

"Who?"

"The woman the Stickman killed and left on the edge of the swamp." I purposely didn't say anything to him regarding the way she was tied and how the wooden stake had been hammered through her. Dewey didn't need those kinds of things in his head. He wasn't like me. Even though our birthdays were days apart, he was, as my mother once put it, emotionally much younger than me.

"How do you know all 'bout this woman and where she turned up?" he asked.

Damn, I hadn't meant to tell him about my mother's files. "I . . . um, I accidentally kind of read my mom's reports 'bout it."

"How do you 'accidentally' read somethin'?"

"They were on the counter in the kitchen and, before I realized what my eyes were doin', they'd already gone through all the information."

Dewey smiled. "I hate accidentally readin' stuff."

What Dewey meant was that he just hated reading stuff whether on accident or on purpose.

"I have a pretty good idea from the description in my mom's report I accidentally read of where it is." *Accidentally* sounded so much better to me than *purposefully*.

We came to a dirt road that veered off left of Hunter Drive and followed it, plunging into a mess of a forest that grew thick and tight on either side of us. Some of the branches hung over the road, and plants and shrubs bunched close up in front of them. The forest blocked the sun, making the road dark. Goose bumps ran up my arms. The darkness felt scary and exciting, like we were entering a whole different world.

"How long are we gonna be at the swamp?" Dewey asked, riding up beside me.

"I dunno. However long it takes for us to find all the clues."

"Didn't your mother already get all the clues?"

This was a hard question for me to answer on account of when I went through the file concerning victim number ten, which was Abilene Williams, I found practically nothing either reported by or noted by my mother. It was almost as though she hadn't been there. But I didn't say that to Dewey. Instead, I answered, "We'll look for things they might've missed. But there is one thing . . ."

"What's that?"

"The scene will probably be delineated"—a word I'd learned a few days ago when I had to look it up in my dictionary—"with police tape. We shouldn't go inside there. We could corrupt the scene." As it was, I hoped we wouldn't have to tell my mother we even visited the *outside* of the scene. I doubted highly she'd be happy to hear about it.

"What does *delineated* mean?"

I let out a breath. "Doesn't matter, Dewey, just don't go past the tape." We came to the opening of the trail I recognized from the description Officer Chris put in his notes. I skidded to a stop. Dewey did the same.

"This it?" he asked.

I nodded. "Should lead us right to the area with that tree."

"How come you know this trail?"

He was so frustrating. "You know it, too, Dewey. We've been down it at least twice I can remember."

"I don't recall ever bein' here before. And I *know* I ain't never seen no happy face tree."

"You have a memory like a goldfish," I said. "It was a while back. Before Preacher Eli returned to Alvin."

"Oh. You sure 'bout this?"

"What part?"

"'Bout going to find some happy face tree on the edge of Leeland Swamp. I'm kinda scared. It's so dark in here. That trail looks even darker. What if the Stickman's around?"

"Dewey, the Stickman's already been and left. That's why there's a crime scene here. He wouldn't come back, that would just be dumb. The police might be lookin' through the swamp for more evidence or somethin'. If he came back, it would just make it more dangerous for him that he might get caught." I thought about that guy from my mother's files, Thomas Kennedy Bradshaw, the one who kept going to the police saying that he was the Stickman. He actually *did* seem to want to get caught, even though the police decided he wasn't the killer. So, I supposed, someone like Thomas Kennedy Bradshaw very well might go back to his crime scenes, hoping to get arrested.

I decided telling Dewey this would only scare him more. Instead, I started for the trail and said, "Come on. It's just a swamp. You'll be fine."

Reluctantly, he followed me. "Okay. What 'bout gators?" he asked.

"What 'bout 'em?"

"They give me the jeebies."

My brow furrowed. "There ain't no gators in Leeland Swamp, Dewey."

"All swamps have gators," he said.

"No, they don't."

"Yes, Abe, they do."

"I ain't arguin' this with you. And we're not goin' into the swamp, anyway. So I don't see why you're so concerned 'bout 'em."

He didn't reply, so I assumed I won that round.

We rode through the soft dirt, each of us on either side of the "wheelbarrow track" I had expected to find from Officer Chris's notes. Then we came to the place where the trail narrowed. This was where Officer Chris decided the Stickman had been forced to leave the wheelbarrow behind and carry Abilene Williams the rest of the way. A thought came into my mind then. It had something to do with the small-trunked trees, brambles, and bushes to the left of the tight path. They reminded me of something, only I couldn't quite put my finger on it. Dewey didn't seem to notice as he got off his bike just as I had.

"We gonna dump our bikes here?" he asked.

I thought this over. "I reckon we should bring 'em to the swamp with us. We leave 'em here, they might get stolen."

So we pushed our bikes down the rest of the path, which, in places, became really tight. I had my bike right of me; Dewey had his on his left. Problem with that was, most of the right edge of the path was overgrown with thistle, briar, blackberry bushes, and prickly shrubs. My bike pretty much saved me from getting caught up in them, but, as Dewey pushed his bike behind me, the vines and branches I passed got pushed forward until my bike cleared them, then they would snap back right into Dewey. Thorny branches kept lashing him like whips. They got caught on his shirt and tore at his skin. I had to stop and help him free himself from them three times. The third one really had him hooked up.

"Stop thrashing," I said. "You're still hooked on the bush." I came back and gently tugged the thorn from his sleeve. "There. Now, just be more careful."

When we finally spilled out of the path, Dewey's right side looked like it had fallen into a bathtub full of mean alley cats.

I laughed.

"Why are you laughin', Abe? It hurts like crazy. Look how much I'm bleedin'." He rubbed his hand over all the flesh wounds in his arm, smearing the blood so his skin became pink. "They really sting."

I shook my head. "You'll be fine. Just let 'em be."

The sun once again shone down on us, and I had to squint to look around us. The air was so humid, and even though we were at the edge of the swamp's green, brackish water, it felt heavy and close. I could taste a rotten dampness in my mouth. Its surface, covered with duckweed, lily pads, reeds, and bulrushes, lay perfectly still. A quietness wrapped around everything like a blanket, and it gave me the willies.

Even though I knew there weren't no gators, there could still be water snakes. A poisonous snake could kill you just as easy as a gator, and some of them might even be able to slither up onto the marshland.

I didn't tell Dewey about the water snakes.

Again I examined the bushes on the left side of the path we just came through, and again something about it seemed weirdly familiar. Dewey apparently didn't have the same feeling.

"Why're you staring at the woods for?" he asked.

"I don't know. Somethin' weird 'bout 'em." Some of them were broken, but it wasn't those ones that tweaked my brain, it was the way the other bushes and small trees were sort of bent away from each other.

About ten feet away, police tape began at the trunk of a cypress and continued on, outlining a fairly big and almost square area. The tree I recognized from the photo was on the far side of the tape, but its trunk was so wide and the carving so big I had no problem making it out from where we were.

"Wow," Dewey said. "There really *is* a happy face tree!"

I ignored him. This was like the third time he'd seen it. Besides, I was much too interested in investigating this real, actual crime scene than worrying about some dumb tree. A white marker lay on the moor near on center of the area outlined in tape, at the foot of a cypress.

"What's that?" Dewey asked, pointing to it.

"I reckon that's where they found her body."

"Creepy," Dewey said.

I had to agree on that point, although I didn't say so.

After taking the bungee off my carrier, I hefted my duffel bag and let my bike fall to the soft ground, where it rattled on top of Dewey's. I started carefully walking around the outside of the taped area, looking all around me for any clues. Dewey followed me, his gaze split between staring at the trees and warily checking the swamp's ominously placid surface.

My insides swarmed with excitement. I had only ever been to one crime scene before (well, actually two, if you count my mother taking me and Carry with her to Miss Sylvie's last year, but we had to stay in the car, so I don't count that one), and that one had changed my life. I never told Dewey about it, not the details, anyway. I didn't think I ever would. The experience just felt very personal to me.

I had hoped this scene would do the same, although I was starting to feel like we might have wasted our time.

The same thought apparently popped into Dewey's mind. "I don't get it, Abe," he said. "What's the point in us comin' all this way if we ain't gonna go inside the actual crime scene?"

"You're thinkin' it all wrong," I replied. "There won't be any clues left inside that tape. The police spent hours going over everythin' to make sure they found everything. What we're hopin' for is that they didn't make the crime-scene boundary big enough."

Dewey frowned. "Sounds pretty lame," he said. "Police aren't dumb. They ain't gonna accidentally tape up a spot that's too small."

"According to the book I just finished, it happens all the time."

"Wow," Dewey said. "The police must be dumber than I thought."

We had almost walked all the way around the scene when Dewey piped up again. "Abe, what are we doin' here?"

I shook my head. "We've been through this, Dewey. We're lookin' for stuff the police might have missed."

"What kind of stuff?"

"I don't know. I won't know until I see it." We came to the edge of the forest and had to turn around and trace the same route back. Again, I went slowly, this time with Dewey in front. I scanned the ground and the trees and everything else around me as we went. The humidity from the swamp started making me feel a little sick, but I didn't want to leave until we found something.

"I think I am remembering bein' here before now," Dewey said. "Only, we never came down that path. We were on the other side of the swamp, weren't we?"

"Yep," I said. I knew eventually it would come to him.

"Wasn't that the day we got lost?"

"Yep."

"Certainly easier now with a path."

"Yep."

"That was the day my arms got so bloody from all the thorny vines and brambles, right?"

I let out a breath. "Yep," I said, watching a drop of blood run down his arm onto the back of his hand.

"How come we didn't take that path back instead of just pushing our way blindly through the woods? Would've been much easier."

I thought about this. We were coming back around the crime scene, and I tried to find the path in the trees and bushes, but I couldn't. Not until we were looking directly at it. "My guess is, we missed it," I said. "It's not easy to see unless you're looking directly at it."

Dewey laughed. "The paths we make are even harder to see. When we just push through and avoid all the big tree trunks, everything springs right back to how it was before we walked through it."

Something like a spotlight turned on in my head. Dewey just brought to mind what I was reminded of when I saw them bushes that ran along the path.

"No, Dewey, you're wrong," I said excitedly, increasing my pace. "The bushes don't snap right back. They kind of do, but never exactly the same as they were before we bent and broke them. Usually, they look like a bear or something forced his way through when we're done."

"What're you so happy 'bout?" he asked as I passed him in my race to get back to the edge of the path.

"Look." I pointed to the bent and flattened undergrowth and the busted branches of some low and spindly trees. The briar and the blackberries subtly curved backward from each other where you could tell they at one time interlaced. "Someone's recently made a path like we always do. Right through here."

"You mean the Stickman?"

I nodded enthusiastically. "I reckon he never left that wheelbarrow behind when the path narrowed, he just pushed it straight through all the brambles and thistles, making his own path. He probably didn't want to carry a dead body all the way to the swamp."

"How come your ma never noticed this?"

That thought had already occurred to me, although my mother seemed to do very little at this site, going by the reports. Pretty much everything was covered by Officer Chris. Still, why hadn't *he* noticed that someone had forged through the woods beside the narrow path? And, just like what usually happens when I ask my brain a question, it came back with an answer.

"I reckon the police didn't see this path for two reasons, Dewey. The first bein' they didn't *need* to. They just assumed because there was a trail, the Stickman used it. They probably didn't care enough 'bout how he got to the crime scene, just that he had. Everything they needed to investigate happened on the edge of the swamp."

"That makes sense, I s'pose. What's the second reason?"

"Second reason, Dewey, is that they ain't thirteen years old. They wouldn't even think of trudging through a bunch of tangled-up briar and bushes and thistles and thorns when a perfectly good path is available."

"So why would the Stickman?"

I let that thought settle in my head until I realized my brain wasn't going to answer that one. "I don't know. Maybe he *had* to use the wheelbarrow. Maybe he couldn't carry the body for some reason. But look, you can tell where he came right through. It's obvious now that I know what I'm looking for. See the way everything's pushed back and forth just a little bit?"

"Just like when we do it," Dewey said.

"Yep. For sure!"

I began walking around the perimeter with the Polaroid camera.

"What're you doin' now?"

"Documentin' stuff. Seein' if there's anythin' else my mom's team could've missed." I glanced around the area. Then I remembered something from *Understanding Forensics:* Crime scenes are three-dimensional, you can't forget to look up and down.

I looked up and saw two crows dive-bombing a hawk. That was interestin' and all, but not really what I was lookin' for. Then, when I looked down, I found something. "Dewey!"

"What?"

"Look at these stones. They almost form a path right to near where the marker for the body is. I reckon the killer used these so he wouldn't leave tracks in the muck."

"Now, how do you know that?"

"Because, look at *that* one." I pointed to the second one in. "It's got part of a footprint on it."

"Don't you mean 'shoe print'?" Dewey asked.

"Whatever," I said and snapped a photo of it. I took photos of other things, too, but nothin' that excited me as much as that shoe print and findin' the killer's *real* path. I went and looked at where he *really* parked that wheelbarrow one last time.

Dewey followed me, coming in close, stepping over some of the bramble and a tangle of strangler fig. He was looking at the blackberry bushes that I figured looked like they were torn apart from embracing each other.

"Man," he said. "This stuff would've really cut up his arms."

"Yeah, but he's probably not a baby like you. Thorns

don't really cut that deep. Only takes a day or two before the marks on your body disappear forever."

Dewey stared intently at one of the blackberry bushes. I had no idea what was so captivating about it.

"What're you doin'?" I asked.

"Abe," he said, his voice slow, with a hint of astonishment to it.

"What?" I answered impatiently.

"Look."

I stepped into the bush a ways and came up beside him, nearly tripping myself into a prickle bush from my shoe getting caught in a web of scrub and vines. As it was, one of the thorny blackberry branches got me pretty good. Now my arm had little rivulets of blood rolling down it, too. "What?" I asked, hearing frustration and anger in my voice.

"Look," he said again.

His eyes were as big as donuts. I followed his gaze to where he carefully held out a blackberry branch with two fingers, each positioned on either side of a particularly sharp-looking thorn. Farther down the vine, a sprout of leaves shot off. It was these leaves that had his attention, and now I saw why.

One of them, a rather big one, looked like it had received a big drop of poster paint.

The splotch was bigger than a quarter, and it was red.

"Do you know what we just found?" he asked.

"I'm not a hundred percent positive, Dewey, but I think I do, yes."

"It's blood," he said.

"Yep," I agreed. "Sure looks that way."

His eyes slowly left the leaf and rose to meet mine. "It's from the Stickman," he said. "We found some of the Stickman's blood!"

I took a deep breath. It certainly looked that way, I had to admit. Now a new thought formed in my head. And that was, how the hell was I going to explain this to my mother?

And once again, this was a question my brain decided to just pass on answering.

CHAPTER 40

Carry and Jonathon sat on the edge of Carry's bed in her bedroom, something Carry's mother only recently allowed. They still had to keep the door partway open. Carry had no idea what was going through her mother's head. If she was going to have sex, she certainly wouldn't do it in her bedroom, especially when everyone else was home. But since her mother had been so good about welcoming Jonathon into the family, Carry decided not to confront her on the issue. She was learning to pick her battles.

Hung around the room, three posters featured pictures of the bands INXS, Guns N' Roses, and Def Leppard. Carry didn't really listen to any of their music anymore—TV was much more important to her now than music—but she had nothing to put up in their place.

Her curtains were pink, matching the comforter on her bed. She had one tall chest of drawers in a corner of the room and a dresser with a half-moon mirror sitting against a wall. Her white closet doors were completely shut. The floor in here was hardwood, the same as it was in Abe's bedroom and the hall. A pile of clothes loomed on the floor, beside an empty laundry basket she had stolen from her mother's room.

"Running away from home?" Jonathon asked, looking at the clothes.

"No, that's just what I wear on a regular basis. It's easier to sift through the pile than to try and pull anything out of my dresser. The only thing not in the pile is underwear and socks."

The light coming in from her window sparkled off the purple gemstone of her promise ring. Constantly, she found her eyes drawn to it. Her mother had had an entirely different opinion when Carry had shown it to her. Carry could tell right away it bothered her. The only thing she said, though, was, "Isn't it a bit early? Aren't you a little young for lifetime promises?"

Jonathon looked at the pile of clothes. "I don't think this has anythin' to do with convenience," he said. "I think you have hoarder tendencies."

She looked at the rest of her room. Other than a stack of books on top of her dresser, it was pretty near spotless. She decided not to argue the point, though.

"Okay," he said, pulling up his legs and crossing them. "So show me."

"Show you what?"

"Your poetry. You said you would."

"I think my words were 'I'll think 'bout it'," she said.

"Well, think about it right now, really fast, and then show me your poems."

"Are you *sure* you want to read them? They really suck, actually."

"I'm sure they don't, and yes, I'm sure I do."

Carry got down on her knees and pulled a box from beneath her bed. It was slightly larger than a shoe box and covered with polka dots of all different sizes and colors. She put it down on the bed between her and Jonathon. "This contains all my poetry and my journal . . ." she said, hesitantly.

"You keep a journal?"

"I used to. Until I met you."

"Why did you stop?"

"Because I became too wrapped up in us. I didn't need to write 'bout the things we did or document 'em. I have them all in my memories."

"Are they good memories?"

"Do you have to ask?"

Jonathon shook his head. "I was just kiddin'. Okay, read me one of your poems."

Carry felt her face flush. "I'm not goin' to read them to you. It's bad enough I'm goin' to show 'em to you."

"Okay, fine. *I'll* read them. Give me one."

"Hang on," Carry said, going through the pages one at a time. "Let me find one that's not completely abysmal." She stopped about ten pages in. "Okay, this one's not *too* terrible. Here." She handed a piece of paper to Jonathon.

" 'Post War'," he read aloud after clearing his throat.

"Don't *read* it," Carry said.

"What do you mean? Of course I'm goin' to read it."

"I mean out loud. Just read it in your head."

"No, good poetry is meant to be read out loud."

"I keep telling you, this isn't good poetry."

"Doesn't matter, I'm reading it out loud anyway." He read:

Post War

I hate waking up alone
With the blankets on my side all thrown this
    way and that
As though they spent the night on a ship
And weathered a thunderstorm
My pillows, one barely on the bed
The other fallen to the floor like a bomb
Then looking over at your side where
    everything's still perfect
Pristine and untouched
And you
All gone

"I told you they were depressing," Carry said.

"It's beautiful," Jonathon said.

Carry felt heat rise to her face. "No, it's lame. I'm a lame poet."

"Let's see some more."

"No, one is all you get."

"Please," Jonathon begged. "Just one more."

Carry huffed. "Okay, *one* more and that's it. I do have to say, though, they sound better with you reading them than they do in my head." She went through the pages in the box again. "Okay, here's another depressin' one. I reckon you'll be all depressed out by the time you finish it. And this is the *last* one you're readin'. Understand?"

"Understood." Jonathon took the paper and began to read. " 'Dead Ends.' Well," he said, "at least the title isn't too depressing." He laughed.

Carry hit him with one of her pillows. "I told you, pretty much *all* my poetry is depressing."

"Fine, let me read it." And so, Jonathon did:

DEAD ENDS

Night settles in like frost on a hillside
The moon's a steel blade in the sky
Surrounded by a twisted band of headlights
Roaming the streets
Each one throws a shadow as you walk
Searching for that little bag of gold
Passing by those who came before
The unlucky ones
The ones you'll never really know
Because you don't even get close enough
Except
Your shadow's not that long
Check where the lines on your palm intersect
One runs north like Interstate 5
The other east like Route 66
But both
Eventually stop
At dead ends

"You definitely have a knack for writing poetry to kill kittens by," Jonathon said.

Carry hit him with her pillow again. "That's not nice."

"No, actually I think you're very talented. Maybe you should just try writing something happy for a change."

"Okay," Carry said. "Maybe I will. Maybe I'll write *you* a poem."

"I'd like that. Maybe somethin' about how fantastic I am." He smiled.

Carry slammed the pillow into his head one more time.

CHAPTER 41

Me and Dewey brought the bloody leaf back to my house. We had been very careful to break the branch and not touch the leaf and to package it properly, the way the book had explained.

We had a slight argument as to whose initials should go on the evidence, mine or Dewey's, on account of *he* actually found the blood but *I* was the one who figured out it was probably the most important piece of evidence left at the entire crime scene.

"Okay," Dewey said. "So, what do we do now?"

I got my forensics book from where it was lying on the table beside my bed. "First thing we need to do is test it to see if it's real blood."

"How do we do that?"

"Something called a 'Luminol Chemiluminescence Test'," I said, reading from the book. I tripped badly over that second word.

"Sounds complicated."

"Actually, it's not. We just take a very small piece of the sample and spray it with one of the fluids that came with the forensics kit. If it's blood, it will glow with a bluish color for thirty seconds or so."

Dewey was picking through the kit that sat on the table we'd set up. "Which liquid?"

I pulled out the empty spray container. "We need to mix a few liquids into the spray bottle." I read the list from *Understanding Forensics* while he got them all ready.

"Okay, now we just need to use the eyedropper to mix 'em," I said after Dewey had extracted them all from the box. "Then we spray a small sample of the blood we found."

Luckily, the leaf had a *lot* of blood on it, so we were able to just tear off a little piece without disturbing the rest. I carefully mixed the solution in the small spray bottle before turning off my bedroom light and drawing my curtains.

"Whatcha doin' all that for?" Dewey asked.

"We need to be able to see it glow," I answered. "Reckon that's easier to do with the lights off."

I moistened a small pad with another chemical from the kit, and we placed the blood sample on it before spraying it. Sure enough, I saw a faint glowing bluish color. "Dewey! Do you see that? It really *is* blood!"

"What did you 'spect it would be, Abe? Of course it's blood."

I suppose he had a point, but still, this was our first attempt at using the stuff from the kit for any sort of serious detective work. It felt good to know something I learned had turned out to be of some importance.

Now a new thought formed in my mind: How were we going to present this bloody leaf to my mother without getting in trouble for investigating an active crime scene? I would be forced to tell her I'd read her files.

Dewey must've had the same thought. "We gotta give it to your ma," he said.

I frowned. "I know. I just don't know . . . What we need to do next is harder than any forensic work I can think of."

"What's that?"

"Sellin' this story to my mom. She's not going to be happy with us."

"But we found a major piece of evidence."

"Doesn't matter. We still went somewhere I'm pretty sure we weren't s'posed to. Not to mention I went through her files. She won't like that one bit."

"But—I don't—"

I cut him off. "Don't try too hard to figure it out, Dewey," I said. "It don't make sense and it won't make sense. That's how it is sometimes when it comes to grown-ups."

CHAPTER 42

It had been two days since Leah found the body of Samantha Hughes on the southern edge of the ravine where the Anikawa ran dark and deep, and the image of the woman's backwardly bent body staked into the riverbank still haunted her. For the past two nights, she'd woken up in sweats, the nightmare lingering like an abandoned cat looking for food.

She'd lost another one, and this one happened right in her search area. Unlike Abilene Williams, victim number ten, Leah couldn't blame anyone else for not stopping the killer. She'd only been moments away from the scene when the Stickman dumped the body.

Moments.

So much can happen in so little time.

Now she sat at her desk, lost in these thoughts, as her eyes roamed the small scene of Main Street she could see out the window on this clear, blue day.

She'd gotten into work around eight this morning, deciding not to even try and go back to sleep when she woke up early. Sleep was the place where dead bodies lay to be found, where killers snatched the lives of victims just before Leah had the chance to catch them.

Sleep made her relive that Independence Day murder. Over and over.

She decided not to give it another chance. And so, she got up, got ready to go, and came to work.

Now it was nine-thirty, and the echoes of her nightmares still refused to stop snapping at her. She felt helpless and useless, like the weight of all the victims fell squarely on her shoulders and, even if this wasn't true, she definitely had to take responsibility for Samantha Hughes.

She had been so close to catching the Stickman. So close, she saw the dust kicked up by his automobile.

But she might as well have been miles away for the good it did her.

The door to the station opened and Chris came inside, his black cropped hair shiny with sweat. "Damn, it's hot out there already," Chris said with a smile. "Not that I'm complainin'. I'll take this over all that rain any day." He saw Leah's face and obviously noticed the detached look in her eyes. "What's the matter?" he asked.

She shook her head. "Nothin', not really." Yesterday she'd been the same, but she had gotten into work late and left early. The whole time, Chris had been busy on the phone and on the computer. She hadn't had any idea what he was working on, nor did she care. Like today, her thoughts had just been consumed by the discovery of Samantha Hughes.

Chris poured a coffee and took his seat. Reaching to a small stack of papers on the other side of his keyboard, he passed it over to her. "Here you go," he said. "Just like you asked."

It took a minute for Leah to pull herself from her dark reverie. "What?" she asked. "What is this?"

He frowned. "Seriously? You don't even remember

the things you call on me to do with my 'special talents'? I'm hurt."

She looked at the top page. It was a report on Stanley Bishop. *Right*. Now it came back to her. She had asked him to get everything he could possibly dig up on the man who called himself "Duck."

"Anythin' interesting?" she asked Chris after clearing the nightmares from her mind.

"Most of it I reckon was already in his file," Chris said. "The things that you're probably most interested in I've gone ahead and highlighted. Everything that happened since the report you gave me was pulled. That consists of a couple of run-ins with the police, the most recent resulting in his being put in Talladega."

Leah flipped through the pages, quickly scanning everything Chris had highlighted in yellow. None of it seemed to apply to the Stickman murders from fifteen years ago, although it was mentioned that he was questioned in regard to the case. Most of the details were left out, though, but she'd already read them in the file her pa had made. "So, nothing came up as being anything suspicious?" she asked Chris, disappointed.

"Well, I reckon there's one thing that'll give you pause," he answered.

"What's that?" She went to the next page. Again, nothing she hadn't expected in the details.

"Look on the *last* page," Chris said. "Remember my gift for unearthing juvie records?"

Leah looked up from the reports and gave him a questioning raise of her eyebrow.

"I reckon if you check out that history, you might find a little something that'll make you at least a mite happy. In fact, it might even make you wanna take a trip out to the Talladega Correctional Institute today rather than waiting any longer."

With a slight increase to the tempo of her pulse, she turned to the last page to see what the hell Chris was talking about. It took her a few seconds to process what it was she was looking at. When she did, two words came to her lips.

"Holy shit," she said.

Chris smiled. "I figured that's what you'd say."

CHAPTER 43

"So, Mr. Bishop," Leah said, setting the manila folder on the steel table in front of her. It contained all the information Chris had dug up on Duck. She had left the station less than an hour after Chris had presented her with his findings, quickly throwing together a photo lineup to show Duck, consisting of the five potential suspects Chris gave her from the Grell Memorial list. Despite what Chris had said about the one not being capable of any recent murders due to his incarceration, Leah saw no harm in including the mug shot anyway. To these, she added two more faces, those being shots of Tommy Stork and Thomas Kennedy Bradshaw—her two Toms. She had a strange feeling in her gut about both of them.

When she'd left for work early this morning, Dan had still been snoring on the sofa, and once she'd made the decision to come out to Talladega, she went back and forth in her mind about whether or not she should call him. She knew if she did, he would insist on tagging along and, although he'd proven useful in the case since coming down, at times he seemed to add needless contention, especially when it came to Gary Carmichael or

Duck. In the end, though, her conscience got the best of her and she decided not calling him was lying. Of course he insisted on joining her. Only now, sitting in the interview room with Duck on one side of her and Dan on the other, she kind of wished she'd refrained from phoning and had just let Dan sleep in.

"I'm back, just as I said I would be," Leah said to Duck.

"I'm fuckin' touched," Duck replied. His hands were cuffed behind his back, just like last time. Only, the comradery Leah had felt last time was gone. Whatever points she'd won by insulting Gary Carmichael had been used up. Or maybe Dan's presence was the reason for Duck's change in disposition. "What's with the ass-hole bein' here?" Duck asked. "I thought we went over this already?"

"He's my partner," Leah said, purposely not glancing away from Duck's eyes. "I'm afraid he's part of the package."

"Well, he wasn't part of my fuckin' package. I read the small print."

Leah sighed. "You said you'd look at some photos for me."

"And *you* said you'd leave Pencil Dick at home."

Leah's mouth tightened into a thin line. "Actually, no. I never said anythin' about Pencil Dick."

In her periphery, Leah saw Dan glance her way as his hands spread apart on the table. His mouth opened, but she was quick to cut off any words he had planned to come out with. "Just ignore him," Leah said. "You're in here with me. He's just here to watch."

Her eyes shot briefly to Dan, and she saw him close his mouth. *Good,* she thought. *Just keep it shut. This time, it's my interview.* Leah felt on fairly steady ground with Duck. Basically, she figured, the key was to pretend to not like everyone he didn't like. Somehow that ingratiated her to him.

Duck laughed, looking at Dan. "What? Pencil Dick finally has no words? I'm impressed. I thought your lips would *never* stop flappin'. Anyway, I reckon we're done here."

He looked up and Leah knew the drill: He was about to whistle for the guard. She yawned, faking boredom. The yawn was real, mind you. She hadn't got much sleep last night with the horrible dreams and all. "Duck," she said. "We've been down this road. I've got the T-shirt back at the station. Now, you gave your word you'd look at photos for me. You aren't one of those fucking guys who goes against his word, are you?"

Duck just stared at her. Leah tried her best to hold his gaze without blinking. Finally, Duck said, "Seriously? You think using the *F* word's goin' to make me do what you want? It doesn't even sound natural comin' out of your mouth."

Dan opened his mouth, but before he could say anything, Duck cut a hard glance his way. "Don't! Not a fuckin' word! I know *you* can say the *F* word, *no problemo*. You can say *lots* of things. I've heard you. Your mouth never stops movin' once it's started, so I think the key here is, *don't start!* I'll tell you what"—he looked back to Leah—"you keep a collar on him and he stays silent, and I'll look at your pictures. But the moment he makes a sound"—he nodded toward Dan—"I'm outta here."

With a deep breath, Leah looked sternly at Dan. "Okay . . . Stanley. I reckon we can do that. Right, Detective Truitt?"

Duck's eyes fixed on Dan. "Don't even answer," he

said. "I don't wanna hear a thing come out of your mouth."

Dan just kept his gaze locked on Duck. Leah was happy he only nodded—slowly—and didn't actually *say* yes.

"Okay. Mr. Bish—" Leah stumbled. "I mean, Stanley, I—"

"Call me Duck. What's with this 'Mr. Bishop' or 'Stanley' bullshit? Lady, you don't know me. That's why you brought up the shit 'bout me keepin' my word. Fact is, I actually have a whole slew of principles I live by. One even happens to be keepin' my freakin' word. But it only applies when I'm not in the presence of pencil dicks like your partner."

"Well, then," Leah said patiently. "I'm glad you've decided to honor your word this time, Mr.—*Duck*. Here." She took the photo lineup she'd put together from the folder on the table and spun it 180 degrees before pushing it across the table to Duck. Then she opened it, revealing the eight photos on the colored Xerox page within. "Can you carefully look over these headshots and tell me if any match the person you met at Grell Memorial? Actually, I'd be happy to know if any look familiar at all, you never—"

Duck was way ahead of her, going through the sheet, nodding at each image. "Never seen him. Never seen him. Never seen him. Never seen her. Never seen her. Never—" And he stopped at the second-to-last photo, the picture of Tommy Stork.

Duck's eyes slowly rose from the table until they met Leah's. "What kind of shit is this?"

"What do you mean?" Leah gave Dan a confused look. Dan just kept watching Duck.

"Why the hell is there a picture of Harry Stork in this? I *told* you. Stork was *not* the Stickman. You guys fucked it all up." He looked back down at the photo and seemed to really examine it for the first time. "What's with the scar on Stork's face? I never saw a—I mean, I seen a lot of pictures of Harry Stork back when he was bein' hunted down. For like a month, pictures were in the paper, on the TV, everywhere. But I ain't never seen one with his face all scarred."

Leah narrowed her eyes, trying to figure out what to make of this reaction. Obviously, her pa had kept things pretty quiet about Stork having an identical twin brother. "That's not Harry Stork," she said at last.

"Fuckin' *hell,* it ain't. That's Harry Stork if I ever saw Harry Stork." Duck fumbled a bit and then said, "All them pictures. I remember Harry Stork. That's his hair. That's his face. Only I ain't never seen no scar across it like that. Somebody cut him bad. Almost got his eye." He looked back up at Leah. "This picture was from around that same time, wasn't it? Durin' all the original Stickman killin's?"

"Yeah, that picture was taken in 1974." Leah looked to Dan, slightly furrowing her brow. She knew why Duck was stumbling. She'd told Dan about it on the drive here. Harry had been locked up for a year in the Mobile County Youth Correctional Institution on May 20, 1959, after being caught breaking and entering a second time, while still on probation for the first. What Chris had discovered and what Duck didn't know Leah knew was that *he* had been tossed into that same institution on March 30 of the same year. Leah had immediately added these points to her timeline directly above Harry's youth incarceration:

Mar 30, 1959—Duck Sentenced a Year and a Half in
Juvie
- Sentenced to Mobile County Youth Correctional
  Institution
- Duck and Harry were together from May 20, 1959–
  May 20, 1960

Duck *knew* Harry. What Leah didn't yet know was
what bearing this factoid had in the Stickman case. It
obviously had *some* importance, as Duck was going out
of his way to make sure he didn't mention ever having
any personal involvement with Harry Stork.

She wondered what Dan was reading from Duck's reaction to Tommy's picture. If he had deciphered anything, Dan was staying thankfully silent. She pulled her
eyes away from Dan and looked back into those of
Duck. "But let me assure you, Duck, in all honesty
that's not a picture of Harry Stork." She swallowed and
decided to push on. "It's his brother."

Duck looked down again at the Xerox. "No freakin'
way," he said slowly. "He's a dead ringer." He followed
that with a dark laugh. "Sorry. Bad choice of words."

"Tommy Stork isn't dead," Leah said. "He's alive
and well."

Duck's eyes narrowed. "What's your point?"

Leah's lips again pressed into a line as she thought
about how to reply. "I'm just sort of . . . thinkin' out
loud here," she said at last, "but I can't help but wonder
by your reaction . . . Did you ever *meet* Harry Stork?"

There was a second's hesitation as Duck's eyes
quickly cut right—away from Dan and away from Leah.
Just enough for Leah to know whatever issued from his
mouth next was going to be a lie. "No," he said. " 'Course

not. I told you. His picture was everywhere. It was just the scar that threw me."

Dan stared at Leah. She could sense how badly he wanted to say something, but she mentally gave him kudos for staying as silent as he had. She actually wished he *could* say something without ending the interview. She would welcome the help. Truth was, she was rapidly running out of things to say. She knew Duck wasn't being honest about meeting Harry, but so what? What did that *mean?* She had no clue. What difference did it make to the case?

She decided it was time to go for a different tack. "All right, Duck, so the rest of the faces . . . You never saw any of them before?"

"They're all nobody to me."

"Except for Stork. You *knew* Stork."

"*Harry* Stork," he said, then immediately corrected. "I mean . . . I . . . knew what Harry *looked* like. From all the coverage during the manhunt. I just . . . I thought the picture was Harry." He looked at it again. "Goddamn freakin' twins or somethin'."

"They are," Leah said.

"What?"

"Twins. They are. Identical twins."

"Ah. That explains it. Identical except for that goddamn gash up his face. That happen in the joint?"

Leah shared another glance with Dan. "No, in a bar fight."

Duck's eyes closed briefly, and he gave her a slight nod. "Broken bottle. Been there. You gotta watch those. They'll fuck you up for the rest of your life. He's lucky he didn't lose that eye."

Leah flipped through the contents of her folder and read some of the notes she'd made concerning what

Chris had given her this morning and what Ethan had told her about Duck being a brief suspect fifteen years ago. "Duck, why didn't you tell me you used to live in Alvin?" she asked. "I told you I was a detective from there."

With a grin, Duck replied, "You never asked me. I make it a practice to only answer what I'm asked. It's done good by me, especially while in *here*. Giving out answers without bein' asked can get you messed up, if you know what I mean."

She didn't, but she just let that go by.

Duck went on anyway. "Last thing I need is to get shanked in the food line."

Leah's voice lowered. "There's . . . You're worried about being knifed? In here?"

Duck guffawed, his laughter pealing off the bare white concrete walls. "Lady, there's shanks *every*where. You know, someone showed me last week how to make one out of a notebook. You know—a motherfuckin' three-ring notebook? This guy could make a fuckin' shank out of one. I mean, what kind of freakin' Martha Stewart home recipe mind even *thinks* of some shit like that? No, when you're on the inside, the last thing you need to do is offer information without bein' asked. You only answer what you's asked, and then only if the person askin' has seniority over you."

"Seniority?"

"You know. If he's in a better 'clique' than you. If he's some freakin' lowlife, you don't give him the time of day. They measure you by those whose questions you answer." He narrowed his eyes again, this time leveling his gaze at Leah. "Remember that. It might come in handy one day." Then he cut his gaze to Dan. "There, Pencil Dick. Some advice. You get that one for free."

"So," Leah said. "Gettin' back to Alvin. How long did you live there?"

Duck shook his head. "I dunno. Five years? Maybe? Might've been seven. Might've been three. I don't remember shit like that."

"But you were there in 1974. When the Stick—when Harry Stork was shot."

Duck gave a quick nod. "I was there. I mean, I wasn't *where* Stork went down, but I was in Alvin."

"What line of work were you in at the time?"

"Lady, if you know I lived in Alvin, you already know the answer to that."

It was true. From what she got from Chris and Ethan, Duck—Stanley Bishop—was mostly unemployed. He had inherited a house from his pa, who passed away in 1972 in Alvin, but sold it a year and a half later and bought a smaller house down in what was now Blue Jay Maples—not far from where Noah Stork lived. That was also when he purchased his yellow '68 Dodge Charger, the car matching the description of the witnesses, something Ethan had stressed was nothing more than a coincidence.

And, like usual, the moment Leah heard the word *coincidence* was the moment she immediately became suspect of the whole thing. Coincidences always disturbed her and, almost always, turned out not to be coincidences at all.

"Did you know Noah Stork?" she asked Duck.

At first, it looked like Duck was going to stumble with another look away, but if he was, he recovered well this time. "No, I thought we just went through that. And I thought you said his name was Tommy or some bullshit like that."

"No," Leah said. "Not the man from the photo. His and Harry's pa, Noah Stork. You moved into his neighborhood after you sold your pa's house."

"Seems to me, you already know the answers to most of what you're askin' me," Duck said. "But no, never heard of nobody named Noah Stork."

"Hmm," Leah mused out loud.

"What the fuck is *hmm?*" Duck asked.

"Just reckonin'," she said. "You must've been almost neighbors."

"Lady, like avoidin' questions, I also avoid my neighbors. I never 'known' any of 'em. At least not on purpose. The last thing anyone wants to do is get to know their neighbors."

"And why's that?"

"Because you and I might be smart enough not to shit where we eat, but sure as hell there's always somebody who doesn't freakin' abide by that rule. And those people'll take you down faster than a coon tryin' to cross the alley in front of your headlights. And just like that coon, there's a good chance you'll smash up your own car tryin' to avoid the collision."

Leah didn't quite understand the metaphor, but she let it slip by. "Something else confuses me, Duck," she said.

Duck looked at Dan. "I thought *you* were the one always confused, Pencil Dick. I guess it's just cops in general." He laughed, a low, almost forced laugh.

"From the old reports, I discovered the police actually questioned you 'bout the old Stickman murders."

Duck had obviously been waiting for this one. His answer came almost immediately. "Yeah? So what? Like I said, you never asked me 'bout it, so I didn't answer. 'Sides, I figured you already knew. That sort of thing had to be in the reports. Looks like I figured right."

"And back then, you denied having anythin' to do with the Stickman, correct?" Leah asked.

Duck's grin grew. "Same as I do now. Wow. Ain't that unbelievable? Maybe there's somethin' to that you oughta think 'bout."

Leah stayed quiet a second before responding. "Problem I'm having, Duck, is that you're sitting here with *inside* information about a crime you were actually *questioned* about fifteen years ago. Your car at the time, a—what was it?"

"I'm sure it's in your report there," Duck said. "Why don't you tell me?"

Leah pretended to read it from the file in front of her. "A yellow sixty-eight Dodge Charger, right? The exact car was described by eyewitnesses as being seen at the crime scene. In fact, the tire imprints matched those found at more than one scene."

Duck shrugged, his smile unwavering. "And just like back then, I'll tell you why that was: just one big coincidence. The eyewitnesses couldn't even agree when it was they'd seen 'my' car. Nor did the police have any idea if those 'tracks' you're talkin' 'bout were from the time the Stickman hammered that wooden stick through his victims. I'd say everythin' 'bout those 'facts' is pretty unreliable." Duck appeared to hold back a laugh. His smile grew. Leah wanted to slap it from his face. She was amazed Dan was still managing not to talk.

"I'm not laughin', Duck," Leah said.

"Well, I am. I had nothin' to do with no murders then, and—in case you haven't noticed"—he looked at the concrete walls around the room—"it'd be kinda hard to be in on anythin' now. You've noticed my silver bracelets?"

Leah looked to Dan and could tell he wanted to talk *so* badly. She almost felt sorry for him. "I got a little problem with all these 'unreliable facts,' Duck," she said.

"What's that?"

"They all seem so coincidental. Fact is, I don't believe in coincidences."

"Then you're right," Duck replied. "You do got yourself a problem." He let out a quiet little laugh. Leah wanted to bludgeon him with her chair.

The dam holding back Dan's words finally burst. "No, you little fuck," he said at last. "*You* got *yourself* a problem. I'm goin' to put my foot up your ass so far you're goin' to have to hire a fuckin' survey crew to pull it out. Do you understand *me?*"

Duck and Dan stared at each other without blinking as seconds ticked by. Leah kept looking between them, wondering who would crack first. Finally, Duck broke the silence with a shrill whistle echoing loudly through the small room.

"Guard!" he hollered. "Guard! We're done in here!"

CHAPTER 44

My mother got home from work quite late. The sky had already turned that purple-orange color it does when the sun drops below the horizon and the first few stars of the evening twinkle overhead. I had expected her home at least an hour ago, but she told me a large part of her day was spent driving with Dan to some place in Talladega and back.

Normally, her being late didn't bother me, but today I had something exciting to show her—the blood we found that might belong to the Stickman. I also wanted to get past the part where I had to tell her I'd been reading her reports and that me and Dewey actually went to the crime scene. The quicker I got that all off my chest, the better, I reckoned.

She had barely got in the door and hadn't even taken off her boots when I started trying to tell her. Of course, I had come up with a million different ways to approach it, only now that I was doing it for real, I forgot every one.

"Okay, okay," she said, as though I was about to show her something I'd spent my day building out of Legos or something. "Just let me get in the door, for cryin' out loud."

"But this is *important,*" I said. "Really important. At least I think so."

I followed her into the kitchen. "Okay, what is it?" she asked, taking a seat at the table. "Why don't you sit down before you start? You seem awfully excited."

Excited wasn't the word. *Nervous* probably fit better. I took a breath and couldn't think of how to start explaining everything to her. I wished I knew what her reaction was going to be before I began. I knew it wouldn't be happy, even if we *did* find a really important clue at the scene.

"You know the person who the Stickman killed all them weeks ago?" I asked her, my words spilling quickly from my mouth. "The one who turned up by Leeland Swamp?"

"Yes," she replied suspiciously. "Although I don't reckon you need to be thinkin' about that. How do you even know where it was? Did those kids talk to you and Dewey again?"

I hesitated, deciding to just ignore her question rather to lie yet again. "Remember the forensics laboratory kit thing you bought me for my birthday?"

"Yes." She smiled. "You've been reading the book for weeks. Did you think I wouldn't notice? I'm glad you finally pulled it out and actually opened the box and took a look at it."

"I did more than that," I said. "Me and Dewey set up a forensics lab in my bedroom."

"Yes, that didn't go by unnoticed, either," she said. "Just remember, I'll want my table back come Thanksgiving. With Dan and Jonathon in the picture now, I reckon we'll be needin' it."

I took a deep breath. She was happy right now. I wished there was any way I could move on in this conversation that would keep her this way. I looked over at the stack of her folders from the Stickman case, still stacked the way I last put them days ago when I finally came to the last one.

"You know those folders?" I asked.

She looked back at them. "Yeah?" she asked slowly with suspicion leaking into her voice.

"I . . . I sorta . . ." My words were coming out awkwardly. I didn't want to admit what I'd done. She was going to be mad. "I . . . I kinda went through and read 'em all."

Her expression changed to one that was a combination of worry and anger. "You did *what,* Abe? You know damn well better than to touch things that aren't yours. Why would you do such a thing?" Then she started almost talking to herself. "I *knew* I shouldn't have brought them home. I should have figured you'd—"

"Mom," I said, "listen. It's okay. That's not what I wanted—"

"It's *not* okay, Abe. You had no right to look through them, nor are you even close to being old enough to read about things like that." She shook her head, completely off-tangent from what I wanted to tell her. "I have no idea what goes through your mind sometimes, you know that? I . . . I don't even know what—"

"Mom!" I said again, only this time she actually heard me.

"What? What the hell did you think I would say about you goin' through my personal stuff? *Police* stuff, yet. You know, between you and your sister, I—"

"Mom!" I said again, hearing the whine in my own voice.

"What?" she snapped.

"That's not the part that's important."

"It is. It is *very* important. I can't trust you, and that is a huge thing, Abe. I—"

Now I started feeling real bad. She never said she couldn't trust me before. "Listen," I said, on the verge of tears. "I'm sorry I went through your stuff. But—"

"But what?" I still saw anger in her eyes.

"But there's more."

"Oh, Christ, how much more do I need to stand? What else did you do? Question suspects?" She laughed an angry laugh I'd never heard from her before. "Let me guess, you and Dewey did somethin' stupid like visit the crime scene or—"

I nodded and she stopped talking.

"What the hell are you noddin' about?"

"We did," I said.

"You did what?" Still her anger was there. In her words and in her eyes. My stomach was sour. I hated disappointing her.

"Me and Dewey. We visited the crime scene."

"Abe!" she hollered, so loud I was happy Carry wasn't home. "Tell me you're kiddin' around. Do you have any idea how easily corruptible some—"

"We didn't go into the scene!" I quickly said. "We stayed outside of the tape. I'm not dumb."

She laughed that angry laugh again, making me feel even worse. "Oh, do *not* tell me how 'not dumb' you are after saying something like that. I—"

"We *found* somethin'," I said, now wishing I hadn't decided to tell her. "Somethin' I reckon might be important."

She stopped and just stared at me for a second. I could tell she was trying to think of what to do or say next.

So I didn't let her decide and just took the lead. "We found some blood. On a leaf. We also saw that the killer didn't leave the wheelbarrow carryin' the body where you—or, I should say, Officer Chris—figured he had in the reports. He pushed it through some bushes. Some of them were prickly, and it was on those bushes we found the blood."

She narrowed her eyes. "What makes you think he went that way with the wheelbarrow?" she asked.

"On account of me and Dewey make paths like that all the time. We know what they look like. The first time you do it, the bushes pretty much spring back to exactly the way they were before, but there are small things that we've noticed that—"

"You *really* found blood?" she asked.

I nodded quickly. "And it's real blood," I said. "I tested it."

"How did you test it?"

"With my forensics kit. What do you think I was learnin' 'bout all that time I was readin'?"

"Show me," she said.

I led her to my room, where the Tupperware container with the leaf and the bloodstain sat on top of the folding table beside one of the microscopes.

"You used my Tupperware for this?"

"Sorry," I said, looking down at the floor.

She examined the leaf. "This small tear—that where you took the sample you tested?"

I nodded, still feeling bad about her saying I'd disappointed her.

"I don't know what to say," she said.

"I'm sorry I read your files," I said.

She paused and said, "You should be. Those were private and *not* your business. What have I told you over and over about your business?"

"That I should mind my own and no one else's?"

"Yeah," she said with a deep sigh. "Something like that."

"Whatcha goin' to do with the leaf?" I asked.

Another sigh came from her lips. "I s'pose I better send it down to Mobile to have it examined. Too late today. I'll get Chris to courier it down first thing in the mornin'. Don't s'pose you found anythin' else?"

"Um, maybe," I said.

"What's that?"

"We think the killer left the wheelbarrow in the prickle bushes and *then* carried Abilene Williams to where he left her by the tree. We think he didn't show footprints on account of he stepped on rocks and boulders most of the way there. We found a partial . . . Is that what you call it?"

"A partial what?"

"Footprint. On one of the rocks. Here, see?" I picked up one of the Polaroids from me and Dewey's forensics table.

My mother took it from me and examined it. "Looks like it could match the ones Chris and Ethan found near the body." She set the photo on top of the Tupperware container. "I'll take this, too."

Her tone was still very curt, and I felt real bad. I examined the hardwood in my floor and tried to think of what to say. Finally, I decided on: "I'm real sorry, Mom."

"I know," she said, giving me a little hug. "I really do. You just—you're too impetuous for your own good."

I nodded, my face pulled into her chest. I didn't know what *impetuous* meant, but I figured, rather than asking, I'd just look it up in my dictionary once we were done talking about it.

CHAPTER 45

Leah and Dan arrived at the station just after half past nine. Dan had brought a few folders from the Strangler case with him, deciding—on Leah's behest—to try and actually work during the day, sober. She noticed as they walked to the station door that he hadn't brought much with him. Expectations obviously weren't high.

She knew Chris had beaten her in because they walked past his car parked on the street. That meant two things. First, coffee would already be made. And second, she could get him to deal with the courier for the blood sample instead of doing it herself. Anytime she could delegate work to Chris was good.

The strawberry smell of the sweetshrubs in front of the station's window almost made Leah forget about the dead woman from three days ago. Almost, but not quite. The body of Samantha Hughes penetrated on that spike still haunted Leah and probably would for a long time to come. Her sleep wouldn't be the same for a while, and nothing she thought of while awake managed to fully replace Samantha Hughes in her mind. Of course, Dan didn't help by continuously telling her "not to take things so personally."

She couldn't help it. It was the way she was pieced together, just like her pa: He had been assembled the exact same way. Ethan once told her that, at times, it was actually a little scary.

"What's that you got there?" Chris asked, nodding to the Tupperware container Leah had in her hand as she and Dan entered the station. At least Abe had been smart enough to store it in a plastic container. She was still angry at him for going through the files and, even worse, visiting the crime scene. He had, however, potentially given her the best lead on the case so far. That was *if* the sample turned out to belong to the Stickman. That was a big "if." For all she knew, it probably belonged to a black bear.

"It's a blood sample," Leah answered.

"From?"

"The crime scene you and Ethan decided to investigate without my help. Looks like you missed somethin' after all."

Chris looked confused. "Where was the sample?"

"Outside your perimeter," Leah said and glanced to Dan.

"When did you find it?" Chris asked.

"I didn't. My boy and his friend did." Chris started to ask another question, but Leah stopped him by holding up her palm. "Don't even ask," she said. "It's a long story and not a happy one, far as I'm concerned. They also claim that there's evidence the wheelbarrow you reported as being parked where the path narrowed actually was pushed onto the edge of where the woods broke by going through the bushes and thickets alongside the trail."

"We'd have seen that if it was true. We'd have seen the wheelbarrow track on the moor."

"Accordin' to Abe, the wheelbarrow was left in a thicket of blackberry bushes and *then* the body must've been carried to where you found it."

"We didn't see footprints indicating that."

"The boys did. At least a partial. Here, take a look."

She handed him the Polaroid shot and Chris squinted at it. "Kind of looks like a boot print."

Leah passed him the photo Chris had taken from that same scene. "What do you think?"

Slowly, he nodded. "Have to admit, could be the same boot."

"Looks to me like the killer made his way to where the body was dumped by steppin' on rocks."

"Okay, then," Chris said. "Answer me this: *Why* would the killer go to the bother of pushing through prickles and thorns and tearing himself apart only to *still* have to carry the victim the last part of the way instead of just parking the wheelbarrow where we said it was parked? The path only went on another fifty yards or so. Maybe not even that. It wasn't like the victim was all that heavy."

This was a question that had lingered in Leah's mind last night while she tossed in her bed trying to get to sleep. She didn't have an answer. "I don't know," she said, finally. "I honestly have no idea why he didn't, but I plan to find out."

With a big breath, Leah produced the blood sample and placed it on Chris's desk. "Here's something else neither of you saw that night."

Chris opened the container and looked at the big red splotch on the leaf. "There's no way we missed something this big," he said. "It wasn't there when we investigated the scene."

"Maybe. Maybe not. Still worth checkin' out." She

looked back at Dan, who had stopped by the doorway to look over the timeline Leah had pinned to the wall. It was the first time she'd seen him take an interest in it. "At any rate," Leah continued speaking to Chris, "I reckon it's worth followin' up on. Can you make sure it's couriered down to Mobile as soon as possible?"

Chris nodded. "I can do that." He hesitated and then asked, "How did your boy know where the crime scene was?"

Leah paused, considering her answer, and decided just to go with the truth. When she had told Dan, he'd pissed her off by almost looking impressed. "He read the stack of files I took home with me."

"Wow," Chris said. "Make you proud?"

"What?" Leah asked, taken aback by his question. "Impressed that my son and his friend have about the same size brains as a dead possum on the road?"

"I don't know," Chris said. "Seems awfully resourceful to me."

"That's what I said," muttered Dan, who was still looking at Leah's timeline on the wall.

"Don't start," Leah said. "Either of you. Just get the courier here, pronto."

"Do you have a mug shot or a photo of Harry Stork handy?" Dan asked Leah. "Or even one of Tommy, although I think Harry's more appropriate."

"Of course I do. One sec." She dragged the stack of file folders to the edge of her desk and began flipping through the pages in the top two, remembering all the "*STORK*" information had been up there. Finding Harry's file, she pulled out the first page with the Xerox photo and handed it to Dan while Chris telephoned the courier saying they had something that needed to be delivered to Mobile today.

He laid it on her desk facing him—so it was upside down to Leah—and, one at a time, took four composites out and laid them beside the small face shot of Harry. He finally decided on one and, after flipping Harry Stork's photo and the composite police drawing toward Leah, said, "What do you think? Close?"

Leah examined the two. There did seem to be similarities, although not enough to make her leap to the conclusion that they were the same man. "Your composite looks older," she said. "The hair's different. And the jawline and cheekbones aren't really the same. The eyes, though. I'll give you those."

"He would be older. This composite was made from a description of the Cahaba River Strangler the night before Christmas in 1982. That's eight years after the original Stickman murders."

"What's your point? Stork's dead."

"I know. Just . . . I've been standing here lookin' at your timeline and can't help but see that it nearly corresponds perfectly with the Strangler. Five years after Harry Stork's shot, the Strangler begins his string of murders up in Birmingham, not even a *month* after you've got Tommy Stork movin' up there."

"But Tommy Stork came back to Alvin at the beginning of this year. You've had a Strangler victim since then, haven't you?"

"No, that's just the thing. We're *overdue* a victim. Meanwhile, this new Stickman comes into play. Just seems a little . . . I dunno. Gives me one of them feelings like electricity skittering on the surface of my skin." He turned to Chris. "Do me a solid? That sample's pretty big. When you courier it to Mobile, can you also send a piece up to my HQ in Birmingham?"

"Certainly."

"I think that's a bit of a reach, don't you?" Leah asked.

"You're allowed to think anything you want," Dan said. "I play my hunches. Besides, it fits your timeline almost perfectly."

Leah smiled, as this was one thing the two of them had in common. She also liked the fact that it was the middle of morning and Dan was not only awake, but his eyes weren't even bloodshot.

And he'd made a hunch based on her timeline.

Then the full impact of his hunch hit her. If Dan's hunch turned out to be right, not only would that make the Stickman and the Strangler the same person, by looking at the timeline there really was only one person he could be.

And that person was Tommy Stork.

CHAPTER 46

On Friday, Leah met with Officer Peter Strident for lunch at Vera's Old West Grill. She showed up exactly at two, as they had discussed. When she walked in, despite not having seen him since she was a teenager, she immediately knew the man sitting by himself against the window was Strident. She remembered his translucent blue eyes, the eyes her pa always said looked like they belonged to an arctic wolf.

Walking across the restaurant floor, Leah approached the man in the light blue button-down shirt and white pants. "Mr. Strident?" she asked.

He looked up and his mouth broke into a smile. Standing, he gave her a small hug. "Leah, it's been so long. Please, call me Peter." He broke their embrace to take a look at her. "You went and grew up. Last time I saw you, you were just a kid."

"Yeah," she said, "I reckon I was still seventeen or eighteen." She laughed. "Got teenagers of my own now. It's a whole different world."

"That's right," Strident said, "you've got a daughter and a son, yes? Here, have a seat." He gestured to the other chair at the table. Leah and he sat down at the same time. She wondered how long he'd been there. The waitress had already filled the goblets with ice water and a menu lay in front of each of them.

"Yeah, my boy's thirteen now, and my daughter's sixteen."

"Wow, where does the time go?" Strident asked, shaking his head. "And it's Abe and . . . um . . . Christine?"

"Caroline," Leah corrected.

Strident pointed to her. "Right. Now I remember. You came on the force when your daddy left, right? In seventy-eight? I kept in contact with him over the years." He frowned. "Well, until he passed. That was, what? Summer of eighty-two?"

Leah took the white napkin from the table and spread it out on her lap, taking the opportunity to look down while her emotions dashed across her face. She gave a little nod. "That's right."

"He was a good man," Strident said, looking out the window, where two girls were riding bicycles. Across the street, a man whose name Leah couldn't remember was sweeping up the sidewalk in front of Raven Lee's Pizzeria, the restaurant owned by the grandfather of Caroline's boyfriend. Alvin had three pizza places, and they all clustered right around this area. Leah figured the town had to have one of the highest pizza-per-capita percentages in the country. Strident went on talking. "Ethan tells me you're a lot like him. Must mean you're a good cop."

Again, Leah felt herself slightly blush. "I don't know. Sometimes I reckon his shoes were a little too big for mine to fill."

"If you didn't have doubts about yourself, you wouldn't be good. Your daddy used to question every decision he ever made. Drove me nuts."

"Really?" Leah knew, of course, what Ethan told her about her pa, how he took everything personally like she did, but Leah had never really fully believed what Ethan said. She figured it was always just part of his "give 'em hell, Tiger" speeches. While she was growing up, her pa had simply been the strongest man in her world. She never questioned his decisions and never thought to wonder whether he did or not. It never crossed her mind that there was any chance of him making a mistake.

Leah's pa retired from the Alvin Police, claiming it was time to face facts. The cancer wasn't going away, and neither was the worsening arthritis in his gun hand. "It's a shame people just sort of wear out," he had told her during that time over tea. "We go from being power-ful to being just . . . insignificant."

He winced when he tried to lift his teacup to his lips. Setting it back down, he decided to use his other hand. Leah squeezed the hand left on the table. "You'll never be insignificant," she said and smiled sadly.

Her pa's eyebrows shot up. "No, not to you. Christ, if only you ran the world." Lowering his voice to a whis-per, he had added, "It would be a much nicer place." With a sigh, he had crossed his legs and continued. "But, un-fortunately, you don't run the world and we need to deal with problems like arthritis and cancer."

Thinking back on it now made Leah wonder if those were really the reasons he left the Alvin Police Force. He worked his last day within six months of shooting Harry Stork. How much of her pa's retirement came from the pain of cancer and arthritis, and how much of it came from second-thinking himself into a guilty con-science?

His "crowning achievement." The death of Harry Stork.

Leah couldn't get Jacqueline Powers's phrase from her *Examiner* article out of her head.

Her pa's "crowning achievement" was quickly boiling down to shooting an otherwise innocent man dead for not dropping an unloaded gun. Had her pa already known this? Was that why he continued taking Stickman case files home for years after his retirement?

Even though Leah knew it was an act of self-defense, it still came with a massive stain being spilled over the incident. Why hadn't her pa gone for one of Stork's legs? His report claimed he'd been trying for Stork's gun arm, but even that didn't really ring true for Leah when she read it. Her pa was a good shot. Stork was only twenty feet away.

Her brain fought as she put the mental picture together. From what she'd read in the reports about that night, there really couldn't be any question. Whether it happened subconsciously or on purpose, her pa had gone for a kill shot.

Leah thought she might be sick.

"You okay?" Strident asked. He had opened his menu and started looking it over while Leah had been running through her thoughts.

"Yeah," Leah said, swallowing hard. "Just . . . I dunno." She decided to change the subject away from her pa. "So, you left Alvin to take a promotion in Mobile? That must've been nice."

Picking up his water glass, Strident took a drink just as she asked her question. He nodded while swallowing and setting the glass back on the table. "Yeah," he said finally. "But don't let them fool you. Lieutenant ain't cushier than detective. It's a lot of work. That's why I went for early retirement six years later. I'd had enough."

"That when you moved up to Selma?"

Another nod. "Yep. It's nice there. Kind of like Alvin, only maybe three times the size. But still, you can get that 'country feeling' if you want to. You know what I mean? Living in Mobile was nuts. I'm not cut out to be city folk. I've really missed Alvin since I've been gone." He looked around the room, likely for a waitress. Only two other tables had people at them. One table already had their food; the other had sat down just after Leah came in. "Who do you have to shoot around here to get some service?" Strident asked with a smile and, for a moment, Leah fell into those blue eyes. She had to exert effort to pull her gaze away. She knew now what her pa had meant.

If Strident noticed, he didn't let on. "Walden still work with you?" he asked. His eyes fell back to the menu in his hands.

It took Leah a moment to even remember the cop Strident was talking about. Otis Walden had replaced Strident when he left in '75. Walden came to Alvin to retire after spending a lot of years working as a sergeant out of Montgomery. But when Strident moved to Mobile hot on the heels of Leah's pa quitting and handing the reins to her in 1975, there was an empty hole to be filled and nobody available to fill it. Somehow, Ethan managed to coerce Otis Walden not only to come out of retirement to join the Alvin Police, but also to be demoted to officer. There was no way Walden made the same money here as he'd been given in Montgomery.

Walden had explained why he'd taken the position to Leah the first week they worked together. He'd said, "I was in retirement for two months. They were the worst two months of my life. And I've had to put up with convicts, drunks, druggies, liars, cheaters, killers, you name it. None of them compare to the hell that is retirement.

When there's nothin' left to do, your mind just sort of ripens and gets ready to fall from the tree. Well, hell, I'd rather be even a beat cop again than have that happen."

Leah liked Otis Walden. He was old and quirky.

Two years later, Walden had tried retirement again when Chris became available to replace him.

"No, he left shortly after I came on board," Leah said, answering his question. "Haven't heard a word from him since. Hope he and his family are well."

Strident grinned. "Me too. He was too old to play cops and robbers when *I* left for Mobile. He was quite the guy. Weirdest sense of humor I've ever encountered in a man. Did you ever hear the pig story?"

Her eyes held his for an instant, and she saw what her father had meant all them years ago when he told her, "Strident's eyes are incredible. Makes him good at inter-rogations. When he looks at you, it's almost like he's looking straight *through* you." Leah felt the effect now, and although his hair and the age spots on his face and hands betrayed all the years that had gone by since she'd last seen him, his eyes were as clear and bright as she ever remembered them back when she was only seventeen.

Leah shook her head and did another look around the restaurant. Finally, a waitress wearing a custom-made Vera's Burgers cowboy hat and the restaurant's uni-form—a denim shirt with tassels, worn dungarees, and brown cowboy boots—came sauntering toward their table. Leah was glad. She really didn't want to hear the "pig story."

The waitress had long black hair, blue eyes, and wore a white apron from her waist to halfway down her thighs. It had three pockets. From one, she pulled a pen and a pad.

"Hi," she said to Leah, and Leah assumed she'd already given the spiel to Strident. "My name's Becky. I'm your waitress today. Have you had a chance to look over the menu?" Her name tag actually said REBECCA, but she suited "Becky" much better.

Strident looked at Leah. "Are their Billy Bob Bacon Burgers as good as they used to be?" he asked.

Leah smiled. "You'd have to ask my son, but he seems to like 'em."

"I'll have one of those, then," Strident said.

"And what would you like to drink?"

He stared at her, and Leah compared the eyes of the two. Both were blue, although Becky's had black flecks, but there was no contest over whose were more captivating. Somehow, when God was giving out eye color, Strident hit the jackpot. "You'll probably laugh at me, but please bring me a Shirley Temple?"

Becky just smiled. "Of course." She turned to Leah. "And for you?"

Leah hadn't even opened her menu. Not that it mattered; she knew most of the choices by heart. "I'll just have one of your Springin' Sportin' whateveryoucallit salads."

"The Springin' Sportin' Rootie Tootie Fabulous Fruit and Gunswallow Greens?" Becky said with a laugh, managing the whole thing without tripping once.

"That's it. And I'm fine with water, thanks."

"All right." Becky finished writing their orders on her pad and tucked it back in the pocket of her waist apron. After taking their menus, she headed back to the kitchen.

"Your pa and I used to come here all the time," Strident said. "Don't think either of us ordered anything close to sounding like the thing you just did."

"They didn't start makin' it until a couple years back. So, I have to ask. A Shirley Temple?" From what pieces and fragments concerning Peter Strident that her brain managed to collate, one was that the man had a penchant for Scotch.

"Yeah," he said, his attention once again going to the view outside. "Age forces you to grow up sometimes. I had a real battle with the bottle for a while. Even while I worked here. But my liver finally began givin' out, and my doctor told me I had to make a choice. Keep drinkin' or wind up dead in a few years. This was just before I went into retirement, and all I could think was, if I die in three years, I worked all that time and got short-changed in the second half where I'm s'posed to start enjoying life."

Leah mulled this over, thinking about Dan. She wondered what his decision would be if faced with a similar fate. The difference between the two was that she doubted Dan even considered retirement at all. He loved being a cop. And he loved drinking, almost as much as he loved being a cop. Again, the thought pinged in her mind that, sooner or later, she'd have to face his habits head-on. At least, seeing Strident ordering a Shirley Temple gave her some bastion of hope for Dan.

Leah tried to remember the last time she'd seen Strident. It would've likely been around the time of the Stickman murders in 1974. Back then, she remembered him having a thin and badly coiffed comb-over. Now the man had little chance of sporting even that. The only hair on his head was at the sides, which curved around his ears, forming sideburns that ran to his lobes. The rest of his head was as shiny as a bowling ball.

She noticed he was staring at her, a rather disconcerting thing on account of those eyes.

"You look good," he said. "Still have that life-light in your eyes. As you go on, and the cases get nastier, sometimes that light goes out. I hope in your case it doesn't. I don't think it ever did for your pa, but then he retired young. But you do, you honestly look really good all grown-up." He smiled and took another drink of ice water.

Leah felt the heat rise to her cheeks. "Thanks. You too."

"No, I don't," he said, smiling. "I look old and bald. But I'm okay with that. My wife hasn't left me yet, so I must be doing something right. Anyway, let's talk about what we came here to discuss. You have some concerns with your pa's old task force?"

The question caught her off guard. She wasn't really sure *what* Strident had planned to discuss over lunch. She had hoped he'd be taking the reins, but now the horses had been handed to her to control.

"I'm just . . . I need to follow every possible lead," she said. "Whoever's doing these new murders *knows* about the letters. We've gotten *two* already. One for each victim. I've found one other person so far on the planet who knows about them, and he's under active investigation, but I really need to question *everyone* with access to that information. How many people are we talkin' about, anyway?"

Strident's gaze seemed to lose its focus as his mind went to work. Leah couldn't tell if he was counting or trying to decide whether or not to even answer.

"Does it matter?" he eventually asked.

"Yeah, I think it does. Remember, somebody on your precious 'task force' leaked the stakes and the stickman drawings to the press. Everyone's fallible. It could've been just a spur-of-the-moment thing, or even an accident. I just need to know if, in the fifteen years since being told the secret, any of your 'trusted' team happened to say something about the letters to anyone, even if it was in a completely benign and offhand way."

Strident's expression didn't change. "They haven't."

"How do you *know?*"

"Because I know. Trust me, they haven't." He tapped his fingers on the table. "There, you got your interview with all of them."

"No, I got a response from you."

"And I represent all of them."

"Did you ask them? *Recently?* What if they just don't want to admit making a slight mistake?"

Something flashed in those strange blue eyes, and Leah thought she might have just offended him. "Nobody has made a mistake," he said slowly, his voice rising to an almost-commanding tone. "The secret is a secret. I wish Ethan hadn't let you or Chris in on it."

"Why?"

"Because I don't *know* the two of you at all. I mean, I know you from when you were a child, but that was years ago. People change over time."

"Not usually, when it comes to their integrity."

Strident's eyes captured hers once more. After a brief silence he responded with one word: "Bingo."

Leah thought about this. "Ethan told me the members of the task force in on the holdback were handpicked by my pa, is that correct?"

Again, Strident seemed to consider this longer than it warranted. "All except for one."

"Well, then, I would say suspicion at least has to fall to that one."

"No," Strident said, his voice remaining matter-of-fact. "I picked that one, and I did it for Ethan *after* your vic turned up three and a half weeks ago. He needed someone down in Mobile to analyze the handwriting to see if the new letter matched the old, and the person we used to have no longer works in Mobile." Leah already knew about Chuck being in what Ethan called his "secret circle." She decided not to let Strident know she knew. Besides, she'd promised Ethan she would tell nobody. In her mind, that even went for people who already knew.

"You mean, he's retired? Have most of them retired? What if one of them developed dementia or something?"

"Leah, you're not listening to me. Nobody's leaked about the letters. If you have someone on your radar who knows all 'bout 'em, well, then, I suggest you take a good long look at him, because he's in a very small classroom and all the students sitting around him are honor students."

With a sigh, Leah thought about Duck and all the coincidences that had lately turned up around him. The biggest hurdle there, though, was the fact that the man couldn't possibly be responsible for these new killings. And, according to Lieutenant Stone from the Talladega Correctional Institution, Duck hadn't had many guests in the last six months. So that left him potentially talking to other inmates; however, the first thing Leah had done was check all the surrounding institutions to see if anybody of interest had been released.

None had.

"Why didn't you just tell me all of this on the phone?" Leah asked Strident. "You surely didn't have to drive all the way from Selma and back to let me know you weren't goin' to tell me anythin'."

"Honestly? I felt you deserved to hear it face-to-face.

I knew you wouldn't be happy, and if I just told you over the phone it would seem like a blow-off. This way, I'm hopin' you'll take me seriously. There has been no leak, Leah. I give you my word on that."

"You're willin' to give me your word that other people didn't let it slip? That's goin' out on a limb."

He nodded. "It is. But I *know* these people. I worked with them for years. You have to understand, this Stickman thing? It's by far not the most damning secrets these folk have been trusted with. These are folk who, if word got out they knew what they knew, their lives could very possibly be in danger, or at least the lives of the people they loved."

That got Leah's mind whirling. Was *that* what Ethan had tried to tell her in that nonsensical conversation she'd had in his office when Chuck called? What could be more secretive than this? Suddenly, scenarios—very *dark* scenarios—began culminating in her mind. They swarmed around in a miasma of shadow, and she closed her eyes while pushing them away.

Becky returned to their table with their orders. She put Dan's Shirley Temple down beside his plate and, grabbing a jug from one of the clean tables, refilled Leah's water goblet.

"I'd already guessed the handwriting expert had to be in on it," she said, trying to sound somewhat less left out of everything. "And I don't appreciate you implying that I can't be trusted."

"I never said anything of the sort."

"Yes, you did. You said you wished Chris and I didn't know."

Strident took a bite of burger and waited until he'd swallowed it to answer. "It's just a case of there bein' too many witches around the cauldron, Leah. As you continue on in your career—especially if you get out of Alvin and become a detective in one of the bigger cities—you're goin' to soon realize there are dirty cops and there are clean cops, and then there's a whole bunch of in-between cops. Unfortunately, the dirty cops far outnumber the squeaky-clean ones. But let me tell you this: When you meet enough of each type, you'll soon be able to know right away where in the spectrum any one of them lies. Your father was born with the knack; I developed it. There's a good chance you inherited it. If not, at least attempt to cultivate it. Because that ability alone will make you stand out from everyone else as bein' an extraordinary police officer, no matter what your 'official' ranking."

After a hesitation while she absorbed all of this, Leah responded, "Wow, that was some speech."

"It wasn't a speech, it was an oration on the current state of law enforcement in America today. I wasn't implying any call to action. Sooner or later, you will figure this out for yourself. If I've saved you a few years by giving you a heads-up, then this trip I made down was by far worth taking."

Leah paused again, seeing the passion in this man's eyes sparkle. The thing he said about the light eventually going out wasn't true of everyone, Leah knew this now. Because it hadn't gone out for him. Somehow he'd made it through the wickedness and kept that glimmer of truth and honesty intact.

"So, after hunting him down for a year and a half fifteen years ago, do you have *any* suggestions or tips on how I should proceed? I think you've managed to settle my concerns over the cops who know about the letters.

But since I have you here for at least another four bites of burger, what do you think should be my number-one priority?"

"That's easy," Strident said, this time while chewing. He waited until he'd swallowed and chased the burger with a drink of his Shirley Temple before telling her the rest. "Your priority should be the same as ours was back then: Find the primary crime scene. Track down the abattoir this man is slaughtering his victims in. Find that, and I guarantee you'll find him."

Leah let out a breath. "But my pa searched for a year and couldn't find it. How can I expect—"

Strident pointed his fork at her, pausing her sentence mid-speech. Leah watched as he swallowed again. "Just because people tell you you're *like* your pa, don't get the wrong idea. You're *not* him. That doesn't make you better and it doesn't make you worse, it just makes you *different*. Just because *he* couldn't find the slaughter-house has no bearing on your ability to. In fact, that may just be your specialty. Who knows? But it's vital you find it because, as we've seen, failure to leave a stone that big unturned can lead to the wrong person taking the fall."

His words spiked through Leah like a bolt of lightning. "You mean, you think my pa shot the wrong guy?"

Strident shook his head. "No, I don't think that at all. I *know* he did. So did he, afterward."

"He told you that?"

"He didn't have to. He spent the rest of his life trying to make reparations for what he'd done. You couldn't have worked closely with the man and *not* have known how he felt about it. Trust me, it's a road you don't ever want to head down. And remember one last thing, and you'll only hear this from me once, okay?"

Leah nodded, not sure she wanted to hear what he was about to say. Deep sorrow, bordering on melancholy, had begun filling her up like mushroom manure being tossed into an empty well.

"Your pa was less than twenty feet away from Harry Stork when he pulled that trigger. I know he had arthritis beginning to develop in his trigger hand, but he was still the best damn shot I knew anywhere. He didn't overcompensate the target. He knew *exactly* what he was doin'."

And with that, the two ate the rest of their meals in relative silence.

CHAPTER 47

After another weekend went by spent with Leah obsessing over how close she'd come to capturing the Stickman, she was ready to go back to work. She was beginning to loathe having time off. Any time spent by herself she spent spinning different stories about how things might've been. Shoulda, woulda, couldas. All meaningless, and all out of her control.

By the time Monday came around, her exhaustion overwhelmed her. With great anticipation she and Dan went in to the station together, someplace where she could find something else to do rather than wallow in her own misery.

"So, what's on the agenda today?" Dan asked, sounding rather chipper. He was still staying up late and still drinking each night, but he seemed to be retiring to the couch a little earlier. From what she could tell based on the bottles the next day, his amount of consumption hadn't really changed, though. Still, she was happy to have him at least somewhat intelligible in the mornings.

Looking at her watch, Leah realized she could only *barely* call it morning. In fifteen minutes, the bells at

First Baptist would ring out noon, the way they always did each day other than Wednesdays and Sundays.

She'd allowed herself to sleep in on account of she knew Chris wasn't coming in to work until at least one, maybe even as late as three. He'd called her just after she got home Friday night and asked if he could take the first half of the day off for "family" reasons. So Leah didn't set her alarm last night and slept near on through to eleven. This probably also explained why Dan didn't look like the ass end of a barrow-pulling donkey the way he did when she got him up out of bed at eight. She couldn't even smell bourbon on him. But then, she wasn't really trying hard to, and he had jumped in the shower for a quick scrub down before they set out.

Chris never actually told Leah what his "family business" was that needed attending to, but she knew his momma was coming down from Arkansas Saturday to stay with him awhile. He went on to complain about how annoying the woman was, how she never stopped fussing about stuff the whole time they were together. "And, man," he had said to Leah, "she can *talk*. You ain't never seen a woman talk like my ma. I just have to keep nodding and saying uh-huh, oh yeah, I see, of course . . . while she just keeps winding and wending sentences, weaving them like they're some sort of tapestry. I never have any idea what she's talking about. And then, there's the fussin'."

"You already told me about the fussin'," Leah had responded.

So today, Leah didn't expect to see his head poke in the door any earlier than two or three. He promised to work late to make up for the time, so Leah figured they all might as well work late. Well, except for Ethan, who might or might not already be in and, in all likelihood, would leave before the clock even made it close to quitting time.

"So, let me ask again. What actually *is* on today's agenda?" Dan asked, opening the door to the station for her. It was unlocked. Ethan actually *had* beat her in.

"Mmm, there's one thing I want to do . . . something I think I *should've* done weeks ago."

"What's that?" Dan went over to the coffee machine while Leah sat at her desk, arranging the stack of file folders.

She started searching for something she knew was in the bottom portion. "Apparently," she said, "at least as far as I can tell from my pa's notes, what clinched Harry Stork's guilt in his eyes came out of a statement given by two eyewitnesses claimin' to have seen Harry's truck at the final crime scene at near on exactly the time Crabtree calculated the body was dumped."

"Crabtree? Who's Crabtree?"

"Sorry," Leah said. "He's our ME. And I just realized he probably wasn't the medical examiner back then."

While Dan spoke, he went through the process of setting up the coffee machine to start brewing. As usual, Ethan never bothered to make coffee. He'd *drink* it, but he wouldn't ever make it. "So, what about these witnesses?" Dan asked. "Something seem fishy in their statements?"

"No, it's not that. The statements are pretty clear. Detailed. I just think it might do some good to talk to them again. See if they remember anything they may have glossed over during their interview."

"You want to interview them *now?* Like, *again?* Fifteen years later?" Dan asked.

"Yeah. I really think it's important to get a fresh take on what they claim to have seen."

"Leah, you do realize it's been fifteen *years,* right? Nothin' these 'eyewitnesses' say will be very reliable anymore. Even if anything they tell you does happen to differ from what they said back then."

Leah held up her palm. "I realize that, Dan. I *do.* But I need to do this for *me.* Because I really need to see all the evidence pointin' to Harry Stork for myself."

"You mean evidence to support your pa taking the shot he took."

She glared up into his eyes. "I mean whatever the hell I want it to mean. This is my case, and if you don't want to come along for the ride, you're damn welcome to stay here and do a crossword puzzle. Just pretend you're Chris."

Leah could tell her sudden burst of anger caught Dan off guard. He threw up both his hands. "No, no, I'm not sayin' anything. You want to go and give folks another interview based on what they saw fifteen years ago, that's fine with me. I won't say another word."

The coffeepot began to sputter. A thin line of black liquid streamed into the waiting pot. Leah stared up into Dan's eyes. After a second, she said, "You're so full of shit." In a low ape of his voice, she went on, "'No, I won't say another word, Leah'." Her voice changed back to normal. "Like you're even capable of goin' even five minutes without saying something. That's just laughable."

Dan smiled. "I do *not* talk like that. You sounded like some gorilla. I mean, some gorilla who could talk."

She shook her head. "You're such an idiot," she said and went back to looking through her files.

* * *

After several coffees and a brief conversation with Ethan, who wanted to know where the hell Chris was, Leah searched the phone books and her online database for a current address and phone number for the two eye-witnesses. All she had were the reports taken fifteen years ago to go on, and when she called one of the numbers, she got a "no longer in service" message and the other one belonged to someone who'd never heard of the woman Leah asked about.

Around two o'clock, Leah had amassed about as much information as she was going to get and had read all the applicable stuff from the files to the point she pretty near had it all memorized. She decided it was time to go and see what new facts she could discover. Tossing Dan a quick glance, she said, "Okay, I think we can head out."

"You're not *still* plannin' on visiting those witnesses, are you?"

"What the hell you think I've been doing since we got here?"

"I was hoping perhaps you were getting a little smarter."

"You really *don't* need to come with me," she said. "Go watch baseball with Ethan. I'm sure he'd love the company. I'll be back 'fore long."

Dan glanced to Ethan's closed office door. "Nah, I think he prefers bein' alone—somethin' I can certainly relate to. Besides, I can't stand baseball."

"It was my pa's favorite sport."

"I'll try not to let that taint my respect for him."

So, after another ten minutes of making sure she had everything she needed, Leah dragged Dan back out to her car. He made it no secret how he felt on the matter, and kept repeating the same thing over and over.

"You sound like a GD mockingbird," Leah quipped as they got into her Bonneville.

"There's just gotta be a better way to spend our time," he said.

"Think of one."

He shrugged. "Play naked Twister?"

She didn't answer that, just cut him a sideways look to let him know she wasn't amused.

"So, who *are* these two eyewitnesses, anyway?" Dan asked, his voice now filled with resignation. "And which one are we goin' to first?"

"Well, there's a slight problem with that question," Leah said, doing up her seat belt. She almost said something when Dan didn't follow suit, but decided just to leave it. Daredevil Dan. She might as well get used to it. Some things weren't going to change.

And again she thought of all that Jim Beam. All those empty bottles in the black bag she'd tucked away in the kitchen closet.

"Oh yeah?" he asked. "What problem is that?"

"Well, after I came up with the great idea to interview them this afternoon, I checked the phone book to make sure they hadn't moved in the past fifteen years."

"Great," Dan said, sarcastically. "And I'm guessin' they have? Where are we headed to? Mobile? Do you honestly think that folk stay in one place over fifteen years? I've probably moved three times in the past dozen."

"Yes, but Dan, I wouldn't be goin' out on a limb and saying you're the 'average' . . . well, anything. You are about the most un-average person I've ever met."

He stared straight out the windshield as she pulled out onto the street. "Thank you," Dan said. "I appreciate that."

She cut him a sideways glance. "I wasn't meaning it to be a compliment."

"Still," he said. "I will take it as one."

With a frustrated smile, she went back to the subject at hand. "See, it turns out one of them witnesses, a Betty-Lou Panders, still *does* live in Alvin. At least I hope it's her. I found one listing for Panders in the phone book and the first initial was *B*."

"Sounds promising," Dan said, that sarcastic edge still annoyingly brushing his voice. "And the second witness? What's their name? And where do they live? Should I have packed for snow? Are we headed to Colorado?"

Leah ignored him, which, on days like today, was hard. Even when he pissed her off, he managed to be funny. Stopping at the intersection, she checked the papers in the file she'd placed down beside her before fastening her belt. She brought the second page from the top up and held it over her steering wheel so she could read and drive at the same time.

"Andrea Reinhardt," she said, checking her rearview mirror.

"Okay, so where's Andrea livin' these days?" Dan asked. "I'm still waiting for you to drop the Colorado bomb on me."

"That's the problem, she could rightly be there. Fact is, I have no idea where she is now. I would've got Chris to track her down for me, but I didn't feel like puttin' this off a few more days."

"Great, he'll love that, I'm sure. So, she wasn't in the phone book, I take it?"

"Nope."

"Then how the hell's *Chris* goin' to be able to find her? He's not some sort of directory assistance wizard or Rolodex mage of voodoo or anything?" When Leah hadn't responded after a second, Dan added, "Is he? I mean, really."

"Watch," she said and unclipped the microphone for her radio, then called in to the station. "Hey, Chris? You in yet?"

Almost an entire minute went by before she got an answer. "Yeah," Chris said, coming on to the other line out of breath. "Just got here."

"Good. I'm with Dan. Listen, we need you to find somebody for me. As quick as a jackrabbit if possible."

Dan looked up at her. "We?" he asked. "I don't think *we* require any such thing." Leah ignored him.

"What do you mean?" Chris asked Leah.

"Means if you can get me her address within the next hour or two, I owe you lunch."

"All right, what do you have for me?"

"Her name's Andrea Reinhardt," she said and then spelled the name out.

Silence followed.

"Chris?" Leah asked. "You still there?"

"Yeah," he said back, the squelch squeaking a bit in the speaker. "I'm waiting for the rest."

"Rest of what?"

"Rest of whatever you've got for me to track her down with."

"That's it. That's all I got. Fifteen years ago she lived in Alvin."

There was a long stretch of silence, and Leah thought she'd lost him. "You really think I'm magic, don't you?" he finally asked.

In the passenger seat, Dan laughed quietly to himself. *Not as quiet as he should be, though,* Leah thought.

"Is there even a Mrs., Ms., or Miss that goes before that name?" Chris asked.

"No, it's been fifteen years. She could very easily be married now and still living here in Alvin."

"Nothing like asking for the impossible."

Another spurt of laughter, this one louder, came from Dan's lips.

"Are you two in cahoots?" Leah asked him.

Dan shook his head, unable to talk he thought this was so funny. "No, it's just like . . . it's like you have no clue."

"Chris," she said back in the microphone, "just see what you can do, all right?"

"Ten-four."

Leah hung the microphone back on the radio. "I swear, one day I'm gonna up and shoot the both of you," she said and turned off of Main Street, heading toward the address she did manage to find in the phone book for Betty-Lou Panders.

Panders lived in one of only a half-dozen houses sitting along a short street south of Main Street called Linda Lane. The houses looked remarkably similar: They were mostly white with sparse decorative trim, had nicely tended yards, and had absolutely no driveway, so there were far more cars parked along either side of the street than there were houses. Leah had to actually park on the cross street, Sweetwater Drive, on account of there being no empty spaces along Linda Lane. The house Betty-Lou Panders hopefully lived in had bright red window boxes overflowing with a variety of colored flowers, mostly purple, yellow, and red.

Leah assumed the sporty, silver two-door Honda parked out front of the house was probably hers, and she was happy that it appeared the woman might actually be home. Hopefully, the *B Panders* from the phone book was indeed the same *B Panders* Leah wanted to see.

She and Dan walked down the edge of the Kentucky sage grass covering the front yard like a blue-green carpet and approached the door, both warily eyeing the BE-WARE OF DOG sign staked into the lawn.

"Great," Dan said, the sarcasm still not gone. "I can think of so many ways this might go bad. The vicious dog sign only adds about a dozen more."

"You could always shoot it," Leah said without even looking at him or slowing her gait.

"Wow, was that a shot at humor?"

Leah walked up the wooden steps that rose to a small porch and the front door, without any indication of a dog so far. Opening the screen door, she knocked on the red wooden door behind it.

"Maybe he's inside," Dan said.

"Who?"

"The killer dog. Or maybe he's sneaky. He could be out here right now, only wearing some sort of camouflage so we don't know it."

Leah just shook her head. "Don't ruin this interview for me."

"I'm not certain it's goin' to be possible for this interview to go any worse than it's headed." He kept glancing behind him and to the sides of the house.

"What're you doin'?" Leah asked.

"Watchin' out for the dog. I hate dogs. Especially ones with teeth."

From inside the house a singsong voice called out, "Coming. Just one moment!"

Leah guessed the woman who answered the door was probably in her early thirties. She had radiant blue eyes—nothing like Strident's, but almost as intense— and short black hair with red highlights. Her bangs were longer and completely red, the same shade as her lipstick. Her black eye makeup along with the hair color made her appear younger than she was, but Leah could see the pinches on the corner of her eyes and the foundation on her face trying to cover the effects of time. She clutched a small gold-colored purse in her left hand. The wide-eyed expression on her face and the fact that she looked ready to go out on a date convinced Leah the woman had been expecting someone else.

"Hello, Miss Panders?" Leah asked.

She gave the slightest of nods as her eyes went from Leah to Dan and back again.

"Betty-Lou Panders?" Dan asked.

"Yeah."

Dan glanced at Leah. "I'm impressed."

Leah almost socked him in the eye. Instead, she just ignored him and spoke to the woman. "I'm sorry," she said. "You look like you're on your way out. We're with the Alvin Police Department."

"Well," Dan added. "*She* is. I'm really just here for the ride."

The woman looked quizzically at Dan. Far more than he was worth looking at.

"Do you have ten minutes, Miss Panders?" Leah asked.

"Um, yeah. Sure. I'm just . . . My boyfriend's picking me up any time. I thought you were him."

"Well, we just need to ask you a few questions about a testimony you gave to one of our officers a while back," Leah said.

Panders's head began to slowly shake. "No, I—"

"It was a *long* while back," Dan said with a stupid grin.

She looked back to Leah. "No, I'm afraid I—"

"It was like *fifteen years* back," Dan said, cutting her off. If his smug smile didn't go away soon, Leah really *would* punch him.

Realization came to Panders's face. "Do you mean that Stickman stuff?"

"Yeah." Leah nodded. "You reported seeing a truck parked at the crime scene belonging to Stork Sanitation and Waste Removal. Do you remember this at all?"

Panders looked unsure, but she nodded. "Yeah. I mean . . . Well, yeah. I remember giving the statement."

"What's wrong?" Dan asked.

"It's just . . . Listen. Am I gonna get in trouble if I tell you something? It's just that . . . Well, back then I was young and I really didn't . . . I just needed money. I didn't think . . . Since then I've become . . . Well, I attend church a lot. In fact, my boyfriend's picking me up to take me to Bible study."

"What are you saying?" Leah asked, narrowing her eyes.

"Back then," Panders said. "I was . . . Well, *we* were asked . . ."

"Who's *we?*" Dan asked.

"Me and Andrea. Someone paid us to say that stuff."

Leah gasped. "You mean . . . you didn't actually *see* Stork's truck parked at the side of the road?"

The woman gave a quick head shake that matched

the nod she gave earlier. "No. I—we, we didn't see *any* truck. Am I in trouble? Because I really don't want to lie, but I really don't want to be in trouble, either."

"No," Leah said.

"Maybe," Dan said, almost at the same time. He flashed a look at Leah that she didn't understand in the least. "Who paid you?" Dan asked Panders.

"I . . . We never got his name. But he gave us each fifty dollars." She paused and looked from one of them to the other. "He *said* we wouldn't get into trouble. Am I in trouble?"

"Where's Andrea Reinhardt?" Leah asked.

The woman gave another quick head shake. "I . . . I have no idea. I haven't seen her in ten years. Why are you asking me this stuff now?"

Dan flashed Leah that same look again. Leah let him take the lead. "Just procedure," Dan said.

"Well, I'm afraid that's all I can tell you."

"So you saw *nothin'?*" Leah asked.

Another fast nod. "Yeah. Listen . . . I really don't want any trouble."

"You're not in trouble," Leah said.

The woman visibly relaxed. "Oh good. For a moment there . . ."

"You just may have inadvertently killed someone," Dan said.

Alarm flooded over the woman's face. Her grip on the purse clenched. Leah saw her knuckles whiten. "What?"

Leah frowned. "Ignore him. He hasn't had lunch yet. Can you describe the man who paid you? Do you think you could give a police sketch artist enough—"

Dan interrupted her. "Leah, it's been fifteen years."

The woman looked at Leah expectantly. "Yeah, I

have no idea what he looked like. He was just this guy. You know? Sort of big. But not so tall. Maybe, I dunno. This high?" She held out a hand about two inches shorter than Leah.

"So big, but short," Dan said. Leah rolled her eyes.

"Yeah."

"What was his hair like?" Dan asked. Leah really was starting to want to take a swing at him. He was now obviously just making fun of her.

"Oh, I dunno. Sort of normal, you know? Like, um . . . normal."

"Okay!" Dan said, with fake exuberance. "Big, short, with normal hair."

"Yeah. No?" Panders gave another quick head shake and looked from Leah to Dan and back again, searching for understanding.

From behind Leah, a car honked.

Panders's face lit up. She beamed a white smile at the driver of a little red Tercel and gave him a quick wave. "That's Richard! I gotta go!" She hesitated, her expression falling a bit. "I mean . . . are we finished?"

Dan let out a big sigh. "Go. Go learn 'bout God."

The woman came out of her house and locked her door, pushing through Leah and Dan in the process. Then, without waiting for them to leave, she tiptoed quickly down the steps and raced across her front yard to her boyfriend's Toyota.

"Learn 'bout truth!" Dan called after her, his hand to his mouth. "I'm sure there's somethin' in that Book 'bout truth!"

But Panders gave no response. She just closed the passenger door after getting into the seat. Her boyfriend hit the gas, and they screeched onto Linda Lane.

"I don't think she heard you," Leah said to Dan.

"Oh, she heard me," he replied. "She's going straight to hell. That's how much she heard me."

Leah gave him a sideways glance. "You know, I'd forgotten just how annoying you really are."

"Then it's a good thing I'm back for a while, ain't it?" Dan asked and then smiled with a face full of white teeth.

During the ride home, Leah radioed back to Chris and told him not to bother working on the impossible any more. Then, once they arrived back at the station, she very carefully put a line through the entry she'd made for June 18, 1974, and June 19, 1974, the dates when Betty-Lou Panders and Andrea Reinhardt claimed to have seen Harry Stork's work truck parked by the side of the road at the crime scene.

CHAPTER 48

Carry and Jonathon were lined up at the Alvin Tri-Plex Cinema for tickets to see *Indiana Jones and the Last Crusade*. The movie had been out since May, but they'd never gotten around to seeing it. She didn't tell Jonathon the truth, that she hadn't ever gotten around to seeing the first one, *Indiana Jones and the Temple of Doom,* in the cinema, either. If she was honest, she'd admit she hadn't actually seen an Indiana Jones movie ever. Somehow she'd managed to dodge that bullet, and look, her life had still managed to turn out okay after all.

She stretched with a big yawn.

It was going to be a long night spent pretending to be all excited to see this newest Indiana Jones installment. In reality, this was the sort of flick Abe and Dewey would've made much better dates for Jonathon to go with. Any way Carry sliced it, Indiana Jones was a boy movie.

Carry didn't like boy movies much.

They got to the theater an hour and a half early. Carry had no idea why. Jonathon had picked her up at five and drove them here without mentioning why they were

going so early. The show didn't start until seven. At first,
Carry thought maybe he was planning on taking her for
supper somewhere first. But he didn't. Not that she *expected* dinner. With Jonathon, she often didn't know
what to expect. All she knew was that, for all intents and
purposes, he was pretty near perfect.

The line they were in to get tickets was long, especially for a Monday. Carry figured most of the people
weren't here for Indiana Jones, though. It had been out
for a while. The big draws at this time were *Lethal
Weapon 2* and the new *Batman* movie starring Michael
Keaton and Jack Nicholson. Honestly? She'd rather be
seeing *Batman*.

Slowly she and Jonathon inched through the line,
going around the turnstile and following the path cordoned off with rope. Carry started to see why they'd
come so early. At the rate tickets were being given out,
they still might not see the trailers before the movie.

And she had a hunch the trailers might be the best
part.

Across the way, four other lines led away from the
snack bar, where the popcorn popped that very bright
yellow color you could never quite get when you made
it at home. The air in here was thick with the smell, and
Carry's stomach gurgled, reminding her that no, Jonathon hadn't picked her up early to take her for dinner.
Just to get in a ridiculous line for tickets to what was
currently the fifth best movie in the theaters. At least
that was what Carry had read in some magazine she was
leafing through a few days ago at the store. She was
pretty sure it was *Cosmopolitan,* although she couldn't
remember seeing a single quiz about sex anywhere

within the pages. So it could very well have been something else.

From beside her, Jonathon inhaled a deep breath through his nose. "Man, that popcorn smells good, eh?"

Carry nodded, hoping his next suggestion would involve buying some once they managed to get through the line. Currently, only four people stood ahead of them.

"You want some?" he asked in a teasing tone.

"I *always* have popcorn when I go to the cinema," she said. "It's a ritual. I reckon something really bad would happen if I ever broke it."

"Like you might go hungry?"

"No, I was thinking more like one of the biblical plagues."

"Nice," Jonathon said. "Which one?"

Carry cocked her head and smiled prettily while she looked at the ceiling thinking about it. "I reckon the plague of lice. They'd infest every sandbox from here right across all of Alabama."

Jonathon laughed. "I see." He held each palm up in front of him, raising and lowering them as he judged what she said. "Plague of lice, or popcorn with movie . . . Plague of lice . . . Popcorn . . . Popcorn . . . Lice." He stopped and smiled at her. "I think we'd better get some popcorn. The lice thing's just too problematic."

Carry grinned and wrapped her arms around him, drawing her face into his chest.

He quickly pushed her away. Before the complaint she had made it to her lips, she realized why he'd broken the hug. The cashier behind the desk was waiting for them. They'd actually made it to the front of the line.

Jonathon proceeded to purchase tickets from a girl

not much older than Carry who wore a black Batman shirt with a gold "bat signal" symbol on the front. Her long brown hair fell straight down on both sides of her shoulders. She looked a little Goth, with dark eye make-up and very light face paint. Carry figured that was about the closest you could get to being Goth and still keep your job at the Tri-Plex. The girl had a brass name tag that read STEPHANIE. Below that were the words *Die Hard,* a movie that came out last year.

"Why does your name badge say *Die Hard*?" Carry asked.

"We're supposed to put our favorite movie," the semi-Goth girl apparently named Stephanie said.

"*Die Hard*'s your favorite movie?" Carry asked skeptically. She didn't mean to make it sound like the movie sucked; she had actually (surprisingly) enjoyed it. She just didn't think it would be the all-time greatest and most favorite flick for a girl who, Carry guessed, was even far more Goth when she wasn't slinging movie tickets at the Tri-Plex.

Stephanie gave Carry a sort of thin-lipped half smile. "Nah, not really. I just needed to come up with something quick. *Die Hard* was like *killin'* in sales back then. So I just said *Die Hard.* Doesn't really matter. It's just for here. It's not like it's my *life* or anything." The smile grew a bit.

"What's your *real* favorite movie?" Jonathon asked. "Or is that a secret?"

Carry glanced to his face, admitting to herself that he *could* be funny sometimes. When he really tried. Mostly, though, he came off a bit corny or campy.

Stephanie leaned forward, and her voice dropped to a whisper. "*The Breakfast Club,*" she said. "But don't tell anyone. I just *adore* Ally Sheedy. I also like *Some Kind of Wonderful,* but only because Mary Stuart Masterson is so hot in it."

Jonathon blinked. "I . . . um, I see. Okay. Haven't seen the second one, and I fell asleep during the first. Isn't that the one where the kids are in detention and suddenly, like halfway through the film, they just break out in weird dance moves for no apparent reason?"

Now Carry gave him her *I'm perturbed* look. In her periphery, she noticed Stephanie casting him the same sort of glare.

"What?" he asked, with a laugh and a shrug.

"They were *bonding,*" Stephanie said.

"You obviously didn't *get* the movie," Carry said.

Jonathon took the tickets from Stephanie. "Obviously not," he said.

Stephanie forced a smile. "Enjoy *Indiana Jones.*" She glanced to Carry. "Such a *boy* movie."

"Okay . . ." Jonathon said.

As he headed for the concession stand, Carry leaned forward and whispered to Stephanie. "Don't worry, I get it. And I loved *Some Kind of Wonderful.* It made me cry."

She doubted she'd get very emotional today, watching Harrison Ford running away from snakes and fleeing giant balls rolling through tunnels.

Jonathon finished buying them food. He slid his wallet into his pocket and turned around, a massive bag of popcorn in one hand, a humongous Coke in the other.

"Are you worried about us having to live in a storm shelter or somethin'?" Carry asked.

"Look at their prices. The next size down is like half

of these and it's only fifty cents' difference. Only an idiot wouldn't buy the extra-large sizes."

"But we're not goin' to eat more than *half* of what you've got. You can barely carry it."

"I'm fine," he said.

"No, you're not," Carry said, watching a small trail of popcorn scatter the floor behind them. The heaping contents of the bag were slowly jumping ship. Carry wrestled the popcorn from his left hand. "Let me take this. You just worry about the Coke. I don't know what the hell you were thinkin'," she said. "I'll be doing nothin' but gettin' up for the toilet if I start drinking that much Coke."

"I was thinking about how much of a bargain I got."

"Why do I suddenly feel like I'm trapped in an Abe and Dewey conversation?" She stared at him a second before adding, "Guess which one you are. And here's a hint: You're *not* Abe."

Jonathon ignored her as he grabbed a handful of napkins and pulled two straws from a dispenser, punching them both through the plastic top on the Coke container.

"Why two?" Carry asked.

"I dunno. I always get two."

"You can't use the bargain excuse here. Straws are free."

"I like having two straws. Besides, we're sharing."

Carry hesitated. "And you're worried about sharin' a straw with me? What do I have, girl cooties?"

"No." He smiled. "It's not that, it's . . ."

She waited for the rest but it never came. "It's . . ." She slowly upturned her hand as she spoke. "It's *what?*"

"I just like having two GD straws, okay? Deal with it."

Carry laughed and tossed her blond curls behind her. "You're funny sometimes."

"I know," he said.

"I don't mean in the 'amusing, ha-ha' sort of way."

"I know."

Almost dropping the napkins and the Coke, Jonathon awkwardly managed to pull their tickets from the front pocket of his jeans and hand them to the ticket taker stationed at the lectern at the beginning of a long and wide hallway.

"Cinema three," he said, ripping the tickets in half and holding out the stubs for Jonathon to keep.

Carry watched Jonathon again juggling with the napkins and the four-hundred-gallon Coke he'd bought. Casually, she reached out with her hand that wasn't holding the popcorn and took the ticket stubs. "I apologize for my boyfriend," Carry said with a smile and a snide glance Jonathon's way. "He's incapable of passing up a bargain. I'm just glad you didn't have a ultra-huge size that was only another fifty cents more, or we'd have had to use a dolly."

The ticket taker laughed.

Carry and Jonathon began walking down the hall to cinema three. "There are starving people in Biafra, you know," Carry said. "Maybe we should send some of our concession goodies over to them."

"Biafra hasn't been Biafra for twenty years."

"You understand my point, though."

Jonathon stopped walking. "It was fifty cents. For *twice* as much."

"More isn't always better, you know."

His eyes narrowed, and his mind obviously whirled

her point around his brain for a brief moment. "In most cases, more actually *is* better," he said at last.

Carry and the popcorn resumed walking, stepping ahead of Jonathon. "Not when it comes to plagues," she called out, not looking back. "Remember that. You don't want to up-size when it comes to plagues."

CHAPTER 49

The day drew on, and without even glancing at the clock, Leah knew she'd been sitting at her desk long enough that the kids would've already made themselves some sort of supper. Then she remembered Jonathon and Caroline were going to a movie tonight. Her eyes rose to the clock. *Damn*. It was going on five o'clock, *much* later than she'd thought.

She reached for her phone to call home and make sure Abe actually *did* fix himself something. Knowing Caroline, she'd probably make Jonathon pick her up early and take her out somewhere for supper.

Leah's fingers had just reached the receiver when the phone rang, scaring her so much her hand jerked back as though she had just touched a hot branding iron.

"Jumpy?" Dan asked from where he sat at Chris's desk beside her. Chris had left for dinner about twenty minutes or so ago. She figured he was likely meeting his momma somewhere, so Leah didn't expect him back soon.

The phones rang again.

"You gonna answer that or what?" Dan asked.

Leah lifted the receiver to her ear. "Alvin Police, De-tective Teal," Leah said.

"Detective Teal? This is Terrance from down here in Mobile?"

"Ah, one of my forensics guys."

"Right. You sent us this blood sample? On this leaf?"

"Yes," Leah said.

"Well, I can tell you it came back zero percent exclu-sive from DNA we got from your victim. Unfortunately, CODIS came back without a hit, too."

"CODIS?"

"Combined DNA Index System. It's a database just recently assembled with DNA profile information, sort of like we do for fingerprints. It's pretty new, so there's *still* a chance the individual who left this blood sample has a record of some sort and just, for whatever reason, didn't have his DNA recorded."

Leah tried to make sense of what Terrance was telling her. "What are some reasons?"

"Well, if he got out of the system ten or more years ago, it's highly likely his DNA profile wouldn't have made it into the database."

Something struck her. "Terrance? Is Harry Stork's DNA in the database?"

"Stork? No. That was back in the mid-seventies, wasn't it?"

"Yeah. Seventy-four. Do you *have* his DNA on file?"

"Um," Terrance muttered, thinking this over. "Yeah. I believe we do. Why?"

"Can you do me a huge favor and see if the sample I sent you matches it?"

Terrance laughed. "You think the blood on this leaf came from a man who's been dead for fifteen years?"

"He's got a brother. I'd at least like to see if it's close."

"Can't you get a sample from the brother? That makes more sense."

"Not really. I don't have enough for a warrant. I'm pretty much just runnin' on speculation."

"Okay, I'll get back to you . . . How's tomorrow? Soon enough? I'll give it to one of my guys to . . . Damn. I forgot, he won't be in until later tomorrow. You might not get a call until after six. You be around still?"

"I can be."

"Okay. I'll make sure Duncan gets it done tomorrow."

"Thanks, Terrance."

Leah hung up the phone. Dan spent the call looking at her with growing anticipation. She shook her head. "The blood came up empty. No matches with coitus."

Dan laughed. "I think you mean CODIS. Combined DNA Index System. Coitus is what we do when the kids are gone for an hour."

Leah smiled. "Oops." But Leah's mind was on other things. One was a question about this DNA database. She wished she knew whom she could exclude as a suspect by knowing whose DNA was on file. For instance, she wouldn't mind at all knowing whether or not Thomas Kennedy Bradshaw's DNA profile was there.

An hour or so later, the phone rang again.

Dan glanced at the clock. "I'm guessing that's gonna be *my* forensics guy."

"Still at work?"

"They work late. There's two of them, and I'm pretty certain they're nocturnal. Like vermin. Actually, there's a lot of similarities between them and vermin, now that I think about it."

Leah answered the phone after the second ring. Sure enough, the voice on the other end asked to speak with Dan Truitt. Leah put the call on hold. "You're right. Someone named Erickson?"

Dan punched the air. "Yes! The whole time you were taking that call, I was sitting here silently praying it was Erickson and not Baker."

"What's wrong with Baker?"

Dan shrugged. "He's just a bit of an asshole." With a flourish, Dan picked up Chris's phone and hit the HOLD button.

"Erickson! How the hell are you?" A pause, then, "Yeah? Well, that should be fun. Man, I haven't been on a road trip for . . . years. What's that?" Another pause, then a laugh. "Well, not *really*. I mean, it involved a road, but that's the only real similar—so, tell me," Dan said, changing subjects mid-sentence, "what did you come up with from that blood sample? And I already know nothing *pinged* on CODIS."

Dan listened for a moment.

"Just because I have mind powers. What did you think?" Dan laughed. "Yeah, Mobile called like two hours ago. Aren't you guys always saying you're the fastest team in Dixie? Apparently Mobile's faster." Another pause. And then Dan transformed right before Leah's eyes. He actually grew serious. "Really?" he asked. "You're not just—" He brought his hand up to his face and leaned his elbow on his desk. "No shit. A hundred, eh? Well, that's pretty inclusive." Another pause. "Okay, thanks. I'll buy you a beer when I get back. Tell Baker I owe him one, too." Another pause and then, "No, he hasn't called . . . Why would he be calling me? Oh. Well, that's great. Sure. Just tell him I already heard it from you. Okay. Thanks again."

Dan gently hung the receiver back up on its cradle and turned his gaze to Leah, his expression nearly unreadable.

"What?" she asked.

"You're not goin' to believe it. I don't know if *I* believe it."

"What?" A small grin came to her lips. She'd never seen this side of Dan before.

"That sample Chris sent up for me on Friday?"

"Yeah?"

"It's a perfect match for the one we had from one of the Cahaba River Strangler scenes. Our guy—the Stickman and the Strangler—they're the *same* guy."

Leah's eyes drifted automatically to her timeline. "No shit," she said.

"And guess what? My lieutenant's supposed to be calling me to say that now that I have an actual *case* to solve down here, I'm welcome to stay until that's all done."

"Really?" She barely heard him, she was so lost in thought about this newest development.

How the hell? The Stickman and the Strangler: the same guy. "But—it doesn't make sense," she said.

"What's that?" Dan asked, leaning back in his chair.

"That the Strangler and the Stickman are the same person."

"Well, unless the Strangler happened to drop by your crime scene a few weeks ago."

"The MOs—" She looked back at Dan. "They're nothing alike."

Dan shrugged. "Maybe that's how they're alike. By not at all."

Leah's forehead furrowed. "What? I don't understand."

"Maybe that's the similarity, the fact that they're so incongruent."

"Does that even make sense to you?"

"Half of what I say doesn't make sense to me. I don't really filter any of my thoughts."

"That explains a lot." Leah's eyes went back to her timeline as she looked at the big empty space in time from Tommy moving to a house just outside of Birmingham in August of 1978 to January of 1989, when he moved back to Alvin. "Did *all* the Strangler murders take place while Tommy lived up north?"

"All the ones we know 'bout," Dan said. "Want me to make some additions to your timeline?"

"Please. I'll let you use my computer. I have the document saved. So—this pretty much seals the case, doesn't it? Don't we pretty much *have* to go with Tommy Stork being the Stickman?" She caught herself and added: "*And* the GD Strangler?" She was still having problems believing they were the same guy. And to think, Dan's first impression was to say maybe there were two Stickman killers—a possibility Leah had been flirting with throughout trying to solve this case. Now it turned out one killer did the work of two. Sort of a flip-flop of Dan's earlier idea.

"Well, it's circumstantial, but, yeah, I have a pretty strong feelin' in my gut that we both know Tommy's our boy. I suppose our next step is to bring him in and question him. Problem is, I don't know that we've got enough to arrest him with. So far, we only have him happening to have been living around the area where we found most of the Strangler victims. It *could* be just a big coincidence. Despite how much you hate 'em."

Leah thought this over. "Let's wait until Terrance down in Mobile gets back to me tomorrow with the blood test."

"That'll still be circumstantial."

"Yeah, but it's one more buckle on the belt."

"Most belts I've ever seen only need one buckle."

"You know what I mean, Dan. If it's a match with Harry, it's just one more of my beloved coincidences."

Dan spent the rest of the evening working on Leah's timeline. By the time Leah was getting ready to go home, it was already growing dark outside the window.

She waited while Dan hung up a newly printed timeline with all of the Cahaba River Strangler information in the right place:

Aug 31, 1978—TOMMY STORK MOVES TO BIRMINGHAM SUBURB

• Noah Stork claims T.S. spent much of his time in Birmingham before move. Unable to offer clue as to why.

Feb 18, 1978—Cahaba River Strangler (CRS): Victim 1

May 20, 1978—CRS: Victim 2

Sept 13, 1978—CRS: Victim 3

Oct 5, 1978—CRS: Victim 4

Nov 27, 1978—CRS: Victim 5

Jan 3, 1979—CRS: Victim 6

May 15, 1979—CRS: Victim 7

Jul 11, 1979—CRS: Victim 8

Dec 27, 1979—CRS: Victim 9 (?)

Mar 3, 1980—CRS: Victim 10

Aug 27, 1980—CRS: Victim 11

Oct 5, 1980—CRS: Victim 12

Nov 30, 1981—CRS: Victim 13

Apr 30, 1982—CRS: Victim 14 (?)
Sept 8, 1982—CRS: Victim 15
Oct 17, 1982—CRS: Victim gets away
Dec 25, 1982—CRS: Victim screams for help, gets away
Feb 6, 1986—CRS: Victim 16
Oct 29, 1986—CRS: Victim gets away
June 4, 1987—CRS: Victim 17
Jan 5, 1988—CRS: Victim 18 (?)
Aug 14, 1988—CRS: Victim gets away
Nov 6, 1988—CRS: Victim gets away
Dec 1, 1988—CRS: Victim 19
Jan 1, 1989—Tommy Stork Moves Back to Alvin

"What are the question marks?" Leah asked.

"Bodies that we didn't find. We only assume they were Strangler victims on account of they were reported missing persons from the area and matched the women the Strangler was fond of."

Then, at the bottom of the timeline, Dan added a quick profile of the killers' "personalities." Reading it over made Leah wonder if that might be the problem—maybe Tommy Stork didn't have schizophrenia. Maybe he had multiple personality disorder.

STICKMAN MO

- Victims black/white and male/female between ages 25–42
- Keeps victim for hours or days before killing and staking
- Backward hog-ties victims (where? primary scene?)

- Kill method: .38 to the back of the skull (1973/74) or 9 mm (1989)
- Spikes dead body, naked from waist up, with picture of stickman
- Took a fifteen-year hiatus from June 16, 1974–June 13, 1989
- Organized. Batting average: 1.000

STRANGLER MO

- Victims only white females between ages 19–38
- Finds victims and takes to murder site immediately
- Strangles victims with rope
- Took a four-year hiatus from Dec 24, 1982–Feb 6, 1986
- Fairly disorganized. Batting average: .769

"You're right about one thing," Dan said. "When the Stickman became the Strangler, he virtually reinvented himself. There's nothing similar between the MOs."

"I know. I don't like it. It's not sitting well with me. Strange that they both took time off."

"Yeah, well, in the Strangler case, I'm pretty sure he got scared. The victim of December 1982 managed to scream loud enough to bring a Good Samaritan running to her rescue with a tire iron. Smashed up the Strangler's hands. That was the beginning of his little four-year 'vacation.' But, also, if you look near the end, that's when all the victims started getting away. It was as though with practice, the Strangler was getting worse at his job."

"With the Stickman, nobody ever got away." Leah frowned. Staring at the list, she tried to find more patterns. Dan stood beside her, apparently doing the same.

"This really isn't sitting very well with me," Leah finally said. "They don't 'feel' like the same person. I wish there were more similarities between the MOs."

Dan's lips formed a thin line as he slowly shook his head. "Problem is, there's nothin' we can do about that. Evidence is evidence. Unless one of our guys is an invited guest to the crime scenes of the other." He laughed.

Leah didn't laugh. "What if that's exactly it?" she asked.

"What?"

"What if they aren't the same person, but somehow work together? Maybe it's exactly what you said. They come out to admire the other's work."

"I think you're makin' it way too complicated," Dan said. "Look, when you have evidence, use it in its simplest context. Almost always, simpler is better. If there's two ways something can turn out and one is crazy-complicated with a bunch of 'what ifs' attached to it and the other is just straightforward simple, go with simple." He raised an eyebrow. "Unless, of course, you find *new* evidence leading you to think it *is* crazy-complicated after all."

CHAPTER 50

The sun had just dropped below the horizon by the time Carry and Jonathon walked out of the movie and found their way back to Jonathon's car. Above them a pumpkin pie stretched wide overhead. Off in the west, a string of stratocumulus clouds pulled apart in the firmament looking like gauze.

Jonathon hadn't stopped talking since the movie let out, almost as though he didn't realize she'd just seen the same film he had, although she hadn't focused on it enough to memorize every line the way he apparently had. More and more he was starting to sound like Abe and Dewey mixed together into some crazy robot version of the two of them that undoubtedly would've been an invention in Dewey's stupid book. *Maybe Jonathon has ADHD,* Carry wondered.

"Maybe I haven't been with you long enough," Carry said, blurting out her words in a rare space of silence, "but do you *always* get this excited over stupid things?"

"Stupid things?" Jonathon asked.

Carry brought her hand to her mouth and smiled at him in mock surprise. "Oops, did I say that out loud? Sorry."

"How can you call Indiana Jones a 'stupid thing'? Harrison Ford was in it. He was Han freakin' Solo."

With a nod, Carry said, "Right. I actually do remember some things. And, yes, I did see *Star Trek* in the theater. I thought he was okay in it."

"*Star Trek*? Did you sniff glue today? Han Solo is from *Star Wars*. You know, the saga? *Star Wars*? The *good* science fiction movies? *Star Trek*'s a flick based around actors older than my grandpa, most of them wearing girdles beneath their uniforms."

Jonathon checked his rearview mirror before backing out of his parking spot and heading up the small road toward Main Street. "*Star Trek*," he said quietly with a chuckle to himself. "You really have no idea, do you?"

"About stupid space movies? No, I don't."

"*Star Wars* reflected the human condition. The first one was a movie full of hope, demonstrating what you can do once you've gone through the proper rite of passage. And yet, what skill ultimately saves the entire rebellion and their not-so-hidden base on Yavin Four?"

Carry blinked, unable to form the concept of this discussion in her mind. "You're really goin' to do this?" she asked.

"Do what?"

"Geek out in front of me. You *know* how much I hate listenin' to my brother and his dweeby friend."

"This is different."

"No, it's the same. Next thing you know, you'll be telling me why Legos will one day save the environment by replacing wood and saving all the trees from being chopped down."

"Let me just finish what I was telling you about *Star Wars* mythology. Think about it—"

"Wait," Carry said, interrupting. "Did you just say 'Star Wars mythology'?"

"Yeah."

"You're comparing Star Wars to, like, the Greek and Roman gods."

"Yes. If you let me continue, I'll show—"

"No."

"No, what?"

"You can't continue. We'd have to break up, and I really don't want to. Please don't disappoint me on this?"

He spoke really fast. "Luke separated from the mother figure—Aunt Beru—when she was killed by the Empire—the Dark Force—and propelled on a journey of mystical training—the Force—to finally—"

"I'm warning you, I'm serious."

Jonathon pulled his eyes off the road and studied her for a moment. He must've read how serious she actually was, because he stopped talking about Star Wars mythology. "Okay," he said. "I'm done. I'm sorry."

"Let me think about your apology awhile. Not sure if it's acceptable."

His eyes narrowed while he tried to decipher whether this had been a joke or not. She knew he couldn't tell.

"Okay," he said finally, and not another word issued from his mouth until they arrived back at Carry's house.

While Jonathon pulled to the roadside to park, Carry rummaged through her purse, feeling more and more like a deranged rodent. "Shit," she said.

"What?"

"My mother's not home yet and the lights are all off, which means my retarded brother isn't home. I heard him say somethin' to Mom this morning about crashing at Dewey's."

"Okay, don't you have a key?"

She paused in her purse-digging to look up at him, once again completely confused by something he'd said. "What do you think I'm looking for right now? Fingernail polish?"

Jonathon shrugged. "I . . . um . . . I didn't . . ." He let out a big breath. "Never mind."

Carry closed her purse and brought her palms down upon it. "Okay, we gotta go to Dewey's and get Abe's key." She looked up the dark street. "I'm not even one hundred percent sure what house he lives in. Shit. Shit shittyity shit."

Jonathon didn't reply. He just looked at her with a smile.

"What?" she asked.

"We don't need to go to Dewey's."

"And . . . why not?"

Jonathon reached across and clicked open his glove box. "How soon things leave your mind. Don't you remember my hobby you asked about?" He pulled out the case that had been on the seat between them on their way to the Greek restaurant. The case containing Jonathon's lock-pick set.

"You're not really goin' to break in to my mother's house?" Carry asked.

"She'll never know." Pulling the key from the ignition, he opened his car door and started to get out. "Come on," he said. "It's my turn to show you something *amazing*."

He was so excited by this prospect he actually didn't come around and open Carry's door. She wasn't so much surprised by this, but by how disappointed it made her feel. With a sigh, she opened her own door and followed him up to the porch.

Jonathon popped the container open and Carry saw the nine silver tools inside. All narrow and thin, looking a lot like the stuff dentists used to make sure they hurt you as much as they could. Each tool had different ends. Some hooked, some went off at sharp angles, some ended at points. Two looked like slender Allen keys.

Putting his hand on the doorknob, Jonathon tried to turn it. It turned, but the door didn't open.

"Always try the door first," he explained. "When I was first learning how to pick locks, I came home early from school and my mother was out. It took me over twenty minutes to pick the dead bolt."

"I don't understand."

"It hadn't *been* locked when I got there. All I did was actually lock it. My ma accidentally left the door unlocked. Took me another fifteen minutes to open the thing again."

Carry laughed. "That's kind of funny."

"Yeah, not so much when you're sweating in four-hundred-degree heat. Anyway, so now I *always* check the door before starting on the locks. In fact, it's a good thing I did, because your knob isn't locked, just your dead bolt."

Carry had no idea you could lock the knob. She wondered if her mother did.

"Do you mind holding this?" Jonathon asked, referring to the container with his picks in it.

Carry held out her hands and he set the open box on top. After looking at the dead bolt for a few seconds, he removed two thin tools from the kit, one with a slightly angled top, the other with a hook.

He gave Carry one last look. "You ready for this?"

"Sure," she said, just very happy to have moved past *Star Wars*.

Gently, he slid one of the tools into the bottom of the dead bolt and slightly turned it.

"What are you doin'?" Carry asked.

"Opening your door. The thing I just stuck in here is called a tension wrench." He jammed the outside end into the ball of the thumb of his left hand to keep it from turning back.

"What does that do?" Carry asked.

"Provides torque."

"I see." She didn't.

"Your dead bolt is a Schlage. So is your knob. They're probably keyed the same. Just sayin'."

"Why?"

"Why what?"

"Why are you telling me that?"

He shrugged. "In case you ever want to lock both of them."

"What's the point?"

"What do you mean?" Jonathon asked.

"If folk can just go buy one of these kits and unlock them anyway, what's the point in ever locking our doors?"

"It takes practice. Not just anybody can do it." With his right hand, Jonathon inserted the hook tool into the top of the keyhole and began working the two up and down and back and forth. He turned his head sideways and brought his ear in close.

"What're you listenin' for?"

"Shh," he shushed.

Carry actually felt put out. She hated being shushed. "Tell me what you're listenin' for."

Jonathon let out a frustrated breath. "Okay, fine. You really wanna know? Your lock is a pin tumbler, which means there's a bunch of key pins held in place by driver pins in a chamber above them. A spring forces down the driver pins. The whole thing's called a pin stack. Your lock is a common Schlage, that I happen to know has five pin stacks. But just to be sure, I just now counted them. That's what I was listenin' to. Once I 'set' all five of them, your dead bolt will unlock."

He went back to work, his ear still close to the lock.

"Why are you still listenin'?" Carry asked.

"As I set each pin, I adjust the tension on the plug with the wrench. That makes the pin holes in the plug mismatch with the pin holes in the casing. So the driver pins won't push right through, locking the key pins. What I'm listening for is the quiet little *ping* sound the driver pins make when they hit the outside of the casin'. Once I hear five *pings*, I'm done."

"And you learned all this . . . *why?* It must've taken up most of your childhood."

"I thought it was cool. And no, I was pretty good about six months after I started practicin'."

A thought had been worrying Carry ever since he started for the door. "Have you . . . did you . . . I mean, we all do stupid things as kids, did you—"

"Are you asking me if I've ever used this to break in to someone's house?"

"Yeah, I s'pose I am. Is that bad?"

"No, just predictable. I've broken into some places, but never to steal stuff. Mostly as pranks. Hang on, let me finish up. I've already set three."

"Seriously?"

"Shh."

This time the shushing didn't annoy Carry near on so much. She stood there watching him, the lock-pick case lying open on her outstretched palms.

She heard a quiet *thunk,* and Jonathon pulled both tools from the dead bolt's keyhole.

"What now?" Carry asked.

He shrugged. "What do you mean?"

"What are you doing now?"

"Nothin', I'm done." He took the case back from her, replaced the two tools he'd taken out, and clicked it closed. Sliding it into the back pocket of his dungarees, he gestured for Carry to open the door.

Cautiously she turned the handle and pushed. And, even though she'd expected it to, when it opened it filled her with a sense of shock and not just a little awe. "I can't believe that's all it takes to break into our house!" she said. "Wait'll I tell my mother."

"She's a detective, Car. I think she knows locks are pickable."

"Yeah, but . . . pickable by a seventeen-year-old kid in, like, a minute? You're a pizza delivery guy, for cripe's sake."

He frowned. "I *used* to be a pizza delivery guy," he corrected. "Now I'm just an out-of-work schmutz with a really groovy girlfriend."

She laughed. "You're not a schmutz. You're the nicest person I know. A good person, even if your hobbies verge on the dark side of the law. What did you mean, you used to break in to places for pranks?"

"Um, stupid stuff, really. Broke into my school a few times, usually during spring or summer break. Got into my church after-hours. The pastor was mighty pissed at me, let me tell you. He was hollerin' fire and brimstone like the devil was handin' it out at a red-light special at Kmart."

"Not First Baptist?"

"No, this was up in Mississip when I still lived with my parents. Jewel City Baptist. Nice little church, actually."

"Why did you break in to it?"

"To get closer to Jesus."

Carry laughed. "Yeah, by breaking the law. That'll do it."

"I didn't break any of Jesus' laws," he said. "Nowhere in the Bible does it say a man can't pick a Weiser dead bolt and two brass Baldwin door handle security locks."

Carry took his hand and led him inside.

"So," he asked. "Are you impressed?"

She turned around beaming. "So impressed I reckon we should put the time we have alone before my mother comes home to good use."

"And how's that?"

"I reckon it involves some cuddling and some kissing."

CHAPTER 51

Leah spent that night tossing and turning in bed. Remarkably, she didn't walk out to the living room to see whether Dan was still awake. She hated interrupting his work, and, if she was completely honest with herself, she wouldn't really like to interrupt his precious drinking. More and more, it was becoming a problem, well, at least to her. Mostly, she thought about it at night, like this, while trying to fall to sleep.

How many bottles of bourbon he'd gone through since coming to her place, she didn't know. She didn't want to know. He was a big boy. He could make his own decisions. Unfortunately, it didn't stop her from worrying about it. But it was far easier to deal with if she didn't see him drinking. As her ma used to say, "Always easier not to look at the bear in the backyard than it is to confront it."

Dan's bourbon was Leah's bear. And she'd almost learned to ignore it. She figured acceptance would come eventually.

But tonight Dan's drinking wasn't the only thing circling 'round her brain. The sudden revelation that the

Stickman and the Cahaba River Strangler were possibly the same person dug away at her. She cleaved to the idea that they still could be separate people, even though the blood of one was found at the kill site of the other.

They don't fit. Everything about the two cases pointed at them being done by different people. Leah couldn't see a single place where anything in the timeline supported the idea that the Strangler was the Stickman, other than the big gap in time while the Stickman murders stopped, during which all the Strangler murders happened. The most shocking things to Leah on Dan's timeline were the facts that not only did the Strangler wait, sometimes an entire year or longer between killings, but he was also far more prolific than the Stickman.

And clumsy.

Five of his final nine attempts at strangling resulted in the victims getting away and, up until then, his record was spotless. What was going on in the end that made him a less effective killer? And why did he go back to being the Stickman? Was it *because* he was having so much trouble as the Strangler?

None of it made any sense. Leah tried her best to push it from her sleepy head.

Problem was, as soon as she did that, something else just replaced it. This time it happened to be the issue of Caroline's Jonathon. Apparently Caroline left her house key in her bedroom and went out to the movies without it. So, when they came back, she'd found herself locked out of the house. But that hadn't stopped her from getting in. Oh no. Apparently, super-sweetie Jonathon had made lock-picking a hobby.

"Isn't that cool?" Caroline had asked Leah after

telling her the whole story. "He has a lock-picking kit and everything. He was through our door in less than a minute."

"The dead bolt?" Leah had asked.

"Yeah. Less than a *minute*."

Leah's daughter must've read Leah's thoughts on her face, because she tried to spin it into something good. "He doesn't break in to houses or nothin' like that. Just his school a couple of times. Oh, and his church. But he said that was to get closer to God."

Closer to God, all right. Closer to the clink, Leah thought as she lay staring at her ceiling. Maybe it was just because she was a cop, but Leah hadn't ever heard of a normal person knowing how to pick a dead bolt in less than a minute. Not unless you counted some of the "normal" ones she'd met on the inside. Turning over, hoping to find a position conducive to sleeping, Leah considered that something like this "lock-picking hobby" was inevitable. She should have seen it coming. Jonathon was too perfect. Him with his "yes, ma'am's and holding open of doors and treating her daughter with nothing but the utmost respect—well, she should've *seen* it. The boy was obviously covering for something. Guilt? Something from his past? Or was he hiding something? Could Caroline's boyfriend possibly have some ulterior motive for falling into her life?

"Oh Leah," she whispered to herself, "you're ridiculous. So he picked your dead bolt. One picked lock doesn't make him a drug dealer."

But she couldn't shake the feeling that lock-picking was like the gateway drug to bigger and better things. And then she chided herself for even having thoughts like that at all. That boy hadn't done one damn thing to deserve her changing her mind on him.

So she did her best to push that one away, too. With a big breath, she tried to relax. But she couldn't. And it wasn't really thoughts of Jonathon she had to blame. If she was honest, being worried about Jonathon was a scapegoat and she knew it. The real tension was all about this Stickman/Strangler stuff.

And Tommy Stork.

Could Tommy really *be* both killers? Or even one?

Granted, the man didn't come off as the tightest bolt in the toolbox, but somehow, in Leah's mind, that made him *less* likely to be the Stickman. Just like Dan had written at the bottom of the timeline, the Stickman was *organized*. *Smart*.

But not the Strangler.

Yet, the Strangler dates matched up exactly with Tommy Stork's moving to Birmingham. And why *Birmingham?* His pa said he'd been going up there often before moving and he hadn't the slightest clue why. The only thing he'd given Leah about it was that he didn't suspect it involved a girl on account of Tommy wasn't really one for girls. Or something like that.

Well, if it wasn't a girl, what was it? She remembered what she had told Dan about bringing Tommy in. They would wait until tomorrow, after hearing whether or not the blood was a match with Harry Stork. Leah made a mental note to put the reason for his move on her list of questions.

And that was all she had. A whole lot of questions.

Shouldn't she feel much closer to breaking the case by now? It had been almost a month since the first of the new Stickman murders. How many more people would have to die before she started piecing things together? How many more could she live with? And that was the biggest problem she had with the Stickman/Strangler epiphany—that it didn't bring her any closer to solving the damn thing. All it did was raise more questions.

She was getting damn sick of all the endless questions.

For once in her life, she actually felt as though she knew exactly what her pa had gone through while on the 1973/'74 Stickman case. At the time, she hadn't really understood the lost look he'd come home with or those times when he'd sit on the sofa with the television on and just sort of "go away." Almost as though he was actually having problems getting back, wandering through thoughts and questions.

That was exactly how she felt now. Only Leah's pa had gone through it for a year and a half. For her, it hadn't even been a whole month. *Oh, Christ,* she thought. *If this goes on even another month,* well—if it did, she had no idea what she'd do. It was almost enough to make her rethink her career, and that was saying something.

Her pa had concluded it all came down to Harry Stork. And from every possible perspective she had tried looking at it, she found every indication that her pa had been wrong. Now, for her, it was all pointing at Harry's brother, Tommy. That scared part of her. Tommy was too close to Harry. What if she made the same mistake her pa did? What if she arrested the wrong man? Would anyone ever figure it out? Would it maybe happen in another fifteen years when the Stickman started killing folk again?

And why hadn't her pa stayed with his suspicion that Tommy Stork was the Stickman? She saw it in the reports. They even interviewed him twice. What had made her pa change his mind and move his suspicions to Harry? Of course, her pa wouldn't have the—in Leah's mind—quite damning entries in the timeline that almost perfectly flanked Tommy's potential career change to the Strangler.

But still, her pa's suspicions had rested on Tommy, if for even a moment. That made Leah feel a bit more confident about hers settling there now. She did wonder, though, what exactly made her pa start focusing on Harry.

Was it the statements of the two women who had been paid off to say Harry's truck was at the murder scene? And who had paid them off? She had to admit, Dan was spot-on in telling her that any details the eyewitness might have known fifteen years ago would be blurred with the passage of time, but surely she'd have remembered if the man had a big scar running across his face, wouldn't she? Tommy Stork wasn't a face you forgot too soon after meeting him.

No, Leah was quite certain Betty-Lou Panders would've mentioned the scar had it been Tommy. So where did that leave them? If Tommy Stork *was* the Stickman and the Strangler, who would be paying off witnesses to fabricate evidence against Harry Stork so he would take the fall for his brother?

Leah pushed all that away and, of course, something else tumbled into its place. This time, the image of Samantha Hughes, victim number eleven. It was a picture that had been popping into Leah's head off and on for the past six days, since she'd found her staked, topless body twisted backward on that wooden stake.

This case should have been solved before now. Samantha Hughes shouldn't have died. And the only person to point the finger at for not having the Stickman in custody was Leah.

She shook her head. If it *did* turn out to be Tommy Stork, then . . . then she'd had ample time to arrest him. She remembered the boots he brought her that she'd photographed. When she got back to the station that day, she'd compared them to the Polaroids taken at the Abilene Williams scene. They hadn't matched. But did that really mean anything? What if Tommy Stork had left one more pair of boots in his closet or wherever the hell he was rummaging that day he came out with the ones he showed to her?

And he *had* lied about the gun. She was practically certain. The only reason to lie is if you're guilty. At least, that was true in Leah's experience.

She lay there well on to two in the morning, posing questions in her brain that had no answers. Why did six of the original nine victims work in the medical industry? Why did Harry Stork have contracts with the hospitals that four of them worked at? And, here was a big one, why did the other two work at Grell Memorial? That was another one of those huge coincidences Leah hated. There was no contract in place between Stork Sanitation and Grell Memorial.

Then, of course, there was the issue of the gun, the Stickman's Smith & Wesson Model 10 chambered .38 caliber. The two slugs the ME pulled out of the victims' skulls matched with it perfectly. If Harry Stork wasn't the Stickman, what the hell was that gun doing in his house? And why did Harry go into hiding for a month after Leah's pa searched his place? Only guilty people run and hide. Unless they think they're being framed. Then innocent people might be driven to hiding.

She second-thought herself for what felt like the millionth time today. Maybe her pa *did* get it right. Maybe back then Harry Stork was the Stickman. She could certainly see why her pa would be led to think so, especially if he had the two statements apparently coming from two independent witnesses. Tire tracks at one or two of the scenes even matched Harry's work truck. But, of course, there were lots of trucks in Alvin. Not only that, but the tracks could've been made a day or two earlier. Still . . .

Leah noticed that every time she thought about there being even the slightest chance of her pa getting the right guy, it seemed to bloom in her chest like wisteria. She *wanted* him to have gotten it right, so badly it was affecting her ability to properly weigh all the evidence. No matter how much it hurt or how uncomfortable it made her, she had to force herself to be less biased. Everything counted on her ability to reason properly. And with a fifteen-year ghost of her father hovering around behind her, she couldn't reason properly at all.

She decided there and then that it didn't matter whether her pa shot a guilty man or an innocent one. What mattered was that she arrested the right man this time around.

Her mind went over the timeline in her memory. The first Stickman murder had happened just over three weeks after Sally-Anne Stork took her own life. From her pa's notes, Leah knew he thought this was what precipitated Harry's mental health to snap, changing him from a man suffering from post-traumatic stress disorder and possibly some level of schizophrenia into a serial killer. It was part of her pa's justification, as she had come to refer to it, that Stork was the murderer.

But Noah had told Leah it was Tommy who'd found his ma's body, not Harry. Certainly this was reinforcement for her suspicion that Tommy might be behind it all. And, although she hadn't ever met Harry Stork, from the reports and the discussions with his pa, Leah was pretty certain Harry wasn't near on as messed up as Tommy. You could tell Tommy wasn't quite right just by talking to him. Of course, you could tell the exact same thing about Thomas Kennedy Bradshaw, a potential suspect Leah hadn't quite let go of yet.

What was it with Bradshaw? Why did she continue to place him on her list of prime suspects?

The worst part of this case was all the damn coincidences. It must've pissed off Leah's pa to no end, on account of Leah knew exactly her pa's stance on coincidences because she had adopted the same notion: There were none. Just like the ocean tides being pulled out by the moon and then released to roll back into shore, effect always followed cause. Everything happened for a reason. Everything *meant* something.

Ethan always told Leah to go with her gut, and her gut was telling her that she'd botched this investigation from the beginning. The "dirty cop" theory was ridiculous. She could see that now. Would she look back on her "Tommy Stork Timeline" in a few days and think the same way about it? Then there was the list of suspects she'd gotten from the Grell Memorial Psychiatric Hospital, nine of which had absolutely no contact info. Could the man claiming to Duck that he was the Stickman be one of those nine?

Leah had brought that list with her everywhere she went, and when she had time, she pulled it out and studied it. Every time she did, something went off in the back of her brain. A beacon or a flare or something. There was something to the list she was missing. She could feel it.

It was the same feeling she had with the video tape on her last big case, the one that ended up tagged as the Maniac Tailor case. The feeling like she was looking right at something and, at the same time, missing it completely.

Currently, the list of thirty-nine names lay folded on Leah's bedside table. Sitting up in her bed, the pillow pushed into her lower back, she reached over and pulled the chain on her bedside lamp. Its yellow light glowed in the early morning darkness. Her clock radio read 2:30. From the living room, she heard a glass *clink* and assumed Dan was getting a refill. She decided she'd done enough soul-searching about Dan's drinking tonight and unfolded the list of names.

What was it about this list? She went over every name and none of them rang any bells. She had never heard of any of these people before. So, where was this feeling coming from?

She wondered whether Tommy Stork had ever been in Grell and concluded that she wouldn't be surprised if he had. Of course, his name wasn't on the list, but it would link him to two of the victims on the Stickman timeline. She decided that was a question best kept for either him or Noah next time she saw them. In fact, another interview with Noah might not be a bad idea. She had some new questions since the last time she'd sat down with him. One being the incorporation of his son Harry's company. Why was it in Noah's name?

Harry Stork.

The Stickman.

The Strangler.

Tommy Stork.

Only Harry Stork had a record. A juvie record, but a record just the same. And what was it Dan had said? Something about being on the inside for a year changing a man. *But,* Leah wondered, *does it change him enough to go from small B&Es to serial killing?* That's a pretty big change.

She remembered reading her pa's report where he'd

transcribed Harry Stork's final words. Something about being set up, being a patsy. How realistic did that scenario come out when Leah played it through in her mind? Sure, the gun could have been planted, which would explain the Ruger Harry had when Leah's pa shot him. But why hadn't Harry dropped the gun? Especially knowing it had no ammunition in the magazine. Maybe Harry was too scared of all the evidence being planted against him. Maybe he thought the possibility of shooting back might be the only thing between him and an escape route that night.

Her door creaked open. It was Dan. She was glad to see he hadn't brought his glass with him. "I saw the light under the door," he said quietly, gesturing to the lamp. "Why are you still awake?"

"Just thinkin'."

"You do that much too much."

Leah smiled.

"You gotta stop thinkin' and get some sleep."

"I know."

"I have an idea, if it helps," Dan said. "One of the victims of the Strangler who got away. She had a pretty good look at the guy. We got our best composite from her. I was thinking maybe we should go see her and show her your photo lineup. See if Tommy sets off any alarms."

"That was years ago." Leah crossed her arms. The list of thirty-nine suspects lay on the bedsheets above her legs. "What happened to your stance on witnesses becoming less useful over time?"

Dan shrugged. "I don't know. And you're right—she never mentioned a scar running up the Strangler's face. I showed you the composite, remember?"

"Yeah, it did have a bit of a resemblance to Tommy, I suppose."

"Only without the scar. Think maybe he covered it up, I dunno, with makeup or something?"

We don't cover our scars very well, she thought. "I don't know. Why would he, unless he *figured* on his victims getting away?"

"Interesting thought."

"Anyway, all I have tonight is interesting thoughts and questions." She yawned. "I really need to get to sleep. I guess we'll go into the station later tomorrow again. I have to wait until after six for my forensics guy in Mobile to get back to me."

Dan looked up. "Sounds good. I have a bit more stuff to get through tonight. You should go to sleep." He crouched by the side of the bed. She rolled in and they shared a quick kiss.

"I don't suppose you have room in there for one more, do you?" Dan said.

Leah let out a sigh. "I told you, I really don't want to have the kids—"

Dan stood up, his knees popping. "I was just kiddin'. Geez. You could've at least pretended you wanted me." He smiled sheepishly.

"I don't need to pretend," Leah said. "I want you. Maybe the kids'll both go out again. Actually, next time Jonathon and Carry have a date somewhere, I'll do my best to get Abe to sleep over at Dewey's. That would give us most of the night."

"I like the way you think. Now, *stop* thinkin' and go to sleep."

"Yes, sir." Leah gave him a salute. "And don't drink too much."

Dan smiled at her as he gently *clicked* the door closed.

Leah turned over for what seemed like the hundredth time and hugged one of her pillows. She was getting overly tired. Finally, she felt herself nodding off, but when she did sleep, it wasn't a sleep full of pleasant dreams. It was a sleep of nightmares. Of stakes being thrust through chests. Of Stickmen. Of Harry Stork. Of Tommy Stork.

And also of Leah's pa.

When she awoke the next morning, she felt as though she hadn't slept a wink. The parts of her dreams she remembered left a queasy, uneasy feeling in her stomach. She got up and put on some coffee, her blue bathrobe wrapped tightly around her. After Dan had left her room and she'd decided they would go into the office later, she'd turned off her alarm clock. Yet another beautiful day presented itself outside.

She walked into the living room and picked up the empty bottle of Jim Beam from where it lay beside the sofa. She brought it into the kitchen and opened the closet, hearing it *clink* against all the other bottles as she put it in the black plastic bag.

The clock on the stove told her it was already eleven o'clock. Pretty soon, even Ethan would be getting in.

Not that she cared. She worked far more hours than she ever got paid for. Besides, so many more important things pressed. Things that *did* matter.

Like catching the son of a bitch who was killing people in her goddamn backyard.

CHAPTER 52

Leah left Dan at home, with him complaining of a headache. He never used the word *hangover,* and the way he tippy-toed around it made Leah strangely angry. She wished he'd just call it what it was. She had started thinking that her hidden spite at his drinking wasn't faring her well. She either had to drop it or confront it. But, like most things in her mind, it didn't drop too well. So she decided to concentrate on something else.

Dan would be in around four, he said. It was currently two. Forensics would be calling her after six, so she had some time. After that, depending on the result, she and Dan might be bringing Tommy Stork in for questioning. She decided that, if they did, she'd do the interrogation. It was her turn. She felt like she'd learned a lot through watching Dan.

She decided to kill the time between now and Dan showing up by going and visiting Noah Stork again. She had a few questions, and she could probably just call him for the answers, but she always felt there was a lot to be gained by talking to people face-to-face.

Once again, the image of Thomas Kennedy Bradshaw came into her mind. Would she ever have gotten the creepy-killer vibe over the phone that she got in real life? She doubted it.

A replay of last night's questions swung around her mind as Leah drove her car through the winding road-ways of Blue Jay Maples. Once again, she managed to get lost before finding Woodpecker Wind. She came to the small break in the woods that denoted Noah Stork's property and parked on the side of the road, just in front of his driveway, which was flanked on either side by the same cavernous ditches that ran along every road in the Maples. The same white Hyundai Excel sat in the drive, where it had been the last time she was there. She wondered if it had even been moved.

Once again, she got out of her car and approached the porch wrapping around the left half of the baby blue house. Just like last time, she marveled at the grounds keeping. The lawn had once again been recently mowed.

Leah figured Noah Stork was a man who knew the value of details.

Before she even made it across the porch, the front door pulled open. "You're back," Noah Stork said, smil-ing.

"I am. I had some further questions for you if you have fifteen minutes?" She noticed he had his shoes on. "Or . . . are you busy? You look like you're on your way out."

After pushing his eyeglasses up his nose, he glanced at his watch, a sparkly gold timepiece. "Got nothin' *but* time," he said, and flashed that same welcoming smile Leah had seen the last time she was there.

"Not expectin' anyone?"

"No, I don't get a lot of company. One of the joys or . . . *quirks,* I guess, of living way out here. I was just taking a little break. Was going to do some weeding in my back vegetable garden, but you are a much more welcome interruption. Please"—he made a sweeping gesture to his open door—"come in. Would you like another sweet tea?"

Stepping inside, Leah shook her head. "No, thank you, I'm fine." This time she didn't wait for him to tell her to leave her boots on. She just did.

"Suit yourself." Stork led her back into the living room, and he sat on the davenport just like before, his right arm going up along the back. She took the same chair she had last time, and, just like before, her eyes went to that wall of books.

Then she noticed something different about the room. On the coffee table sat a silver and black typewriter with a piece of paper rolled halfway through it. There was a pile on either side of the machine. The one on the right was about two inches thick and upside down. She could see typewritten letters through the paper.

"You're writing?" she asked.

"I am," Stork said and, taking his arm off the back of the davenport, used it to lift the translucent red cup from where it stood in front of the stack of—Leah assumed— *blank* pages on the left of the typewriter. He took a big drink from the cup and put it back down. "You *sure* you don't want any of this tea? It might be the best batch I've made."

She smiled. "I'm sure. Thank you, though. So, what're you writing?"

Stork's arm went back to the top of the davenport. "Oh, I've been working on that off and on a couple of years now. It's a 'work in progress' type of thing. I don't know if it will ever be done." He laughed.

"Is it a book?"

He pushed his glasses back up his nose before returning his right arm to the back of the davenport. "Yeah. It's . . . I don't really know what it is at this point, I've been at it for so long. I think my original premise has changed a dozen times."

"Can I see?"

Leaning forward, Stork's arm once again left the davenport to grab the upside-down two-inch stack of paper. He handed it across the table to Leah. "It's still a first draft. Don't expect too much." He chuckled.

Leah admired the thickness. "It's impressive without even readin' it. I guess being around all these"—she gestured to the wall of bookshelves—"all day is an inspiration?"

"Well, maybe that's it. I just feel you should do something on this planet during your life that will maybe outlive you. You know, leave some sort of legacy."

Leah nodded. She looked down at the title page.

JOSHUA JUDGES

A View into the Split and Fractured Psycho-analytical Mind

by Noah Stork

"I'm guessing with a title like this, it's not a mystery or anything like that?"

Another laugh from Noah. "No, nothing like that. It's really rather dry, to be honest. It's sort of a portrait of my relationship with my son."

"I see," Leah said, still looking at the top page. "Tommy?"

"Yes."

"'Joshua Judges'?" She looked over at Stork. "Why 'Joshua Judges'?"

"Well, as you undoubtedly know, the term on one level refers to the two books that appear in sequence in the Old Testament, but that's only a small part of why I chose the title—the cleverness of turning the book of Judges into a verb." He smiled. "Something you may not be aware of is how much debate there's been about those two particular works. Especially by historians and theologians."

"No, I had no idea." Leah flipped over the top page and started reading the first page of the manuscript, which happened to be the beginning of the book's introduction. It explained how the book was a *". . . tightly written scientific treatise on the treatment, causes, and effects of mental conditions such as bipolar disorder, schizophrenia, dissociative identity disorder, and other spectrum disorders, focusing also on how these disorders manifest from infancy through to adulthood . . ."*

Leah tried scanning the text quickly, but found it too difficult to grasp unless she slowed down and read it word by word. Obviously, the man she was interviewing got well-educated somewhere. It looked in places like the typewriter ribbon needed changing. Every second or third character was printed much lighter than the rest, giving the work a very arduous feel to it, almost as though the letters were straining to stay on the page. That was when she realized the typewriter wasn't even electric.

"You typed all this with a manual typewriter?" she asked, looking up.

"Yes. I have a fascination with old mechanical devices."

"It must have taken you forever."

"Like I said, you're looking at around two years' worth of work. But let me just get back to the title for a moment. Both books in the Bible recall the tale of Israel settling in the land of Canaan and what happened during their first two centuries there," he said. "If you divide Joshua in half, the first half describes the Israelites' arrival and early battles, and the second details how the land was divided among Israel's tribes. Joshua concludes with the people committing themselves into a covenant with God."

"What does that have to do with mental disorders?" she asked.

"Well, it's a metaphor, you see. Take schizophrenia, for example. Like the Israelites, schizophrenia settles in to the patient and almost literally divides the psyche up through a process that, once you've seen it, can only be described as war."

"I see."

"If one gives Joshua and Judges just a cursory reading, it is quite simple to take them as just a sequential discussion of Israel becoming a dominant force in Canaan."

Leah felt slightly embarrassed that she didn't know the Bible well enough to even have an opinion. She found Stork immensely fascinating, though. "And they aren't?" she asked.

He laughed. "Hardly. Joshua dies and is buried at the end of the first book, then Judges goes on to describe a plethora of defeats and setbacks of the Israelites, implying that these trials occurred after Joshua's death. Judges even opens with the phrase, 'After the death of Joshua . . . ' which reinforces this notion."

"Okay," Leah said, still staring into his eyes.

He took another sip of sweet tea. "Well, the second

chapter of Judges surprises the careful reader," Stork continued. "Joshua is not only back, but he's leading the Israelites during these conflicts, only to later die, leaving many historians to wonder whether the stories actually overlap somehow."

Leah narrowed her eyes, still wondering what this had to do with schizophrenia. She was amazed someone would even know these sort of things. Well, other than people like Reverend Matthew from First Baptist who got paid to know this stuff. "I see," she said.

"Looking closer at the books reveals a more complex situation, actually, one that raises questions both historical and theological, not only about reliability as history, but also discerning the very essence of Israel's entry into Palestine. Debates on the issue range from those who deny absolutely any historical validity to those insisting every detail is absolutely accurate. Some deny any possibility of anything miraculous happening, while others use the idea of the inerrancy of Scripture to assert complete accuracy."

"Sounds confusing," Leah said. She could not imagine reading even the introduction of Noah's book and understanding it. She really wondered who would ever want to publish such a book, but she kept that question to herself.

"Oh, it is," Noah said. "There is a lot more about those two books I could tell you, but that is enough that, if you understand even a bit of what I've said, you can relate schizophrenia or dissociative identity disorder or any myriad spectrum disorders to the metaphor and understand a bit of what goes on when it activates in a person. Not only is something like schizophrenia akin to being privy to a circuitous argument of this sort, but it also causes the brain to be thrown into episodes where reliability of the senses and a solid knowledge of the essence of reality are thrown into question. In other words, much like Joshua and Judges, the mind contradicts itself. Also, as with the Scriptures, there is debate over whether schizophrenia is a single mental disorder or a number of separate syndromes. Hence the term *spectrum disorder*."

"I see. It's a rather complex metaphor."

"It is. But the book isn't an easy read, either." He laughed. "And then there is also another context in that, by writing a book about mental disorders in the first place, I am automatically taking on one side of the argument. So, in essence, I am judging. So, yes, you could say the title is a sort of triple entendre."

Leah nodded. "Dissociative identity disorder . . . That's . . ."

Noah nodded, too, and finished her sentence. "Multiple personality disorder. Right. One just sounds more pretentious, so I use that." Another laugh.

Leah remembered her thought yesterday concerning the Stickman and the Strangler being the same person but different personalities. "So," she said, "as far as the metaphor goes, *you're* Joshua. You're the one judging."

"Yes," he said, smiling, light gleaming off his glasses. "Exactly."

Leah stood and handed him back his manuscript pages before returning to her chair. Stork put them back facedown beside the typewriter.

"How do you know so much about mental disorders?" she asked.

"Mainly from living with Tommy," he said.

"Tommy is diagnosed as . . . ?" Even though she already knew, it seemed like the right place to ask this question.

"Schizophrenia, but if you consider all the disorders to be on a spectrum, there isn't a whole lot of difference—chemically—between schizophrenia and . . . dissociative identity disorder, for instance."

"Wow. I had no idea."

"Few people do. That's why I'm writing the book."

She gestured to the manuscript. "You've obviously spent a lot of time thinking about Tommy's condition. You've done a lot of research?"

He frowned. "Yes, I wish I didn't know so much, to be honest. But when you live with someone suffering from a mental illness for as long as Tommy and I were under this roof, you can't help but see all the different sides of the thing. And, of course, the more I saw, the more I wanted to learn, so I own many books on the subject."

"What behavioral patterns do you think have resulted from his . . . disorder?"

Stork sat back on the davenport. "Well, Detective, that's a complex question, and you really need to know my son to understand. Symptoms of schizophrenia are many. They can include hallucinations, delusions, disorganized thinking, and unintelligible speech. Sometimes thought patterns can be broken before they complete, which results in many quick changes of behavior or strange shifting of topics while talking. Most people suffering from schizophrenia go through social withdrawal and lose motivation and judgment abilities. Their ability to read common social cues becomes hindered. Usually there is an emotional response to the disorder, or, at times, a complete lack of emotional response. Many, like my Tommy, refuse to accept they even have the illness, which complicates the issue because they often refuse treatment."

Leah leaned forward. "Tommy told me he didn't think he was schizophrenic. He said *you* were, actually."

Stork smiled. "Common deflection for sufferers. No, I show none of the signs. Sufferers of schizophrenia have difficulty holding jobs, and their long-term memory and attention span both become affected. Even the speed their brain functions at can be impaired."

"I see." Her eyes glanced down to the typewriter. "Be hard to write while suffering from bad long-term memory and attention symptoms, eh?"

Still smiling, Stork nodded. "Yes, Detective. Nearly impossible."

"After doing so much research into it, do you think your son's diagnosis was right? Aren't these things sort of hard to diagnose?"

"Again"—he nodded—"yes, because of the spectrum they lie on. Each disorder can take on some of the qualities of another one, depending on situations and even age. As far as Tommy's diagnosis, I believe it's good *enough*. What I mean by that, Detective, is that his diagnosis allows his psychiatrist to prescribe medication that keeps his condition in check. The medication is similar across the spectrum. So even if I see indications in Tommy that his condition might lean toward being dissociative identity disorder, it doesn't really matter, providing the medication works with those symptoms, too. It's more the prescription that's important. Not the name of the disorder. If you understand?"

Leah nodded. "Do you think he actually does lean toward having dissociative identity disorder?"

Noah once again put his right arm up on the davenport's back. "I think there are traits to his illness that indicate he may suffer at least some symptoms that one is more apt to see in someone with dissociative identity disorder than schizophrenia, yes. But I see the opposite, too. It's all one big gray area, Detective."

"I think I read somewhere that these sorts of disorders are genetic. Is that true?"

The question seemed to momentarily flummox Stork. "Some researchers believe the *tendency* to something like schizophrenia can be transferred through heredity, yes. There has been evidence of the disorder running in families."

"What about Harry?" Leah asked. "Did he ever show signs of having it? Maybe that's what happened while he was stationed in—"

Stork cut her off. "No. Not Harry. I told you last time you came here, Harry had PTSD from whatever he went through over there."

"What about your wife?" For a moment, Leah forgot her name, but managed to remember just in time to add it onto her sentence. "Sally-Anne. Do you think that might've—"

"No," Stork said, again rather abruptly. "No, no, Detective. Not my Sally. She . . . she had other problems. She just couldn't cope with seeing her boys . . . well, you know."

"I have a question regarding Harry's business, Stork Sanitation and Waste Removal?"

Noah brought his arm down and his fingers went to his chin. "Yes?"

"From what I can tell, the company was incorporated in your name. Can you tell me why you did that?"

"It's pretty simple, really. With Harry's condition, it just made more sense for me to own the company. We weren't sure if he was going to get worse or better, and so my wife and I decided it would be best if I handled all the 'corporate' items." He spoke with his hand as he said all of this, finally dropping it into his lap with his other one.

Leah had her pad out and was taking notes. "Thanks. So, obviously, you know a lot about the business."

"A fair bit, yes."

"Such as all the contracts with medical institutions around southern Alabama? Going through the records in our files, I found some a couple hours' drive away. Was it feasible to do work and have to spend that much time drivin'?"

"You're talking about the big clients. Yes, Detective, they paid quite a bit for Harry's services. And yes, it took a lot of his time. Sometimes it was too much for just one person. He actually offered a job to Tommy, but, of course, Tommy had no desire to work. He's been like that all his life. So, I wound up working for Harry kind of"—he lowered his voice as he said the next part—"under the table, if you know what I mean."

Leah wrote this down on her notepad. "How often would you say you did that?"

Stork looked up at the ceiling. "There were only a few times. Maybe a half dozen. Maybe a little more. I didn't really keep track."

"But you did the books."

He nodded. "I did, but I didn't keep track of when I helped him. Like I said, I wasn't 'officially' hired."

Leah nodded and jotted down some more notes.

"Now, I understand that on June twentieth of 1974, your house was broken into?"

His hand moved back to his chin. "Yes. Someone broke the window in Tommy's bedroom. Made the hole big enough to reach inside and unlock it. I'm assuming after that, he crawled through."

"Right. I read the statement you made to police.

Why do you say you're 'assuming' the vandal crawled through?"

"Because, and this should also be in the report, nothing was taken. At least nothing I could find."

Leah narrowed her eyes. "I see. So, why do you think someone broke a window and came into your house?"

"I honestly can't answer that, Detective."

"Did your insurance cover the window?"

Stork shook his head. "It wasn't worth involving them for. I got it fixed out of pocket."

"You're aware, Mr. Stork, that when the police searched your son Harry's house, they found a Smith and Wesson Model Ten handgun that matched the murder weapon used on at least two victims and likely on all nine?"

"I am aware that's what they claim, yes."

"'That's what they claim'? Do you contest that claim?"

Noah Stork took a deep breath. "Detective, I do not think my son Harry was a serial killer. To the best of my knowledge, Harry didn't own a gun. Since returning from the war, he actually loathed them. It was a trigger for his PTSD. I cannot tell you where that gun police found in his house came from. I will tell you this, though: I believe Harry was set up. I mean, nobody wants to admit their kid might be a cold-blooded murderer, but this is more than that. In Harry's condition, he was *incapable* of performing the atrocities he's been blamed for."

"Well, the night your son died, he definitely did have a firearm in his possession. He refused to lower it, and that's why the detective was forced to fire on him."

"Your father," Noah clarified.

Leah swallowed. "My pa, yes. Harry wouldn't drop his gun. If he had, he'd still be alive."

"You don't know that. He'd have gone into the system. Nobody knows what might have happened once he was on the inside."

"Have you . . . You sound like you're speaking from experience."

"Only the experience of reading, Detective. No, I have no police record. You surprise me, I would think you'd have looked that up."

Leah smiled. "We only check out the suspicious people, Mr. Stork. Do you, yourself, own a gun?"

"I don't," he said, shaking his head. "No."

"What about your son Tommy?"

"Tommy?" He gave a little laugh. "I highly doubt it. If he did, I wager he'd have hocked it long before now. But he might. You can never tell with Tommy. I don't pretend to know what goes on in that boy's head."

Leah's eyes cut to the stack of written manuscript pages on the coffee table. *But you do seem to know the inside of his head. In fact, you judge him. Or, at least, Joshua does.* She made some more notes. "I see. For what reason *might* Tommy own a gun?"

Stork shrugged. "I can't answer that. Maybe . . ." He shook his head. "I don't know. Tommy isn't one for talking much unless it's with specific intent, such as for borrowing money or needing a lift somewhere. But I can't imagine anything good coming of him having a firearm. He's . . . unpredictable at best."

"He doesn't drive?" Leah's eyebrow went up on reflex. She remembered that pomegranate red Ford Fairlane in his yard the day she interviewed him.

Again Stork closed his eyes. "I never know. Sometimes he apparently *has* a car, other times he mysteriously does not. Again, I do not claim to know what goes on inside the boy's mind."

And again, Leah glanced at the upside-down manuscript on the table.

Noah shook his head slowly and continued talking about Tommy. "I can read about his disorders all I want, but that will only allow me to understand the *disorder,* not *him*. I do feel he may have elements of dissociative identity disorder, which complicates things dramatically. I only say this because there are days when I do not know the person I am speaking to. It's like he's a totally different man."

"You mean, like multiple personalities?"

Stork shrugged and upturned his right palm. "I don't know, Detective. Maybe."

"What was Tommy's childhood like?"

"The person you should be asking is my wife, but unfortunately, as you know, that's impossible. But she did most of the job of raising our children. I was away with work much of the time. And we moved around a lot. Georgia, Nebraska, North Carolina, even other parts of Alabama, such as Annistan."

"What did you do for work that took all your time?"

Noah put his right arm once again up on the back of the davenport. "I was a door-to-door salesman most of my life, Detective. It's not a job I would recommend for anyone."

"No?"

"Detective, the general public are boors. Any job that throws you into a public arena—especially one where you're forced to try to *sell* them something—is one you want to run away from screaming."

"How long did you do it for?"

"It felt like a lifetime." He looked up at the ceiling as he calculated. "Let's see. I quit when we moved here. That would've been 1964."

"What did you do after that?"

He laughed. "As little as possible. No, I actually worked here in the library for ten years before I retired, which was right around the time I lost my wife. One was the effect of the other, you see. And then, of course, I lost Harry . . ." For a moment, something like anger flashed in his eyes.

"You know," Leah said, "the detective who shot Harry . . . my pa . . . he gave him many chances to drop his weapon."

"You mean the weapon that was empty of ammunition?"

"My pa had no idea it was empty. He only knew somebody had a firearm aimed at him."

"I thought Harry yelled out something about being a set-up patsy?"

"How did . . . ?"

Noah closed his eyes. "It's a small town, Detective. Secrets don't keep well in small towns."

"Well, it wasn't a secret," Leah said. "He did yell somethin' to that effect."

"Then why was he shot? Obviously, he felt the pressure of being set up. Not a single bone in my body believes Harry brought that gun into his house. Somebody *else* put it there."

"Who?"

Stork shrugged.

"My pa had no recourse but to shoot him."

"In the heart."

"He was aiming for his arm."

"Was he? Was he *that* bad of a shot? Listen, Detective, pretend the man that pulled the trigger that night *wasn't* your pa. Pretend it was just some detective you didn't know. Would you still be defending him like this?"

Leah opened her mouth but said nothing. Closing it again, she flipped through her notes. "I think I'm done here. Thank you." Her words came out clipped, but that was the best she could do.

"Very well," Noah said, coming to his feet. He picked up the cup from the coffee table and drank the rest of his tea down. "Now I guess I'll get back to my book. Good thing Sally-Anne's not around for this. Writing is an extremely harsh mistress." He laughed again.

After putting her notepad back in her pocket, Leah walked outside to the porch. She then made her way down the driveway to her car out on the street. Part of her hated Noah Stork at that moment, but another part shared his perplexity about his son's death. He had made her wonder if what he'd said was right. If it had been another man, other than her pa, reporting that Harry didn't drop his weapon while hollering about his innocence, would she have questioned it? She didn't know.

That thought turned rancid in her stomach.

CHAPTER 53

Leah's day turned into a hard one as she drove back to the station. Ever since last night, she couldn't keep bad thoughts from cycling in her head. She finally managed to let go of what Noah Stork had told her, about how if it hadn't been her pa she wouldn't have been so quick to wash him of any guilt. With that gone, now her mind settled on Samantha Hughes and how the girl had been dumped less than a city block from where she'd been. Right inside her search area of the Anikawa. So close, she actually saw the dust of the vehicle pulling away.

But not the vehicle.

Any other day—if it had still been raining, even—there wouldn't have been near enough dust kicked up to hide the getaway car completely. Or truck. She didn't even know that much.

It wasn't something she could just let go. It was too painful. Because of her, the Stickman was still out there and, in due time, because of her he would kill again. That part of the equation didn't change. One thing Leah was sure of: He had to be stopped. It didn't matter if this was the same Stickman from fifteen years ago or not. It didn't matter that her pa might've killed an innocent man. None of these things mattered.

The only thing that really mattered was that she put an end to it all.

Tommy Stork.

The Stickman.

The Strangler.

Were those all the pieces of the puzzle? If so, why did that leave so many questions? How *had* the Stickman known that Ethan would happen to drop in to the station on the Fourth to place a bet with his bookie? How could anyone have known that? Was he somehow watching the station? Did he have the phones bugged?

All those notions felt slightly ridiculous.

She tried to think of something else, so her mind moved on to Dan. She remembered the night she thought she'd fallen in love with Dan Truitt. New Year's Eve of last year. She wondered now, sometimes, how strong that love really was. Could she love him forever? When Billy died, she had felt he was her soul mate and that she would never feel the same way about anyone else.

And she never had.

Not even about Dan Truitt. But what she was feeling for Dan was *something* like love, only different from the love she had had for Billy. At that moment she realized that you could never love two people the same way. It wouldn't work. Everyone deserved a unique type of love, tailor-made for them. With that fact came the realization that she very well could continue to love Dan Truitt forever.

Dan didn't replace Billy, but he augmented a space in Leah's life where Billy had been. And her feelings grew from the role he played as her lover.

It was good. It was the way Leah suspected nature had intended it.

Her thoughts went back to the Stickman murders.

Deep down, she knew the truth. There was too much evidence not to accept it. Whoever was killing folk now was most likely also responsible for the other nine people fifteen years ago. And for all the Cahaba River Strangler victims. Leah had known the truth for some time now, only she hadn't wanted to face it. And now, for the first time, she did.

Her pa had shot the wrong man.

His legacy, his biggest case, as reported by the *Alvin Examiner,* was a fraud. He'd screwed it up. He got caught up in the wrong evidence, like the gun they found in Harry Stork's house. Leah had no question about it anymore. That gun was planted. The only big questions now were: Why was Harry Stork set up? Who set him up? And how, exactly, was he set up?

Was it all Tommy's doing? Did he pay off Betty-Lou Panders and Andrea Reinhardt? If so, how could Betty-Lou not have remembered that scar on his face?

Thinking all this just frustrated Leah. The answers didn't light up the way they were supposed to.

Leah pulled up to the curb in front of the station and got out of her car. Dan was already there. She knew this because she had to park behind his green Nova.

She walked to the station door going over the conversation she and Dan had yesterday about Tommy Stork. She was pretty sure when Mobile called this evening, they would be telling her the blood sample matched against Harry Stork. If so, there wasn't much, other than evidence, between pinning Tommy as the Stickman and the Strangler and putting him away for life. Or, she supposed, for death. That would be a decision made by twelve of his peers.

She laughed at that thought. Like any of them would be as stupid as Tommy came off.

But her stomach didn't like it. She didn't know why, but something still ate at her. There were so many questions—not big questions, just unanswered questions. Outstanding things that even putting Tommy in the killer's seat didn't answer or fix.

But they *had* to. Tommy *was* the killer. She was sure of it. *Dan* was sure of it.

Throughout all her pa's reports and statements and notes was one constant theme. One constant question. Where was the primary crime scene? The slaughterhouse? Find the primary crime scene and everything would tumble into place. He had intimated—no, even more than that. *Insisted*—that the primary crime scene was the key to unlocking the whole case.

But he'd never found it.

Now Leah's thoughts about Tommy Stork brought with them the memory of that old abandoned barn across the street from his house and two fields away, a hulking husk of a building that, in her mind's eye, appeared openmouthed, hollow, and still. Waiting for a second chance, as though it were a hyena that had just caught the taste of death for the first time.

Why haven't I thought of it before? Now that she did, it brought her back to almost two years ago, when she took down the Cornstalk Killer. *Why hadn't the building tweaked that memory when I first saw it?*

Everything seemed to be passing by her unnoticed. What was going on? She usually ran on gut instinct. Well, this time around, her gut wasn't doing her or anyone any good.

Her bottom teeth pushed hard against her top. Something about those thirty-nine suspects from Grell had her on edge. Tommy didn't fit with them. His name should be on that list. And surely Duck would've remembered the scar. After seeing his reaction to the photo lineup, there was no way he'd ever even heard of Tommy before then. And how *did* Duck fit into everything? He *knew* about the holdback. Someone either really did tell him or he was part of the bigger picture.

The bigger picture. Was that what Leah wasn't seeing?

It was four-thirty when Leah sat down at her desk. Chris was there today, so Dan was relegated to a chair at the coffee table. It was either that or a seat in the interview room. She gave him the choice.

"Hey!" Dan said. "Either of you guys want coffee? Just made a fresh pot! Yummy, yummy coffee." He held the half-filled pot up above his head as the coffee inside sloshed from side to side.

Leah just smiled at him. It was like putting him at the kids' table on Thanksgiving.

CHAPTER 54

My mother wasn't home yet, at least I hadn't heard her come in. Carry and Jonathon were in the living room watching television. The set was so loud, I could hear it from way down here in my room, and my door was even mostly closed.

As far as my mother knowing I went through her files, she seemed okay about it now. I think she was only mad for a couple of hours. As usual, it was the right decision to do it behind her back. She would never have told me I could read them if I'd asked her, and almost always the punishment wasn't near on as bad as I thought it would be.

The stack was still on the counter. I had figured once she knew I was reading them that she'd take them in to work, but she told me she had two copies of everything so she could work from home just as easily as from the station, and, besides, I had already *finished* going through them. She didn't seem too concerned with me making another pass if I decided to.

Of course, I had known my mother wouldn't approve of me reading all about a real serial killer. She no doubt thought it might somehow affect me badly to read all the details of how the victims were killed and then moved to a secondary scene where he did even more stuff to their dead bodies. Thinking back to it, I realized I had sort of skimmed over the really bad stuff. I wondered if maybe my mother was right. Maybe I really shouldn't have looked through all those files and reports.

Oh well, too late now.

Anyway, once I'd started I couldn't stop. Something about it all fascinated me in a way nothing had before. I felt like those reports and stuff had a long, invisible arm that reached out with an invisible hand that grabbed me by my shirt and tugged me toward the kitchen every time I found myself home alone. Even the more boring stuff that didn't talk about blood or death or any of that still really interested me.

I liked reading about all the clues and I especially liked it when I found something that my grandpa scribbled down. It was almost like he had come back from the grave to spend some time with me at the kitchen table, telling me all about one of his biggest cases.

I looked around my bedroom, realizing how much I still missed my grandpa. I missed him even more than I missed my pa, but I think that was on account of my pa dying before I really got a chance to know him. I barely remembered what he looked like, and I suspected the memories I could find with him were more than likely from the shoe box full of his pictures that my mother gave me and not real memories from back when I was two.

For the first time ever I wondered if maybe I was lucky my pa died when he did and that he wasn't a big part of my life, because then I would probably miss him as much as I missed my grandpa and that might be too much missing for me to take.

I thought about Noah Stork from my mother's file and wondered how much he missed his son Harry, even though Harry might've killed all those folk and did those horrible things to their bodies. I bet his pa probably still loved him and missed him. I didn't know for sure. Did you stop loving people when you found out they did terrible, awful stuff to other people?

Maybe.

Suddenly I was happy that nobody I was close to was a serial killer. I thought about my mother and what would happen if I found out she had been just shooting folk for no reason. Would I no longer love her? I didn't think I could ever not love my mother, no matter what she did. But maybe if she had been a serial killer, it would make missing her all the worse, because I would have to force myself to just remember the good things and that would be a lot of work, especially at night when I was lying by myself in bed.

I wondered why my mother wasn't in yet. I guessed this new Stickman case was to blame. It came into her life and now it took all her attention trying to solving it. That's what my mother was like.

I would say one thing: Having Dan here was starting to wear on me. I knew my mother loved him and all, but he was one of the most irritating people I think I'd ever met. I was sure Carry would even agree with me on that point.

Carry was miffed because she wasn't allowed in the living room after eleven at night since Dan was sleeping in there, which was a dumb reason, really, because I didn't think Dan went to bed until it was morning. I based this fact on having heard him a number of times when I got up in the middle of the night to use the bathroom. One time I heard him rustling paper. Another time he was humming or something. And I could always see the faint glow of lamplight shining into the dining room if I looked down the hall and through the kitchen.

I could tell Carry didn't like the situation. She complained about it practically every night. She even complained about it when she didn't have to, like last night, when I went around the house telling everyone I was going to bed.

My mother and Dan were sitting at the kitchen table discussing something important, probably related to the Stickman case. I knew it was important and something she didn't want me to hear about on account of how quiet they were talking and how they completely stopped when I emerged in the kitchen from the hall.

"I'm goin' to bed," I had said.

Dan held up his hand and pointed at me with his index finger while his thumb pretended to be the gun's hammer. "Have a good one, *poncho,*" he'd said. I had no idea what "poncho" meant. Probably just another one of those dumb things he was always saying. His stupid jokes really got on my nerves sometimes, but I put up with them for my mother's sake.

"Come give me a hug," my mother said, and I walked to the other side of the table and wrapped my arms around her neck. "Sleep well," she said.

Then I walked into the living room to make sure Carry and Jonathon knew I was going to bed, too.

Jonathon sat at the far end of the sofa with his arm up across the back and Carry was somehow sprawled across him and most of the rest of the couch with her back pressed hard against Jonathon's chest. From where I stood, it looked incredibly uncomfortable. "Let me guess," Carry said when she saw me. "Mother wants you to tell me it's eleven o'clock and Jonathon has to leave and I have to get out of Dan's precious bedroom."

I shook my head. "I just came in to tell y'all I'm headin' to bed."

"Why do I care if you're going to bed?" Carry asked.

"Good night," Jonathon said, like a normal person.

"Are you goin' to start coming out of your room to let everyone know when you're 'bout to go pee? Seems like the next logical step," Carry said.

I shook my head again. "Nope. Just when I'm goin' to sleep."

"You're strange."

"I'm just glad he didn't come in to tell you it's eleven," Jonathon said and smiled. As awkwardly as possible, he wrapped his arm around her neck and pulled her back. She lifted her head and Jonathon kissed her forehead.

I didn't think I would ever understand the point of dating someone. It just made you do stupid things that looked dumb to everyone around you.

Far as I could tell, Dan pretty much stayed up all night. I would have guessed this even without waking up and hearing him based on the fact that he never got out of bed before two in the afternoon. Well, sometimes he did, but not on most days. Like today. He got up at pretty near exactly two today. Nobody I knew slept until two in the afternoon, except last year when Carry spent the majority of her summer break sleeping.

I don't think Carry minded having to leave the television at eleven, though, because eleven o'clock was also the time when Jonathon had to go home. I got the feeling she didn't like doing stuff without him anymore, television-watching included. When school got out for summer break, my mother alerted Carry to the new summer rules, one of which was an extension in time before Jonathon had to go home each night. While school was in, he had to leave by nine. Now that school was out, he could stay until eleven.

This summer Carry seemed happier than all the others I could remember. Jonathon brought her happiness with him when they met. I was glad to see her smiling so much. She even treated me better now that she had a boyfriend. She rarely yelled at me or anything, and I couldn't even remember the last time she called me "ass face." All in all, Jonathon made things easier for everyone. Besides, I liked him, too. He always got excited when Dewey would tell him about one of his lame inventions, only it wasn't that fake excited thing that adults usually did. Jonathon actually seemed really excited, like he wanted to help me and Dewey build whatever Dewey had drawn. Even I never got that excited about any of Dewey's inventions—mainly on account of them hardly ever working.

I got off my bed and left the memories of going to sleep last night on my pillow. Leaving my room, I walked down the hall to the kitchen, hearing the television louder than ever.

That big stack of folders still loomed, this time from the edge of the kitchen table. Part of me wished I hadn't gotten through them so fast so I would have some left to read now. I was just about to flip through a few when Carry appeared.

Quickly, I snatched my hands back away from the files. "Hi, Carry!" I said. "How are you doin'? Why are you out here? I mean, um, instead of, you know, in there?" I started off talking fast, but by the end I was stammering and slowing down like cars passing a really bad accident on the freeway. Everyone always looked because they'd just spent an hour in bumper-to-bumper traffic and they figured that was worth at least a good two-minute look at the car wreck.

Carry stood there staring at me. "What the hell are you doing?"

"Nothin'," I said really quickly, accidentally glancing at the folders sitting on the table, beckoning to me.

"You're just weird," she said.

"Where's Mom?" I asked.

"Still at work, I guess."

I glanced out the window. The sun had already fallen behind Mr. Farrow's house, and the sky had a purple band across it. "Isn't she late?" I asked. "Did she phone?"

Carry narrowed her eyes at me. "Why would she call? She's not, like, thirteen or anythin'." Carry started going through cupboards. I had no idea what she was looking for, but she stopped when she found the Kool-Aid packets. She pulled out three. "Jonathon!" she hollered out to the living room. "What kind of Kool-Aid do you want? Grape, lime, or orange?"

She waited, but instead of yelling back, Jonathon walked into the kitchen. He was wearing pajama pants.

"Are you spending the night?" I asked.

He didn't answer. Carry did. "No, he's not spending the night. What's wrong with you? Where would he sleep? Dan has to have his living-room alone time so he can get drunk and do word-search puzzles."

Jonathon laughed.

"Why is he in pajama pants?"

"Because they're comfortable. He leaves them here."

It was weird talking about Jonathon as though he wasn't right there in the room.

I thought over what Carry said about Dan. "Does he really get drunk? Dan, I mean. Does he?" I asked. This didn't sound like a good thing to me. I wondered whether my mother knew.

Carry just looked at me a second and then said, "Duh."

"How do you know? You aren't allowed in the living room once he goes in there to work."

She set the Kool-Aid packets down on the counter beside the white jug and walked over to the closet on the other side of the kitchen table. "Well, if the smell the next day didn't prove it, these would probably be a dead giveaway."

As she pulled open the closet, I saw a black garbage bag slumped on the floor beside all of our galoshes. "What's that?" I asked. The bag was far from being full and the top folded in on the rest, so I couldn't see inside.

Carry found the opening and gathered it all into her grip, then lifted the bag onto the kitchen table across from where my mother's files, reports, and notes about the Stickman case all sat neatly stacked. My mother had obviously finished going through them, too, as she used to keep her place by setting a ninety-degree break between the stuff she'd read and the stuff still to go.

As Carry set the bag down on the table, it responded with a few loud *clunks*. "Take a look," she said.

I walked over and opened the bag just as Carry turned on the light above the table. Inside the bag were a bunch of empty bottles, all with the same label. I pulled one of them out and looked at it under the light, reading the label out loud. "Jim Beam. Kentucky straight bourbon. The best bourbon since 1795." Fourteen more bottles rolled around the bottom of the bag, hitting one another with more *clunks* as I counted them.

"Fourteen bottles?" I asked Carry, who was back beside the counter where the juice jug and Kool-Aid packets waited.

"That's it?" she replied. "I'm surprised."

Jonathon leaned against the fridge, his arms crossed. He had yet to say a word. His lips made a thin line, not really smiling and not really frowning.

"Isn't fourteen bottles a *lot?*" I asked, still looking at Jonathon. Carry was being snarky. I could hear it in her voice.

But instead of answering me, he looked across the kitchen at Carry. "I dunno," he said. "What do you think, Carry? Is fourteen bottles a lot?"

"Depends, I s'pose."

"On what?" I asked.

"On who's drinking 'em. I'm guessin' for Dan, fourteen bottles is just 'bout right. I reckon there'll be one more by the time I get up tomorrow."

"But," I said, "isn't . . . These are big bottles."

"Liter bottles," Jonathon said. I had no idea what that meant or whether he was agreeing with me about them being big or not. He turned his head back to Carry. "How many nights has he been here so far?"

Carry looked up. "Um, let me see." She started counting silently on her fingers. When she got to three, she started out loud. "Three, four . . ." She kept going right up to twenty-seven. "Twenty-eight, if you count tonight."

"So he's averaging half a bottle a night. I don't know, Abe. You reckon that's still a lot?" Jonathon asked.

"Seems like it to me. You ever try some?"

Jonathon smiled at Carry. I didn't understand why.

"Well," Carry said. "Tell him. He asked you a question."

"Yeah, Abe. I have. Not a lot, but my grandfather sometimes gives me some."

"Could you drink a half a liter in a night?"

Jonathon smiled wider and he laughed. "If I wanted to wake up in the ditch two days later, maybe. No, I get pretty smashed on two double shots."

Carry grimaced. "That's how you drink it? Straight?"

With a nod, Jonathon answered, "That's how my grandpa does, so that's how I do. He doesn't let me have it very often. I think I've drunk with him maybe three times. And to answer your question, Abe, *yes,* half of a liter a night *is* a lot. Especially if it goes on twenty-eight nights in a row."

I looked to Carry, worried. "Do you reckon Mom knows?"

She laughed. "Who do you think is tryin' to hide them in a black garbage bag in the kitchen closet?" She looked to Jonathon. "I'll say one thing about my mother. She might be a good detective in the way she figures stuff out and finds things, but she'd make a terrible criminal. She doesn't even know how to keep her boyfriend's drinkin' problem hidden. All this does is make it look like she's ashamed of him."

"Maybe she is," Jonathon said.

Carry put her arms up in the air. "Well, it's her issue. I'm not goin' anywhere near it. Now, where was I?" She spotted the Kool-Aid packets and started picking them back up off the counter. When she had them all, she held them out in a fan to Jonathon. "Pick one. Grape, lime, or orange?"

"First," Jonathon said, "Kool-Aid doesn't come in flavors. It comes in colors. They all taste the same."

"No, they don't," I said.

"Yes, they do."

He was crazy. I told him so.

"Okay," he said. "Call me crazy, but they all taste the same to me." He glanced back to Carry. His body hadn't moved. His arms were still crossed. He still leaned against the fridge.

"Well, just pick one," she said.

"It doesn't matter."

"It does to me."

"Then you pick one."

"I'm asking *you* to. Are you saying what I want isn't important?"

I couldn't believe this was becoming such a big issue. I wasn't sure whether they were serious or not. I half-expected them to start screaming at each other and then break up over stupid Kool-Aid packets.

"Okay," Jonathon said. "I pick the middle one. Green."

Carry nodded. "Fine. Lime."

"No, green."

"You can call it whatever you like." Ripping off the top of the packet, she poured the green powder into the jug and then scrunched the packet up into a ball. Then she hefted the sugar from the cupboard and poured a whole lot of that in, too. With a groan, Carry struggled under the weight of all that sugar to lift the jug by its handle as she sidestepped to the sink, using her left hand to open the cupboard beneath it so she could drop the scrunched-up packet into the garbage can.

Setting the jug onto the sink's aluminum bottom, she let the water run cold for a bit into the other side of the sink before she swiveled the faucet over and let the water pour into the jug.

"Do you like Dan?" I asked Carry.

"What?" she asked. The water was loud.

"He asked you if you like Dan," Jonathon said for me.

Carry sort of smiled and took a deep breath. "I dunno. He's okay, I guess. I like Mom being happy, and he makes her happy, so I s'pose, yeah. I guess I like him okay. Why? Don't you?"

I should have seen that one coming before I asked. I had no idea what to say, so I took the advice my mother gave me once: If you don't know how to answer a question, just be as honest as you can. "I guess he's all right. He gets a little annoying with his stupid jokes sometimes."

"Oh yeah, I didn't say he wasn't annoyin'. I just said I like how he makes Mom happy."

"Do you think we should talk to Mom 'bout these bottles?" I asked.

Carry turned off the faucet and stared at me. "No," she said firmly. "I think that's a terrible idea. All you'll do is put Mom in an awkward spot where she either has to lie to you or 'fess up to herself 'bout somethin' I'm pretty sure she's doing her best to ignore." She lifted the jug from the sink and set it down on the counter, placing the top on it.

"What do you mean?" I asked.

Carry frowned and rolled her eyes.

"No, no, Carry," Jonathon said calmly. "He asked you what you mean. Clarify for him." I couldn't figure out what Jonathon was doing. He had been acting weird ever since we started talking about Dan.

"Look," Carry said to me. "You're probably not old enough to understand this, but Mom's hiding spot for his bottles was so not a good spot that there wasn't any way we were the ones she was hiding them bottles from." She turned to Jonathon. "Does that make sense?"

Jonathon smiled. "Don't ask me. Ask him. I *know* where you're going with this."

I shook my head. I had no idea where she was going. "I don't get it."

"Mom just wanted them bottles out of sight from *her*. She didn't even think 'bout you or me finding 'em. She just didn't want to keep them anywhere *she'd* have to be seeing 'em all the time, constantly being reminded of the one bad thing in her perfect relationship. Remember, Dan's the first guy she's ever dated since Pa died. How long ago was that?"

I shrugged. "I dunno, I was only two."

"Do the math, then. Thirteen minus two. So, it's been like eleven years. First guy in eleven years, and she's found herself ass-over-teakettle in love with him. The last thing she wants to face is that there might be parts of him she didn't expect would turn out to be so bad when she first started dating him, and now her heart's completely invested. She doesn't want to even consider that she might've made a mistake." Carry was reaching up into the cupboard on the other side of the plates and bowls, going for the glasses. She looked back at Jonathon. "You're havin' some, right?"

"Sure."

Then, surprisingly, she looked to me. "What 'bout you?"

I nearly fell off the chair I was leaning on. "Sure!" I said.

"Anyway," Carry said, bringing down three glasses and setting them in a row on the counter, "Mom put those bottles in that bag and hid the bag in the closet so *she* wouldn't find 'em. So I reckon you better put 'em back where they were before she gets home."

Jonathon stopped leaning and now just stood. His hands went into the pockets of his pajama pants, and he rose up on his toes. I just noticed he had bare feet. "Hey, you, um, got any chips or anythin'?" he asked Carry.

Carry opened the corner cupboard again. That was where my mother stored all the snacky food on days she went shopping. The snacky food usually lasted one, maybe two days before me and Carry ate it. It had been almost a week since my mother bought groceries. I knew as well as Carry did that there was nothing in that cupboard but old, stale crackers.

"Not that I can see," she said. "Oh, hey, do you like crackers?"

"Don't," I said.

"What?"

"Don't make him eat the crackers."

"Why?"

"They've been there since Christmas."

"Seriously?" Jonathon asked. Then to Carry, he said, "You were goin' to give me six-month-old crackers? *Seriously?*"

She laughed. "I would've stopped you before you actually put one in your mouth."

"No, you wouldn't, I can tell by your face! You were goin' to watch me eat crackers from Christmas!"

"Actually," I said, "I think they were from the Christmas before last."

"They were not," Carry said.

"I don't care," Jonathon said. "You're evil."

"Tell you what I'll do," Carry said. "After we're done with our Kool-Aid, let's walk down to Harrison's Five-and-Dime and buy you some chips. Consider it a peace offering for fiddling with the idea of possibly giving you food poisonin'."

Jonathon pushed his hands up over his face, continuing upward into his hair. He groaned. "Oh, I really don't feel like getting dressed again before I have to leave."

Carry smiled. "That's fine, I'll just go. You don't have to come. You do a lot for me. Consider it my turn."

"You sure? I mean, I'd let you take my car, but you don't have a license."

"I'm sure."

"No, here's what we'll do," Jonathon said. "I'll drive and just leave my pajamas on. You can run in and—"

"Stop!" Carry said. "I told you I'd go and that's it. I'm goin'. It's a beautiful night out there."

"All right. You win. How long will you be?"

"I dunno. It's not far. Probably thirty minutes. Maybe a bit longer. I want to drink my Kool-Aid first, though."

I placed the bottle from my hand back in the bottom of the bag with the others and closed up the top. All that glass was heavier than I thought. I used two hands to drag them off the table and put the bag back into the closet beside all our rubber boots. I closed the door.

"Good job," Carry said, picking up two of the glasses, which were now filled with green Kool-Aid I was near on positive tasted like lime. But if my mother could fool herself about Dan's drinking by hiding the bottles away somewhere she knew not to look at, then maybe we were all susceptible to thinking things were different than they really were. Maybe I tasted lime when I drank green Kool-Aid because my mind expected green liquid to taste like lime.

I thought me and Dewey should do a blind taste-test with a bunch of different colors of Kool-Aid, just to see what happened.

Jonathon had followed Carry and the two glasses in her hand back to the living room. The jug still stood on the counter beside the sink. I put it in the fridge and went back to the counter for my glass. Closing my eyes, I tried to convince myself it was full of purple Kool-Aid. I kept concentrating on it until my mind only saw purple water in the glass I was holding.

Then I brought it to my lips and tipped it up.

As soon as the Kool-Aid touched my tongue, the picture in my mind shifted to green and all I could taste was lime. I wasn't certain which came first, the taste or the change to the image I had been trying to hold in my head. It annoyed me.

Then I realized how much it didn't really matter whether the Kool-Aid all tasted the same to everyone but me. Besides, that wasn't what was really annoying me. My eyes automatically cut back to the closed closet door on the other side of the table, and I couldn't help but wonder if my mother maybe closed her eyes, forcing her mind to picture the closet empty except for all them boots. Just because I couldn't make my Kool-Aid taste different by picturing it a different color in my mind didn't mean my mother couldn't make that bag full of bottles disappear by convincing herself it wasn't there.

Maybe she was just better at it than me.

CHAPTER 55

Leah's call from Mobile didn't come in until after eight o'clock. Chris had gone home at five sharp, and Ethan left maybe a half hour after Chris. Leah and Dan were just about to call it a day when the phone rang.

"That can't be the forensics guy," Leah said. "It's my kids, probably wondering where the hell I am."

Dan shrugged. "One easy way to find out."

Leah answered the call. It was Chuck, one of the cops Leah was pretty sure was in the secret circle.

"Chuck, what do you have for me?"

"Hey, Miss Leah. First, I want to apologize for calling so late. I'm actually surprised y'all are even around to answer the phone."

"We are nothing if not faithful," Leah said.

Chuck gave a little laugh. "Anyway, you wanted us to test this blood sample you sent against Harry Stork?"

"Yeah."

"Okay, I did that, not really expecting to get a hit from a new blood sample against a fifteen-years-gone dead man."

Leah felt her adrenaline increase. "But you did? It matches?"

"Sure as hell does. Positive match against Harry Stork. Came out 99.97 percent inclusive. Now, just tell me again, what made you even think this blood would match a dead guy from fifteen years ago? I really need some clarification here."

"Terrance didn't tell you?" Leah asked.

"Tell me what?"

"Oh." Leah laughed. "Harry Stork has a brother. The sample's gotta be from him."

She picked up a pen that was beside her keyboard and quickly wrote on a piece of paper: *Blood positive match for Harry Stork. 99.97 percent inclusive*. She held it up for Dan to read.

Dan made a gun with his index finger and thumb and pretended to shoot the timeline they had hanging on the wall.

Even though this was the outcome she'd expected, hearing it in real life brought a weird sensation of relief with it. All the puzzle pieces finally fell into place. Well, most of them did. The important ones, anyway.

"Okay . . ." Chuck said, tentatively. "But without testing the sample against the brother, I can't make you a guarantee that it is necessarily his blood. Likely? Yes. But I doubt it's enough to get you a warrant if that's what you're looking for."

"I'll worry 'bout that," Leah said.

Dan was looking at her, trying to gauge both sides of her conversation from her face. Leah covered the mouthpiece on the phone and whispered to him, "He won't commit to it being Tommy's blood, but says it's very likely. I'm okay with 'very likely.'"

"So, that's it, then?" Chuck asked. "Anythin' else I can do for you?"

"No, I think that's it. Thank you, Chuck. I appreciate you puttin' in the time to get this to me today."

"I live to serve," Chuck said.

Leah hung up the phone.

"So," Dan said, "I suppose Tommy Stork just jumped to number one on the suspect hit parade?"

"He's been there for some time, to be perfectly straight." *Yeah. Tommy Stork right along with Thomas Kennedy Bradshaw.* Leah supposed this just eliminated Bradshaw completely, which meant when she interviewed him that morning he was just acting weird on account of him actually just being weird.

That was one of those thoughts that didn't settle properly in Leah's stomach. People reacted more than they acted. Their reactions almost always pointed to some fact. And if you didn't understand their reaction, then you weren't privy to the fact that drove it.

"So, what's our next step?" Dan asked.

"I say we go pick Tommy Stork up now. Bring him in for questionin'."

"We really only have vague circumstantial evidence on him."

"If we play it properly, maybe we can get him to believe we have more?"

Dan narrowed his eyes. "What do you mean?"

"Well, we can probably fill in some of the blanks ourselves. Then tell him we have proof of the facts."

"Are you saying to lie to a potential serial killer suspect?" Dan asked. "The audacity."

Leah laughed. "I'm sure, between the two of us, we can make this work. We're allowed to bring him in for questioning without a dump truck full of evidence."

". . . and you're right. Nobody said we weren't allowed to lie a little." He thought this over. "Okay, let's go get him. We'll figure out the details on the way."

Leah glanced at the clock. It was just past eight-thirty. Outside, twilight was unraveling in a deep purple and blue dress.

Dan made it to the door first. He turned the handle and held it open for Leah. She was just about to walk through when she noticed something on the step outside.

A white envelope with the name *Leah Fowler* scribbled across the front in what was becoming familiar handwriting.

"Oh no," she said. "Not now. Not goddamn now."

Dan leaned over and plucked it up. "It's for you," he said, gravely.

With deep breaths, Leah leaned against the doorjamb as Dan passed her a pair of latex gloves. Snapping them on, she carefully tore open the letter. Inside was a single piece of paper folded in thirds. She removed the paper and unfolded it, knowing exactly what she'd see.

Only . . . it wasn't exactly what she'd expected at all. This note was different from any other she'd ever heard of coming into the station.

There wasn't a single stickman or stickwoman, there were three: a tall woman with some sort of badge on her chest, a shorter woman, and an even shorter man. The tall woman and the short man were both drawn in black felt marker. The middle one, the girl, was in red.

It took a good second for everything to sink in, a good second before Leah knew what she was looking at.

"Oh my God," she said, her breath catching on the words.

"What?"

"It all just ramped up," she said, her eyes glued to the

page. "It's . . . I didn't think it could *get* any more personal. But—" The sting of tears ached behind her eyes. She couldn't stop them. She felt the first one roll down her cheek.

She handed the paper to Dan. "It's Caroline," she said in a whisper. "That bastard's goin' after my daughter."

Written on the page was Cherry Park Forest, with a time of 11:30 P.M. There were also two initials on the bottom right of the page: *T.S.* Only, unlike the *H.S.* letter her pa had received fifteen years ago, this one looked, at least to Leah, like it was written by the same person who wrote all the rest.

Why would Tommy Stork initial his own letter? Did he know they were onto him? She reflexively looked around the station. Could it be bugged? Again, she didn't find that a conceivable proposition.

"There's no way we can search that forest in three hours. That forest is *huge*." Cherry Park Forest hugged the southern bank of Cornflower Lake, and extended all the way north to First Road. There had to be five or six square miles of forest to go through.

It would be near on impossible.

Dan held out his hand, palm down. "Okay, just take a breath for a moment. As far as you know, Caroline's at home, isn't she?"

Leah looked at the clock. She and Jonathon would be on the sofa watching television for at least another two hours.

"Call her," Dan said, his voice straining to be calm.

Leah picked up the telephone receiver and quickly dialed her home number. "Abe," she said when her son answered, "put Caroline on. Do it quick, it's an emergency."

Abe told her Caroline wasn't home. She'd gone to the store.

"Is Jonathon with her?" Leah knew she was sounding panicky, but she *was* panicked.

"No, Jonathon's here. What's going on?"

"Put Jonathon on."

"Mom, what's going on?"

"Goddamnit, Abe, just do what you're told for once without asking so many bloody questions!"

Jonathon came on the line.

"Jonathon," Leah said. "Where's Carry?"

There was a hesitation before he spoke. "She just went for a walk to the mercantile. Why? Is something wrong?"

"I . . . I don't know."

"She should be back anytime. She said she'd be a half hour or so."

"Listen, Jonathon," Leah said, trying to remain calm. "I think Caroline may be in danger. Can you go pick her up and drive her to the station? I'll be in my car and meet you up halfway. How long ago did she leave?"

"Um, I don't know." His voice started quavering. *Shit,* Leah thought. She'd panicked him. "Maybe forty-five minutes? I'll get in my car right now and find her for you. What kind of danger?"

Leah ignored his question. "Forty-five minutes? Just to go to the goddamn store? Damn it!" Desperately, she tried to clear her mind so she could think. "Never mind. I'll go pick her up myself. Which store was she headed to? Harrison's Five-and-Dime?"

"I believe so, yes. What's going on, ma'am?"

"I'll explain later," Leah said. "Right now I just gotta go get her. I'm sure she's fine." But Leah heard her own voice as the words came out. The words sounded fake and made-up. No doubt Jonathon heard it, too. They both knew nothing was fine.

"Oh my God," Jonathon said. "Does this have somethin' to do with the Stickman?"

"Just let me go find her before anyone else does, okay?" Leah said and hung up the phone.

Dan was waiting for Leah to get off the call and give him an update. "She's gone," Leah said, her voice cracking. *Goddammit,* she thought. *You have to hold it together. Now more than ever.* "He's after my baby girl."

Shushing her, Dan quietly asked, "Where? Where has she gone?"

Leah stared at the floor, slowly shaking her head. She opened her mouth, but no words came out. It was like she had lost the ability to speak. After a moment, when she finally managed to say anything, the words came out in a squeak. "She went to the store. Said she'd only be thirty minutes." Her eyes rose up to meet Dan's. "That was pretty near an hour ago." No matter how much she fought against it, Leah couldn't keep the image of Samantha Hughes from popping into her mind, except instead of seeing the woman's face on that staked, twisted body, she saw Caroline's. And instead of being stuck in the clay on the edge of the Anikawa, Caroline was staked to the damp trails running maze-like throughout Cherry Park Forest. Staked and twisted with a big 9 mm bullet hole in the back of her head. Leah trembled all over. Her fingers began to twitch. She couldn't hold it together much longer. "I . . . I have to go find my daughter," she said in a whisper.

Dan moved closer, but she held up her palm, telling him to stay put. If he hugged her now, she would lose it for certain.

"Dammit, I *knew* it was Tommy," she whispered. "Why didn't I bring him in earlier today?"

She saw Dan swallow. "Don't start with the shoulda, woulda, couldas. Not now. Now you need to focus," he said.

She stared into his eyes, looking at him washed out from her tears. "I *knew* it, Dan. I *knew* Tommy Stork was our killer. I think he was always the Stickman, even fifteen years ago. He's . . . he's got schizophrenia and . . . and from what I gathered from his pa, some sort of multiple personality disorder. I don't know why he's . . . and last night . . . we both *knew* he fit perfectly into the timeline. Why the hell didn't we—"

Dan shushed her and wrapped her in a hug. "No!" she said, pulling free. "I have to go pick up my baby. He won't have gotten her yet. She's still fine."

"We have to call Chris and Ethan in," Dan said.

"You call them. I'm goin' to get my daughter."

"You can't drive. You're way too upset."

"Dan!" she said, firmly. "I'm goin'. You're staying here and calling Chris and Ethan. I'm goin' to look for my daughter!"

Dan held up his palms in surrender.

Leah exited the station, leaving the door open behind her. Jumping behind the wheel, she slammed the car door closed behind her. A second later, her tires spun, squealing on the still sun-warm asphalt as she pulled out onto Main Street and made a U-turn back toward Hunter Road beneath a velvet field of starlight.

CHAPTER 56

Leah drove down Hunter Road and up Main Street and then backtracked to Cottonwood Lane. For near on thirty minutes she searched the area around Mr. Harrison's Five-and-Dime, going back and forth over the path Caroline would've taken to get there. She kept jumping at shadows in the night. Every time she turned a corner, her headlights would sweep across something like a tree or a telephone pole and Leah's heart would leap, thinking for sure it was Caroline. But it wasn't. Three times she did the circuit before Leah finally resigned herself to the fact that her daughter was missing.

Chris had already radioed her twice. He and Ethan had made it in to the station ten or fifteen minutes ago. From what she knew, the three of them—Dan, Chris, and Ethan—were on their way to Tommy Stork's.

Leah had already told Dan her theory about the barn across the street from Stork's house possibly being a good bet on the primary crime scene. That was, if it really was abandoned. From where she stood, she didn't know how good of a look she'd gotten at it. She knew what it looked like in her memory, but she also knew how deceiving that could be.

On so many levels.

"Christ," she said to herself. "We should've just gone and checked out that barn *then*." They'd had two hours to wait for that six o'clock call to come in at eight-twenty or whatever the hell time it was.

Goddammit, Chuck. If you'd have called when you were supposed to, we'd have Tommy at the station being interviewed right now and Caroline would be safe and sound in front of that television.

Chris radioed again to tell her they had made it to Tommy's shack on Rodman Road. Tommy didn't an-swer his door, so they went in anyway. Leah guessed Ethan likely booted the door down, unless Chris had the battering ram in his squad car. Chris told her the house was empty and nothing seemed disturbed. That was when Leah reminded them of the barn across the street.

"I'm heading up now," Leah said. "I shouldn't be more than ten or fifteen minutes." She struggled with wanting to tell them to wait for her. This was *her* daugh-ter. She should be the one to save her. But yet . . .

"We can handle this, Leah." Chris said.

"I think . . . I don't know, Chris. Do what you can. Just . . . be safe. And find Caroline." She still wished they were all there. Who knew what that place looked like inside? It might be a death trap. Not only that, but—"Tommy might not be working alone," she said, think-ing of the two MOs for the Stickman and the Strangler that Dan had put at the end of his adjusted timeline. Two personalities. Two people? Or one very messed-up per-son?

When she'd stumbled through this with Chris, he'd finally stopped her and told her they would start looking up and down Rodman Road. He told her not to worry. They would find the primary scene. They would make sure nothing happened to her daughter. And, he insisted, if she stopped talking and just started driving, she'd be there already.

"Okay," she said right before ending the call. "I'm turning on to Rodman now. Just have to come up and around. There's no GD streetlights up here. Makes it hard to go over seventy."

Dan came on the radio. "Seventy? Are you nuts? Leah, slow down. We want *everyone* to live through this."

She shook her head. *Doesn't he get it?* Sometimes he could make her so mad. "Tell Chris I'll be there in ten minutes."

"Got it," Dan said. "And Leah, listen. We're goin' to find her. She's goin' to be okay."

Leah hung the microphone back on the radio, thinking, *Don't make promises you can't keep.* Her mind began filling with memories of all the different times she'd told parents or spouses exactly what Dan had just said to her. *Don't worry. It's all going to be fine. I'll find her. I'll bring her home safely.* Of course, sometimes she did, but not always. And when she didn't, when those loved ones either showed up dead or didn't show up at all, Leah had to somehow face those same people she'd made those promises to and tell them she'd lied. She hadn't been able to keep their babies safe.

This time, it was *her* baby, and Dan had just said exactly what she'd said all those times when she'd been wrong. Those times when she'd lied.

The tears came again, streaming down her face. Without Dan watching, she didn't feel compelled to hold them back. She turned and started toward Tommy Stork's house, feeling overwhelmed and empty. Lost.

"You can do this," she said to herself. "And you will."

The clock on her dash read 9:25 P.M.

Rodman Road twisted abruptly to the left and began a slow arc past farmland and ranch land. Leah knew Tommy Stork lived about three-quarters of the way to the end of the road, where it joined up with Pineview Drive. She couldn't be more than five minutes away at the speed she was going. One thing was for sure: She was happy all that rain had stopped so she didn't have to worry about hydroplaning at seventy miles per hour.

As she drove, Leah's mind drifted through her interview weeks ago with Tommy Stork. She analyzed every word she could remember him saying, trying to remember if there was any hint of where he might be hiding Caroline if her guess about the barn turned out to be wrong. But the more she thought, the more she panicked, and the more everything just sort of galloped away from her like a wild horse heading over a hill.

Always, it came back to that image of Caroline staked in the forest with a bullet hole in the back of her head.

Leah pounded the steering wheel. "No! No! No!"

Then she thought about the list of the thirty-nine suspects she'd gotten from Grell, and once again there was that feeling, as if she was missing something. She'd looked at that thing so much she had practically memorized every name, but still she hadn't figured out what tugged at her about it. The folded list was still in her front pocket.

She came up the gentle rise and, under the light of the half-moon and the twisted band of stars twinkling far above the road, she could pretty much see where Stork's shotgun shack probably stood on the edge of the road another four or five miles away in this land of nothing but fields and farmhouses and tractors and hay bales and the edges of forests way off in the distance. One farmhouse had a single, solitary light on outside. No lights in the windows. It looked frightened, waiting for its people to come home.

What she could make out perfectly was the ominous sight of the barn she'd snuck a look at that day she'd interviewed Tommy. It slowly rose on the horizon against a backdrop of constellations as she came up the gentle hill, growing more ominous as it grew taller. The yellow moon shone onto the structure's wood, making it look far darker and far more gray than she remembered it being. Now it was almost black and possibly charred. Either it was the light of this weird night, or the barn may have been in a fire. From where she was, the wood around the entranceway looked crusted, and the doors stood at obvious angles to their hinges.

They were, however, closed, and from what Leah thought she could see under the light of all the little stars, they were tied shut with either a rope or a chain. Or it could just be a shadow. Above them, the door of the hayloft hung open, and as Leah got closer, she could even make out a small heap of scattered hay in the moon's white and bone-like light. It looked like it wanted to escape out the mouth of that door. *That grass must be older and drier than a Kentucky sand weevil,* Leah thought.

Now that she was closer, there could be no mistake. Fire had wrought the damage to that barn. Destroyed the sheathing. It was no longer in use, as Leah had suspected. Probably had been abandoned for years. The scraped wooden doors looked like a mouth with a cyclopean loft for an eye. And, to Leah, that mouth shouted out in pain.

Could her daughter really be tied up inside that building? Was she even still alive? Leah shivered and pulled her attention back to the road. She didn't want to think about Caroline being anywhere near that barn. Especially not on a dead, dark night like tonight.

She had moved to slow, and sickness filled Leah's stomach. She felt like she might vomit. If it wasn't for her, Caroline would have been safe. But the Stickman wanted things to be as personal as possible.

Dammit. You knew *it was Tommy. You* knew.

She unclipped the microphone from her car radio and called for Chris, hoping to God he and Ethan weren't out of his car already searching on foot.

"Chris, you there? Chris? Chris, it's Leah?" She wanted to tell him she was there. Get them all ready to rush the farmhouse at once. There was a long duration of silence, and then . . . nothing. No response.

"Goddammit!" she screamed.

Pulling the microphone up by its cord from where she had dropped it onto the car's floorboard, Leah tried to call again. "Chris! Chris, goddammit. Chris, come in. Are you there? Chris!"

Just then, the big car phone she had mounted beneath the dash sprang to life. She jumped at the sound of it ringing. Leah put her hand on her chest. "Holy shit," she whispered, trying to catch her breath.

She let the microphone to the radio go again and picked up the phone. "Leah Teal," she said.

"Hi, ma'am? It's Jonathon. Sorry to call you on your car phone. I just wanted to—"

She didn't hear the rest of what Jonathon said on account of right then her radio started squawking. "Leah! It's Chris. Sorry, we were out of the car. Just heard you as we were walking back up. Leah?"

Quickly she scooped up the microphone and started talking. "I'm here."

"You're where?" Chris asked.

"I'm at Tommy Stork's," she said, trying to keep the panic out of her voice. "Well, I'm coming up now. What's the plan? Any sign of Caroline?"

"You told us to wait for you, didn't you?"

Her brain scrambled for an answer. "Yeah. I did. Okay, I'm right here. I see you." She clipped the radio's microphone back in place and picked up the car phone from where she'd laid it on the seat.

"Hi, Jonathon. Listen, I . . . Jonathon? You there?"

She waited for his voice, but it never came. All she heard was dead air.

CHAPTER 57

I watched Jonathon begin to become unhinged as he talked to my mother on the phone. Something was wrong, and from what I could hear, it had something to do with Carry.

They hadn't talked long, and now Jonathon just sat there with the phone against his ear, not saying a thing. I didn't know if my mother was talking or what. It seemed like he was just waiting.

After about a minute, he put the phone receiver back on its cradle without so much as a good-bye. He turned to me, and I didn't like what I saw in his eyes at all. They reminded me too much of some eyes I'd seen a couple of years ago. Those ones had belonged to a dead girl.

"What is it?" I asked quietly. "Are you all right?" My whole body was tense. I felt my calf muscles cramp up like they did when me and Dewey went on long bike rides. "How come you never said good-bye?"

He swallowed and looked slightly away from me. Like he couldn't stand to look in my eyes. That scared me more than ever. "It's . . . it's . . . ." He fumbled for the words.

"It's what?" I asked.

"Your ma was on the radio, talkin' to Chris." Jonathon's voice sounded hollow, like he was at one end of the cardboard tubes that come out of the insides of wrapping paper at Christmastime. Only this was a long tube, and even with my ear pushed right up against my end, I could barely hear him. "I . . . I heard enough," he murmured.

"What was she talkin' to Officer Chris about? What do you mean, you heard enough?"

"It's . . . your sis—Carry . . . She's gone missing."

My legs wobbled beneath me. I quickly backed to one of the kitchen chairs and sat down. I figured it was either that or the floor. Staring at Jonathon, I could tell my eyes were wide. All I wanted him to do next was tell me everything would be okay and Carry would be fine and I'd get over my sudden seasickness.

And when that didn't come, I felt something else well up inside me. It burned like fire, and I knew what it was on account of it happened just like this near on a year ago when I was out front playing sword fight with Dewey and old Preacher Eli dropped by. That afternoon I'd been so mad I broke my wooden sword over my knee.

This time I just wanted Jonathon to tell me the truth. All of it. Exactly how he heard it.

"Tell me what you heard," I said, my voice sounding muffled on account of it coming out from behind my teeth.

He was on the sofa with his head in his hands. "I don't know . . ." he said, and I heard tears in his words and just then I felt bad about being so angry. I hoped he didn't know I'd got like that. It wasn't because of him, it was because of all them people in my mother's files. All

those dead people, and for what? It was such a waste.
None of them deserved to die.

And surely my sister didn't.

"Tell me what you heard?" I whispered. "Please?" I
crawled off the chair and sort of walked over to the sofa
on my hands and knees. I touched Jonathon's shoulder.
He still had his head in his hands.

Jonathon took a big breath, raising his head from his
hands. I saw his chest go all the way out and back in
again. His eyes drifted to me. "I really don't know, Abe.
But I think Carry's in trouble. I . . . I've gotta go help
her."

"What kind of trouble?"

Something happened then that had never happened
before. As I watched from my vantage point kneeling on
the carpet, something sparked in Jonathon's eyes that I
never in a million years thought I'd ever see. I thought I
had gotten angry, but my anger only lasted a minute and
it was little kid anger, I could see that now. Because
Jonathon's face—the way it changed—scared me more
than I had been scared in an awful long time. And that
was saying something. Jonathon had looked away right
when the anger hit, but his eyes came back to mine now
and that anger was still there, red and fierce, and yet, at
the same time, something small and precious, maybe
blue and sad, also gripped him.

I reckon that was the first time in my life I ever fully
understood the word *tragic*. At that moment, Jonathon
terrified me.

He took some deep breaths. When he talked to me
again, his calmness was back. "I'm sorry, Abe. Look, I
honestly don't know any more than you do about what's
goin' on. As soon as I do, you'll be the first to know."
He put his hand on my shoulder. "*Capiche?*"

I shrugged. "Sure," I said sadly. I didn't even bother to ask him what *capiche* meant.

Jonathon ran through the house to Carry's room, where he changed out of his pajama pants and into the shorts he'd been wearing earlier in record time. I never saw him act like this before. Ever.

He sat on a dining room chair, putting on his shoes. I'd never understand people who did up their laces. Just seemed like a waste of time and energy.

Jonathon looked up after putting on shoe number one. He clutched my upper arm. "Abe, listen. Do you have a phone book? The White Pages?"

"What for?" I asked. I knew we had a phone book, but I had no idea where it might be.

For a moment I thought he was going to get angry again. I even flinched, but he caught himself. "Hey, hey . . ." he said. "It's okay. I'm okay now. Listen, I overheard your ma saying something to Chris about them having to get to some guy named Tommy Stork. I'm sure that's what she said. My guess is that they think *he's* got her. I really have to get there to help. So I'll ask you again. Do you have a phone book?" He spoke that last sentence really slowly.

I felt my eyes go wide as saucers at this news. "Tommy Stork's the Stickman?" I asked, hearin' my own excitement in my voice. I felt bad right away for gettin' worked up over somethin' when Carry was in such danger.

He tilted his head at me. "You . . . *know* who Tommy Stork is? And I said nothin' about the Stickman. What's goin' on, Abe?"

Of course I knew who Tommy Stork was, I'd been studying my mother's files on this case probably near on as much as she had. "I . . . well . . ." I decided there was no point in lying. Besides, my mother already knew. It only got better from there. "I kinda spent two weeks goin' through my mom's files and readin' 'bout the case."

Concern fell over Jonathon. "Reading what about the case, exactly?"

"Well, I pretty near have to say I"—I scratched the back of my neck, which had suddenly gotten very itchy—"I pretty much read all of it."

Now it was his turn for his eyes to go wide. "You read it *all?* What the hell were you thinkin'? Your ma's gonna turn into a ballistic missile when she finds out!"

My eyes dropped to the shag carpet. "She already knows."

"That you read them *all?* And she's okay with that?"

I looked back at him and nodded. "Yeah. I mean, not completely okay, but she took it a lot better than I expected."

"She took it a lot freakin' better than I expected, too," he said. "Now, Abe, we have to focus. I *need* a phone book."

"No, you don't," I said. "I can tell you exactly where Tommy Stork lives."

"You know?"

"Well, not off by heart, but there's a report on him in one of the top three folders in the kitchen with his address written on it."

While he finished tying up his second shoe, I raced to the kitchen and rifled through the files. Sure enough, Tommy Stork's report was right where I remembered it. Outside the window the night looked pitch-black. I wished everyone was at home right now, watching TV together. All cozy in the living room. Heck, I'd even settle for having to spend the night listening to Dan.

Just before I handed Jonathon Tommy Stork's report, I looked at the address on it. "Oh, maybe he moved."

"What do you mean?" That concern had fallen back again.

"I didn't notice before, but my mom has written a different address beside it. He's on Woodpecker Wind."

"Not wind, Abe. Wind. Like Blind, only with a *W*. And I know where that is. It's down there in Blue Jay Maples. Me and some buddies used to race all around them roads when we first got our licenses. Kind of stupid thinking back on it now, though. Anyway, I have to go, Abe." He gave me a hug. Jonathon had never hugged me before, and now I was more scared than ever.

He pointed at me after opening the door. "Be brave, you got that, young man? Your sister needs you to be brave."

I just nodded. I had no idea what to say to something like that.

Before he closed the door, he said one more thing to me. "You stay put, you got that? No matter what. You don't leave this house."

Again, I nodded in silence.

"I'm serious, Abe."

So was I. Where the hell did he think I'd want to go, out to find the Stickman myself? I thought the whole lot of them were crazy, especially Jonathon. At least my mother got paid for doing stupid things.

Jonathon pulled the door closed, and immediately I was cast in shadow.

I stood there, all alone in the darkness, and started to cry.

Somehow, that felt just right.

CHAPTER 58

It was all too familiar as Leah came right up the road to Tommy Stork's shotgun shack. Like a play she'd seen from outside the theater, but it was loud enough that she heard practically every line of it.

Darkness had rolled in fast since she'd left the police station. It was a clear sky and the moon was cut in half, looking like it just came out of a celestial ice cream scoop. *Yeah, sure,* thought Leah. *And the stars are all candy sprinkles.*

She wasn't in the mood for ice cream and candy.

The letter with the *T.S.,* exactly like the one Chris said came when Leah's pa shot out Harry Stork's heart. Only, everyone seemed quite sure this letter was in the same handwriting as the last two. Was that more evidence pointing at this being a different Stickman? Leah had pretty much exhausted that theory. She was sick of even running through all the ridiculous scenarios it would take to completely exonerate her pa. She had to admit, first to his memory and then to herself, he'd made a mistake. That was all it was. An honest mistake.

But it was one of them mistakes there was no coming back from.

She pulled her Bonneville to the side of the road a ways before Tommy's shack. The other two cars—Dan's and Chris's squad car—were parked along the same side, only farther up. Nobody had parked right in front of the house. That wasn't something you were taught in cop school, just something you worked out for yourself, which was probably the definition of common sense. You didn't want to announce to the world that you were there for Tommy, and you didn't want your vehicle to be a target if he started thinking he was at the shooting range.

She walked all the way up, past Tommy's property, to where the three men were gathered around the squad car. At least two lights were turned on inside of Tommy's shack. Their light seemed to come out of the windows at crazy angles, giving the place a sort of fun house atmosphere.

"Why'd you leave the lights on?" Leah asked.

"I'm not paying the electrical," Ethan said. "And he's jackrabbitted out of here."

Leah jerked a thumb behind her. "That Fairmont in the yard's his. *It's* still here, so I doubt he's far. I only met Tommy Stork once, but he didn't peg me as the type of guy who went on too many nature hikes." The Milky Way continued shining across the sky overhead. Any other time, it would have looked beautiful. Tonight, it reminded Leah of a noose.

"Well, I reckon him being close is good news for us," Ethan said. "Because he ain't in that shack. It may have been blacker than the ace of spades when we went in, but I went through every square inch of that place. That puts my dollar on your hunch 'bout that barn. You know, I've been lookin' at it. It's not a good place. I can *feel* it.

And it feels, I dunno. Like it *knows* we're here and it's watching us."

Leah frowned. "Let me tell you, somethin'. I certainly understand when something feels somehow 'off.'" She felt the exact same way every time she pulled that sheet out of her pocket with the list of the thirty-nine suspects from Grell Memorial. She wondered if she'd ever figure out that one.

The trunk to Chris's squad car was open, its lights brightening up that small part of the road. Ethan walked back and pulled out three walkie-talkies. He handed one to Dan and one to Leah.

"What about me?" Chris asked.

"You won't need one. You're on my team."

"Okay, well, I'll carry it."

Ethan showed no sign of handing it over. "You're on my team, I said. You don't *run* my team. *I* run my team. You're the guy who doesn't get to talk on the walkie-talkie."

"Why don't we have four?" Chris asked.

"Because only three of us work at the goddamn department! Now, come here, all of you." Leaving the trunk open, Ethan walked to the front of Chris's car, where they all gathered around the hood and bent over.

It almost felt like a damn football huddle to Leah. Everyone blocked out a lot of the night's light, and now she couldn't see her GD hand two feet in front of her face.

"Now, listen," Ethan said. "There's two ways to do this. The right way and the wrong way. We're gonna make damn sure we do it the right way, you hear?"

Leah cast a glance over to Tommy's shack. The door sat askew on the frame, barely holding on to the top hinge. A very large boot hole went almost near on all the way through. She'd predicted right. That would've been Ethan.

"Now, none of us have put eyes on the rest of that structure," Ethan continued. "I'm willin' to bet there's some windows in the back—probably missing some glass—and at least one side door, possibly two. Now, the part that makes this whole thing hard is that there hayloft."

They all turned and took a look at the rotted wood and broken clapboards barely standing in the gentle breeze. The light of the half moon caught the edge of the hayloft and lit up the opening like a cold white spike. That was why Leah could see the hay so well. But that light came to an abrupt end. It went in one solid line, from the bright moon to a shivering black.

"What's so hard about the hayloft?" Chris asked.

"If he's got her up there? We'll be like over-plump turkeys late for the dinner party. He'll have nothin' but clear shots at all of us, and we can't see shit all. For that matter, how the hell would we even get up there, even if we somehow managed to get that close without him seein' us?"

He waited for Chris to speak, but after a moment of silence, Ethan gave up. He squinted in the darkness, trying to get a better look. "Can any of you tell if those front doors are locked?"

"I think there's a rope or a chain running through the hasps," Leah said. "At least that's what I reckoned I saw when I pulled up. Might've been a shadow or somethin'."

"Doesn't mean they're locked. I wouldn't think the whole place, the way it stands, is even worth as much as a lock."

"True," Dan said, raising his eyebrows. He'd come

up along beside Leah and now caught her attention discreetly. "How are you holdin' up?" he whispered.

She closed her eyes and smiled sadly with a nod. "I'm keepin' in there."

His arm went around her. "Good girl. We'll figure this out."

And all Leah could think was, *Please don't promise, please don't promise. For God's sake, please don't promise.*

"So I say we do it this way," Ethan said, laying out a plan Leah was near on positive he was making up on the fly. "Two of us will take those front doors, *providing* they're not locked. I want the other two to each go around on either side. Leah, you take the left. Dan, you . . . the other one."

"The right?"

Ethan nodded. "If there turns out to be no other way in and those front doors are locked, well, then . . . we have another problem."

"Which is?" Chris asked.

"Same as the problem with the goddamn hayloft, Chris. We shoot out those locks, we may as well just paint a target on our bloody foreheads."

Chris went stone-faced.

"All right," Ethan said. "I'm guessin' at least one of you's gonna find a doorway. I'm guessin' if there even *is* still a door attached to the doorway, that it will likely be unlocked. I want you both to radio me back and tell me the situation. I won't be goin' in those front doors . . . and neither will Chris . . . until we hear 'bout your situations."

"Okay," Dan said, clipping his walkie-talkie to his belt. "What if all the doors are unlocked and we hit the place and find nobody inside?"

Ethan sneered at him. "Yeah, you always gotta be the one jackass who takes the party out of the parade, ain't you? *If* that happens, we must assume our killer is up in that hayloft."

"There's probably a ladder," Chris said.

Ethan just shook his head at him. "You really think you're gonna climb a ladder after bustin' into an old barn that probably echoes like the call of some banshee wolf and have the guy holed up in the hayloft *not* hear you? And then, you think you're goin' to climb up twenty feet on some rickety ladder and somehow take this guy by surprise?"

Chris went back to being stone-faced.

"One last thing," Ethan said. "Before anyone tries the doors or anythin' else, remember what I told you. There's a smart way of doing this, and then there's the stupid way. We're goin' to settle on doing things the smart way. So, I would like Leah and Dan to please walk all the way around the left side of the structure, and me and Chris will go around the right until we all meet at the back. Then we'll have a much better idea of what we're lookin' at here. And if—Jesus, I hesitate to even say this—but if you find a window and you feel it's safe, try to sneak a peek inside so you can get a better read on our situation. Y'all got that?"

Everyone but Leah nodded. She was too busy fighting off bad thoughts. The realization had fully come to her that this was *real*. All this was really happening. Since she'd seen the Stickman's letter, she'd been in a cloudy daze. Now everything hit her like a dump truck. All of it. All at once. Hard and fast.

Her body trembled. She could be moments away from seeing her baby girl lying tied up or worse . . . Closing her eyes, she struggled not to think about the "or worse" possibility. Choking her thoughts back, she noticed Dan staring.

"What is it?" he asked. "You okay?"

Her tears returned. "I don't know, Dan. I really . . . I don't. I don't know. I'm not sure I can do this."

Dan glanced at Ethan and Chris already starting for the barn. "Yes, you *can* do this," he said quietly. "You can. Just try not to think the worst."

She took a big breath.

"We okay?" Ethan asked, turning around from about twenty paces up.

"We're good," Dan answered. He looked back into Leah's eyes, lowering his voice. "Yeah, we're good. We're gonna be all right."

Leah wiped the tears from her face and steeled herself, even though her head felt like she was in an evil carnival from some horror movie where every step you take just springs a new trap. Her mind kept flashing through all the times she hadn't been quick enough to stop the killer, starting with Samantha Hughes and going all the way back to the Cornstalk Killer case and Ruby Mae Vickers over a decade ago. So much blood. So many bodies. Her pulse began to race again. *What if Caroline* . . . No. She stopped that thought right in its tracks. She needed to calm down. She needed control.

Something happened then that caused Leah to look back the way they had come, back to the three cars parked on the edge of the road, each one at least a block and a half away from Tommy's shotgun shack. Back to that row of forest way off in the distance looking like a line of giant sentries in the night, with a half-dozen fields bridging the space between her and them, the darkness painting the fields into lakes. And back to that ramshackle shotgun house that Leah really would have no problem firing a bullet straight through. That house with the door barely hanging on, like some soccer kid's tooth after getting kicked in the mouth with a pair of cleats during practice. And those crazy lamps the guys had left on.

The house looked like it was grinning at her. And she hated that grin.

But it wasn't the grin that made her look back. She didn't know what it was. A sound, maybe? A bird? There were no cars on the road, other than theirs. But something made her turn back. Maybe it was her gut instinct. Maybe it had finally decided to return.

Or maybe it was that voice she always heard. The one that never really answered her questions but just brought her peace. That voice that sounded like her pa's.

Whatever it was, she most certainly did turn back, and, in that second, just as her eyes drifted across Tommy's shack, she saw movement inside. Something blurred across the spray of lamplight coming screeching through the cockeyed space left open by that dangling door.

Now everyone was at least two dozen paces in front of her, all approaching the barn just as quiet as cats. But there was no point in being quiet anymore. Tommy Stork obviously knew they were there. He'd managed to get out of his house and hide until . . . until Leah had led them on a wild-goose chase.

"He's in his house!" Leah shouted. "He's back in his goddamn house! He's *seen* us!"

CHAPTER 59

Jonathon's car bounced over the small rise on his way down Maple Drive toward Blue Jay Maples. As the car's suspension descended, he heard the hood slam down hard, but he so didn't care about his car right now. All he could think of was Carry and whether or not she was okay. He should never have let her go for that snack run on her own. The worst part? He wasn't even hungry. And that was then. Now, the way his stomach felt? He didn't expect he'd ever eat again.

The drive was a wash of outside house lights streaking by him in the dark. His vision had pretty near tunneled to nothing but the patch of road ahead of him. And his mind was clearer than he remembered it being in a long time. It felt like a clock. That inevitability of time sooner or later catching up with wherever you thought you could run and feel safe.

He and Carry had even joked about her ma putting in another curfew like she had while searching for the Cornstalk Killer, and Jonathon had told her this one was different because this time the killer was going for older people, not kids. But why would Jonathon ever trust a cold-blooded killer not to throw a changeup pitch at him? The man was mad. By nature, he was unpredictable.

And Jonathon and Carry had laughed. With the strength of dragons. With that thought, Jonathon thought back through all the tales he'd read over the years, starting with fairy tales when he was a child and progressing into high fantasy novels as he got older.

There was a thing about dragons. He realized it now.

No matter how big their roar or how sharp their teeth, they always turned out to have a soft spot, somewhere.

Maybe it wasn't him and Carry who were the dragons at all. Maybe it was the Stickman. This Tommy Stork or whatever his name was. He was the one with the princess. He was the one whose tower Jonathon was now speeding toward as he took the turnoff into Blue Jay Maples.

Luckily for him, he'd spent a lot of time driving around these streets. When he first got his license, he and two of his friends would come out here at night and "rat race" each other around the S-shaped streets, without caring about their speed or even their headlights. The cops never came out this far, they knew that.

Of course, back then Jonathon had thought they were invincible. That they always would be.

Now the world seemed nothing but fragile, as though made from blown glass, and all it would take would be one careless person to let it slip from their fingers and fall to the floor.

He wasn't ready to let go of Carry yet. He would save her.

He just wasn't quite sure how that was going to happen. Despite the dry roads, as Jonathon took a hard left onto Mockingbird Lane, his back tires spun out in the loose dirt as his front barely managed to find purchase on the gravel of the new road. His Sentra near on fish-tailed into one of the big gulleys scooped out of the ground at the edge of all the roads down here. He was driving too fast. He had to slow down. He couldn't help Carry if he wound up dead before even getting to her.

And the night certainly didn't help. It had been easy driving down here: The streets he took had sporadic sodium lights along them, and the vast stretch of stars along with the moon coming up on his left had provided him with lots of light. Now, though, inside these narrow roads carved through the muddled and knotted woods like crazy fjords, there were no streetlights—well, hardly any—and the tall birches and maples scrunched together by all the tangle wood and strangler fig blocked out most of the natural light.

But Jonathon's thoughts were too overcome with saving his girlfriend to be scared about his driving.

But . . . And with that "but" came all the second-guessing. What did he plan to do, anyway? He wasn't a cop. What did he honestly expect to do? He had no idea, he just knew that Carry, wherever she was, was in trouble. How much? Well, judging from her ma's reaction to everything, Jonathon figured a swampful. And it didn't matter that he didn't know how he was going to help yet. When the time came, he just would. That was the way fate worked, the way his grandpa always told him it did. And if something were to happen to Carry and he hadn't tried to help? How could he ever live with himself again? That would be impossible.

So he calmed his mind, knowing he'd taken the only real course of action available to him.

Mockingbird Lane twisted a hard left, and then, not even forty feet later, bent into an almost ninety-degree right. *Whoever made these roads, they should be the ones in trouble,* he thought.

He was now on Chickadee, a road he was pretty sure accessed Woodpecker Wind just over a mile down its curvy path. One thing Jonathon knew and was thankful for was the fact that he had a good memory. At least, he hoped it was good as he slammed the wheel left again and then right, thinking that he had to have gone a mile by now.

Where was that road?

On the verge of pulling a U-turn, he saw a light just beyond the turn up another half mile or so ahead. Most intersections in this bird land did have streetlights: one of them at every intersection, which meant one light every two or three miles of careening between these deadly, crazy ditches. At least it could be a light. The sharp banking turn obscured most of it, but he thought he had made out a streetlight between the boughs of the dozens of trees between. He lost it now as he continued toward it. It could've just been a spattering of shorter trees on one side of the road allowing the white rays of the moon to shine down and briefly catch some leaves. His heart sank now, as he got closer to the turn and saw no other sign of brightness.

Then, just as he pulled a tight left and gravel sprayed out from his tires as the rear of his Sentra spun around, the light slid into view, shining down over his silver Nissan like the light of heaven beaming down on the saints. Snatching a quick look at the road sign, Jonathon's hope swelled. It read WOODPECKER WIND, just as he'd remembered.

Accelerating, he chanced the higher speed based on this road not being as curvy as the rest. There were no houses for the first mile at least, and then he came to one on his right. A white house with a picket fence. Slowing down, Jonathon strained to see the number on the side of the house, but ivy covered the black numbers. Luckily, the porch light was on, and he was able to make out the last of them. It was a four, which told Jonathon enough.

According to the report Abe had given him from Leah's files, the house number she'd written in was 749. Jonathon knew, no matter what the first two numbers of this white house might be, it wasn't Tommy Stork's. It wasn't even on the right side of the road.

At least another mile of twists and turns went by before Jonathon passed the next house, this one much older than the last, and not in good repair. He only saw a glimpse of it streaking past. He didn't even bother slowing down for it—it was still on the wrong side of the road.

Then, maybe three-quarters of a mile later, Jonathon could see the woods start to break, which either meant it was somewhere loggers had been clear-cutting or it was another piece of property, this time coming up on his right, the same side Tommy Stork lived on.

He slowed down as he came closer, but not too slow. Just in case this Stork guy was watching, Jonathon didn't want to look suspicious. He kept his speed around thirty-five, a speed he figured most folk would think reasonable for tonight in this dense wood on these vicious roads under the black grip of all these trees.

It was still too fast. He'd missed the house number. The house was blue, and the numbers had been white. He *thought* the last two had been a four and a nine, which was close enough for Jonathon to pull over to the edge of the road and park his car. He'd head back on foot, just in case it was Stork's house. If it wasn't, he'd be sure to drive even slower past the next one.

Locking his car, he ran as silently as possible, staying on the roadside where the ground was hard dirt rather than on the road, where his shoes would kick up gravel.

Coming to the clearing, he saw the blue house with the white porch and shutters and decided to just keep jogging quietly by so he could get a look at the house number. He hoped someone going for a little run way down here wouldn't be too out of the ordinary if he was spotted.

He did his best to keep his eyes focused in front of him while just grabbing occasional glances to the numbers by the door.

Sure enough, he'd found the place. A little blue clapboard house, prettier than all get-out, with a nice lawn and what looked to be a newly painted detached garage. A white Hyundai Excel was parked in the driveway. Looked like Tommy Stork was home. Probably a good sign.

Jonathon kept jogging until the trees once again separated him from any line of sight back to Stork's property. Then he slowed to a stop and thought about his next move.

One thing struck him immediately. Where the hell was Carry's ma and the other cops from the Alvin station? Surely they had to have beat him here. Maybe they were even more concerned than he was about being seen. Maybe they were hiding, each posted somewhere back in the woods on either side of the crazy killer's house.

He figured he'd find out soon enough.

A thought ran through his head. *What drives a man living in a nice, pretty house with a big, fancy porch and a well-kept lawn and gardens to take people from right out of life and then take their lives?* He shook his head. Was Carry somewhere inside that little blue home that wouldn't look out of place on one of the covers of all them *Life* magazines Jonathon's grandpa kept on the toilet? Norman Rockwell, that was the name of the guy who painted a lot of them. Jonathon couldn't see it. The place was too nice. It actually *reminded* Jonathon of his grandpa's place.

But this was the address Miss Leah had written on the report. This had to be where Tommy Stork lived, didn't it? Panic raced through Jonathon's veins as the thought struck him that maybe she hadn't written it as a replacement address. Maybe she had just been on the phone and needed somewhere to jot something down.

Still hiding out of sight from anywhere on the property, Jonathon thought about the detached garage with the new paint job. And the more he thought about it, the more he doubted there was anywhere else more likely to be the sort of place crazy people like Tommy Stork would bring his victims to. Carry was in that garage. She had to be. Somehow, Jonathon just knew it.

Standing on the roadside, Jonathon surveyed the area around him. The trees on the other side of the ravine-like ditch stood side by side like sentinels all the way down to where the area opened onto the garage and that house. Mostly, here, were still oak and birch, but also a lot of Douglas fir, their boughs weighed heavily down with Spanish moss. Between the trees, thickets of shrubs, vines, and prickly bushes grew up and around like razor wire on top of a security fence. He became aware of the smell of the woods. It saturated the air like one of them deodorizers his ma used to put in the bathroom. Jonathon thought he could taste the tree sap from where he stood.

Stepping back three or four big steps, he took a running leap across the culvert to the narrow edge of land on the other side leading to the wall of forest. He fell at least three feet short of his target, and struggled to climb up the clumpy black edge of the ditch. Twice he tried digging his feet and fingers into the dirt lining the trench, only to have it crumble in his hands, sending him backward, and, one time, tumbling onto his back into the culvert's bowled bottom.

"You're just lucky you didn't hit your head," he whispered to himself, taking note of a mighty big boulder a foot away from where he'd landed. He cleared that thought and tried going up the side again, this time determined to make it. His foot went deep into the loam and came down on something solid—another rock, perhaps. Whatever it was, it provided some much welcome leverage. Reaching up with his right hand, his fingers wrapped around a twist of vine he found hanging down from above. It wasn't until Jonathon had started coming up, hand over hand on that vine as though it were a climbing rope, that he realized it was covered in blade-sharp thorns. Warm rivulets of blood from his palms began dripping down his fists and continued down his forearms.

But he felt no pain as he hefted his right leg up onto the edge of the ground. Even the smell of the trees had disappeared. As he rolled onto his side and then his back, freed from Dante's dark pit of hell, Jonathon's only thoughts whirled around Carry.

CHAPTER 60

After Leah hollered, everyone came running back. Dan reached her first.

"You saw Tommy?" he asked. "What 'bout your daughter?"

"I don't know. I only saw Tommy. At least I reckon—" Now that the moment had passed, she started doubting herself. It had happened so quick . . . What if she *hadn't* actually seen somebody? Now all her goddamn yelling would have alerted Tommy they were about to close in on the barn. Now he'd have no choice but to . . .

"Leah!" Dan yelled almost straight into her face, scaring the bejeezus out of her. "What's goin' on? Did you see him or not?"

She looked back at the shack. Everything seemed to be running in slow motion, almost as if they were all under water. Ethan said something, but it just sounded like bubbles. Chris even said something, Leah thought. She didn't care. All she cared about was going over what had just transpired in her mind. Had she seen someone? Or was it just a trick of the light? Or had she simply *wanted* to see someone so bad that her brain had tried to do her a favor?

"What?" Leah asked, her senses reeling. She felt confused, then she felt herself falling.

Dan grabbed her before she hit the ground. Then, cautiously, he set her down there for safekeeping.

"So, we're actually *not* okay," Ethan said, walking up and slightly huffing and puffing.

"Guess not," Dan said. He looked down at Leah. "Well, ball's in your court. Did you see him or didn't you?"

Leah took several deep breaths. She studied Tommy's shack for another sign of movement, but, of course, there was none. "Yes," she said at last. "I did. I saw him. He's in the house."

"You're sure?" Ethan said.

"Yes." Leah got up off the dusty ground and brushed her pants with her hands.

"Okay, slight change in plans." Dan turned to Leah. "You're stayin' in the car. I don't care what car you pick to stay in, but you're waitin' for us in one."

"No," Leah said, shaking her head. "I'm not."

"You just practically fainted."

"But I didn't. I'm fine now. I'm doing this. I'm coming with you."

Ethan let out a big breath. "This is a *mistake,* Leah. This is what I meant about not doin' anything stupid. *This* . . . this minute here? *This* is stupid."

"I don't care. He's got my daughter, and I'm coming!" She marched ahead of everyone else, unclipping her gun from its holster on her way.

"Wait a minute!" Ethan called out, slowly and resignedly. "We still need a . . ." He stopped. She wasn't listening. Dan and Chris came up on either side of him. ". . . a plan," Ethan finished, matter-of-factly. "Or has everyone just decided to wing it today?"

The guys started asking each other what the hell was going on. "Is she just goin' to march straight in there and shoot Stork dead where he stands?" Chris asked.

"I God well hope not," Ethan said. "This whole thing's bad enough already. Don't need some bloody renegade cop goin' off all vigilante." But he didn't dare shout out to her. He didn't want to compromise her position.

She did stop walking, though. Right when she reached Chris's car. The others quickly caught up.

"Okay," Leah said, still worked up. "Here's the thing. Maybe Caroline's in the barn, maybe she's not. If she's in there, there's two possibilities. One, she's dead. And two, she's alive. As long as we don't let Stork back across the road, that doesn't change. Her fate is sealed. Therefore, we take Stork down at his house. Good plan?" She looked straight at Ethan.

Ethan raised a hand. "I have a question."

"What?" she asked histrionically.

"What if Caroline's in his goddamn house?"

"You just searched the house."

"Yes. And when I did, Stork wasn't there, either. If he's back, she could be, too."

It was the wrong thing to say. Dan knew the minute he saw her reaction. She was hell-bent on moving again. "You're right," she said, this time actually pulling her gun. "We assume Caroline's in the house." She popped the cylinder on her revolver, made sure all six chambers were full, snapped it back in place, and gave it a spin.

"Wait!" Dan yelled, going for her arm to hold her back. "This is *not* how you want to approach this! For Christ's sake, Leah, just think for a minute."

"Tell Ethan I've got the back door. I'd advise you and Chris to start clearing rooms."

Dan stopped walking beside her as they came to the

front of the house. "You sure 'bout this?" he called out as she continued to the back, getting lost in the shadows of the darkness.

"I'm not sure about nothin' right now." She was breathing heavy. Her words came out in clumps.

Leah took her position by the back door, wondering if this was how her pa felt that night with Harry Stork. She could taste bile at the back of her throat. Unlike her father fifteen years ago, Leah didn't have the luxury of a blow horn. "Tommy Stork!" she screamed. "We know you're inside! We have the house surrounded! Your only move is to surrender. Give up the girl and come out peacefully, and you won't be killed!" On that note, she pulled back the hammer on her Smith & Wesson 686.

Seconds went by as nothing happened. Not even a curtain fluttered on the small window by the back of the house. "Tommy!" Leah yelled again. "This is your last chance. You have to the count of five. One . . . two . . . three . . . four . . . five!" She grabbed the walkie-talkie from where she'd stuffed it into her pocket. "Okay, Ethan!" she screamed into it. "Make your move!" It would occur to her later that she probably didn't need the walkie-talkie.

Then came three hard slams as Ethan's boot undoubtedly took the door right off the house this time. Leah heard Dan and Chris run inside. "Room one, clear!" Dan shouted.

"Room two, clear!" Chris shouted.

Dammit, Leah thought. *He's hiding inside. We need to flush him out.*

"Don't forget to check behind furniture and under beds and inside closets!" Leah yelled.

"He's in the bathroom!" Chris yelled.

Then, right on the heels of that, she heard Dan scream,

"He's makin' a run for the back door, and he's armed! Repeat: He's armed!"

Leah crouched down low with her weapon still in her hand. Her fingers were shaking, she could see it by the moonlight glittering off the barrel of her Smitty.

Suddenly, the back door opened and out burst Tommy Stork. Leah's eyes immediately went to the piece in his left hand. The light of the moon shimmered over the barrel. She thought it looked like a Beretta, like the 92 Harry Stork had wielded the night he made a move very similar to the one his brother just did.

"Wait!" he shouted, out of breath. "You got the wrong guy."

"Yeah, I've heard that one before!" Leah yelled. "Drop your weapon! And where the hell's my baby girl?"

The weapon stayed gripped tightly in his hand. "I don't know what you're talking 'bout. You got the wrong guy! I've been set up." His gun definitely was a Beretta. Either the same one Harry had, or maybe a 96. Either way . . . *shit.* Now was not the time for thoughts to start churning in her head again. The next second could be her last.

"Drop the weapon!" Leah screamed once more. "I'm not telling you again!"

But just like the last time she warned him, he didn't obey. It was like he wasn't even aware he was holding it.

It's the wrong gun. She was absolutely positive there were no Beretta 92s or Beretta 96s that chambered 9 mm. None that she'd ever heard of, anyway. Then some new thoughts crept into Leah's overclocked mind. She realized what had caught the attention of her subconscious about the list of thirty-nine suspects. It was one of the names. Originally, only the surname had *pinged* because it was an unusual name and she'd heard it twice over the course of days. *Delford*. Someone on the list had the last name of *Delford*. And someone *else* had the last name of Delford: Sally-Anne—Noah's wife. *Shit*. No wonder her brain had been performing mental gymnastics to get her attention. The name on the list was Joshua Delford. *Joshua*. The same name Noah used in his book.

"Tommy!" Leah yelled. "Wait!" She held up both her palms, letting her gun swing around her finger. "Now, please, put your gun down." She said this quietly and calmly, but inside her head, pieces were clicking.

And as soon as they started, they didn't stop. Everything began coming together. Noah wasn't judging Tommy at all. Joshua was judging Noah. And it was Noah who hated the military for what they supposedly did to Harry, but it wasn't really the military he was targeting. She went back to that first interview she'd had with him. It was the doctors and the hospitals. Hospitals Harry Stork worked at and where he, occasionally, brought his dad along to help.

She figured out the asterisks on those jobs. She hadn't known if Harry Stork had put them there or her pa. Now she knew the truth: Neither of them had. That was Noah, reminding himself about which shifts Harry paid him for illegally under the table.

She hadn't run a medical report or any kind of report on Noah Stork, but she was willing to bet he'd built the alias and used it every time he was admitted to a hospital. Back when he started, they didn't even have computers and databases in place. Nobody would've ever known. Leah doubted even the Social Security numbers were ever really used. Nobody expected someone to use an alias while being admitted to a hospital. Why would they? Only, Noah was a lot smarter than anyone knew. He obviously felt one day that the cover might come in handy.

Leah realized Tommy still had his Beretta trained on her. "Tommy, it's over. I know you're the wrong guy."

"You're just fuckin' with my head now!" he screamed.

"No," she said quietly with a quick shake of her head. "No, I'm not. Please put the gun down before you do something really dumb."

Back in the sixties, hardly anyone worried about any sort of identity theft, never mind creating identities for no apparent reason. Noah could even have a passport issued under the name Joshua Delford. It wouldn't surprise Leah at all.

"It wasn't me," Tommy said, the weapon coming dangerously around, its barrel quivering.

"I know!" Leah said. "Please just throw your gun out onto the ground. I know it wasn't you. Nothing's goin' to happen to you."

Another thought flew into Leah's mind. This one was the clincher. The blood sample . . .

"Tommy," she said. "I can tell you don't want this to go any further. Put the gun down now." His green eyes caught the icicle light of the moon and held it for an instant. That was when Leah knew he'd made a decision. Not that it mattered. With her hands above her head and her weapon dangling from her index finger, she couldn't defend herself no matter what happened.

But she knew then she didn't have to. She knew he wasn't going to do anything stupid. With a deep breath, Tommy looked at the gun one last time before making his next move. Leah held her breath, waiting to see what that move would be.

Behind Tommy, Dan was coming up fast.

"No, don't!" Leah yelled to Dan, but it was too late. He tackled Tommy Stork right off the back porch of his shack. A gunshot rang out into the fresh Alabama air, followed by the smell of cordite. A dozen birds from the trees surrounding the area exploded into the sky, racing over the top of the shack, almost looking like bats in this godforsaken night.

Dan looked up from where he was lying on top of Tommy and disarming him. "You didn't really just tell me not to do that, did you? The man had a gun on you. He's a killer!"

Leah's chest heaved as more and more puzzle pieces fit together. Her timeline was right, only she'd had the wrong name on it. Tommy Stork was as innocent as his brother, Harry, had been. Neither of them were the Stickman.

Catching her breath, Leah shook her head emphatically. "It's not him. It's not Tommy. And it wasn't Harry."

Now Dan seemed angry. "Then tell me, who in the name of hell is it?"

"Their pa," she said, near on dying from exhaustion. "It's their goddamn pa." Her words disappeared into the night's shadows, heard by nobody but herself.

CHAPTER 61

Making it onto his feet, Jonathon began walking the narrow path between the trees and the ditch toward Stork's property line. All the while, he stayed as quiet as he could, trying hard not to dwell on the bad feeling wrapping around his insides on account of he still had seen no sign of Miss Leah and her team.

When he got to where the woods broke, he squatted down and put his head out slowly for a look at the garage standing there in the stark moonlight. It was the same baby blue of the house, only with that bright sheen you got after just painting something. He couldn't see any lights. Lucky for him, he had the moon. If it had still been raining . . . Well, if it had still been raining, his silver Nissan Sentra would've probably been swallowed by one of them ditches on the edge of some bird street long before he managed to get there.

The garage had a pull-up door that was white. Jonathon had no way of knowing whether it was locked or not. Garage door locks were usually automatic and done from the inside. They weren't something he could pick.

It didn't matter. He wasn't about to go pull up the

door anyway. He could just imagine throwing that door up, its metal wheels rattling and roaring against their steel track as the thing slowed to a nice stop at the top. No, he'd be better off just going up and kicking it and yelling out, "Hey, it's me! Come so you can kill me, too!"

He chanced looking a bit more. The house had a dim light on somewhere inside it. He could see it glowing faintly through the living room picture window. But that was it. The rest of the rooms he had window views of were dark as the porch. Same went for the garage. Luckily, the moon and the stars allowed him to view the garage's side well enough to know there wasn't a door or window on it. At least not on the side he could see.

With a few deep breaths, Jonathon decided his next move would be from where he stood now to that side of the garage. The blind side. Mentally, he counted to three, then dashed across the bit of yard separating him from his target. He moved low and fast and, far as he could tell, silently. The short, healthy grass took care of that, and he was thankful for it.

His nerves had caught up with him as he finally came to a stop halfway down the wall and pressed his back to it. He allowed himself time to catch his breath fully and calm down before thinking his next thought.

Now, he cautioned a look around the corner to the back of the building.

Behind the garage, a small garden bloomed chock-full of pansies, tulips, and daffodils, their colors faded with the waning light, making them look like old photographs. Just like everything else Jonathon had seen about this place, the flowers and the garden didn't fit the picture for him. They didn't belong in this place of death. It made him wonder if they reflected their owner.

Likely Stork didn't fit the world, either. His life must be a constant juxtaposition. He was the ultimate human non sequitur. Jonathon's heart pounded, jackhammering his ribs, feeling like a fully stretched water balloon ready to burst. Sweat trickled down the side of his head.

Pulling the front of his gray T-shirt from his Dockers, Jonathon used it to wipe his face dry. With a glance toward the front of the building, making sure he wasn't in danger of being caught, he took another look around the back, spotting the two white motion-activated security spotlights with the controller box between them up in the peak of the garage's roof.

The lights did nothing to slow Jonathon's racing heart as he slowly ducked his head back behind the wall.

He still hadn't really seen the back side of the garage. He needed to know if there was a door or a window or . . . whatever . . . but now he had an even bigger problem. How would he get past those lights?

Jonathon had interesting hobbies. He knew this to be true. Home, school, and church security being a big one. He felt his back pocket, double-checking that his lock-pick set was still with him. He'd slid it into his pocket as soon as he got in the car back at Carry's. Now, even if there actually *did* turn out to be a door, he was in a tight spot on account of those lights.

But he *did* know a thing or two about how the motion-activated part of the security lights worked. They ran on a system known as PIR, a term describing the passive infrared light they used to detect movement. Everyone called them "motion detectors," but the fact was, they didn't detect motion at all. What they did was look for changes in temperature, running on the theory that an abrupt change in temperature (especially one going up to somewhere around a human body's skin temperature) would be evidence of an intruder, and so the lights would come on. Then, after five to fifteen minutes, depending on how they were set, they'd go back off again.

The idea was to make a potential crook think someone had spotted him or heard him and turned on the light. Jonathon's problem wasn't that he was afraid of the lights, he was afraid of there being a window in the back of the garage that might allow someone else to see the light if it came on.

He actually knew a great deal about PIR. The way it worked was, internally, the lights watched the area in a three-dimensional cone-shaped pattern it divided up into little cubes. Each of the cubes was measured for temperature, and any dramatic shift in temperature from one cube to an adjacent cube would activate the lights. Due to the nature of their workings, in *theory* it should be possible to outsmart them by moving really slowly and allowing the lights time to "get used to" a very gradual change in temperature. But, for the kind of speed he needed, Jonathon didn't have the time nor the patience.

Because of the cone-shaped pattern and the fact that these particular lights were placed about ten or eleven feet above the ground, Jonathon had a bit of breathing room. It explained why he hadn't already tripped them. They probably wouldn't see him at the garage's corner until he either walked out a yard or came closer.

He wasn't entirely sure how confident he was in those facts, though. So, when he decided to take another look, he sent up a small prayer to the god of whoever ruled over electric lighting to do him a solid.

With that done, he took one more glance, attempting to see everything on the garage's back side. He moved slowly, even though he knew it wasn't slowly enough. If he was in one of those light's field of view, he was a dead man.

He kept moving a little farther out, his eyes darting from the back of the garage to the lights hanging at the peak, thinking every inch would be the one that killed him. But they didn't turn on, and he got enough around to fully see the back wall.

Quite close to where he was stood a door, closed and, he suspected, locked. No dead bolt on it. The door handle looked like a Schlage and appeared to be a bolt lock. A bolt lock had a tiny version of a dead bolt—a spindle, really—that retracted from the door frame when it was open, but otherwise kept it tightly closed and in the hasp and strike plate.

On the other side of the wall was a window. From inside, a dim light shone through the glass, forming a stretched square on the ground between the garage and the garden. It was faint and flickery, almost like the garage was being lit with a lantern. There were no curtains on the window.

But what really got Jonathon's attention was the white wooden apparatus hanging on the outside wall between the top of the door and the PIR lights: a ladder.

If Jonathon could get the ladder, he could conceivably get on the garage's roof and adjust the lights so they pointed anywhere but behind the garage guarding that window and door.

Jonathon had seen enough of the garage on his jog across the front of the property to know that the final side was just like the one he now hid behind. Nothing but blue wooden siding ran along it. No window, no door. Alas, no ladder.

Thoughts began uncontrollably unrolling in his brain. How fast could he get that lock open? Fast enough that the light coming on wouldn't matter? Not a chance. Could he pull down the ladder without making any noise? He doubted it. He might be able to do it fairly quietly. But that didn't matter. He couldn't possibly get to it without first stepping into the watchful eye of the security lights.

And the worst thought of all followed those. While he was out there, unable to decide what to do, Carry was—as far as he guessed—just beyond the wall, praying for her life. That was, *if* she was still alive.

That was a thought he really couldn't afford to entertain, so he dropped it and dropped it fast.

And just then, his savior appeared, coming through the garden, pushing aside pansies as its little paws delicately tread through the soft dirt. Jonathon wondered if maybe someone had heard his prayers after all.

A brown and black bobtail, probably out looking for mice, appeared from a bouquet of tulips. First his feline face, then the white tufts at the end of his front paws, and finally his gray tail with a long white tip.

Immediately Jonathon heard the security lamps' *click,* and the yard and garden behind the garage were bathed in white light. The white end of the cat's tail snapped straight up at attention. He ducked back behind the shadow of the garage's side wall and waited.

It wasn't long. Maybe five or ten seconds—until Jonathon heard the door being unlocked and swinging open. He really hoped that cat hadn't darted away. If it had, this might end up just as bad as if Jonathon had tripped the lights himself. He kept perfectly still, feeling sweat run down his face and one bead race down his arm. Everything in his brain told him to run as he stood there motionless, waiting for an indication of what to do.

Then, in the silence, he heard a small "mew."

The cat had stayed. Jonathon let out a huge breath

he'd been holding far too long as he listened to a dispute between the cat and, he assumed, Tommy Stork.

"Go away," he heard a man's voice whisper from around the corner. "Go!"

Then the door clicked closed again, and again Jonathon heard the lock.

Pulling up his shirt from where it still hung untucked, he dried the sweat off his face again. It was time to get to work. He had five to fifteen minutes, depending on how those lights were set, to get that ladder down from the roof without drawing any attention to himself either through noise or the view through the window.

The ladder was up on two white metal hooks screwed into the back wall. Standing at the outside of the door, Jonathon reached up and was able to grab the bottom but not the top. Carefully, he brought the end down, stopping just short of the angle of the ladder coming into view of the window. The ladder wasn't light, and to keep the end up high enough, Jonathon could only slightly bend his elbows. It gave him no leverage. He couldn't possibly just lift the whole thing up by this one end.

Sweat streamed into his eyes. *It might as well be the middle of the goddamn day*, he thought, placing one end of the ladder back on the hook. He pulled off his T-shirt and used it like a rag to dry the sweat off his face, neck, and under his arms. When he was finished, he tossed it to the ground.

From inside the garage came the chilling sound of Carry sobbing.

It doesn't matter, he thought. *I don't have time for it to matter. Just do it. Just get it over with.*

He brought the ladder's edge down again, this time letting it fall past the window's glass. Jonathon had no choice. If Stork noticed it, then fate had decided to cut him a raw deal.

Even with his hands now on both sides of the ladder, it took all the strength in his lower back to pivot the thing up and over the other hook. Then he almost let it fall back against the glass. Sweat poured from his hair and his arms while he scrunched up his face in pain, trying to keep the wooden edge of the ladder from slamming into the glass.

He was just about to fumble it when he used every bit of strength he had left to twist it outward, spinning it away from the window. It flew from his hands as it crunched onto the ground. In Jonathon's ears, it was one of the loudest sounds he'd ever heard.

Standing there, frozen with fear, he listened, waiting for the door to yank open.

But all he heard was Carry's crying. She was louder now, and he wondered if that helped conceal the ladder's heavy landing. With a big breath, he decided not to overthink it and slid the ladder along the grass until it was well past the window. As he did, he noticed it was older than he'd thought. The boards making up the sides were cracked, and in one place, a new board had been nailed across where it had almost split in two. Even some of the rungs looked ready to go.

At this point, he wasn't about to let that concern him.

Pulling the ladder open to lengthen it, he set one end on the grass between the forest and the shadowed wall and gently let the other end set down on the bottom of the garage's roof. With slow, careful, and deliberate steps, he made his way up, rung by rung, hoping the thing didn't crack on him. Not because he'd get hurt, but because the sound would alert Stork to his presence.

He felt a surge of relief when his left foot came in

contact with the garage's shingles. With very slow steps, being careful not to shift his weight too suddenly and cause the ceiling joists to creak, he walked up the roof's slopes and across to the peak. Once there, he got on his knees and, being ever so careful not to put his hand anywhere in front of the square plastic motion sensors, he positioned each light so that it stared harmlessly outward at the middle of the tangled mess of trees making up the forest on the other side of the garden.

Returning to the ladder, he gave it one look before deciding he was better off just to jump.

CHAPTER 62

Dan and Tommy landed in the grass, and Dan seized the wrist of the hand holding the gun while simultaneously bringing his own gun up to the side of Tommy's head. Tommy's gun had been the one that fired the shot, but it was an accidental shot that went off into nowhere.

"You thought you could get away with this?" Dan asked, not even sounding winded. "With being the Stickman and the Cahaba River Strangler? Well, you're killin' days end here. Tell me where the girl is, or so help me God, I'll shoot you where you lie."

"I . . . don't . . . know . . . please . . . ?" Stork's voice came out in gasps. The wind had been knocked from his lungs when Dan hit him, and he was trying to get it back.

"Dan!" Leah shouted. "No! He doesn't know. He's not the Stickman! We got the wrong guy." As soon as she said it, the irony hit her. This could've turned out exactly like the Harry Stork murder did fifteen years ago.

While she talked, Ethan came around and helped Dan off of Tommy Stork after taking the gun from Stork's loosened grip. Dan slowly got up, leaving Stork gasping in the mud. "It wasn't me," he said quietly.

"I know," Leah said. "I know. It was your goddamn pa."

"What do you mean?" Dan asked as Ethan brought Stork's arms around behind and slapped on the cuffs.

"The blood. The blood should have been a hundred percent match to Harry Stork's if it was Tommy's. They're identical twins. They have—had—identical DNA. But the blood, it wasn't . . . The match wasn't one hundred percent. It was ninety-nine point nine . . . whatever. The blood *can't* belong to Tommy."

She saw revelation wash over Dan and she nodded vigorously. He was probably going through the same thing she just had, the moment when everything started making sense, when all the pieces of the picture started lining up, and once it started, it just kept going.

Ethan looked up, but his expression was more one of pride. Almost as though he was silently telling Leah, *See? I knew you could do it.* Dan, on the other hand, started connecting the dots. She could see it happening right there, plain as the moon frowning down.

"Exactly," she said without him saying a word. "The blood's not from him, it's from his pa, Noah. Noah Stork *is* the Stickman. And, I guess, the Strangler. And that's why he knows so goddamn much about mental illnesses. He's got one. Actually, I think he's probably got many, but one's gotta be something like dissociative identity disorder."

Dan looked confused. "Dis—" he started.

"Multiple personalities. He's like that woman in that movie." She couldn't remember the name of the movie. It didn't matter. "Come on! Let's go."

Dan raced after her. "Wait," he said. "Let's take my car. I'll drive!"

She stopped and turned back for just long enough to snap, "Like hell you will!"

CHAPTER 63

After landing fairly quietly on the lush grass between Stork's garage and the woods, Jonathon left the ladder where it was, up against the roof. It was actually well-hidden here in the shadows. Likely the absence of it from the back wall would give it away faster than a casual glance back here.

Jonathon didn't like leaving this side of the garage. He felt safer here with the wild forest only a couple of yards away and the bony light of the moon blocking him out than he did anywhere else. Other than being slightly more hidden, being here really *wasn't* any safer than anywhere else, but something about those clutching trees and bushes made him think that if anything started to happen, he could just dive in to the underbrush and lose himself.

Then he heard something, something that tore a hole right into him. From the other side of the wall, Carry, whose sobs had been growing since Jonathon had arrived, gave out a shriek.

Oh, dear Christ, Jonathon thought. *Not now. Not when I've come this far.*

In one way, hearing Carry had bolstered him. She

still lived. But in another, having never heard her cry before, he felt as though he could crumple right into the lawn at his feet.

He shook the thought away. Now he had to finish this. It didn't matter what had happened to Miss Leah and those other guys, it was all down to Jonathon. And he could do it. He thought about his grandpa and whispered to himself, "Indian blood, my friend. Indian blood." He remembered all his grandpa's stories and thought that, after tonight, he'd have a good story of his own.

Keeping down, he crept around the back of the barn. It was more open here, and he felt more exposed. Not only that, the moon was near on its way to being right overhead, and it focused down on him like a searchlight.

The cat he owed so much to had disappeared. Not that he blamed it.

Feeling something rise in his throat from all the stress roiling in his stomach, Jonathon slowly lifted his head to peer in the window.

And, for the first time, Jonathon got a look at the man who would kill the girl whom Jonathon loved, someone who, according to the police report Abe had given him, was named Tommy Stork.

Stork didn't see him. He wasn't interested in the window. And, for a moment, Jonathon's heart slowed down and he almost relaxed. He knew where Stork was, and as long as he did, he was safe. He could take his time. Then he saw something else in that garage, and his relief quickly disappeared in a flurry of adrenaline.

It was Carry. She lay on the floor on her side, just a few feet away from where Stork stood. Her arms and ankles were pulled backward where they'd all been hogtied together. On top of this, she wasn't wearing a shirt or even her bra. Jonathon felt a surge of heat rise in his body. If that animal in there had laid even a finger on her, it would be the last chance he'd ever have to do it again. Jonathon would make *sure* of that.

The irony of what he just thought about Tommy Stork wasn't at all clear to him, of course, because he had no way of knowing the man he now watched speaking something to Carry wasn't Tommy Stork at all, or that Tommy Stork had already lost two of his fingers in a construction mishap. Nor did Jonathon have any way of knowing that, at that very moment, Leah, Dan, Chris, and Ethan were driving to his position, hopefully in time to throw a monkey wrench into the way this dizzyingly terrifying night was unfolding.

Jonathon allowed himself another second to gaze from his vista. Carry appeared in shadow, slightly behind a tall, narrow table that sat ninety degrees from a workbench that ran the length of the wall beneath the window. The light in the garage was dim and, indeed, flickery. Only two fluorescent lights were installed along the bottom of the ceiling joists, the inside of the garage being unfinished, and of the two, only the dual bulbs in the far one by the door actually worked. The other, the unit closest to Jonathon, had one dead bulb and another with that annoying flicker. Jonathon figured that bulb didn't have long to live.

So, it's a race, he thought, *between a fluorescent bulb and the girl of my dreams.*

Carry's chest heaved with deep breaths. The way she was tied pushed out her abdomen and obviously made it hard to inhale far. When she blew out, it all came with a continual sob that practically broke Jonathon's heart every time. His insides felt as cold and dead as the cement floor Carry couldn't get up from.

While Jonathon appraised the situation, his eyes constantly went back to Stork, waiting for him to telegraph any sort of move or a turn of the head. Jonathon knew Carry's only chance of survival was now left with him, and he wouldn't go down that easily. At the far end of the garage, as though waiting to be packed up, Jonathon made out the shadows of what looked like some tools. One stood on its head, either a sledgehammer or an ax or something to that effect. Beside it, something else that Jonathon couldn't make out leaned against the inside wall.

Then he saw something about that wall and the others that almost made him vomit.

The long wall, the one Jonathon had felt safest hiding behind, was nearly completely covered with what looked like a dark brown paint, shot from one of them paint guns he'd played with once at someone's birthday party he'd been invited to. Now, Jonathon couldn't remember whose party it was, but he certainly remembered those guns. They weren't real, but they were close enough for him. Even though the company hosting the event made everyone wear goggles, Jonathon took a shot to his upper cheek, and it hurt so much he'd had to sit out the next two rounds. The green paint that impacted him splattered up over his goggles and down around his neck in a pattern pretty similar to the "paint" he was seeing now.

He felt himself retch when he realized this was the room all of the Stickman victims had been killed in. He looked at the wall across from that one, the one Stork and Carry waited alongside, and saw more of those faded patterns. Only, near on halfway between him and the door, there were two splatters that weren't faded at all. Even the fluorescents glimmered in the bright red explosive bursts that looked even fresher than the blue paint on the outside of the garage.

None of the splatters rose to more than four, maybe four and a half feet from the floor. The victims were all shot sitting down or, more likely, Jonathon surmised, while tied up backward the way Carry was now. It was all too gruesome and, finally, Jonathon had to duck away. Not because he worried Stork was going to glance out the window and see him, but because the thought occurred to him that the way the blood was situated made it appear to be a strangely macabre wainscoting.

Jonathon realized one thing: For him to successfully save Carry, it was integral that he control his mind. Already, it was breaking free of its cage far too easily, and the really hard part hadn't even started yet. Crouched down beneath the window, he did a visualization technique his grandfather had taught him, claiming it originally came from a great Indian shaman.

This was one of the stories Jonathon never knew whether to believe or not, but the fact remained that it did help clear his mind and calm him down. Thinking only of his breath, he let all other thoughts flow down a river in his mind. He gave them none of his attention, only assured himself that the thought had happened and then he let it go, like a dandelion seed floating on a late September breeze. Soon, fewer and fewer thoughts came down that river, until all he saw was the gently ebbing and flowing of the water. No longer did he even feel his breath.

Just like always, something happened then. From out of the woods following the slowly curving river, came a bear. Always it was the same bear. His power animal, as his grandpa said. "Not everyone gets a bear, you know," he had told Jonathon the first time he'd managed to get that far into the exercise. "You should feel very proud to have that bear."

"What do others get?" Jonathon had asked when the visualization was over.

"One never knows. Some get a frog. Some a beaver." His grandpa laughed. "I know one who even got a coyote."

"Why is that funny?"

His grandpa stopped laughing. "Coyote is not a good power animal. He is a trickster. Having a coyote for your animal makes you weak and a sham. A charlatan."

"What is your animal?" Jonathon asked quietly, unsure of how apropos the question was.

"What do you think?"

He considered the question, his eyes falling to one of the wooden masks on the wall of the room. "An eagle?"

His grandpa raised one eyebrow. "No, but you're close."

Jonathon shook his head. He could think of nothing close to an eagle. "A hawk, then?"

"No." His grandpa laughed. "What's my name?"

Then it came to him. His grandpa's power animal was a raven.

"Is a raven good? What does it mean?"

Light came to his grandpa's eyes. "Raven is very good. He is a master of time and space, and he can fold each together to put you in the right moment at exactly the right time."

"For what?"

His grandpa raised an index finger. "That's part of it. You don't know. Raven knows, only. He has a plan already set out. Raven stands for rebirth, recovery, a sort of renewal of one's soul. He can heal and cast light where there is only darkness."

"Wow, that's a lot." Jonathon dropped his gaze. Suddenly his bear didn't seem all that fantastic anymore.

His grandpa's hand gripped his shoulder. "What made you change just now?"

"I dunno," Jonathon said, trying not to sound disappointed. His eyes lifted to his grandpa's. "What does a bear do?"

His grandpa's eyes grew wide and clear. "Bear is fierce, a protector. He is the embodiment of the Great Spirit. And don't forget, your animal has his own constellation. Remember? The Great Bear?"

Jonathon smiled. He certainly did, a group of stars otherwise known as Ursa Major. The Big Dipper formed from his neck and body.

"He learns quick, too," Jonathon's grandpa added, "and is by far the most fearsome hunter in the woods."

"Really?" Jonathon had asked, a little perkier but dubious of this last claim. His eyes narrowed. "What about tigers?"

His grandpa had waved the question away. "Oh, tiger's good, too. But you are bear!"

Now, Jonathon stood on one side of the river and across from him stood the bear, up on his hind legs. Almost the same height, they stayed silent, staring into each other's eyes. The water no longer flowed. Gentle ripples in an otherwise mirrored surface caught the rays of sunlight beaming warmly upon them. Jonathon made out the bright flashes from the corners of his eyes.

The bear's voice filled Jonathon's head. "She needs you. Your courage has brought you this far. You must protect her, as I protect my cubs. Think of her as your cub, and you'll become the most dangerous animal in the world."

With that, the voice left Jonathon's mind, and the

bear got back down on four legs, turned, and lumbered slowly back into the woods, the bushes and trees closing up behind him, leaving not a trace of his path.

Jonathon opened his eyes, still sitting squatted beneath the garage window. Carry's crying still reverberated through the walls, but Jonathon was no longer panicked about them. He knew what he had to do. And he needed to be careful and slow to do it right.

Then, Carry's sobbing stopped and, although her voice still sounded chilled and wet, she asked Stork something. The words were too muffled by the wooden siding for Jonathon to make them out, but Stork's answer came through loud and clear. "Don't worry, honey," he quipped, his voice strangely bell-like. "This will all be over soon enough. And it won't even be painful, I promise. It's really just one quick shot. In and out in no time."

Carry fell into a trio of shrieks, each louder than the other. So loud, Jonathon made a quick look around to see if anyone had heard. Then he remembered that the closest house he knew of was at least a mile away. That was precisely why Stork lived way down here, Jonathon was sure of it.

When her cries finished, she said something else Jonathon couldn't hear.

"Oh, all right," he replied. "I suppose so, but just this once." Jonathon heard the man moving, but didn't dare chance another look.

He heard footsteps quietly walk across the garage's cement floor. Then came the loud sound of the garage door being pulled up on its steel tracks and Jonathon jumped. At first he thought Stork had opened this back door right beside where Jonathon hid, crouched on the lawn. Jonathon couldn't believe how loud that front door really was.

He decided to quickly make another visual. When he did, he almost crapped himself. Stork was outside but turned around, his face looking directly toward the back of the garage where the top of Jonathon's head poked up above the bottom of the window's glass.

"Shit!" Jonathon said, quickly ducking and flipping around, his back pressed tightly against the siding between the window and the door. "He saw me! Goddamnit!" The only good part about all of this was that Jonathon hadn't seen a gun anywhere.

At least not yet.

Then followed the sound of the door being rolled right down until the final shuddering when it came to the end. After that, Jonathon heard no more except Carry's faint sobs from inside the garage. From everywhere else, the lawn, the forest's perimeter, and the back of the house, cicadas filled up the night with their song, which, to Jonathon, sounded way too similar to a dentist's drill.

With panic still coursing through him, Jonathon stood there, trying to hear around the cicadas for any trace of footsteps on the lawn walking down either side of the garage. He heard none, but then, he, too, was able to walk on Stork's lush grass without making any noise. Finally, he decided to make the first move. Stork had enough time to be waiting just around one of the sides.

Jonathon picked the one he knew, the one that made him feel almost comfortable and, again keeping low, spun quickly around, his fists ready to fight.

Stork wasn't there. Quickly, Jonathon ran around the back of the garage, staying lower than the window, and checked the other side. Stork wasn't there, either. But then, while Jonathon started high-fiving himself in his head for not actually being seen, he heard the sound of Stork's house door being closed.

Jonathon's eyes grew as his adrenaline picked up. He jogged in place for a second, blowing on his palms before rubbing them together. This was his chance, and he wasn't sure he'd ever get another. This one felt pretty much like a gift from his friend, the old bear.

Going around the back of the garage again, Jonathon inspected the knob on the white back door. Indeed, the lock was a Schlage. That was good. It shouldn't take him more than a minute—probably more like thirty seconds—to get in.

"Of course, there's always the chance he's got a heavy-duty latch with a giant-sized Abloy padlock hanging off the end on the inside," he whispered to himself, then remembered what his bear had said. *Just think about saving Carry. Nothing else matters.*

Whoever had installed the door handle had gone to the bother of putting a pretty heavy-duty striker plate on the door frame. Without that plate, there was a chance the old credit card slide trick might have worked. It worked a lot more often than Jonathon suspected most people thought. Bend your card slightly, insert it between the door and the jamb—above the door latch—and bring it down on an angle, working it against the latch until, *voilà!* The card literally opened the door for you. Jonathon didn't have a credit card, but his student card would've probably worked. It had worked before.

First things first, though. He had to check to see whether the door was even locked. Wrapping his fingers around the knob, he slowly began to turn it, whispering what wouldn't be the last in a series of small prayers tonight, this one going out to the patron saint of whomever they had in charge of door security.

It turned in his hand, and Jonathon felt his heart swell right up into his chest as he kept turning until . . .

He couldn't anymore. Truth be told, it turned maybe one or two degrees before the lock stopped it from going anywhere else. "You guys need to fire that saint and replace him with someone who knows his job better," he whispered, pulling his lock-pick set from his back pocket.

"Okay," he said, giving the handle another quick once-over. "Common Schlage back door lock with bolt pin." As far as door locks went, it was pretty skookum. Top of the line, really. But still, it would be the same on the inside as near on every other bolted door lock he'd opened: same pin and tumbler hardware with five pin stacks. He wondered why whoever installed it had opted out of putting in a dead bolt, too? Oh well, this just made everything that much faster. He hoped Tommy Stork's bathroom visit or wherever he went would take at least a bit of time.

Sweat had collected on his forehead again and was running down the sides of his face. Under his arms, he was soaked. Fumbling in the shed's shadow, he managed to find his gray T-shirt where he'd tossed it on the grass and used it again to dry himself off. Easier to work the lock without wet fingers.

How much time did he have until Stork returned? He did some rough calculations in his head. One minute for the lock, maybe two since he was working under pressure. Actually he scratched that and said three, since that was by far the worst case. If he couldn't be in after three minutes, he'd hang up his lock-picking hat for good.

Then what? Seconds to reach Carry. Freeing her was

another thing entirely. If that *was* an ax he'd made out at the end of the garage, it might be sharp enough to cut her ropes, but it wouldn't be his first choice, that was for sure. He hadn't been able to see the workbench really well, but usually benches like that came with tools. Maybe a small handsaw or, wonders of all wonders, some aviator shears. Stork had a nice place. Kept his gardens well. Shears wouldn't be entirely out of the question.

Anyway, worst case would be around seven minutes to get Carry free and on her feet. So, totaled, that all gave him a worst case of ten minutes. Did he have that kind of time? He seriously doubted it. But what else could he do?

Besides, he just realized he'd wasted an entire minute at least thinking about all of it when he should have just been doing and not thinking.

Opening the small case in his hand, he plucked out the tension wrench just as he became aware of something else. The wrench in his right hand and the case sitting open on his left palm were moving. No, not moving, trembling. Despite his thoughts staying out of the game, the rest of his body was scared shitless. "No," he whispered. "You can't possibly do this if you're jittery. You have to stop shaking." He breathed in deeply and slowly let it out, hoping to whatever God was watching that his body would calm down.

But the more he tried, the more he thought about it, the more he felt the uncontrollable panic rise inside him, and the more he shook. He had to do this, though. Somehow. In the next minute, his hands were vibrating so badly he wouldn't have been able to pick even the simplest of locks.

Frustrated and angry at himself, he stood there, the

sweat once again returning worse than ever, even as the night had cooled. He stood there helpless before the door, as important seconds ticked away beneath a garish-white half moon.

He felt alone.

There wasn't even time to go back to the bear.

CHAPTER 64

Leah raced her Bonneville up and across acres of forest toward Blue Jay Maples, where all the streets had names like birds and they wound and wended their way through dense woods with gaping ditches dug out on either side, because on one of those windy roads squatted a baby blue house with white shutters belonging to Noah Stork. And Leah distinctly remembered the detached garage recently painted huddling in the trees a ways back and alongside the home. She felt her teeth grind together as she considered how much of a bet she would offer that it was in that very garage that Noah Stork had executed all them victims.

All this time, for fifteen years, that garage had just crouched there, lonely and empty, full of the memories of screams and bloodshed, with absolutely nobody giving it a second's thought. It was right out there, and nobody had a clue. Even she had walked right past it four times on her way in and out during her visits to Noah Stork, and never once had she even regarded the garage with any interest.

Her gut feelings no longer worked. And that scared the hell out of her.

The primary crime scene. Noah Stork's bloody blue garage.

But Leah knew sometimes the best hiding places were right out in the open, in plain sight. All it took was a bit of gumption and luck. Or, in this case, she suspected, something closer to narcissism and arrogance. The profile she'd been putting together in her head for Noah Stork during the drive had led her to believe that megalomania could probably be added to the list of the man's other obvious attributes.

Well, today, whatever had kept Noah Stork's "hobbies" secret for so long, just got its card punched. Leah knew he had her little girl in that garage. Now that they were getting closer, as she slid around snaky turns and rumbled over rocky roads, she began to actually *feel* her daughter. There was no doubt this time. Leah knew, once they got to Stork's house, she'd find Caroline. The only worry now was what state her daughter would be in when that happened.

"Was it possibly about slowing down a mite? Because I think if it was, you might want to pay that voice some attention."

Leah glanced over and shook her head. Now *he* was telling *her* that *she* drove recklessly? As usual, he was ridiculous.

One way or another, though, tonight Leah would avenge her pa's legacy and make right a travesty that had occurred fifteen years ago. That part felt right, and for once parts of this case settled well in her stomach. The only real questions still unanswered for Leah, other than a few small ones, were: Who had set up Harry Stork? Noah? Could he really have done that? Of the two twins, Leah got the sense that Harry was by far the favored child. And once that question was answered, the next best one—if the answer to the first one didn't turn out to be Noah—was why? And of course, a third one fell after those two: How, exactly, was he set up, anyway?

Leah had the beginnings of a hunch on how to go about finding the answers, and she liked where it was coming from: either her spleen or her gut. Either one was close enough.

Tommy Stork was handcuffed in the back of Chris's squad car. They figured bringing him with them was the only way to guarantee he wouldn't run off and call his pa, tipping him off about the cops coming his way. Besides, he wasn't innocent. He might not have killed anyone, but he'd trained a gun on an officer of the law, refused to relinquish his weapon when commanded to do so, and hell, he even lied about having the gun in the first place. No, things weren't going to come out all roses and carnations for Tommy Stork, either.

Or he'll cop an insanity plea and get off easy.

Leah didn't care. She didn't hate Tommy. Not the way she hated Noah right now. It was a boiling and spitting and greasy hate that filled her right to the top. Probably not the sort of hate she'd want to hang on to for much longer than it took to take Noah Stork down, but for now she just rolled with it.

"Susan B. Anthony for your thoughts," Dan asked, obviously seeing the thoughts rattling behind her eyes. The siren sound wasn't turned on, but she had the red and blue on her dash. It spun around, washing the interior of the car and the trees flying by in a dazzling array of colors.

"Nothin'," she responded. "Just keepin' the wheels between the culverts. You know what? I'd like to have two minutes in one of them interrogation booths with whoever designed these roads along with a lead pipe or somethin' to that effect."

Dan forced a laugh, but nothing about it was genuine. He was worried, too. *And hopefully not,* Leah thought, *about finally getting his hands on the Cahaba River Strangler.* Right now the semantics of what Noah Stork did no longer mattered. All that Leah cared about was saving a life so precious to her.

Dan's grip on her Bonneville's handhold had been white-knuckled ever since they'd entered Blue Jay Maples, but now, as Leah tore around these Byzantine roads with thickly knotted woods streaming by outside, she actually felt how unsettled he was.

She came to a now-familiar turn and slowed enough to take one hand off the wheel and pull the siren off the dash.

"What're you doin'?" Dan asked. "Now you won't be able to see anythin'."

"Noah Stork lives on this road. I don't want him havin' any hints that he might be gettin' a few more for company tonight."

Dan didn't answer, but he did shift uncomfortably on the seat.

The road took a hard left and then a hard right. Leah accelerated into both turns, her back tires spitting up rocks like Cronos regurgitating his children. She took the right way too hard and lost control as the back end swung her around like a weather vane, the car coming to a stop pointing almost entirely in the wrong direction.

Maybe I really should have let Dan drive.

She felt Dan about to say probably more or less her exact thought, when she held up her index finger and said, "Not a word."

Slowly and gingerly, she pulled the car back around,

being very careful of the black shadows swallowing up the night on the edge of the road, and got the car going the right way again.

Her car continued to sputter rocks and squeal out patches as Leah went through each turn, growing closer and closer to that little blue clapboard house where so much death had lingered for far too long.

CHAPTER 65

Jonathon's shaking hadn't gone away. And he didn't know what to do.

He just stood there behind Tommy Stork's detached garage, the T-wrench in one hand, the rest of his picks in the case resting on the other, and waited. He had no idea what he was waiting *for,* though. A sign from God maybe? Jonathon wasn't a regular attender of church, so he wondered how much attention God even paid to someone who'd maybe set foot in a nave half a dozen times in his entire life, not counting the times he broke into Jewel City Baptist up in Mississippi. Besides, he bet even with church, the good Lord looked past people with lock-pick sets in their back pockets.

Jonathon's head was a mess. Every time he tried to think rationally, his brain just went nuts and figured any second he'd hear the door to Stork's house open and out the man would come, destroying what was probably Jonathon's only chance to save Carry.

Finally he couldn't take it anymore. Setting the T-wrench on the grass with the rest of his set, he picked up his shirt and dried himself off again. Then, hoping he wasn't being too loud, he did six jumping jacks, trying to loosen himself up. While he jumped, he fully extended his hands and fingers, shaking them out. "It's okay," he whispered. "Everything's okay. This is just another lock."

He did this three times before he finally felt it start to work. He'd calmed himself down enough that the trembling had lessened substantially. Now, if he could just stay this calm, he'd probably be okay. Unfortunately, it took wasting more precious time to arrive at this state.

Thinking of time brought back thoughts of Stork coming out of his house again. "Don't!" Jonathon snapped, louder than he'd intended. He dropped to a whisper and continued the demand of his subconscious. "Don't even *consider* thinkin' about it," he whispered again.

Picking up his tools, he grabbed another one from the box and left the rest of them on the ground inside their open case.

Lock-picking really wasn't a hard skill to master. Even to call it a skill rendered it almost funny. No, it was more like a knack. Once you got it, you just always knew how to do it. People always thought Jonathon had to have practiced a lot to be that good, but the truth was, it all boiled down to two things: your sense of hearing and your sense of touch.

Because you couldn't see inside the cylinder, those two senses were really all anyone had to work with and, like anything, the more locks you picked, the better you got at it. Your ability to "feel" what was going on inside that tiny vault grew faster than your ability to hear it, but being good involved honing both of those senses.

Sliding the torque wrench into the bottom of the keyhole, he turned the knob again until it stopped. Then he jammed in the wrench and kept pressure on it with the ball of his left hand.

While he did this, he continued thinking about how he'd learned his technique many years ago, when he was still a tween. Thinking about that kept the panicked shaky thoughts at bay.

Jonathon had spent maybe six months practicing a half hour or so a day before he felt good enough at it to call himself a lock picker. He practiced using various old locks people gave him, and when he couldn't find anything else to try with, there were always working locks on his doors. His own and his neighbors.

He quickly learned many people's work schedules.

Not that he opened anyone's houses with less-than-noble intentions. He just opened them for the sake of seeing if he could. Then he'd lock them again. He only messed up once, and he still blamed it on the lock being his first pin and tumbler with *seven* pins. He'd managed to get it open, but when Terry-Lee Grant drove in her driveway after a long day of working behind the concession stand at Wheelie's Roller Derby, he was still standing on her porch trying to get the damn thing locked again.

Of course she thought he was trying to break in. So Jonathon had to explain to some very dubious policemen that he only did it for fun and wasn't really trying to get into Miss Terry-Lee's house. The only thing sitting in his favor was the fact that he *had* managed to unlock the dead bolt and nobody could find any evidence of him coming inside.

He figured the cops just chalked him up to being crazy. That was fine by him. Better than probation, that was for sure.

With the torque wrench in and everything steady, he gently turned the knob, first counterclockwise then clockwise. He had to know which way the knob turned to open the door; otherwise, if he turned it wrong after setting all the pins, the tension would give and all the driver pins would simply push back into the plug. And that would mean starting all over. From scratch.

The secret to understanding which way the knob turned was by feeling the subtle difference in each direction. He turned it counterclockwise and the lock stopped him almost immediately. It felt "hard." Jonathon tried the other way and, to most people, it would probably feel the same, but it didn't. To Jonathon there was a distinguishable difference. Turning clockwise made the knob "give a little." It felt "soft."

Now Jonathon knew. For this knob, you turned clockwise to open it.

This was really the only talent it took, being able to feel slight changes in tension. Otherwise, it was just an exercise in patience and tenacity. Again, he was reminded it was more of a knack than anything else.

As he did, he considered that not everyone who learned about his "knack" immediately filled with the fright of him stealing everything they owned one night while they went to the movies. No, there was a whole other group that, as soon as they saw what Jonathon could do. This was especially true when it came to the No. 15 Master Lock.

Master brought this particular lock on the TV show *Fight Back* in 1983, claiming it was unbreakable. On the show, each lock survived two rounds shot at it dead-center with a high-caliber rifle without opening. Somehow, this impressed everyone and proved Master was right. Nothing could break through their new product.

Well, Jonathon showed how he could pick a No. 15 fresh out of the package in thirty-seven seconds, *count-*

ing the time it took to tear open the package. Some people watching this had a sort of evil "epiphany moment," when a kind of darkness enveloped them and their minds immediately began concocting complex schemes for Jonathon. In the past few years, he'd been asked to rob banks, break into liquor stores, open safety deposit boxes, you name it.

But Jonathon's interest was only in lock-picking, not owning a lot of useless junk he'd have to try to pawn in shops that would know damn well by the second or third time he came in that he wasn't just "cleaning out his basement."

He believed his obsession with lock-picking stemmed from an early fascination he'd developed for solving things early in his life. His grandfather used to carve and construct wooden puzzles, usually involving a polished wooden ball on a string, that had to be solved by shifting a series of odd geometric obstacles, each appearing way too small for anything to go anywhere. They always started out feeling impossible, but as long as he never gave up, eventually Jonathon solved them.

That was when his enchantment for his grandpa set in, too. As Jonathon often thought, solving the puzzles was tough. How hard must it be to come *up* with them?

If he could only see me now, Jonathon thought. Then he seriously considered it. What *would* he say to do if he were here?

"Get to goddamn work," Jonathon answered quietly. He'd tell Jonathon he had no choice. Nobody else was here. At the end of the day, the cavalry wasn't coming.

The thinking helped. Jonathon's hands had been steady while he first counted the pins, verifying there were five, and then started methodically working each one, from back to front, pushing up the key pins to release the driver pins. This, of course, pushed back on their springs, always increasing the pressure.

And he always kept tightening everything with the torque wrench.

So far, two driver pins had cleared the shear line—the point where the plug and upper compartment of the cylinder meet—and as each one had, he adjusted the tension and listened carefully. All he needed to hear was that quiet little *ting!* as the driver pin fell down onto the casing. If there was any real skill in all of this, it was in the tension adjustment. For each pin, you had to work it and get a feel for whether it was too tight or too loose. You couldn't really tell until you got the key pin all the way up.

Jonathon figured he was about fifty seconds in, when the third of the five pins fell into place. This wouldn't be breaking any of his records, but better safe than sorry, he figured. He readjusted the T-wrench and worked on the fourth pin, pushing it up and gauging the pressure of the spring, figuring how much tension he needed for it to clear.

His sweating had returned. First on his face and hair, then his arms, but now his hands were getting moist. This was dangerous. He couldn't just stop and wipe them off. He'd lose all the work he'd done, so he pressed on, hoping Stork would stay in his house just a little while longer. What the hell did he go in there for anyway? To watch TV? It felt like an eternity had gone by since he'd left Carry all bound up and alone on that hard concrete floor.

Worried his grip on the wrench might slip from the sweat, he tried sliding the end of the tension wrench deeper into his thumb. It didn't work. His hands had been sweatier than he thought. The wrench slipped, right across the inside of his palm, before falling near on completely out of the lock. It dangled from the keyhole like a broken flagpole, and Jonathon didn't need to be told what that meant: All five pins were back in place in the bottom compartment of the plug.

He took a deep breath and considered giving up.

He had to start over.

He didn't want to start over.

It was too much. Time had to be running out.

Using his shirt once more, this time he made sure he cleaned every bit of sweat from his skin he could find. A faint breeze had picked up the smell of the pansies and tulips growing behind him, and it felt a little cooler against his bare chest. But it wasn't the heat causing him to sweat, it was his nerves. Christ, usually he could've gotten through five of these locks by now.

He collected himself, got his bearings, and did what he had to do. He had no choice but to start over, working from back to front, this time with the T-wrench practically driven into the side of his thumb.

It went faster this time. Maybe because he was so annoyed with himself. But, one by one, the driver pins cleared the shear line until Jonathon came to the final one. He paused for a breath and wiped his forehead with the back of his right hand.

Then he set to finish.

He pushed the last pin up and felt the plug turn, just a bit. He needed more tension. Ever so slowly, he adjusted the wrench while continuing to work that last pin with his hook pick. He held his breath as he felt it go farther and farther back.

And then . . .

And then he heard the wonderful quiet *click* of that

last driver pin falling down on the casing. With a twist of the T-wrench, he spun the knob around and the bolt lock opened.

Letting go of his breath, his panic about Stork returning came back. How long had that taken him? Four, five, maybe six minutes? Way too long, that was for sure.

From all around him, the sound of those damn cicadas sang out into the night, combining with the flowery smell of summer. He wished he could be anywhere else right now. Anywhere. He figured he couldn't find a place worse than being behind the door you just unlocked that belonged to the garage of a serial killer holding your girl hostage.

Whatever made him think he could do this?

He didn't give that thought a chance to settle. Instead, he quickly picked up his box, put the two tools away, snapped it back shut, and slid it back into his pocket. He stopped again, listening for Stork's house door, but heard nothing except those cicadas. Even Carry's whimpering seemed to have faded.

Four crows flew from the trees behind him, cawing loudly. Jonathon jumped, and that was all it took to bring his fear and his trembling back full-tilt. He hated himself for it, but what could he do?

Slowly, he pulled the door open and stepped inside the garage of death.

The door made no noise, and Jonathon was careful to step gently onto the floor, but somehow Carry knew someone had come in the back. The thin table was blocking her from the back door and she struggled, kicking herself around it far enough to see what was going on. When she saw Jonathon, she froze. For what felt like an eternity, they both stared into each other's eyes, fearful and wondrous.

Then her face lit up, the dim and flickering fluorescent lights shining in her blue eyes. Jonathon saw tear streaks on her face, and new tears standing in her eyes. Her lips, a soft pink, broke into a smile. "Jonathon!" she said, much too loud.

Jonathon held his index finger to his lips and whispered, "Be quiet." He glanced at her body. "Where's your shirt?" he asked.

She shook her head. "I don't know. I was blindfolded when he brought me in. Listen, you—"

Her voice grew louder. She was going to alert Stork at this rate. Once again, Jonathon quietly reminded her to keep quiet.

Her fear slid back on her. "You can't be in here!" she whispered anxiously. "If he catches you, he'll kill you, too!"

His finger returned to his lips and he shushed her. Then he asked, "Where did he go?"

"To get me a glass of water," Carry whispered back.

He'd been gone a pretty fair stretch of time to just be fetching water. He was doing something else in that house, something Jonathon didn't even want to imagine. What he needed was a plan. The faster, the better.

He quickly scanned the workbench for something to cut through the rope binding Carry's ankles and wrists together behind her back. He couldn't find anything. His heart skipped a beat for a moment when he found a wooden box full of gardening supplies. He really wanted a pair of shears or even a dead-bolt cutter. Christ, he'd settle for a box cutter at this point.

A pegboard hung on the wall adjacent to the window with handheld power tools assembled on it. He looked them up and down. Two drills, a router, a biscuit joiner, and a circular saw. He briefly considered the saw, but knew it would be far too dangerous. Besides, the sound of an electric saw going off in this quiet corner of the world would not be inconspicuous by any means.

Jonathon scrambled for an idea. The garage door was firmly closed. Opening it would cause a ruckus far bigger than it would take to bring Stork running. Besides, the way she'd been hog-tied all backward like that— Jonathon worried he might not be able to carry her.

If Stork only went for water, he wasn't going to be gone long. Jonathon couldn't go back outside. He'd never get another chance like this.

That was when he remembered the ax or the sledgehammer or whatever it was sitting on its head at the far end of the garage by the door. He marched over, pleading for it to be an ax and to be a sharp one at that.

Half his wish came true. It was an ax, and the thing propped up against the wall beside it was a wooden stake with a stickman drawing stapled to its top. Jonathon didn't have to look at the paper. He knew what he'd see. A stickman with hair that turned up on both sides of its face and two circles on its chest where breasts should be.

The stickman was meant to be Carry, and the stake was to be pounded through her chest somewhere in the dark trails of Cherry Park Forest. And even all that wouldn't be the thing that killed her. He remembered enough from the killings fifteen years ago to know that the police figured the victims were already dead by the time they were dumped at the crime scene. The real death happened someplace they'd never managed to find back then. A place Jonathon once saw a newspaper refer to as the "Stickman's slaughterhouse." An abattoir. Jonathon knew, as he stood under the only working fluorescent light in the garage, that he'd found that place.

From in here, the dried bloodstains telling stories dating as far back as 1973 hit him even more vividly than they had through the window. And then there were the two across the room. The ones that weren't a burnt sienna color from fading over time, the two that looked like someone had just shot the wall with a goddamn paint gun.

He felt bile roil inside him. Fought to keep it from coming up his throat. He retched, but managed to hold everything down. He grabbed the top of the ax's handle and dragged the head down the cement floor to where Carry lay, her face turned away toward the open back door, her eyes streaming tears and her body jerking, as quietly, she cried to herself.

Jonathon knelt down beside her and felt the ax's blade with the inside of his palm. It wasn't that sharp. It would take a while to get through the rope.

He made a quick look around from his lower position now on the floor. Beneath the tool bench were two cabinets, both made of hardwood left unfinished. Jonathon guessed they were homemade. The smaller of the two had a camping cooler tucked away on top of it. The larger one stood beside the other, much larger and much wider. He wondered how far back it went.

He didn't see any more tools. Nothing to cut through the rope. He would have to go with the ax.

"Okay," he whispered, bringing it around so he could talk to Carry face-to-face. "I'm goin' to use this to cut your rope and free you. Then we'll run out and head straight for the woods. They're deep and thick and dark. Stork will never find us."

"Where's my mother?" Carry asked, confused.

Jonathon shushed her again.

"But does she—"

Jonathon shushed her again, cutting her off as he worked the blade of the ax against the edge of the rope. "I'll tell you everything once we're safely away from Tommy Stork."

Carry gave him a weird look. "Who's *Tommy* Stork?"

The ax wasn't making much headway. A few strands of string had split, but Jonathon really felt like he was getting nowhere. "Stork's the maniac who just left to get you water."

Carry started to say something else, but this time Jonathon actually snapped at her. "For Christ's sake. Be quiet until we're out of here."

It worked. She stopped talking. Jonathon wished he had the same control with this ax as he did with her.

"Shit, this isn't workin'."

"Don't you have to swing it?" she asked.

"What? Are you nuts? How accurate do you think I am with an ax? I'll cut your goddamn hand off or worse. Christ, I could split your back right open."

"Okay," Carry said, sounding almost calm. "Bad idea."

"No," Jonathon said, "we're gonna have—" He stopped talking. Carry's head rose from the floor, her eyes steeped in fear. Jonathon could tell she was about to speak, so he shushed her without even giving her the chance.

He had to think, but there was no point in thinking. They'd run out of time and they both knew it the moment they heard the sound of Stork's front door closing, followed by his footsteps coming across the porch.

"Shit!" Jonathon whispered.

"Chop off my hand!" Carry said. "Go ahead! Do it! Just get me untied. I don't care 'bout my damn hand!"

"Shh," Jonathon said. "Let me think before we do something that drastic."

"Jonathon! Trust me! We *need* drastic! Cut off my goddamn hand!"

But there was no time even for that. Stork was right in front of the garage. His footsteps stopped as he bent down. They were completely out of time.

Any second now, that garage door would come sailing up, and then, all hell would break loose.

CHAPTER 66

"I'm gonna try home again, see if she made it back there, maybe." Leah said, lifting the heavy phone again.

As soon as she'd said it, she could tell Dan didn't concur with her brainy idea. He let out a big sigh, in fact.

"What?" she asked.

"First, you're doing sixty-five down these rabbit trails, just askin' to wipe us out into one of those damn hell pits. And second, don't you think Caroline would've called *you* if she was home?"

"I'll slow down while I'm talkin' if that makes you happier."

Dan ran his hand through his hair. The hand not hanging onto the car for dear life.

"Think about it, Leah. At the very least, Jonathon would've called you. I mean, maybe I can see your boy, or even your daughter, neglectin' something like that, but that Jonathon kid seems to actually have most of his shit together."

She looked at him sideways for as long as she possibly could without going off the road. When she spoke again, it was with a voice tempered with, well, temper.

"First off, you sanctimonious bastard, where do you get off putting down my kids? I'll have you know, Abe's a pretty smart button. Do I have to remind you that *he* was the one who found the blood that solved the case you guys couldn't make any headway on for ten goddamn years? And how many of you tried? No, it took the genius of my thirteen-year-old to finally make the break that might bring the Cahaba River Strangler to justice!"

Dan held up his palm. Again, the one not keeping him in his seat. "Okay," he said, "you're right. I apologize. I was way off-base. The kid's smart as a . . ." He drifted off, apparently trying rapidly to think of a comparison "Smart as a goddamn bullwhip. That's what he is. A bullwhip! The minute he gets out of school, I'm goin' to offer him a job."

"He's going to college, Dan."

"Okay, the minute he's out of college."

Leah checked her anger, noticing it was displaced. Something else was weighing on her. "And . . ." she started.

"And?" Dan asked. "And what?"

"And I have recent reason to wonder about Jonathon. Doesn't he come off a little 'too' nice to you? Like, too perfect?"

"Now you're persecuting people for bein' nice? You know, given time, I think you'd start to suspect every single person in this county of somethin'." He gave out a little laugh. "Maybe, just maybe, you've actually met a genuinely nice guy for the first time ever."

"He picks locks."

"What?"

She nodded. "He picks locks. For fun. Has a whole kit and everythin'. They came home the other night and Caroline had forgotten her key and he said, 'Now don't you worry your pretty little head about it,' and he pulled out his lock-picking kit and went ahead and picked my dead bolt. Caroline said he did it in a blink."

"How fast is a blink?" Dan asked.

"I don't know. A minute, maybe? Maybe five? Dan, that's not the point. The point ended with, 'And he picked my dead bolt.'"

Dan rubbed his chin and watched the forest whipping by in a big blur of shadowy green. "Really, eh?" he asked. "Jonathon. Hmm. Kid has more depth than I expected. Maybe I should be offering *him* a job. Before he goes and bats for the dark side."

"Don't goof with it, Dan," Leah chided. "I don't even want to *think* what some of his *other* 'hobbies' might be. You know, because 'stealing cars' didn't pop into my mind immediately after Caroline orated her little tale about my dead bolt."

A weird grin came to Dan's face. "You really do scamper to the worst possible case about everything, don't you? Anyway, don't think about shit like that. If you want us to call home, fine. But *I'll* make the call. You concentrate on staying between the gulleys."

Leah knew Dan was right. Calling home was just stupid. She would have heard if Caroline had returned. But that was—

"Make the call." She glanced at him, then back at the road. "I know, I *know!* It's crazy, but I need you to make the call."

"Fine, makin' the call." He picked up the phone and had to hold it almost an arm's length from his eyes to read the buttons. "Are these written in Braille?"

"You didn't bring your glasses?" It had surprised her that until recently, she'd had no idea Dan even wore glasses to read.

"I'm good," he said, and started hitting buttons. "Eight six four eight, right?" he asked.

"What?"

"Your number. I knew the first three."

"Yeah, you got them all."

He held the phone to his ear and waited for the call to go through.

Leah wasn't as patient as him. "What's goin' on?"

"Jesus, woman, it has to *ring?*"

"It isn't ringin'?"

Dan nodded. "Has done. Twice now."

"Where is everybody?"

Dan kept waiting for someone to answer.

"Goddammit!" Leah said, hitting her steering wheel. "Where the hell are those kids?"

Dan lifted a finger at her, cutting her off. "Ah, uh, hi, Abe. How are you?"

"Is Carry back?" Leah asked over top of him.

"Hang on," Dan said, and put his hand over the receiver. "Just be patient."

"Patient?"

Dan spoke into the phone. "No, Abe, not yet. Listen, can I speak to Jonathon?"

A pocket of silence went by, and Leah figured he was waiting for Jonathon to take the phone, but his face was a strange mess of confusion and fear. "What do you mean . . . ? He what?" Dan raised his volume, clearly agitated. "When? How long ago?" Another pause while Dan pressed his left hand to the side of his head. "What address? How did you—"

Finally, he hung up, his face ashen.

Leah's heart was beating a syncopated rhythm as she waited impatiently for Dan to say something. "What?" she asked. "What is it? What's goin' on?"

"He . . . Jonathon . . . Man, this even sounds nuts . . . but . . ."

"But what?" Leah was ready to hear that the world was ending the way Dan was going on.

When he spoke, it turned out she was right. It was. "It's Jonathon," he said. "He's gone."

"Gone where?"

Their eyes gripped each other's. "Gone to save Carry."

Time went by without either of them saying a word until finally Leah shook her head as though trying to clear a mess of puzzle pieces somebody just dumped on her brain with no finished picture to go with it. "What do you mean, Dan? What do you mean, he's gone to save Carry? He doesn't know where to go. Last time I talked to him, even *I* didn't know where to go."

"That's just it. He overheard you tell Chris that Tommy Stork was the Stickman."

"And? He never showed up at Tommy's place. Tommy was the *last* guy, Dan. Big ol' redneck with a Fairlane. Remember? If he gets there now, it hardly matters."

"Leah," Dan said, his eyes going to the road. "Abe gave him Tommy's address."

"How does Abe even—" But she realized he might know. He did read through all her files. "Even still. Nobody's at Tommy's. It's not like—"

"Abe gave him Tommy's report from 1974."

"I still don't—" She was about to say the word *understand* when suddenly she did. She remembered scribbling Noah's address on Tommy's record because that was the first report she'd got to and, at the time, it really hadn't mattered. It was only a backup address in case she needed it.

Her mouth fell open. "So, when Abe gave Jonathon Tommy's address, it was actually . . ."

"It was actually *Noah*'s address. Jonathon's at Noah Stork's house."

"Thinkin' he's at Tommy's." Her words came slow and mechanical, almost as though she were taking orders at a drive-through. "This is the worst night of my life. And that's countin' bein' woken up at two A.M. to find out my husband had just been yanked from my life on account of a head-on collision. You know how bad a morning like that can be? This night's even worse."

Dan didn't respond. He just stared at the road and gently nodded his head. Leah got the feeling he really might be able to relate to something like that. Although the two of them talked a fair bit, there were certain things—more concepts than actual subjects—that, when they came out or the conversation swerved their way, Dan would back down and gently change topics. Leah never pushed it. She felt, though, on some level, Dan had wounds. He hid them well, mainly through sarcasm and what he counted for wit. He did a good job at appearing strong from the outside.

Even dragons have soft spots, she thought, considering whether maybe Dan was more a case of muddy waters running deep.

She wondered how deep, remembering all them empty Jim Beam bottles she'd stuffed into that garbage sack squirreled away in the kitchen closet.

That morning of the Fourth, as they'd walked up to the station, what was it he had told her about his drinking? She tried thinking back. It was the morning of the day she'd found Samantha Hughes's half-naked body staked on the edge of the Anikawa. That part she had no problem recalling, and she doubted she would for a long, long time.

She remembered now. He'd said he *had* to drink, and

that when he didn't, the world was way too crazy. Drinking made it tolerable enough to concentrate on one horrible thing at a time. He told her it kept the monsters from all charging through his head at once.

That morning, she'd ignored her gut reaction, which was to tell him those were just weaselly excuses and justifications so he didn't feel bad for having a problem he didn't want to face.

All his points had done was make him sound like a coward.

But now, in this hollow, harmful, dark, and deadly night of emptiness, she started to wonder what, exactly, Dan Truitt's monsters really looked like. Maybe they were the real reason he drank, the *real* things he was scared of.

Maybe he wasn't a coward at all, just a pragmatist.

She decided one day she would press him to answer her. To tell her all about the crazy monsters lurking in his head. A day like that could bring them closer.

It could also change her life, possibly forever.

CHAPTER 67

Jonathon's heart kicked into overdrive. The way it was pumping tonight, he almost worried it might wear out. Knowing Stork was about to pull the garage door up had him scrambling. His body tingled with adrenaline from his fight-or-flight instinct kicking in. It wasn't much of a decision. Stork had a gun. Jonathon didn't even have a shirt. He was going for flight.

He quickly looked around. There was the back door, which he had closed behind him, but that would cut him off from Carry and he'd never get a second chance. Besides, he doubted he'd even have enough time to run around the table to get through the door and close it before Stork was inside.

Thoughts whirled in his head, out of his control. Destiny played out in Jonathon's hands, turning it over, showing a queen high bluff. He couldn't win. On the verge of resigning to fate, his brain suddenly made a decision for him, pulling his attention to those cabinets, the short one with the cooler on top and that big, wide one that looked as though it could be as deep as the workbench above it.

Jonathon shuffled over and pulled the door open, ex-

pecting to find it full of shelves or tools or something.
What he saw surprised him.

The cabinet was empty. A big empty box. He still
wasn't sure he'd fit, but he was going to damn well try.
Squatting down, he sort of sidestepped in, feeling the
lock-pick kit in his back pocket bending against the cabinet and jamming into him. He pulled it out and tried
again.

Across the garage, the handle of the garage door rattled as Stork's hand wrapped around it.

Jonathon squeezed as hard as he could, managing to
get his head in with his neck bent painfully forward.

The garage door squeaked. Any minute it would rise.

Jonathon was in the cabinet, but the door was still
wide open. There was no pull on the inside. He looked
over at Carry, now almost out of view because of the
solid side of the narrow table she'd wiggled around
when Jonathon entered.

He had to close the door.

The garage door started to rise, just as Jonathon
pulled out one of the sharp-hooked tools from his pick
collection. Throwing his bent-up arm out, he jammed
the pick into the door's back, plunging it a half inch into
the soft pine. He began pulling the door closed, slowly
and gently so the pick stayed in the wood.

He had it halfway closed as the garage door began
rolling up.

That was when Jonathon saw it. Stork's ax, lying on
its side on the concrete floor inches from the rope binding Carry's arms and legs. There was no possible way
Stork wasn't going to see it.

Jonathon's mind screamed at him to close the door.

But the ax . . .

There was no time for the ax. Jonathon continued

pulling the door gently closed even as the garage door clanked all the way open and he heard Stork step inside. "Miss me?" he asked Carry, his words echoing in the unfinished interior, bouncing off those bloodstained walls.

Jonathon got the cabinet door completely closed as he heard Stork's footsteps come closer. He made it. *Just.* His heart sounded loud, so loud he hoped Stork wouldn't hear it, hoped he was only hearing it from inside his body. He took some deep breaths and worked the lock-pick tool out of the wood and placed it back in its container, having to feel around in the dark.

The temperature in the pitch-black cupboard already had risen since Jonathon got inside. Sweat streamed down his naked chest and abdominals. His hair was soon soaked, and sweat ran down his face and into his eyes. He couldn't wipe it. He was in a position where he couldn't move a muscle. He just hoped to Jesus nothing would cramp up.

"What's this?" Stork asked, sounding glib. "You moved." There was a pause and then, "You weren't thinking of trying for the door, were you? You realize you wouldn't even get over the footing tied up the way you are."

After a few seconds, Stork spoke again.

"Here," Stork said. Jonathon wished he knew what was going on. "Now you're spillin'," Stork said. "Just slow down. All right, that's better." Jonathon figured it was the water he'd been fetching for her. "Okay," Stork said finally. "That's it. Now, no more whining."

Stork's heavy footfalls sounded as though he was walking away again, and then Jonathon heard why as the heavy garage door rolled back down its metal tracks and slammed shut when it got to the bottom.

The footfalls came back. Jonathon had a good idea

what was coming next. That ax was just lying there for all the world to see. And just as he expected, all the world that mattered saw it now.

"What's this?" Stork asked, his voice changing to a clipped whisper. It was as though Jonathon heard the devil himself speaking beyond the walls and door of the cabinet.

There was more silence, and then Jonathon jumped, banging his head on the top of the cabinet as Stork's voice went into a scream. "How did you get this!"

Carry stayed silent.

"I asked you . . ." And Jonathon assumed he'd grabbed her by her hair, lifting her face from the concrete because of the painful yelp she let out. "Where. Did. You. Get. *This?*"

Carry continued her painful shrieks, and Jonathon's muscles tightened. It was his fault she was in pain. He'd left the ax on the floor. Stupid, stupid, stupid. The sweat and the heat of the cabinet were becoming too much. He wondered how airtight the space was. He felt dizzy. That could be from a lot of things, though.

"I asked you a question!" Stork barked again. But Carry said nothing.

Jonathon guessed Stork's next move was to look at the rope tying her ankles and wrists together, since he then asked her, "Who did this? You couldn't have! There's no way! Who helped you?"

Carry still said nothing. Then she yelled out even louder in pain. It took every ounce of energy Jonathon had to try to stay calm and not come out of the cabinet too early.

"Who? Who got this ax and tried cutting you free? Where is he?" Stork's voice was still loud, commanding.

Jonathon wished he could see anything that was going on, because a huge pocket of silence followed. He once again heard Stork's footsteps on the concrete, and Carry's quiet sobs returned.

He wished he knew what Stork was doing. Whatever it was, Jonathon really hoped it didn't involve his gun.

CHAPTER 68

Leah and Dan reached Noah Stork's house before Chris and Ethan got there in the squad car. Leah figured that was how it would work out. She'd had at least some experience of getting through Blue Jay Maples recently. Chris hadn't. And from her experience, Chris wasn't a confident driver. He'd never take those turns as fast as she had.

"Where's the bastard's house?" Dan asked. They'd been bumping down Woodpecker Wind for two or three miles. She'd already told him it would be coming up on their left.

"You can't see it until you're almost on top of it," she said, slowing down after hearing her own words. "It's just sort of dug out of the woods." She slowed down.

"What're you doin'?" Dan asked.

"I think we're almost there."

"You *think* or you know?"

"This sort of looks familiar, and the woods seem to be thinning as they go around the corner."

"I don't see Jonathon's car," Dan said.

"Maybe he couldn't find it."

"Yeah, maybe," Dan said, sarcastically.

"I barely found it the first time I came here."

"*That* doesn't surprise me. So, what do we do now?"

Leah pulled over to a stop just before she could see where the trees broke for Noah Stork's property line. The two exited the vehicle and crossed the road to where the side of the woods lined the deep ditch of Wood-pecker Wind.

The culvert followed the road like a pit of some giant eel. From outside her car, it even looked bigger and the night here, strangled off by all the trees, gave so little light, when Leah looked down she couldn't trust she was even seeing the bottom.

"Who the hell designed this roadwork?" Dan asked. "The Marquis de Sade?"

"It is strange, isn't it?" Leah looked across the ditch to the narrow edge of land, a mix of short weeds and witchgrass that followed along between the culvert and the thick wall of the woods. "We need to get over there. If we stay on this side, we'll open ourselves up too much by the time we reach his house."

"Great," Dan said. "How close are we to Stork's property line?"

"I don't know. A hundred yards?"

"A hundred *yards?*" Dan asked. "Why didn't you pull closer? Do you have any idea how far a hundred yards is?"

"Not really," Leah answered. "I'm not good with measurements."

"A hundred yards is a goddamn football field."

"Okay, then more like thirty? Maybe? Twenty? Fifty?" She shook her head. This was just wasting time. "Look, I have no idea. We just need to get over this gap-ing hole."

"I'm wondering if it gets narrower in places."

Leah shook her head. "It doesn't. I've been down here a *lot* recently."

Dan licked his lips, the area around them probably feeling stubbly, a move Leah had witnessed him making before, usually when he was thinking hard on something.

"How far across you reckon that is?" he asked Leah, and then immediately added, "Never mind. I forgot who I was asking." He let out a little laugh. "A hundred yards."

"Thirty sounds more reasonable. I'm pretty sure it's thirty."

"Well, from this edge of the trench to the other's gotta be three, I'm guessing. How deep is this thing? I'm not certain I can even see the bottom. You've been here during the day, haven't you?"

"Yeah, but I didn't look in the ditches."

Dan backed up a few paces. "Well, we gotta do what we gotta do."

"Wait," Leah said. "Can you actually jump three meters? That's, like, nine feet."

"Truthfully?"

"Yeah."

"Not a chance. But I'm hoping to get far enough that I can grab something on the other side of the channel. Just in case the thing is like a ravine and goes down thirty feet or something."

"What if it does and you don't?"

"Then my advice? Take your chances with his driveway instead of following me to my death."

That wasn't a very comforting thought.

"See you on the other side," Dan said with a smile and a salute. Then he ran for the edge of the culvert, taking wide strides and growing quickly in speed. Leah heard his pants shuffle as he left their edge and sailed for the next. Quickly, she went closer as she saw him coming down.

He was right, he didn't make it to the edge, but he did land on the sloped bank on the other side. And he did manage to stop himself from continuing on down the slope.

"You okay?" Leah asked.

"Little winded. Good news, though." The dirt beneath his shoes broke and he began sliding down with it. In a blur his left arm came up and around, his fingers grabbing around some vines and shrubs hanging over from where they grew up on the edge of the trench.

"Shit!" Dan said.

"What?"

"Goddamn prickles. Can't any part of this just be easy? I had to go and grab a thunderwood vine?"

"Is it really thunderwood?"

"I don't know for sure. Too goddamn dark to make out any details, but I'm pretty sure."

"It's poisonous."

"I know! Don't you think I know?"

"You'll swell up and get pustules. Eventually they'll erupt with pus."

"You don't know how big a goddamn football field is, but you know every fucking fact about the plant sending painful throbs down my arm? Will you just jump in here! I'm not letting go. I can use it to get us both up. You won't have to touch it!"

"I thought you had good news?"

"I did before I grabbed this goddamn plant and felt its thorns embed themselves in my hand. The good news is, the ditch isn't that deep. Maybe fifteen feet. You'll be fine as long as you make this side somewhere. Dirt's nice and soft." He winced and Leah knew the pain in his arm was getting worse.

She went back on the street a little farther than he had, then made a run for the ditch.

"Make sure you land left of me. There's more of this goddamn plant to the right."

She came down almost on top of him. He managed to do a spin-turn enough so most of her body landed in the loamy dirt beside him.

"Nice jump," he said, his teeth clenched.

"Okay, what now?"

"Climb onto me. Climb onto my shoulders and then pull yourself up onto the edge."

"You'll be able to hold us both? Won't the vine break?"

He shook his head. "It's thunderwood. It's thick and the plant's roots are like anchors. Hurry up, I can't hold myself and you all day."

She did as he said, first pulling herself up his arm and then putting her boot against his side while leveraging with his head. All very awkward, especially since she had to keep a watchful eye on the thunderwood. That was the last thing she needed.

For her final act of indiscretion, she had to put one foot on Dan's head in order to get high enough to pull up to the edge. When she finally scrambled up onto the narrow strip of land between the woods and the ditch, she was so winded she could hardly breathe. She lay down on her back inhaling deeply, staring at the stars.

"Look, don't relax yet," Dan said, his voice coming over the edge of the trench. "I need you to pull me up."

She turned over and crawled back toward him. Keeping most of her body on the path, she bent down, her breasts crushing against the top inside of the culvert. Reaching down, her right hand grabbed his.

"Okay, pull," he said, his other hand still gripping the thunderwood.

She managed to get him up about two feet higher. "Now what?" she asked.

"Just hold me for one minute. You're goin' to feel all my weight. Ready?"

"Yeah," she said.

Flexing his arm, Dan pulled hard on the thunderwood. Leah couldn't even imagine the pain he must've been in. Then he jerked himself up, letting go of the vine. Leah tightened her grip, hoping he wouldn't pull her right in with him.

At the top of his pull, his left hand once again wrapped around the thorny vine and she heard him grunt. But he was higher now. Only two feet from the edge.

She could hear him breathing. "You okay?" she asked.

"Never been better," he said, out of breath. "Okay, we have to do that one more time."

And they did. This time Dan re-grasped the vine almost at its base, well over the edge. From there, he dug his feet into the sloping dirt on the edge of the culvert and leveraged himself up and over the top.

They both lay on their backs, breathing heavily. Dan kept bringing his right hand over to scratch his left.

"You shouldn't scratch it," Leah said.

"Don't," Dan said. "Don't even start." He scratched some more.

"You'll only make it worse," she said.

Finally, they both stood up. "I'll tell you one thing," Dan said.

"What's that?"

"We better make sure the property's clear from pryin' eyes before the other two get here, because there's *no* way Ethan's making it over that ditch."

Leah didn't answer. It wasn't the sort of thing that required an answer.

They walked along their narrow strip of ground flanked by the woods on their left and the abyss on their right. Dan kept scratching his left upper arm. "I hate thunderwood," he said.

Leah could see the trees starting to break. They'd made it halfway around the bend in the road. She'd been right, Noah Stork's property line would be in sight anytime now.

"We're almost there," she said.

They came a little more around the curve, and Leah could suddenly make out what it was she'd been watching the harsh, white glow of the moon glittering off of for the past twenty feet. And, although she had somewhat expected it, actually seeing it here was a completely different thing. All her muscles went tense. She tasted iron in the back of her throat.

Parked along the roadside, also far enough back not to be seen from Stork's property, was Jonathon's silver 1982 Nissan Sentra. If not for the moonlight, it would be practically invisible in the shadows.

"Shit," Leah said.

Dan followed her gaze, figuring out what he was looking at much faster than Leah had. "You knew it would be here."

"I was holding out for hope."

Dan looked at her. "On a night like this? Good luck."

They both got down and sneaked a peek around the corner into Noah Stork's yard. Leah was happy to see his white Hyundai still parked in the driveway.

"Have you seen the ladder yet?" Dan asked.

"What lad—" But then she did see it, although it was near on invisible between the side of the garage and the thickly trunked oaks towering toward the sky. "I see it."

"Any guesses?" Dan whispered.

Leah thought about it. Why would there be a ladder heading to the roof of the garage? "Maybe Stork was cleaning his eaves earlier?"

"Garage has no eaves. Guess again."

"I can't. I can't think of any reason."

"What about Jonathon?"

"You think he's on the roof? Has to be around the other side then."

"Why would he be on the roof?" Dan asked.

"How the hell should I know? *You're* the one who said—"

"I was posing the question to both of us." He glanced at Jonathon's silver car. "Why is he parked on the other side of the house, anyway?"

Leah shrugged. "Must've come a different way. Probably knows this area better than me. Wouldn't take much. He probably had a shortcut."

"Great. That's all we need. Gives him even more time to fuck himself."

Leah knew she hadn't covered her reaction to Dan's comment. Somehow, she'd pushed Jonathon's danger out of her mind. Now it came back, full-swing.

Dan took a deep breath and let it out. "He's probably okay," he said unconvincingly. "He's street-smart."

Leah's eyes narrowed. "Last time you called him book-smart. Which is he?"

"That was before you told me he could pick locks."

The static sound of a walkie-talkie blurted from Dan's belt. Quickly, he grabbed a knob and turned down the volume before bringing the microphone to his lips. "Hey," he said. "You guys here?"

Ethan's big voice came out of the speaker, sounding like he was standing in a giant tin. "Yup," he said. "Parked right behind you. How the hell do we cross this bloody ravine?"

Dan couldn't help but laugh a bit. "You don't. You just follow the road the same direction you were driving. You'll come to Stork's property about forty feet down. His driveway bridges your 'ravine.'"

"That safe?" Ethan asked.

"Doesn't look like anyone's watchin' the front. I think you'll be fine."

"Where are you two?"

"We'll be standing just off in the woods right beside the driveway. We'll wait for you here."

It didn't take long for Ethan and Chris to make it to the driveway and then hastily step across the lawn into the shadows with Leah and Dan.

"Whose silver Sentra is that?" Chris asked.

Leah let out a big breath. "It belongs to Caroline's insanely stupid but extremely valiant boyfriend."

"You mean he's gone in there to save her?" Ethan asked.

"Don't see him out here, do you?"

"Don't be a smart-ass."

"Sorry, I'm just worried. And now I'm worried about *two* kids, not just one."

Leah glanced up at Ethan. "Tommy in the back of the squad car?"

"Oh yeah," he said without looking her way.

"Good. If this goes the way I think it will, we can let him go after. No sense charging him. He's too dumb to get it, anyway."

Chris stood from where he was crouched watching the house and garage and turned around. "What's the plan?" he asked. "And I assume we've all noticed the ladder?"

"I was just thinking that same question," Dan said. "About the plan, I mean. We already brainstormed the ladder. We got nothin'."

"The garage," Leah said. "It's gotta be the primary crime scene."

"You said the same thing about that creepy barn," Chris said.

"This time I'm sure. Christ, look at the place. What are our options? It's either the garage or the house."

"Why not the house?" Ethan asked. "Just for the sake of argument."

Leah stared at him. "My pa used to refer to the primary scene as 'the slaughterhouse.' I've been inside Noah's place. There ain't no way he's slaughtering people in there. It's so clean you could eat off the toilet. I think we can safely add obsessive-compulsive disorder onto the growing list of mental issues I'm mentally compiling for the man. He's clean to the point of irritation. Freaky clean."

Ethan let out a breath. "I'm havin' a problem with Jonathon," he said.

"What's that?" Leah asked.

"I don't *hear* anythin'. He must've gotten here almost an hour ago. Wouldn't you reckon whatever he planned to do once he got here he'd have already done?"

A cloud of fear passed over Leah's face. "You mean, maybe he's—"

Ethan quickly shook his head. "If Jonathon was dead, Carry'd be screaming something fierce."

Something caught in Leah's throat before her words tumbled out. "Well, then, what if—"

Ethan shook his head again. "Then our friend Noah Stork would be on his way to Cherry Park Forest. He's gotta know he's latched himself onto some pretty hot properties. My guess is that he'd want to get this over with sooner rather than later. Unless he wants to get caught. Maybe that's it. Maybe this is his last stand."

"God, I hope not. You're makin' it sound like the Battle of the Little Bighorn."

"Yeah, except Stork ain't no Crazy Chief."

Dan snorted. "He ain't even Custer. Let's go see what's on the other side of that—"

He stopped as the front door of Stork's house swung open. "Everybody back up," Dan whispered, scratching his arm.

They did and Leah watched from between two looping blackberry vines as Noah Stork walked across his porch and down the steps to his driveway. He was carrying a yellow cup in his right hand and Leah wondered what was inside it.

"Look at his boots," Dan whispered as Stork came around the front of his car, which was backed into the driveway, the same as it had been both times Leah had paid him a visit.

Stork's boots were black and rose about three-quarters of the way up his thighs. He got to the front of the garage, grabbed the handle, and then stopped. He was looking down at his boots, and Leah now noticed one not being tied. Setting down the yellow cup on one of the concrete path stones that led back to the driveway, Noah Stork tightened the laces starting from the bottom, awkwardly doing it with only his right hand. He worked all the way to the top of the boot and even managed to tie a double bow, all one-handed.

Leah and Dan shared a confused glance. "Must be something wrong with his left hand or arm or something," Dan whispered.

Leah thought back to her encounters with Stork. That first interview, when he fixed her iced tea. Something about the way he'd gotten the iced tea, one glass at a time, had struck her odd. Now she realized he only used one arm. Even when he was on the davenport, it was always his right arm up along the top. And yet—he could *type*. She'd seen his manuscript. That was a lot of typing for a one-handed job.

Then she remembered the inconsistencies in the darkness of the characters. Half were significantly lighter than the others. She'd bet dollars to donuts the light ones came from his left hand.

A bunch of other things started taking on a recognizable shape. This explained why he didn't just carry Abilene Williams through the narrow path. He simply didn't have the ability. It also explained the drag marks they'd found between where Leah suspected he'd parked to where Samantha Hughes's body was staked by the Anikawa.

Except—from what she remembered, there were no weird anomalies in the case from fifteen years ago. Could this be a new injury, or was she wrong about thinking this Stickman was the same guy from fifteen years ago? Suddenly her pa's theory about Harry Stork started looking okay again.

She wanted to point all this out to Dan, but now was definitely not the time.

Stork turned slightly to grab the garage door handle, and Leah immediately recognized the bulge in the back of his black dress shorts, covered by the white button-down shirt he hadn't tucked in. The bulge became less conspicuous as he stood, pulling the garage door up with his right hand as he did so.

"He's packing," Dan said, again in a whisper.

When he bent back down to get the water still on the stone, the gun in his pants once again revealed itself. A sour sickness filled Leah's stomach. She suddenly felt as though she might get sick.

The garage door stayed open as he went over to the shadow of something lying on the floor. Leah tried to wrap her head around the fact that the shadow she was seeing was probably her daughter. He held her head up and helped her drink whatever was in the yellow cup. The thought made Leah shiver.

Leah quickly glanced around the rest of the garage, most of which was in darkness. A bright fluorescent light fixture running across the front of the ceiling threw everything else in shadows. She did see a window and a standard door on the back wall.

"I bet Jonathon's outside that back door," she whispered to Dan just as Stork came back and pulled the big metal door down with a *clang*.

"If he is, I hope he knows Stork just came inside."

"I suggest we break into two teams," Leah said to all of them. "Dan and I will go around to the back side of the garage. Ethan—"

The sound of someone screaming from inside the garage not only cut Leah off short, but she almost jumped out of her skin. It was so loud she had no problem making out the words.

"Where did you get this!" screamed the voice.

"Is that Stork?" Dan whispered to Leah, but she shushed him. She'd only heard Stork speak in his normal, quiet, almost pensive tones. She wasn't sure whether it was him or not. Leah started to relax, thinking that was all they were going to get, when right then more loud words erupted from behind the garage door.

"I asked you a question!" Yeah, Leah figured, that could very well be Stork.

The hollering went on. "Who did this? You couldn't have! There's no way! Who helped you?"

It was Noah Stork. Leah was pretty much sure of it. Besides, who else could it be? They'd just seen everything in that garage. If another man had been skulking around, she'd have spotted him.

Leah looked to Dan. Did that mean Jonathon was in there? Did that mean he was still alive? It could mean any—

Another scream stopped her thoughts: "Who? Who got this ax and tried cutting you free? Where is he?"

Dan looked at Leah and whispered, "He said 'ax,' right? We all heard 'ax'?" He looked from face to face but nobody paid him any attention.

They waited another couple of minutes, but no more words were said loud enough to hear them this vantage point behind the corner of the forest.

"This change our plan at all?" Dan asked Leah.

"No, I think it just expedites it." She glanced to Ethan. "Dan and I take the rear. You guys have the front. That's pretty much the plan. Oh, and if you get the chance, go for a head shot. I'll stand up in any court and testify you were going for his arm but overcompensated."

"And got him in the head?" Chris asked. "That's a lot of overcompensating."

Leah didn't look at him. "Yeah, well, that sorta shows you how I'm feeling right about now."

CHAPTER 69

Leah and Dan crept around to the back of the garage, both walking around the ladder instead of under it like Leah had expected Dan to do. The back of the garage was just how Leah thought it would be, with the closed white door and the almost-square window. What she didn't see was any sign of Jonathon.

"Wait," Dan whispered. "Spoke too soon." Reaching down, he picked up a gray T-shirt that had been balled on the grass. He shook it out and held it in front of him. "Jonathon's?" he asked Leah.

She nodded, trying to think things through. Why was Jonathon's T-shirt outside instead of on him, wherever he happened to be?

"Maybe he thought he would come off more valiant if he rescued her naked from the waist up?"

Leah glared at him. "Okay, you know what?" she whispered. "There are times when I don't mind your funny little quips, but now is *not* one of them. Please don't test me on this. Understood?"

Dan's lips formed a tight line. He nodded.

"Good." Leah went over to the window and snuck a glance inside, her first instinct to look at the walls and test her primary crime scene theory. Test came back gruesomely positive. "I think I'm goin' to be sick," she said. The dark splatter stains covered and, in places, smeared along the walls and floor.

Dan came up and shushed her. "This glass is only single-pane thick," he whispered. "He'll easily hear us if we're not extremely quiet." Dan looked back at the flower garden lit by the half moon.

"Seems strange that a psychopathic killer can make such beautiful things. Maybe underneath all them mental illnesses, he's just a fragile—"

Leah's glare snapped toward him. "Do *not* say anythin' good about this man to me. I'm serious, Dan. I plan on killin' him, and I don't need anythin' about that dragging my conscience down."

Even though she'd whispered, he shushed her again. "What if we get a chance to take him alive?"

She opened the clip on her holster. "There's only one way I'm takin' this son of a bitch," she said. "And I'm doing it for me, for my pa, and for Caroline. Shit, even for Jonathon. If I reckoned I could get a proper shot off through this window, I'd take it right now."

"Think about what you just said before you do anything rash," Dan whispered. "It's not our duty to kill unless it's our only option."

"I give two shits about my goddamn duty, Dan. This man deserves death."

Quietly, Dan asked, "Like Harry Stork did?"

Leah felt her face explode to red. "Do *not* do that to me, Dan. Do *not!* You have no right!"

"Okay," he whispered, raising his palm. "Just quiet down, or it won't matter anyhow."

"Where the hell's Jonathon?" Leah asked, going back to the window.

Dan shrugged. "Maybe inside?"

"We saw inside. He wasn't there. Try the door. See if it's locked."

Gingerly, Dan put his hand on the knob and gave it a slow turn. It didn't stop. "It's unlocked."

"God *damn* it!" Leah whispered through her teeth. "Then he *is* in there. But where?"

Ethan's voice cut through the walkie-talkie static. Dan quickly lowered the volume and stepped around to the side of the garage where the ladder still stood. Leah followed. "What's goin' on?" Ethan asked.

"We found Jonathon's shirt and the back door's unlocked. We figure that's his handiwork, but there's no sign of him. We reckon he must already be inside."

"I didn't see him when that door was open."

"Yeah, us either. But it's really all we can think of."

"What do you mean, you found the boy's shirt?"

"Exactly that. It was lying in a ball on the grass."

"Why would he take his shirt off?" Ethan asked.

"You ponder that," Dan said. "We'll get back to you once we decide our move." He clipped the walkie-talkie back to his belt. "Okay," he said to Leah. "We don't have lots of options. I suggest we take the door and go in with guns up. He won't expect the door to be unlocked, we'll have the element of surprise."

Leah thought this over, then shook her head. "He's too close to Caroline and she's supine and motionless. She'd be a sitting duck."

Dan sighed. "Okay, I'm actually not against your idea of shooting through the window."

"What time is it?" Leah asked Dan.

Dan checked his watch. "Eleven-oh-five."

"Shit, that means he has twenty-five minutes to kill her, let her bleed out, put her in his car, drive her to Cherry

Park Forest, and drag her somewhere to stake. He's gotta be thinkin' about leavin' anytime now. I'd say we have five minutes, on the outside."

"It's gonna have to be the window shot."

Leah took another peek. Noah Stork was now kneeling beside Caroline, his back to the window. All Leah could see was the top of his head above the narrow table blocking the view.

"He's way too close to her now, and I don't have a direct shot anyway."

Dan came up beside her just as Noah briefly stood, pulling a Glock 19 from the back of his pants.

"Shit!" Leah snapped.

Noah knelt back down beside Caroline, whose head, if Leah had things visualized correctly, was facing away.

"We have to!" Dan said. "It's now or never."

"Dan, I have no shot."

"Then we hit the door. Do it that way."

Just then, Caroline must've felt the barrel of the Glock press against the back of her head on account of she started to scream.

"No! No! Please don't!" Her words were flooded with tears.

"Hit the door!" Leah yelled, stumbling over Dan. "Now!"

CHAPTER 70

Still stuck in the cramped cabinet, Jonathon listened as Carry's cries increased. His heart was thundering against his chest. He knew he had to make a move and he had to do it soon. Where the hell was Miss Leah and the rest of the police? They certainly weren't going to make it in time to do anything.

"Now," he heard Stork say, "this part. This is where you start cryin'."

Then he heard the slider of a gun.

Then Carry started to scream.

Jonathon didn't even pay attention to her words. Running on full adrenaline, he kicked open the cabinet door and pushed himself out. His legs complained from being bent so long, but he forced them to stand. Forced them to move.

He stumbled over the narrow table but managed to see Stork bent over Caroline with the barrel of a gun pressed to the back of her head. The noise Jonathon made coming out of the cabinet made Stork snap his attention over his shoulder. Surprise filled his eyes as Jonathon heaved the table out of his way and practically dove at Stork.

It didn't take long for Stork to react, though. His gun hand came away from Caroline's head and he spun his body around and began leveling his weapon at Jonathon.

Jonathon was on the verge of launching himself at the man, when he realized the gun was pointed directly at his chest. Fear overcame his adrenaline and Jonathon froze. The surprise in Stork's face melted away as a grim smile took its place.

"My, my," he said, his gun steady in his grip. "What have we here? Somebody's Romeo?"

"Jonathon!" Carry screamed. "Run! Get the hell out of here!" Her voice sounded raw. Her body began to convulse as she broke into tears. "Please," she said, quieter. "Please don't hurt him. Just let him go? Please?" The words broke into more sobs.

"I won't hurt him much," Stork said, matter-of-factly. "Just enough to kill him."

CHAPTER 71

Leah and Dan were on the verge of going through the door when a cacophony of noise from inside brought Leah back to the window. Jonathon now moved through the garage, tackling the table, trying to make his way to Stork. At first, Leah thought he'd done it. Thought he was going to tackle Stork before Stork even knew what hit him, but that damn table was giving him too many problems. Finally, Jonathon just threw it aside, but by then it was too late. The surprise factor no longer worked for Jonathon. And Stork had now managed to wheel around and point his Glock right at Jonathon's chest.

Now Jonathon just stood there, probably scrambling for an idea of what to do next. Leah was doing the same.

Finally, she looked to Dan. "Radio Ethan. Tell them to open the garage door."

"Okay . . ." Dan said. "Why?"

"It will distract Stork enough to get us in through there." She pointed to the door.

"Sounds like a plan. Let's hope it's a good one."

Dan went around the side again and radioed Ethan. He came back and told Leah to be ready to go on three.

It wasn't even two when the rattle and tumble of the big garage door's wheels echoed through the room as Ethan and Chris brought the door up.

Without even making noise, Leah and Dan opened the back door. Dan went in first.

By the time Leah was inside, Stork's gun was no longer pointed at Jonathon, it was trained on Ethan, who stood out brightly on account of the fluorescent lights above his head.

Ethan had his .38 out and pointed right back at Stork. Only difference was, Ethan used both his hands to grip his gun, and Leah knew now that for Stork, this wasn't an option.

"Drop it, Stork!" Ethan said.

Slowly, Stork stood from his crouch, never once taking his eyes or aim away from Ethan. Leah wasn't even sure if he knew she and Dan were inside yet.

They both took a firing stance as Stork said to Ethan, "You're my biggest threat, therefore, you go first."

Just then Chris stepped out of the night's shadows and came in under the lights. His gun was gripped the same as Ethan's. They stood about seven feet apart.

"Now you got a decision to make," Chris said. "You get one of us, we get you."

"Actually, the decision's even more complicated than that," Dan said.

From Stork's reaction Leah realized he'd had no idea they were there. Now his head snapped in their direction, and he found himself being sighted down the barrel of four weapons.

Something flickered behind Stork's eyes. An idea, perhaps.

Stepping back, Stork grabbed Jonathon and pointed his gun to the side of Jonathon's head. "Okay, you guys all get a shot and kill me four times. I only get one. And it's for Romeo here. As they say, all is fair in love and war." He was smiling. Leah wanted so badly to shoot that smile off of his crazy goddamn face.

Leah looked down at Caroline, lying tied up on her side, gently sobbing. She could only see Leah and Dan from her position. "Mom?" she asked. "Mom, what's goin' on?"

"Just work stuff," Leah said. "We're getting you out of here."

"Where's Jonathon?" Carry asked, her voice on the brink of hysteria.

"He's fine, baby," Leah said, taking a step forward. "He's safe."

Stork let out a laugh. "A strange definition of the word *safe* you have, my dear. But do me a favor and take a step back."

Leah didn't move.

Stork screamed. "Do it! Do it right now, or so help me I'll blow his goddamn head off!"

Leah stepped back.

"So you have friends, little girl. And this one's a pesky one. Like a cockroach. They get into everything, too. I assume you were the one who moved my ax?" Even though his words were directed at Jonathon, he never stopped looking at the cops, his eyes going from one to the next to the next and to the next. And all four of them had their weapons trained directly his way.

He smiled. "I know, you all want a piece of me right

now. Well, you can have it, but only on one condition. And that's that I get Romeo. Quid pro quo. You shoot me, I shoot him. As they say in Babylon, 'An eye for an eye . . .' Well, you know the rest."

"It doesn't have to go that way," Dan said. "We can still all walk out of here alive. Just lower your weapon."

Stork let out a little laugh. "Don't you see? This was going to be my last one anyway. I can't do it anymore. I'm not physically able. I can't even lift someone as light as your daughter without pain shooting through my arm. Besides, I'm tired of it all. All the killing, all the screaming. All the pressure."

"What pressure?" Leah asked. She wanted a shot so bad.

"In my head. Pressure. I have to do this, I have to do that. I'm sick of being a slave to my brain. I welcome death." He cut a quick glance to Jonathon. "What about you, Romeo? How welcoming are you to death? If I were you, I'd start making my peace real soon now." As he finished his speech, his gaze went back to Dan.

"Stork," Dan said with incredible calm. "See this gun I'm holding? It's a DoubleTap Derringer loaded with .45-caliber ACPs with two rounds already chambered. I know, awfully nice of my lieutenant to let me carry such a piece. But I want you to realize this 'thing' I have pointed at you right now has the capability to kill you twice before you even realize I squeezed the trigger. I suggest you lower your weapon now and not make me prove it."

Leah often wondered what kind of gun Dan had. It was different from any she'd seen before, with two barrels lined up vertically.

"Noah," Dan said.

"Who *are* you?" Noah asked. "The group's 'spokes-man'? Why have I never seen you before?"

Dan took one hand off his weapon, stepped forward, and extended his hand. "Dan Truitt, detective out of Birmingham. I—"

"Go back where you were!" Stork screamed, freaking out. "I swear I will pull this trigger!"

Dan looked to Leah. "Not the most polite guy I've ever met. I thought you said he made you sweet tea?"

Leah shrugged. "Must've been a good day."

Stork looked back and forth between them. "Just fuckin' shut up!"

Dan sighed. "Look, you say you're tired of being sick. You don't have to die to fix that. There are medications that will work. You just haven't found them yet. Think back to the night you lost Harry. You went five years without killin' anyone. If you did it then, you can do it now. You don't *have* to be an executioner all the time."

"I'm not *an* executioner," Noah hollered back at least twice as loud as Dan was. "I'm *the* executioner. I'm the Stickman. I'm the Strangler." He paused, as though he was letting this sink in.

"We know, Noah," Dan said. "We figured it out. It took a thirteen-year-old boy to do it, but we figured it out. Why do you think I said 'five' years and not 'fifteen'?"

Stork obviously decided none of that mattered. "I went to sleep for five years," he said. "Goddamn doctors and their medication. They just lull you into a walking coma. So I stopped taking their meds, and lo and behold, I woke up. I managed my way outside of the box, and from here, I can see it all now. The cover-ups, the conspiracies, how the medical community links to the military, how everything leads to everything else in one big connection. I'm more lucid now than I've ever been."

"I think I have a shot," Dan whispered to Leah.

"No!" she whispered back. "He's too close to Jonathon. He'll blow his head apart."

"I'm a good shot," Dan said. "And the muzzle velocity of this pistol is nothin' short of truly amazing." Leah couldn't believe how calm he was.

Leah thought hard. They had to do something mighty quick. Stork had a loaded, chambered pistol, its barrel pointed six inches from Jonathon's temple.

"Try it," Stork said. "Take your shot."

"Shit, he heard me," Dan whispered to Leah.

"Of course I heard you. Do you think I'm deaf?"

"Don't do anything rash, Stork. We *will* shoot. You don't need to die today."

Then Noah Stork began quoting Shakespeare. Leah knew it was Shakespeare because it happened to be from one of the two plays they had to learn for high school English. "By heaven," he said, theatrically, "I will tear thee joint by joint and strew this hungry church-yard with thy limbs. The time and my intents are savage, wild, more fierce and more inexorable far than empty tigers or the roaring sea."

Leah remembered the speech and where it came in the play—right before Romeo died. Then she realized why Stork had quoted it, but that realization came too late. Noah Stork had just told Jonathon good-bye.

"No!" Leah screamed. "No! Don't!"

Everything felt like it was moving in slow motion as, without any sign of emotion, the Stickman, the Strangler, and the man named Noah Stork gently squeezed the trigger on his 9 mm semi-automatic.

The garage exploded with the massive sound of gunshots. Leah thought she heard three near on simultaneously. Instinctively, her eyes closed from the intensity of the noise. Everything went black. The room filled with the smell of cordite.

CHAPTER 72

Leah opened her eyes as the echo of gunfire died away, only to be replaced by Caroline's screaming.

Jonathon's body collapsed, crumpling and tumbling onto the concrete floor. He wound up falling on his side, his head lying in clear view of Caroline. Blood pooled rapidly around his head before tributaries formed, taking it away from the growing red lake. Caroline's screams were wicked. They filled the garage, and, Leah suspected, even the neighbors a mile up the road must be able to hear them. The top part of Jonathon's skull seemed to detach slightly from the other. Leah had to look away. Unfortunately, because of how she was bound, Caroline couldn't. She sounded like a wild animal being butchered.

The two shots from Dan's gun had blown Stork backward against the wall, putting two new splatter patterns across the unfinished wall. Dan's gun made two obvious bullet holes in Stork's body, one in the chest and one slightly lower.

For a moment, Stork stood there, his back against the wall, his gun still held in the hand of his outstretched right arm, his left arm dangling useless at his side. Something about him reminded Leah of a scarecrow. Or a crucifix.

Then, horrifically, his lips formed a smile and a small laugh escaped his throat. He spoke, and his voice sounded like dust. "Poor Romeo," he said.

Leah mistakenly thought Stork was going to live. That was when she took aim and squeezed a shot off herself, this one going straight through Stork's heart.

He slid down the wall, leaving a trail of fresh red in his wake. Reaching the floor, he looked like he'd sat down for a nap with his head tilted forward. Around him and from under his legs, bright red pools of blood began to form.

Caroline still stared at what was left of Jonathon's head. His eyes were wide open and almost seemed focused on her as she sobbed, screaming between chest heaves. "Why did you kill him?" she yelled to the dead man sitting behind her. "Why? Why him?"

But the Stickman couldn't answer, because he was dead.

And this time, he was staying that way.

CHAPTER 73

All Carry did now was cry, all the time.

She had to go to therapy and everything. I heard my mother talking to Dan about it. They said that when the medical examiner came to take the bodies away, Carry wouldn't get off of Jonathon. My mother finally had to pick her up and carry her to a car. She kept screaming with tears streaming down her face as she watched them "bag and tag" him, an expression I remembered from the book I'd read. I guess that meant Jonathon was evidence now, too. Funny, how all that forensics stuff meant so much to me before, and now it just seems so far away and pointless.

But all Carry does is cry. And screams. She bursts into screams a lot. Things like, "Why did he have to die?" and "It's not fair!" Well, actually, to be honest, she usually yells it a bit more like, "It ain't fucking fair!"

The first time I heard her scream out the *F* word, I thought my mother would come down the hall and throw a fit at her, but she didn't. In fact, I don't think she even said anything about it. I guess when you're so sad you can't control what you say, then it's okay to break some of the rules. I don't know.

Sometimes she'll start screaming in the middle of the night, and it jolts me awake, but I don't get mad. You don't get mad at people when they are filled up with sadness. I didn't even need my mother to tell me that.

Dewey was really sad when I told him what happened. I think he may have even cried, but he tried to hide it so I won't ever ask him. He definitely took it hard. It's been two days, and he hasn't been over or called or nothing. I miss Dewey, but right now I'm kind of glad it's just me, my mother, and Carry. Well, I guess Dan's here, too, but I don't notice him much. Carry stays in her room so the TV stays off and, I guess, I have been pretty much staying in my room, too.

I sure do miss Jonathon. I miss everything about him. He bought me and Dewey lady fingers for the Fourth all on his own because he wanted to be nice. Nobody told him to. In fact, by her reaction to him giving them to us, I don't think Carry even knew.

Yeah, I sure do miss him.

Want to know a secret? Well, it's not really a secret. I'm not ashamed of it or anything, I just . . . I don't know. It's kind of weird. But I've been crying a lot, too. The thing is, though, I'm not entirely sure what I'm crying about. Sometimes I think I'm crying for Jonathon on account of him dying, but then other times it feels like I'm crying for me since I don't get to see him anymore. And other times? I feel like I'm crying for Carry, although I think Carry does enough crying for all of us.

Everything's different now. It's not even like when my grandpa died. Things were different after that, but . . . well, it was different.

Today, I asked my mother when things would go back to normal.

"They may never go back to the way you remember them, Abe," she said. We were both sitting on my bed.

I told her I didn't like that answer. "What about Carry?" I asked then. "Will she ever be normal again?"

My mother thought this over. "Your sister's been through a lot, Abe. Everyone handles death differently, and you have to remember, she loved Jonathon. She loved him and she watched him die right in front of her. These kind of things affect you forever."

"You mean like when I looked into the eyes of Mary Ann Dailey when she was lying beneath that willow?"

Concern fell over my mother's face. "You still remember that?"

I nodded.

"Do you have nightmares about it?"

I shrugged. "I don't know. I don't usually remember my dreams."

She reached out and tucked a lock of my hair back behind my ear. "How often do you think about that?" she asked.

"I dunno," I said. "All the time. I ain't never seen anythin' like it."

My mother seemed to consider this. "Do you wish you hadn't seen her that day?"

I shook my head. "I'm glad I did."

My mother looked puzzled. "Why?"

I looked into her eyes. "On account of everybody else there were just police doin' their jobs. Nobody 'cept maybe you really cared about her just lyin' there, and you were too busy really anyway. 'Sides, you're a grown-up. Mary Ann Dailey needed someone her own age—well, closer to her age, anyway. She needed someone she could tell her story to who would understand."

My mother looked even more puzzled. "What do you

mean?" she asked, her eyes narrowing. "Understand what? What story?"

"The story of her life. The story of how it ended. How she never got to do everything she thought she would on account of her life being taken away so early. See, I understood this. I was meant to. And it's not a bad story, it's one that makes you happy for everything you have and everything you get to do. And it was good that I was the one who saw her, because I know, no matter what, I ain't never gonna forget her."

My mother took a big breath and kind of looked away at the microscopes still standing on that fold-out table. "Did you tell Dewey all this?" she asked.

I shook my head.

"Why not?"

"He wouldn't understand, or he'd make me clarify it so much that it would lose its meaning. I don't ever want to lose the feeling that comes with the memory."

"It's a good feeling?"

I shook my head. "No, it's a horrible, scary feeling."

Her jaw tightened. "Then why do you want to keep it?"

"Because I think there are still much more things I can learn from it. I reckon it's the sort of thing you have to mull over for a lifetime and you might still not understand it completely."

"How do you feel about Jonathon's death?"

"I miss him. He was a nice guy."

She paused, and it felt like she was thinking real hard on something. "What sort of feeling do you have with this memory, Abe?"

"I don't rightly know. I think it's still forming itself, to be honest. I don't feel bad, not like I did for Mary Ann Dailey."

"Really? How come?"

I gave this a moment's thought. "I reckon it's because Jonathon always seemed so happy. I don't think he missed out on a lot, even though he died so young. Life for him was simple. The simpler things are, the better they are, I believe. Folk always try to complicate life too much."

She placed her hand on my knee. "Are you worried about your sister?"

I blinked, thinking this had to be a trick question. "Of course I am. She's goin' to be all right, though, right?"

My mother took another big breath. "I think so, Abe. There's a process she has to go through. No telling how long it will take, though."

"What kind of process?"

"It's called the 'grieving process.' It has five steps."

"And Carry's gotta go through all five? How long is each step?"

My mother softly shook her head. "It's always different for everybody. And she might not go through all five, or she might go through some many times before she's ready."

"Ready for what?"

"To face the world again."

I wondered about my next question, whether or not I might upset my mother, but I decided to ask it anyway. "Did you go through these steps when Pa died?"

Her eyes went back to them microscopes. "Yes, Abe. I did."

"And how long did it take you?"

Her chest expanded, and a big sigh came out. "I'm not sure."

"How come you ain't sure?"

"Because I reckon in some ways I'm still going through them."

"Still?" I asked. "What about Dan?"

She looked at my floor. "Dan's a good person. He treats me well."

"Do you love him?" I asked.

She gave me a look that made me wish I hadn't asked. When she spoke, she stumbled over her words. "Um . . . you know what? Yeah." She smiled. "Yeah, I reckon I do."

I smiled back, not because I liked Dan so much, but because my mother seemed happy. Then I had a thought that made my smile disappear.

"What's wrong?" my mother asked.

I rubbed my nose. "You reckon he drinks too much?"

Her eyes widened slightly. She really didn't expect me to ask that, and I wondered if maybe I'd get lectured for not minding my business. "Um . . . well, let me ask you that question, Abe. Do *you* reckon he drinks too much?"

"He averages a half liter of Jim Beam a night," I said. "That seems like a lot. To me, at least."

Her eyes narrowed again. "How do you know so exactly the amount he drinks?"

"Carry showed me where you've been putting all the empty bottles."

My mother's lips pressed into a line. She bounced her feet off my floor. "Is that right?" she asked, not looking at me.

"Was you tryin' to hide them? Carry said you were."

Her eyes met mine. "Y'all had a discussion about this?"

I frowned. "Sort of. Carry said you weren't hidin' them from us, though."

"I wasn't? Who was I hiding them from, then?"

"Carry figured you was hidin' them from yourself. So you didn't have to deal with it."

My mother looked away, her head gently nodding. "That's what she reckoned?"

I nodded.

My mother patted my knee again. "Your sister's goin' to be fine. She's bright. Even brighter than I ever gave her credit for."

CHAPTER 74

"Duck," Leah said, sitting back comfortably in her chair. She spoke quietly, so her voice didn't slam around on the screaming white concrete walls. In places, the paint was peeling. Leah didn't like these rooms. They reminded her of death. *Death that comes silently into the night and leaves behind its unmistakable teeth marks*. That was what these walls said. They warned you. Warned you about getting in the way of death's teeth marks.

Leah cleared her throat and spoke slightly louder. "Duck," she said again. "I'm back." She was back at the Talladega Correctional Institute, this time without Dan. It didn't make Duck look any more happy to see her.

"Where's Pencil Dick?"

"He had to head back to his own station. It's up north."

"Thought you were partners?"

"We are. We were." She hesitated and then finished with, "We are."

"Kind of long-distance partners, ain't you?"

Leah just watched that ball sail over the plate. She wasn't going to let herself be riled up by Duck or anyone else. After what she had been through, she was happy just to have another day with her daughter safe and sound. "It's a work in progress," she finally said.

Duck narrowed his eyes as the revelation came to him. "No! Don't tell me. You and . . . and . . . Pencil Dick?"

"It's really not."

"What?"

"Like a pencil."

Duck looked panicked. Started shaking his head. "No! I don't want to hear actual *details*. This is freakin' worse than solitary!"

Leah smiled. "You know why I'm here?"

"No, but I'm sure you're goin' to tell me. You're almost as bad as *he* was, the way your mouth never stops movin'."

"I'm here on account of I know what you did."

Duck shook his head. "And, lady, as usual, I ain't got no fuckin' idea what you're talking 'bout."

"You lied to me, Duck. You said you never met Harry Stork, but you did. In fact, if I'm correct, you knew him well."

"Listen, lady, I already told you, I—"

She raised her hand to quiet him. "No, you lied. You told me you never met Harry Stork whereas the truth was, you did. And you knew him almost *intimately* well."

"I don't even wanna *know* what you mean by *that*," Duck said.

"Okay, well, I may never know *how* well you knew him, but from August 1959 until July 1960, you guys spent time together in juvie. Now, you're goin' to tell me that was all just coincidence, too? And you never actually *met* him?"

Duck just shrugged. "You can make up any shit you want."

"I don't have to make shit up, Duck. The shit's all over the place. I'm just pickin' it up and lookin' at it."

Duck closed his eyes and shook his head.

"Problem is, Duck, you left some evidence behind you. After Harry Stork's house was raided by the police, it was never put up for auction. In fact, nobody has ever been inside it since."

"Lady, what the fuck does this have to do with—"

"Until we went back in again. Last week. See, after all the pieces fell into place about Noah Stork, it got me thinkin'. The man showed a lot of compassion toward both his sons, but especially toward Harry. Made me wonder why someone like that would let their kid take the fall. Fact is, he didn't, did he, Duck?"

Duck's handcuffs rattled. "Once again, lady, I have no idea where you're—"

"The one thing you didn't lie about, Duck, was having anythin' to do with the Stickman killin's. Fact is, they started a good eight months, maybe even a year, before you came into the picture. Before you ever met Noah Stork at Grell Memorial Psychiatric Hospital in Montgomery."

Duck looked like he was going to speak, but he didn't. Then, "I told you, I don't know nobody named—"

"Oh, you do. Only when you first met him, his name was Joshua Delford. You knew right away, though, didn't you? The resemblance is uncanny. Those boys got a lot of their old man's genes. But it was Noah—or Joshua, if you prefer—who told you about the signature, right, Duck?"

"Lady." Duck laughed. "This is a fuckin' *reach*."

"No, Duck, it ain't. Because you remembered Harry

and knew Harry might be useful. But what really clicked with you was hearing about how the Stickman did it. And what he did. Something deep in the reptilian part of your brain *liked* it. In fact, you liked it so much you sold your house in Calvert and bought a different house just miles away from where Noah Stork lived, in what is now Blue Jay Maples. Back then, it was just the boonies with nothin' but logging roads running through it. Why would anyone move to a godawful place like that, unless they had some kind of ulterior motive? And you had one, all right: You wanted to keep *tabs* on Noah Stork so you could 'discover' his victims, just like the police."

"This is some sick and twisted shit you're spoutin', lady."

"Mmm," Leah said. "I'm afraid on that point, we agree. Because deep down, you're no killer, are you, Duck? But you like the *idea* of killin'. You're like the Son of Sam, only without the actual drive to pull the trigger. Maybe you're just too much of a pussy?"

Leah heard his handcuffs rattle again. Moisture had collected on Duck's cropped hair. "Lady! Nobody *ever* calls me a pussy. You don't have any *freakin' idea* who you're—"

"Well, whatever the reason, you didn't like actually killin' no one. At least not that I could find. You just liked to 'see' the victims afterward. What did it do for you, Duck? Give you some kind of thrill? Did you masturbate at the crime scenes?"

Duck looked away to the white wall at his right. A trickle of sweat ran from his blond hair down the left side of his face, curving around the outer edge of his ear.

"That really *is* some fucked-up, twisted shit, as you said, Duck."

"You have no proof of nothin'," Duck said.

"Oh wait. We're comin' to that. The part where we go back into Harry's house fifteen years later. But don't let me spoil it."

Duck locked eyes with her for an instant, and if Leah hadn't known until then, now she knew for sure. Duck was guilty. She was firing on all his cylinders, and his motor was revving up. He was actually shaking.

"Anyway, one thing you never suspected when you broke in to Noah Stork's house and stole the gun was that he would call the authorities."

Duck studied her. Luckily, she hadn't got to the part where she had to lie, yet. She could tell the truth and not stumble. She just hoped she could brace herself all the way through. Getting a confession hung on it.

"He did, Duck. He called us. Well, I wasn't there at the time, but an officer by the name of Strident went out to his place, and he was showed how the bedroom window—Tommy's window—had been broken enough for a hand to get through and open it completely. Nothin' was reported as stolen, though. Makes one wonder why Stork even bothered reporting it."

Something shimmered in Duck's eyes, and Leah knew he was wondering the same thing. He looked at her as though trying to size up whether she was pulling this stuff right out of her ass or not. She wasn't. Not yet. This part really happened.

"But I know what *was* taken and, for obvious reasons, not reported. Noah's .38 Special. Smith & Wesson. Does that sound familiar to you?"

"Lady, like I said, you ain't got—"

"Then why are you sweating so much, Duck? Why are you trembling? Surely you—"

A shrill whistle came from the other side of the table. "Guard! Guard!" Duck called out. "We're done in here. Guard!"

"Nobody's coming, Duck. They all know the truth. How the police were closing in on Noah and how you panicked. You didn't want to see it all go away. You didn't want Noah to be caught. So you framed Harry, knowing that with what little we had in the way of DNA and blood matching back then would trigger a match close enough to assuage any police officer's doubts. You paid off two 'eyewitnesses' for pretending to see Harry Stork. You even made sure they picked *Tommy* out of a photo lineup before Harry Stork was ever on anyone's radar, knowing that the police would make the connection because they were monozygotic twins. That, and the fact that the witnesses reported Tommy as the man, only nobody remembered seeing the scar on his face—*that* led the police to Harry.

"Then you planted the gun in Harry's house. One thing forensics *could* do in 1974 was match a round to a gun, and you *knew* we had at least one bullet in evidence. You knew on account of you broke into our shop and stole all the Stickman case files from where they sat on Joe Fowler's desk. So you knew you needed to plant a murder weapon.

"Four weeks later, police received their final Stickman letter, only this one didn't come from Noah Stork, it came from you. And just so nobody was fooled, you even put Harry Stork's initials on it. *H.S.,* the final Stickman victim."

"This is freakin' incredible," Duck said, regaining some of his composure. "I feel like I'm watching a freakin' movie. Nobody's goin' to believe this story."

"No? Harry did. At least he believed *your* version of

it. You visited him just before putting the gun in his house. You told him you broke into our shop and saw the reports. The reports that said we were after *him*. You psyched him out enough that you knew he'd run. Knew he'd hide. What choice did he have? Then, a day or two later, his house was raided, and the police came forward saying they found the weapon in the home of Harry Stork and issued a statewide manhunt. Sounding familiar yet, Duck?"

"Not at all. You're crazy." He sounded calm, but sweat dripped from his chin. He kept trying to wipe it away with his orange sleeve, but he couldn't quite get it all.

Leah was closing in for the final blow, and she only hoped he kept believing her. So far, it had been easy, because so far she hadn't lied. Lies were coming, though. And when they did, she had better be able to act it all out because Duck's confession depended on it.

"So, after telling Harry if it ever came down to it, the evidence would put him away for life or even maybe get him the death penalty, you said to make sure he shot first. You drilled that into his mind. Problem was, Harry wasn't a killer. He didn't even buy bullets for the gun. The magazine was empty when he burst out of that shack."

Duck's hand trembled. If only sweating and twitching would stand up in court, this would all be over.

"And so, Harry Stork died for the Stickman killin's. And that ended them. Probably, you thought, forever."

She waited to hear something back, but Duck remained silent.

"What you didn't know, though, Duck, was that Noah Stork continued. It took a handful of years, but the urge to kill came back. Only this time, he decided to change things up. Probably, he thought, the Stickman case was closed. They solved the crime. No point in stirring up any old witch pots. I mean, that's what you thought, right? That getting Harry put away or killed would be enough of a signal to make Noah Stork go into hiding? Don't feel bad. He did. He did for years until that urge came back. And when it did, he reinvented himself.

"As the Cahaba River Strangler."

Duck's eyes went wide and gripped Leah's. She had him.

"You know what started Noah Stork and the Stickman killin's? It was the death of his ex-wife. She killed herself, Duck. Granted, the family was a little messed up. Noah Stork has—had—schizophrenia, which, of course, you knew about. What you don't know is that he handed a lot of that down to his kids. Sure, being in Vietnam set Harry off, but Tommy was diagnosed early. Neither of them were as bad as Noah, though. Yet nobody knew. Not about Noah. They only knew about Joshua Delford. But it was the death of his wife, Sally-Anne, that finally pushed Noah Stork's diseased mind over the edge. Started him on the Stickman murders. What you probably *don't* know, and the ironic part, is that the killin's were targeted. Not the first few, but the rest. They were targeted at people working in hospitals. People whom Noah Stork would run into while helping out his son Harry with his cleaning business. So, in a way, Harry *was* involved. You just never knew. And, of course, neither did he."

Duck stayed silent. His eyes darted from hers to the tabletop. Sweat continued dripping off his chin and down his neck. The upper part of his uniform was getting wet, the soaked orange taking on almost the color of dried blood.

"I know what you're wondering. Why did the Stick-man killin's start up again if Noah Stork was getting all his killin' enjoyment out as the Cahaba River Strangler? I know. This one stumped me for a long time. Then it came to me. And once again, there's some irony here. Not sure how well-read you are, but I don't want you to miss it. Surely Noah Stork wouldn't have. Me, Duck. I'm the reason. I was interviewed in the *Alvin Examiner* in an article that ran about three weeks ago now. In the article I talked about my pa—my father. Who was as fine a police officer as there ever was one. Any idea who that was, Duck? He's dead now."

Duck almost imperceptibly shook his head.

"Joe Fowler," Leah said. "My *pa*. That's right, Duck. How strange is the world now? My pa shot Harry Stork. *My* pa. Until that article ran, Noah Stork had no idea I even existed, never mind that I became a cop in my pa's footsteps. It was enough to bring the Stickman back out of hidin'. And that's why, this time 'round, the letters were comin' to *me*. Not Joe Fowler, but Leah Fowler. And Noah Stork knew damn well I went by Teal, but he just used 'Fowler' to get to me. And to raise the stakes of the game."

"This story"—Duck laughed, shaking his head— "nobody's ever goin' to believe—"

"You might be right, Duck. If it wasn't for the final proof we needed to wrap everythin' up." Here it went. This was where she had to sell it as best she could. Just a couple of little lies. A couple of little leaps of logic she'd made and was pretty confident were on the money.

"Remember I told you, nobody's stepped foot in Harry's house since the day it was searched?" she asked him. "The place was like a museum, Duck. Everything exactly as they left it in 1974. Only, back then they didn't have the technology we have now. They didn't have such a thing as 'latent fingerprints.' Know what latent prints are, Duck? Latent prints are fingerprints that are not visible to the naked eye, but do exist."

She let this sink in while Duck tried to look everywhere but at her.

"You see, the person leaving the print would never see it. In fact, in 1974, nobody would ever see it. But these days, we have the ability to bring them out. Using all sorts of things I don't even pretend to understand, we can find latent prints as easily if they were patent prints. Oh, in case you aren't well-versed in the forensics lingo, patent prints are normal, everyday fingerprints you can see without the use of magnesium powders, chemicals, or ultraviolet radiation. Anyway, when our forensics guys searched the house for latent prints, Duck, guess what they found?"

He slowly lifted his eyes from the tabletop to hers.

"Go on, guess," Leah said. "Please? Just take one wild guess?"

Duck looked back down.

"They found some! Isn't that *great,* Duck? Fifteen years after the fact, we are able to find prints we couldn't back then. How wonderful is that? And guess who those prints belong to? Come on. I'll give you three guesses. Oh, and I'll also tell you one of them came off of the .38 that was planted in Harry's house. Aren't you goin' to guess?"

Duck didn't move. His sweat continued to run. She wasn't sure, but she thought she'd sold it. Everything now depended on what happened next.

She remembered back to the article she'd read in *Scientific American* while she and Dan had waited for Gary Carmichael's receptionist to get off the phone that day.

"There's something else, too, Duck. I don't know how well-versed you might be in cutting-edge forensic technology these days, but have you ever heard of an 'electron microscope'?" Leah put all her thought into making sure she came off deadly serious.

Duck didn't answer her question.

"Yeah, I hadn't, either, until my forensics guy mentioned it to me. Apparently, using this microscope they can now bounce electrons off of teensy-tiny grains of metal and look at what's called a 'backscatter pattern.' Now, I don't even pretend to understand the science, but from what my guy said, this 'backscatter pattern' is like a fingerprint. It contains all sorts of information about the metal and its history."

She tried to read Duck's face. She couldn't tell whether he was buying it.

"So," she continued, "let's say someone punched that metal with some sort of code—or number. Perhaps a serial number? And then, somehow, that number got taken off, maybe it was ground off, or sanded off. Doesn't matter how. Doesn't matter. What's important is that the backscatter pattern from this microscope bouncing electrons off the atoms in the gun's metal allows forensic scientists to make out what those numbers were, even though they'd all been filed away."

She gave this a moment to sink in. Sweat continued coming down the sides of Duck's face and neck.

"Duck," she said, lowering her voice almost to a whisper. "I know where Harry got that Berretta from. I know who that gun was, and still is, registered to."

His eyes slowly closed. When they opened again, they stared straight at her. Duck looked like a heavyweight boxer coming out for round ten and realizing he's got nothing left, that the next jab would be all it would take to knock him down, like he just wanted to get it over with.

Leah kept her voice quiet. "I can help you, Duck. If you confess, I can make sure you get off fairly easy. Remember how I did it last time, with Carmichael? I can do it again. But if you make me push this through the system . . . well, I'm afraid there won't be anything I can do."

She waited. Duck didn't move. Just trembled. She wished she could read his thoughts. Doubt circled in her mind like vultures over a dead corpse. Had she oversold it? It didn't really matter, anyway. By his reaction, she knew she was right. Really, that was justice enough after all this time. It would just have been nice, though, if only for the memory of her pa—

"What do you want me to do?" Duck said quietly, his eyes reaching up to hers.

"All I want is for you to tell me the truth," Leah said calmly and smiled.

CHAPTER 75

"So, Duck confessed to setting up Harry Stork?" Dan asked Leah. They were sitting in Leah's living room at opposite ends of Leah's sofa. Two wineglasses and a bottle of cabernet sat on the table. Dan's glass was almost empty. Leah's was pretty near full. They'd been sitting there for less than ten minutes.

"He did."

"And you didn't take me along?" He shook his head. "I would've loved to see him squirm."

"I don't know if I could've done it with you there. I'm not a good liar."

Dan's eyes widened. "You lied? *You? Say* it ain't so."

Leah laughed. "I had to. I had to make him think we had him dead to rights. Well, we kinda do, but I wanted to make *sure* of it. Besides, I thought we were allowed to lie."

Dan finished his glass and poured himself a new one. He went to top off Leah's but noticed none of hers was missing. "Are you even drinking?" he asked.

"I drink a little slow."

"Apparently. In the same way Boy George is a little gay."

Leah lifted her glass and made a show of taking a sip.

"I knew I could count on you." Dan smiled. "So, where were we?"

"About lying bein' okay."

"Ah, you actually do have to watch yourself there. The rules are a bit sticky."

"How so?"

"I think the wording is something like, 'A police officer can use deception in an investigation so long as the deception doesn't result in coercion sufficient to make someone confess to a crime they did not commit.'"

"So I was fine, then." The sun had just gone down, and with the windows open, the room flooded with a purple-orange from the night sky.

"You were fine as long as Duck is guilty."

"You think there's a chance he isn't?"

Dan waved that question away. "I think everyone's guilty. Just makes things easier. Covers all my tracks. So, there's still some things I'm a bit hazy on, probably because I never went through that towering stack of files you and your son read." He smiled at his little dig at the end. The man really thought he was funny.

"You mean my son, who solved the case you've been working on for ten years?"

Dan swallowed a gulp of wine. "That'd be the one, yes."

"Well, what do you want to know?"

"Why did Noah go back to being the Stickman after fifteen years? Especially when he had such a good gig as the Strangler?"

"Took me a bit to figure that one out, too. Turns out the answer had been literally staring at the side of my head all day while I worked."

Dan looked at her questioningly.

"The interview I did in the *Examiner*. I talked about my pa being Joe Fowler and how his most important case was hunting down the Stickman. Noah Stork read the article and became aware Joe had a daughter working his old job in Alvin. I guess the temptation was just too great to resist."

"I see. Wow, fame really does come fraught with danger. I thought those bleeding-heart actors not wanting the paparazzi to bother them were just being whiny."

Leah smiled. "That's actually how Noah Stork knew Ethan was goin' to be in the office early the morning of the Fourth."

Dan shook his head. "Sorry, you just lost me. Could be all the wine."

She knew he was kidding. She was just happy she'd managed to keep it at only wine for Dan's last night before heading back to Birmingham. "The interview I gave in the paper. I say right in it that I work most holidays like the Fourth, and that it makes for a long day on account of I usually check in to the office early in the morning before hitting the streets."

"Wow, so the letter actually was meant to be found by you."

"Pretty sure, yep."

Leah pulled two file folders from the coffee table. She'd picked them up at work yesterday on her way back from her visit with Duck. Included in the folders was a background check, a medical report, and all the other items Chris thought were pertinent for Noah Stork.

"What's that?" Dan asked.

"Stuff Chris pulled for me about Noah Stork. I picked it up at the station yesterday on my way back from Talladega."

"Anything surprisin'?"

"A little, yeah. The man retired from the army after twenty-two years of service."

"I thought he was crazy?"

"Oh, he is. But I think it's the kind of crazy that might work in your favor in some environments. He even participated in D-day with the Five Hundred and Seventh, as part of the Eighty-Second Airborne Division."

"So, he jumped out of planes?"

Leah nodded. "Hence the jump boots. Also, the original Stickman gun, the Smith and Wesson Model Ten—it's possible that came back from the war with him. Back then, the gun was known as a Smith and Wesson Victory."

"Nice," Dan said. "No serial numbers on that gun, right?"

"No, you're thinking of the Beretta Ninety-Two Harry had when he died. The Model Ten wasn't registered."

"I see. So, what was with his arm? Something else he brought home from the military?"

"Appears so." She read from the report, trying to paraphrase. "He received a Purple Heart for his action in Operation Varsity, where his team dropped behind enemy lines. They were under fire, and someone from his own platoon fired a shot that severed part of his left deltoid muscle. It's all very medical mumbo jumbo. Something called compartment syndrome."

"Compartment syndrome? Never heard of it. And he was shot by one of his *own* guys?"

"Yeah, apparently they had to investigate the incident before he was given the Purple Heart. But whatever this compartment syndrome is, it's not something easily treated. Stork's condition grew worse through the years. Which is why—"

"Which is why he had it out for the medical community. This also explains why his victims seemed to be getting better at running from the Strangler in his later years."

"And the fact that the Stickman had problems carrying victim number ten down that short path," Leah added, "not to mention the drag marks I found left by Samantha Hughes. I'm pretty sure that, whatever his condition was, probably something like arthritis set into it not long ago. My pa had arthritis in his gun hand the last few years he worked on the force. It wasn't a pretty sight to watch him pretendin' to be just as good as ever."

Dan nodded gravely.

"But with Stork," Leah went on, "I should have seen it. I interviewed him twice, and, now that I think back, he never used his left hand or arm for nothin'. Funny I didn't pick up on it at the time. He obviously had mobility in his left hand, though, since he did use it to type, but even his typing was affected. And I saw that and *still* nothin' clicked."

"Typing?" Dan finished the last of his glass and re-filled. He topped off Leah's.

"Stork was writing a book on mental illnesses."

"How apropos."

"Yeah, well, if he hadn't died, he'd probably have a nice quiet place to write. That is if they didn't give him the death penalty."

"That's a big if."

"And one we'll never know. Can't say I'm too broken up about that." Leah took a sip of wine. "I think this syndrome thing is why he took a break between being the Stickman and becoming the Strangler."

"Actually, that's a good point," Dan said. "Why did Tommy Stork's move north correspond so well with the start of the Strangler murders?"

"On that point, I can only guess. But consider it an educated guess."

"Okay. Shoot."

"First, the reason Tommy Stork hung out around Birmingham so much was because that was where his ma was buried. That was why he moved there, to be closer to her. I reckon finding her that day when she took all the pills was really hard on him."

"Wow. He just went from potential serial killer to momma's boy in my head. Quite the transition."

"Anyway," Leah said, making googly eyes at him, "if you'd let me finish, it's no secret that there wasn't any love lost between Tommy and his pa. In fact, looking back at my interviews with Noah Stork, I think he might've originally planned to let Tommy take the fall for both the Stickman and the Strangler. I have found a pattern, though, going through the Strangler incidents you listed on my timeline."

"*Our* timeline," Dan interjected. "But let's not split hairs."

"Okay, *our* timeline. Noah Stork had a compulsion to record things. When we searched his house the night he killed Jonathon, we found an abundance of journals and stuff. His own mind seemed to fascinate him."

"Wow, I think I can actually relate to that. So, you're saying he journaled about being a serial killer?"

Leah set down her wine and leaned back on the sofa. "No, nothing that obvious, but he did talk about all the times when he tried to visit Tommy and make some sort of peace."

"Let me guess," Dan said. "That never went well?"

Leah shook her head. "Never. In fact, he'd usually leave all riled up. And those dates correspond almost exactly to the victim dates you put on *our* timeline." She fell quiet then and looked away.

"What just happened?" Dan asked. "What's wrong?"

"Just . . . it's . . . all this time and you know?" She looked up at him. "My pa really did shoot the wrong guy."

Dan spread his palms open and touched his fingertips together. "He was a good man. He did good work. I doubt he made any more mistakes than anyone else. Probably a lot less."

Quietly, she nodded, her eyes looking at the TV that wasn't turned on. "It's just . . . somehow it makes everything seem so . . . *random* and useless."

"I thought you didn't believe in 'random'?"

She let out a big breath and took another sip of wine. "You know, when I was fifteen, he was my *world*. That man meant *everything* to me. He could do no wrong."

"You know Leah, he did a lot of right."

She nodded, her eyes back on the TV. She remembered what Strident had said. Something about Ethan telling him they were a lot alike, she and her pa, and how that must make her a good cop.

Did it? She used to love being compared to him. But now . . . ?

Was that the real issue that was bothering her? That if he could be capable of making such a mistake, was she capable of it, too?

Ethan had told her that her pa spent the later parts of his life still going over that case. The Stickman. Harry Stork. Her pa had *known*. He *must've*. He'd known he made a mistake. And somehow, he lived with it.

Life went on.

And that's where Leah's problem was. She didn't know if she *could* live with it. She wasn't sure life would still go on at all.

As she'd said to Strident, she had some mighty big shoes to fill.

"Wow. Hey, what time do you have?" Dan asked, breaking the silence.

Leah checked her watch. "Just past midnight."

"How 'bout we make out for a bit? Abe's at Dewey's for the night."

"Yeah, but Caroline's in her room."

"I can be quiet. Besides, she never comes out."

"I don't know."

"I'm leaving tomorrow."

Leah just half-smiled at him.

"Okay, then," Dan said. "How 'bout just some heavy petting?"

Leah downed the rest of her wine and scooted over beside him on the sofa. "Okay," she said. "Heavy petting I can do."

CHAPTER 76

Leah knocked on Caroline's bedroom door. "Is it okay if I come in, honey?" She took the lack of an answer as it being all right. Slowly, she opened the door and saw Caroline lying on her bed, her tearstained face turned toward the window where, outside, the sky had just begun to grow purple as twilight began setting in.

Sitting on the edge of her daughter's bed, Leah ran her hands through Caroline's hair.

"Would it help if I told you I know how you feel?" Leah asked.

"Why, Mom?" Caroline asked. "Why did he have to die?"

"I don't know, honey. It's a question nobody can really answer. What's important is that you don't ever forget him."

"How could I ever forget him? I *loved* him, Mom."

Leah wrapped her arms around her daughter. "I know you did. He was a great guy."

She started crying hard. "What is it?" Leah asked.

"He gave me a promise ring."

Leah smiled. "I know."

Caroline looked up briefly. "He broke his promise."

"No, no. That's not how you look at this. He died trying to save your life."

"I know," she said, getting a small handle on her tears. "But . . . I even wrote him a poem. I was going to give it to him when I got back from the five-and-dime that night. I *waited* because I was worried he might not like it. Now I wish I'd have just given him the stupid thing when he got here." She began crying. "He never got to read it."

"Can I see it?"

Caroline nodded through her tears. "Yeah." She picked up a piece of paper with writing on it from her bedside table and held it out for Leah.

"Read it to me," Leah said instead of taking it. "I think it would be cathartic for you."

Caroline sniffled, trying to hold the tears back. "Are you sure? I don't know if I can."

"Try."

Caroline cleared her throat, but Leah still heard the tears when she spoke. "Okay," Caroline said, "but you probably won't like it. It's not very good."

"Let me do my own judging, okay?"

Caroline nodded and began to read, stopping several times to choke back her sobs.

MY BREATH AND YOUR HEART

> Helpless
> I was balanced
> On love's razor-sharp edge
> Stumbling and tumbling
> With each word that you said
> Falling so deep

> I caught my breath and your heart
> Holding them both
> Until the Fates, life, or time
> One day tear us apart

"That's it," Caroline said. "It's not very long or nothin'."

"It's beautiful, Caroline. He would've loved it."

Caroline had a black string around her neck with something wooden hanging from it. Leah saw it swinging as her daughter put the poem back where she'd been keeping it.

"Is that new?" Leah asked.

"What?"

"This." Leah plucked it up with her fingers. It was some sort of carving.

"Jonathon's grandpa gave it to me," Carry explained. "It's a hummingbird." The tears came back even stronger. "It's supposed to bring good luck."

Leah gave a big sigh. "Well, in a way it worked."

Caroline pulled away, looking at Leah incredulously. "How can you even *say* that?"

"Honey, because *you're* still here. And I think you may have Jonathon to thank for that."

Another sniffle from Caroline. "But he'll never get to read my poem because now he's gone." She was racked with sobs again. "I don't know how I keep crying. You'd think I'd run out of tears."

"No, tears are something you never seem to run out of. I know. I cried near on every day for six years after your pa was killed."

"How did you get past it?"

"Sooner or later, you will stop thinking about the bad

parts, him being shot and all, and those memories get replaced by all the good things you did together while he
was still here. But it's goin' to take some time."

"So, for now I just lie here cryin'?"

"If that's what it takes." Leah nodded. "Just remember
that me, and even Abe, are here for you if you need us."

Caroline sniffled. "Thanks, Mom," she said, returning the hug her mother held her in. "I just miss him so
much."

"I understand that. I still miss your pa every single
day. But trust me, with time, the missing becomes easier. Sooner or later you will move on with your life."

Caroline's chest heaved as she took a big breath and
slowly let it out. "Right now, I can't imagine life without Jonathon." She rubbed her eyes.

"I know."

"We saw each other practically every day."

"I know."

Caroline's sobs came back. "Mom, I miss him *so*
much. It's like there's a hole in my heart that won't ever
be filled again."

"It will, honey. It just takes time."

Leah looked out Caroline's bedroom window. The
purplish sky had started to turn that deep midnight-blue
color you always see at the day's end. A few stars had
begun to shine, twinkling in the vast stretch of dark
blue. How far away were they? *The universe is so big,
it's easy to get lost.*

One day, Caroline would be okay with Jonathon's
death. Maybe not in months, maybe it would take years,
but once that day came, Leah's daughter would once
again see the world's beauty instead of just its brutality.
She might even look up at the night's first stars with a
secret wish, the way she did when she was younger.

Now, Leah made her own wish on the stars, that her daughter would make it through this soon. It made everything feel just a mite better.

But there were some things that didn't heal, things you couldn't come back from, and Leah thought that was the most tragic part of Caroline's losing Jonathon— that her world would be forever changed. The Stickman had returned and taken three victims with him.

Leah now considered, in a way, there were four.

Everyone grew up eventually, but Caroline had just been forced to do so early. The naïveté she held tightly to that made life safe had been lost. This brought tears to Leah's eyes, because that naïveté could never be brought back. Like Jonathon, it was gone from Caroline forever.

A deep sadness fell over Leah's heart.

She had failed to protect her butterfly; instead she had touched its wings.

ACKNOWLEDGMENTS

Since *Dream with Little Angels,* each new book feels a little more solid and real to me than the last, and I owe a lot of that to the following people, without whom *Sticks and Stones* would've been a different book.

As always, a debt of gratitude goes out to my agent, Adrienne Rosado, for her tenacity and diligence. If there is any agent as fine as she, I know not of them.

And to my editor, the colossal John Scognamiglio, who serves as a navigational beacon when the skies darken and the waves crash. This time around, I want to especially thank him for allowing me to come in at nearly double my contracted word count so I could tell this story the way I wanted it to be told.

Also to Jeffery Deaver, Michael Connelly, Brian Michael Bendis, and Warren Ellis, for raising the bar so freaking high, inspiring me to aim my own standards at the stars.

A nod to Claudia Lacunza at Easy DNA for her help in making sure I got that part of the science right.

Applause for Yvonne Rupert for giving Raven Lee Emerson a story to tell.

Also, big thanks go to cochise1872, whose real name I never managed to find out. (I tried, man. Honestly, I really did.) His online posts taught me everything I needed to know about lock-picking and made me realize there's absolutely no point in locking my doors anymore.

Once again, Mark Leland put himself at my disposal for all things police procedural and deadly. One day, maybe we'll hit the firing range, Mark. I seem to believe you offered something like that once upon a time. . . .

A tip of the hat goes out to Natalie Pierson, whom I somehow managed to coerce into becoming my research assistant for this book.

And I'd be fraught not to mention all the help I receive from the Chilliwack Writers' Group, a group consisting of Mary Keane, Garth Pettersen, Ken Loomes, Terri McKee, Fran Brown, and Wendy Foster. On that same note, I'd like to send out props to all my friends at Writers Village University. You're all a swell bunch of folks, and my life's better for having you in it.

Finally, a big thank-you to all of you readers out there, for continuing to stick with me and support my work. Without you, I'd still be back writing novels purely for the entertainment of me and my cats. And frankly, the cats are terribly harsh critics.

Michael Hiebert
British Columbia, Canada
June 2016

Oh, and just in case y'all might be wonderin' . . . The Oakland A's swept the San Francisco Giants in a demoralizing four-game win to take the 1989 World Series, despite having to put up with a magnitude 6.9 earthquake hitting the field just minutes before the start of game three.

In other words, Leah won twenty bucks.

Connect with U s

Visit us online at
KensingtonBooks.com
to read more from your favorite authors, see books
by series, view reading group guides, and more.

Join us on social media

for sneak peeks, chances to win books and prize packs,
and to share your thoughts with other readers.

facebook.com/kensingtonpublishing
twitter.com/kensingtonbooks

Tell us what you think!

To share your thoughts, submit a review,
or sign up for our eNewsletters, please visit:
KensingtonBooks.com/TellUs.